D1250745

THE WALKING DEAD

ALL OUT WAR
AP EDITION

created by Robert Kirkman

image comics presents

The Walking Dead
all out war ap edition

ROBERT KIRKMAN
creator, writer

CHARLIE ADLARD
penciler, cover

RUS WOOTON
letterer

SEAN MACKIEWICZ
editor

special thanks to
STEFANO GAUDIANO

THE WALKING DEAD, ALL OUT WAR AP EDITION. First Printing. Published by Image Comics, Inc., Office of publication: 2001 Center Street, 6th Floor, Berkeley, California 94704. Copyright © 2014 Robert Kirkman, LLC. Originally published in single magazine form as THE WALKING DEAD #115-126. All rights reserved. THE WALKING DEAD™ (including all prominent characters featured herein), its logo and all character likenesses are trademarks of Robert Kirkman, LLC, unless otherwise noted. Image Comics® and its logos are registered trademarks of Image Comics, Inc. Skybound Entertainment and its logos are © and ™ of Skybound Entertainment, LLC. No part of this publication may be reproduced or transmitted, in any form or by any means (except for short excerpts for review purposes) without the express written permission of Image Comics, Inc. All names, characters, events and locales in this publication are entirely fictional. Any resemblance to actual persons (living or dead), events or places, without satiric intent, is coincidental. PRINTED IN CANADA. ISBN: 978-1-63215-038-7.

For international inquiries: foreign@skybound.com.   For licensing inquiries: contact@skybound.com.

All Out War

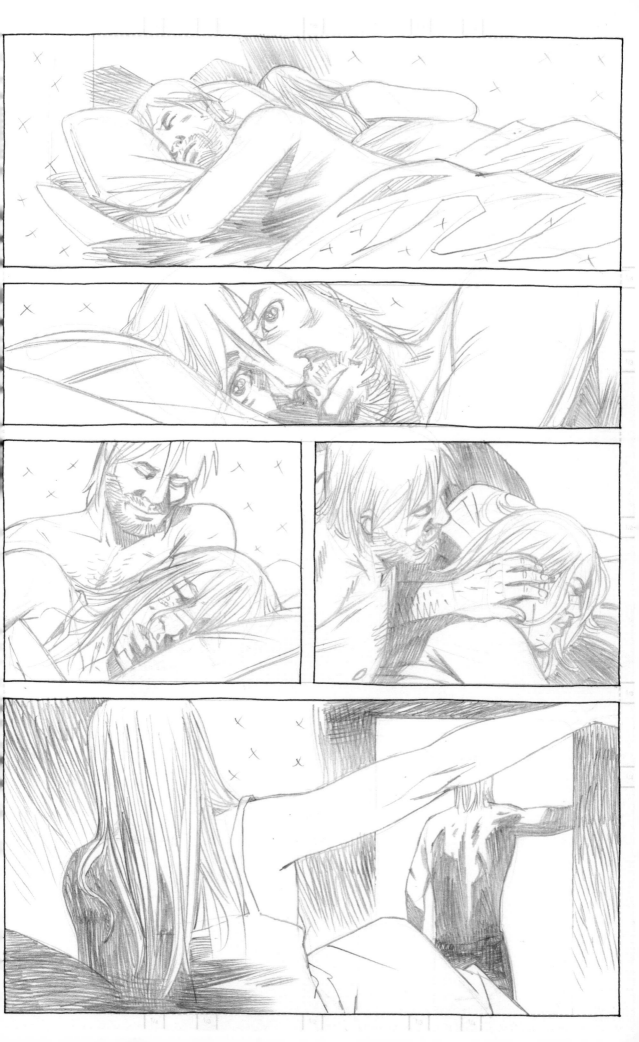

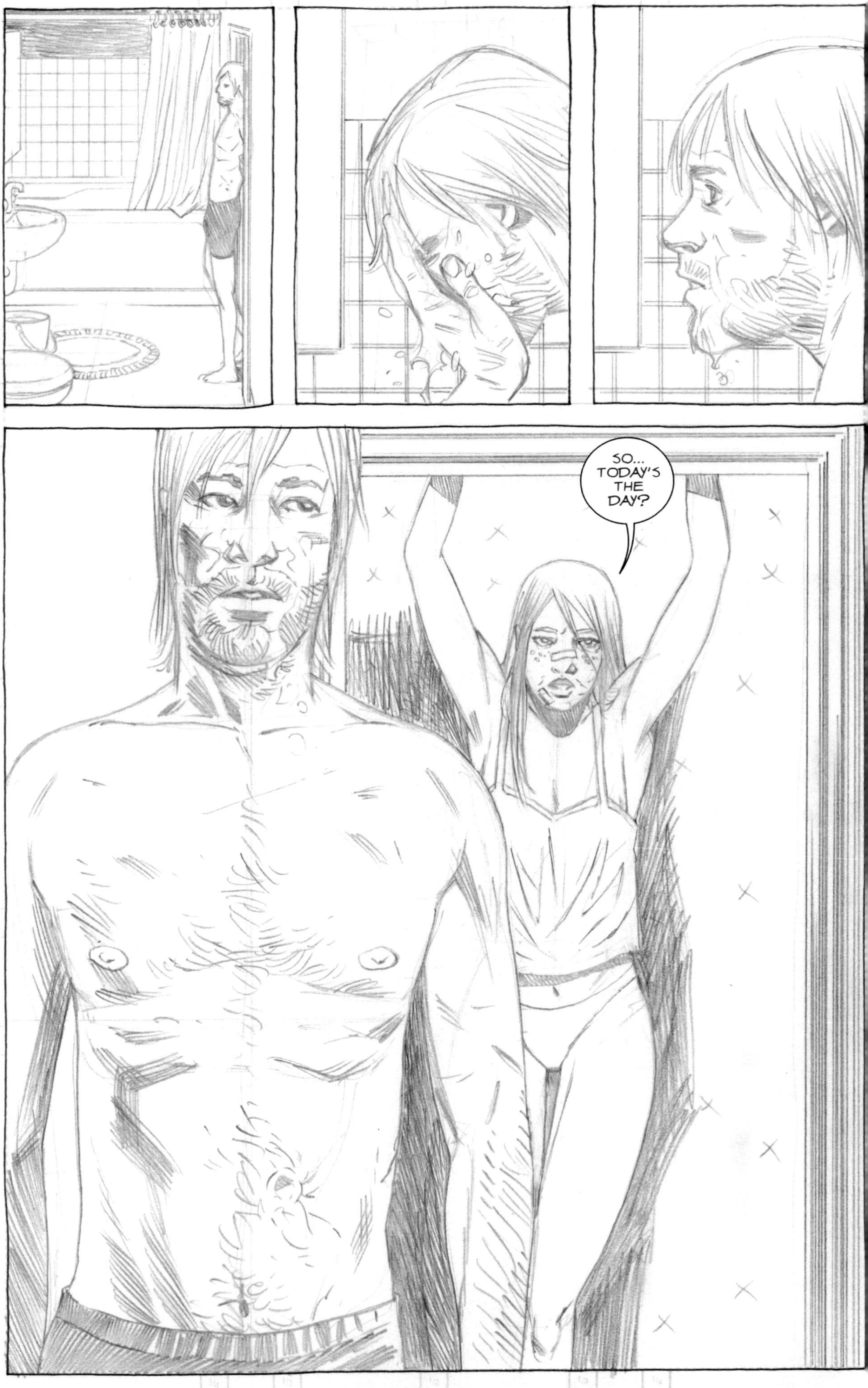
SO... TODAY'S THE DAY?

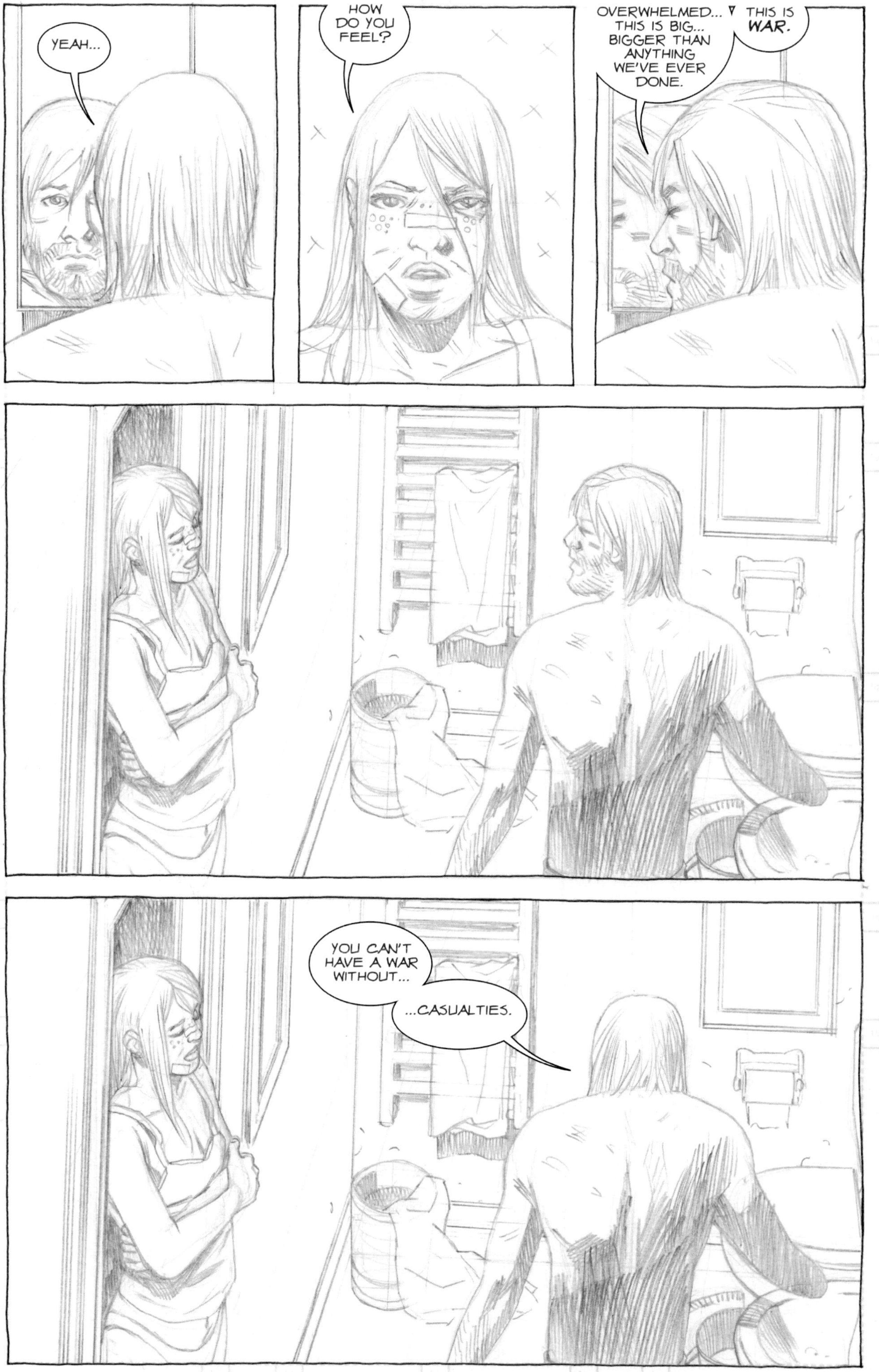
YEAH...
HOW DO YOU FEEL?
OVERWHELMED... THIS IS BIG... BIGGER THAN ANYTHING WE'VE EVER DONE.
THIS IS WAR.
YOU CAN'T HAVE A WAR WITHOUT...
...CASUALTIES.

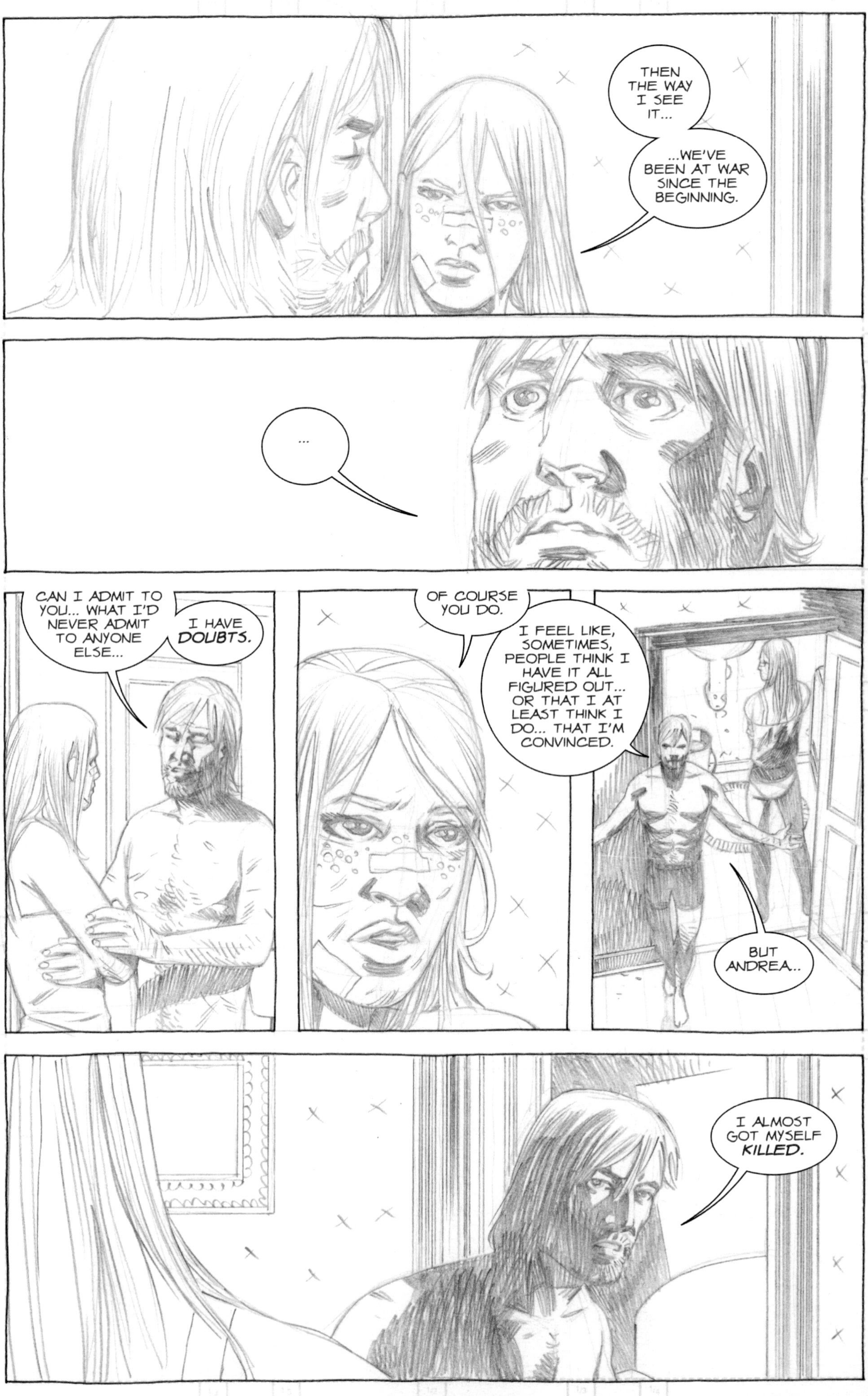
THEN THE WAY I SEE IT...
...WE'VE BEEN AT WAR SINCE THE BEGINNING.
...
CAN I ADMIT TO YOU... WHAT I'D NEVER ADMIT TO ANYONE ELSE...
I HAVE *DOUBTS.*
OF COURSE YOU DO.
I FEEL LIKE, SOMETIMES, PEOPLE THINK I HAVE IT ALL FIGURED OUT... OR THAT I AT LEAST THINK I DO... THAT I'M CONVINCED.
BUT ANDREA..
I ALMOST GOT MYSELF *KILLED.*

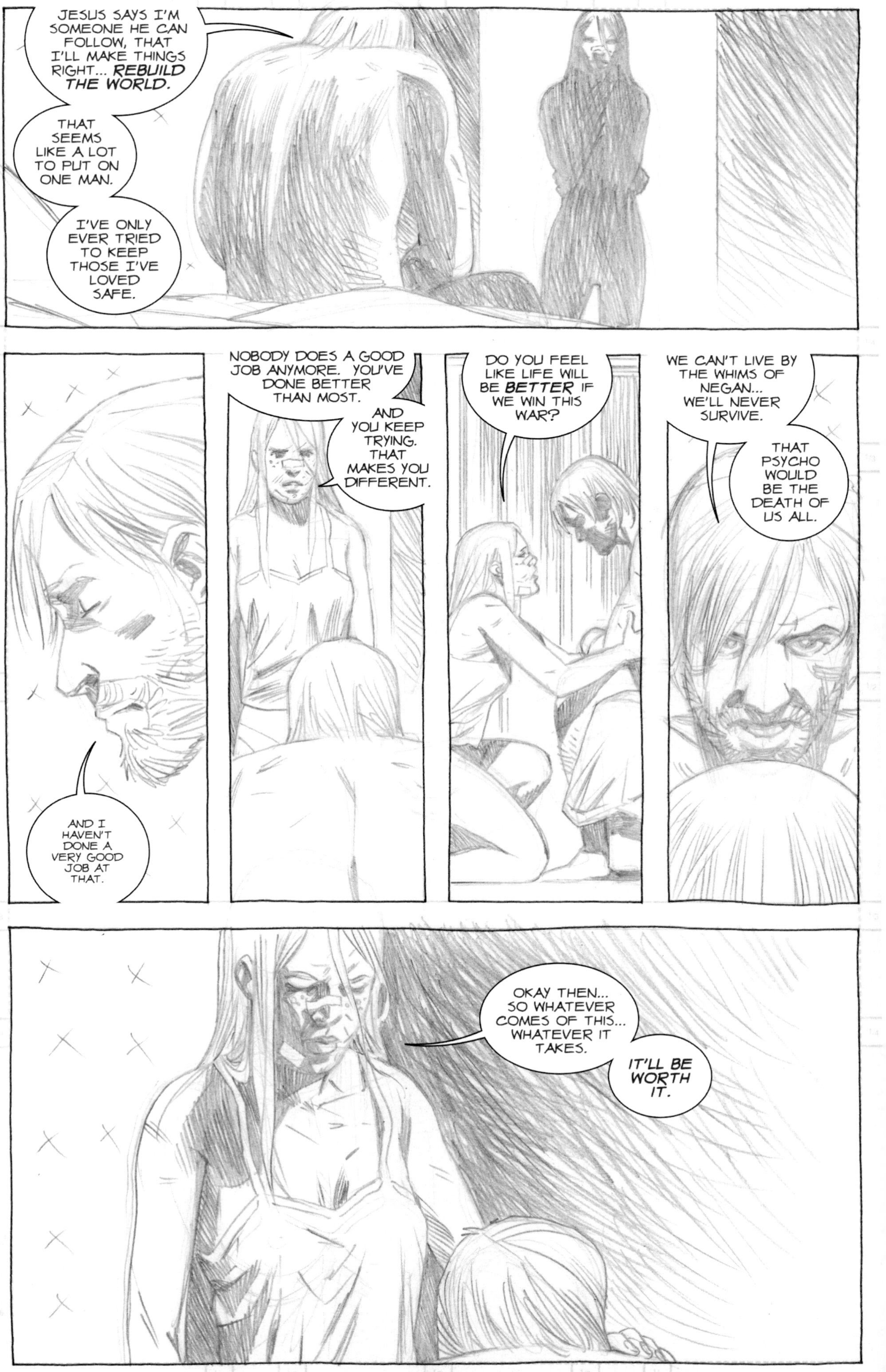
JESUS SAYS I'M SOMEONE HE CAN FOLLOW, THAT I'LL MAKE THINGS RIGHT... REBUILD THE WORLD.
THAT SEEMS LIKE A LOT TO PUT ON ONE MAN.
I'VE ONLY EVER TRIED TO KEEP THOSE I'VE LOVED SAFE.
AND I HAVEN'T DONE A VERY GOOD JOB AT THAT.
NOBODY DOES A GOOD JOB ANYMORE. YOU'VE DONE BETTER THAN MOST.
AND YOU KEEP TRYING. THAT MAKES YOU DIFFERENT.
DO YOU FEEL LIKE LIFE WILL BE BETTER IF WE WIN THIS WAR?
WE CAN'T LIVE BY THE WHIMS OF NEGAN... WE'LL NEVER SURVIVE.
THAT PSYCHO WOULD BE THE DEATH OF US ALL.
OKAY THEN... SO WHATEVER COMES OF THIS... WHATEVER IT TAKES.
IT'LL BE WORTH IT.

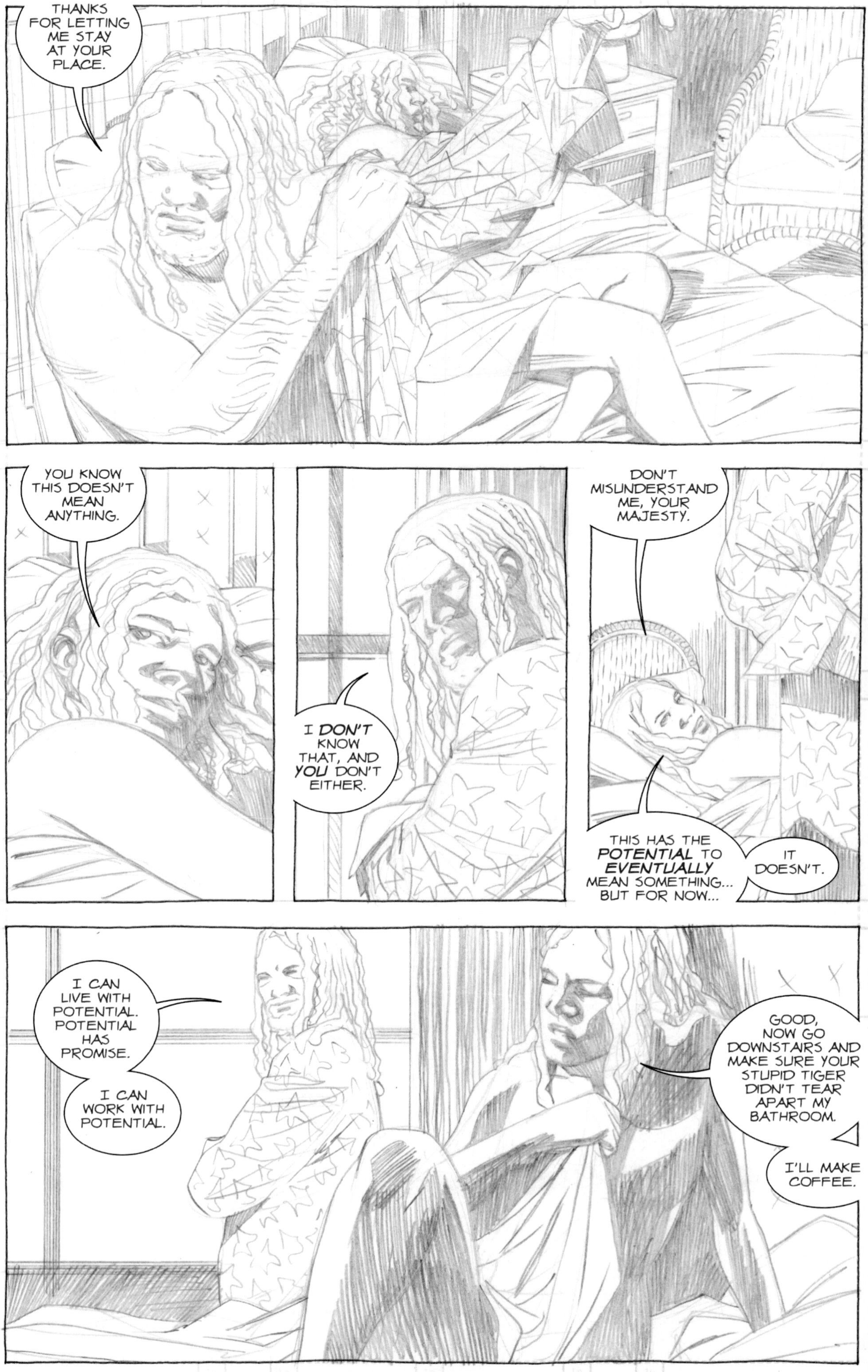
THANKS FOR LETTING ME STAY AT YOUR PLACE.
YOU KNOW THIS DOESN'T MEAN ANYTHING.
I DON'T KNOW THAT, AND YOU DON'T EITHER.
DON'T MISUNDERSTAND ME, YOUR MAJESTY.
THIS HAS THE POTENTIAL TO EVENTUALLY MEAN SOMETHING... BUT FOR NOW...
IT DOESN'T.
I CAN LIVE WITH POTENTIAL. POTENTIAL HAS PROMISE.
I CAN WORK WITH POTENTIAL.
GOOD, NOW GO DOWNSTAIRS AND MAKE SURE YOUR STUPID TIGER DIDN'T TEAR APART MY BATHROOM.
I'LL MAKE COFFEE.

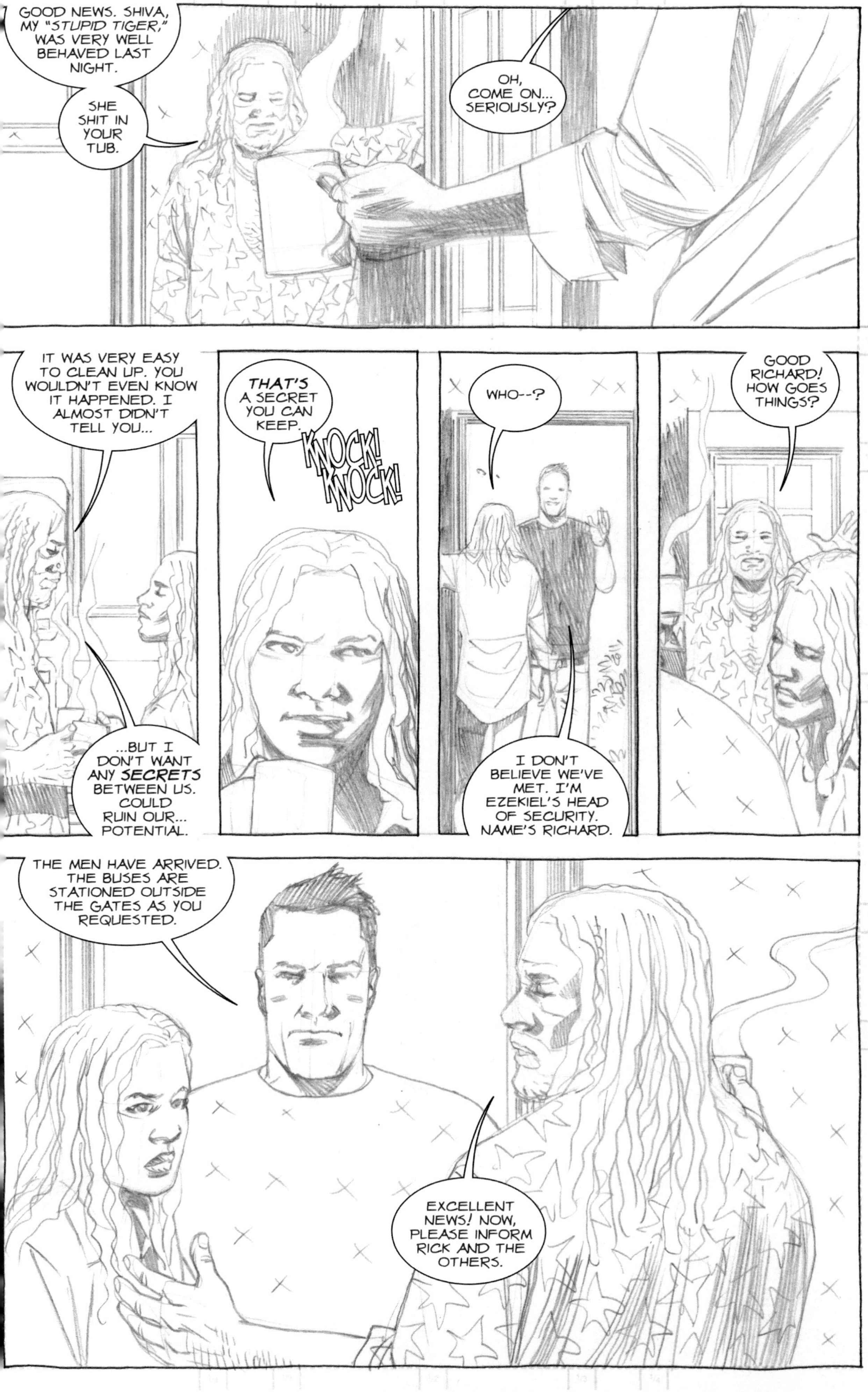
GOOD NEWS. SHIVA, MY "STUPID TIGER," WAS VERY WELL BEHAVED LAST NIGHT.
SHE SHIT IN YOUR TUB.
OH, COME ON... SERIOUSLY?
IT WAS VERY EASY TO CLEAN UP. YOU WOULDN'T EVEN KNOW IT HAPPENED. I ALMOST DIDN'T TELL YOU...
...BUT I DON'T WANT ANY SECRETS BETWEEN US. COULD RUIN OUR... POTENTIAL.
THAT'S A SECRET YOU CAN KEEP.
KNOCK! KNOCK!
WHO--?
I DON'T BELIEVE WE'VE MET. I'M EZEKIEL'S HEAD OF SECURITY. NAME'S RICHARD.
GOOD RICHARD! HOW GOES THINGS?
THE MEN HAVE ARRIVED. THE BUSES ARE STATIONED OUTSIDE THE GATES AS YOU REQUESTED.
EXCELLENT NEWS! NOW, PLEASE INFORM RICK AND THE OTHERS.

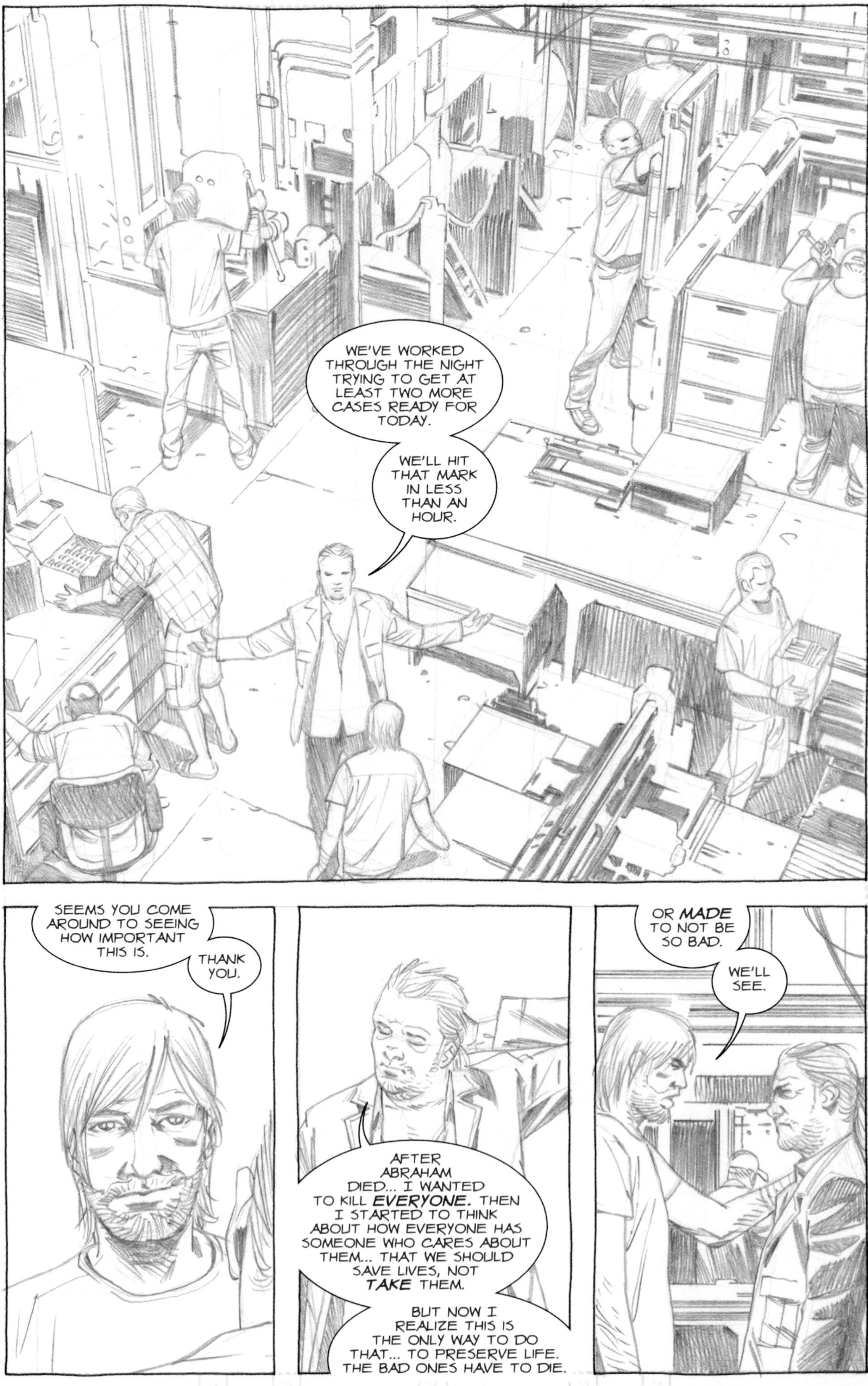
WE'VE WORKED THROUGH THE NIGHT TRYING TO GET AT LEAST TWO MORE CASES READY FOR TODAY.
WE'LL HIT THAT MARK IN LESS THAN AN HOUR.
SEEMS YOU COME AROUND TO SEEING HOW IMPORTANT THIS IS.
THANK YOU.
AFTER ABRAHAM DIED... I WANTED TO KILL EVERYONE. THEN I STARTED TO THINK ABOUT HOW EVERYONE HAS SOMEONE WHO CARES ABOUT THEM... THAT WE SHOULD SAVE LIVES, NOT TAKE THEM.
BUT NOW I REALIZE THIS IS THE ONLY WAY TO DO THAT... TO PRESERVE LIFE. THE BAD ONES HAVE TO DIE.
OR MADE TO NOT BE SO BAD.
WE'LL SEE.

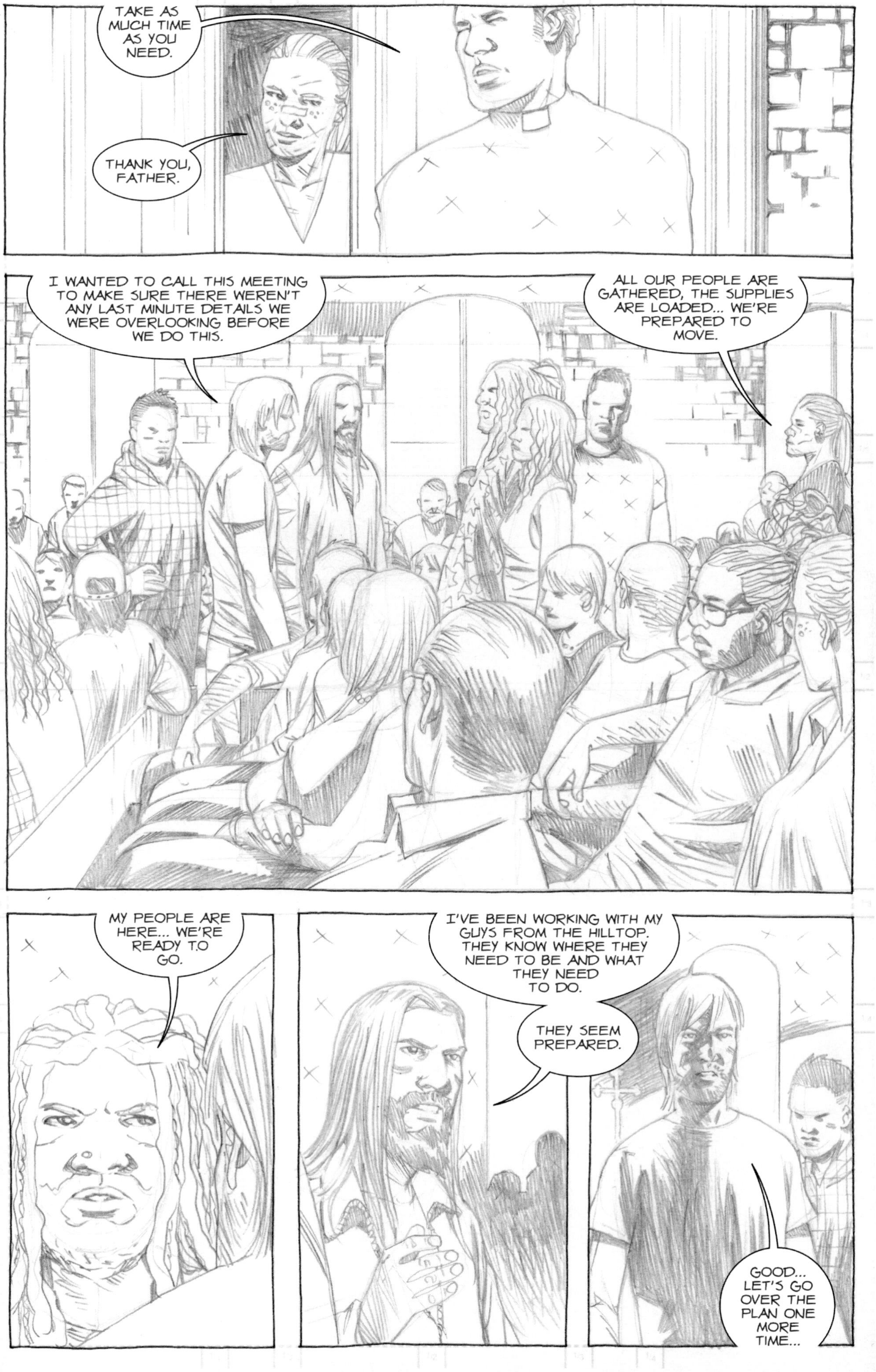

TAKE AS MUCH TIME AS YOU NEED.
THANK YOU, FATHER.
I WANTED TO CALL THIS MEETING TO MAKE SURE THERE WEREN'T ANY LAST MINUTE DETAILS WE WERE OVERLOOKING BEFORE WE DO THIS.
ALL OUR PEOPLE ARE GATHERED, THE SUPPLIES ARE LOADED... WE'RE PREPARED TO MOVE.
MY PEOPLE ARE HERE... WE'RE READY T.O GO.
I'VE BEEN WORKING WITH MY GUYS FROM THE HILLTOP. THEY KNOW WHERE THEY NEED TO BE AND WHAT THEY NEED TO DO.
THEY SEEM PREPARED.
GOOD... LET'S GO OVER THE PLAN ONE MORE TIME...

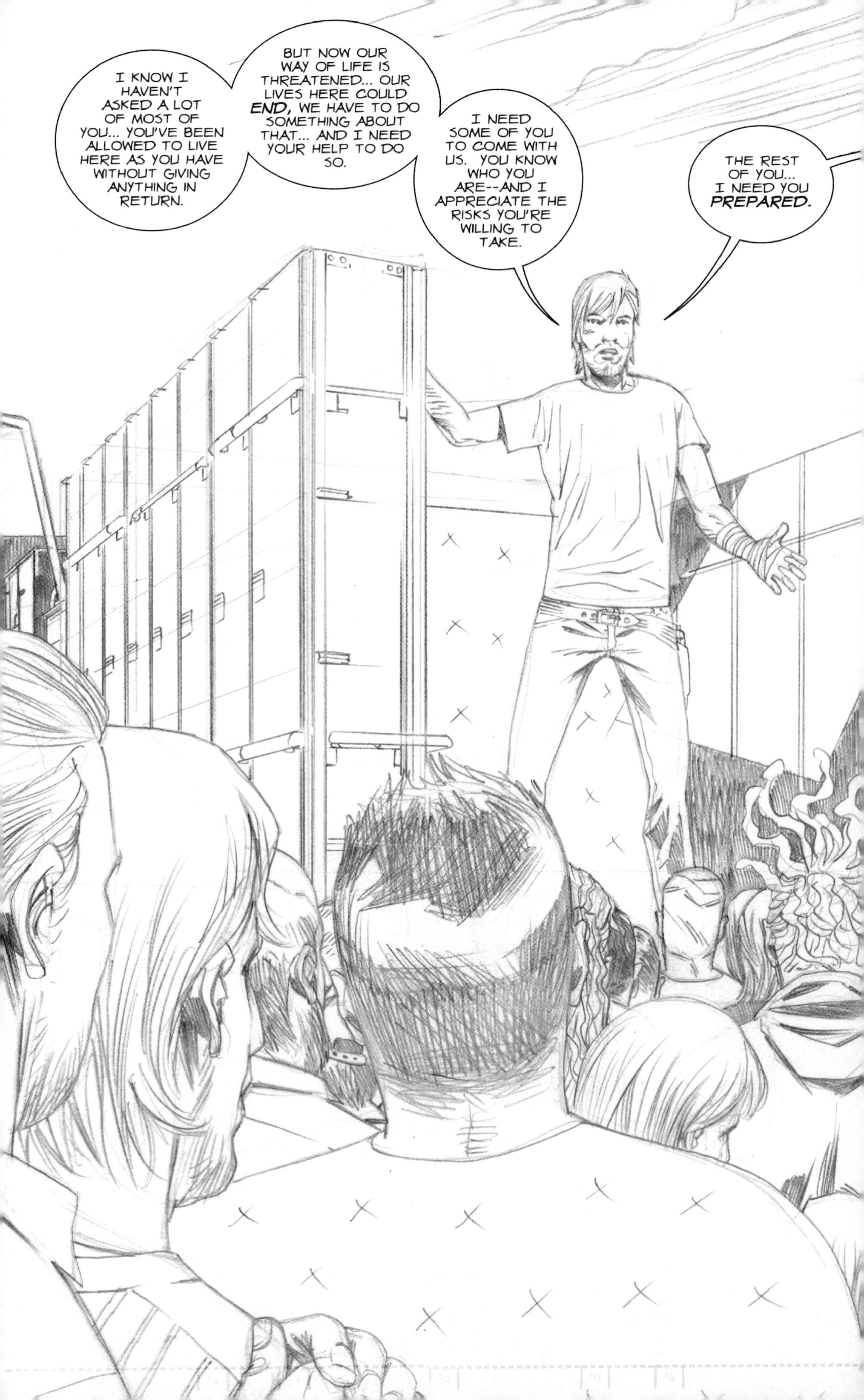
I KNOW I HAVEN'T ASKED A LOT OF MOST OF YOU... YOU'VE BEEN ALLOWED TO LIVE HERE AS YOU HAVE WITHOUT GIVING ANYTHING IN RETURN.
BUT NOW OUR WAY OF LIFE IS THREATENED... OUR LIVES HERE COULD **END,** WE HAVE TO DO SOMETHING ABOUT THAT... AND I NEED YOUR HELP TO DO SO.
I NEED SOME OF YOU TO COME WITH US. YOU KNOW WHO YOU ARE--AND I APPRECIATE THE RISKS YOU'RE WILLING TO TAKE.
THE REST OF YOU... I NEED YOU ***PREPARED.***

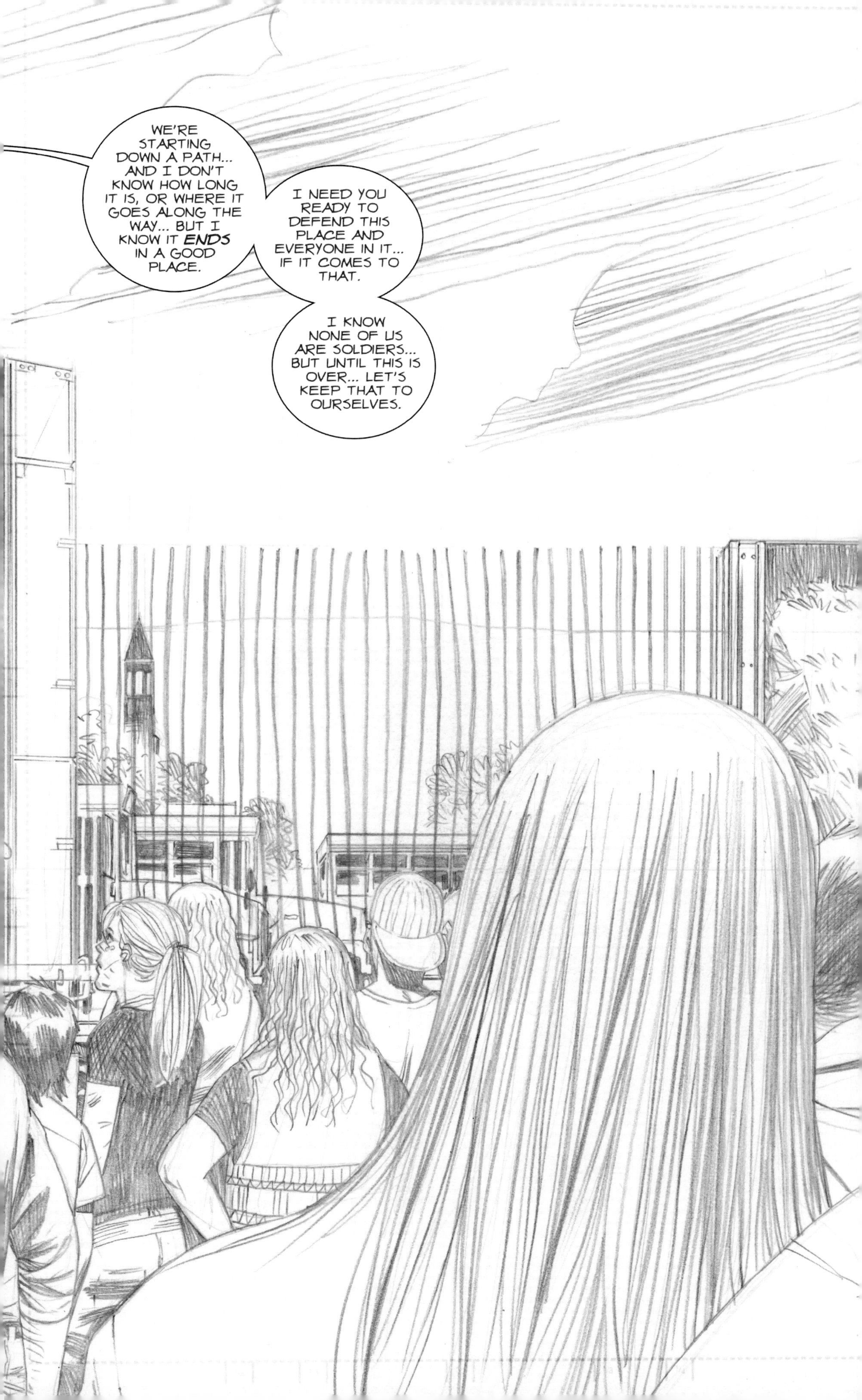
WE'RE STARTING DOWN A PATH... AND I DON'T KNOW HOW LONG IT IS, OR WHERE IT GOES ALONG THE WAY... BUT I KNOW IT **ENDS** IN A GOOD PLACE.
I NEED YOU READY TO DEFEND THIS PLACE AND EVERYONE IN IT... IF IT COMES TO THAT.
I KNOW NONE OF US ARE SOLDIERS... BUT UNTIL THIS IS OVER... LET'S KEEP THAT TO OURSELVES.

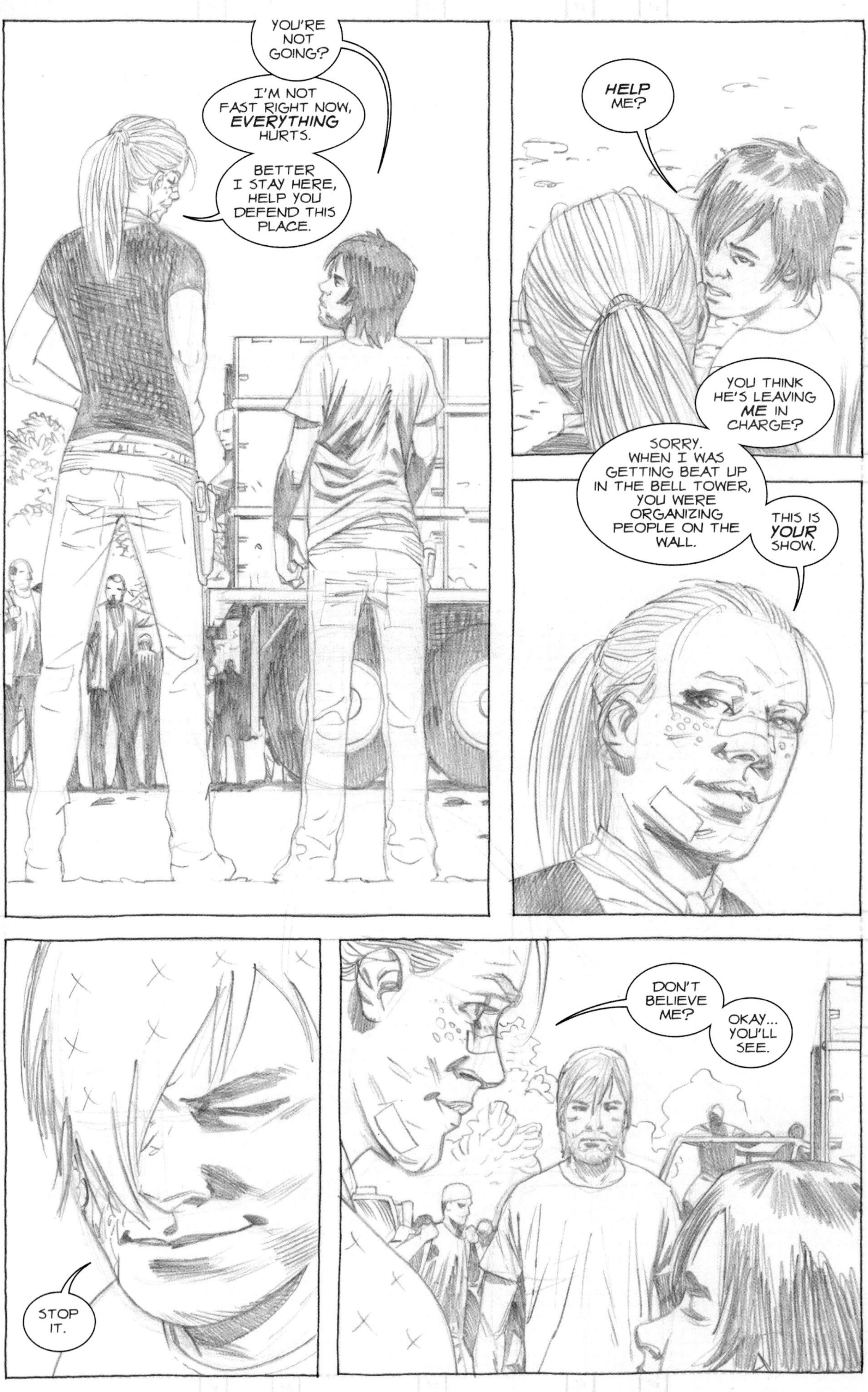
YOU'RE NOT GOING?
I'M NOT FAST RIGHT NOW, EVERYTHING HURTS.
BETTER I STAY HERE, HELP YOU DEFEND THIS PLACE.
HELP ME?
YOU THINK HE'S LEAVING ME IN CHARGE?
SORRY. WHEN I WAS GETTING BEAT UP IN THE BELL TOWER, YOU WERE ORGANIZING PEOPLE ON THE WALL.
THIS IS YOUR SHOW.
STOP IT.
DON'T BELIEVE ME?
OKAY... YOU'LL SEE.

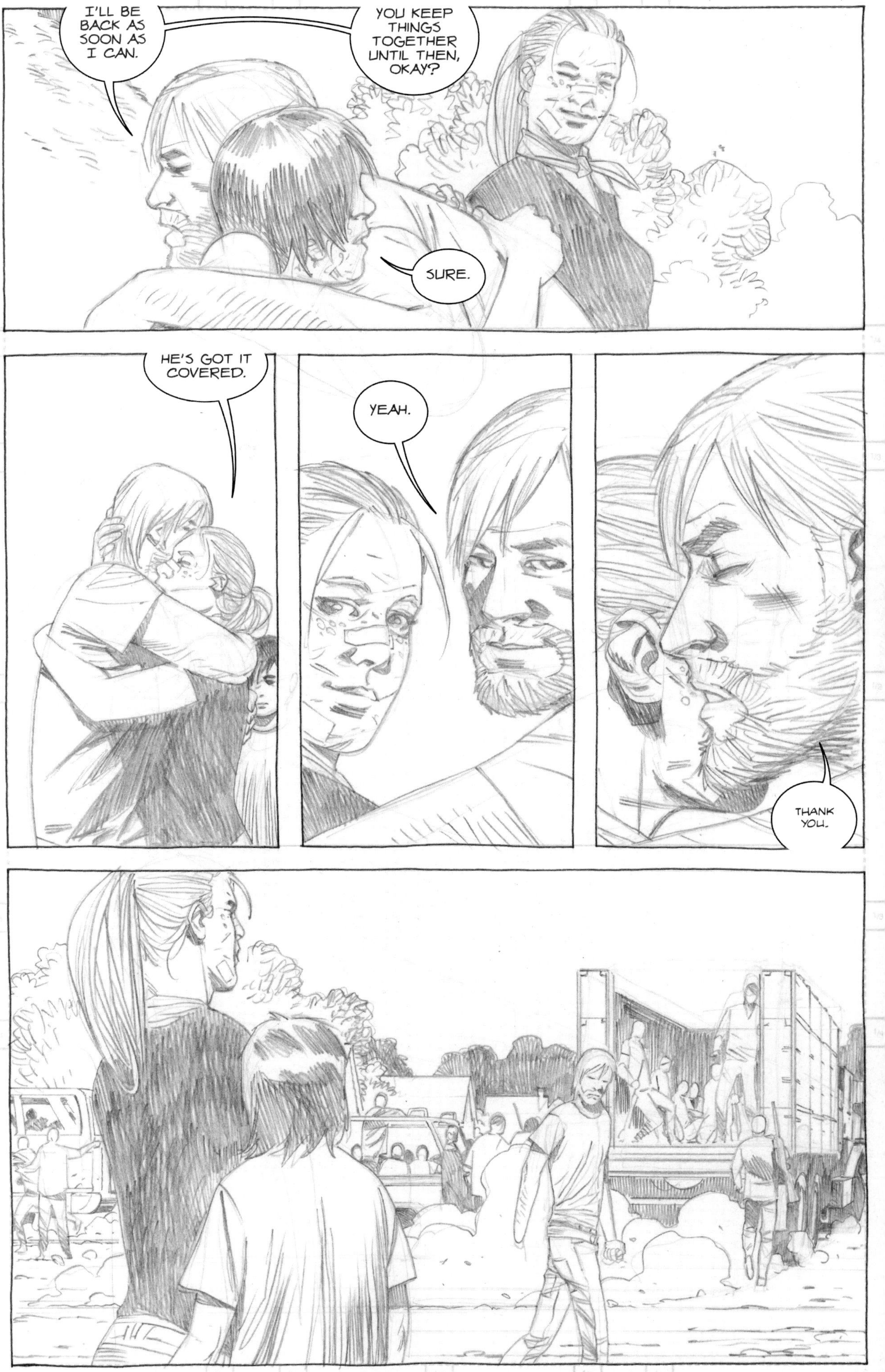
I'LL BE BACK AS SOON AS I CAN.
YOU KEEP THINGS TOGETHER UNTIL THEN, OKAY?
SURE.
HE'S GOT IT COVERED.
YEAH.
THANK YOU.

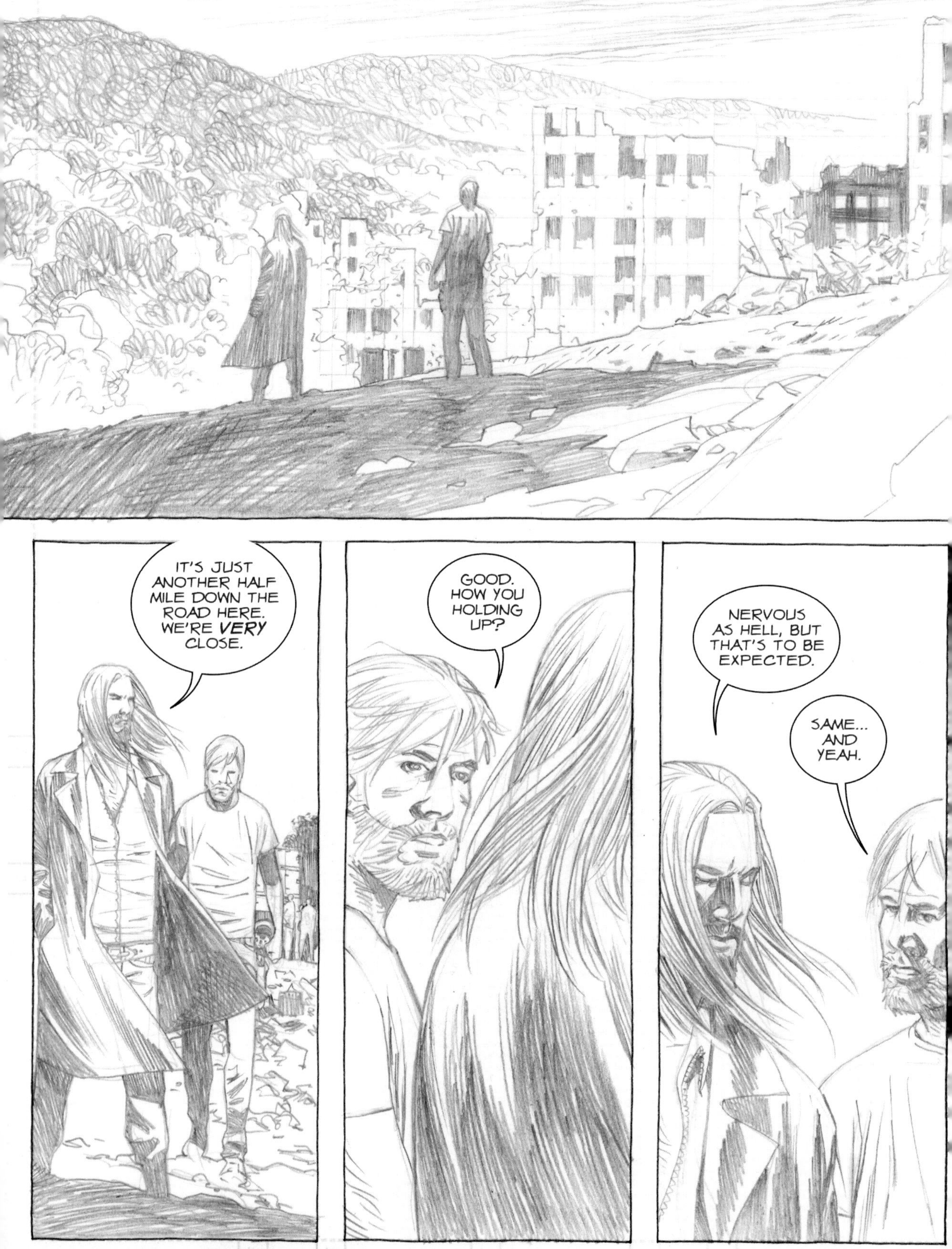
IT'S JUST ANOTHER HALF MILE DOWN THE ROAD HERE. WE'RE VERY CLOSE.
GOOD. HOW YOU HOLDING UP?
NERVOUS AS HELL, BUT THAT'S TO BE EXPECTED.
SAME... AND YEAH.

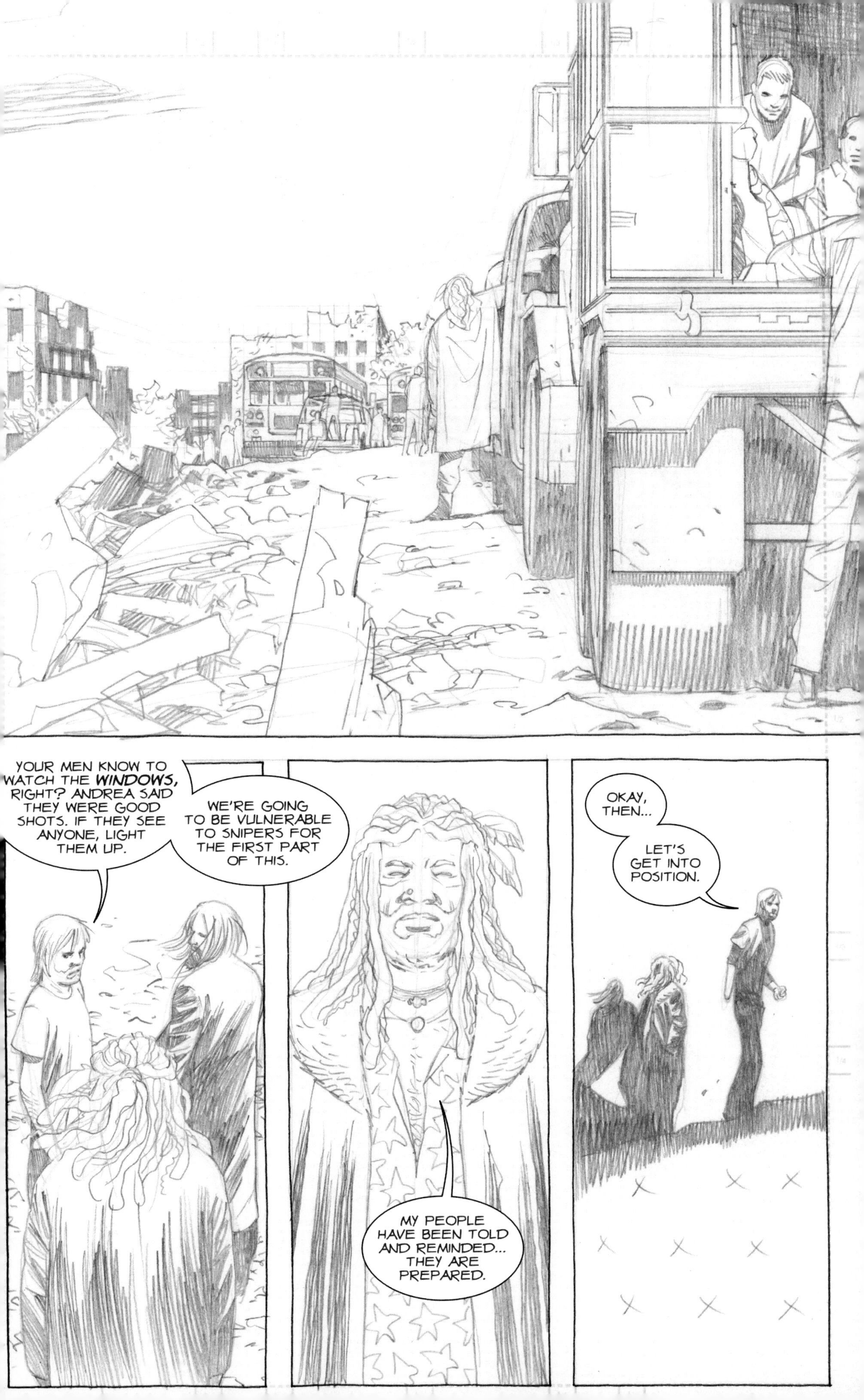
YOUR MEN KNOW TO WATCH THE WINDOWS, RIGHT? ANDREA SAID THEY WERE GOOD SHOTS. IF THEY SEE ANYONE, LIGHT THEM UP.
WE'RE GOING TO BE VULNERABLE TO SNIPERS FOR THE FIRST PART OF THIS.
MY PEOPLE HAVE BEEN TOLD AND REMINDED... THEY ARE PREPARED.
OKAY, THEN...
LET'S GET INTO POSITION.

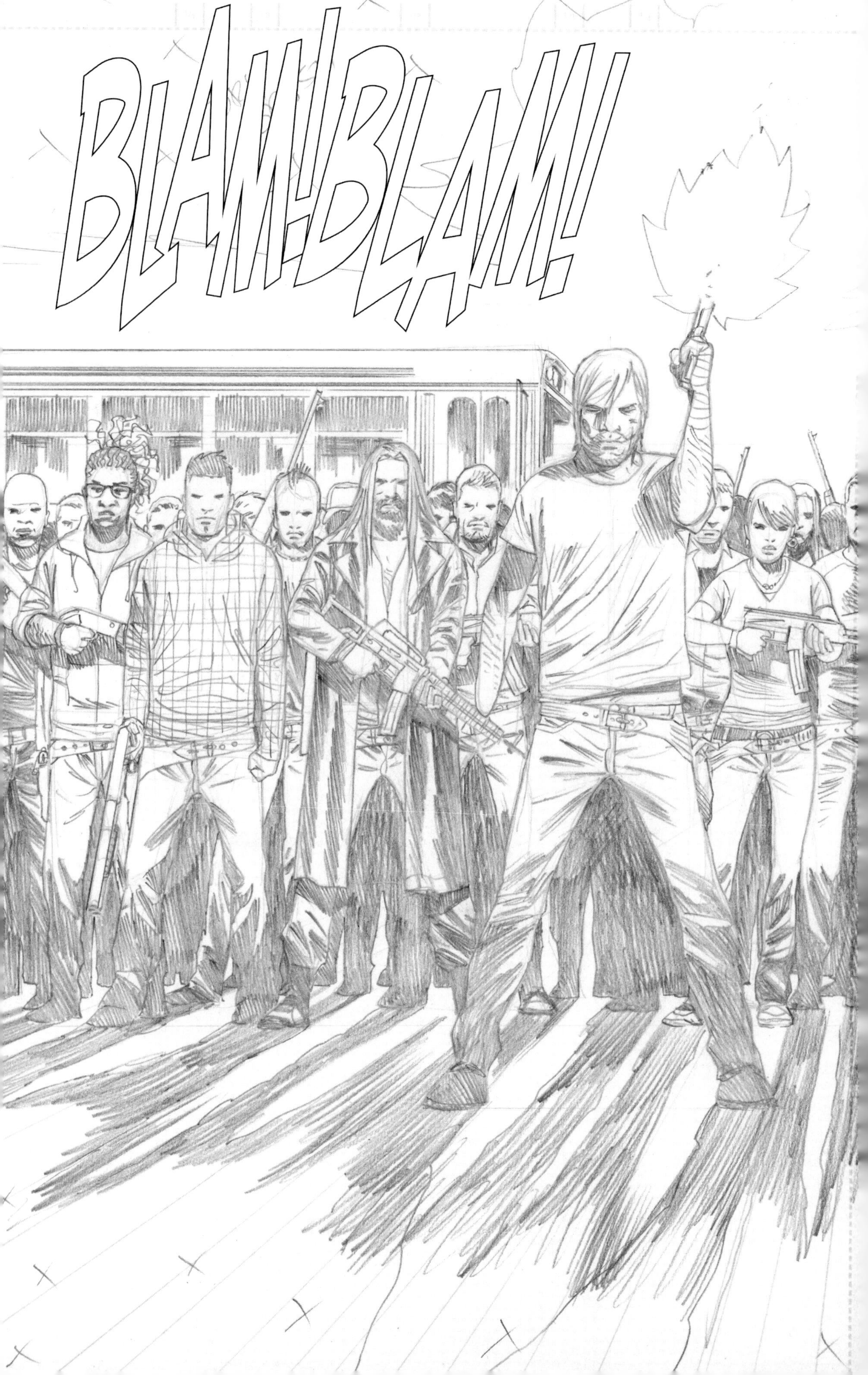
BLAM! BLAM!

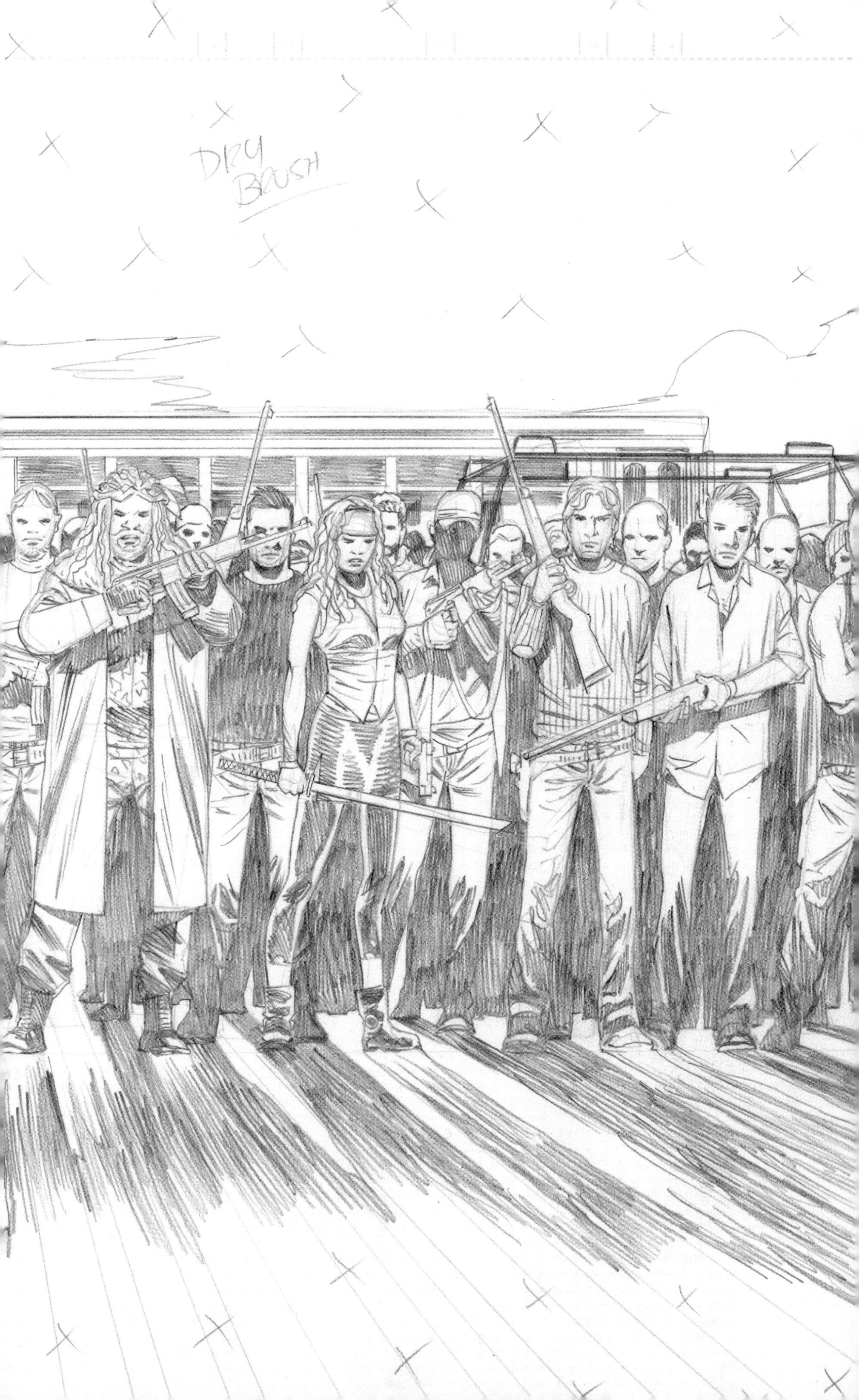
DRY BRUSH

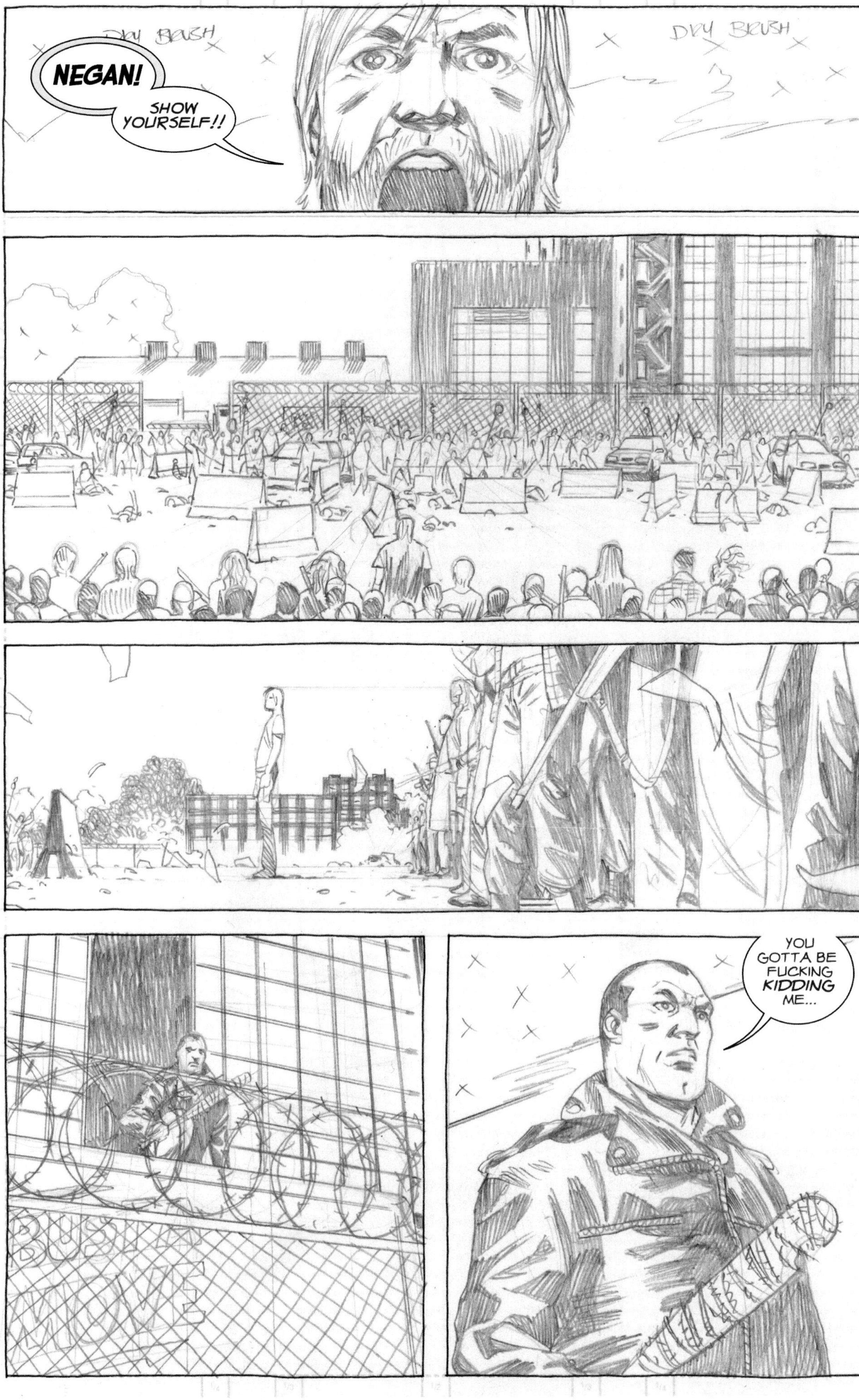
DRY BRUSH
DRY BRUSH
NEGAN!
SHOW YOURSELF!!
YOU GOTTA BE FUCKING KIDDING ME...

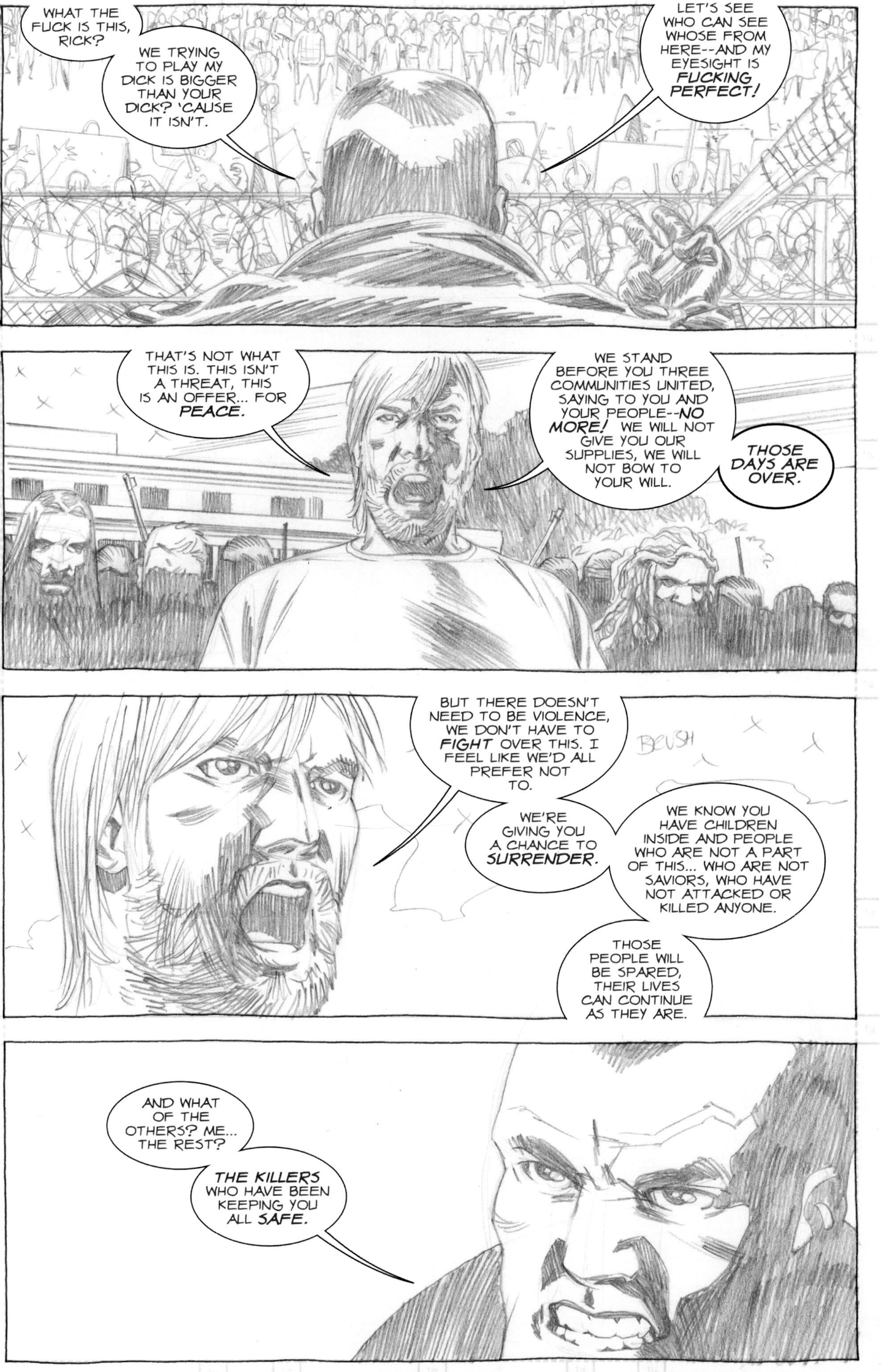
WHAT THE FUCK IS THIS, RICK?
WE TRYING TO PLAY MY DICK IS BIGGER THAN YOUR DICK? 'CAUSE IT ISN'T.
LET'S SEE WHO CAN SEE WHOSE FROM HERE--AND MY EYESIGHT IS FUCKING PERFECT!
THAT'S NOT WHAT THIS IS. THIS ISN'T A THREAT, THIS IS AN OFFER... FOR PEACE.
WE STAND BEFORE YOU THREE COMMUNITIES UNITED, SAYING TO YOU AND YOUR PEOPLE--NO MORE! WE WILL NOT GIVE YOU OUR SUPPLIES, WE WILL NOT BOW TO YOUR WILL.
THOSE DAYS ARE OVER.
BUT THERE DOESN'T NEED TO BE VIOLENCE, WE DON'T HAVE TO FIGHT OVER THIS. I FEEL LIKE WE'D ALL PREFER NOT TO.
BRUSH
WE'RE GIVING YOU A CHANCE TO SURRENDER.
WE KNOW YOU HAVE CHILDREN INSIDE AND PEOPLE WHO ARE NOT A PART OF THIS... WHO ARE NOT SAVIORS, WHO HAVE NOT ATTACKED OR KILLED ANYONE.
THOSE PEOPLE WILL BE SPARED, THEIR LIVES CAN CONTINUE AS THEY ARE.
AND WHAT OF THE OTHERS? ME... THE REST?
THE KILLERS WHO HAVE BEEN KEEPING YOU ALL SAFE.

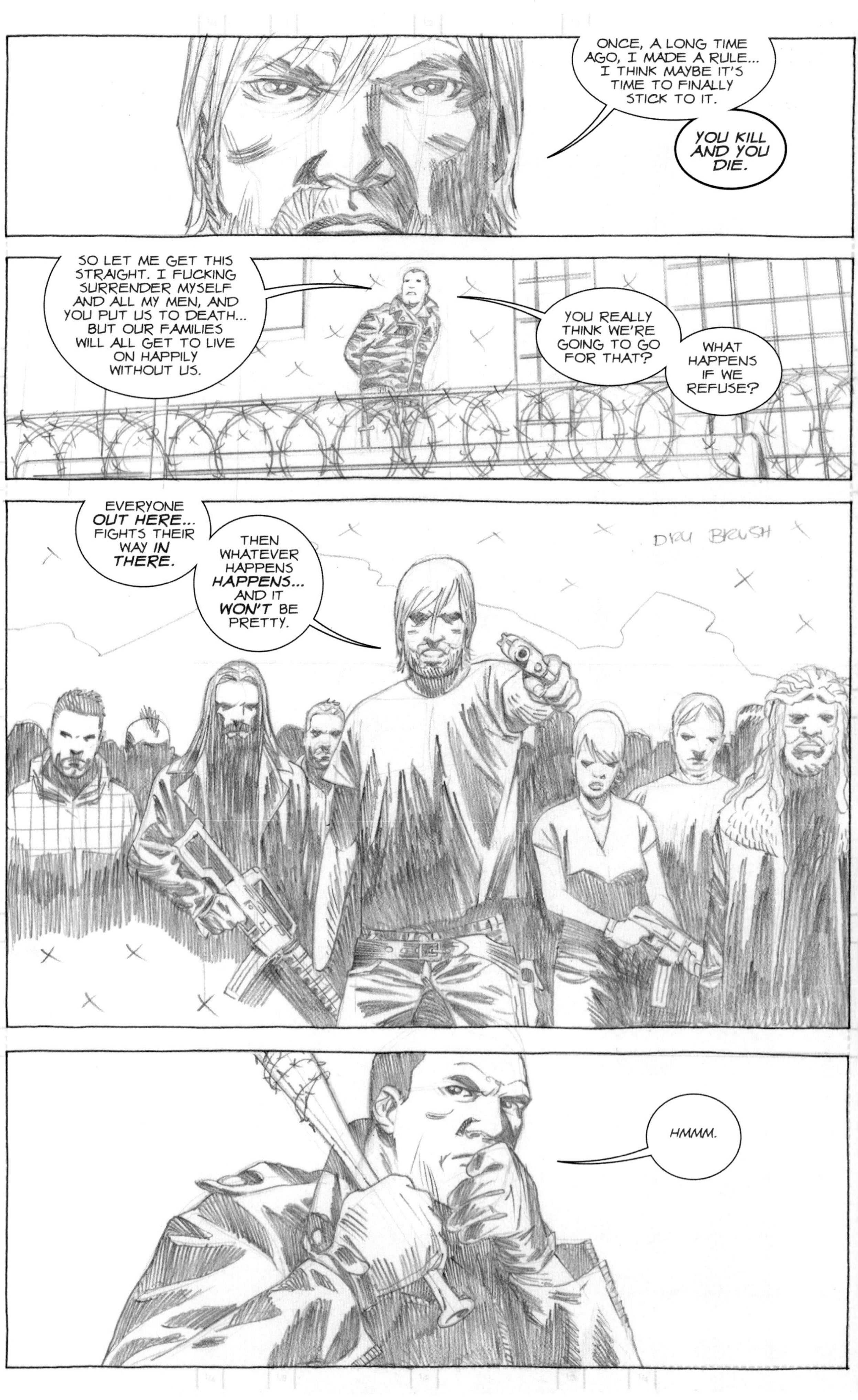
ONCE, A LONG TIME AGO, I MADE A RULE... I THINK MAYBE IT'S TIME TO FINALLY STICK TO IT.
YOU KILL AND YOU DIE.
SO LET ME GET THIS STRAIGHT. I FUCKING SURRENDER MYSELF AND ALL MY MEN, AND YOU PUT US TO DEATH... BUT OUR FAMILIES WILL ALL GET TO LIVE ON HAPPILY WITHOUT US.
YOU REALLY THINK WE'RE GOING TO GO FOR THAT?
WHAT HAPPENS IF WE REFUSE?
EVERYONE OUT HERE... FIGHTS THEIR WAY IN THERE.
THEN WHATEVER HAPPENS HAPPENS... AND IT WON'T BE PRETTY.
DRY BRUSH
HMMM.

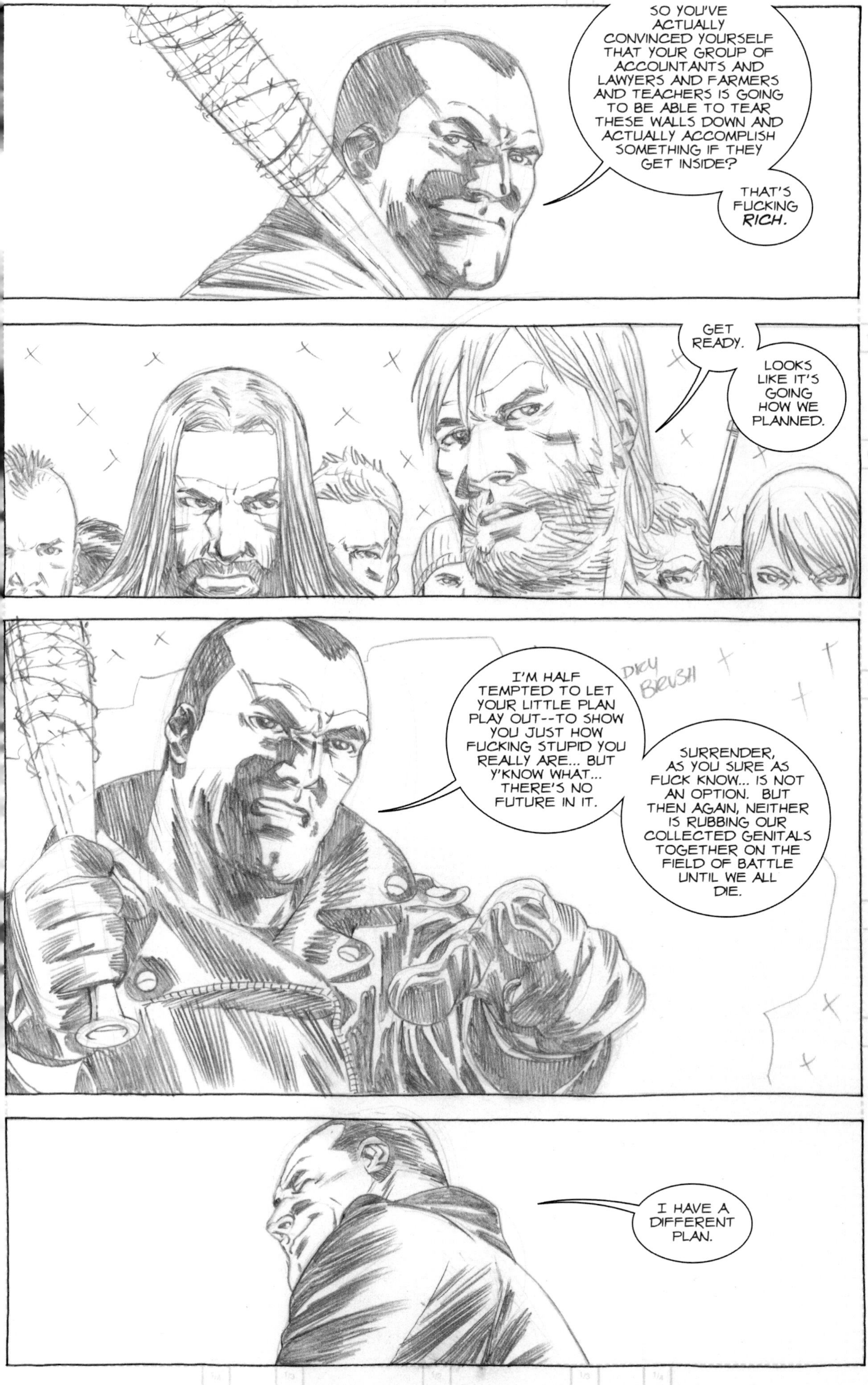
SO YOU'VE ACTUALLY CONVINCED YOURSELF THAT YOUR GROUP OF ACCOUNTANTS AND LAWYERS AND FARMERS AND TEACHERS IS GOING TO BE ABLE TO TEAR THESE WALLS DOWN AND ACTUALLY ACCOMPLISH SOMETHING IF THEY GET INSIDE?
THAT'S FUCKING *RICH.*
GET READY.
LOOKS LIKE IT'S GOING HOW WE PLANNED.
I'M HALF TEMPTED TO LET YOUR LITTLE PLAN PLAY OUT--TO SHOW YOU JUST HOW FUCKING STUPID YOU REALLY ARE... BUT Y'KNOW WHAT... THERE'S NO FUTURE IN IT.
DRY BRUSH
SURRENDER, AS YOU SURE AS FUCK KNOW... IS NOT AN OPTION. BUT THEN AGAIN, NEITHER IS RUBBING OUR COLLECTED GENITALS TOGETHER ON THE FIELD OF BATTLE UNTIL WE ALL DIE.
I HAVE A DIFFERENT PLAN.

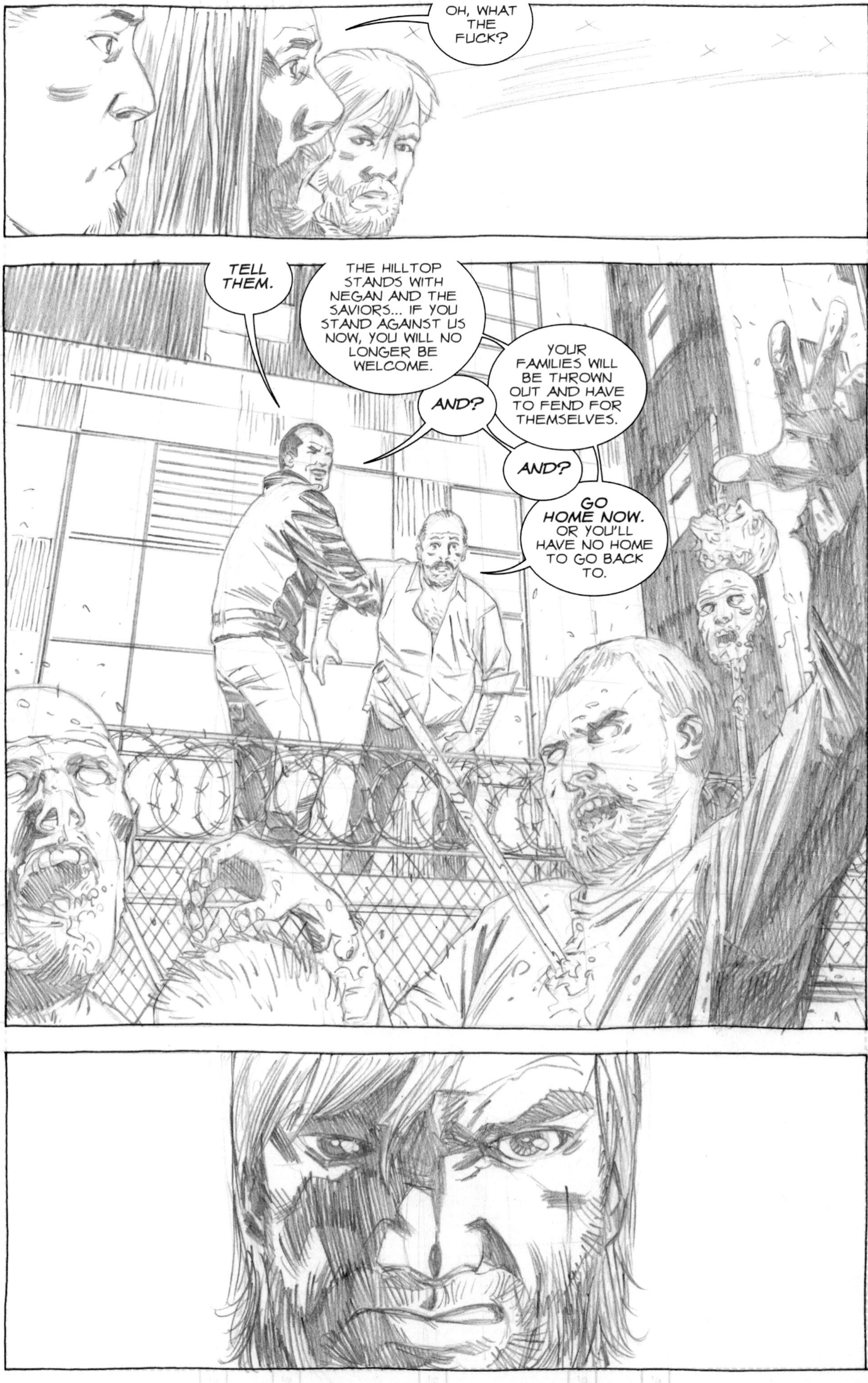
OH, WHAT THE FUCK?
TELL THEM.
THE HILLTOP STANDS WITH NEGAN AND THE SAVIORS... IF YOU STAND AGAINST US NOW, YOU WILL NO LONGER BE WELCOME.
AND?
YOUR FAMILIES WILL BE THROWN OUT AND HAVE TO FEND FOR THEMSELVES.
AND?
GO HOME NOW. OR YOU'LL HAVE NO HOME TO GO BACK TO.

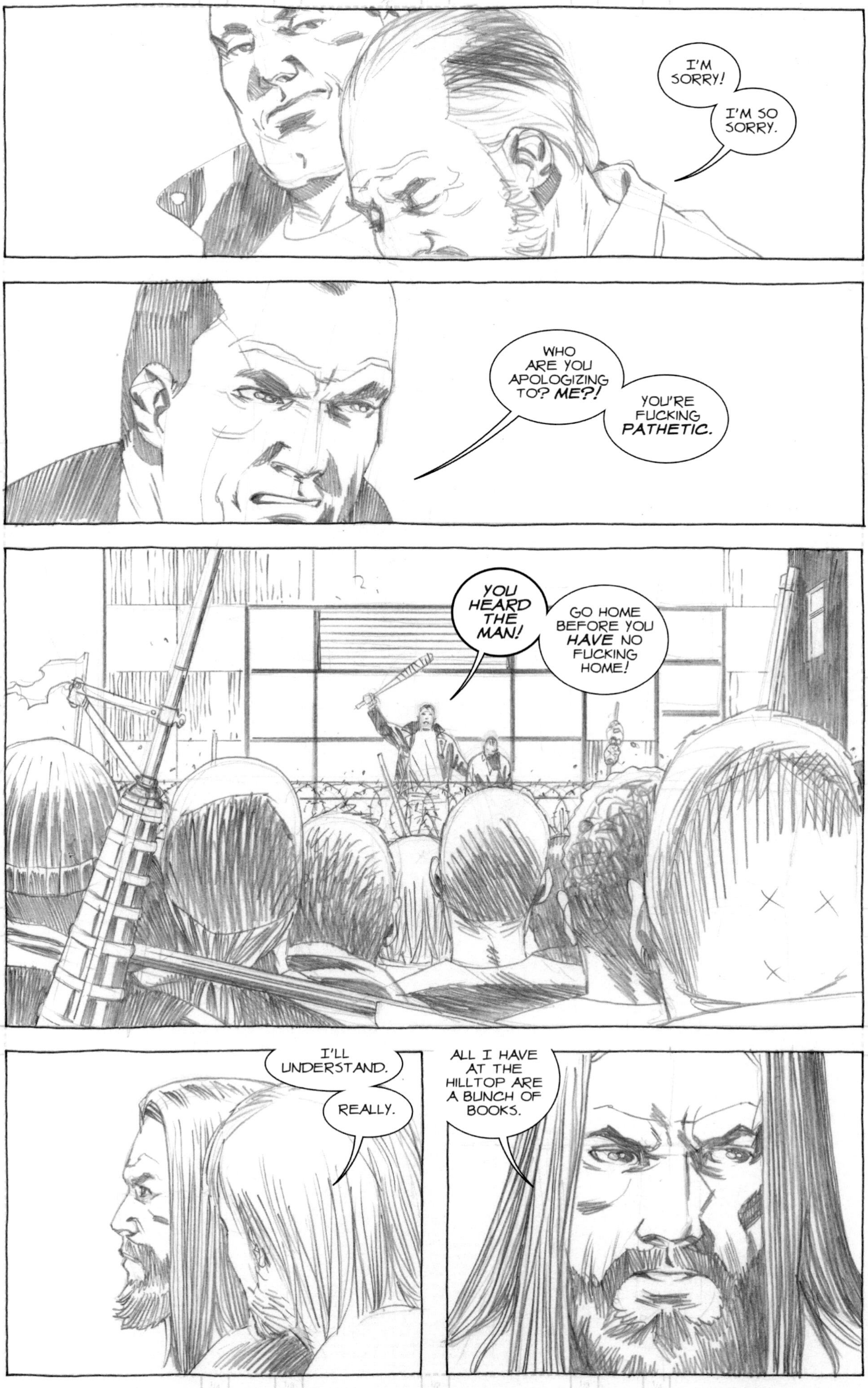
I'M SORRY!
I'M SO SORRY.
WHO ARE YOU APOLOGIZING TO? ME?!
YOU'RE FUCKING PATHETIC.
YOU HEARD THE MAN!
GO HOME BEFORE YOU HAVE NO FUCKING HOME!
I'LL UNDERSTAND.
REALLY.
ALL I HAVE AT THE HILLTOP ARE A BUNCH OF BOOKS.

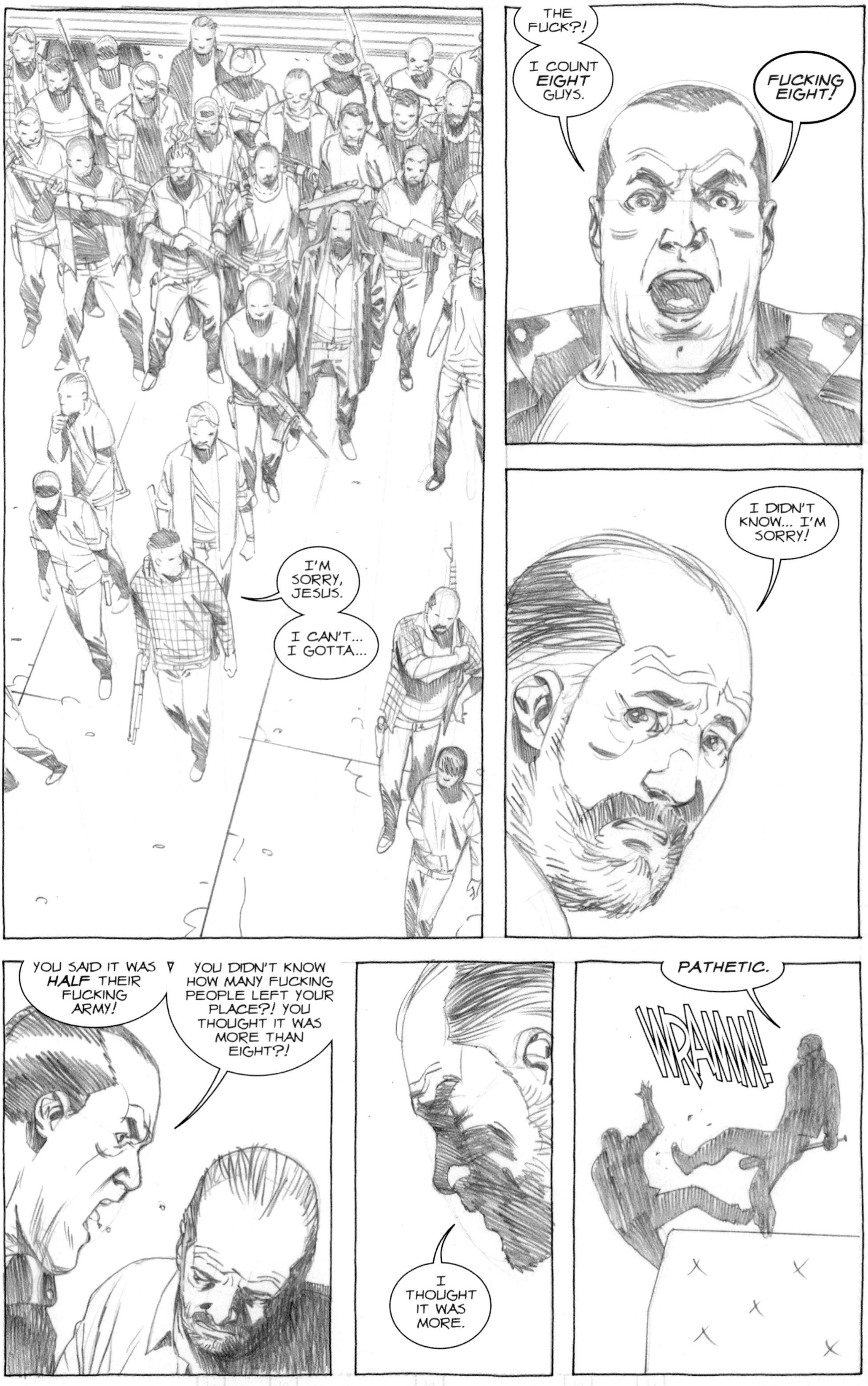
I'M SORRY, JESUS.
I CAN'T... I GOTTA...
THE FUCK?!
I COUNT EIGHT GUYS.
FUCKING EIGHT!
I DIDN'T KNOW... I'M SORRY!
YOU SAID IT WAS HALF THEIR FUCKING ARMY!
YOU DIDN'T KNOW HOW MANY FUCKING PEOPLE LEFT YOUR PLACE?! YOU THOUGHT IT WAS MORE THAN EIGHT?!
I THOUGHT IT WAS MORE.
PATHETIC.
WRANNN!

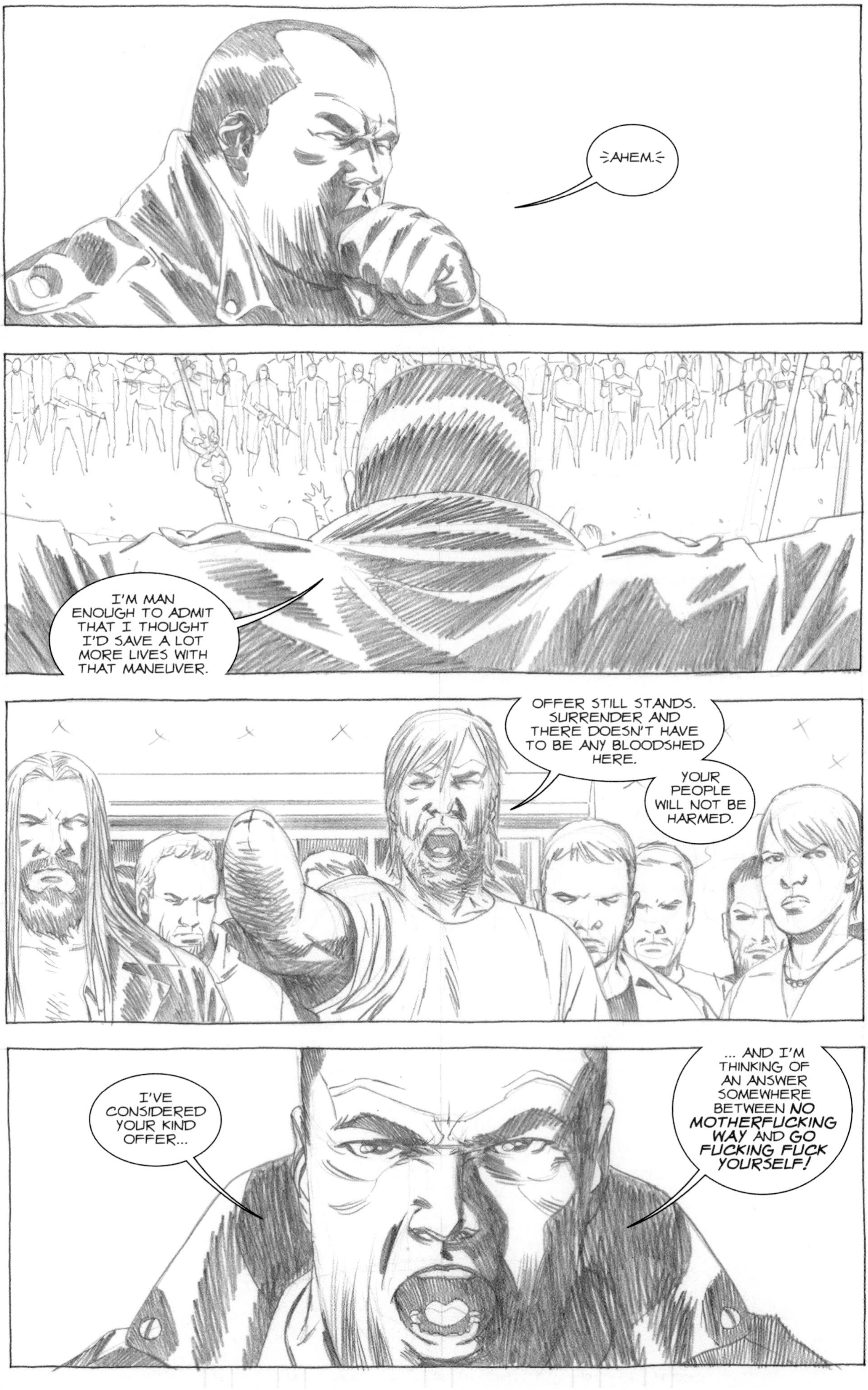
AHEM.
I'M MAN ENOUGH TO ADMIT THAT I THOUGHT I'D SAVE A LOT MORE LIVES WITH THAT MANEUVER.
OFFER STILL STANDS. SURRENDER AND THERE DOESN'T HAVE TO BE ANY BLOODSHED HERE.
YOUR PEOPLE WILL NOT BE HARMED.
I'VE CONSIDERED YOUR KIND OFFER...
... AND I'M THINKING OF AN ANSWER SOMEWHERE BETWEEN NO MOTHERFUCKING WAY AND GO FUCKING FUCK YOURSELF!

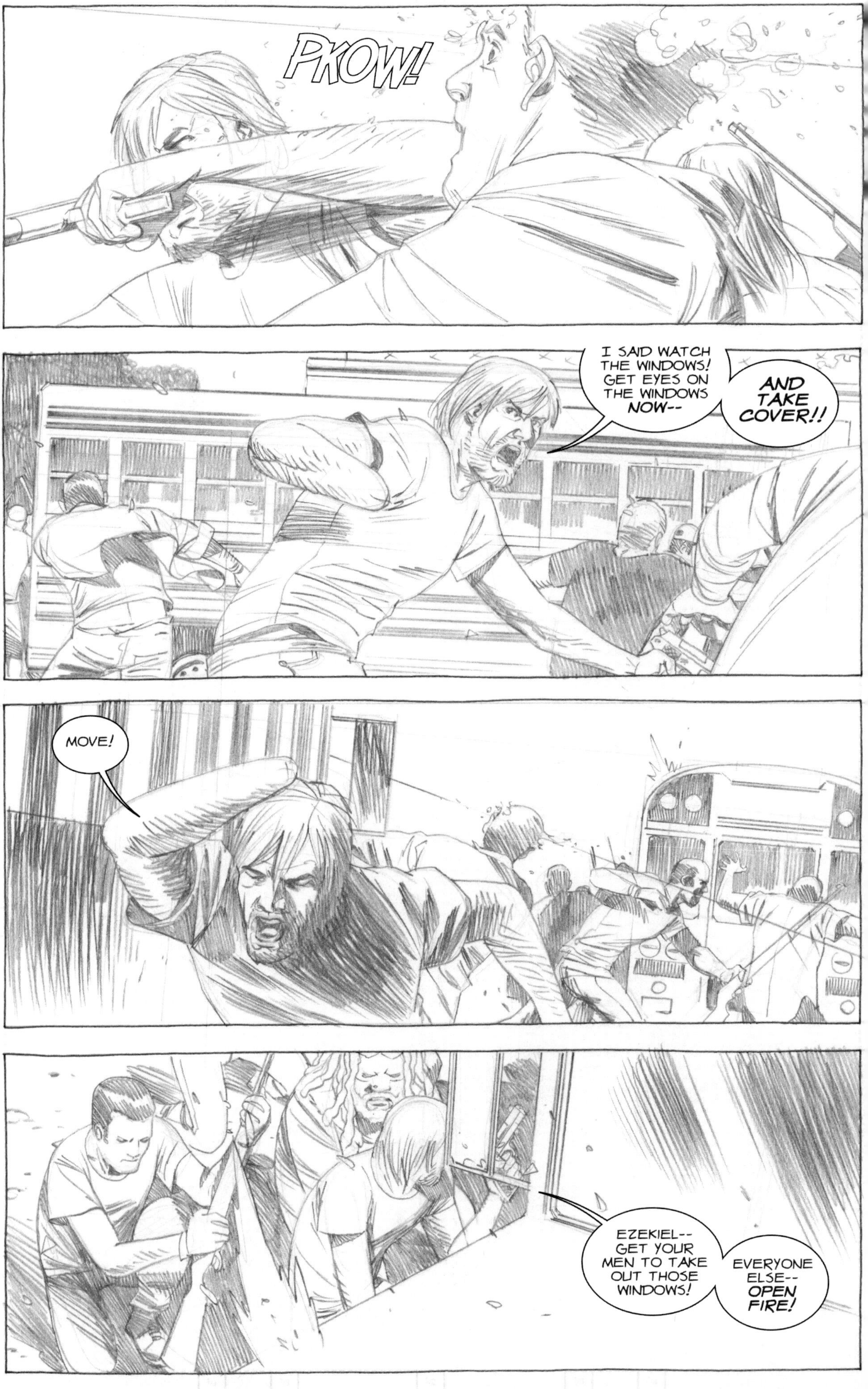
PKOW!
I SAID WATCH THE WINDOWS! GET EYES ON THE WINDOWS NOW--
AND TAKE COVER!!
MOVE!
EZEKIEL-- GET YOUR MEN TO TAKE OUT THOSE WINDOWS!
EVERYONE ELSE-- OPEN FIRE!

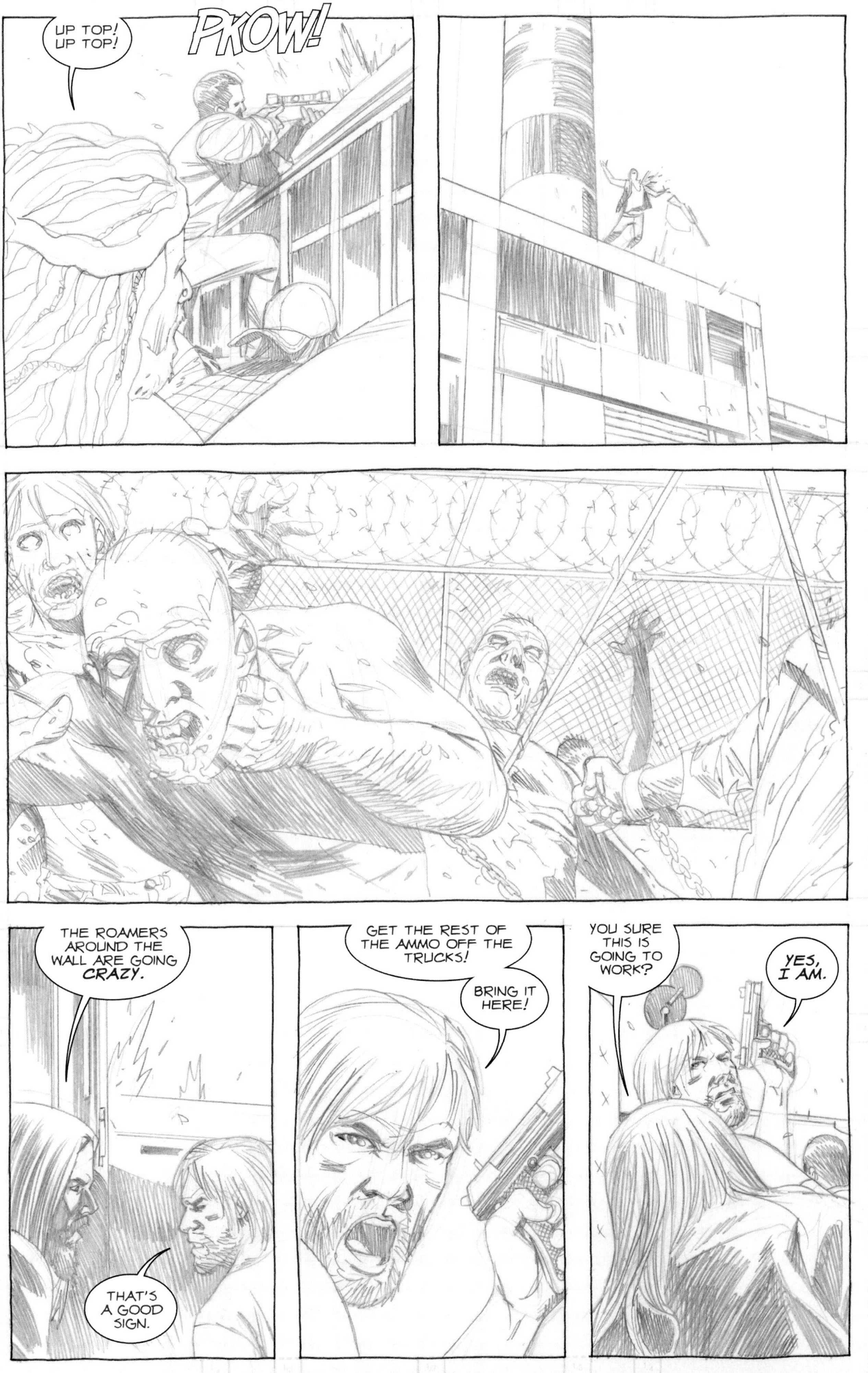
UP TOP! UP TOP!
PKOW!
THE ROAMERS AROUND THE WALL ARE GOING CRAZY.
THAT'S A GOOD SIGN.
GET THE REST OF THE AMMO OFF THE TRUCKS!
BRING IT HERE!
YOU SURE THIS IS GOING TO WORK?
YES, I AM.

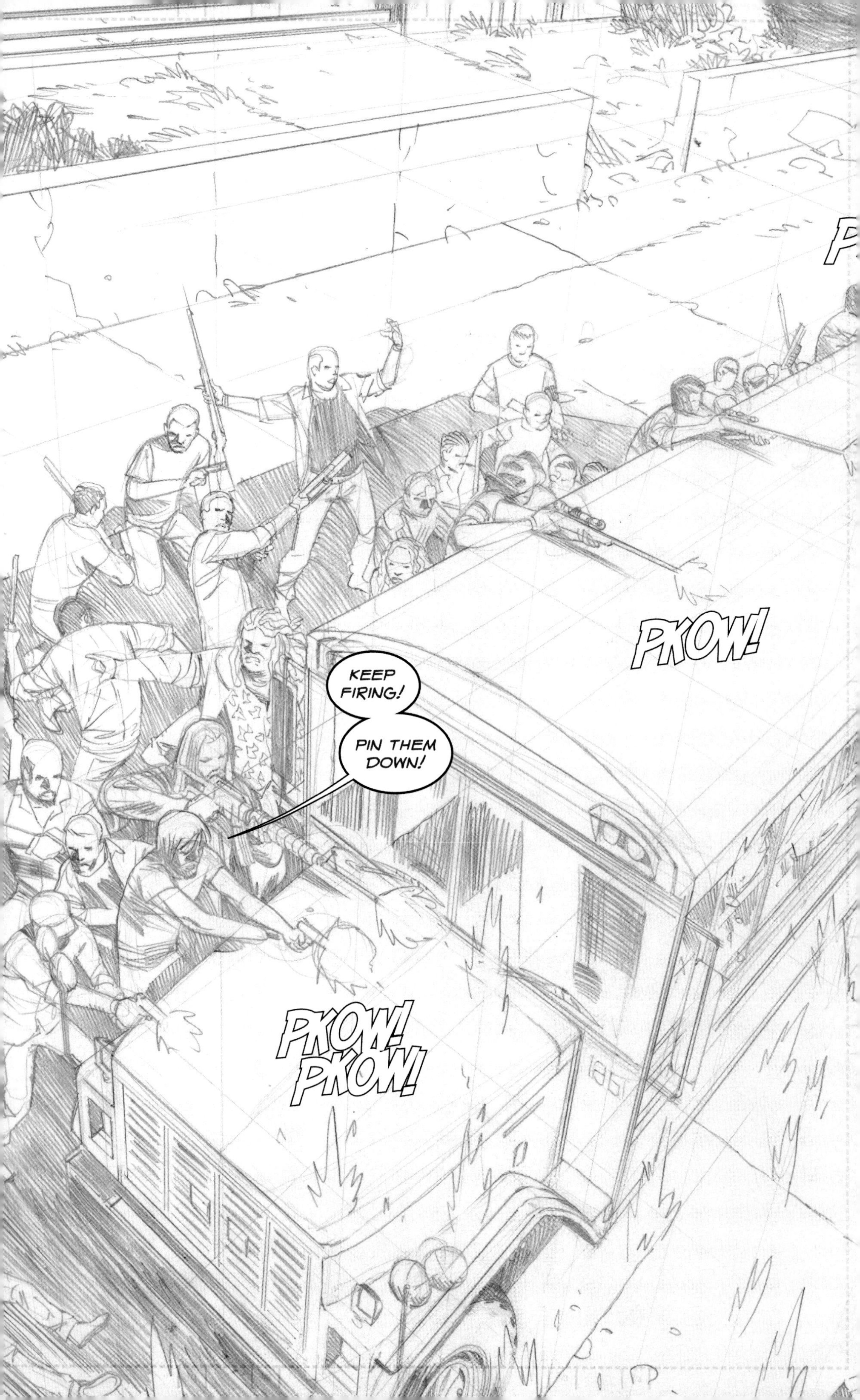

PKOW!
KEEP FIRING!
PIN THEM DOWN!
PKOW! PKOW!

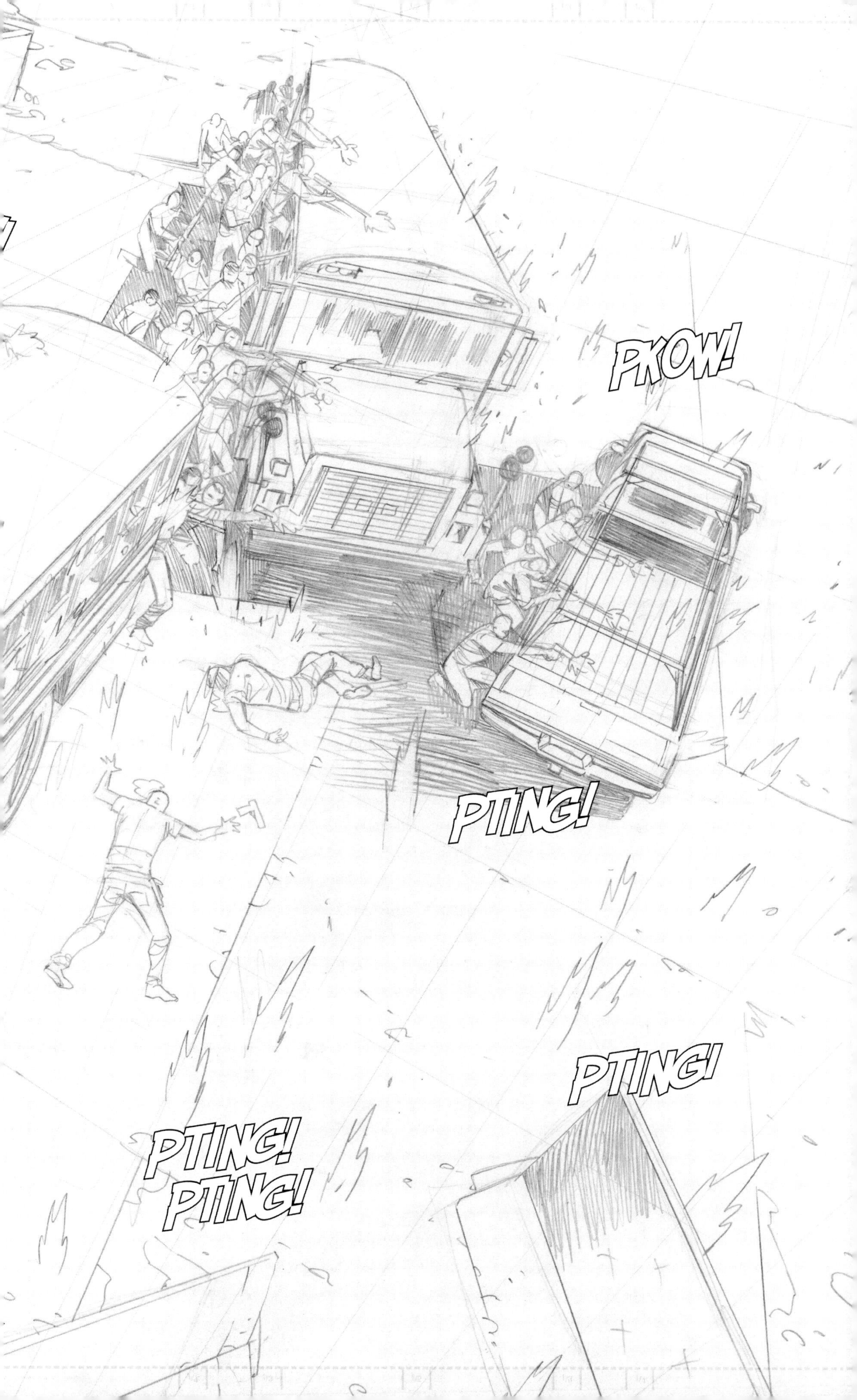
PKOW!
PTING!
PTING!
PTING!
PTING!

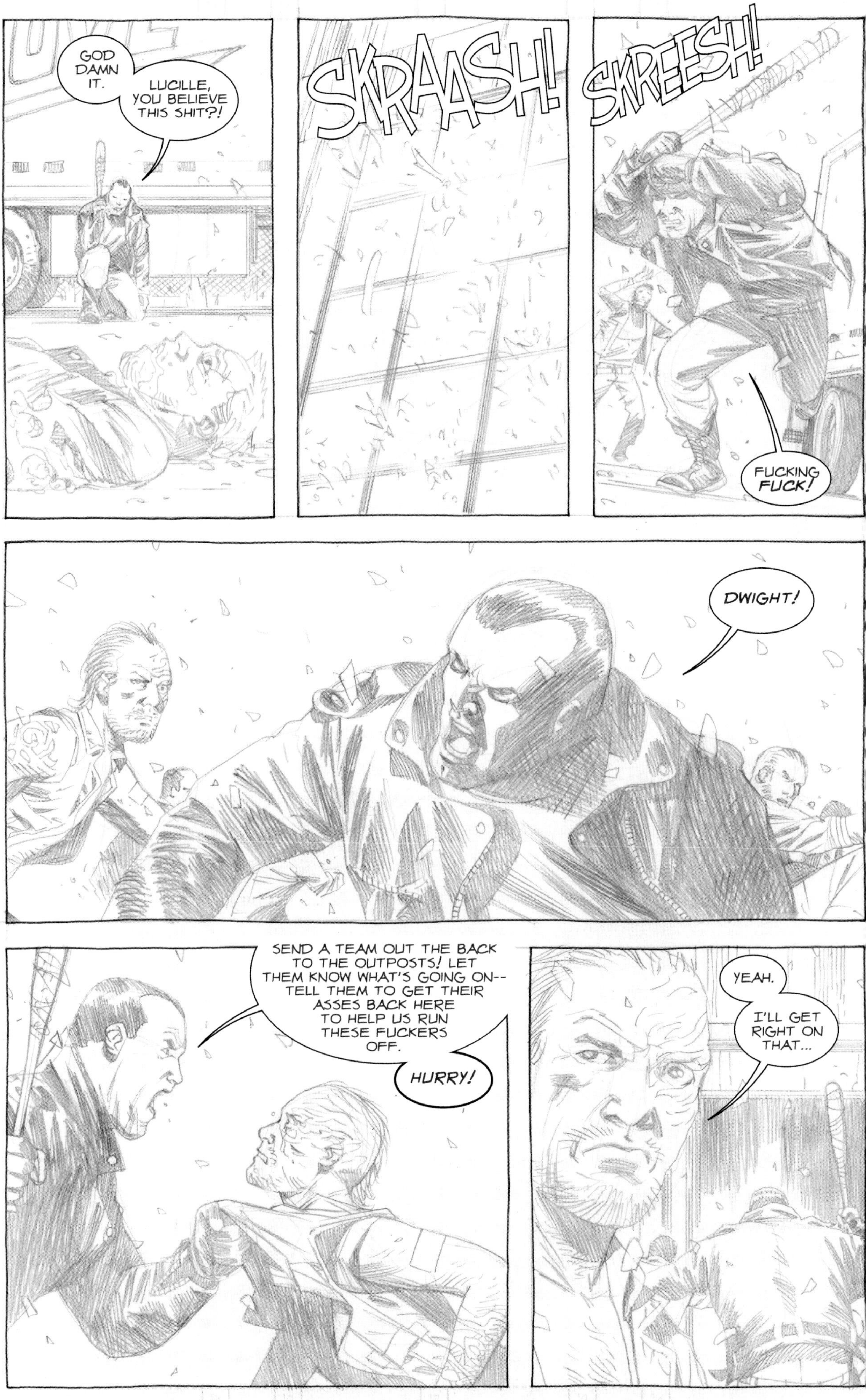

GOD DAMN IT.
LUCILLE, YOU BELIEVE THIS SHIT?!
SKRAASH!
SKREESH!
FUCKING FUCK!
DWIGHT!
SEND A TEAM OUT THE BACK TO THE OUTPOSTS! LET THEM KNOW WHAT'S GOING ON-- TELL THEM TO GET THEIR ASSES BACK HERE TO HELP US RUN THESE FUCKERS OFF.
HURRY!
YEAH.
I'LL GET RIGHT ON THAT...

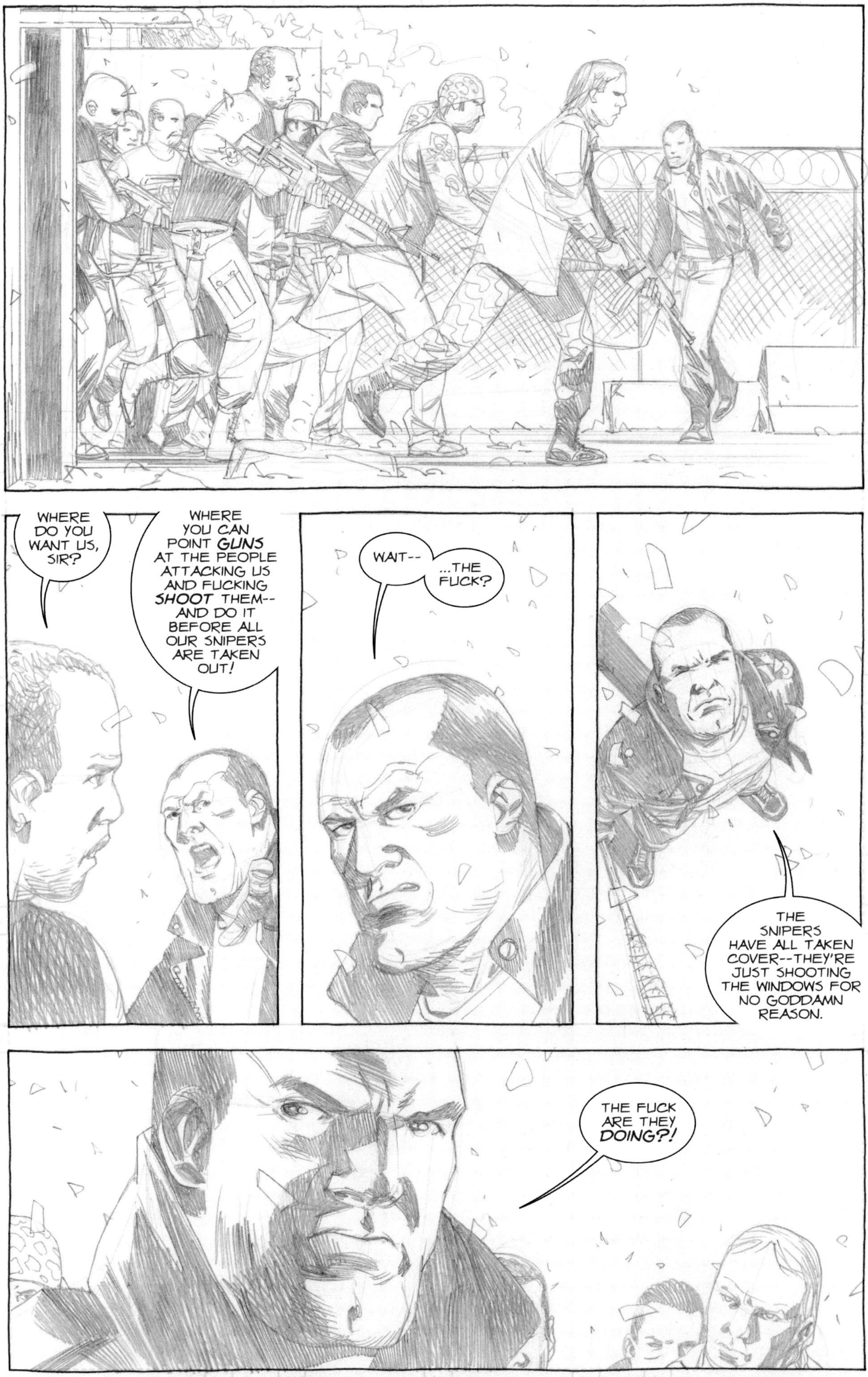
WHERE DO YOU WANT US, SIR?
WHERE YOU CAN POINT GUNS AT THE PEOPLE ATTACKING US AND FUCKING SHOOT THEM-- AND DO IT BEFORE ALL OUR SNIPERS ARE TAKEN OUT!
WAIT--
...THE FUCK?
THE SNIPERS HAVE ALL TAKEN COVER--THEY'RE JUST SHOOTING THE WINDOWS FOR NO GODDAMN REASON.
THE FUCK ARE THEY DOING?!

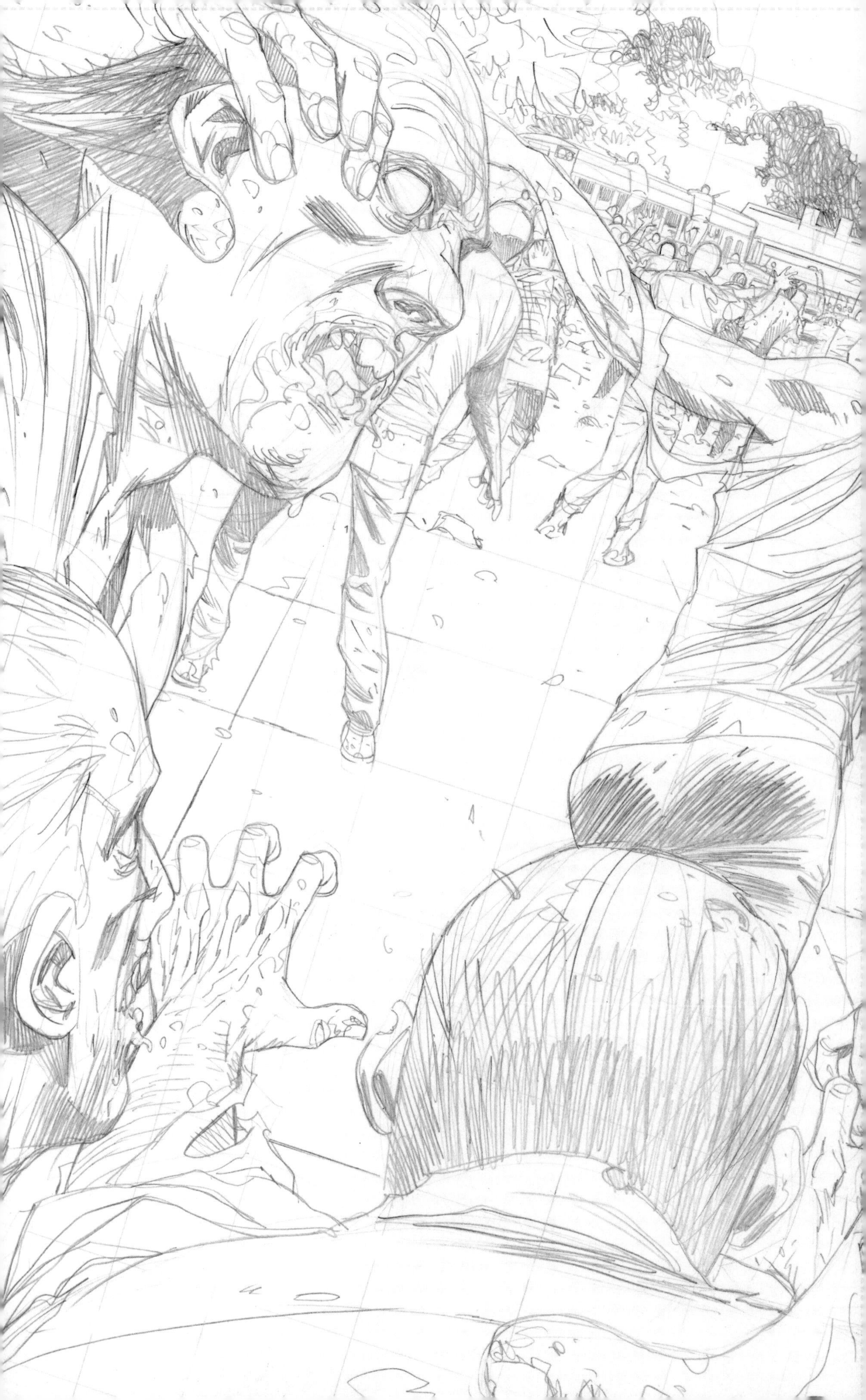

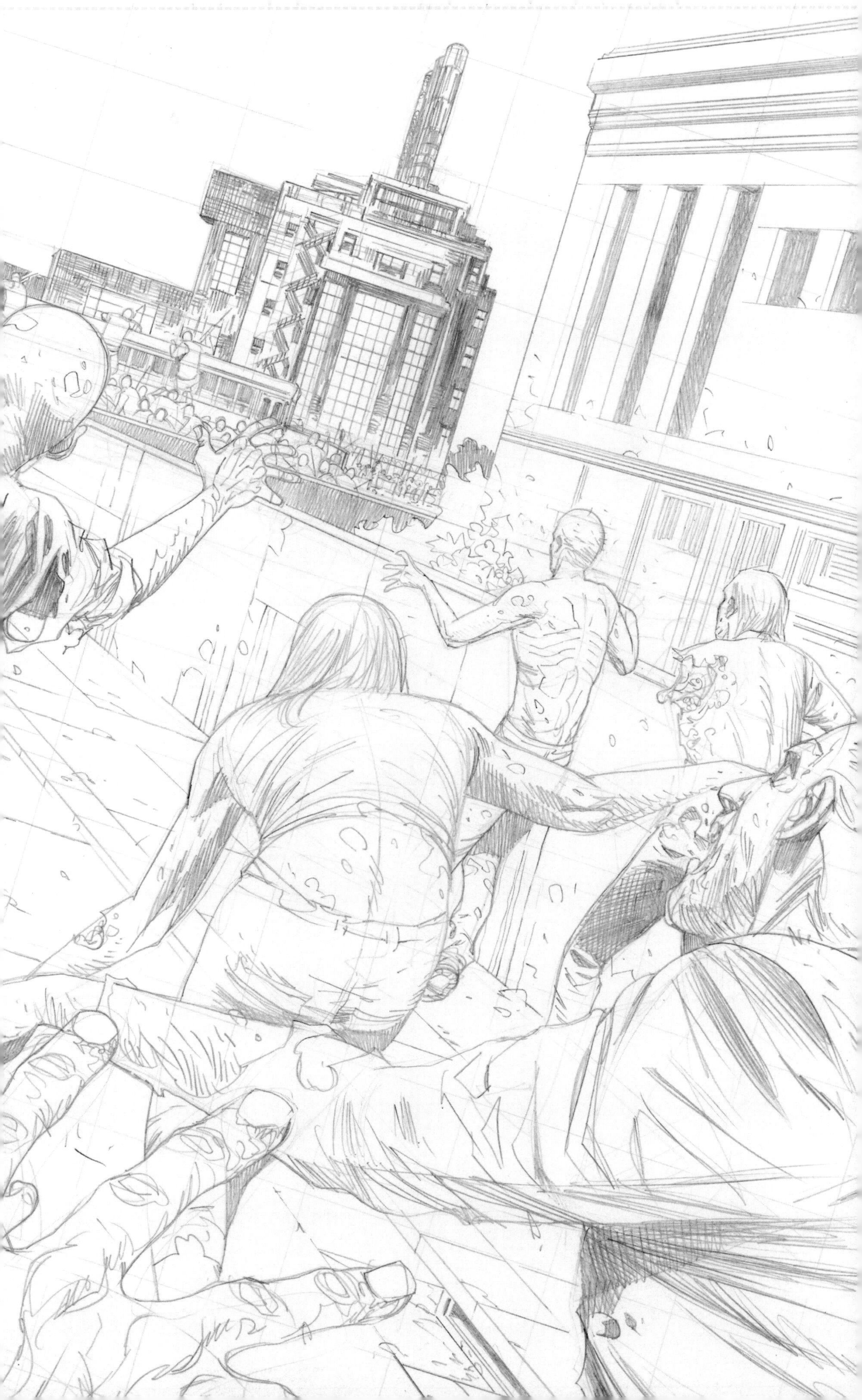

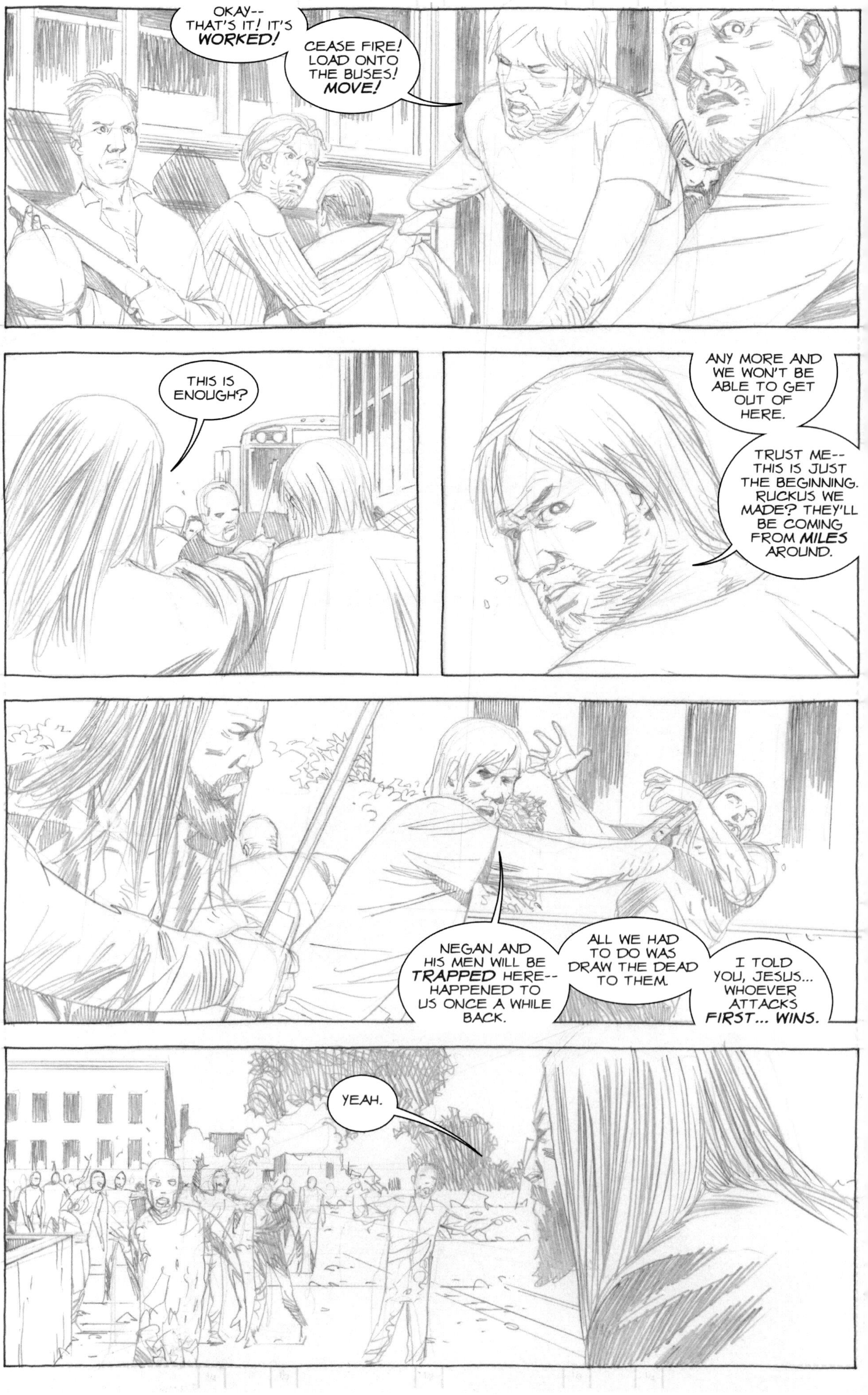
OKAY-- THAT'S IT! IT'S WORKED!
CEASE FIRE! LOAD ONTO THE BUSES! MOVE!
THIS IS ENOUGH?
ANY MORE AND WE WON'T BE ABLE TO GET OUT OF HERE.
TRUST ME-- THIS IS JUST THE BEGINNING. RUCKUS WE MADE? THEY'LL BE COMING FROM MILES AROUND.
NEGAN AND HIS MEN WILL BE TRAPPED HERE-- HAPPENED TO US ONCE A WHILE BACK.
ALL WE HAD TO DO WAS DRAW THE DEAD TO THEM.
I TOLD YOU, JESUS... WHOEVER ATTACKS FIRST... WINS.
YEAH.

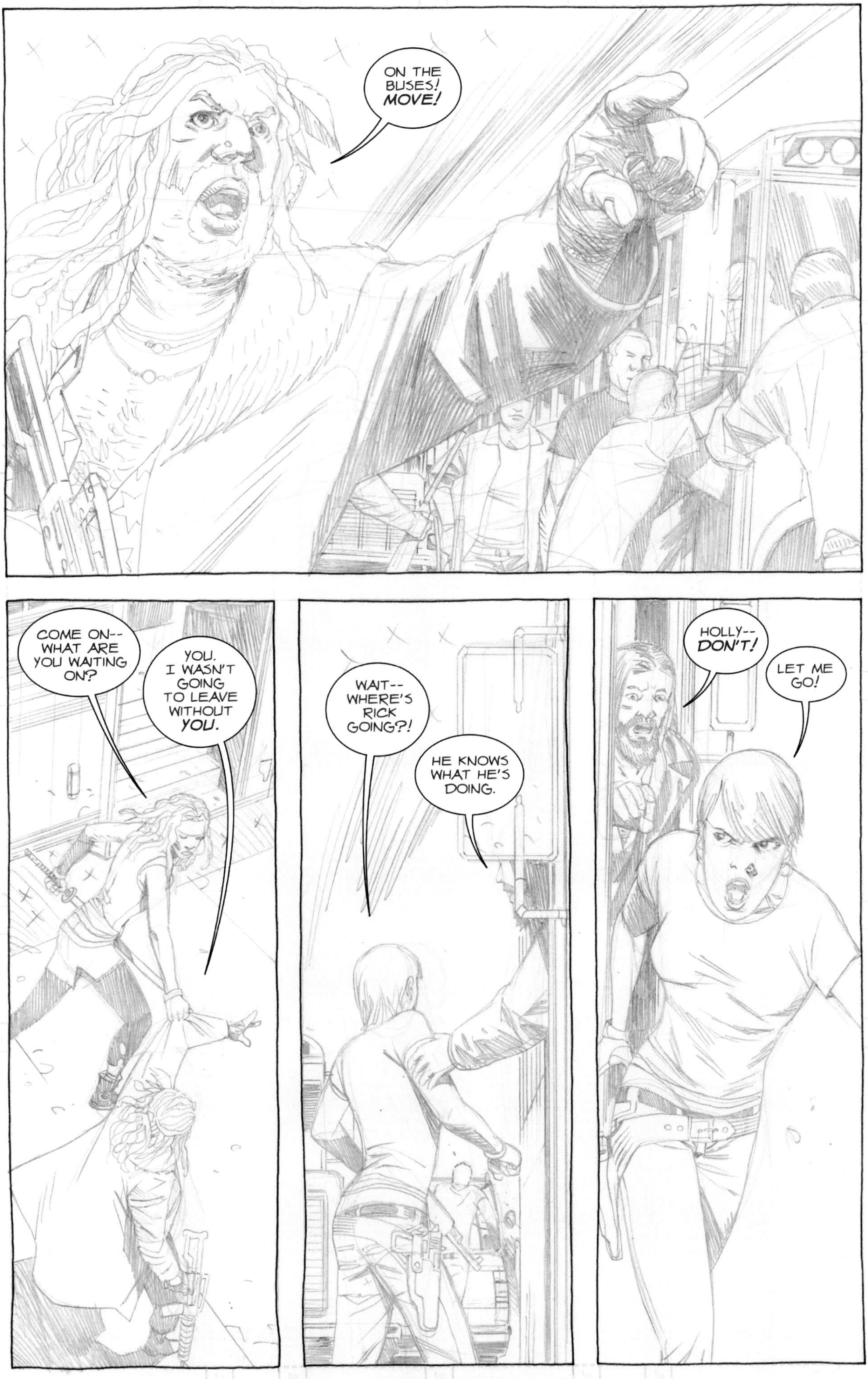
ON THE BUSES! MOVE!
COME ON-- WHAT ARE YOU WAITING ON?
YOU. I WASN'T GOING TO LEAVE WITHOUT YOU.
WAIT-- WHERE'S RICK GOING?!
HE KNOWS WHAT HE'S DOING.
HOLLY-- DON'T!
LET ME GO!

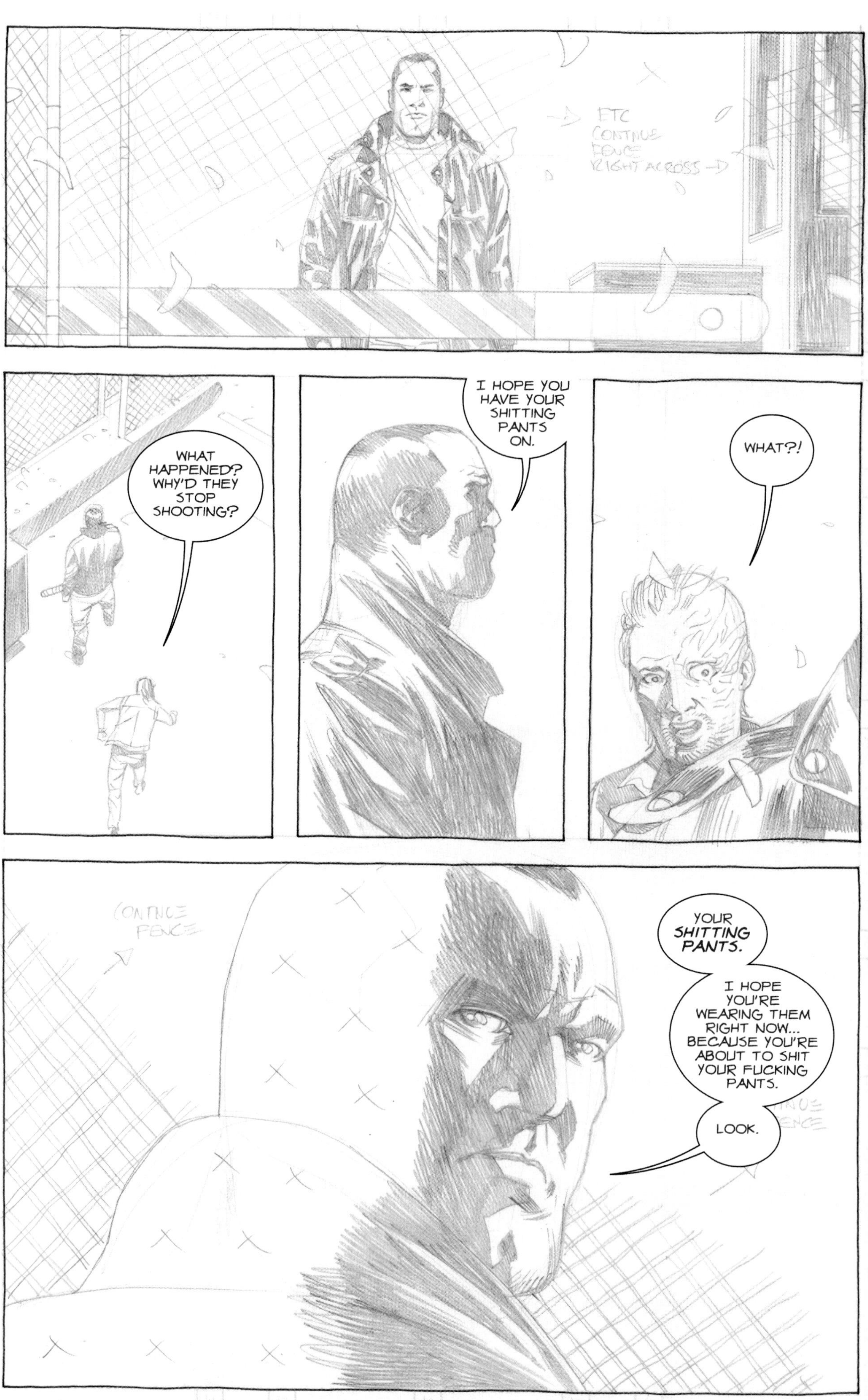
WHAT HAPPENED? WHY'D THEY STOP SHOOTING?
I HOPE YOU HAVE YOUR SHITTING PANTS ON.
WHAT?!
YOUR *SHITTING PANTS.*
I HOPE YOU'RE WEARING THEM RIGHT NOW... BECAUSE YOU'RE ABOUT TO SHIT YOUR FUCKING PANTS.
LOOK.

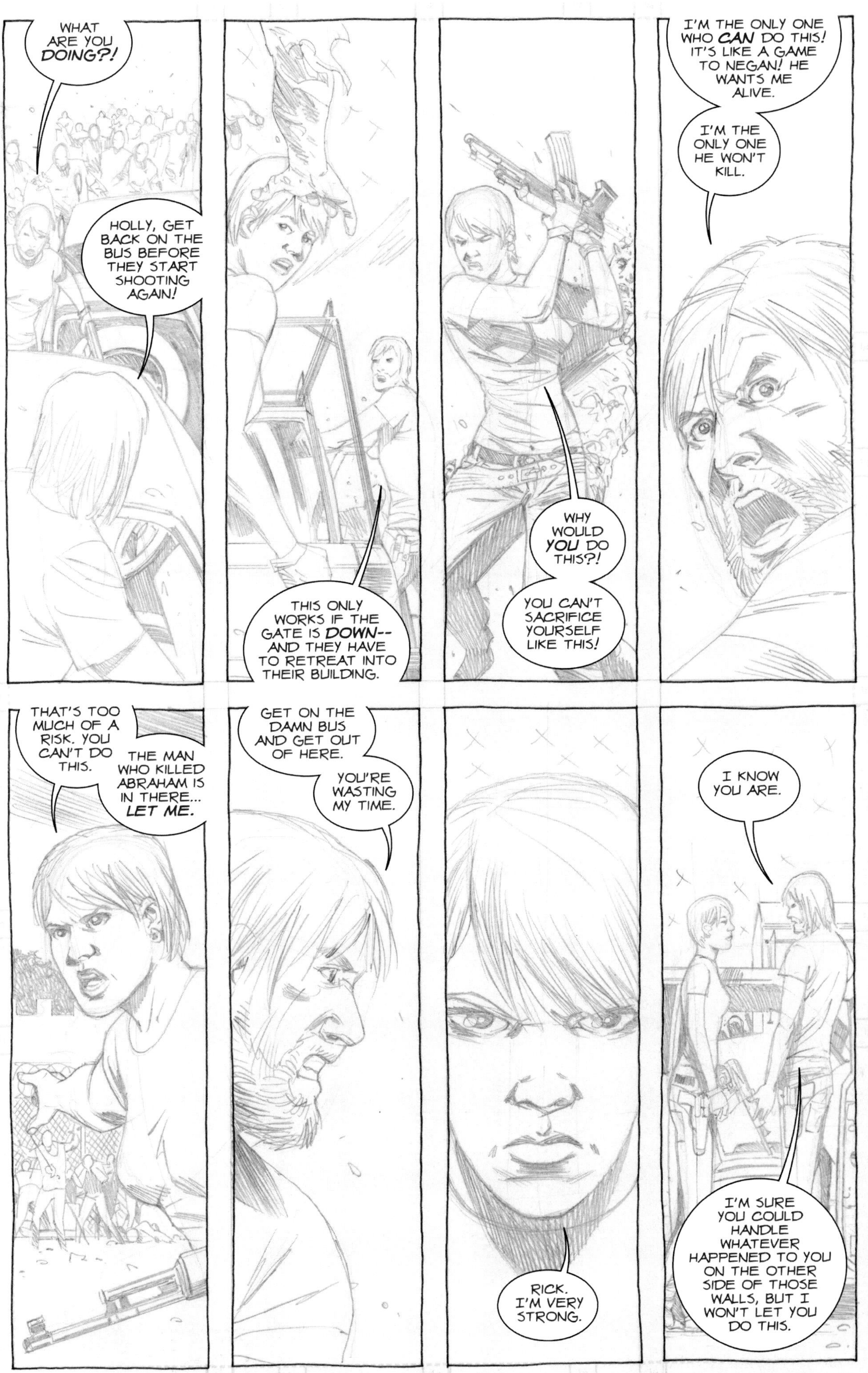
WHAT ARE YOU DOING?!
HOLLY, GET BACK ON THE BUS BEFORE THEY START SHOOTING AGAIN!
THIS ONLY WORKS IF THE GATE IS DOWN-- AND THEY HAVE TO RETREAT INTO THEIR BUILDING.
WHY WOULD YOU DO THIS?!
YOU CAN'T SACRIFICE YOURSELF LIKE THIS!
I'M THE ONLY ONE WHO CAN DO THIS! IT'S LIKE A GAME TO NEGAN! HE WANTS ME ALIVE.
I'M THE ONLY ONE HE WON'T KILL.
THAT'S TOO MUCH OF A RISK. YOU CAN'T DO THIS.
THE MAN WHO KILLED ABRAHAM IS IN THERE... LET ME.
GET ON THE DAMN BUS AND GET OUT OF HERE.
YOU'RE WASTING MY TIME.
RICK. I'M VERY STRONG.
I KNOW YOU ARE.
I'M SURE YOU COULD HANDLE WHATEVER HAPPENED TO YOU ON THE OTHER SIDE OF THOSE WALLS, BUT I WON'T LET YOU DO THIS.

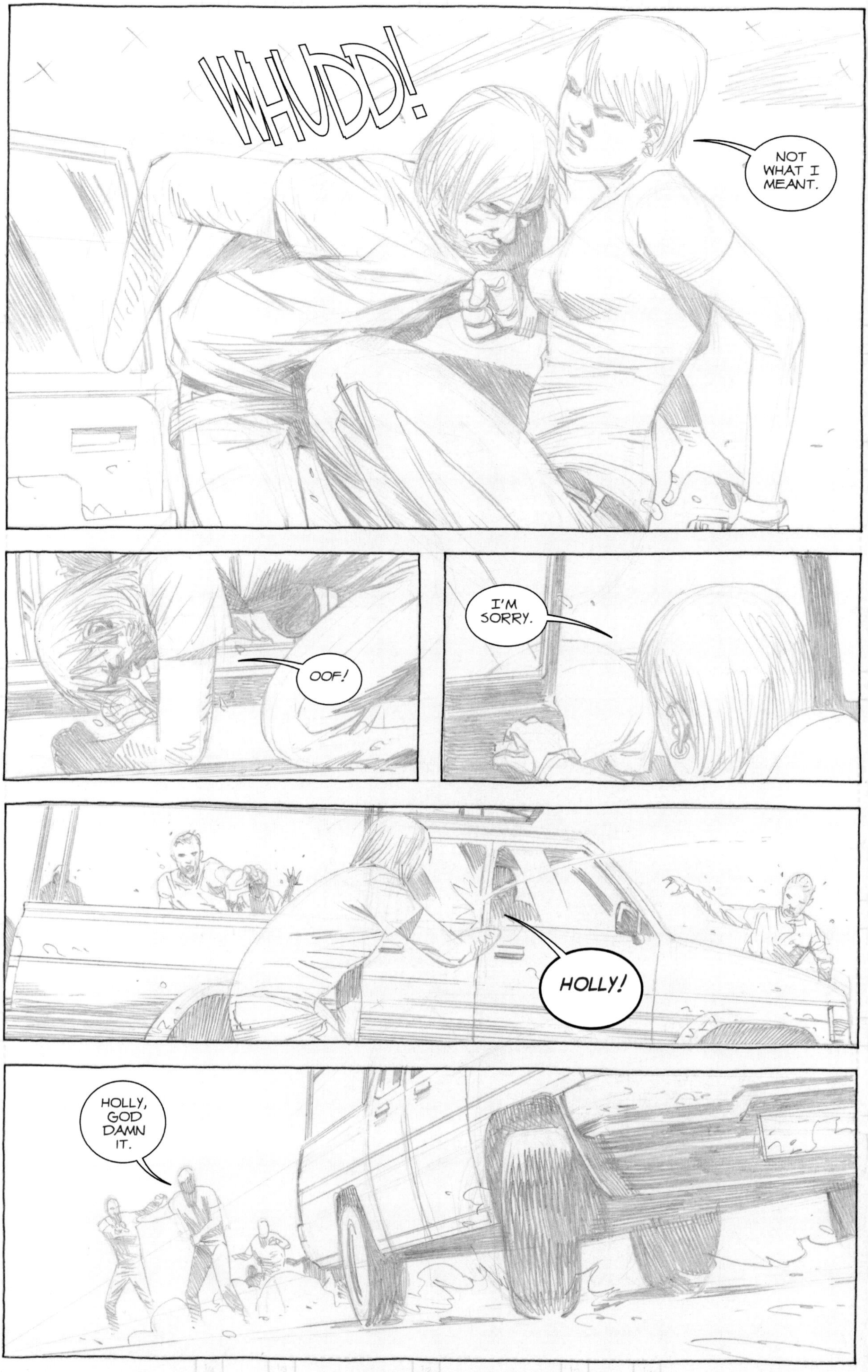
WHUDD!
NOT WHAT I MEANT.
OOF!
I'M SORRY.
HOLLY!
HOLLY, GOD DAMN IT.

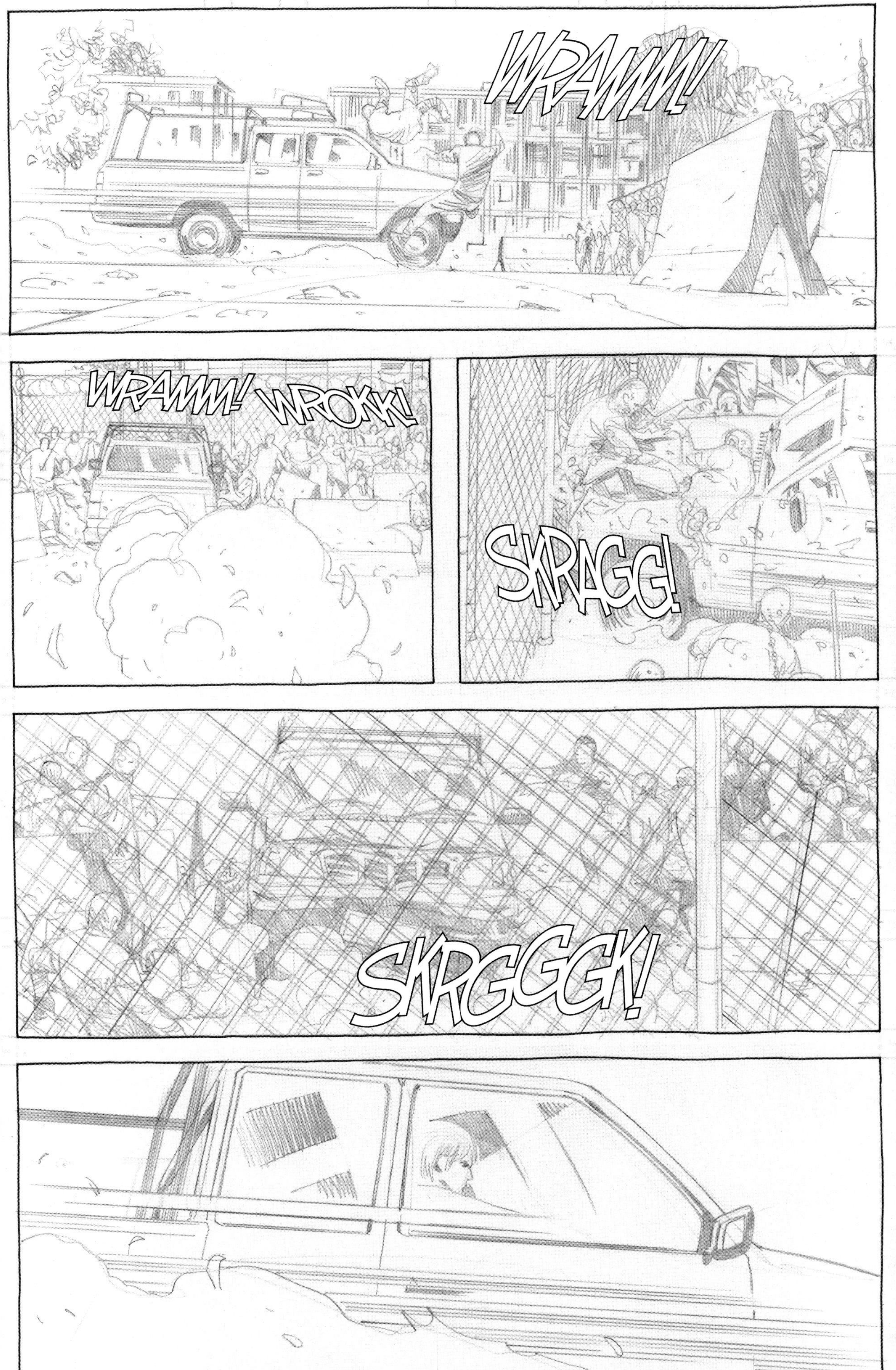
WRAMMM!
WRAMMM!
WROKK!
SKRAGG!
SKRGGGK!

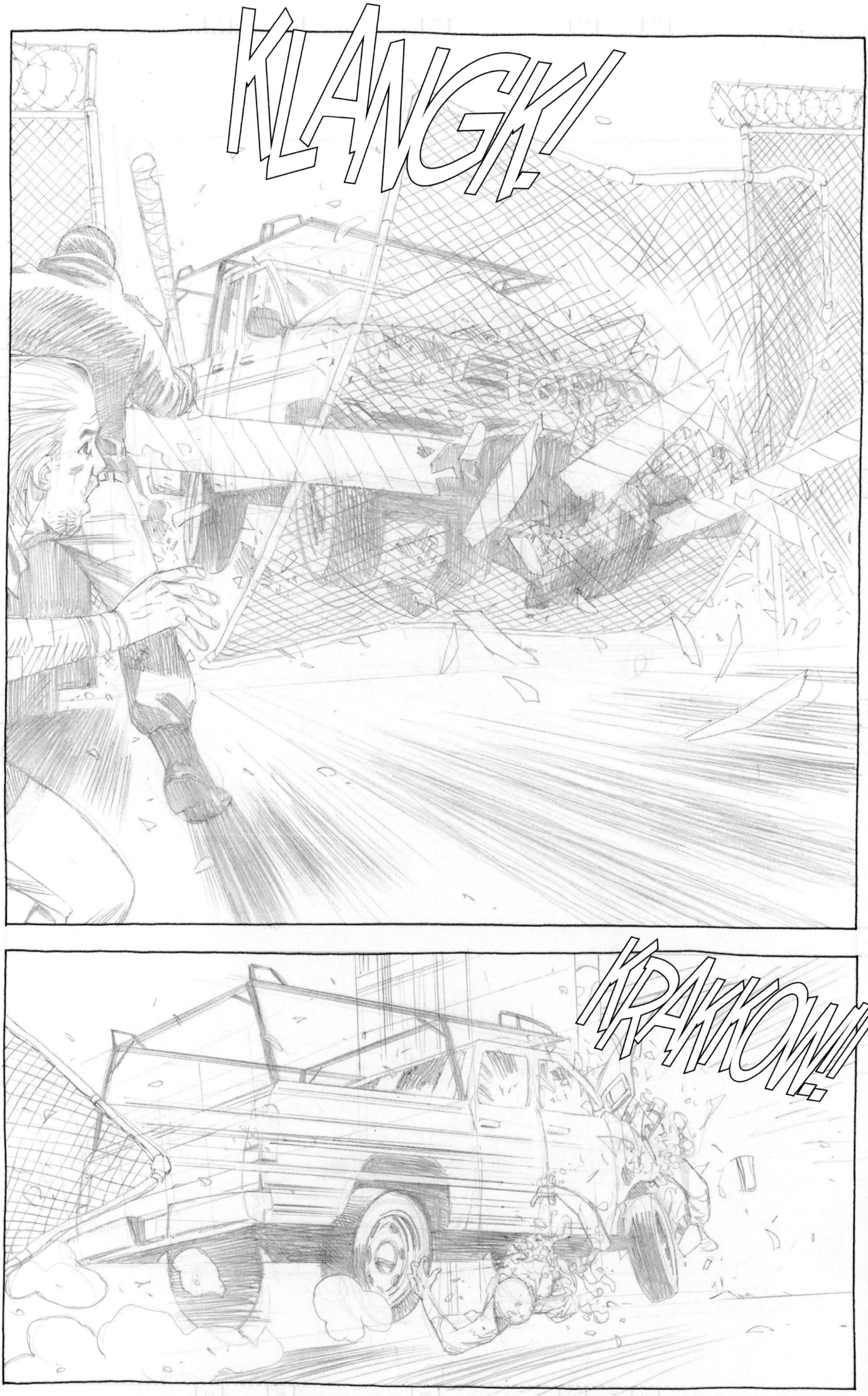
KLANGK!
KRAKKOW!!!

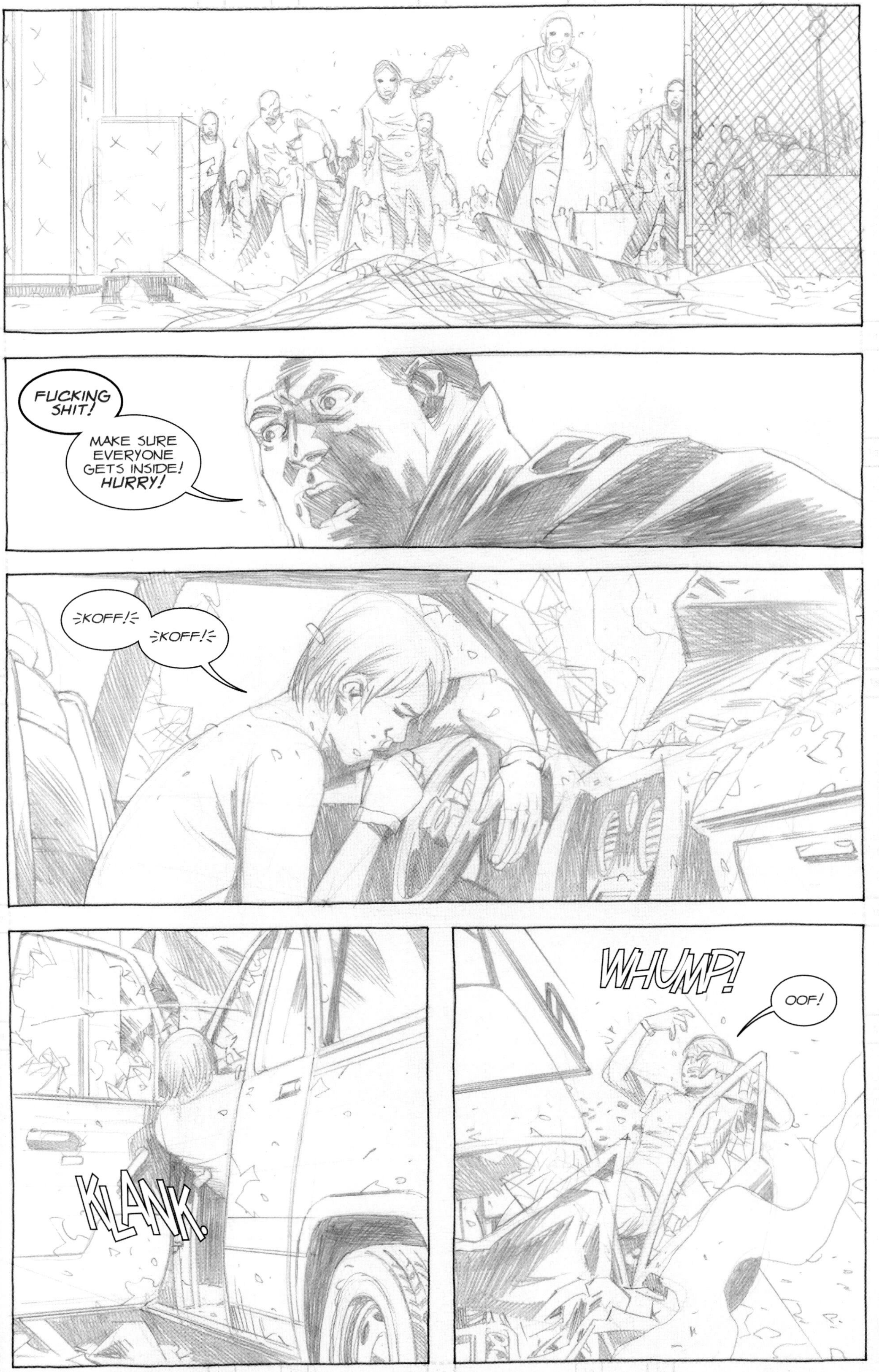
FUCKING SHIT!
MAKE SURE EVERYONE GETS INSIDE! HURRY!
KOFF!
KOFF!
KLANK.
WHUMP!
OOF!

GAH!
WRAMM!
YOU THINK I'D LET YOU GET OFF THAT FUCKING EASY, DID YOU?
NO FUCKING WAY, SISTER.

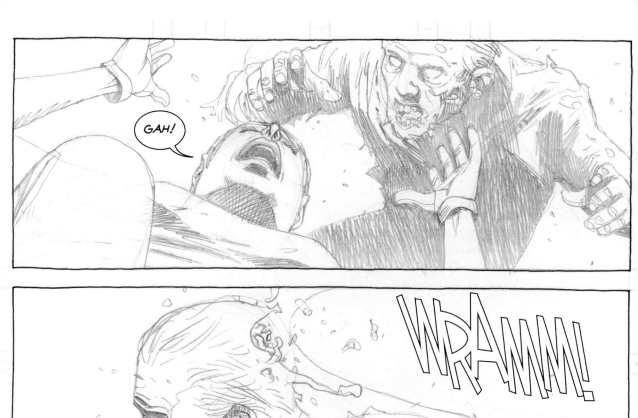

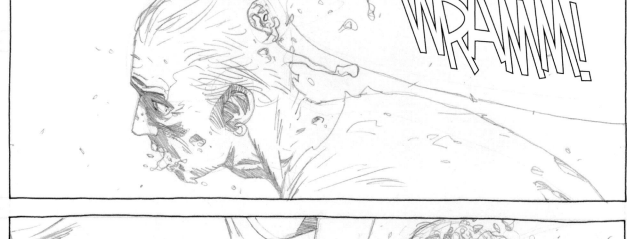

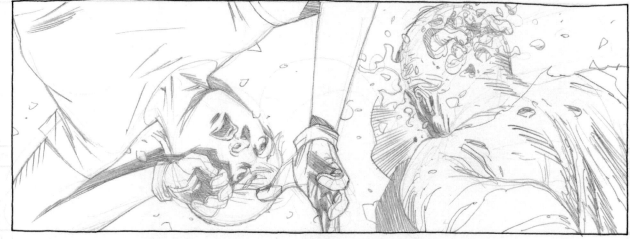

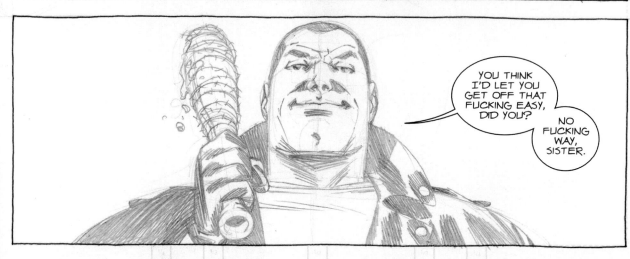

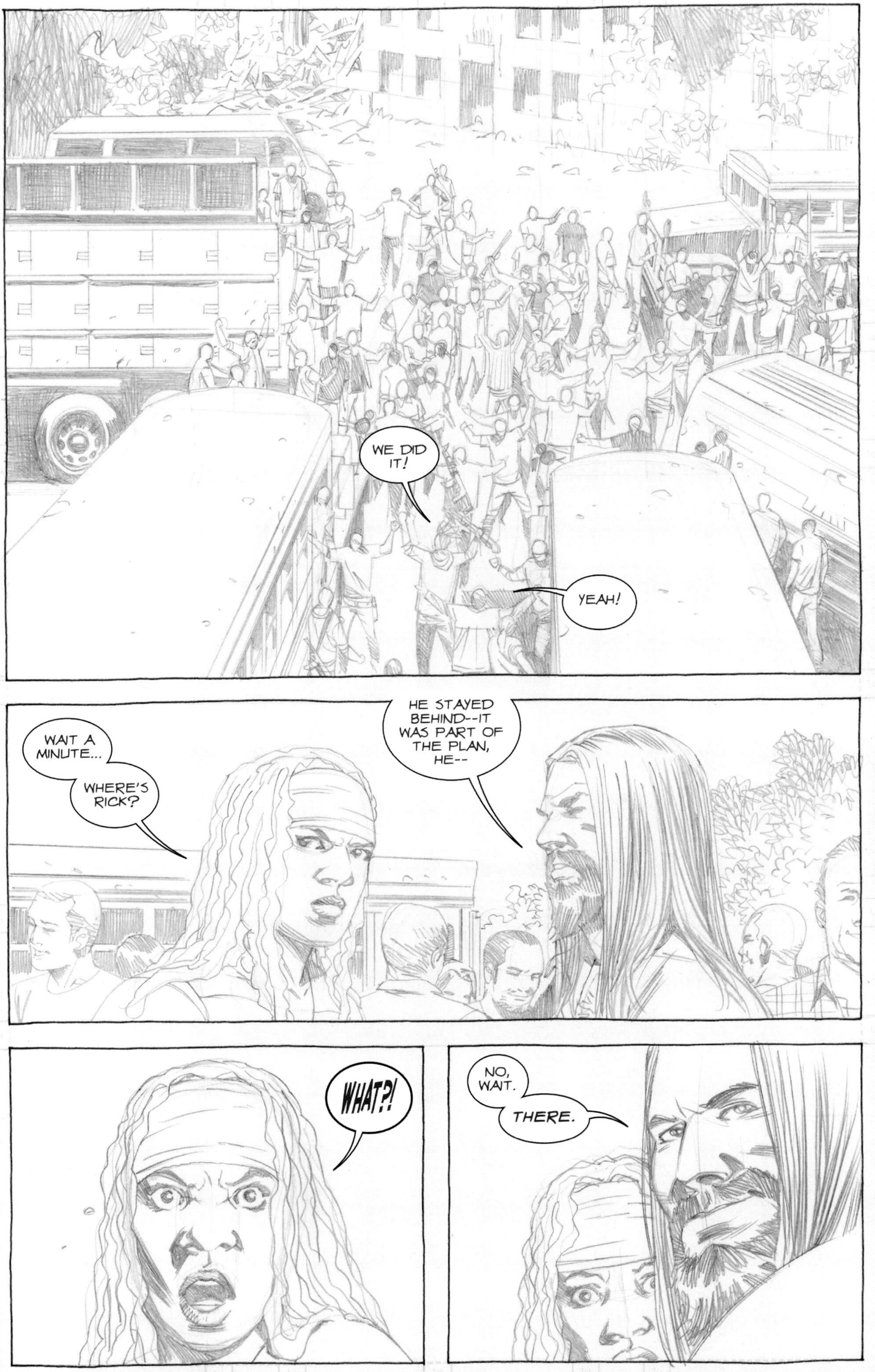
WE DID IT!
YEAH!
WAIT A MINUTE...
WHERE'S RICK?
HE STAYED BEHIND--IT WAS PART OF THE PLAN, HE--
WHAT?!
NO, WAIT.
THERE.

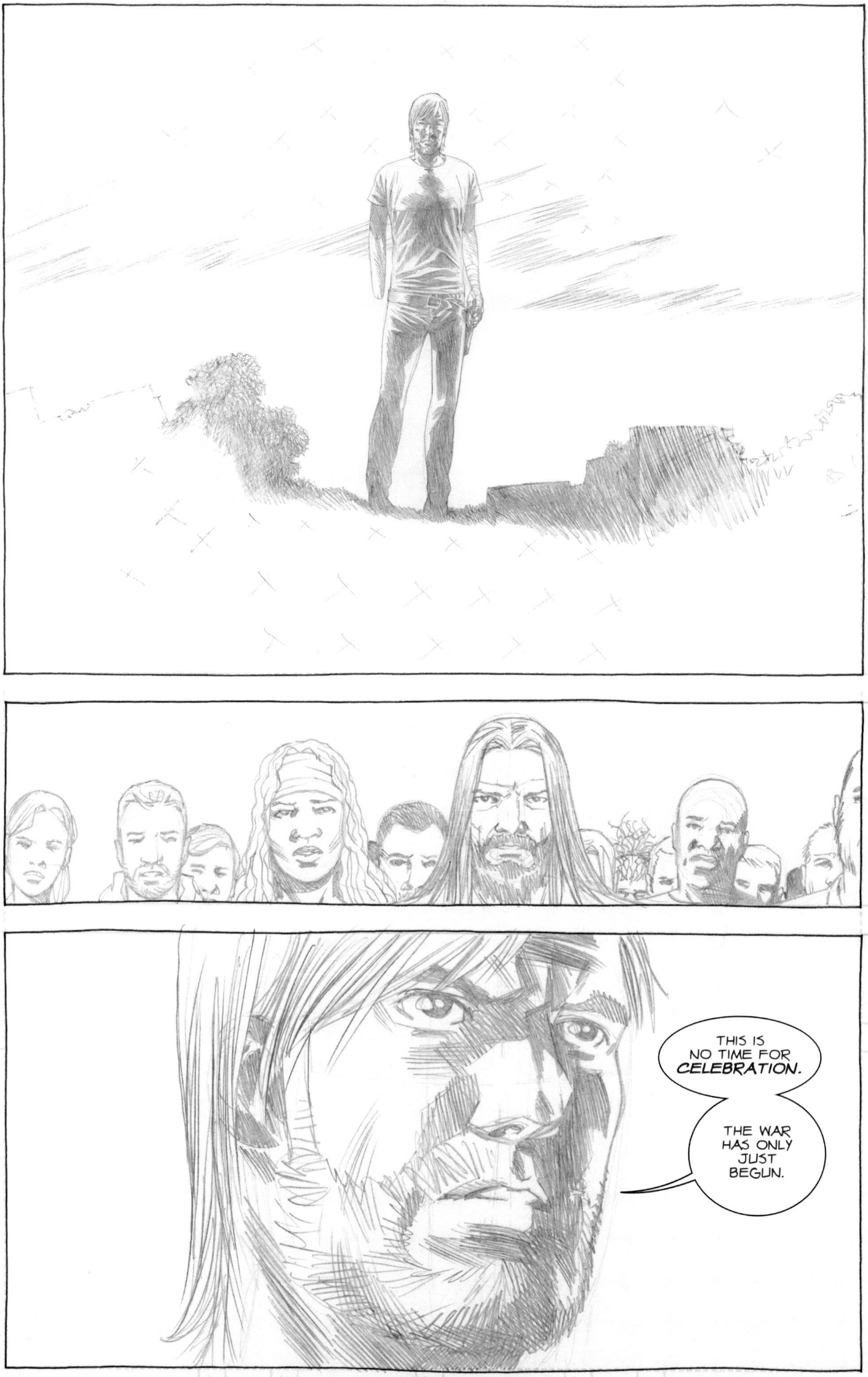
THIS IS NO TIME FOR CELEBRATION.
THE WAR HAS ONLY JUST BEGUN.

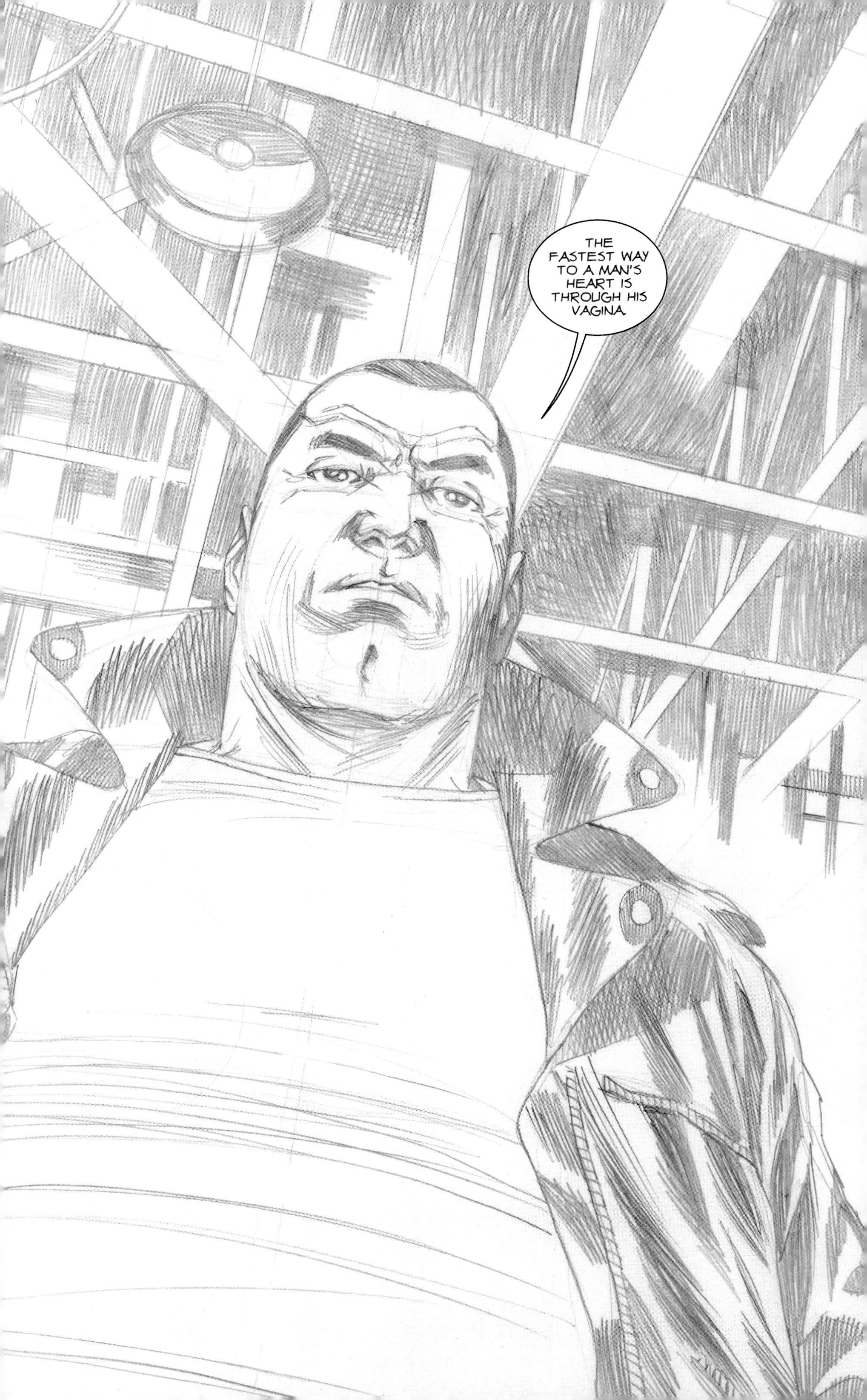
THE FASTEST WAY TO A MAN'S HEART IS THROUGH HIS VAGINA.

A LOT OF PEOPLE SAY IT'S THE STOMACH. THAT'S THE SAYING... BUT THAT'S FUCKING *STUPID*.

MEN LIKE TO EAT, SURE. BUT DO *ALL* MEN PLACE THAT MUCH IMPORTANCE ON THEIR NEXT MEAL?

YOU COOK A MEAN MEATLOAF AND SO YOU'VE FUCKING *GOT* THEM WRAPPED AROUND YOUR LITTLE FUCKING FINGER?

NO GODDAMN WAY.

MEN LOVE TO *FUCK*.

ALL MEN.

EVERY GODDAMN ONE OF THEM. YOUNG, OLD, FAT, THIN, SMART, DUMB, ALIVE, DEAD... *ALL MEN*.

AFTER A WHILE, A CERTAIN KIND OF MAN... MEN LIKE RICK GRIMES, THEY FIND ONE VAGINA THEY *REALLY* ENJOY BEING INSIDE. THAT BECOMES *THEIR* VAGINA.

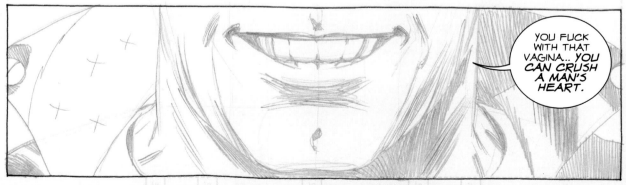

YOU FUCK WITH THAT VAGINA... *YOU CAN CRUSH A MAN'S HEART*.

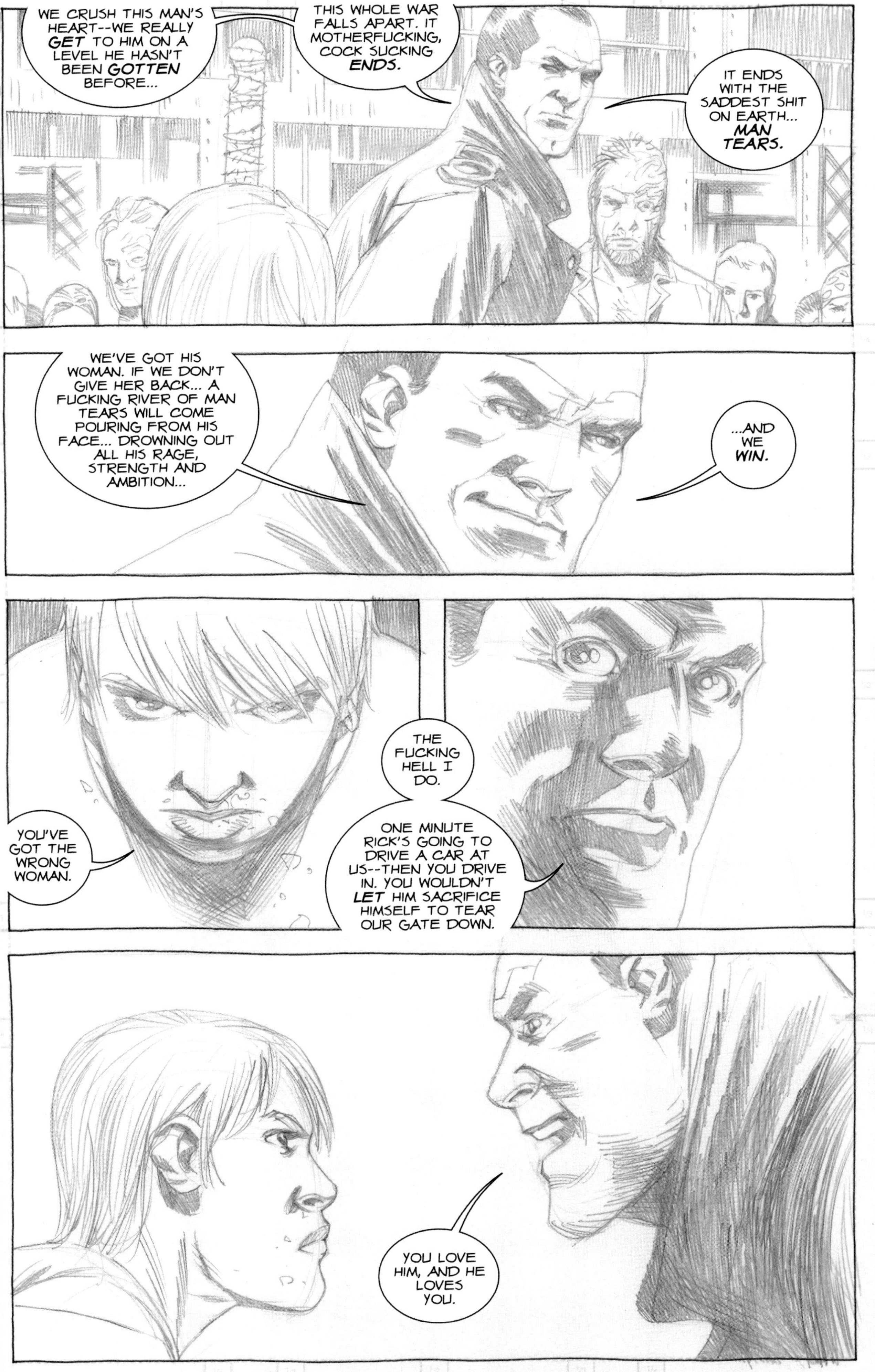
WE CRUSH THIS MAN'S HEART--WE REALLY **GET** TO HIM ON A LEVEL HE HASN'T BEEN **GOTTEN** BEFORE...
THIS WHOLE WAR FALLS APART. IT MOTHERFUCKING, COCK SUCKING ***ENDS.***
IT ENDS WITH THE SADDEST SHIT ON EARTH... ***MAN TEARS.***
WE'VE GOT HIS WOMAN. IF WE DON'T GIVE HER BACK... A FUCKING RIVER OF MAN TEARS WILL COME POURING FROM HIS FACE... DROWNING OUT ALL HIS RAGE, STRENGTH AND AMBITION...
...AND WE ***WIN.***
YOU'VE GOT THE WRONG WOMAN.
THE FUCKING HELL I DO.
ONE MINUTE RICK'S GOING TO DRIVE A CAR AT US--THEN YOU DRIVE IN. YOU WOULDN'T ***LET*** HIM SACRIFICE HIMSELF TO TEAR OUR GATE DOWN.
YOU LOVE HIM, AND HE LOVES YOU.

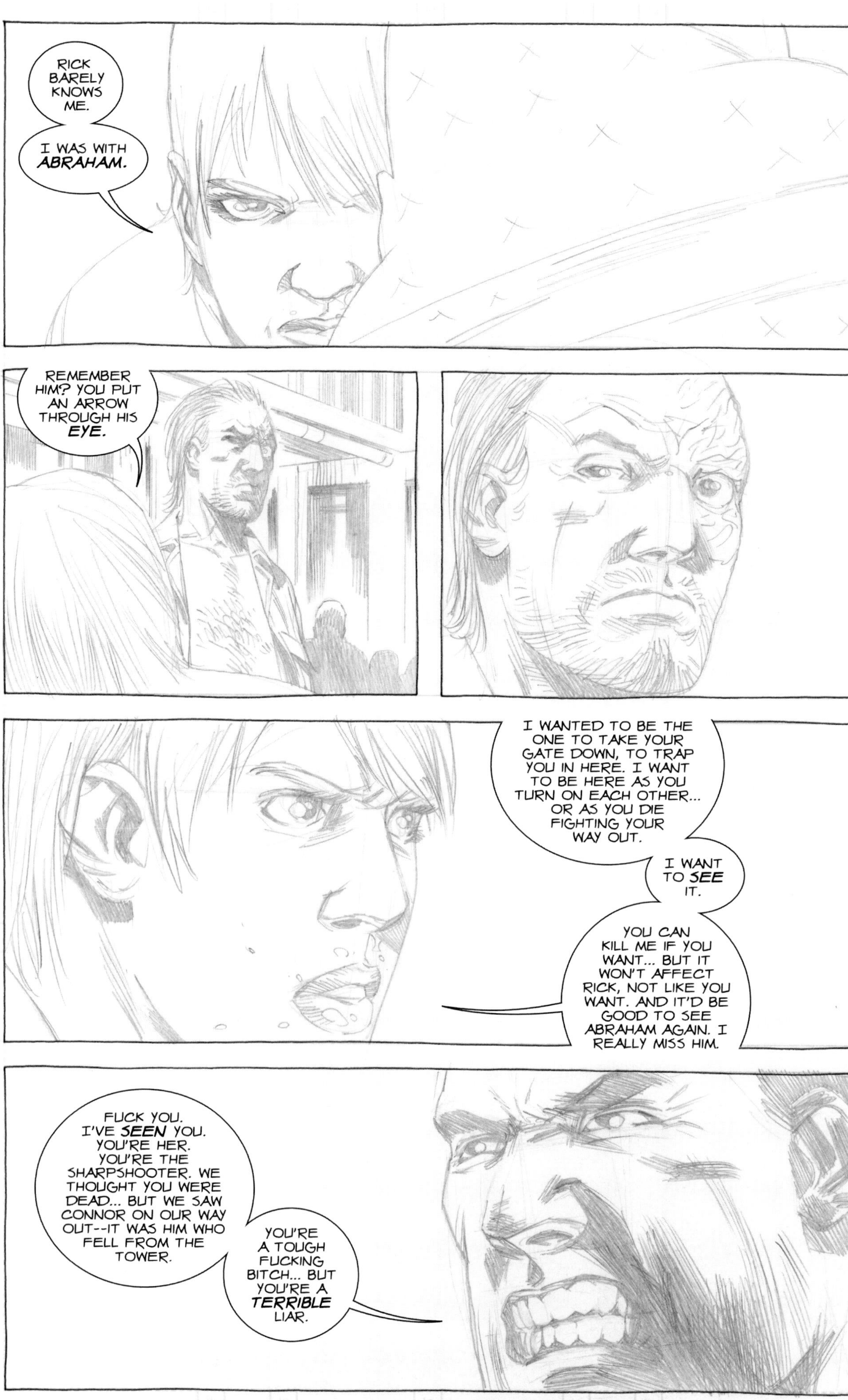
RICK BARELY KNOWS ME.
I WAS WITH ABRAHAM.
REMEMBER HIM? YOU PUT AN ARROW THROUGH HIS EYE.
I WANTED TO BE THE ONE TO TAKE YOUR GATE DOWN, TO TRAP YOU IN HERE. I WANT TO BE HERE AS YOU TURN ON EACH OTHER... OR AS YOU DIE FIGHTING YOUR WAY OUT.
I WANT TO SEE IT.
YOU CAN KILL ME IF YOU WANT... BUT IT WON'T AFFECT RICK, NOT LIKE YOU WANT. AND IT'D BE GOOD TO SEE ABRAHAM AGAIN. I REALLY MISS HIM.
FUCK YOU. I'VE SEEN YOU. YOU'RE HER. YOU'RE THE SHARPSHOOTER. WE THOUGHT YOU WERE DEAD... BUT WE SAW CONNOR ON OUR WAY OUT--IT WAS HIM WHO FELL FROM THE TOWER.
YOU'RE A TOUGH FUCKING BITCH... BUT YOU'RE A TERRIBLE LIAR.

ANDREA GOT THE SHIT BEAT OUT OF HER BEFORE SHE THREW YOUR GUY OUT THE WINDOW.

SHE'S BACK AT HOME, HEALING. YOU REALLY THINK SHE'D GET OUT OF THAT BELL TOWER UNSCATHED?

TRUST ME, I'VE GOT A COUPLE CUP SIZES ON HER.

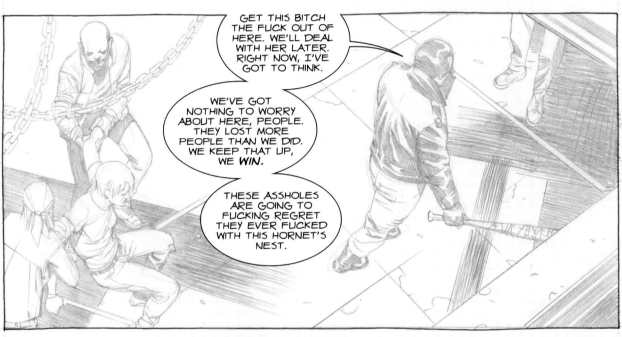

GET THIS BITCH THE FUCK OUT OF HERE. WE'LL DEAL WITH HER LATER. RIGHT NOW, I'VE GOT TO THINK.

WE'VE GOT NOTHING TO WORRY ABOUT HERE, PEOPLE. THEY LOST MORE PEOPLE THAN WE DID. WE KEEP THAT UP, WE **WIN.**

THESE ASSHOLES ARE GOING TO FUCKING REGRET THEY EVER FUCKED WITH THIS HORNET'S NEST.

YOU WANT ME TO PREP THE MEETING ROOM? ARE YOU GOING TO PLAN A STRIKE AGAINST THEM?

IF WE MOVE FAST, THEY'LL NEVER EXPECT IT.

NO, CARSON. NOT YET.

WE HAVE MORE *PRESSING* MATTERS TO ATTEND TO.

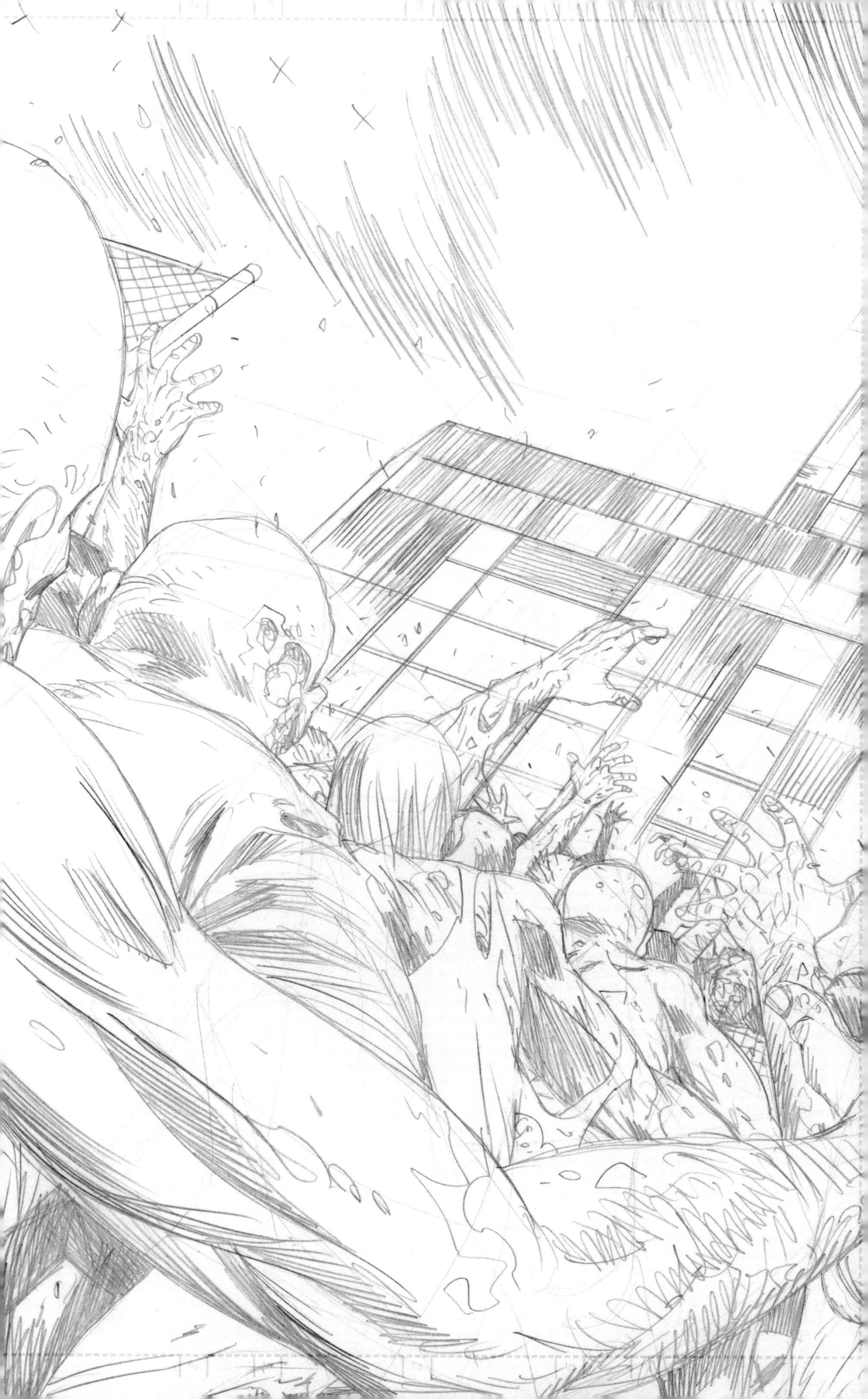

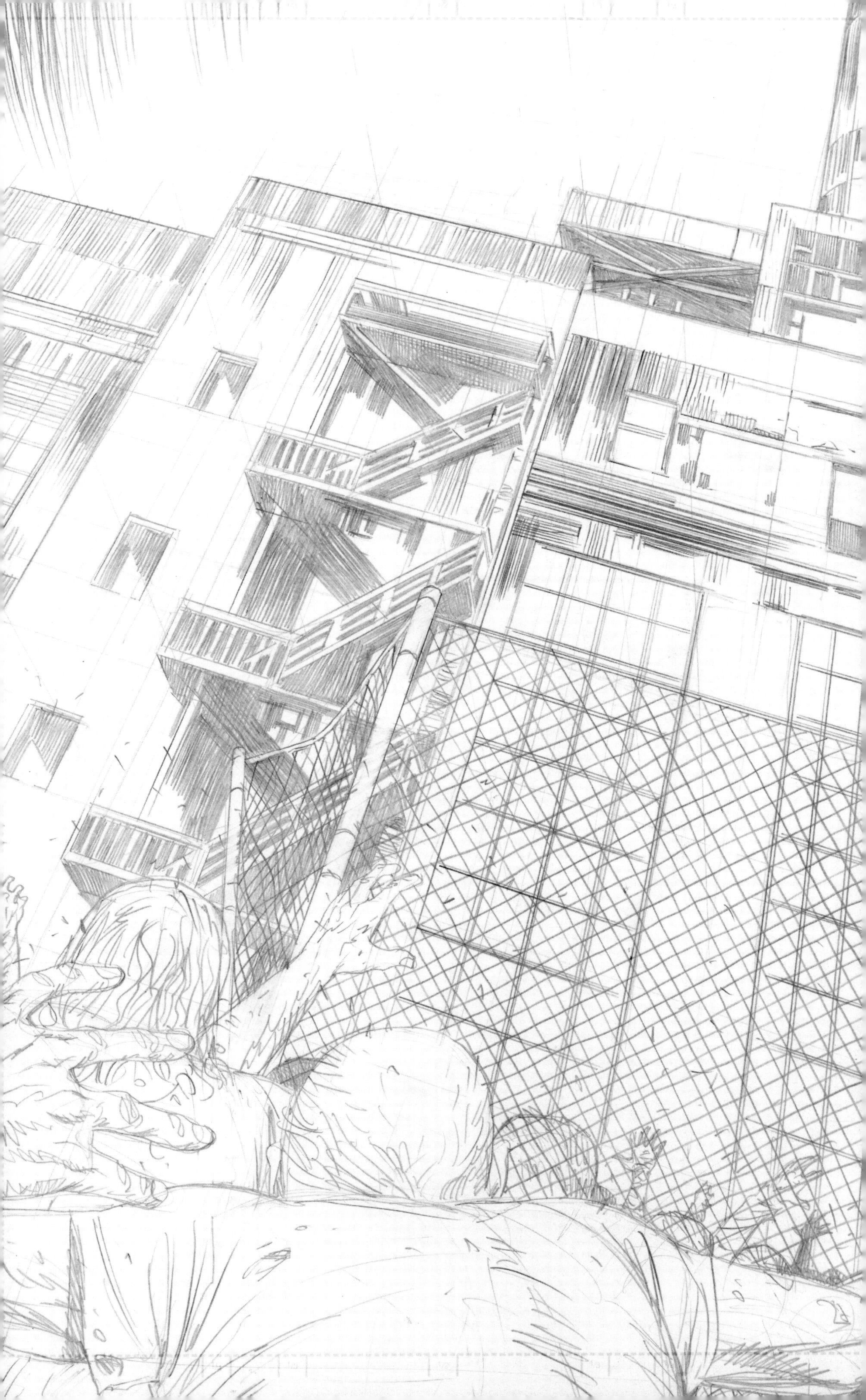

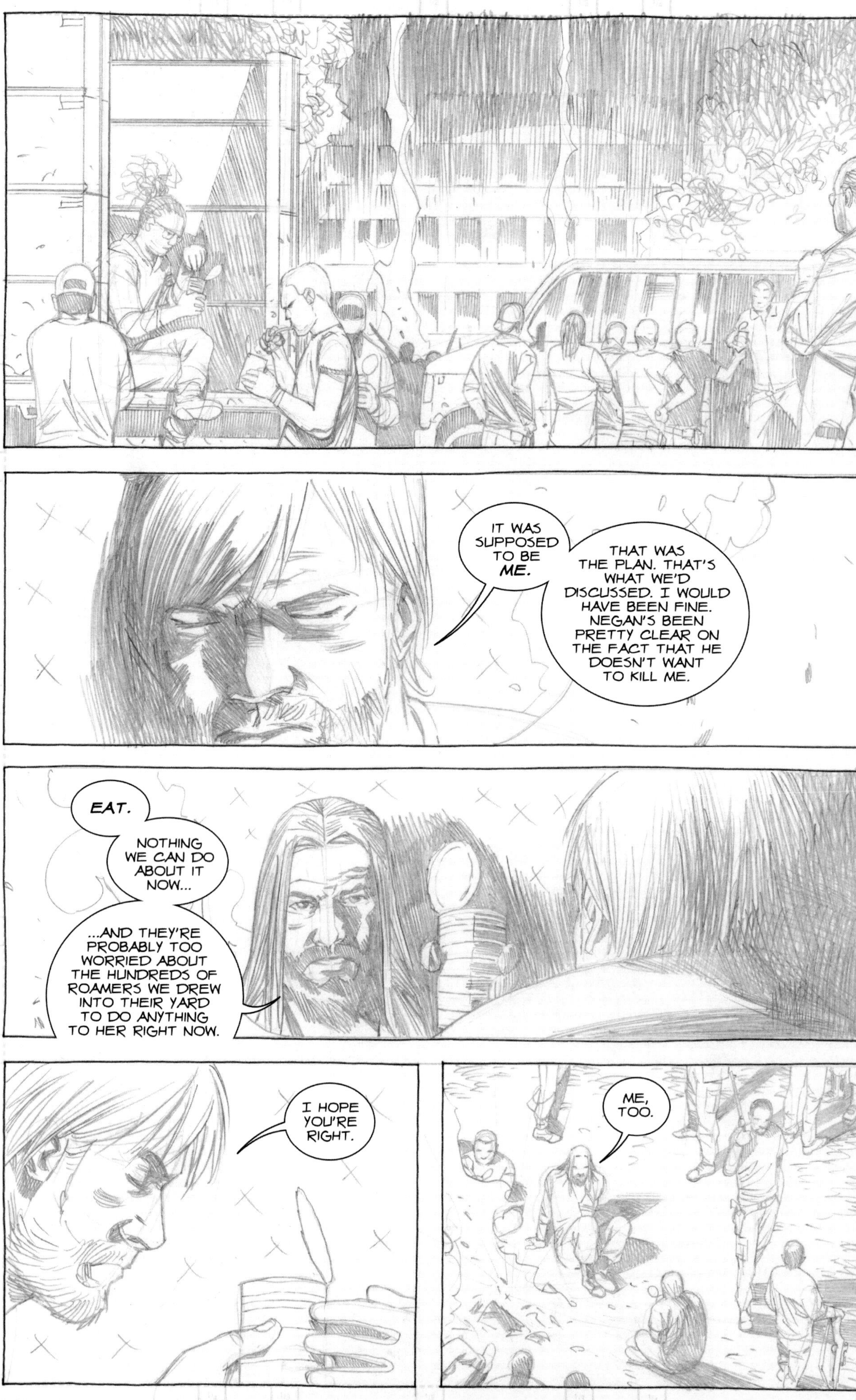
IT WAS SUPPOSED TO BE ME.
THAT WAS THE PLAN. THAT'S WHAT WE'D DISCUSSED. I WOULD HAVE BEEN FINE. NEGAN'S BEEN PRETTY CLEAR ON THE FACT THAT HE DOESN'T WANT TO KILL ME.
EAT.
NOTHING WE CAN DO ABOUT IT NOW...
...AND THEY'RE PROBABLY TOO WORRIED ABOUT THE HUNDREDS OF ROAMERS WE DREW INTO THEIR YARD TO DO ANYTHING TO HER RIGHT NOW.
I HOPE YOU'RE RIGHT.
ME, TOO.

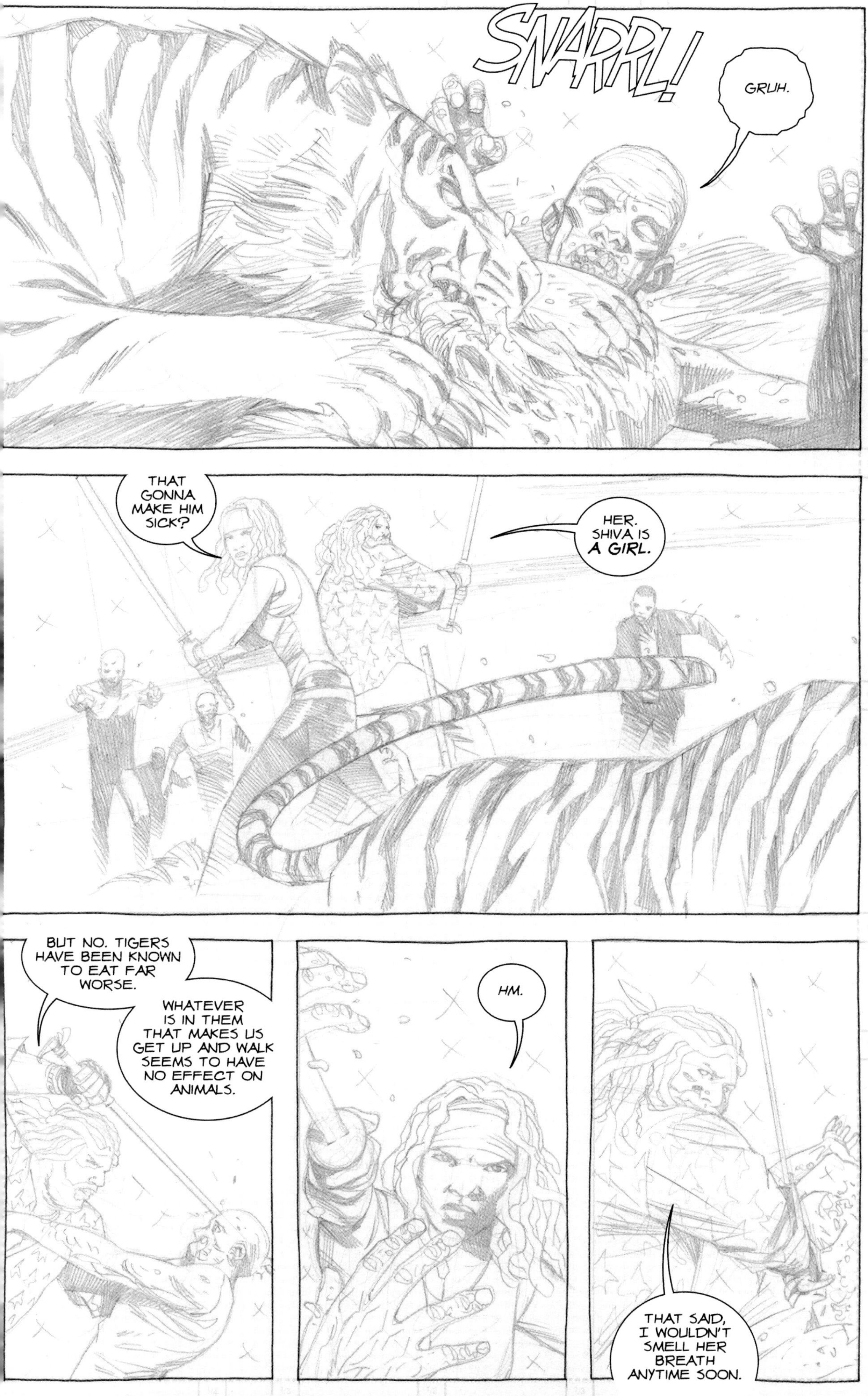
SNARRL!
GRUH.
THAT GONNA MAKE HIM SICK?
HER. SHIVA IS A GIRL.
BUT NO. TIGERS HAVE BEEN KNOWN TO EAT FAR WORSE.
WHATEVER IS IN THEM THAT MAKES US GET UP AND WALK SEEMS TO HAVE NO EFFECT ON ANIMALS.
HM.
THAT SAID, I WOULDN'T SMELL HER BREATH ANYTIME SOON.

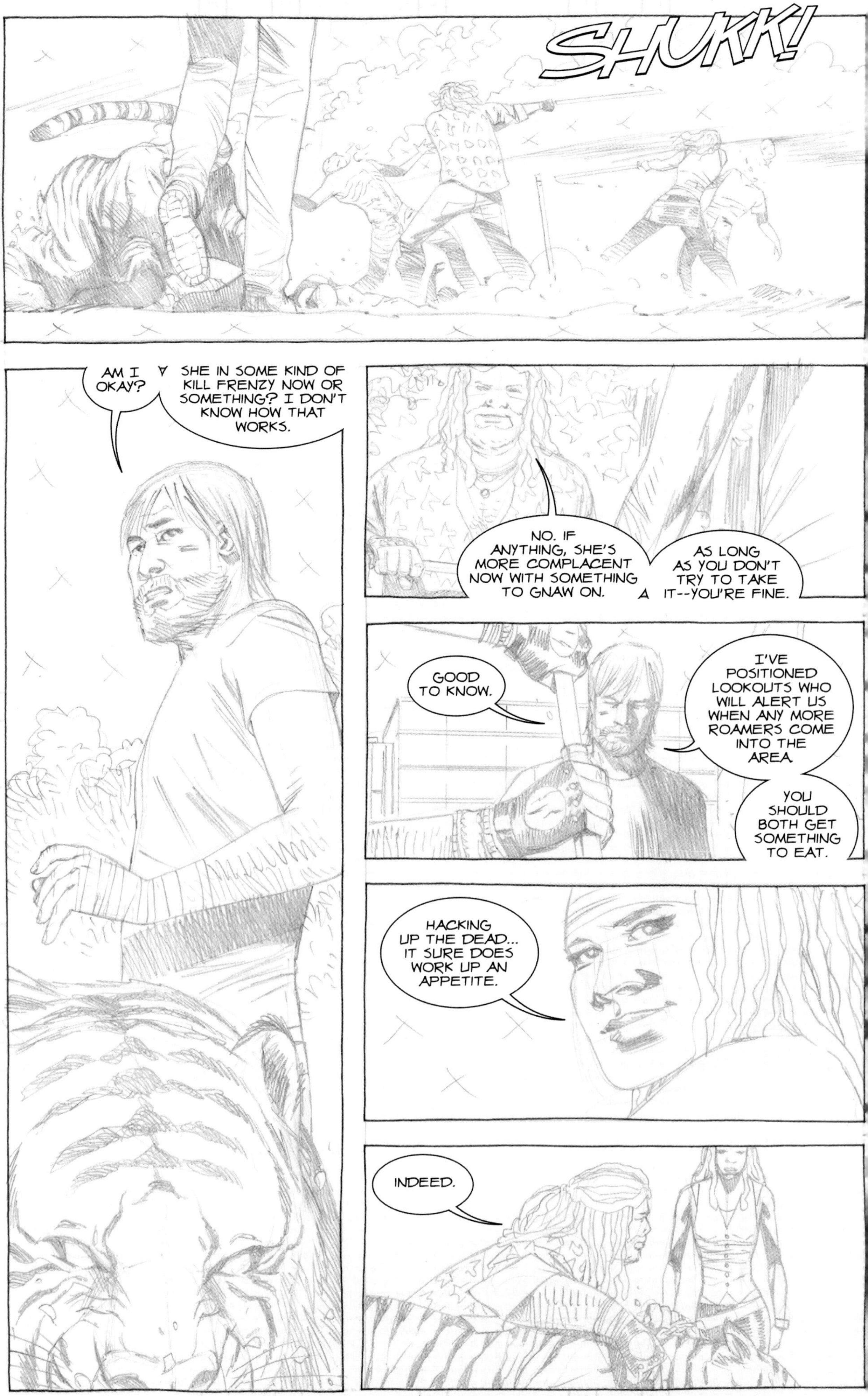
SHUKK!
AM I OKAY?
SHE IN SOME KIND OF KILL FRENZY NOW OR SOMETHING? I DON'T KNOW HOW THAT WORKS.
NO. IF ANYTHING, SHE'S MORE COMPLACENT NOW WITH SOMETHING TO GNAW ON.
AS LONG AS YOU DON'T TRY TO TAKE IT--YOU'RE FINE.
GOOD TO KNOW.
I'VE POSITIONED LOOKOUTS WHO WILL ALERT US WHEN ANY MORE ROAMERS COME INTO THE AREA.
YOU SHOULD BOTH GET SOMETHING TO EAT.
HACKING UP THE DEAD... IT SURE DOES WORK UP AN APPETITE.
INDEED.

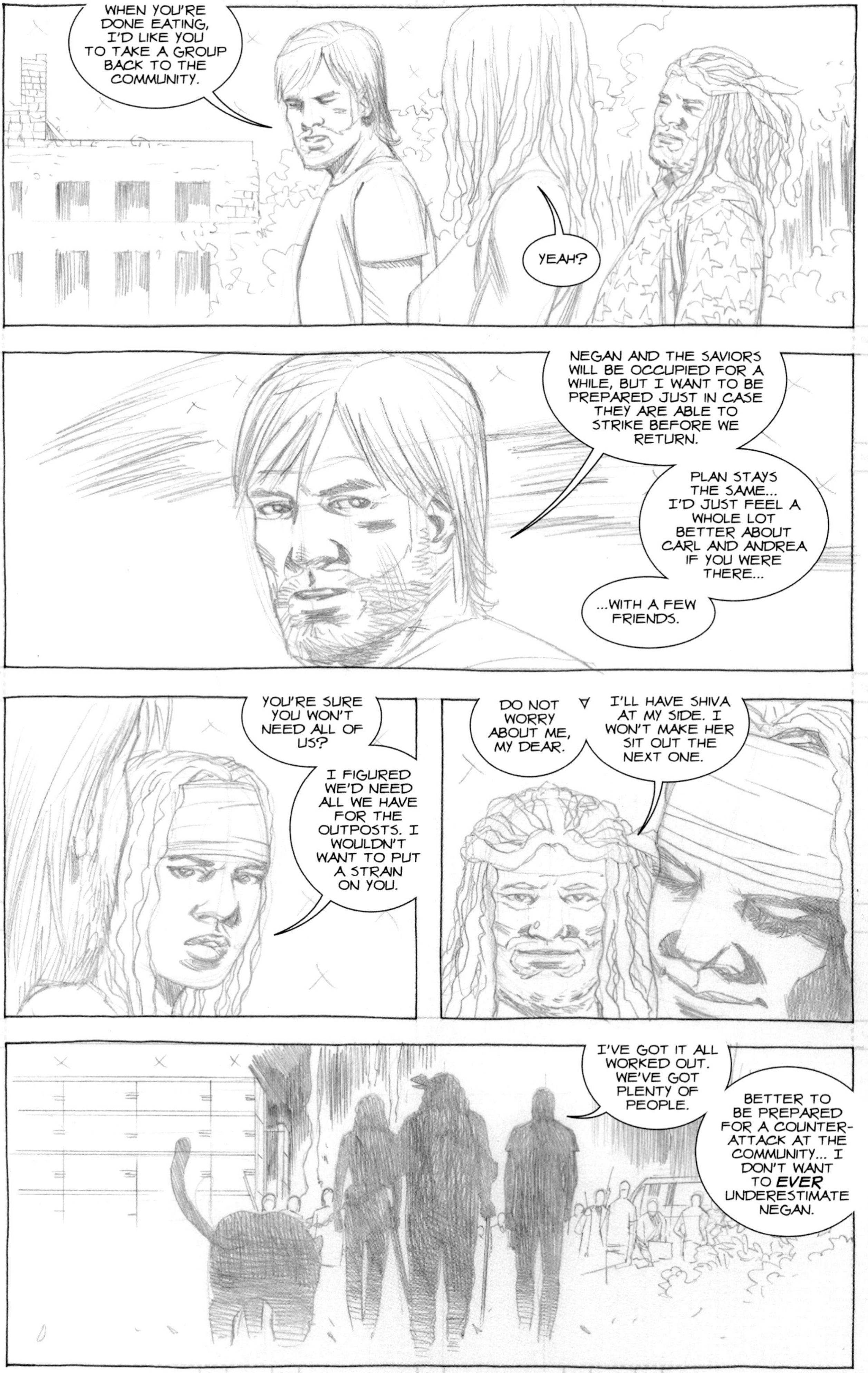
WHEN YOU'RE DONE EATING, I'D LIKE YOU TO TAKE A GROUP BACK TO THE COMMUNITY.
YEAH?
NEGAN AND THE SAVIORS WILL BE OCCUPIED FOR A WHILE, BUT I WANT TO BE PREPARED JUST IN CASE THEY ARE ABLE TO STRIKE BEFORE WE RETURN.
PLAN STAYS THE SAME... I'D JUST FEEL A WHOLE LOT BETTER ABOUT CARL AND ANDREA IF YOU WERE THERE...
...WITH A FEW FRIENDS.
YOU'RE SURE YOU WON'T NEED ALL OF US?
I FIGURED WE'D NEED ALL WE HAVE FOR THE OUTPOSTS. I WOULDN'T WANT TO PUT A STRAIN ON YOU.
DO NOT WORRY ABOUT ME, MY DEAR.
I'LL HAVE SHIVA AT MY SIDE. I WON'T MAKE HER SIT OUT THE NEXT ONE.
I'VE GOT IT ALL WORKED OUT. WE'VE GOT PLENTY OF PEOPLE.
BETTER TO BE PREPARED FOR A COUNTER-ATTACK AT THE COMMUNITY... I DON'T WANT TO ***EVER*** UNDERESTIMATE NEGAN.

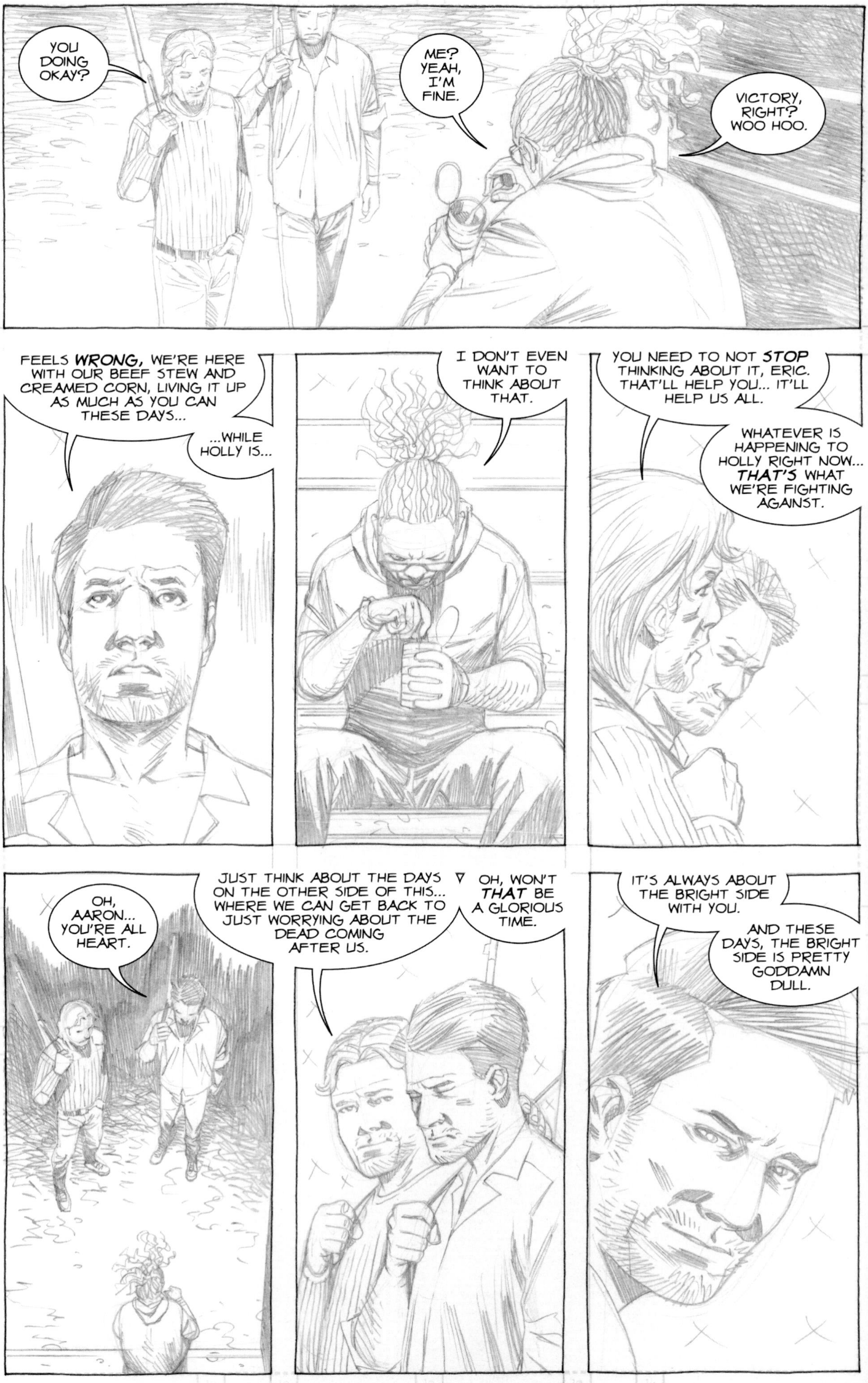
YOU DOING OKAY?
ME? YEAH, I'M FINE.
VICTORY, RIGHT? WOO HOO.
FEELS WRONG, WE'RE HERE WITH OUR BEEF STEW AND CREAMED CORN, LIVING IT UP AS MUCH AS YOU CAN THESE DAYS...
...WHILE HOLLY IS...
I DON'T EVEN WANT TO THINK ABOUT THAT.
YOU NEED TO NOT STOP THINKING ABOUT IT, ERIC. THAT'LL HELP YOU... IT'LL HELP US ALL.
WHATEVER IS HAPPENING TO HOLLY RIGHT NOW... THAT'S WHAT WE'RE FIGHTING AGAINST.
OH, AARON... YOU'RE ALL HEART.
JUST THINK ABOUT THE DAYS ON THE OTHER SIDE OF THIS... WHERE WE CAN GET BACK TO JUST WORRYING ABOUT THE DEAD COMING AFTER US.
OH, WON'T THAT BE A GLORIOUS TIME.
IT'S ALWAYS ABOUT THE BRIGHT SIDE WITH YOU.
AND THESE DAYS, THE BRIGHT SIDE IS PRETTY GODDAMN DULL.

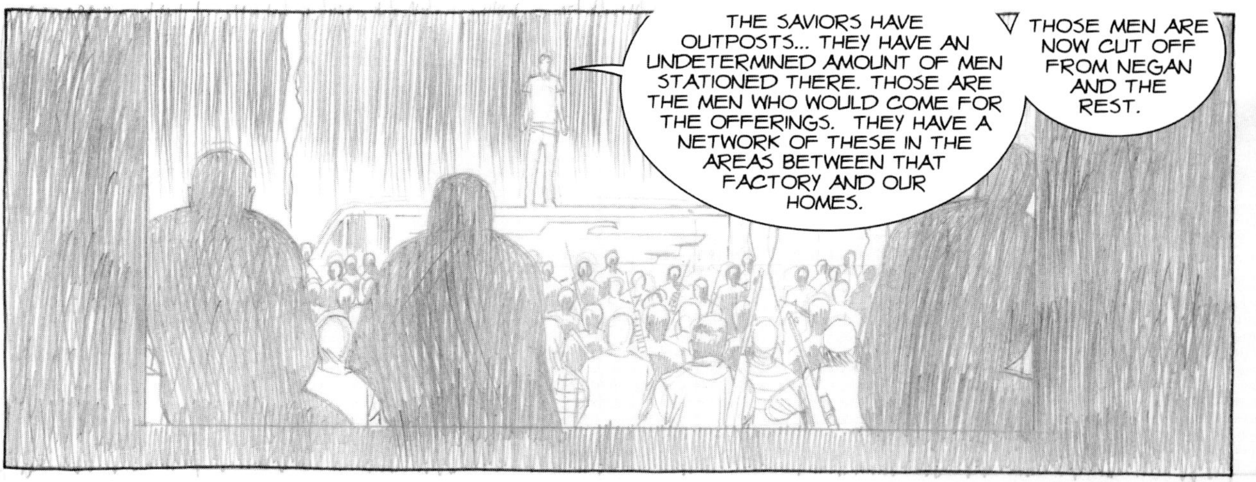
THE SAVIORS HAVE OUTPOSTS... THEY HAVE AN UNDETERMINED AMOUNT OF MEN STATIONED THERE. THOSE ARE THE MEN WHO WOULD COME FOR THE OFFERINGS. THEY HAVE A NETWORK OF THESE IN THE AREAS BETWEEN THAT FACTORY AND OUR HOMES.
THOSE MEN ARE NOW CUT OFF FROM NEGAN AND THE REST.

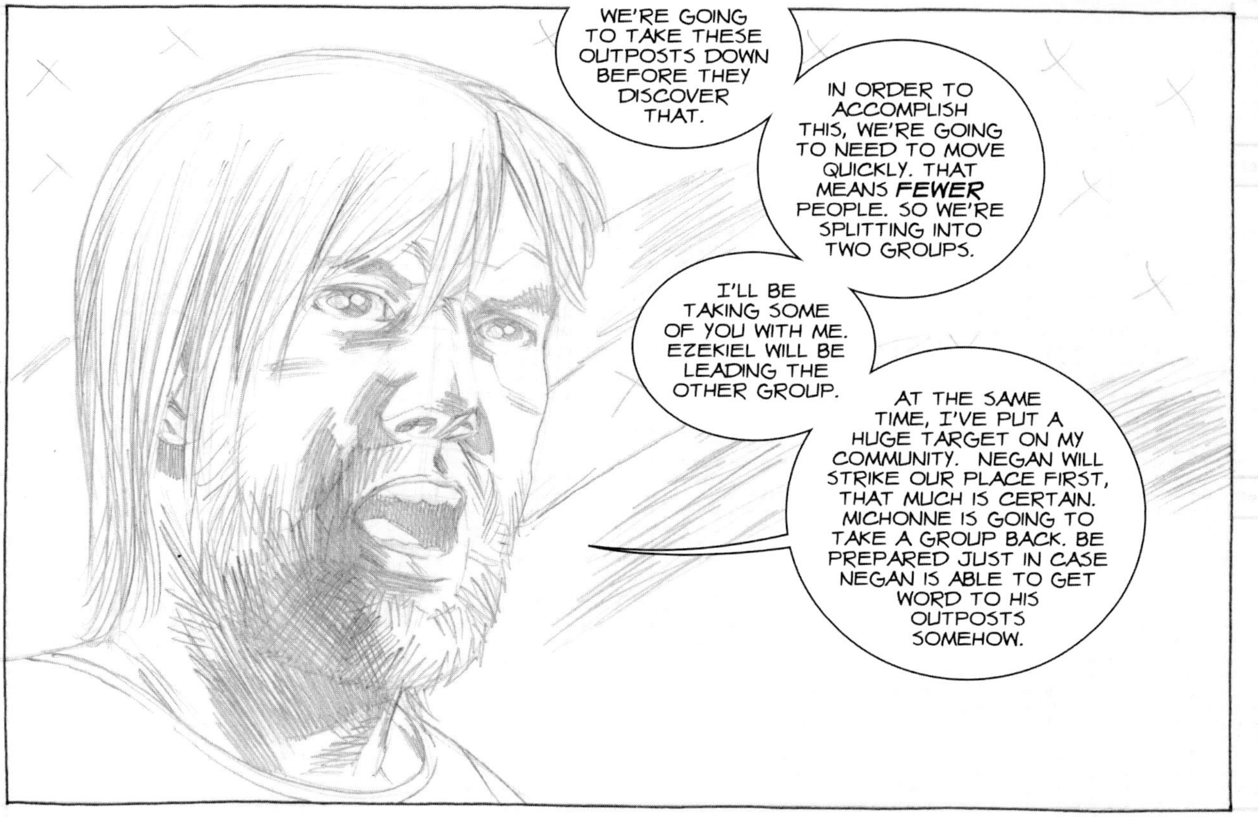
WE'RE GOING TO TAKE THESE OUTPOSTS DOWN BEFORE THEY DISCOVER THAT.
IN ORDER TO ACCOMPLISH THIS, WE'RE GOING TO NEED TO MOVE QUICKLY. THAT MEANS ***FEWER*** PEOPLE. SO WE'RE SPLITTING INTO TWO GROUPS.
I'LL BE TAKING SOME OF YOU WITH ME. EZEKIEL WILL BE LEADING THE OTHER GROUP.
AT THE SAME TIME, I'VE PUT A HUGE TARGET ON MY COMMUNITY. NEGAN WILL STRIKE OUR PLACE FIRST, THAT MUCH IS CERTAIN. MICHONNE IS GOING TO TAKE A GROUP BACK. BE PREPARED JUST IN CASE NEGAN IS ABLE TO GET WORD TO HIS OUTPOSTS SOMEHOW.

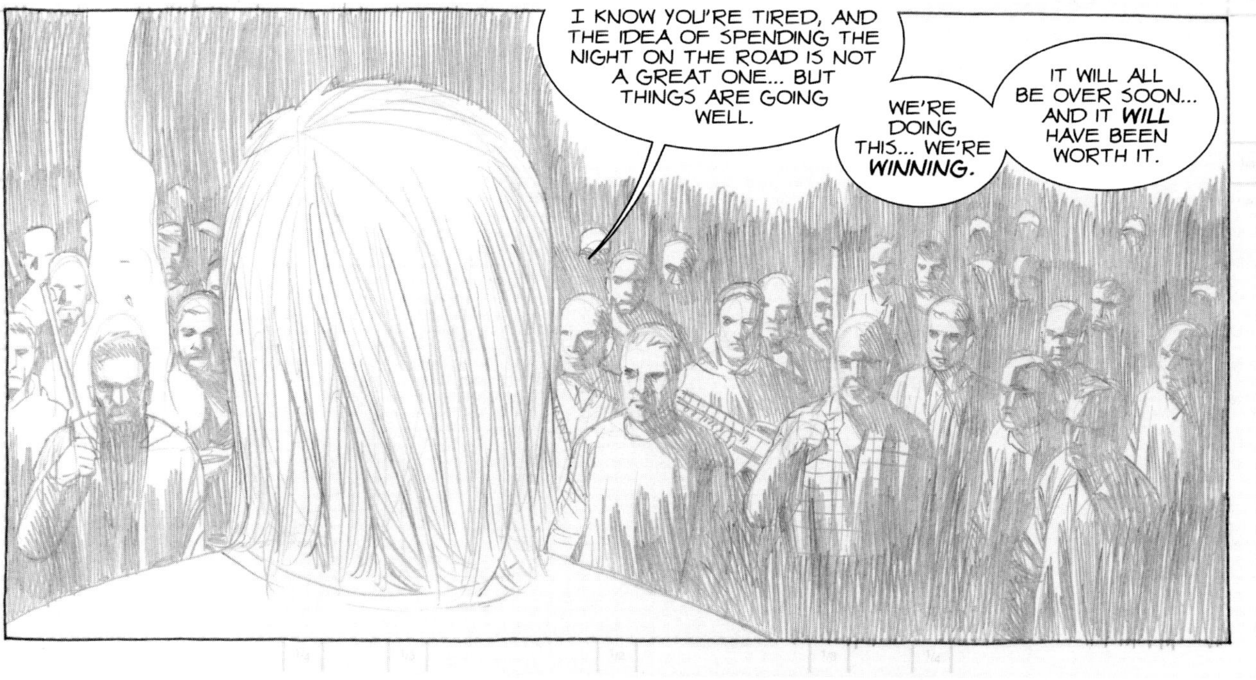
I KNOW YOU'RE TIRED, AND THE IDEA OF SPENDING THE NIGHT ON THE ROAD IS NOT A GREAT ONE... BUT THINGS ARE GOING WELL.
WE'RE DOING THIS... WE'RE ***WINNING.***
IT WILL ALL BE OVER SOON... AND IT ***WILL*** HAVE BEEN WORTH IT.

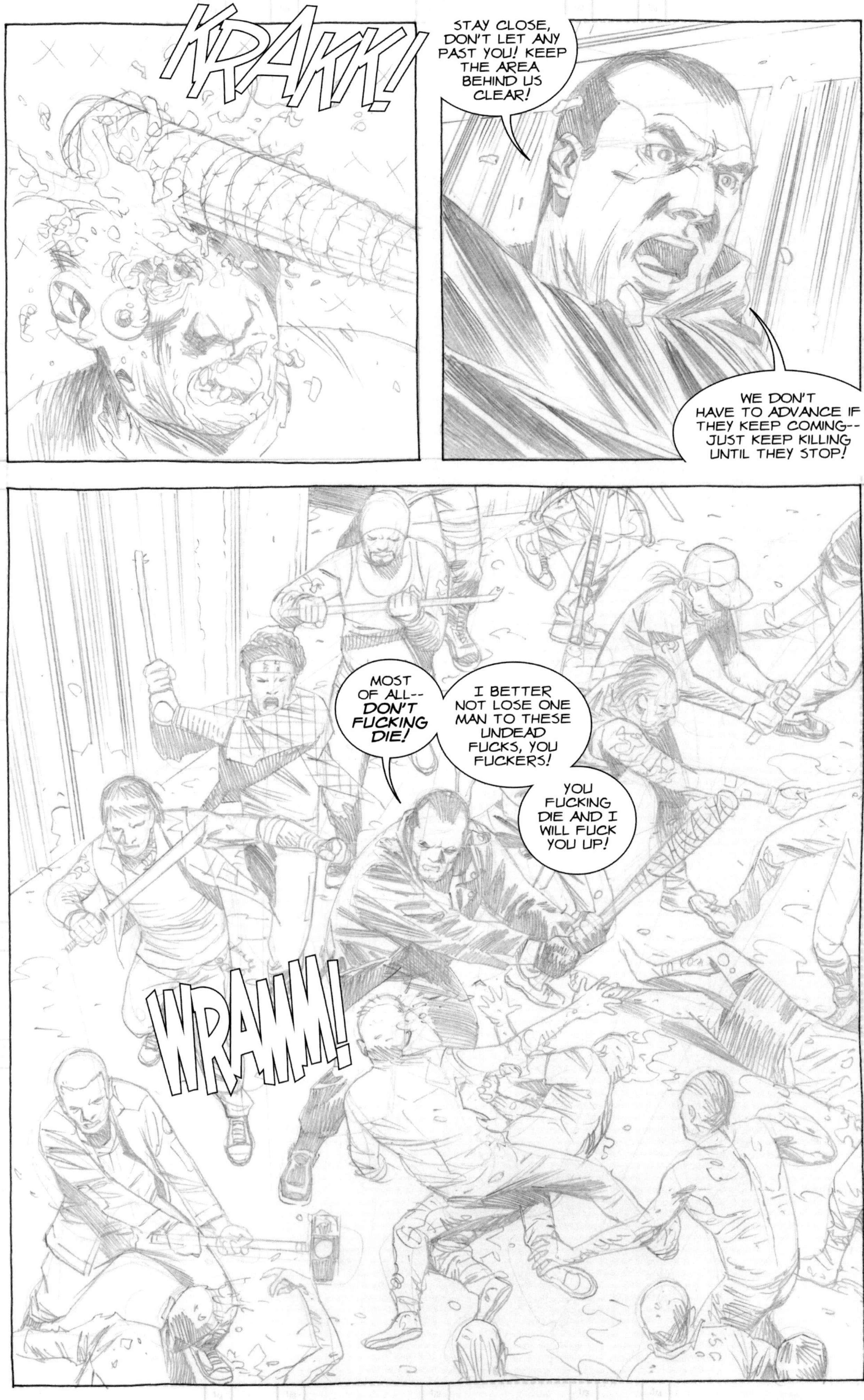
KRAKK!
STAY CLOSE, DON'T LET ANY PAST YOU! KEEP THE AREA BEHIND US CLEAR!
WE DON'T HAVE TO ADVANCE IF THEY KEEP COMING-- JUST KEEP KILLING UNTIL THEY STOP!
MOST OF ALL-- DON'T FUCKING DIE!
I BETTER NOT LOSE ONE MAN TO THESE UNDEAD FUCKS, YOU FUCKERS!
YOU FUCKING DIE AND I WILL FUCK YOU UP!
WRAMM!

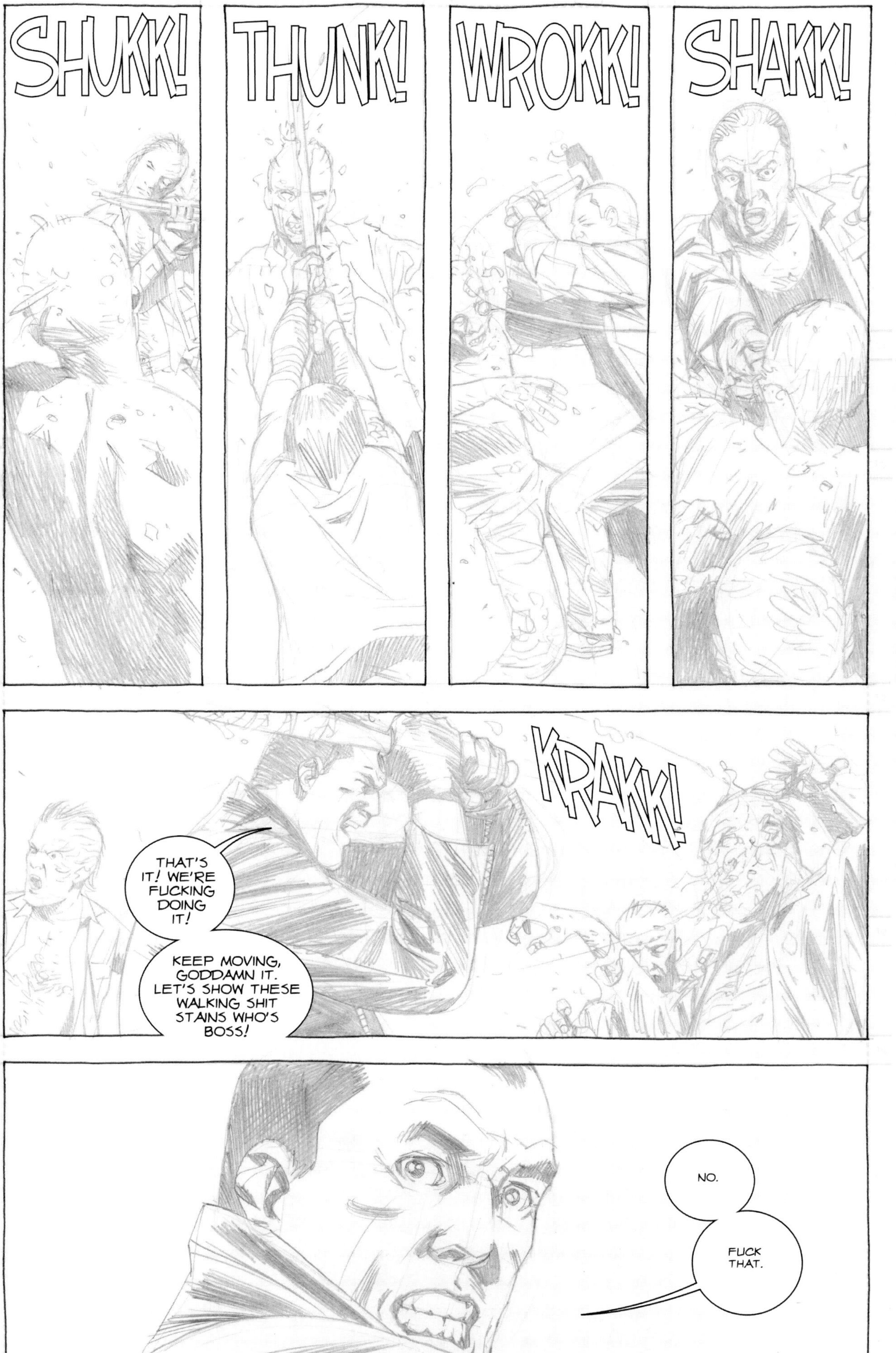
SHUKK!
THUNK!
WROKK!
SHAKK!
KRAKK!
THAT'S IT! WE'RE FUCKING DOING IT!
KEEP MOVING, GODDAMN IT. LET'S SHOW THESE WALKING SHIT STAINS WHO'S BOSS!
NO.
FUCK THAT.

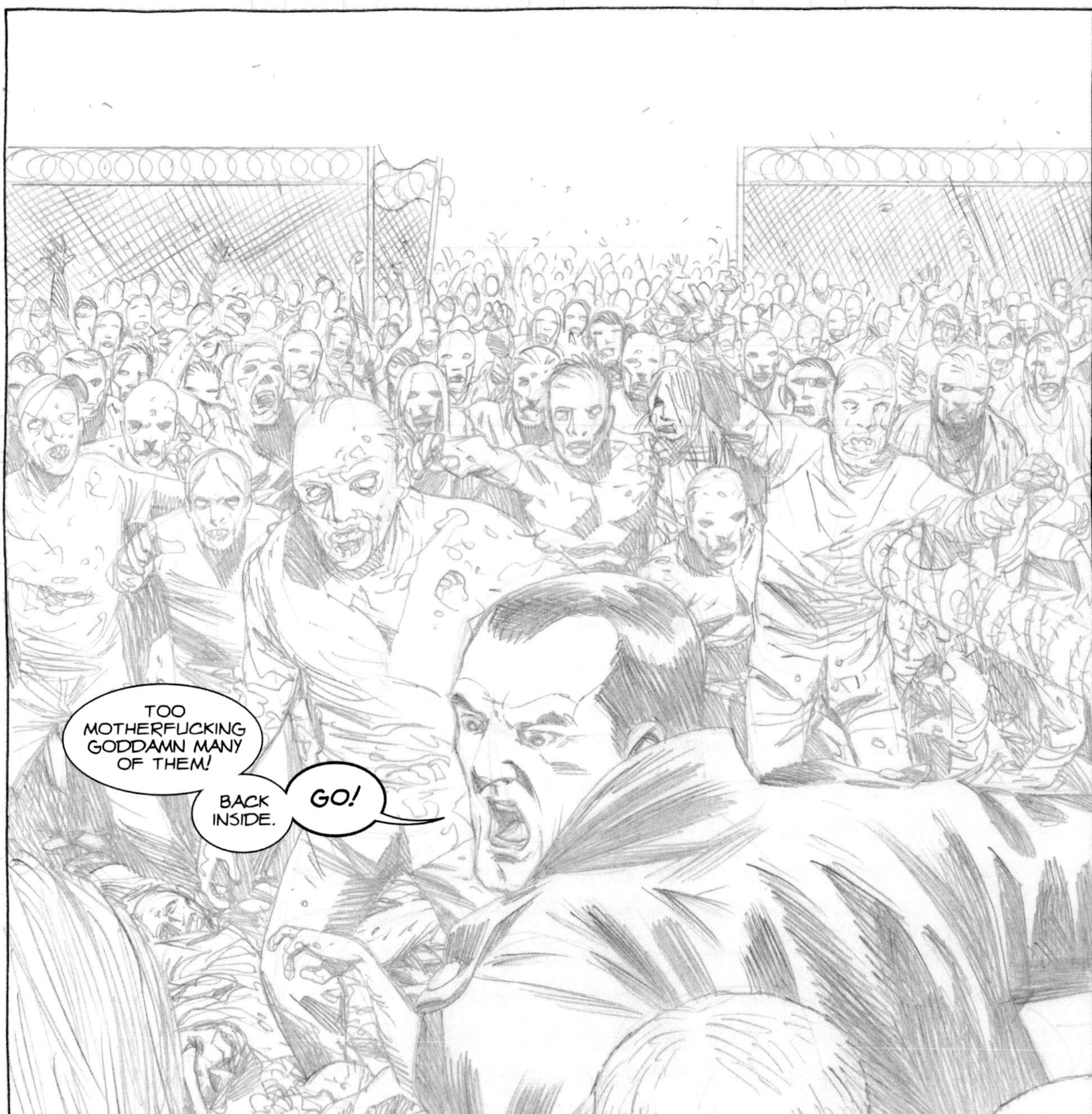
TOO MOTHERFUCKING GODDAMN MANY OF THEM!
BACK INSIDE.
GO!

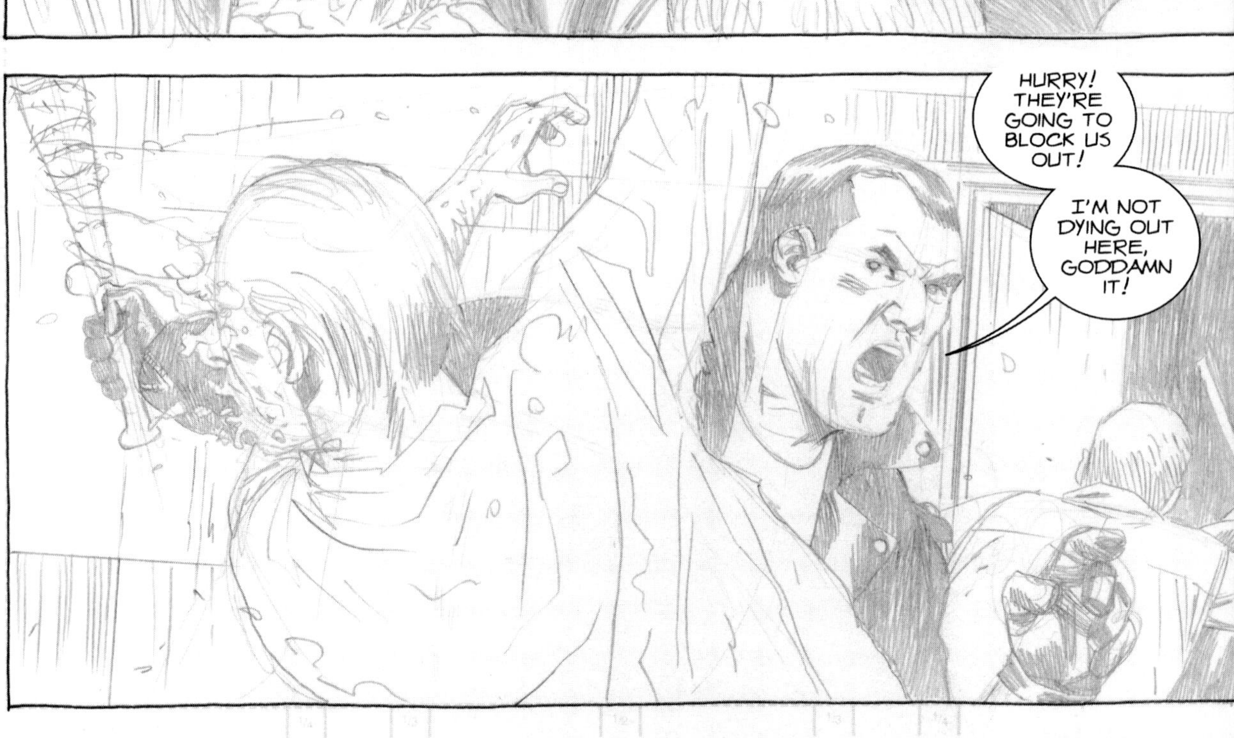
HURRY! THEY'RE GOING TO BLOCK US OUT!
I'M NOT DYING OUT HERE, GODDAMN IT!

CLOSE THE FUCKING DOOR! **NOW!**

CHOOM!

I WANT A TEAM OUT THERE EVERY TWO FUCKING HOURS. KILL AS MANY AS YOU CAN, RUN INSIDE, WAIT FOR THEM TO CALM DOWN.

GET OUR SMART FUCKERS TOGETHER. THERE'S GOTTA BE A WAY TO THIN THESE SHITHEADS OUT FROM A FUCKING DISTANCE. DROP SOME BIG ROCKS ON THEM OR SOME SHIT.

FUCKING FIGURE IT OUT.

WE CAN'T BE TRAPPED IN HERE FOR MORE THAN A DAY. THAT HAPPENS... **WE'RE DEAD.**

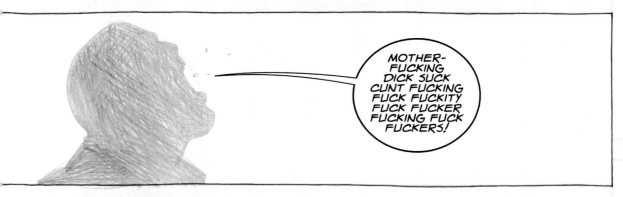

MOTHER-FUCKING DICK SUCK CUNT FUCKING FUCK FUCKITY FUCK FUCKER FUCKING FUCK FUCKERS!

FUCK.

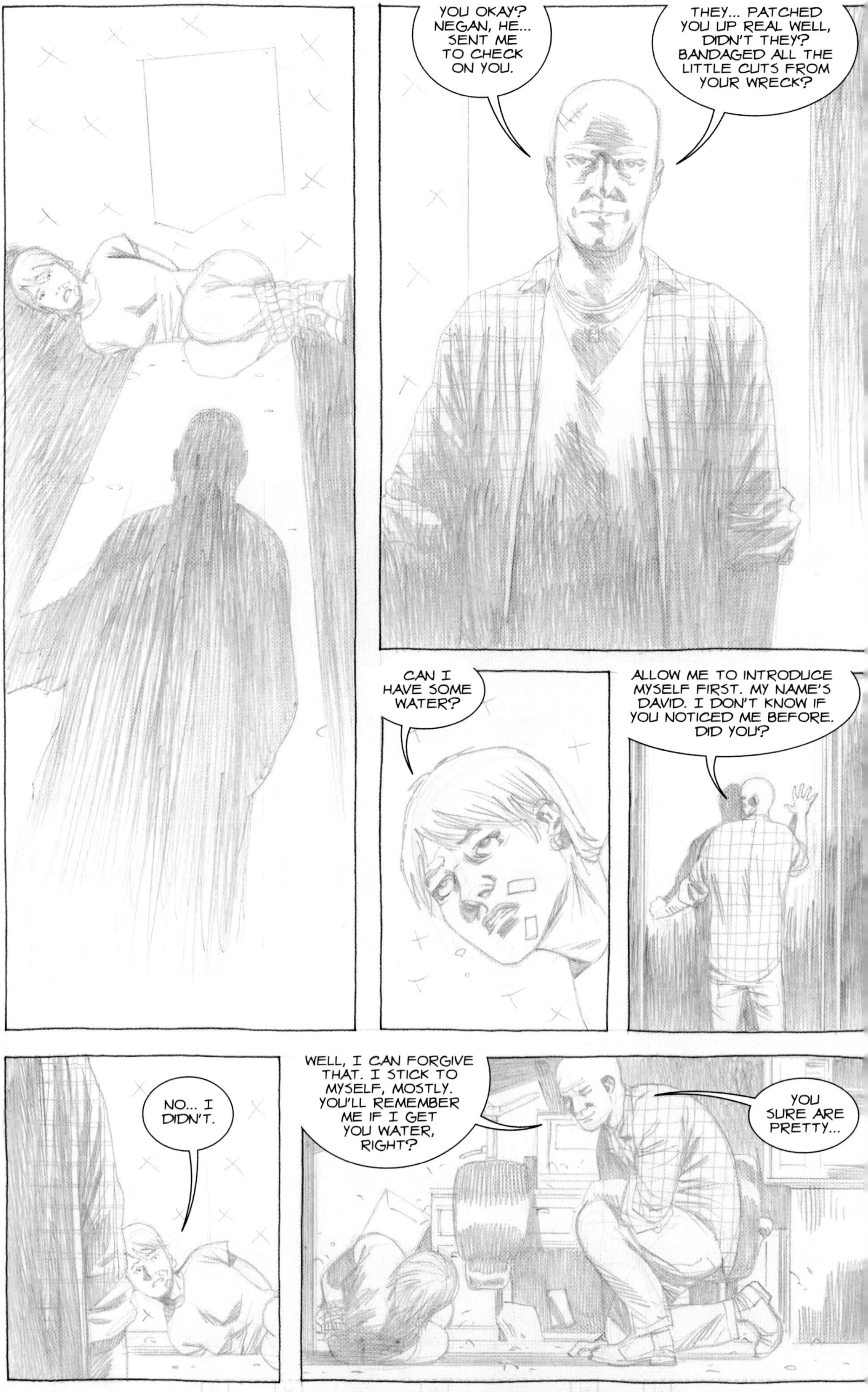
YOU OKAY? NEGAN, HE... SENT ME TO CHECK ON YOU.
THEY... PATCHED YOU UP REAL WELL, DIDN'T THEY? BANDAGED ALL THE LITTLE CUTS FROM YOUR WRECK?
CAN I HAVE SOME WATER?
ALLOW ME TO INTRODUCE MYSELF FIRST. MY NAME'S DAVID. I DON'T KNOW IF YOU NOTICED ME BEFORE. DID YOU?
NO... I DIDN'T.
WELL, I CAN FORGIVE THAT. I STICK TO MYSELF, MOSTLY. YOU'LL REMEMBER ME IF I GET YOU WATER, RIGHT?
YOU SURE ARE PRETTY...

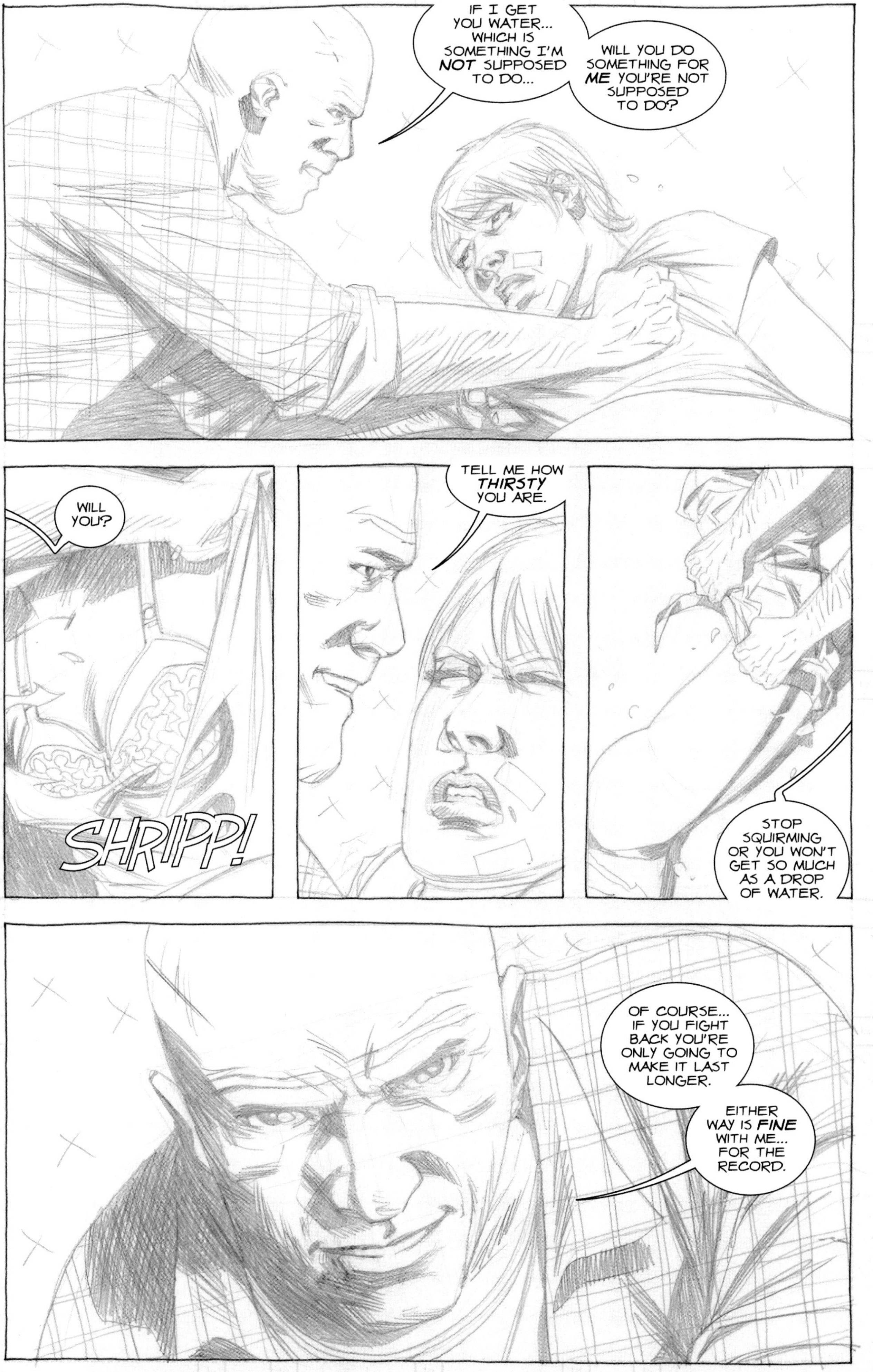
IF I GET YOU WATER... WHICH IS SOMETHING I'M NOT SUPPOSED TO DO...
WILL YOU DO SOMETHING FOR ME YOU'RE NOT SUPPOSED TO DO?
WILL YOU?
SHRIPP!
TELL ME HOW THIRSTY YOU ARE.
STOP SQUIRMING OR YOU WON'T GET SO MUCH AS A DROP OF WATER.
OF COURSE... IF YOU FIGHT BACK YOU'RE ONLY GOING TO MAKE IT LAST LONGER.
EITHER WAY IS FINE WITH ME... FOR THE RECORD.

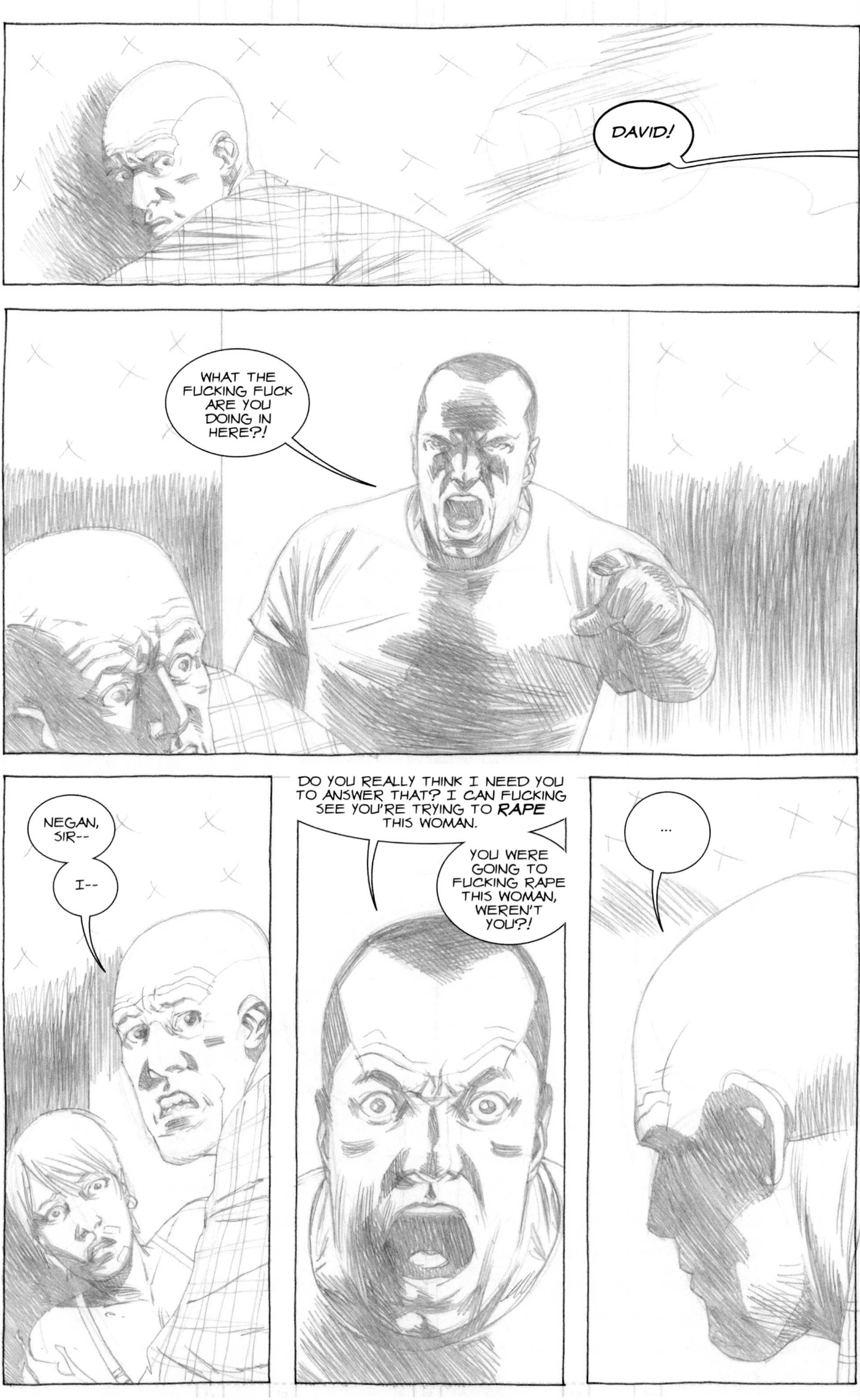
DAVID!
WHAT THE FUCKING FUCK ARE YOU DOING IN HERE?!
NEGAN, SIR--
I--
DO YOU REALLY THINK I NEED YOU TO ANSWER THAT? I CAN FUCKING SEE YOU'RE TRYING TO *RAPE* THIS WOMAN.
YOU WERE GOING TO FUCKING RAPE THIS WOMAN, WEREN'T YOU?!
...

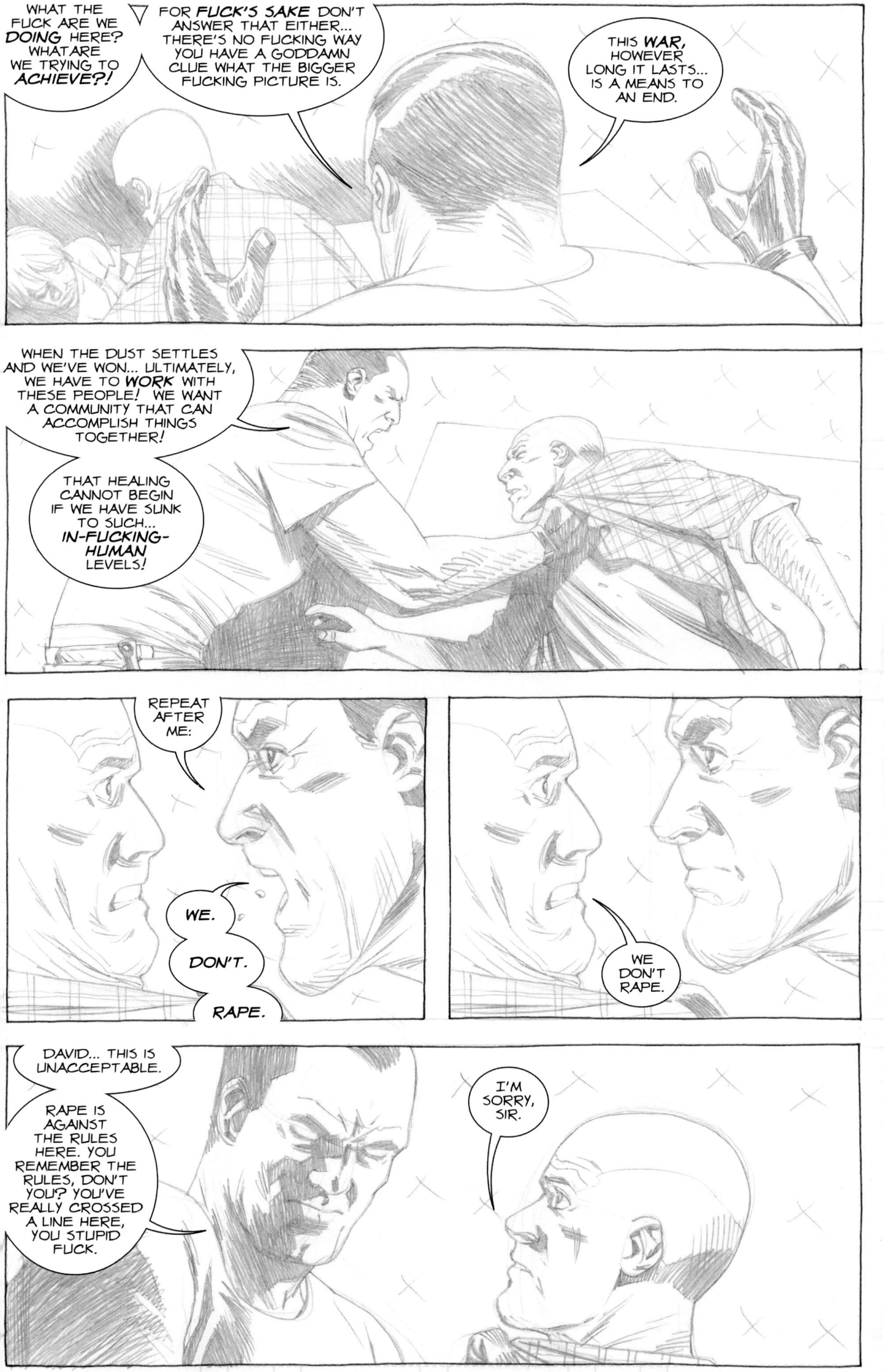
WHAT THE FUCK ARE WE DOING HERE? WHATARE WE TRYING TO ACHIEVE?!
FOR FUCK'S SAKE DON'T ANSWER THAT EITHER... THERE'S NO FUCKING WAY YOU HAVE A GODDAMN CLUE WHAT THE BIGGER FUCKING PICTURE IS.
THIS WAR, HOWEVER LONG IT LASTS... IS A MEANS TO AN END.
WHEN THE DUST SETTLES AND WE'VE WON... ULTIMATELY, WE HAVE TO WORK WITH THESE PEOPLE! WE WANT A COMMUNITY THAT CAN ACCOMPLISH THINGS TOGETHER!
THAT HEALING CANNOT BEGIN IF WE HAVE SUNK TO SUCH... IN-FUCKING-HUMAN LEVELS!
REPEAT AFTER ME:
WE.
DON'T.
RAPE.
WE DON'T RAPE.
DAVID... THIS IS UNACCEPTABLE.
RAPE IS AGAINST THE RULES HERE. YOU REMEMBER THE RULES, DON'T YOU? YOU'VE REALLY CROSSED A LINE HERE, YOU STUPID FUCK.
I'M SORRY, SIR.

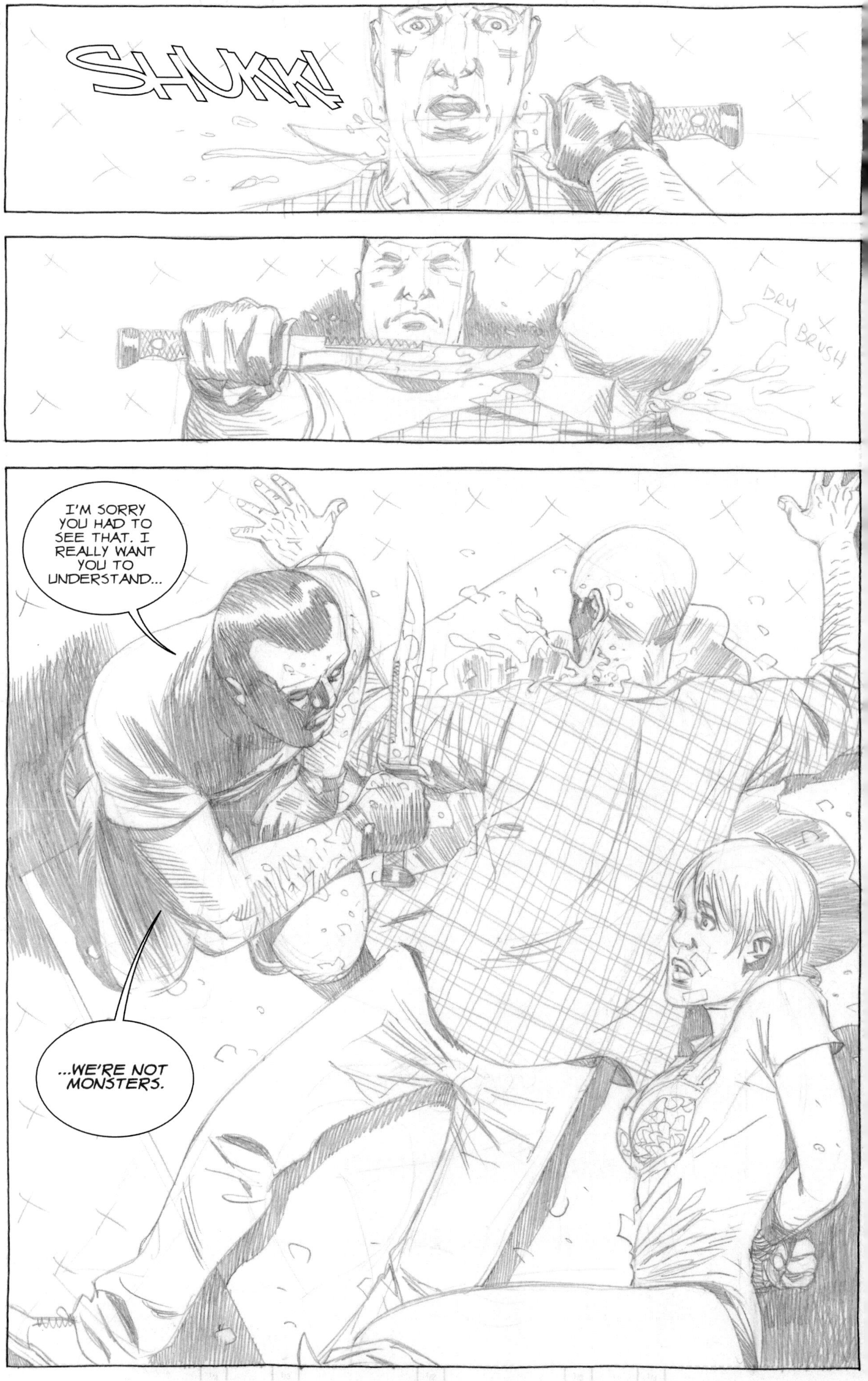
SHUKK!
DRY BRUSH
I'M SORRY YOU HAD TO SEE THAT. I REALLY WANT YOU TO UNDERSTAND...
...WE'RE NOT MONSTERS.

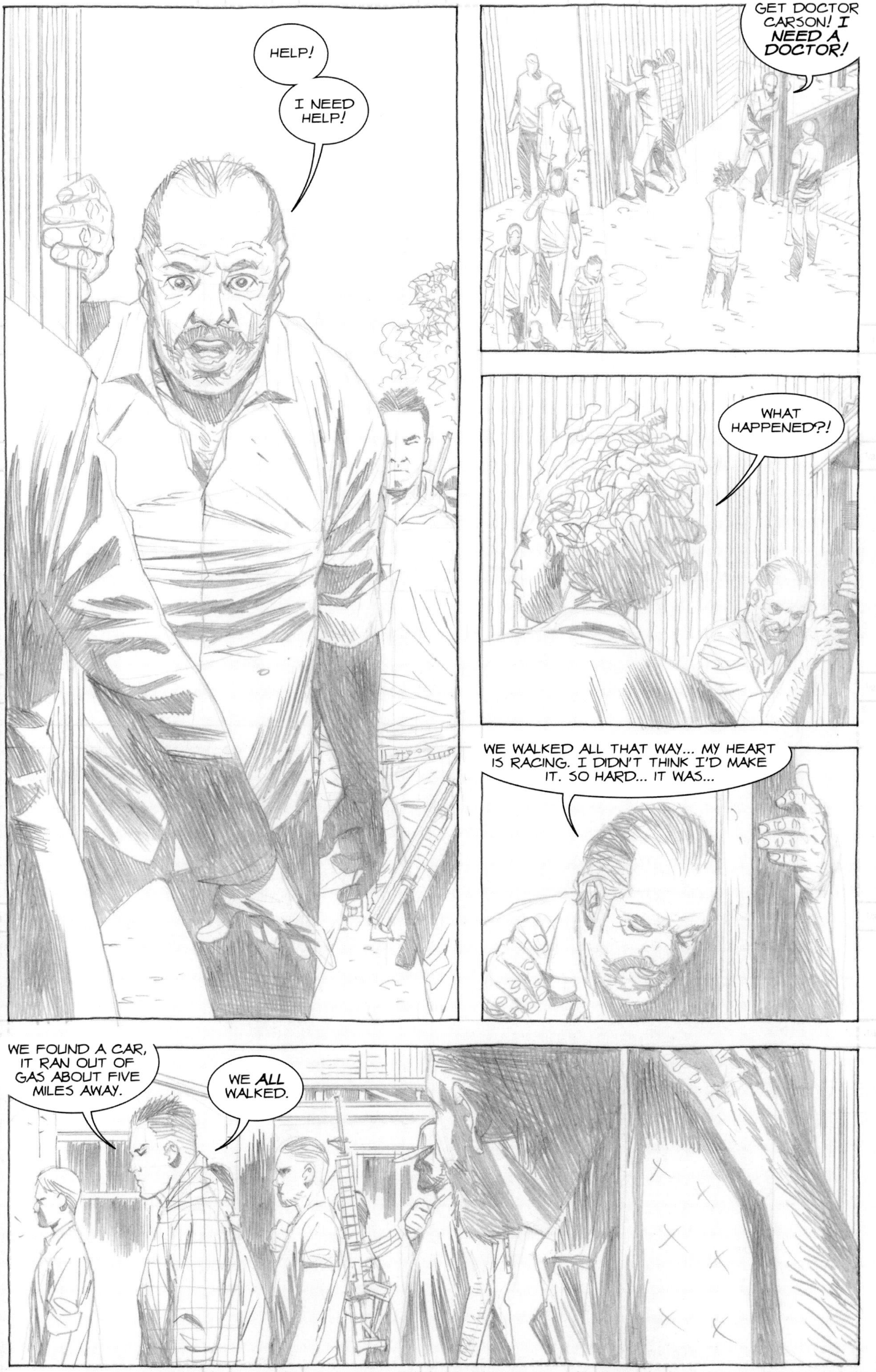
HELP!
I NEED HELP!
GET DOCTOR CARSON! I NEED A DOCTOR!
WHAT HAPPENED?!
WE WALKED ALL THAT WAY... MY HEART IS RACING. I DIDN'T THINK I'D MAKE IT. SO HARD... IT WAS...
WE FOUND A CAR, IT RAN OUT OF GAS ABOUT FIVE MILES AWAY.
WE ALL WALKED.

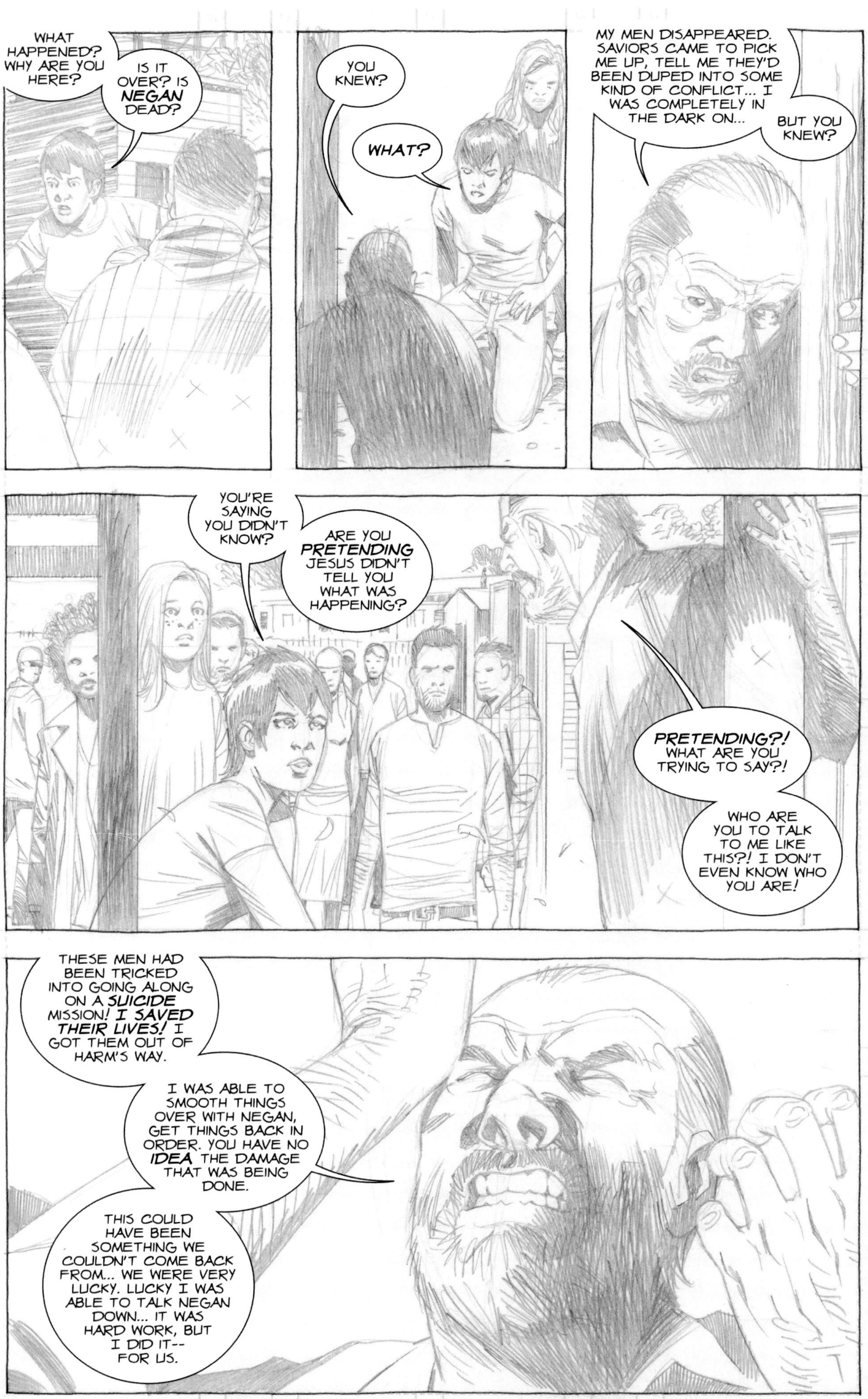
WHAT HAPPENED? WHY ARE YOU HERE?
IS IT OVER? IS NEGAN DEAD?
YOU KNEW?
WHAT?
MY MEN DISAPPEARED. SAVIORS CAME TO PICK ME UP, TELL ME THEY'D BEEN DUPED INTO SOME KIND OF CONFLICT... I WAS COMPLETELY IN THE DARK ON...
BUT YOU KNEW?
YOU'RE SAYING YOU DIDN'T KNOW?
ARE YOU PRETENDING JESUS DIDN'T TELL YOU WHAT WAS HAPPENING?
PRETENDING?! WHAT ARE YOU TRYING TO SAY?!
WHO ARE YOU TO TALK TO ME LIKE THIS?! I DON'T EVEN KNOW WHO YOU ARE!
THESE MEN HAD BEEN TRICKED INTO GOING ALONG ON A SUICIDE MISSION! I SAVED THEIR LIVES! I GOT THEM OUT OF HARM'S WAY.
I WAS ABLE TO SMOOTH THINGS OVER WITH NEGAN, GET THINGS BACK IN ORDER. YOU HAVE NO IDEA THE DAMAGE THAT WAS BEING DONE.
THIS COULD HAVE BEEN SOMETHING WE COULDN'T COME BACK FROM... WE WERE VERY LUCKY. LUCKY I WAS ABLE TO TALK NEGAN DOWN... IT WAS HARD WORK, BUT I DID IT-- FOR US.

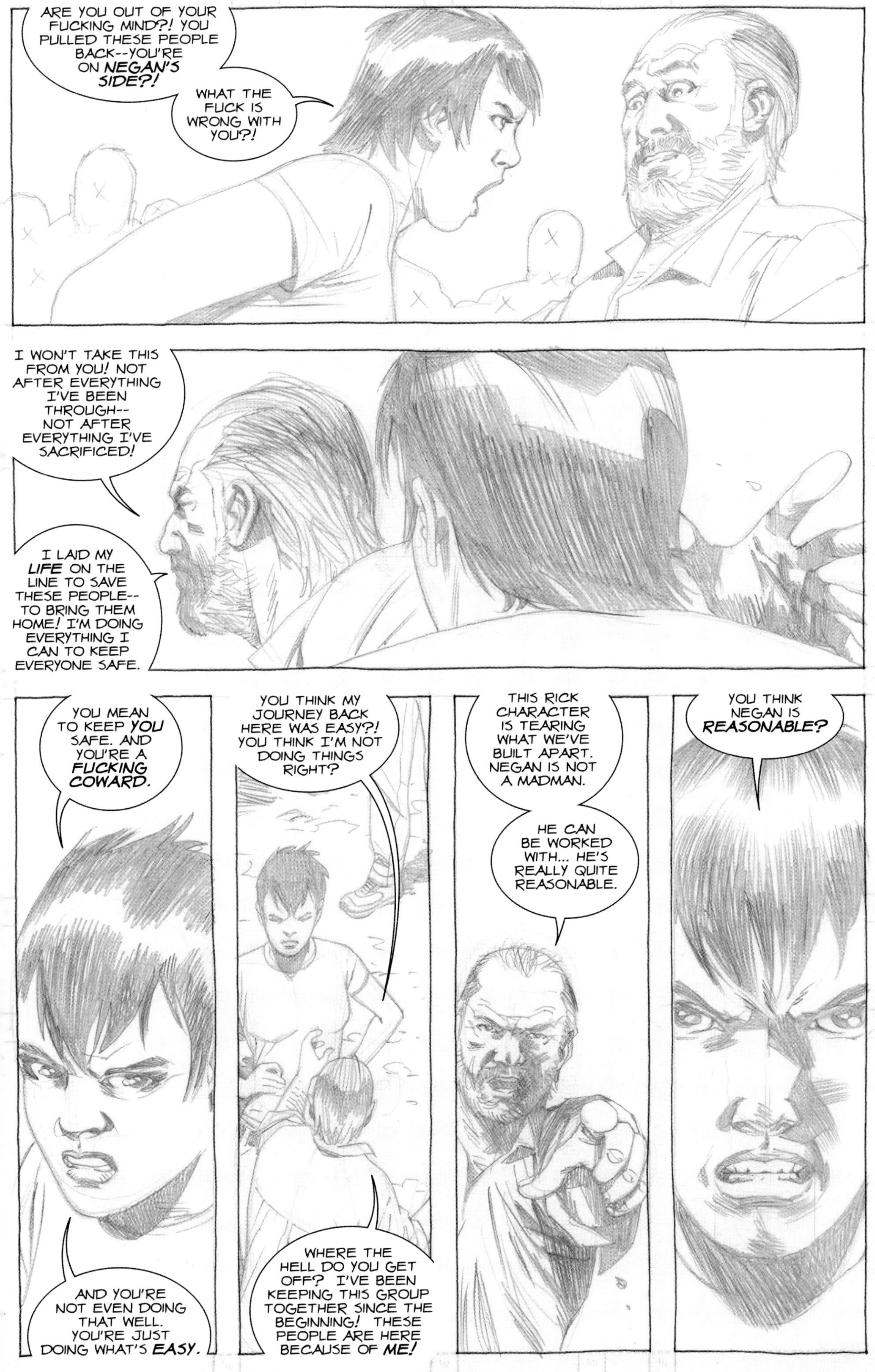
ARE YOU OUT OF YOUR FUCKING MIND?! YOU PULLED THESE PEOPLE BACK--YOU'RE ON NEGAN'S SIDE?!
WHAT THE FUCK IS WRONG WITH YOU?!
I WON'T TAKE THIS FROM YOU! NOT AFTER EVERYTHING I'VE BEEN THROUGH-- NOT AFTER EVERYTHING I'VE SACRIFICED!
I LAID MY LIFE ON THE LINE TO SAVE THESE PEOPLE-- TO BRING THEM HOME! I'M DOING EVERYTHING I CAN TO KEEP EVERYONE SAFE.
YOU MEAN TO KEEP YOU SAFE. AND YOU'RE A FUCKING COWARD.
AND YOU'RE NOT EVEN DOING THAT WELL. YOU'RE JUST DOING WHAT'S EASY.
YOU THINK MY JOURNEY BACK HERE WAS EASY?! YOU THINK I'M NOT DOING THINGS RIGHT?
WHERE THE HELL DO YOU GET OFF? I'VE BEEN KEEPING THIS GROUP TOGETHER SINCE THE BEGINNING! THESE PEOPLE ARE HERE BECAUSE OF ME!
THIS RICK CHARACTER IS TEARING WHAT WE'VE BUILT APART. NEGAN IS NOT A MADMAN.
HE CAN BE WORKED WITH... HE'S REALLY QUITE REASONABLE.
YOU THINK NEGAN IS REASONABLE?

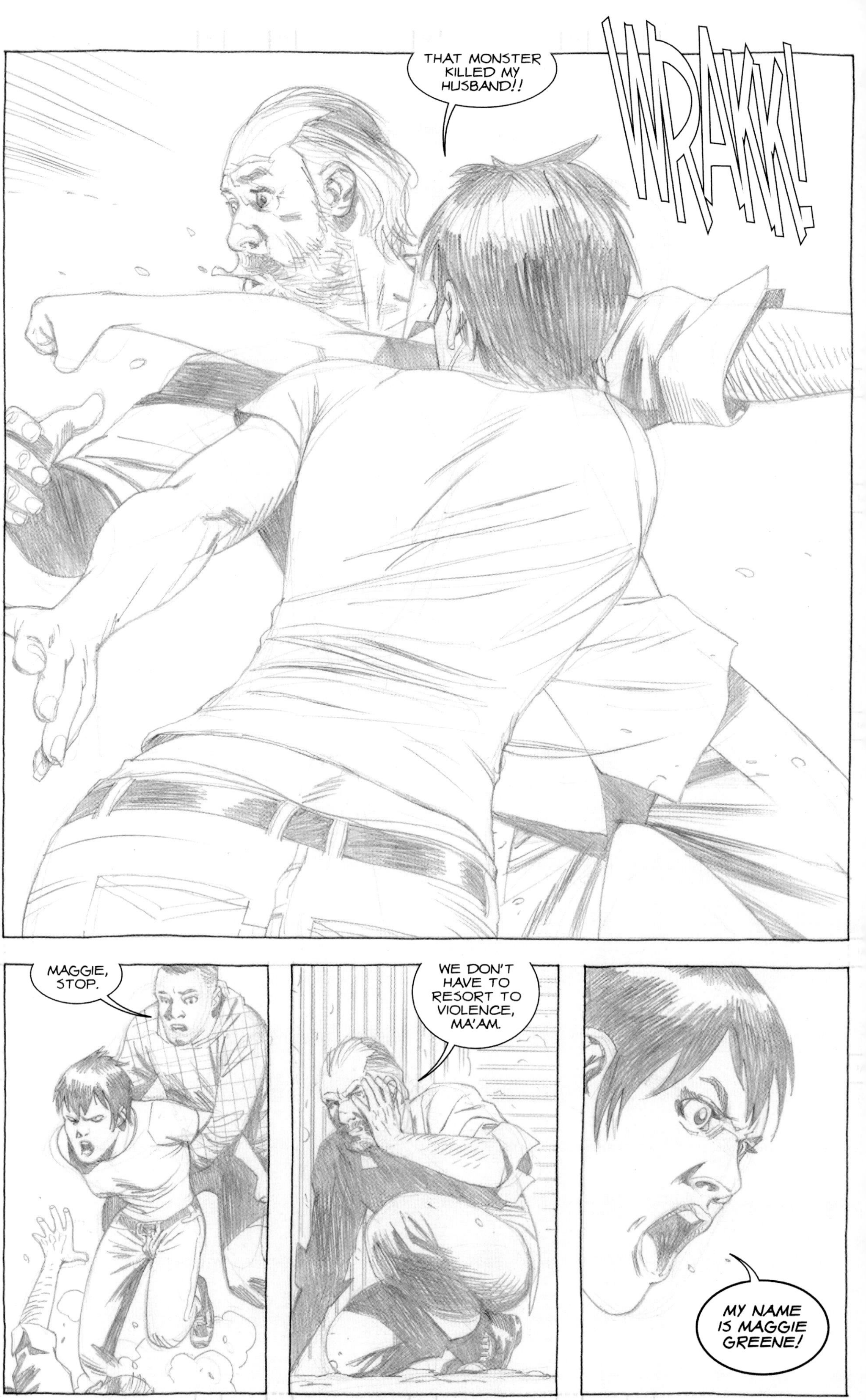
THAT MONSTER KILLED MY HUSBAND!!
WRAKK!
MAGGIE, STOP.
WE DON'T HAVE TO RESORT TO VIOLENCE, MA'AM.
MY NAME IS MAGGIE GREENE!

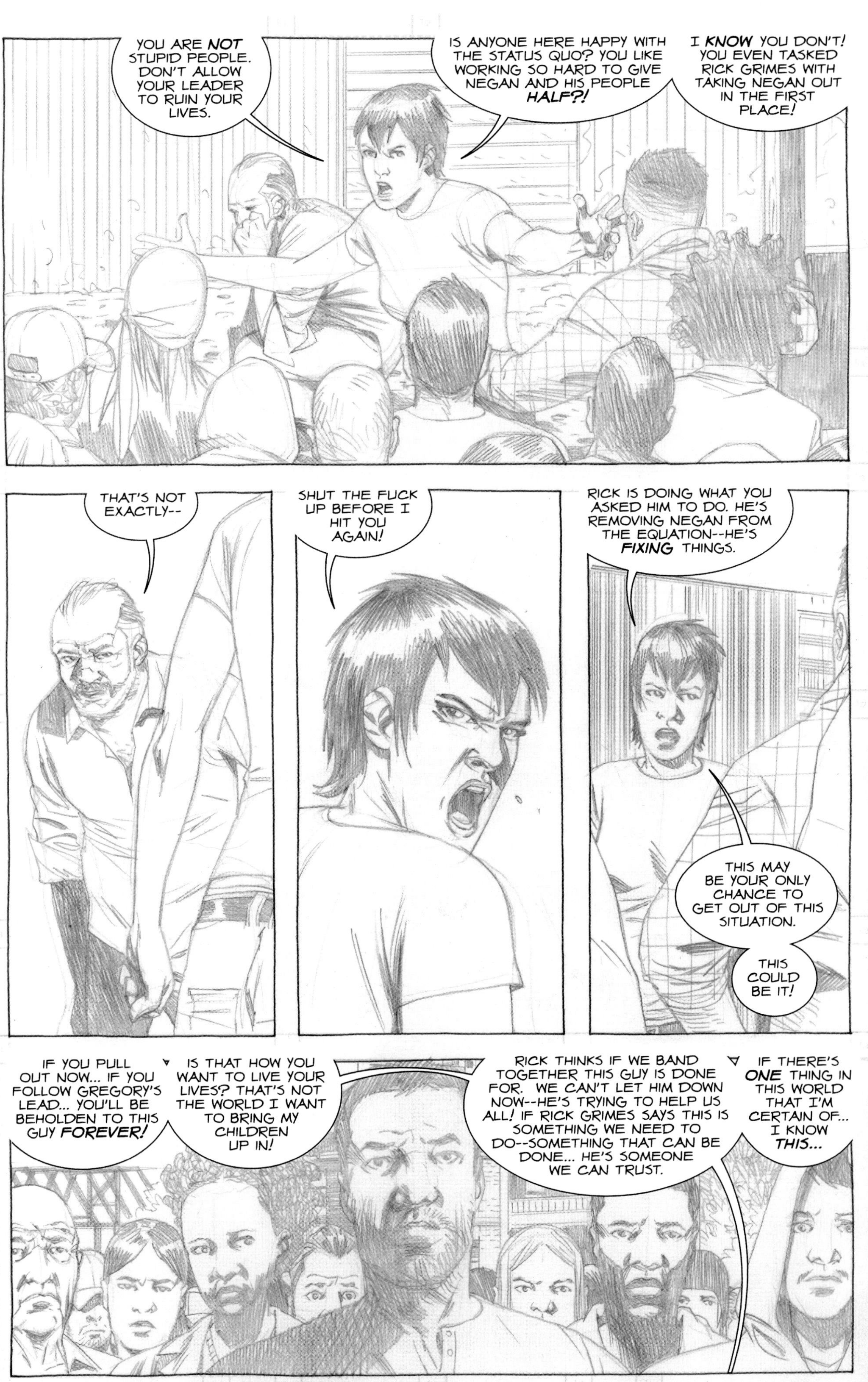

YOU ARE NOT STUPID PEOPLE. DON'T ALLOW YOUR LEADER TO RUIN YOUR LIVES.
IS ANYONE HERE HAPPY WITH THE STATUS QUO? YOU LIKE WORKING SO HARD TO GIVE NEGAN AND HIS PEOPLE HALF?!
I KNOW YOU DON'T! YOU EVEN TASKED RICK GRIMES WITH TAKING NEGAN OUT IN THE FIRST PLACE!
THAT'S NOT EXACTLY--
SHUT THE FUCK UP BEFORE I HIT YOU AGAIN!
RICK IS DOING WHAT YOU ASKED HIM TO DO. HE'S REMOVING NEGAN FROM THE EQUATION--HE'S FIXING THINGS.
THIS MAY BE YOUR ONLY CHANCE TO GET OUT OF THIS SITUATION.
THIS COULD BE IT!
IF YOU PULL OUT NOW... IF YOU FOLLOW GREGORY'S LEAD... YOU'LL BE BEHOLDEN TO THIS GUY FOREVER!
IS THAT HOW YOU WANT TO LIVE YOUR LIVES? THAT'S NOT THE WORLD I WANT TO BRING MY CHILDREN UP IN!
RICK THINKS IF WE BAND TOGETHER THIS GUY IS DONE FOR. WE CAN'T LET HIM DOWN NOW--HE'S TRYING TO HELP US ALL! IF RICK GRIMES SAYS THIS IS SOMETHING WE NEED TO DO--SOMETHING THAT CAN BE DONE... HE'S SOMEONE WE CAN TRUST.
IF THERE'S ONE THING IN THIS WORLD THAT I'M CERTAIN OF... I KNOW THIS...

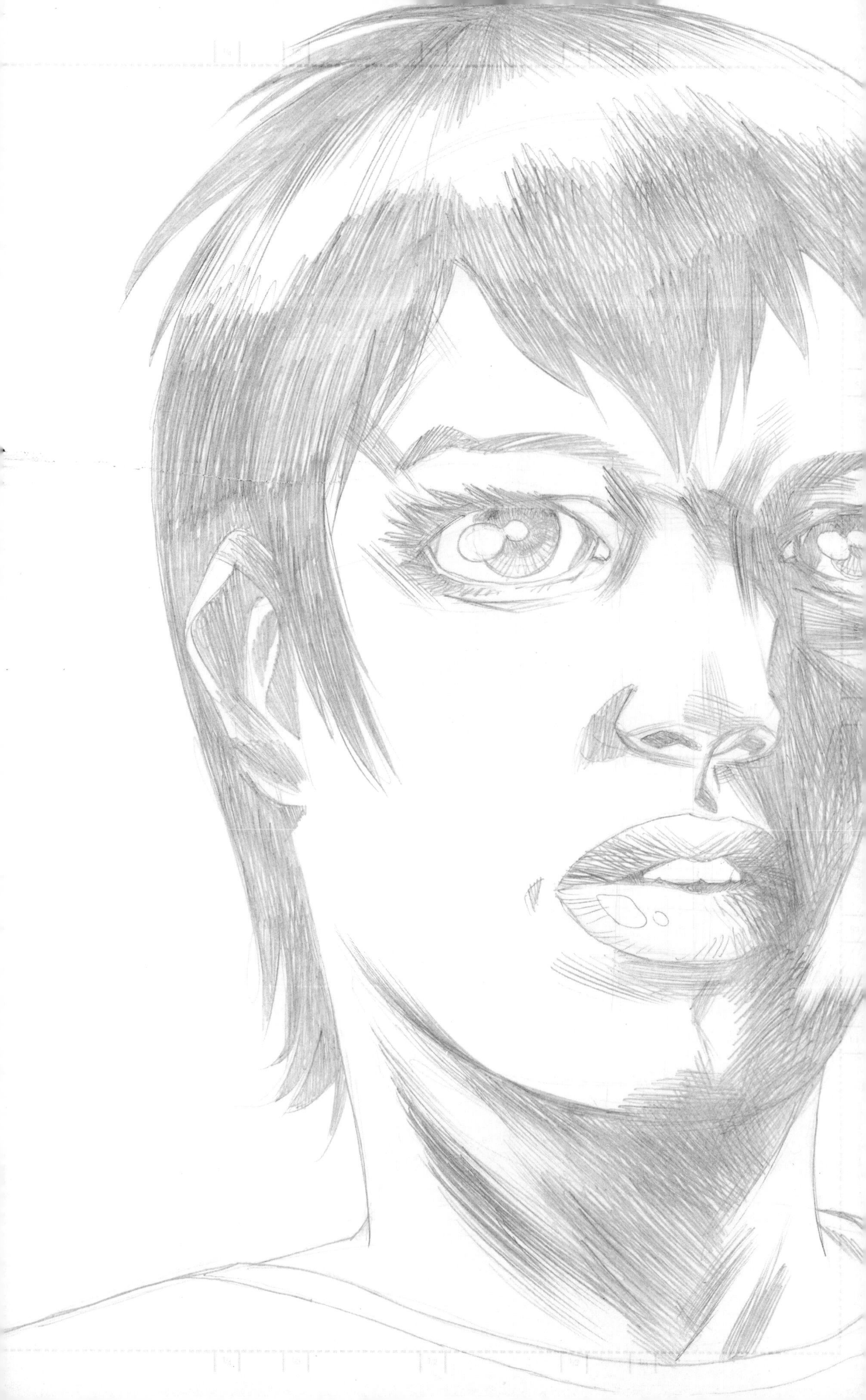

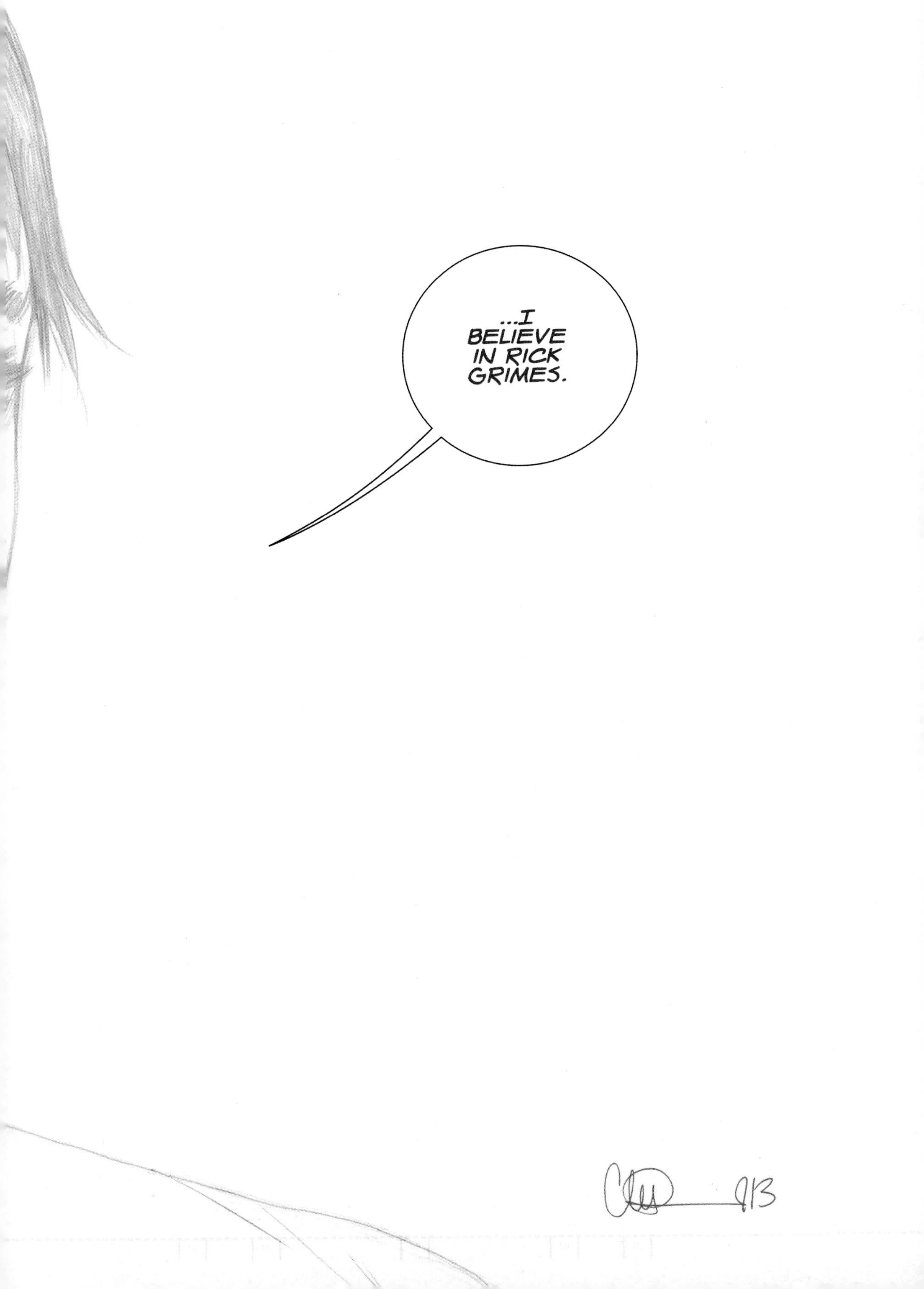
...I BELIEVE IN RICK GRIMES.

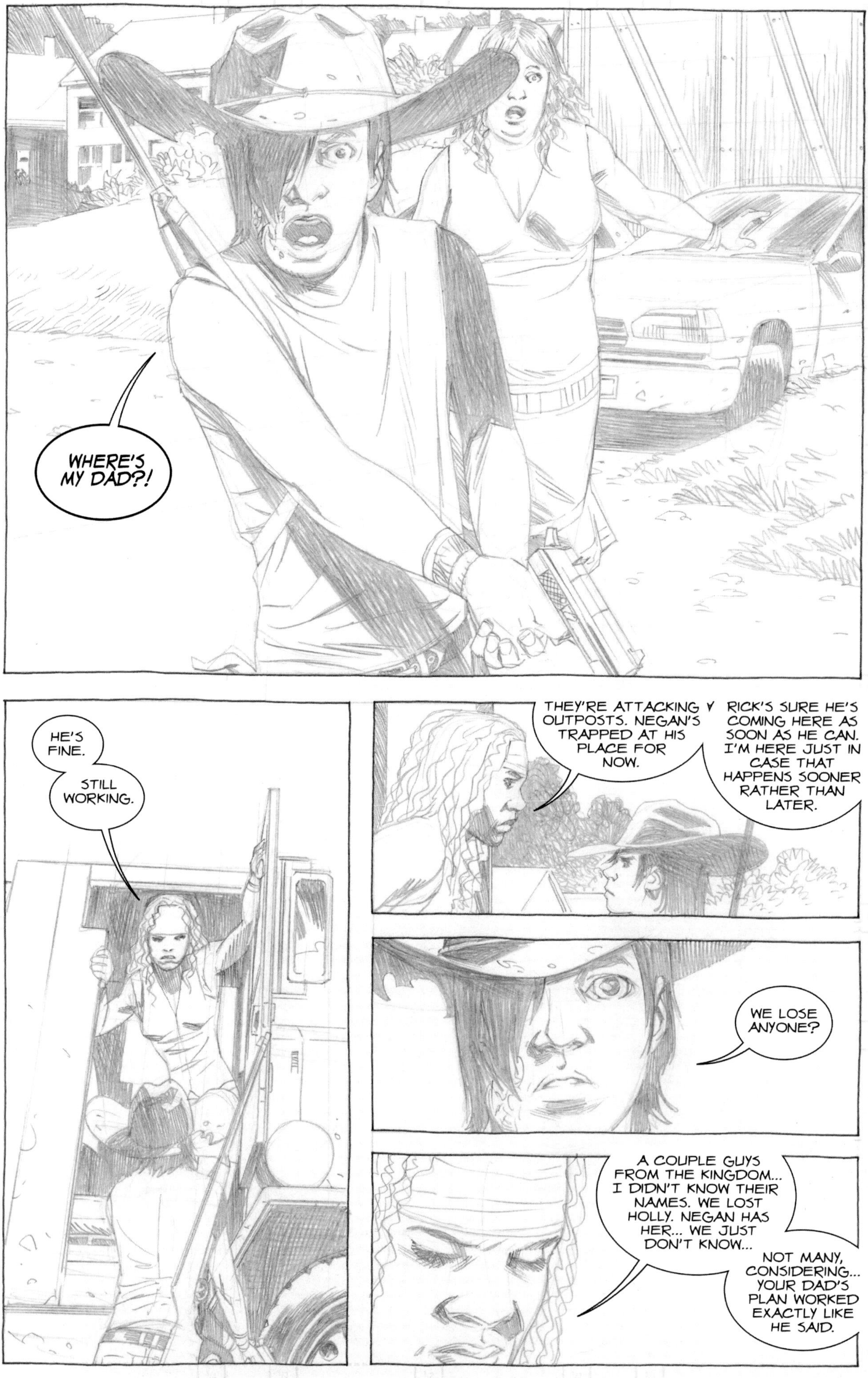
WHERE'S MY DAD?!
HE'S FINE.
STILL WORKING.
THEY'RE ATTACKING Y OUTPOSTS. NEGAN'S TRAPPED AT HIS PLACE FOR NOW.
RICK'S SURE HE'S COMING HERE AS SOON AS HE CAN. I'M HERE JUST IN CASE THAT HAPPENS SOONER RATHER THAN LATER.
WE LOSE ANYONE?
A COUPLE GUYS FROM THE KINGDOM... I DIDN'T KNOW THEIR NAMES. WE LOST HOLLY. NEGAN HAS HER... WE JUST DON'T KNOW...
NOT MANY, CONSIDERING... YOUR DAD'S PLAN WORKED EXACTLY LIKE HE SAID.

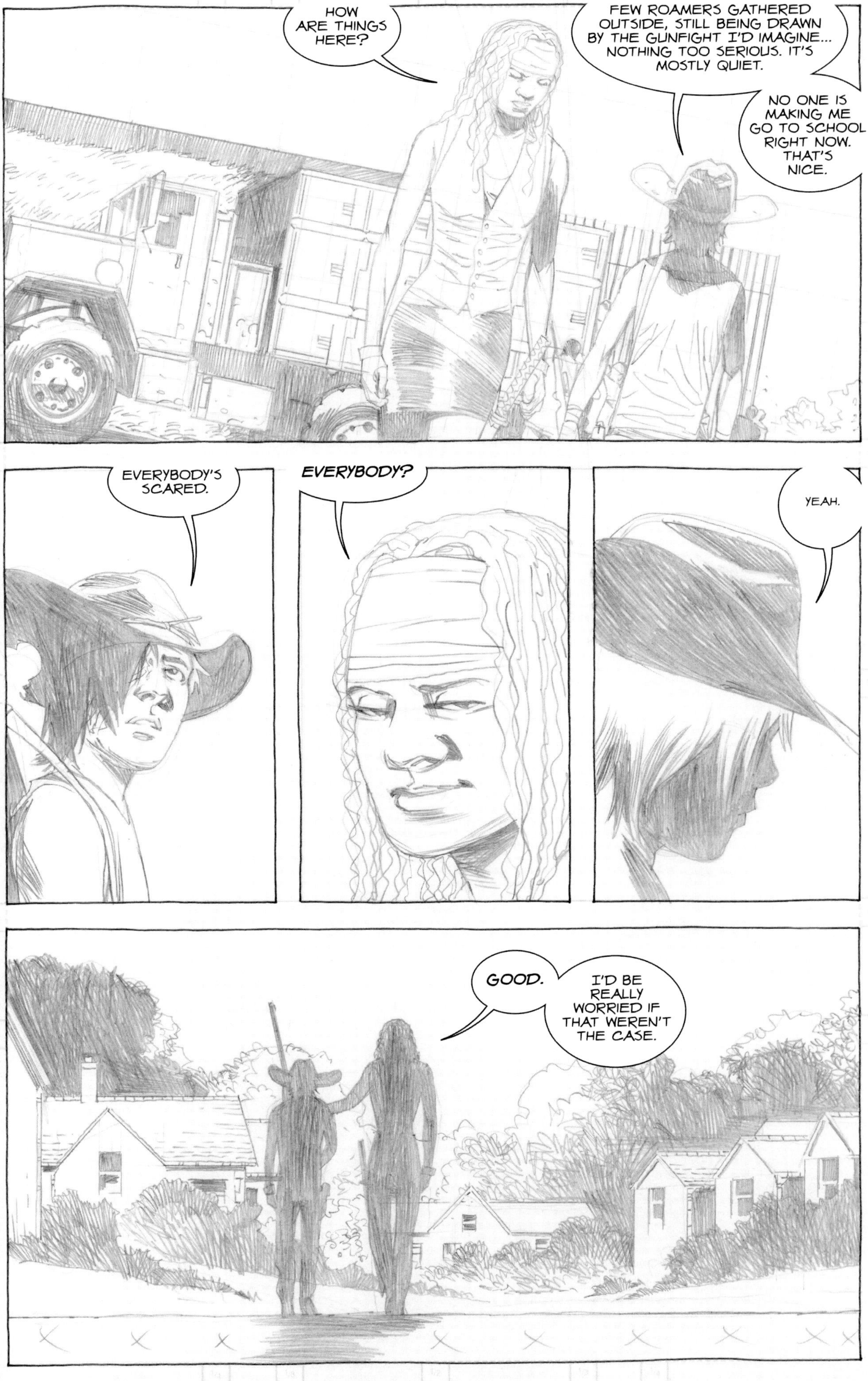
HOW ARE THINGS HERE?
FEW ROAMERS GATHERED OUTSIDE, STILL BEING DRAWN BY THE GUNFIGHT I'D IMAGINE... NOTHING TOO SERIOUS. IT'S MOSTLY QUIET.
NO ONE IS MAKING ME GO TO SCHOOL RIGHT NOW. THAT'S NICE.
EVERYBODY'S SCARED.
EVERYBODY?
YEAH.
GOOD.
I'D BE REALLY WORRIED IF THAT WEREN'T THE CASE.

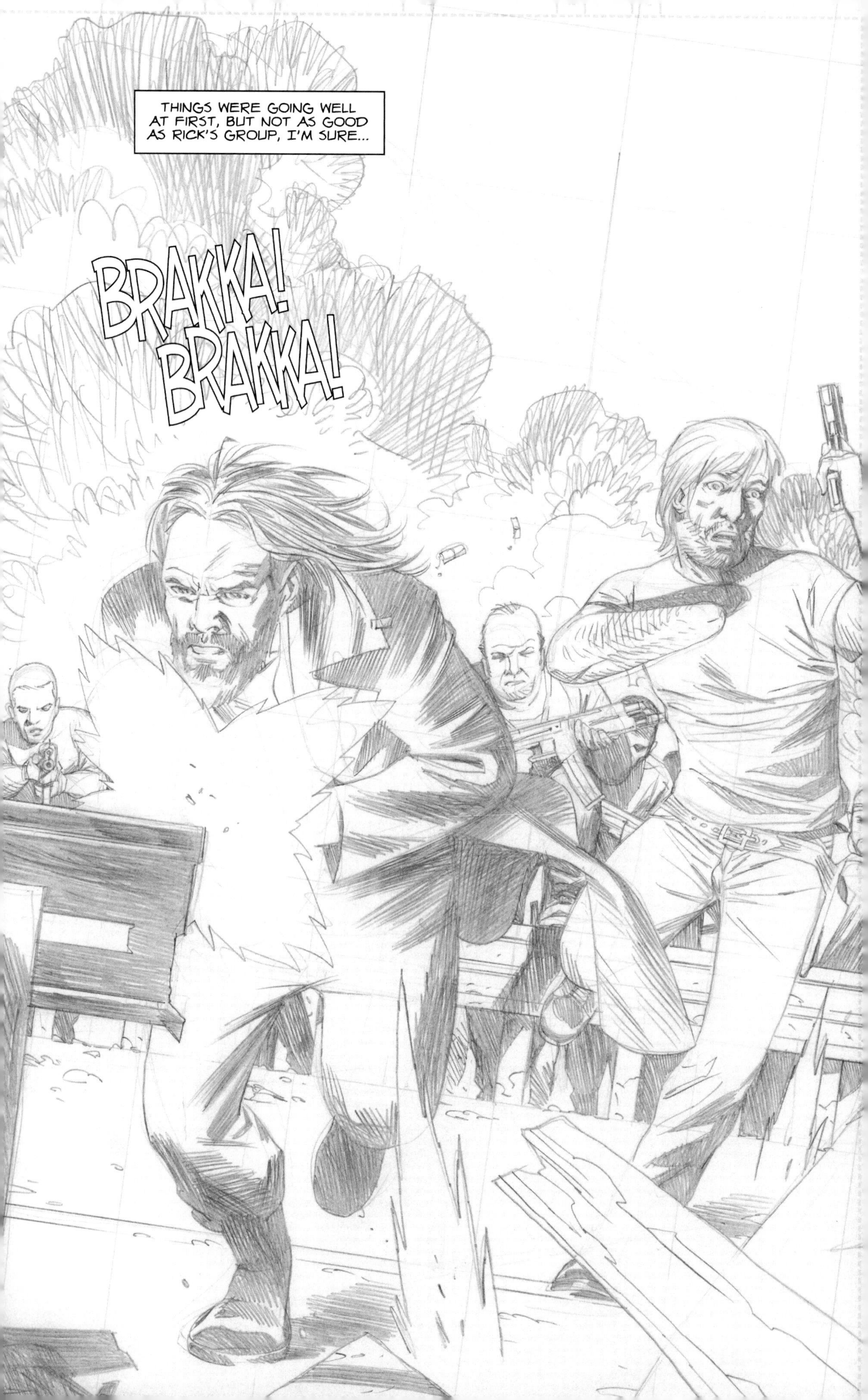
THINGS WERE GOING WELL AT FIRST, BUT NOT AS GOOD AS RICK'S GROUP, I'M SURE...
BRAKKA! BRAKKA!

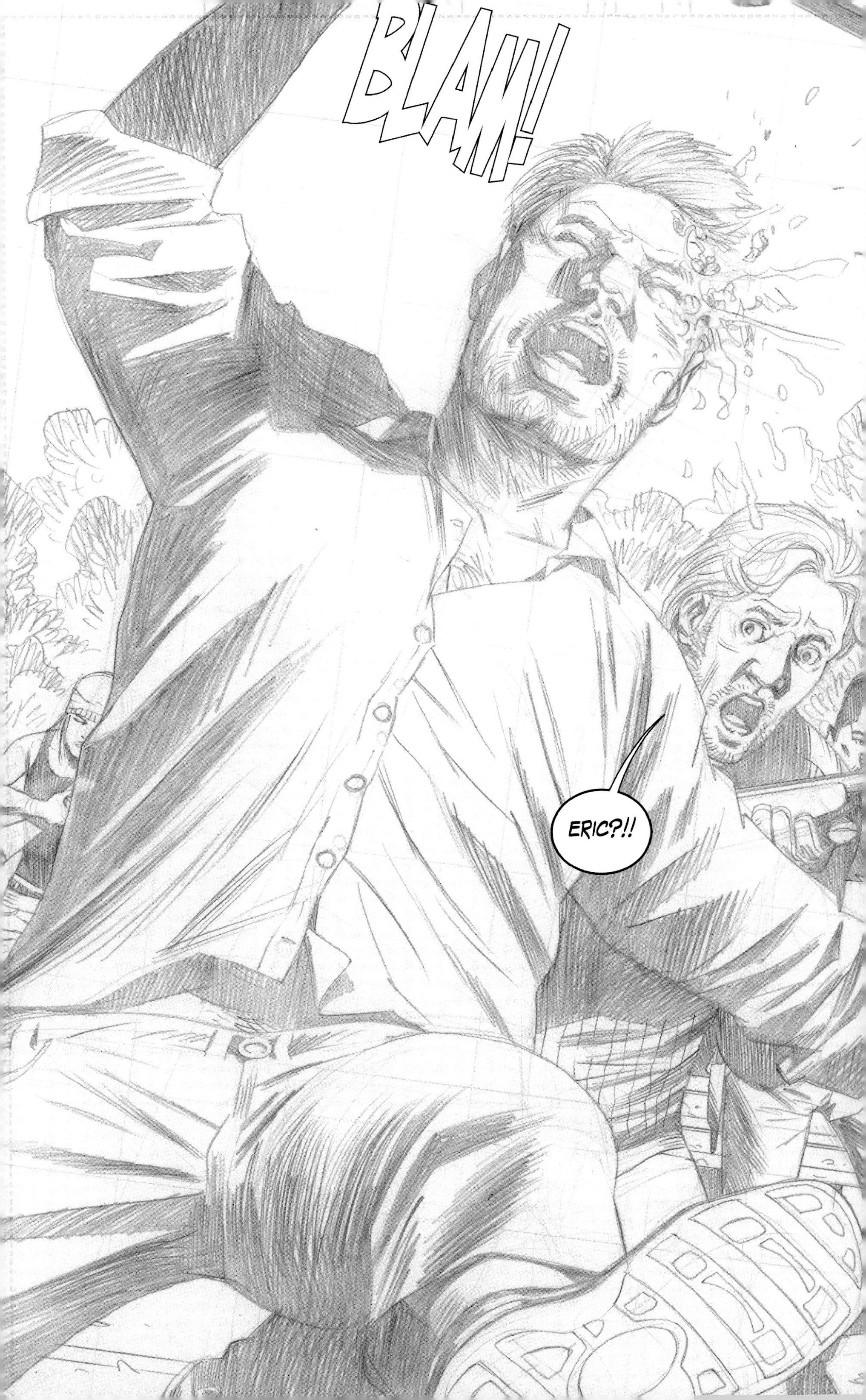
BLAM!
ERIC?!!

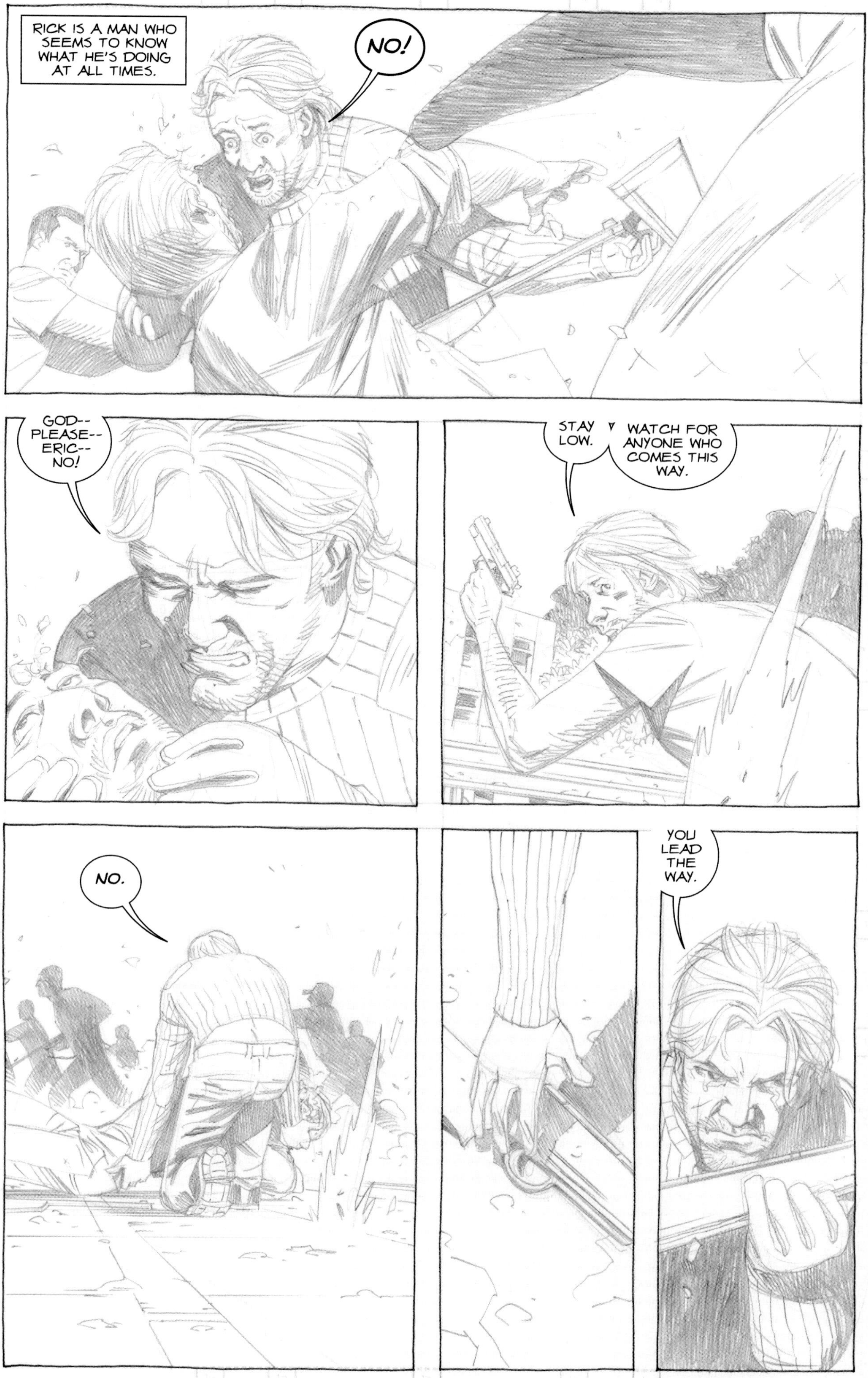
RICK IS A MAN WHO SEEMS TO KNOW WHAT HE'S DOING AT ALL TIMES.
NO!
GOD-- PLEASE-- ERIC-- NO!
STAY LOW.
WATCH FOR ANYONE WHO COMES THIS WAY.
NO.
YOU LEAD THE WAY.

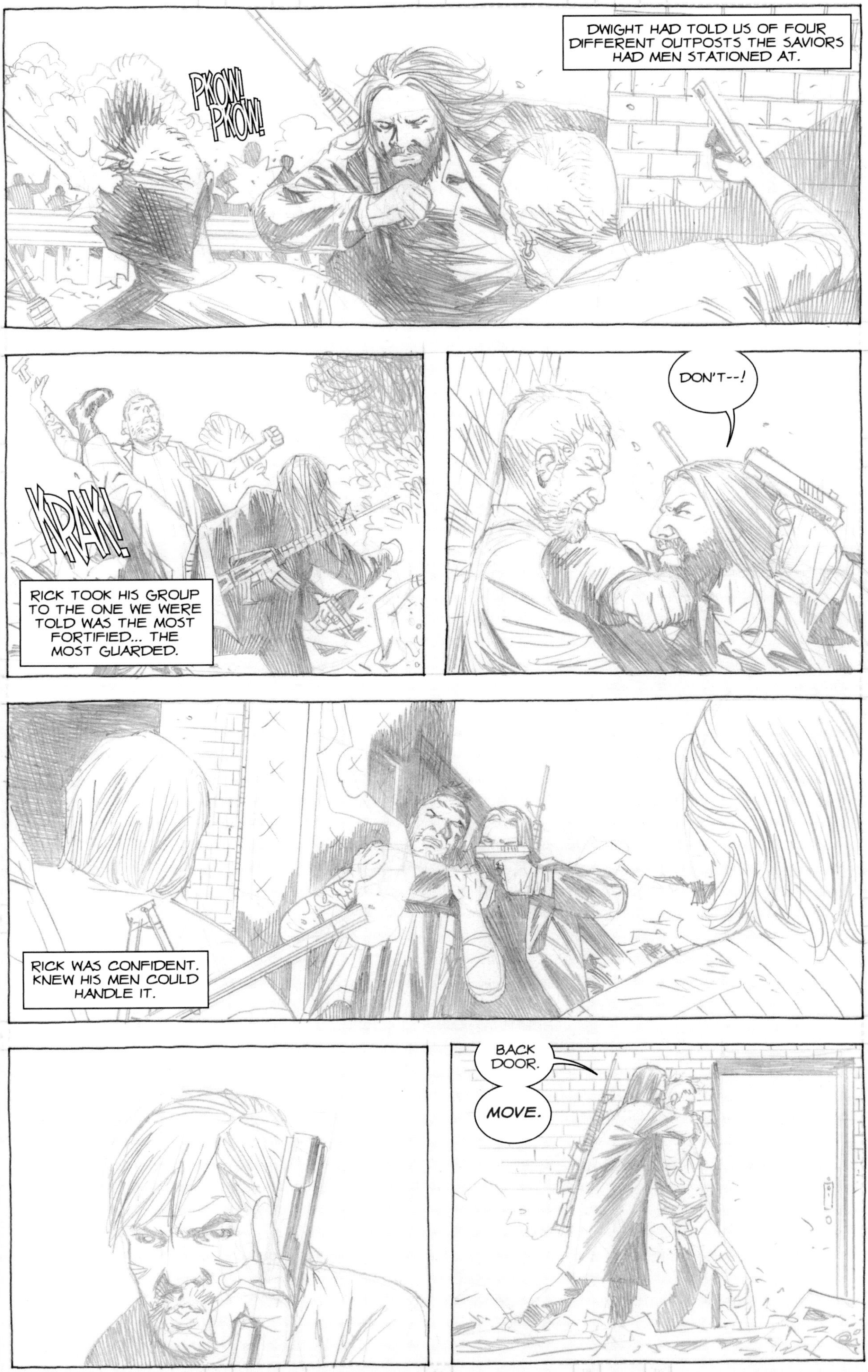
DWIGHT HAD TOLD US OF FOUR DIFFERENT OUTPOSTS THE SAVIORS HAD MEN STATIONED AT.
PKOW! PKOW!
KRAK!
RICK TOOK HIS GROUP TO THE ONE WE WERE TOLD WAS THE MOST FORTIFIED... THE MOST GUARDED.
DON'T--!
RICK WAS CONFIDENT. KNEW HIS MEN COULD HANDLE IT.
BACK DOOR.
MOVE.

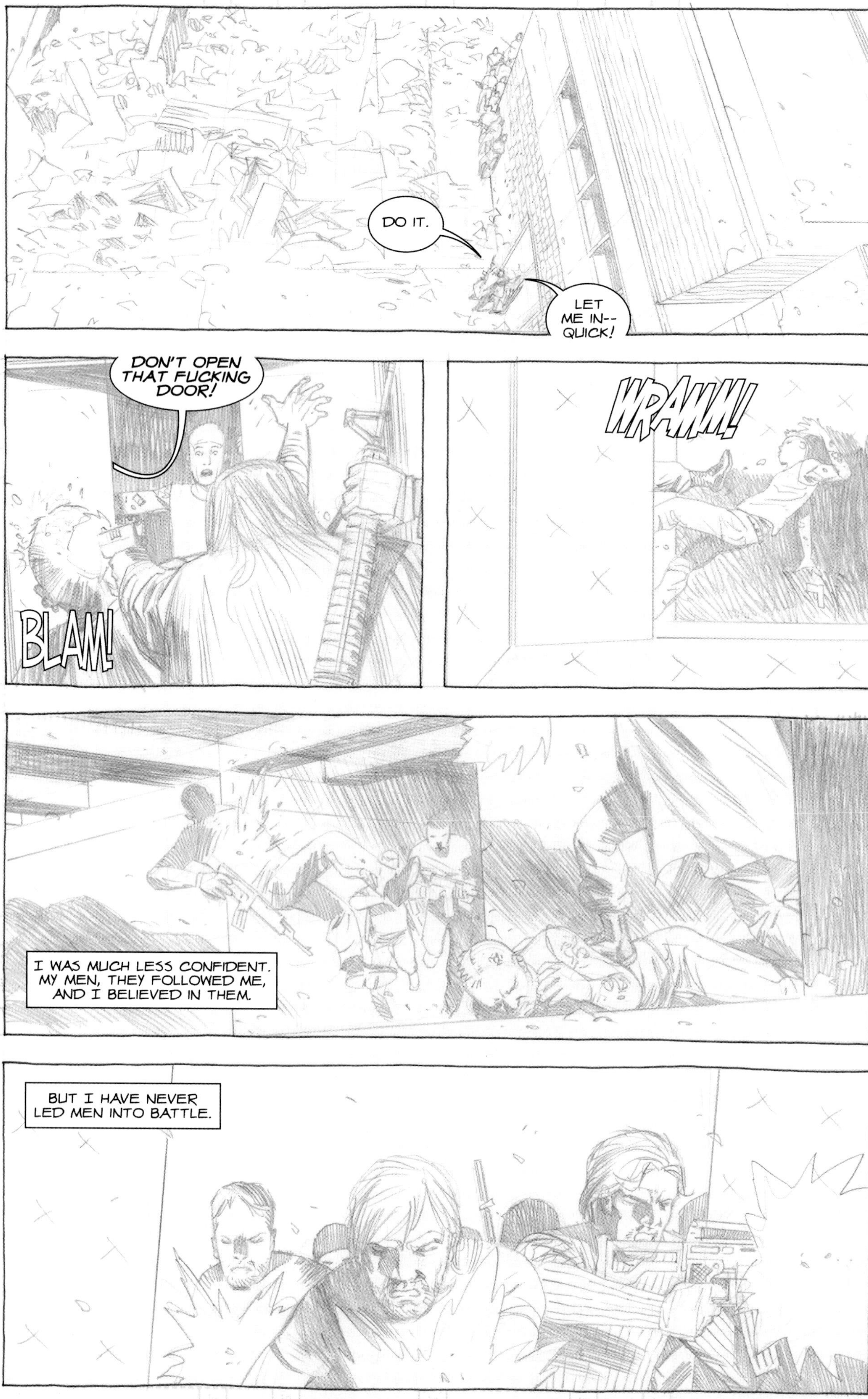
DO IT.
LET ME IN-- QUICK!
DON'T OPEN THAT FUCKING DOOR!
BLAM!
WRAMM!
I WAS MUCH LESS CONFIDENT. MY MEN, THEY FOLLOWED ME, AND I BELIEVED IN THEM.
BUT I HAVE NEVER LED MEN INTO BATTLE.

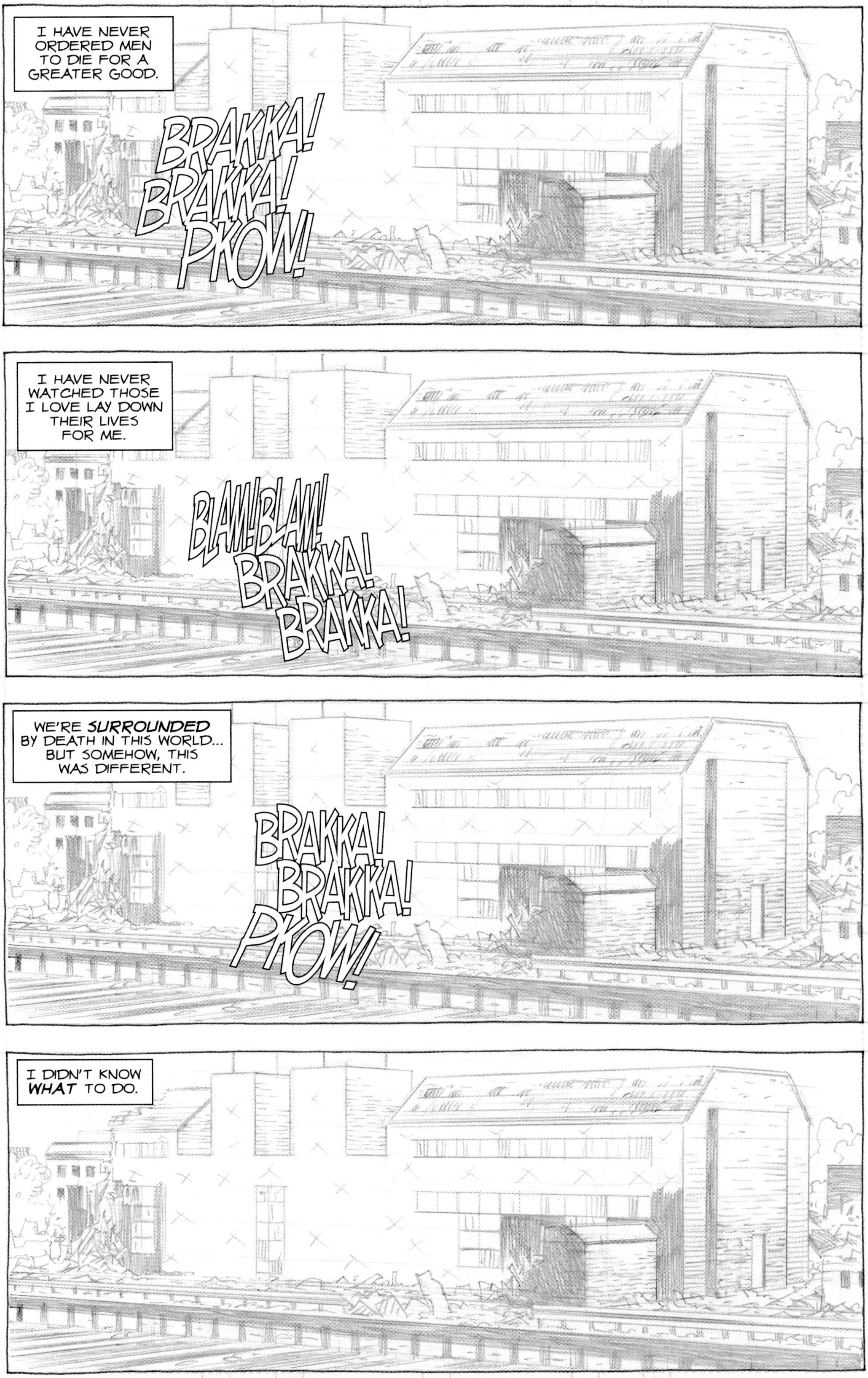
I HAVE NEVER ORDERED MEN TO DIE FOR A GREATER GOOD.
BRAKKA! BRAKKA! PKOW!
I HAVE NEVER WATCHED THOSE I LOVE LAY DOWN THEIR LIVES FOR ME.
BLAM! BLAM! BRAKKA! BRAKKA!
WE'RE SURROUNDED BY DEATH IN THIS WORLD... BUT SOMEHOW, THIS WAS DIFFERENT.
BRAKKA! BRAKKA! PKOW!
I DIDN'T KNOW WHAT TO DO.

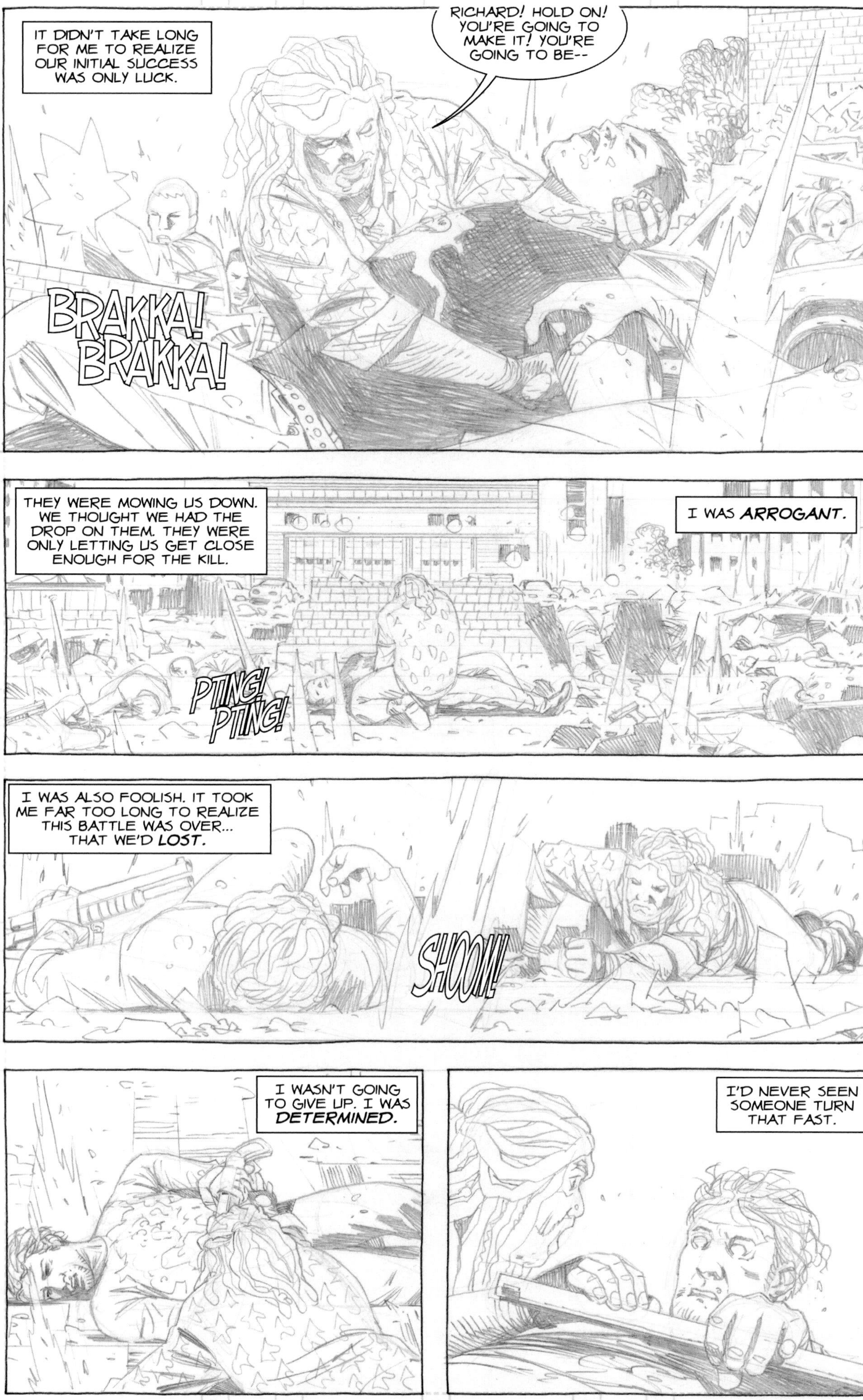

IT DIDN'T TAKE LONG FOR ME TO REALIZE OUR INITIAL SUCCESS WAS ONLY LUCK.
RICHARD! HOLD ON! YOU'RE GOING TO MAKE IT! YOU'RE GOING TO BE--
BRAKKA! BRAKKA!
THEY WERE MOWING US DOWN. WE THOUGHT WE HAD THE DROP ON THEM. THEY WERE ONLY LETTING US GET CLOSE ENOUGH FOR THE KILL.
I WAS ARROGANT.
PTING! PTING!
I WAS ALSO FOOLISH. IT TOOK ME FAR TOO LONG TO REALIZE THIS BATTLE WAS OVER... THAT WE'D LOST.
SHOOM!
I WASN'T GOING TO GIVE UP. I WAS DETERMINED.
I'D NEVER SEEN SOMEONE TURN THAT FAST.

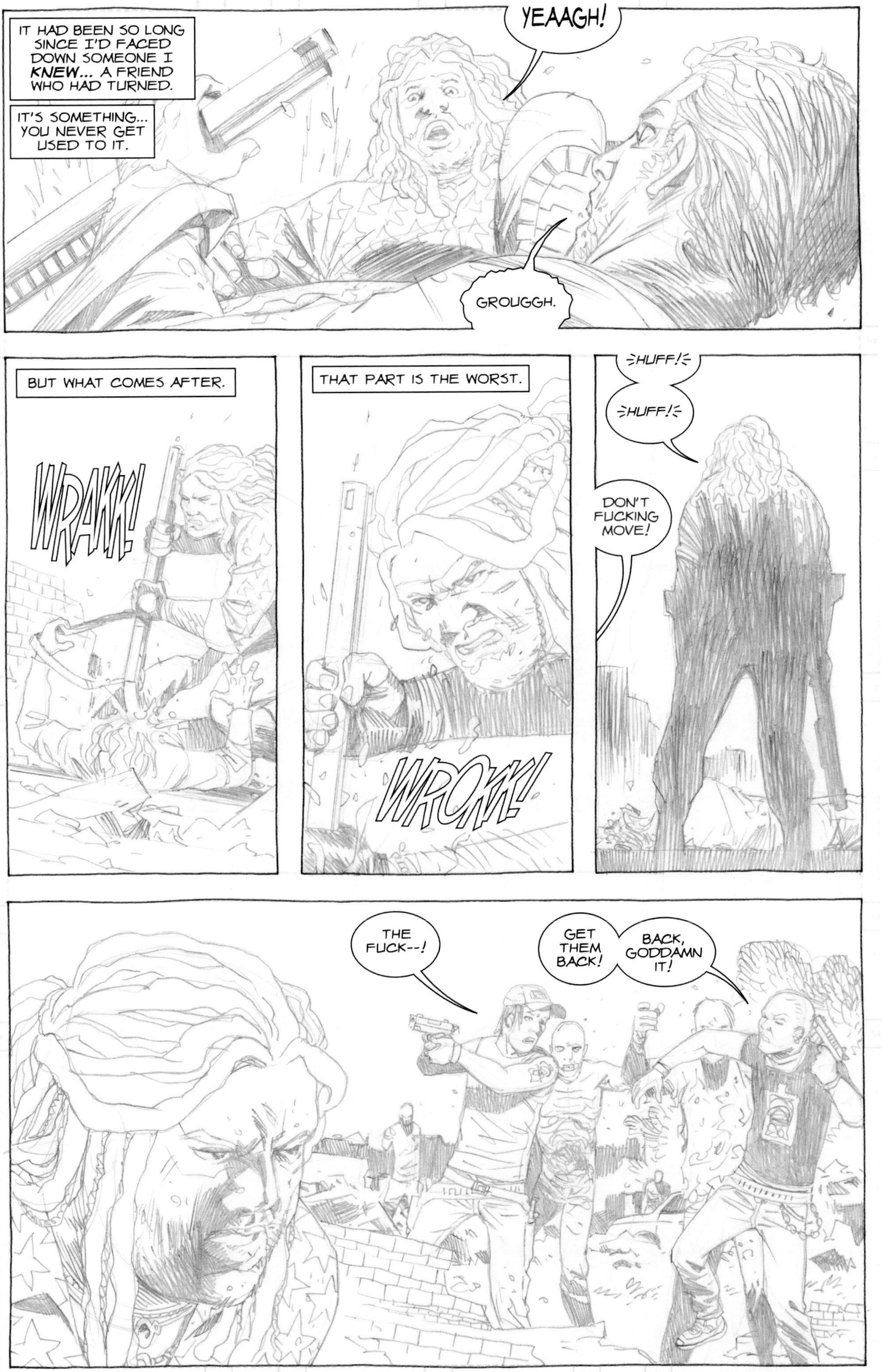
IT HAD BEEN SO LONG SINCE I'D FACED DOWN SOMEONE I **KNEW...** A FRIEND WHO HAD TURNED.
IT'S SOMETHING... YOU NEVER GET USED TO IT.
YEAAGH!
GROUGGH.
BUT WHAT COMES AFTER.
WRAKK!
THAT PART IS THE WORST.
WROKK!
HUFF!
HUFF!
DON'T FUCKING MOVE!
THE FUCK--!
GET THEM BACK!
BACK, GODDAMN IT!

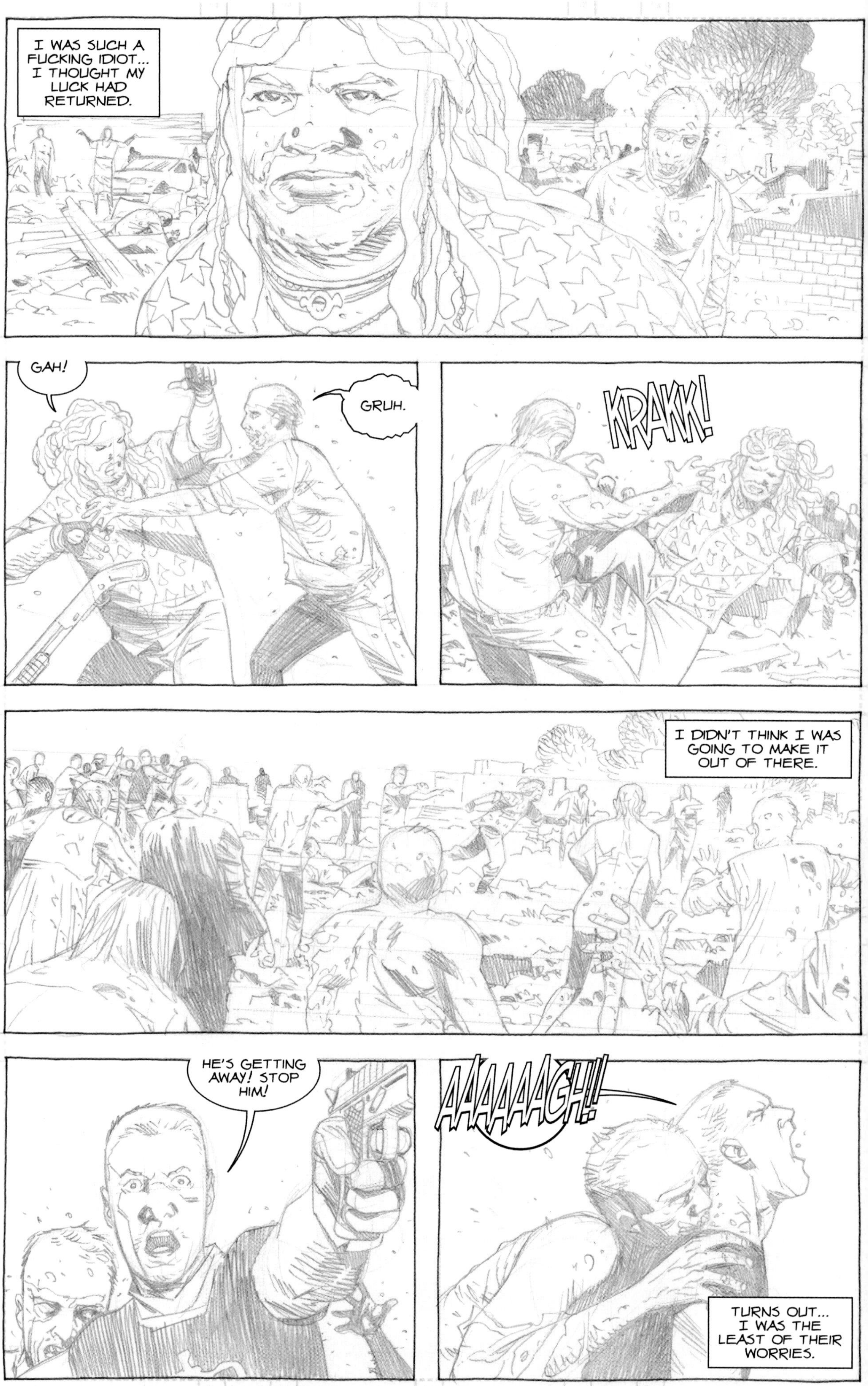
I WAS SUCH A FUCKING IDIOT... I THOUGHT MY LUCK HAD RETURNED.
GAH!
GRUH.
KRAKK!
I DIDN'T THINK I WAS GOING TO MAKE IT OUT OF THERE.
HE'S GETTING AWAY! STOP HIM!
AAAAAAGH!!
TURNS OUT... I WAS THE LEAST OF THEIR WORRIES.

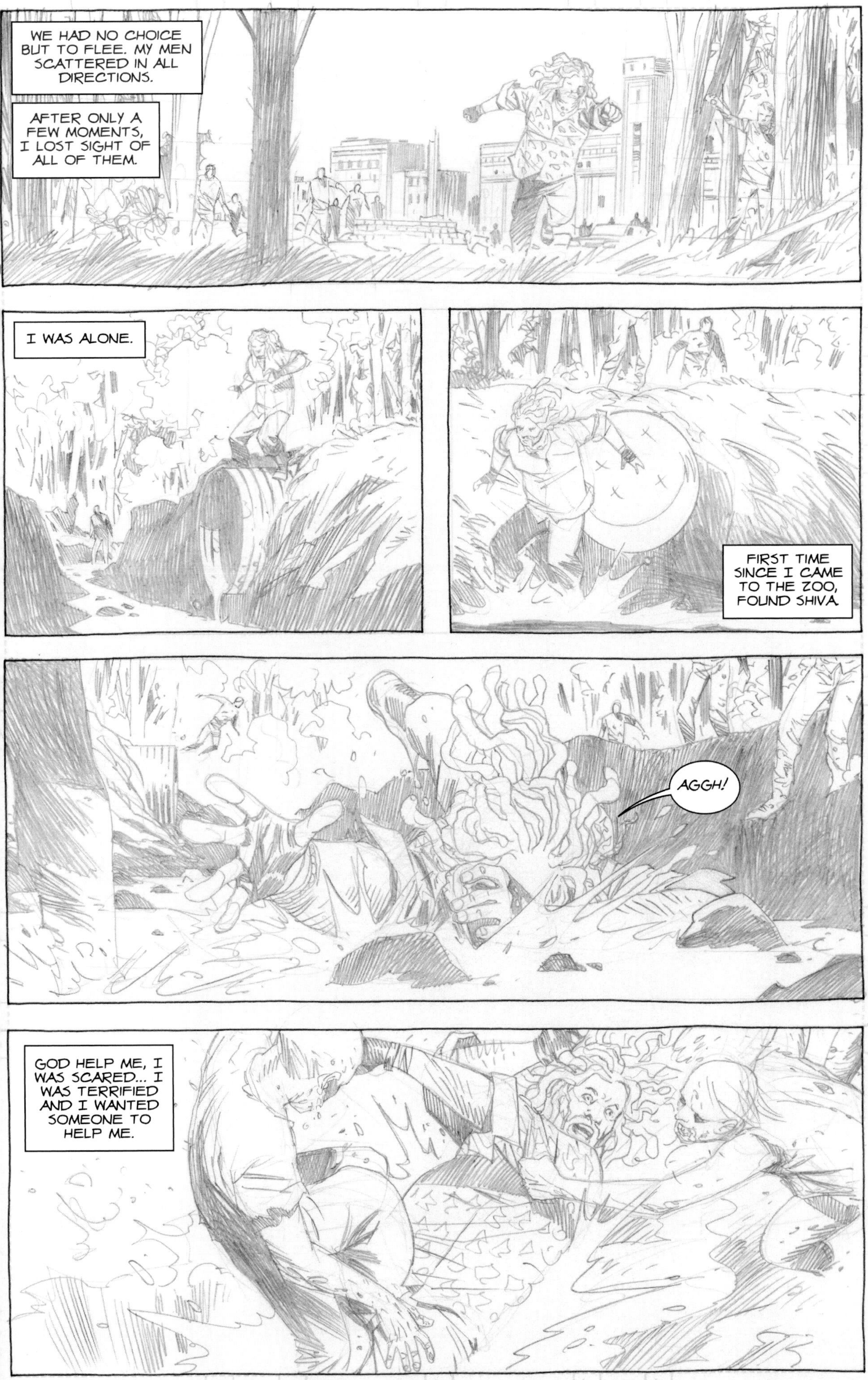
WE HAD NO CHOICE BUT TO FLEE. MY MEN SCATTERED IN ALL DIRECTIONS.
AFTER ONLY A FEW MOMENTS, I LOST SIGHT OF ALL OF THEM.
I WAS ALONE.
FIRST TIME SINCE I CAME TO THE ZOO, FOUND SHIVA.
AGGH!
GOD HELP ME, I WAS SCARED... I WAS TERRIFIED AND I WANTED SOMEONE TO HELP ME.

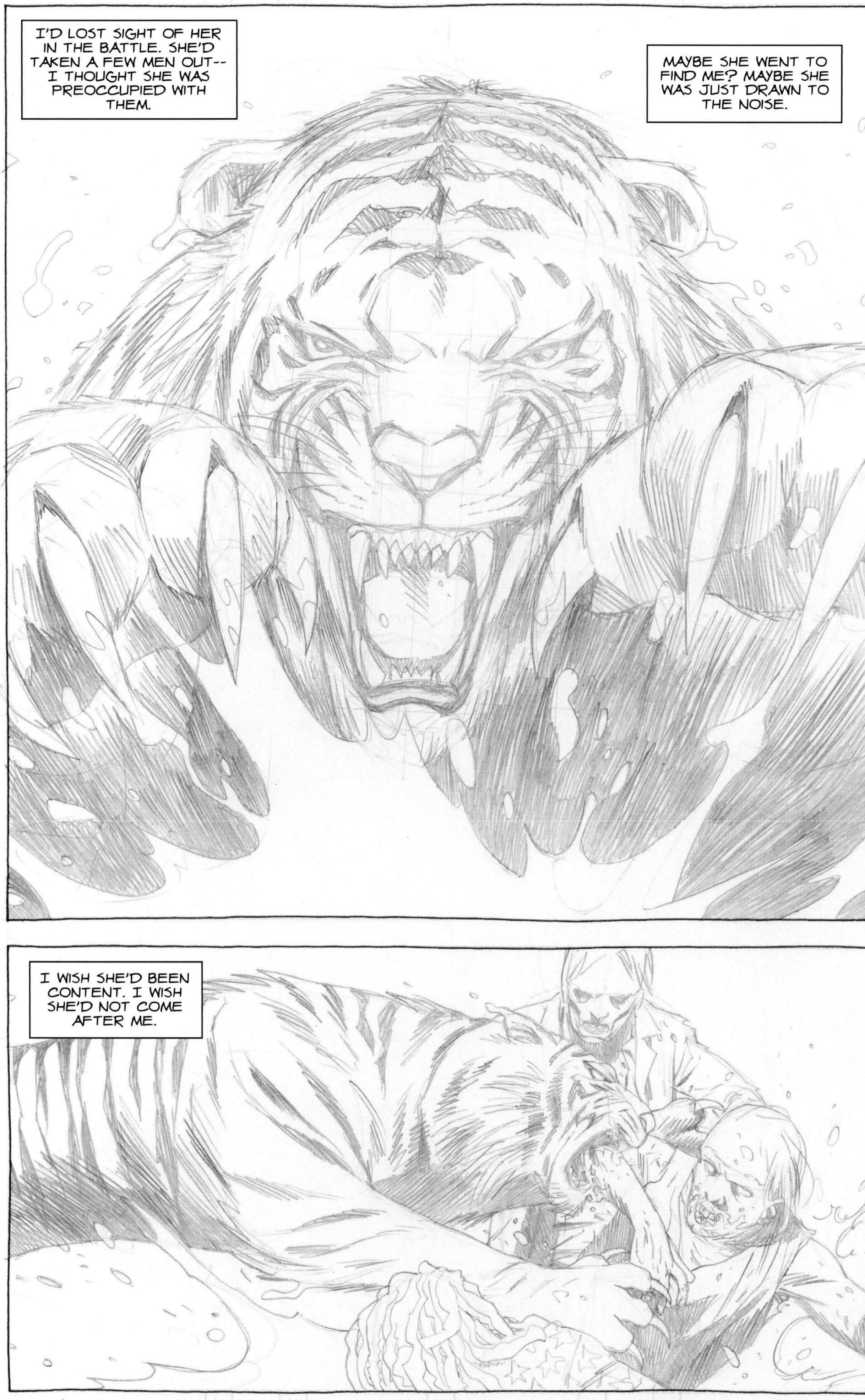
I'D LOST SIGHT OF HER IN THE BATTLE. SHE'D TAKEN A FEW MEN OUT-- I THOUGHT SHE WAS PREOCCUPIED WITH THEM.
MAYBE SHE WENT TO FIND ME? MAYBE SHE WAS JUST DRAWN TO THE NOISE.
I WISH SHE'D BEEN CONTENT. I WISH SHE'D NOT COME AFTER ME.

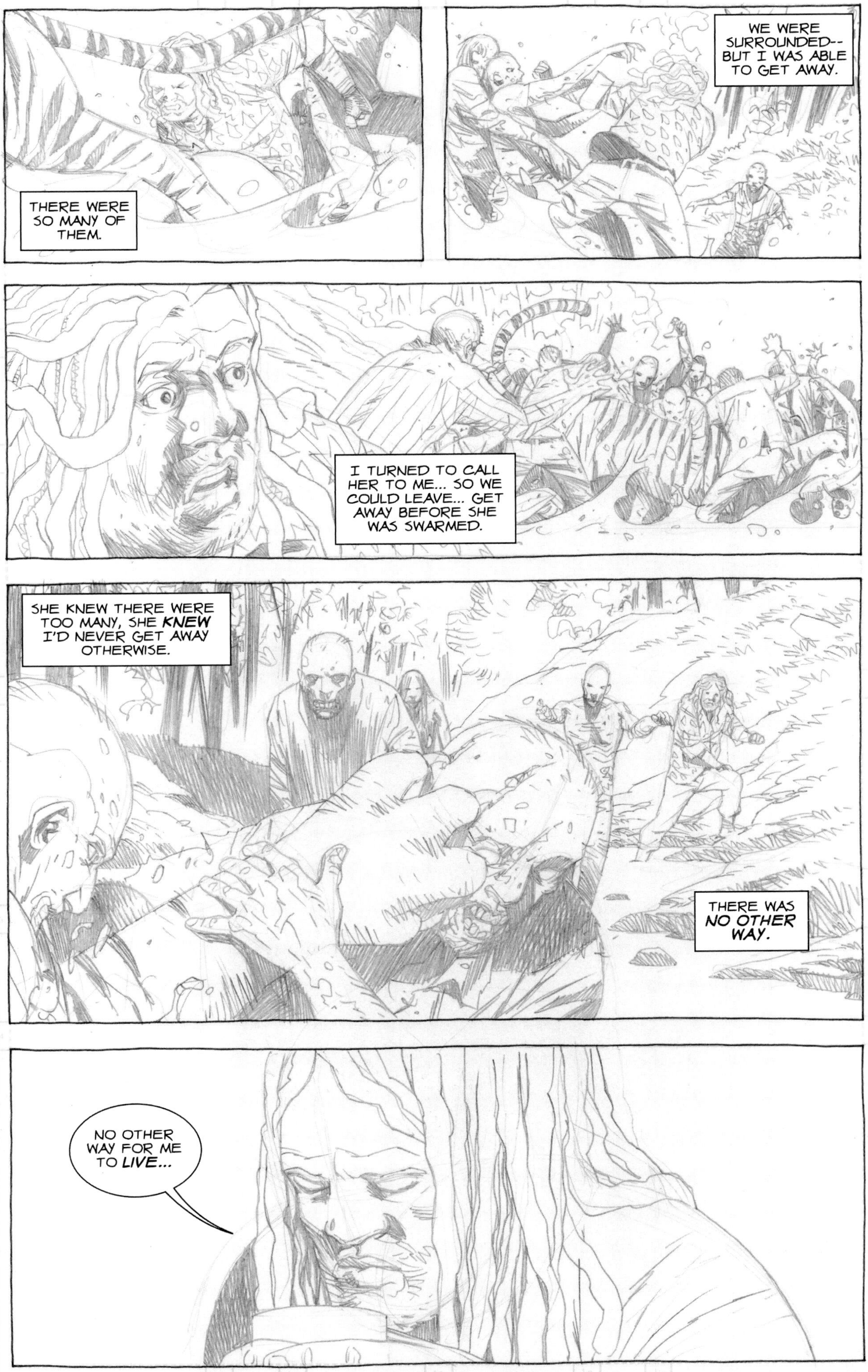
THERE WERE SO MANY OF THEM.
WE WERE SURROUNDED-- BUT I WAS ABLE TO GET AWAY.
I TURNED TO CALL HER TO ME... SO WE COULD LEAVE... GET AWAY BEFORE SHE WAS SWARMED.
SHE KNEW THERE WERE TOO MANY, SHE KNEW I'D NEVER GET AWAY OTHERWISE.
THERE WAS NO OTHER WAY.
NO OTHER WAY FOR ME TO LIVE...

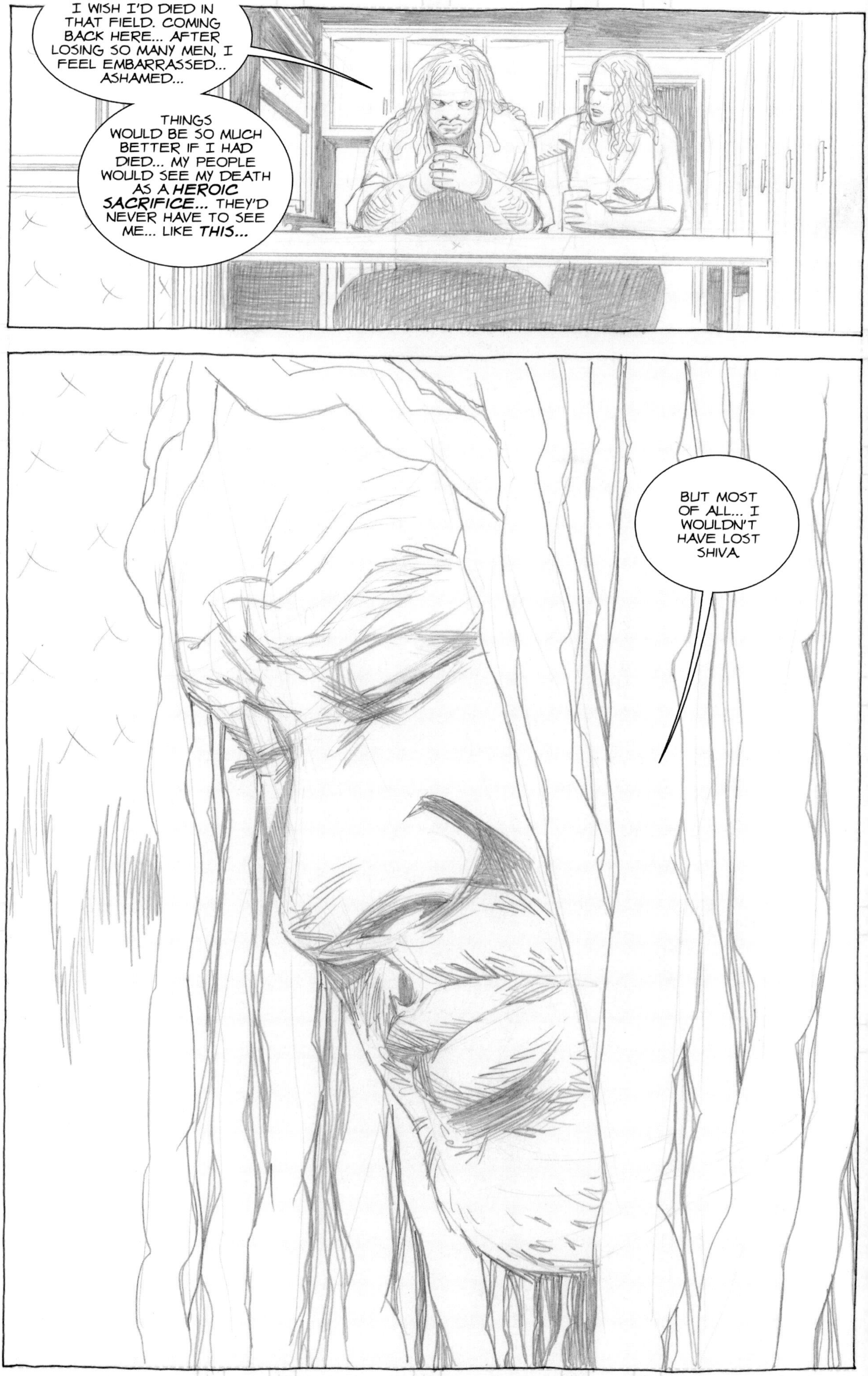
I WISH I'D DIED IN THAT FIELD. COMING BACK HERE... AFTER LOSING SO MANY MEN, I FEEL EMBARRASSED... ASHAMED...
THINGS WOULD BE SO MUCH BETTER IF I HAD DIED... MY PEOPLE WOULD SEE MY DEATH AS A HEROIC SACRIFICE... THEY'D NEVER HAVE TO SEE ME... LIKE THIS...
BUT MOST OF ALL... I WOULDN'T HAVE LOST SHIVA.

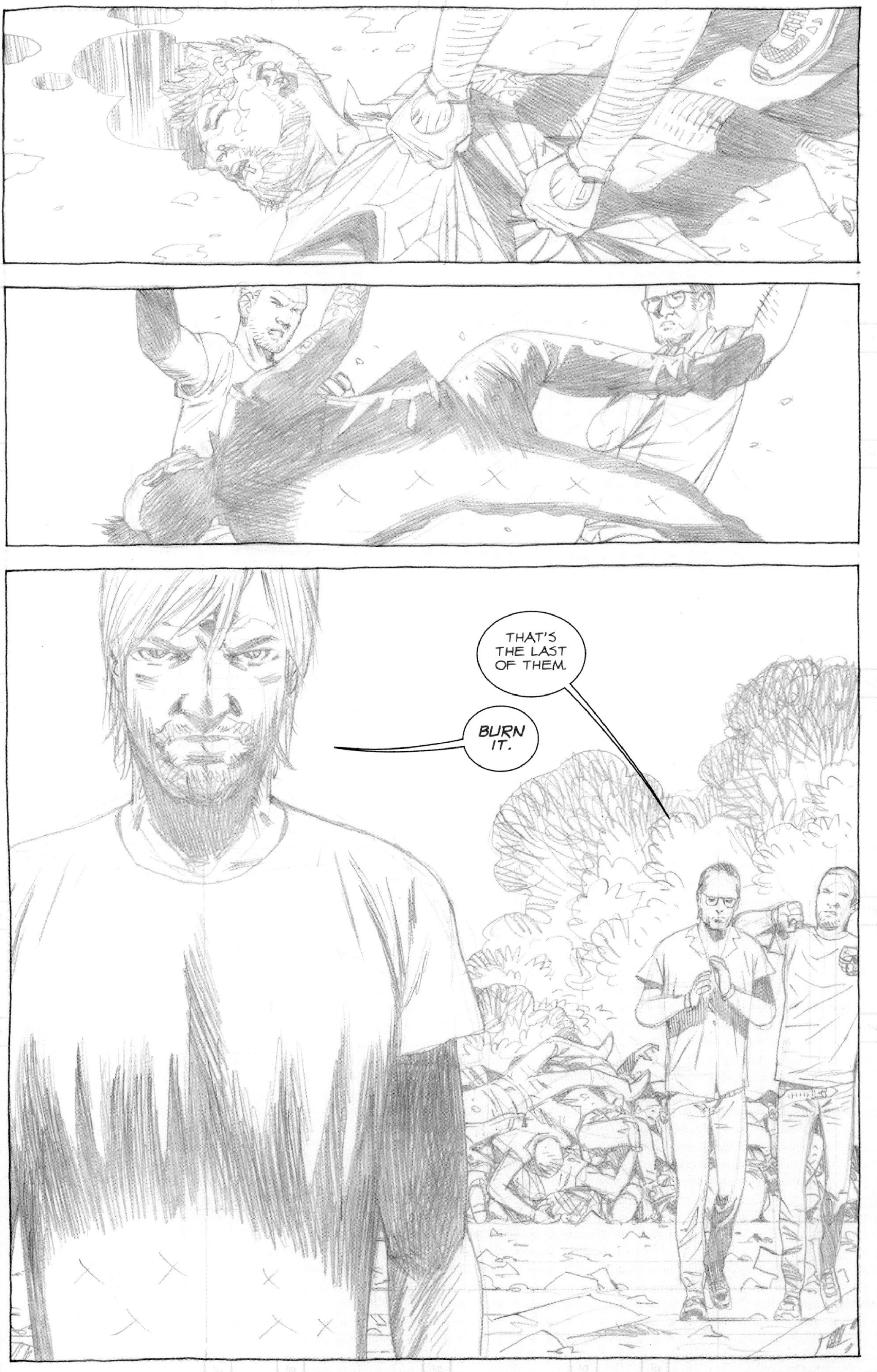
BURN IT.
THAT'S THE LAST OF THEM.

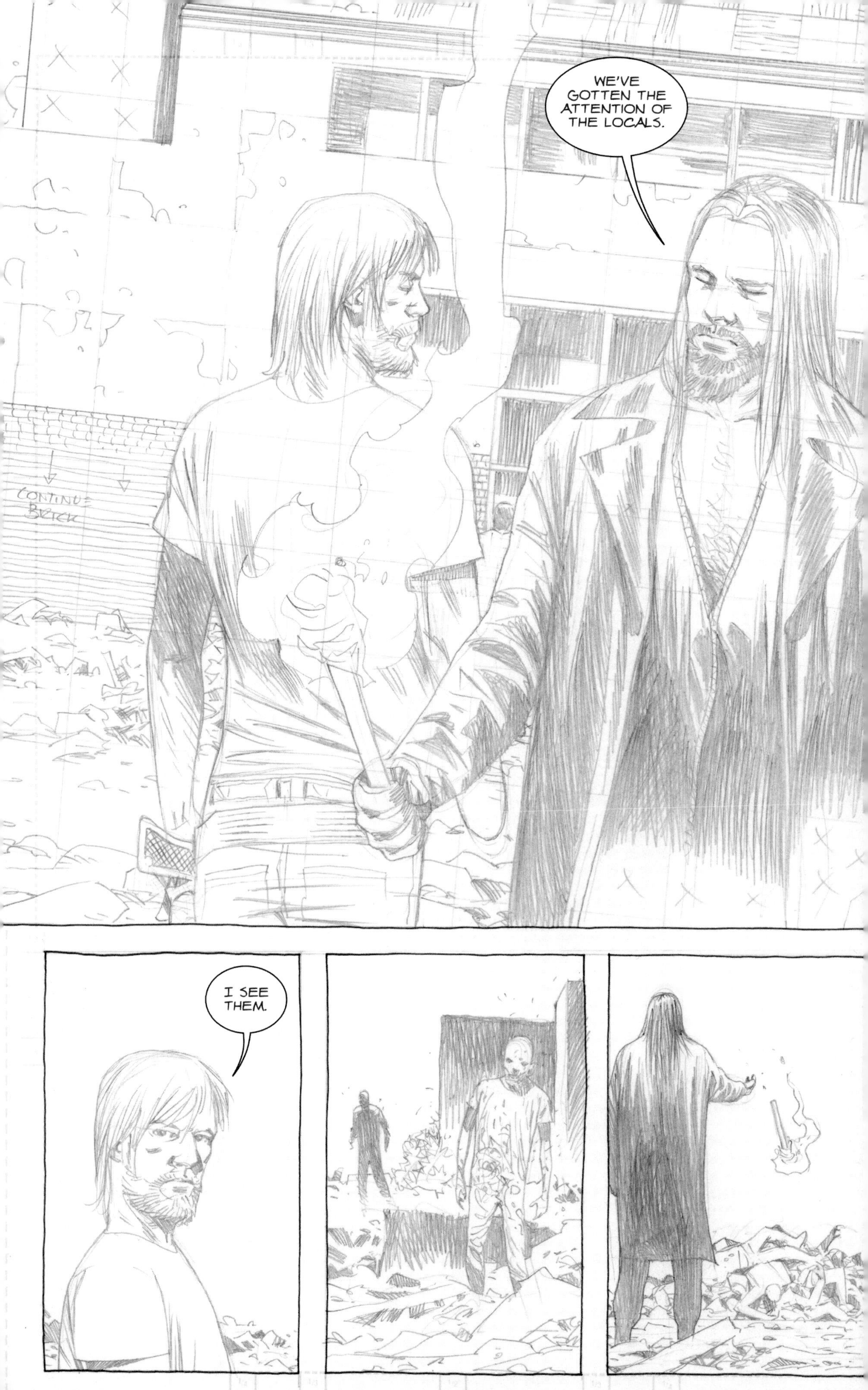
WE'VE GOTTEN THE ATTENTION OF THE LOCALS.
CONTINUE BRICK
I SEE THEM.

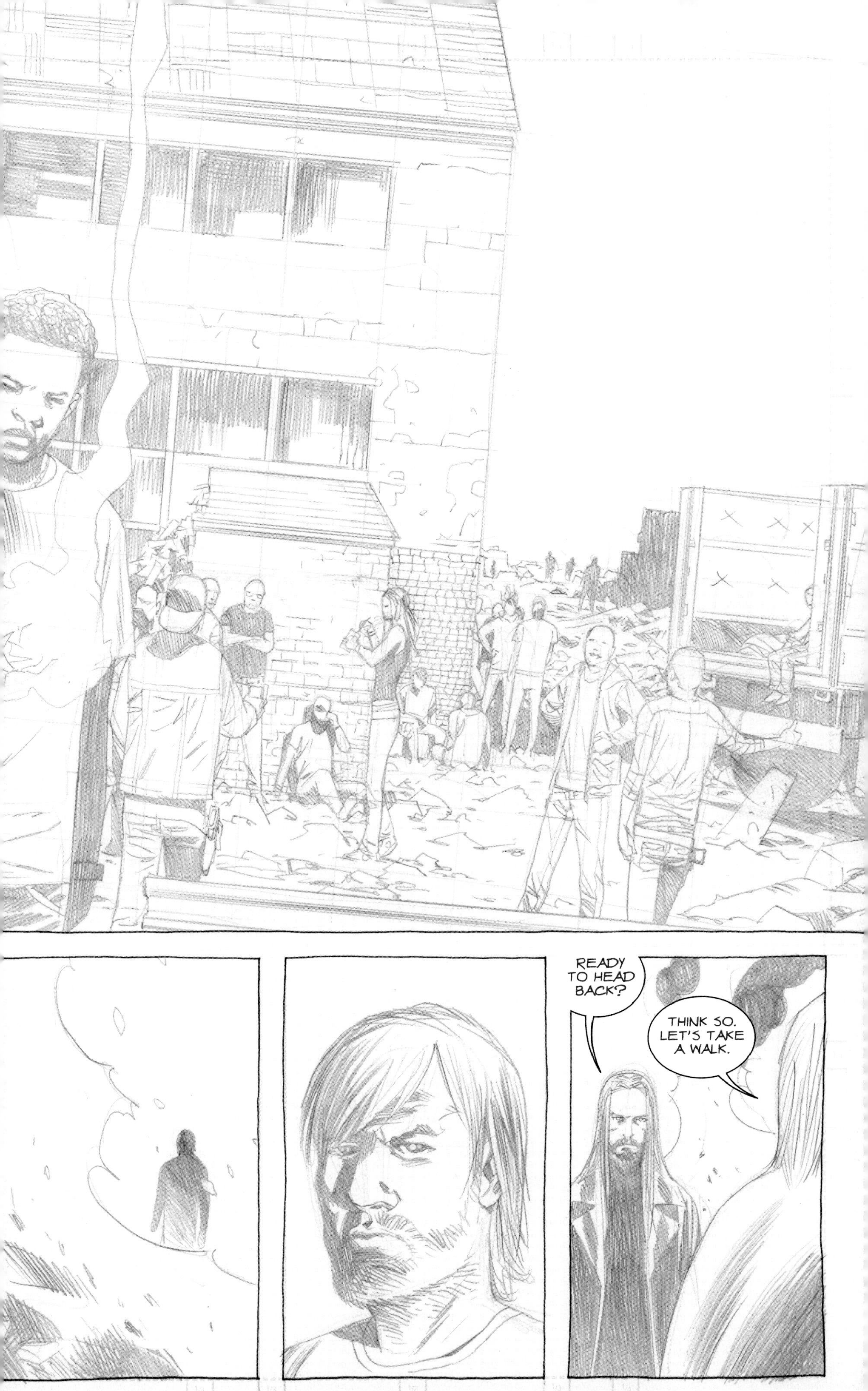
READY TO HEAD BACK?
THINK SO. LET'S TAKE A WALK.

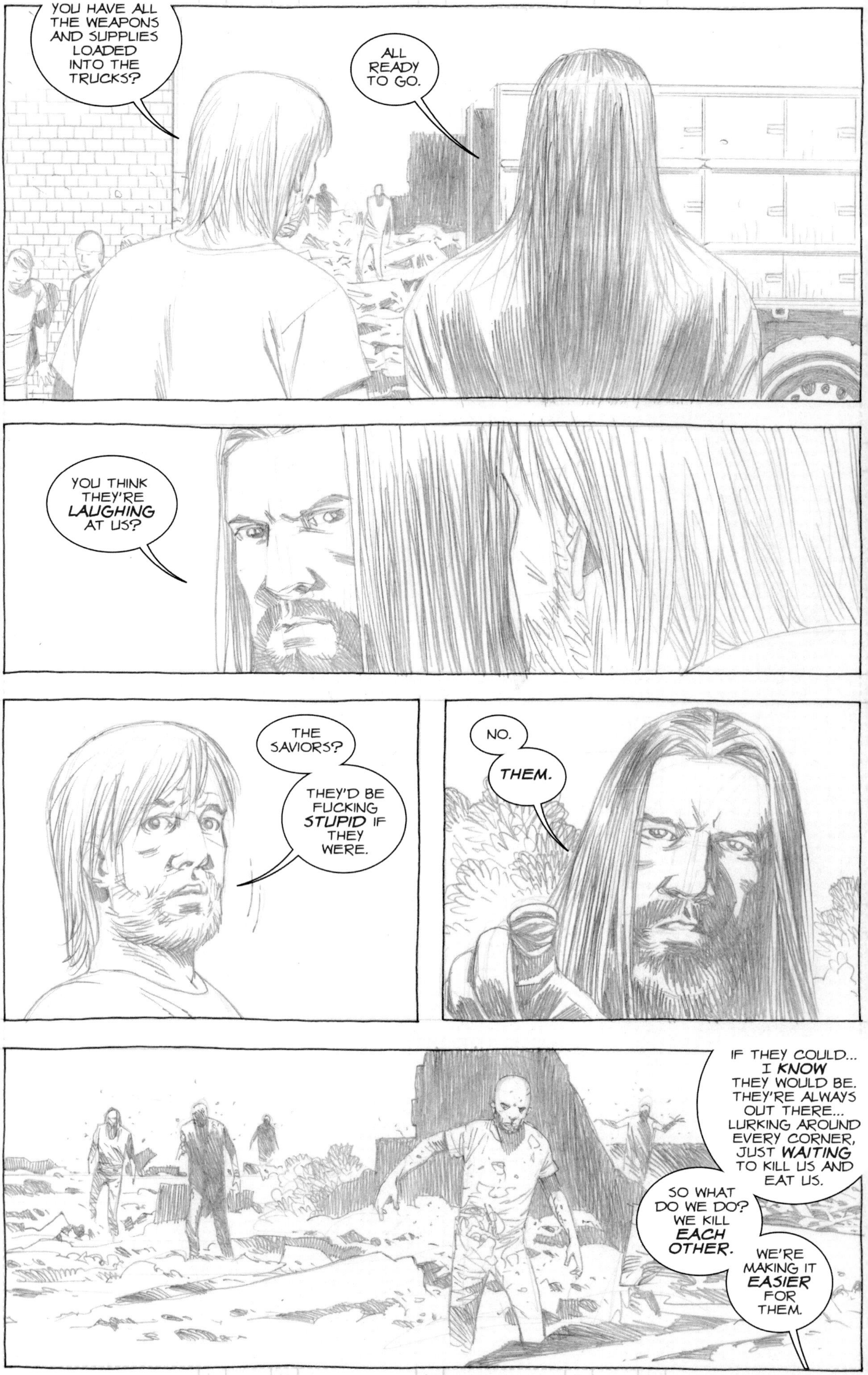
YOU HAVE ALL THE WEAPONS AND SUPPLIES LOADED INTO THE TRUCKS?
ALL READY TO GO.
YOU THINK THEY'RE LAUGHING AT US?
THE SAVIORS?
THEY'D BE FUCKING STUPID IF THEY WERE.
NO.
THEM.
IF THEY COULD... I KNOW THEY WOULD BE. THEY'RE ALWAYS OUT THERE... LURKING AROUND EVERY CORNER, JUST WAITING TO KILL US AND EAT US.
SO WHAT DO WE DO? WE KILL EACH OTHER.
WE'RE MAKING IT EASIER FOR THEM.

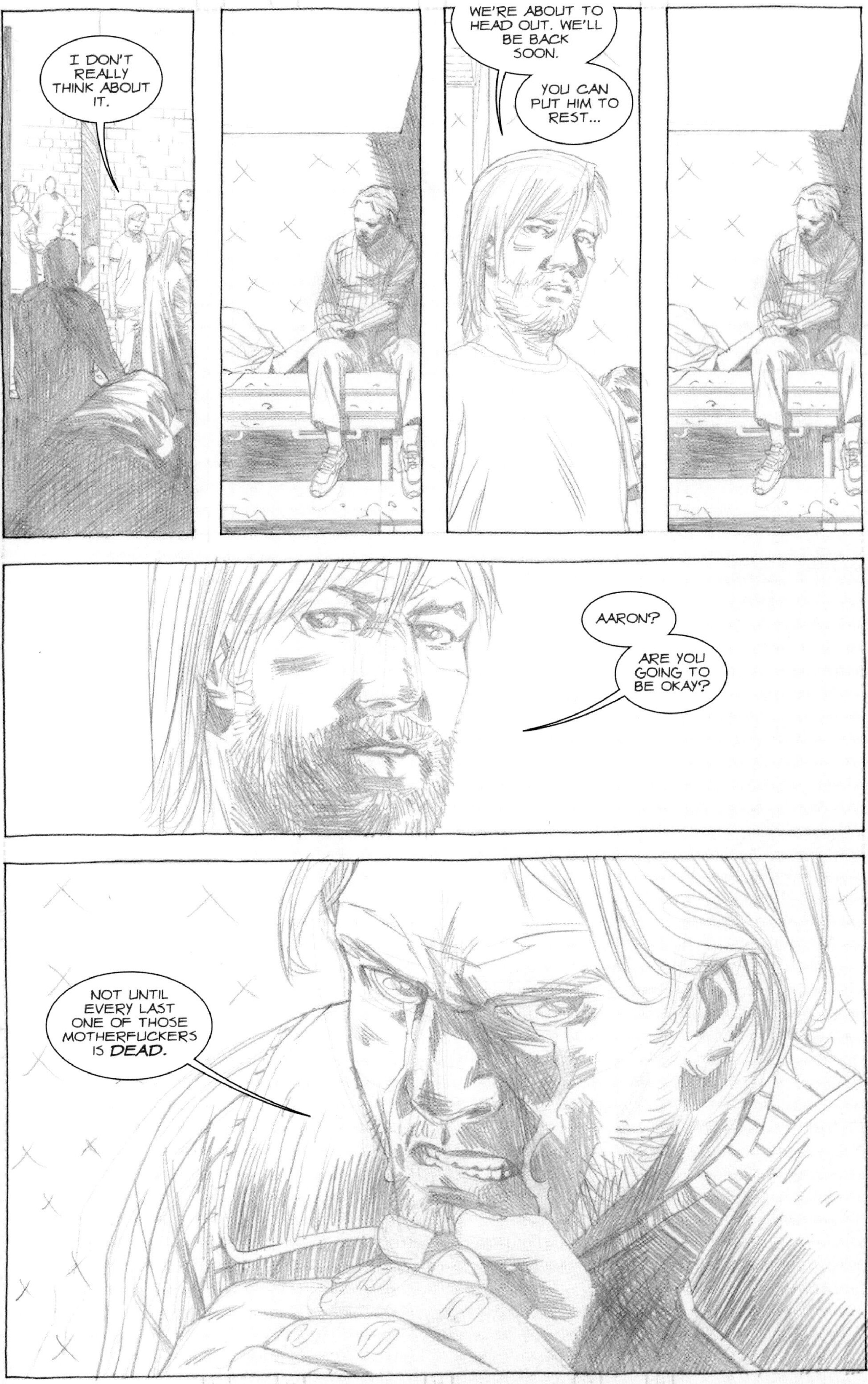
I DON'T REALLY THINK ABOUT IT.
WE'RE ABOUT TO HEAD OUT. WE'LL BE BACK SOON.
YOU CAN PUT HIM TO REST...
AARON?
ARE YOU GOING TO BE OKAY?
NOT UNTIL EVERY LAST ONE OF THOSE MOTHERFUCKERS IS DEAD.

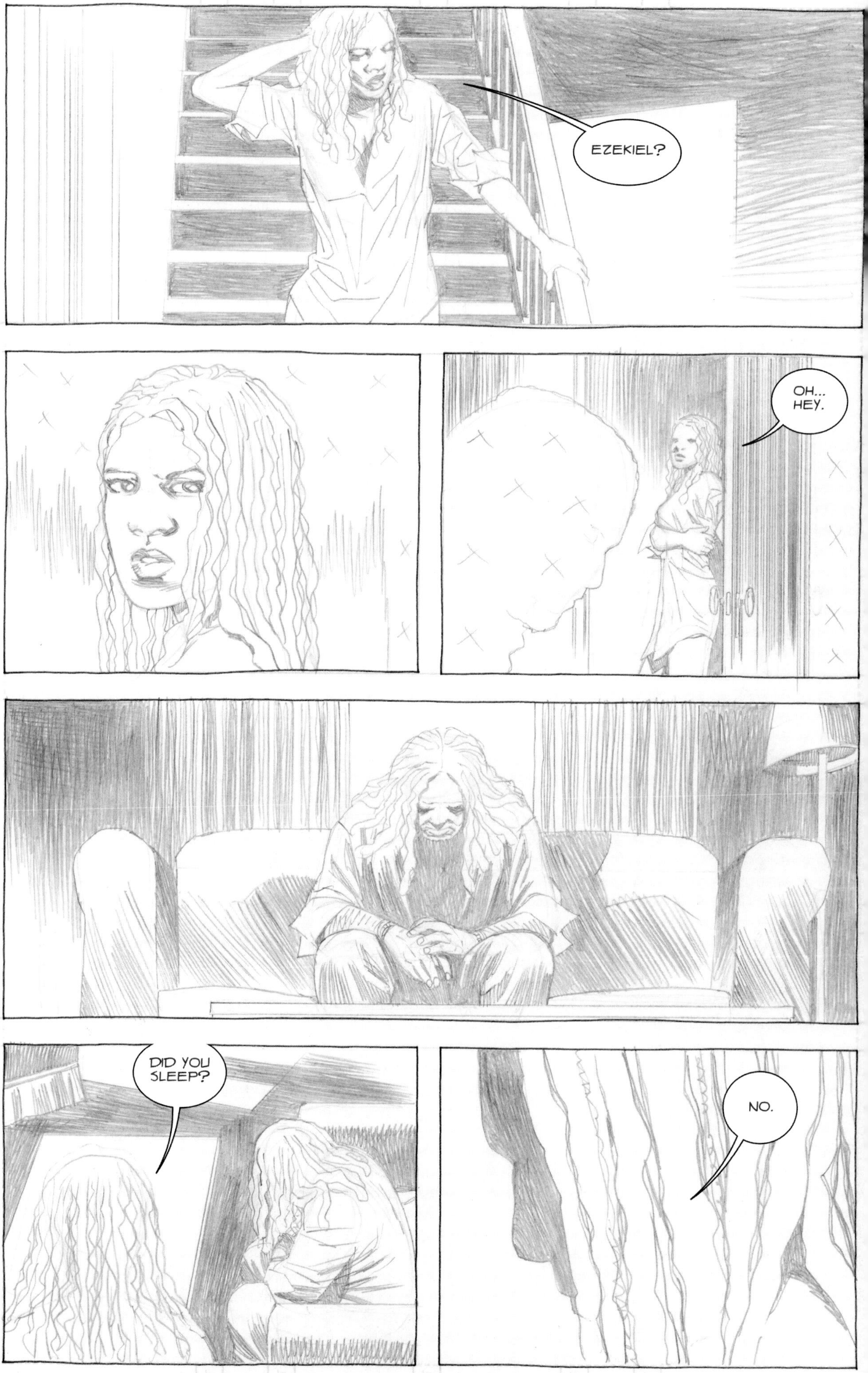
EZEKIEL?
OH... HEY.
DID YOU SLEEP?
NO.

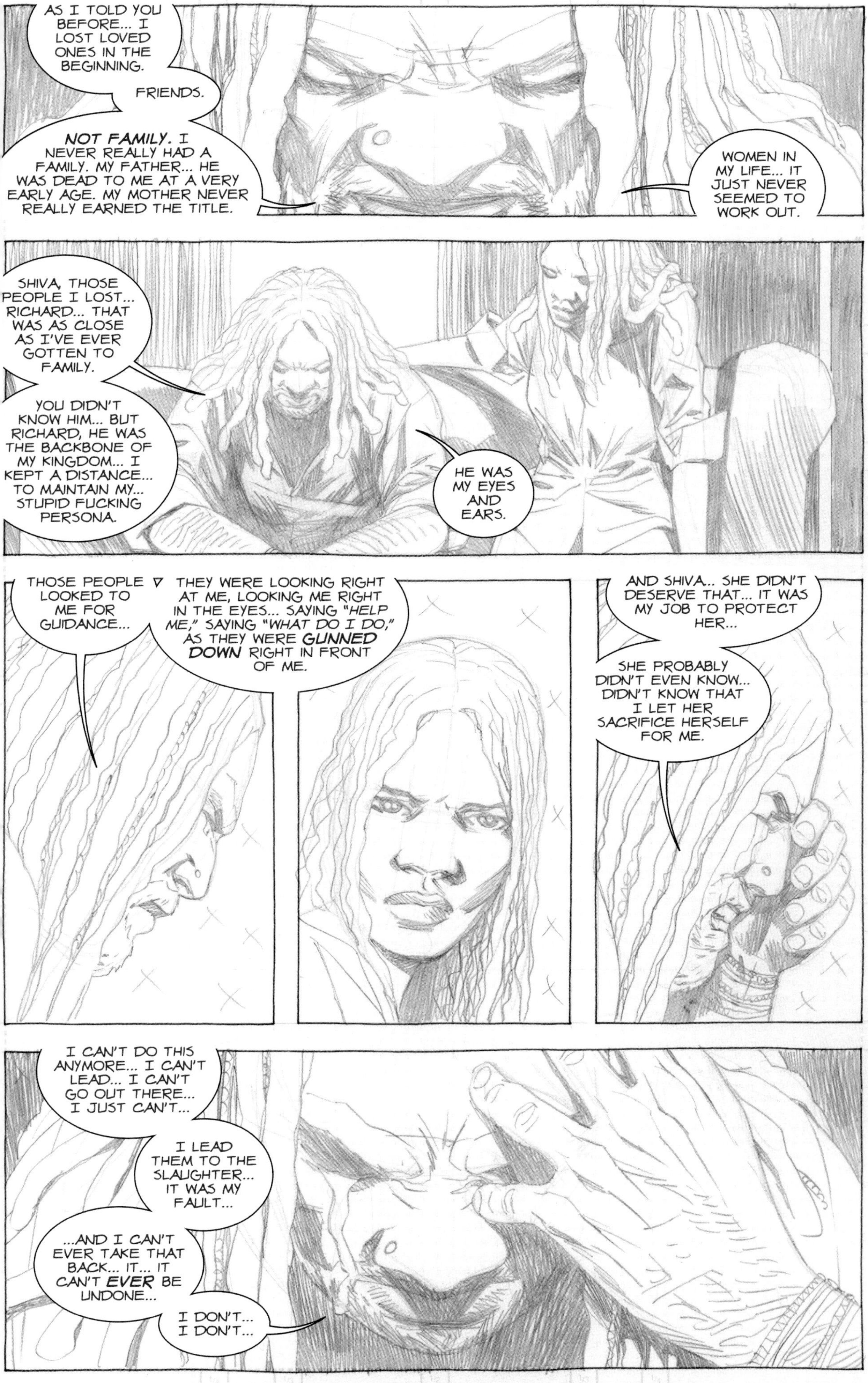
AS I TOLD YOU BEFORE... I LOST LOVED ONES IN THE BEGINNING.
FRIENDS.
NOT FAMILY. I NEVER REALLY HAD A FAMILY. MY FATHER... HE WAS DEAD TO ME AT A VERY EARLY AGE. MY MOTHER NEVER REALLY EARNED THE TITLE.
WOMEN IN MY LIFE... IT JUST NEVER SEEMED TO WORK OUT.
SHIVA, THOSE PEOPLE I LOST... RICHARD... THAT WAS AS CLOSE AS I'VE EVER GOTTEN TO FAMILY.
YOU DIDN'T KNOW HIM... BUT RICHARD, HE WAS THE BACKBONE OF MY KINGDOM... I KEPT A DISTANCE... TO MAINTAIN MY... STUPID FUCKING PERSONA.
HE WAS MY EYES AND EARS.
THOSE PEOPLE LOOKED TO ME FOR GUIDANCE...
THEY WERE LOOKING RIGHT AT ME, LOOKING ME RIGHT IN THE EYES... SAYING "HELP ME," SAYING "WHAT DO I DO," AS THEY WERE GUNNED DOWN RIGHT IN FRONT OF ME.
AND SHIVA... SHE DIDN'T DESERVE THAT... IT WAS MY JOB TO PROTECT HER...
SHE PROBABLY DIDN'T EVEN KNOW... DIDN'T KNOW THAT I LET HER SACRIFICE HERSELF FOR ME.
I CAN'T DO THIS ANYMORE... I CAN'T LEAD... I CAN'T GO OUT THERE... I JUST CAN'T...
I LEAD THEM TO THE SLAUGHTER... IT WAS MY FAULT...
...AND I CAN'T EVER TAKE THAT BACK... IT... IT CAN'T EVER BE UNDONE...
I DON'T... I DON'T...

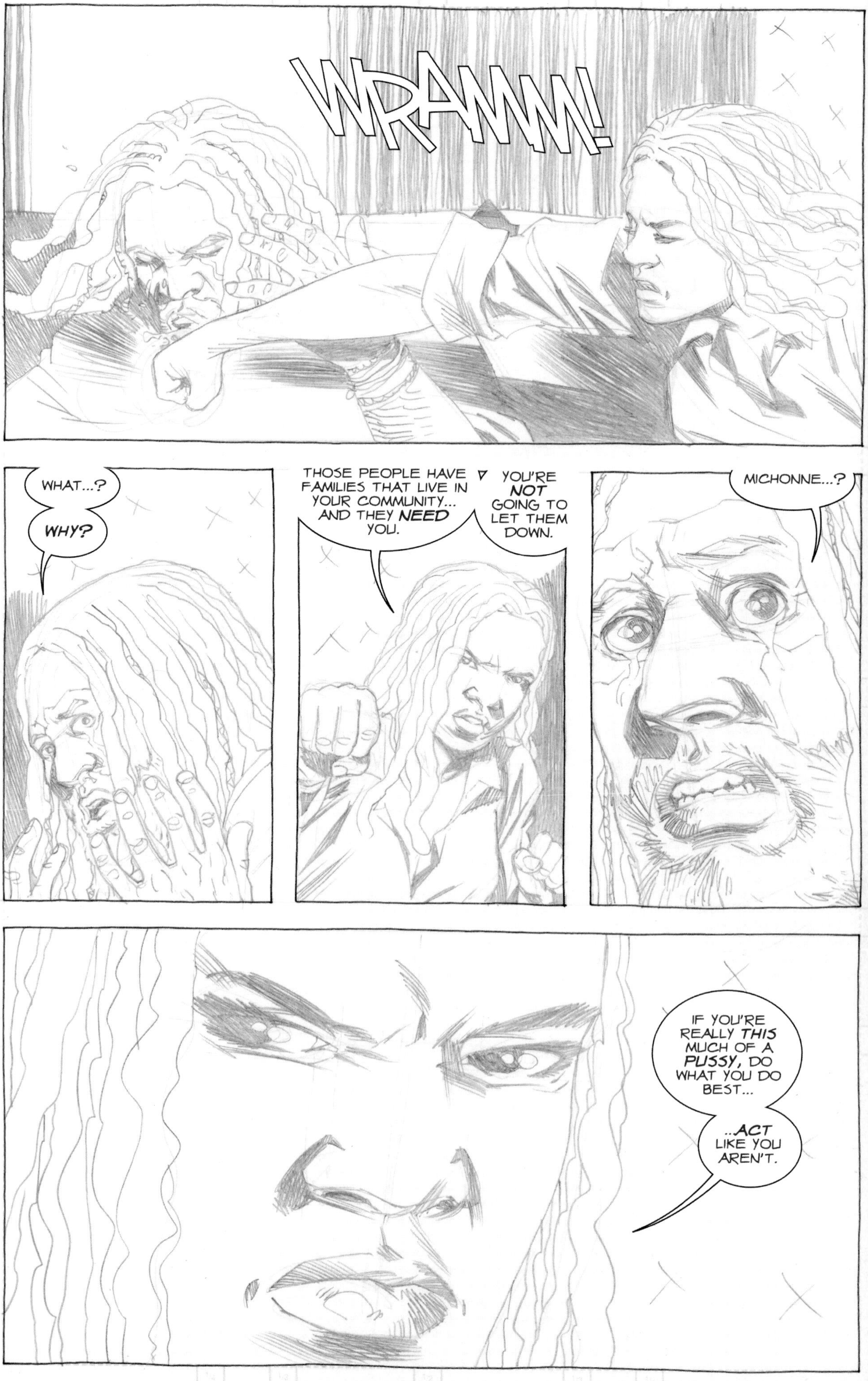
WRAMM!
WHAT...?
WHY?
THOSE PEOPLE HAVE FAMILIES THAT LIVE IN YOUR COMMUNITY... AND THEY NEED YOU.
YOU'RE NOT GOING TO LET THEM DOWN.
MICHONNE...?
IF YOU'RE REALLY THIS MUCH OF A PUSSY, DO WHAT YOU DO BEST...
...ACT LIKE YOU AREN'T.

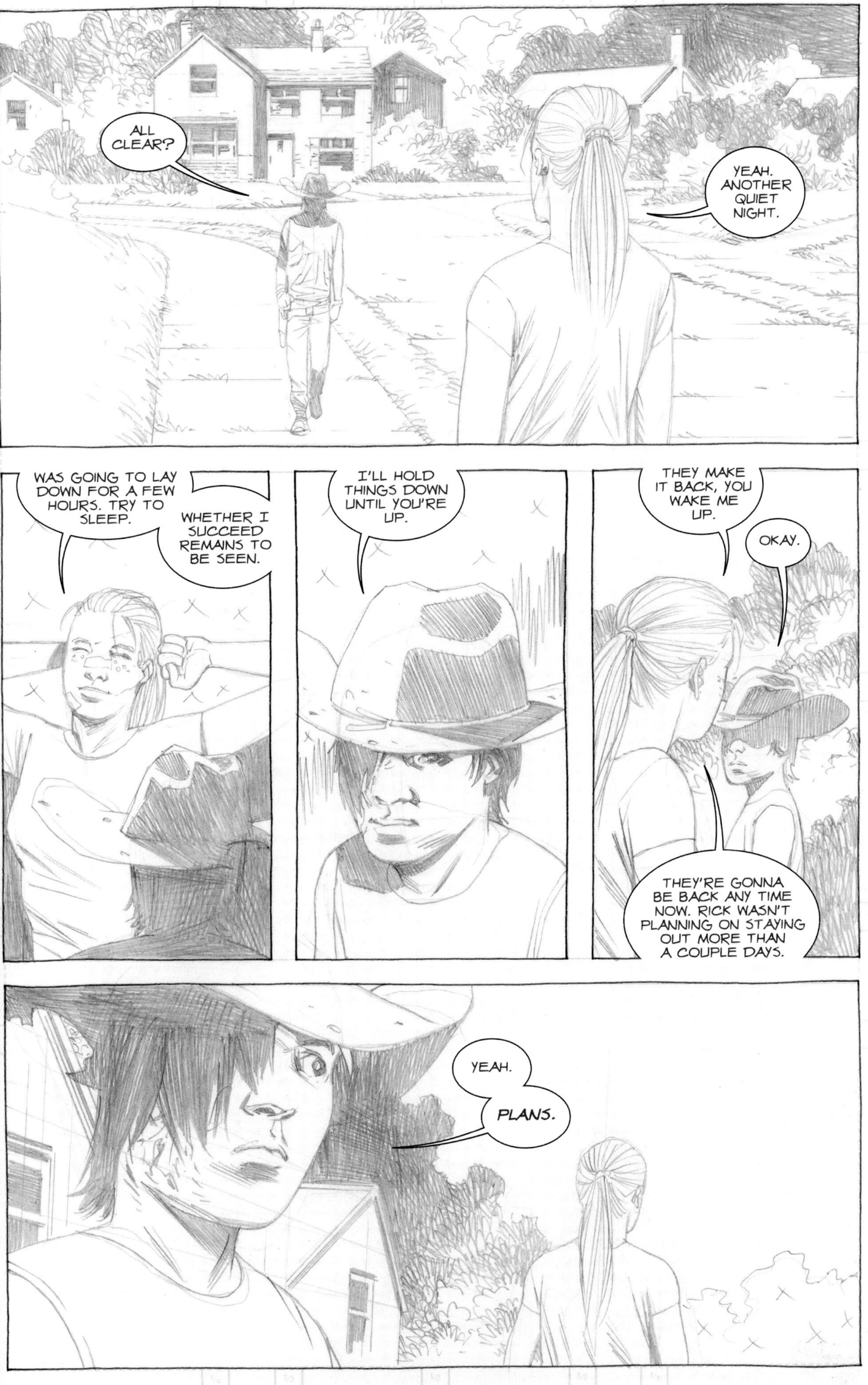
ALL CLEAR?
YEAH. ANOTHER QUIET NIGHT.
WAS GOING TO LAY DOWN FOR A FEW HOURS. TRY TO SLEEP.
WHETHER I SUCCEED REMAINS TO BE SEEN.
I'LL HOLD THINGS DOWN UNTIL YOU'RE UP.
THEY MAKE IT BACK, YOU WAKE ME UP.
OKAY.
THEY'RE GONNA BE BACK ANY TIME NOW. RICK WASN'T PLANNING ON STAYING OUT MORE THAN A COUPLE DAYS.
YEAH.
PLANS.

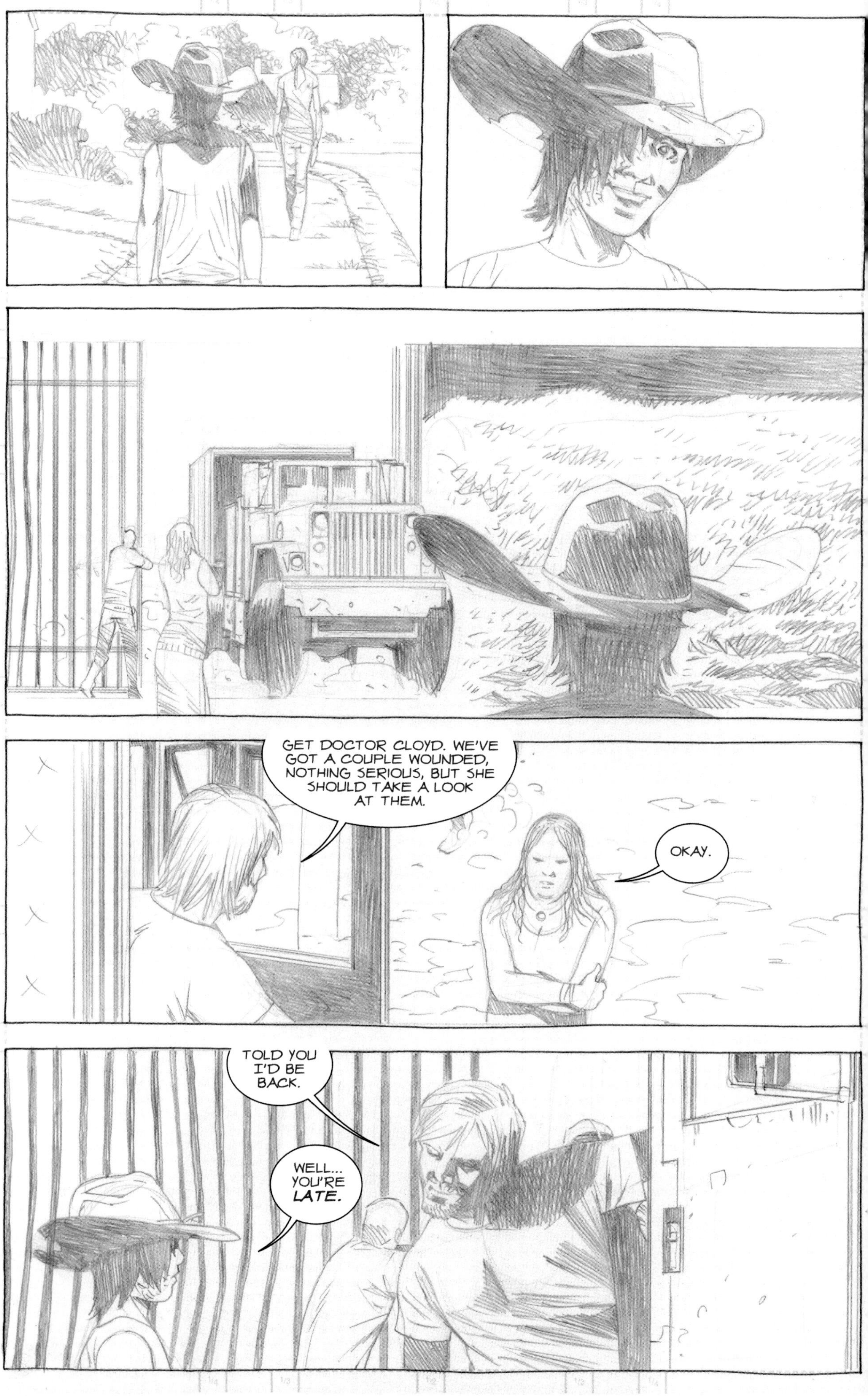

GET DOCTOR CLOYD. WE'VE GOT A COUPLE WOUNDED, NOTHING SERIOUS, BUT SHE SHOULD TAKE A LOOK AT THEM.
OKAY.
TOLD YOU I'D BE BACK.
WELL... YOU'RE *LATE.*

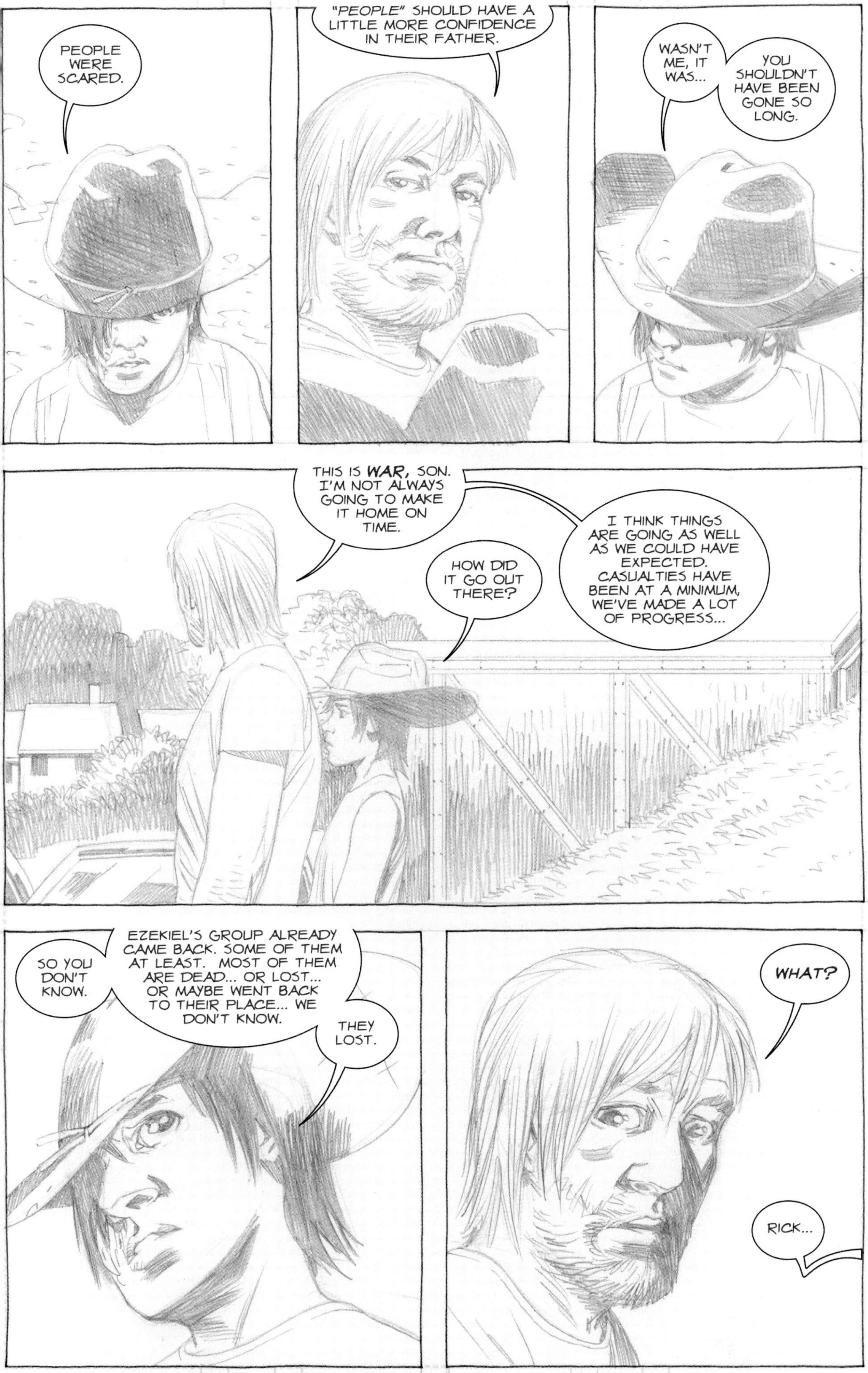
PEOPLE WERE SCARED.
"PEOPLE" SHOULD HAVE A LITTLE MORE CONFIDENCE IN THEIR FATHER.
WASN'T ME, IT WAS...
YOU SHOULDN'T HAVE BEEN GONE SO LONG.
THIS IS WAR, SON. I'M NOT ALWAYS GOING TO MAKE IT HOME ON TIME.
HOW DID IT GO OUT THERE?
I THINK THINGS ARE GOING AS WELL AS WE COULD HAVE EXPECTED. CASUALTIES HAVE BEEN AT A MINIMUM, WE'VE MADE A LOT OF PROGRESS...
SO YOU DON'T KNOW.
EZEKIEL'S GROUP ALREADY CAME BACK. SOME OF THEM AT LEAST. MOST OF THEM ARE DEAD... OR LOST... OR MAYBE WENT BACK TO THEIR PLACE... WE DON'T KNOW.
THEY LOST.
WHAT?
RICK...

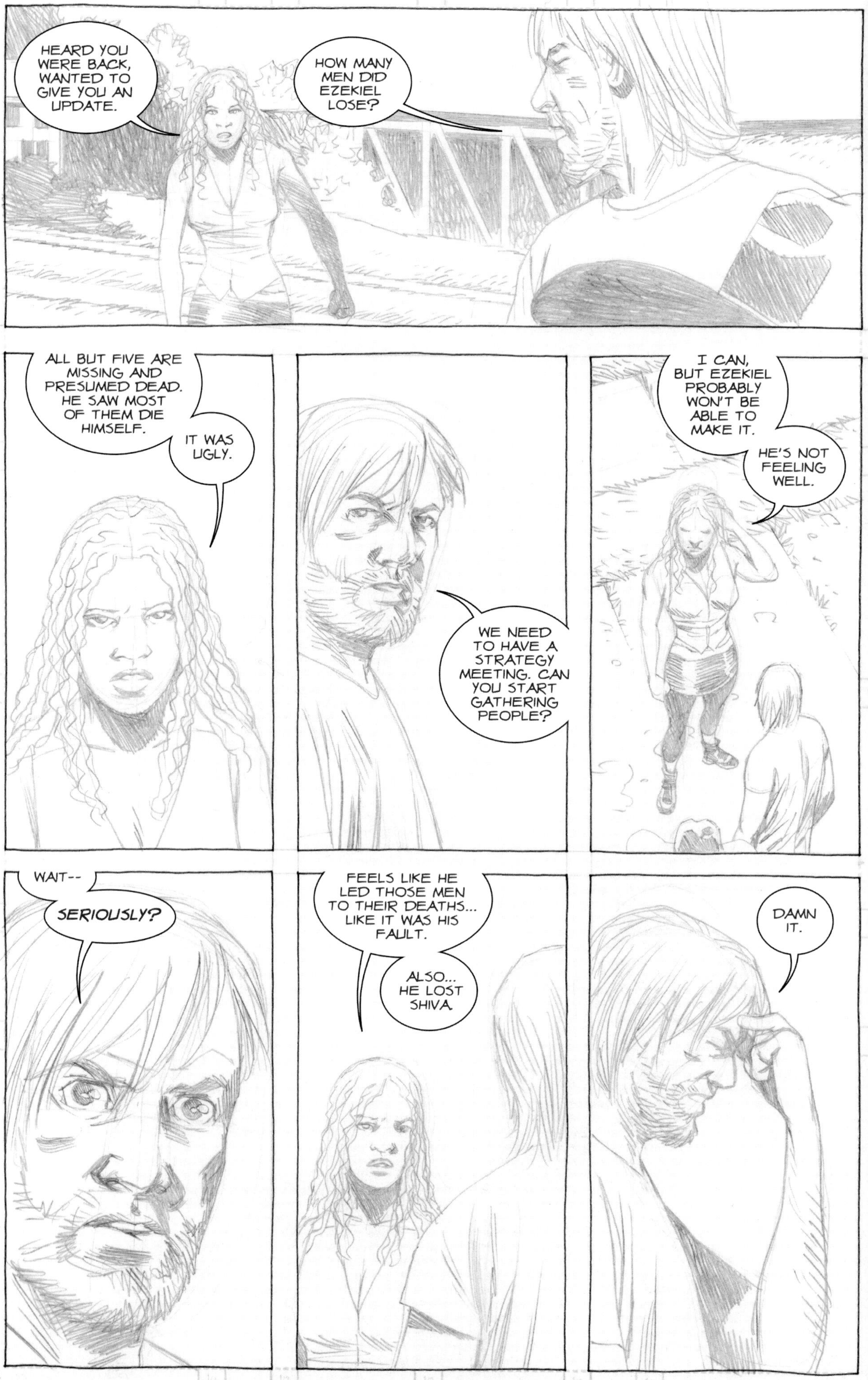
HEARD YOU WERE BACK, WANTED TO GIVE YOU AN UPDATE.
HOW MANY MEN DID EZEKIEL LOSE?
ALL BUT FIVE ARE MISSING AND PRESUMED DEAD. HE SAW MOST OF THEM DIE HIMSELF.
IT WAS UGLY.
WE NEED TO HAVE A STRATEGY MEETING. CAN YOU START GATHERING PEOPLE?
I CAN, BUT EZEKIEL PROBABLY WON'T BE ABLE TO MAKE IT.
HE'S NOT FEELING WELL.
WAIT--
SERIOUSLY?
FEELS LIKE HE LED THOSE MEN TO THEIR DEATHS... LIKE IT WAS HIS FAULT.
ALSO... HE LOST SHIVA.
DAMN IT.

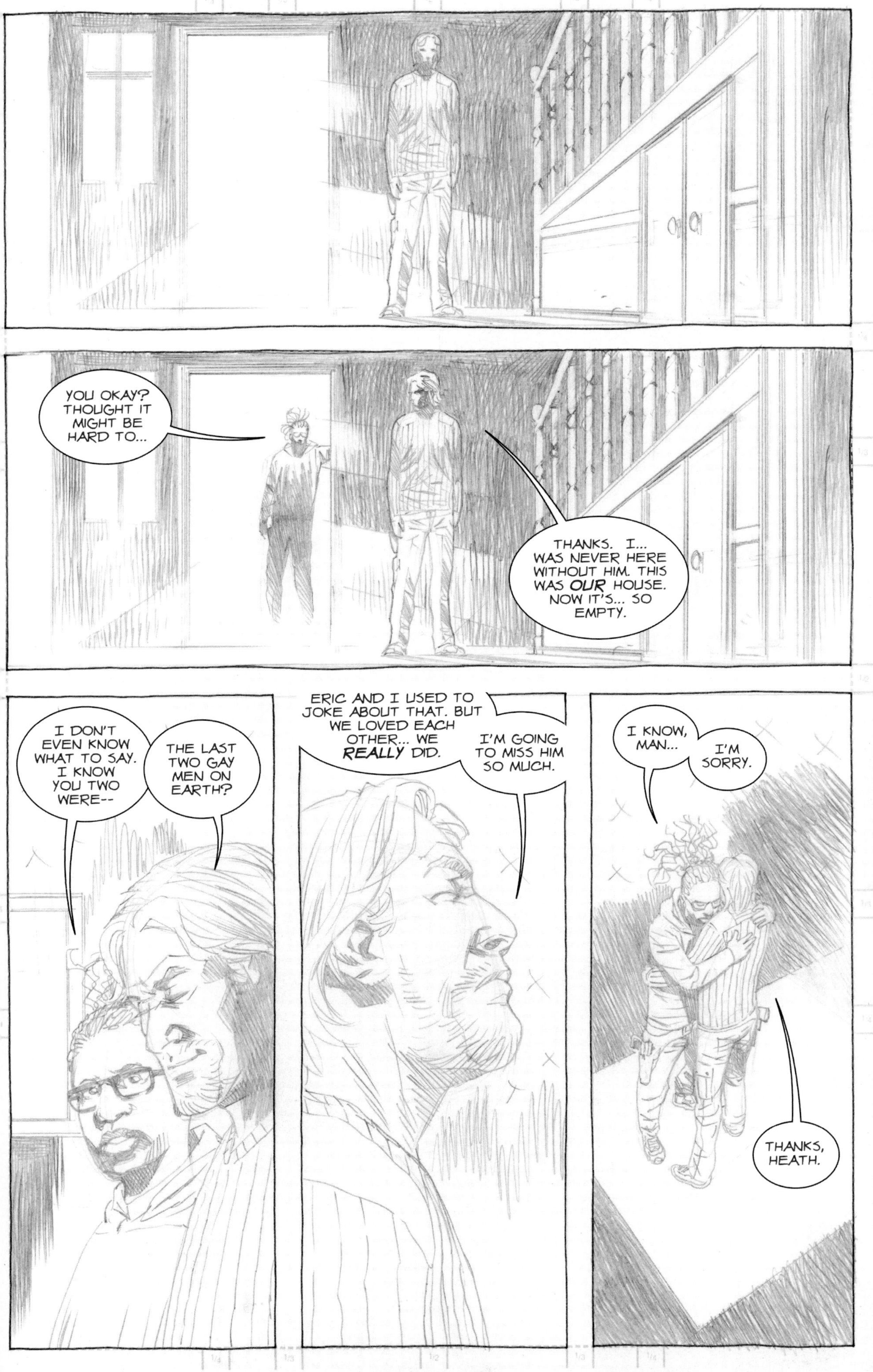
YOU OKAY? THOUGHT IT MIGHT BE HARD TO...
THANKS. I... WAS NEVER HERE WITHOUT HIM. THIS WAS OUR HOUSE. NOW IT'S... SO EMPTY.
I DON'T EVEN KNOW WHAT TO SAY. I KNOW YOU TWO WERE--
THE LAST TWO GAY MEN ON EARTH?
ERIC AND I USED TO JOKE ABOUT THAT. BUT WE LOVED EACH OTHER... WE REALLY DID.
I'M GOING TO MISS HIM SO MUCH.
I KNOW, MAN...
I'M SORRY.
THANKS, HEATH.

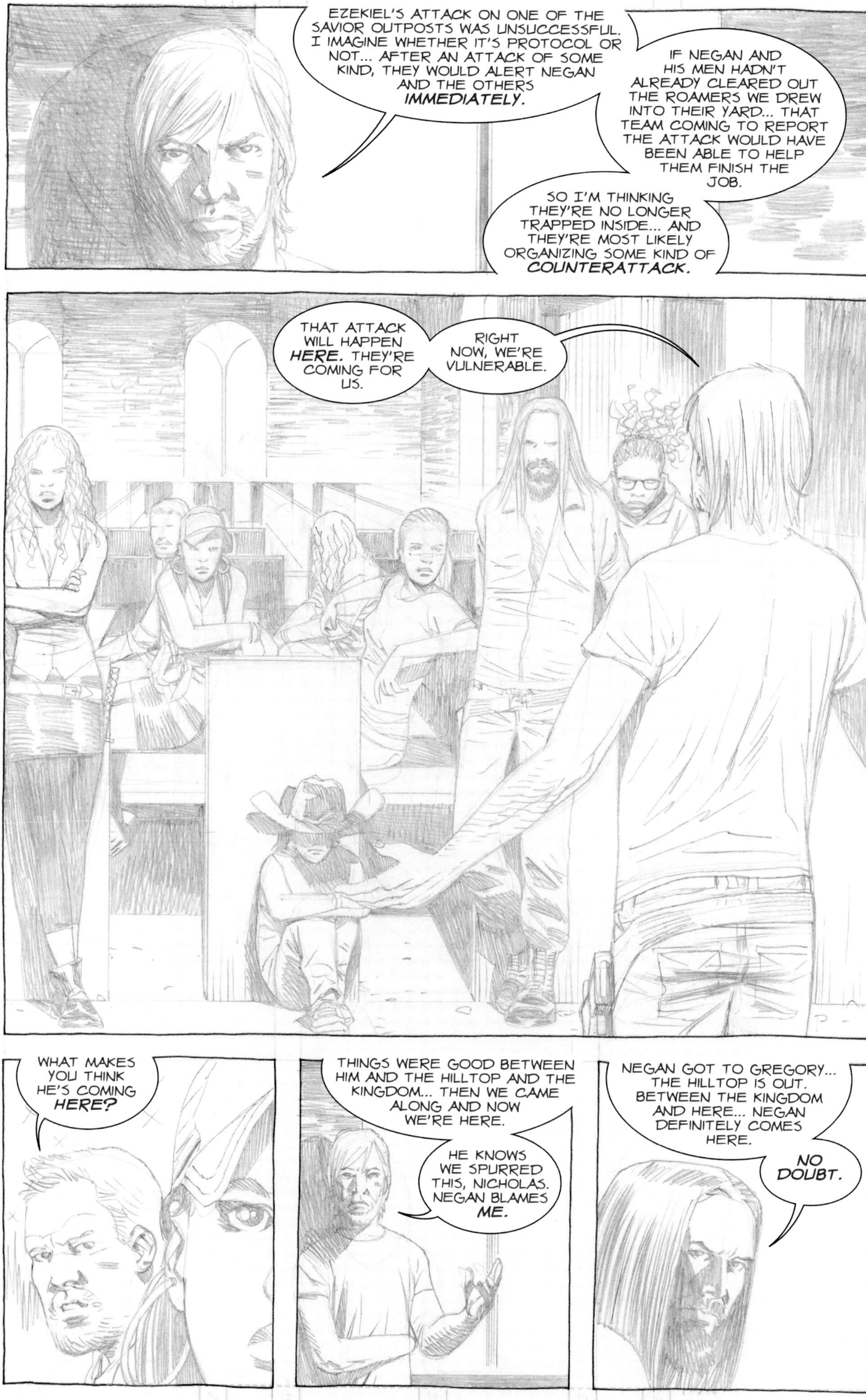
EZEKIEL'S ATTACK ON ONE OF THE SAVIOR OUTPOSTS WAS UNSUCCESSFUL. I IMAGINE WHETHER IT'S PROTOCOL OR NOT... AFTER AN ATTACK OF SOME KIND, THEY WOULD ALERT NEGAN AND THE OTHERS IMMEDIATELY.
IF NEGAN AND HIS MEN HADN'T ALREADY CLEARED OUT THE ROAMERS WE DREW INTO THEIR YARD... THAT TEAM COMING TO REPORT THE ATTACK WOULD HAVE BEEN ABLE TO HELP THEM FINISH THE JOB.
SO I'M THINKING THEY'RE NO LONGER TRAPPED INSIDE... AND THEY'RE MOST LIKELY ORGANIZING SOME KIND OF COUNTERATTACK.
THAT ATTACK WILL HAPPEN HERE. THEY'RE COMING FOR US.
RIGHT NOW, WE'RE VULNERABLE.
WHAT MAKES YOU THINK HE'S COMING HERE?
THINGS WERE GOOD BETWEEN HIM AND THE HILLTOP AND THE KINGDOM... THEN WE CAME ALONG AND NOW WE'RE HERE.
HE KNOWS WE SPURRED THIS, NICHOLAS. NEGAN BLAMES ME.
NEGAN GOT TO GREGORY... THE HILLTOP IS OUT. BETWEEN THE KINGDOM AND HERE... NEGAN DEFINITELY COMES HERE.
NO DOUBT.

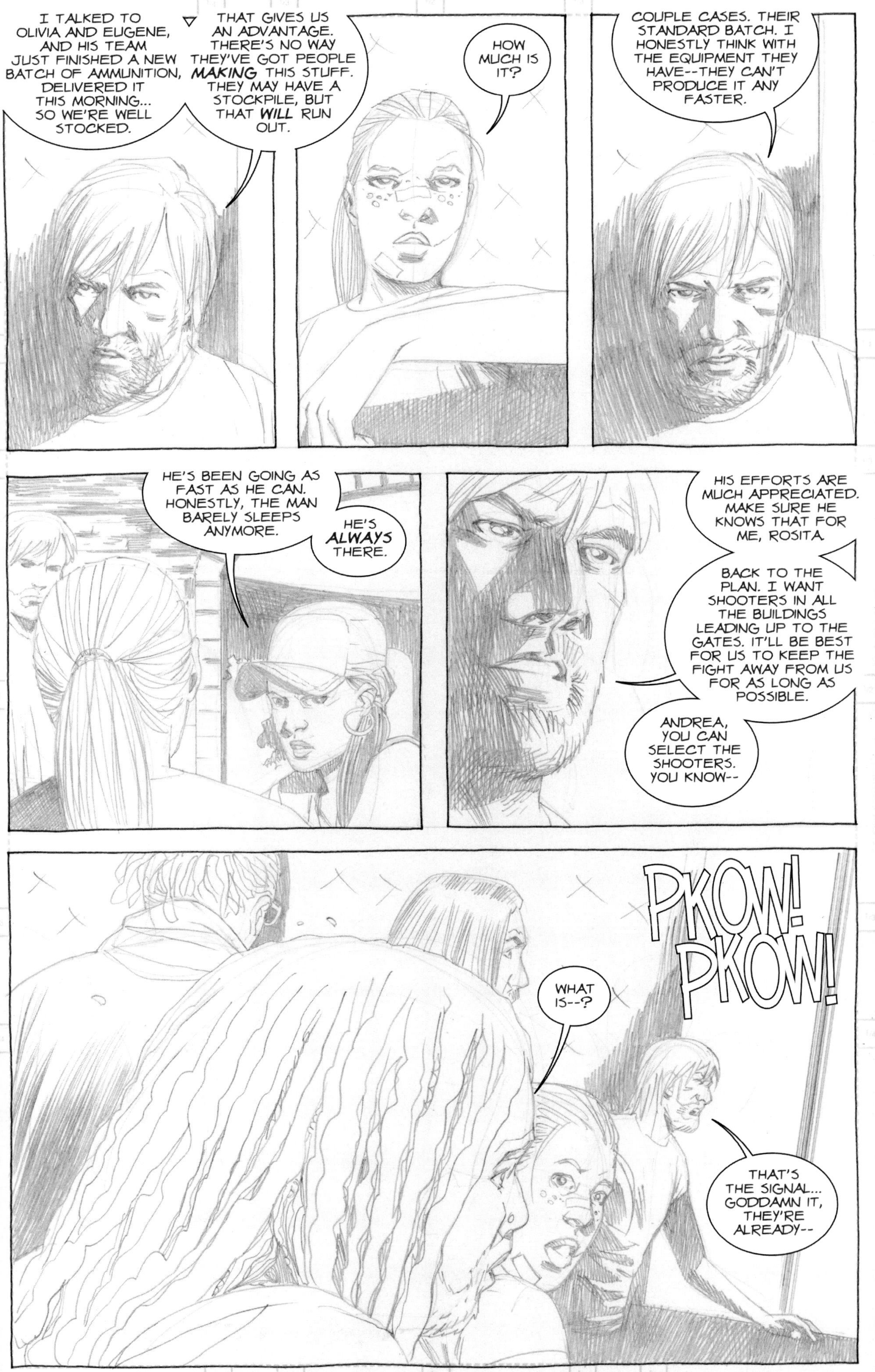
I TALKED TO OLIVIA AND EUGENE, AND HIS TEAM JUST FINISHED A NEW BATCH OF AMMUNITION, DELIVERED IT THIS MORNING... SO WE'RE WELL STOCKED.
THAT GIVES US AN ADVANTAGE. THERE'S NO WAY THEY'VE GOT PEOPLE MAKING THIS STUFF. THEY MAY HAVE A STOCKPILE, BUT THAT WILL RUN OUT.
HOW MUCH IS IT?
COUPLE CASES. THEIR STANDARD BATCH. I HONESTLY THINK WITH THE EQUIPMENT THEY HAVE--THEY CAN'T PRODUCE IT ANY FASTER.
HE'S BEEN GOING AS FAST AS HE CAN. HONESTLY, THE MAN BARELY SLEEPS ANYMORE.
HE'S ALWAYS THERE.
HIS EFFORTS ARE MUCH APPRECIATED. MAKE SURE HE KNOWS THAT FOR ME, ROSITA.
BACK TO THE PLAN. I WANT SHOOTERS IN ALL THE BUILDINGS LEADING UP TO THE GATES. IT'LL BE BEST FOR US TO KEEP THE FIGHT AWAY FROM US FOR AS LONG AS POSSIBLE.
ANDREA, YOU CAN SELECT THE SHOOTERS. YOU KNOW--
PKOW! PKOW!
WHAT IS--?
THAT'S THE SIGNAL... GODDAMN IT, THEY'RE ALREADY--

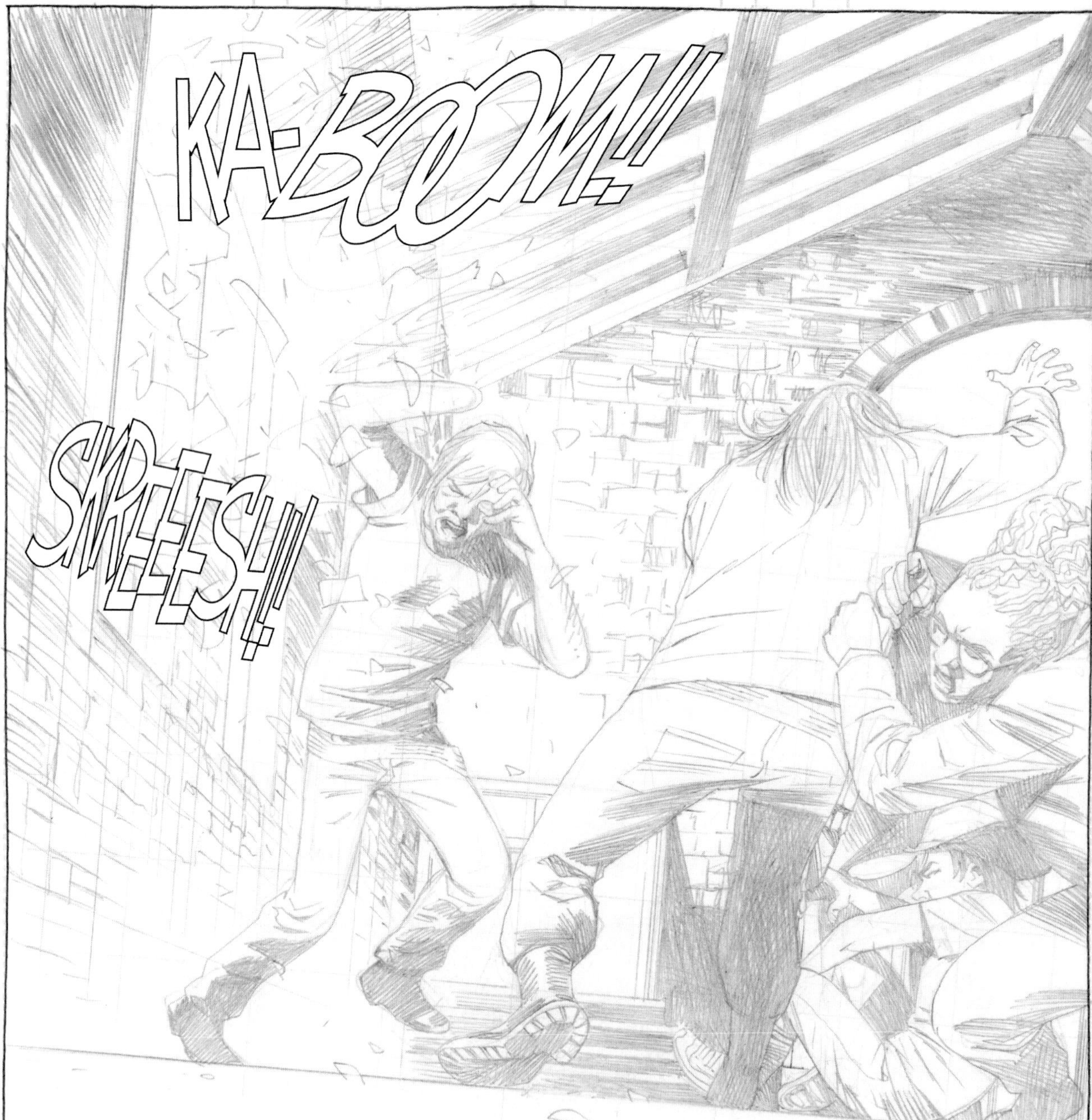
KA-BOOM!!
SKREEEESH!!

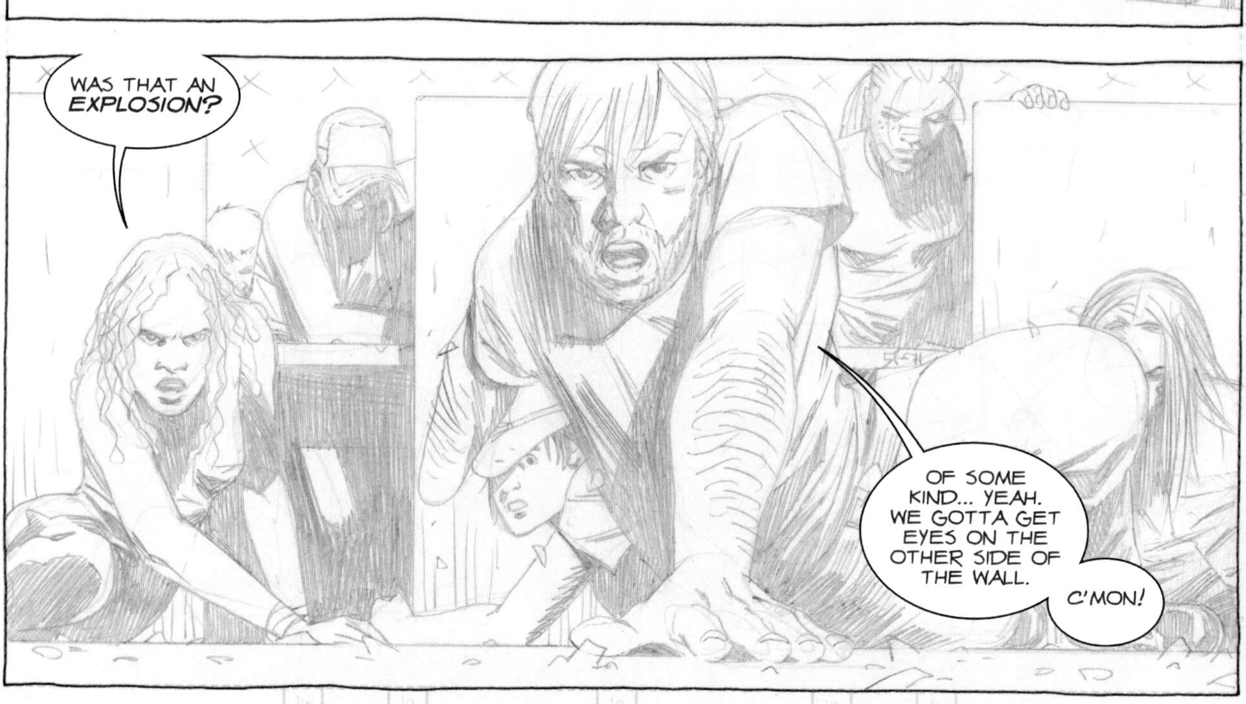
WAS THAT AN EXPLOSION?
OF SOME KIND... YEAH. WE GOTTA GET EYES ON THE OTHER SIDE OF THE WALL.
C'MON!

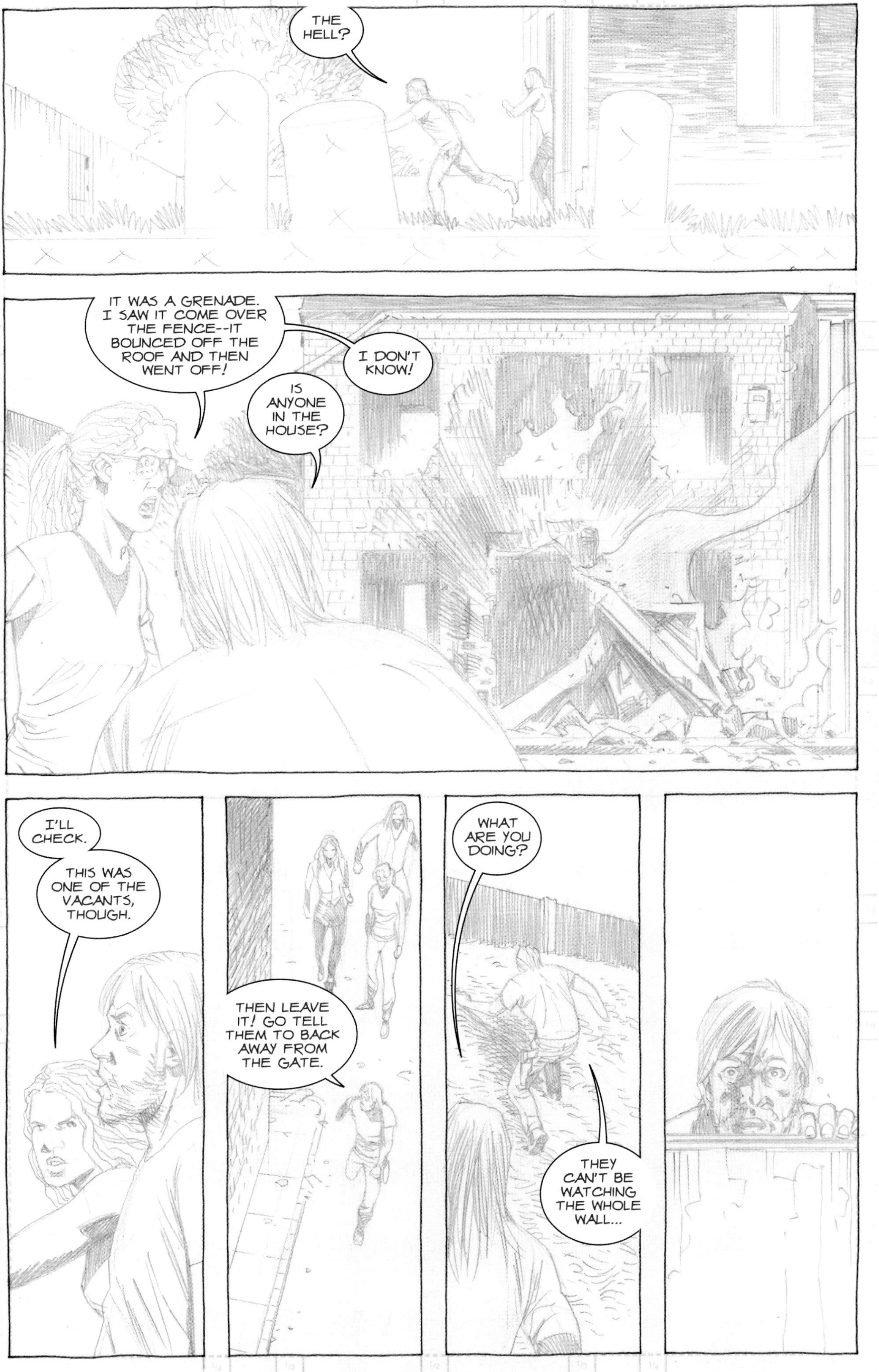
THE HELL?
IT WAS A GRENADE. I SAW IT COME OVER THE FENCE--IT BOUNCED OFF THE ROOF AND THEN WENT OFF!
I DON'T KNOW!
IS ANYONE IN THE HOUSE?
I'LL CHECK.
THIS WAS ONE OF THE VACANTS, THOUGH.
THEN LEAVE IT! GO TELL THEM TO BACK AWAY FROM THE GATE.
WHAT ARE YOU DOING?
THEY CAN'T BE WATCHING THE WHOLE WALL...

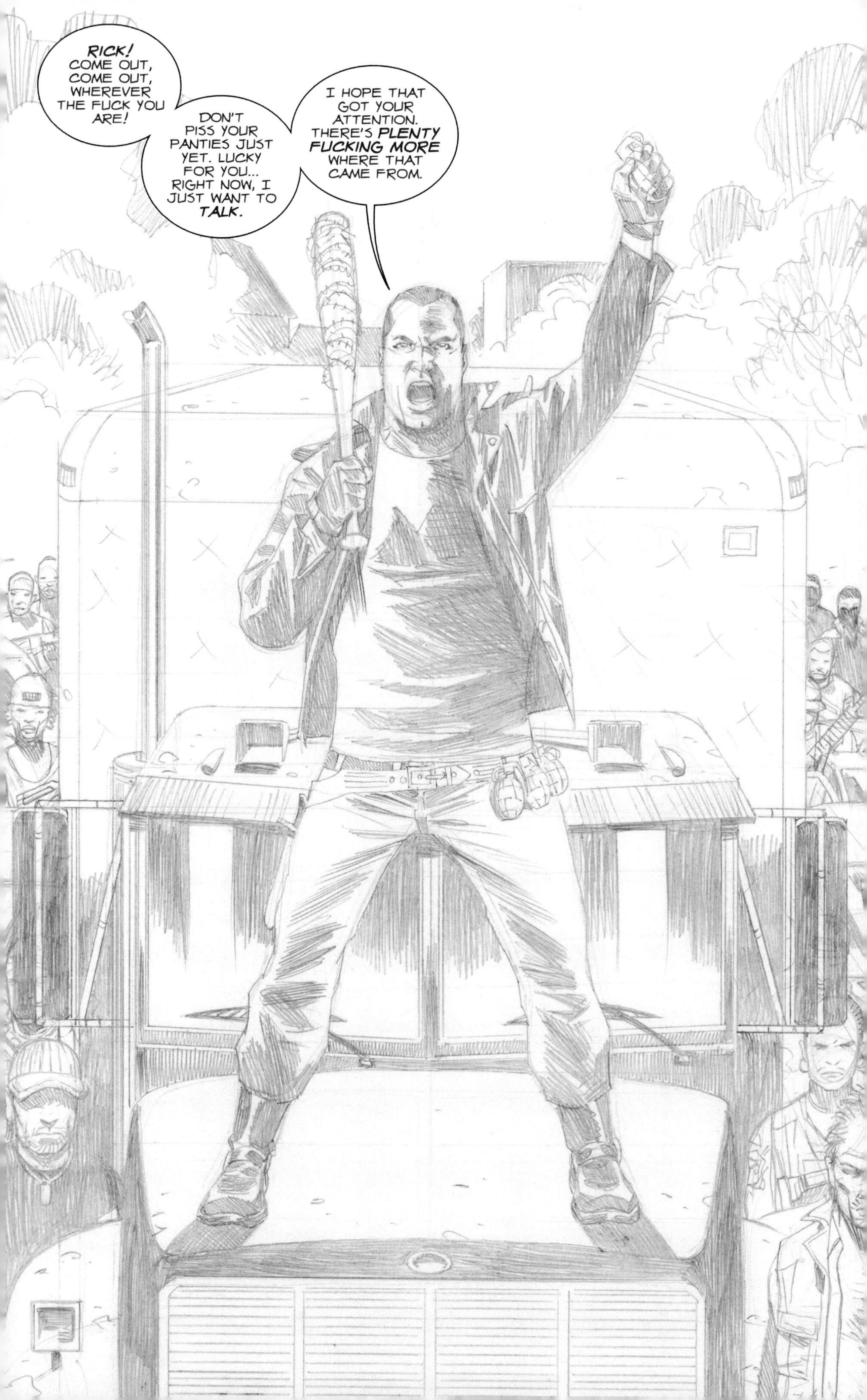
RICK! COME OUT, COME OUT, WHEREVER THE FUCK YOU ARE!
DON'T PISS YOUR PANTIES JUST YET. LUCKY FOR YOU... RIGHT NOW, I JUST WANT TO TALK.
I HOPE THAT GOT YOUR ATTENTION. THERE'S PLENTY FUCKING MORE WHERE THAT CAME FROM.

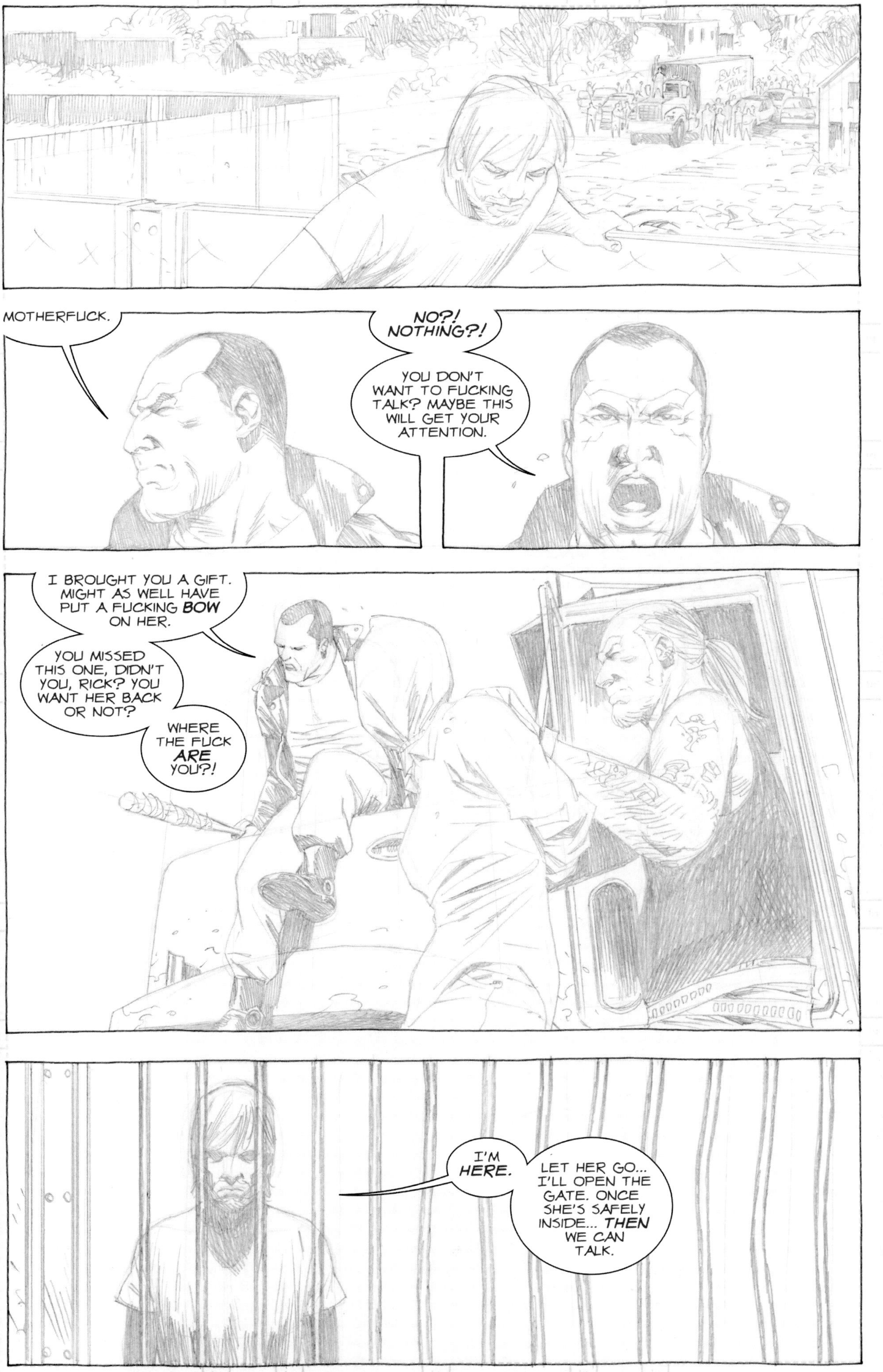

MOTHERFUCK.
NO?! NOTHING?!
YOU DON'T WANT TO FUCKING TALK? MAYBE THIS WILL GET YOUR ATTENTION.
I BROUGHT YOU A GIFT. MIGHT AS WELL HAVE PUT A FUCKING BOW ON HER.
YOU MISSED THIS ONE, DIDN'T YOU, RICK? YOU WANT HER BACK OR NOT?
WHERE THE FUCK ARE YOU?!
I'M HERE.
LET HER GO... I'LL OPEN THE GATE. ONCE SHE'S SAFELY INSIDE... THEN WE CAN TALK.

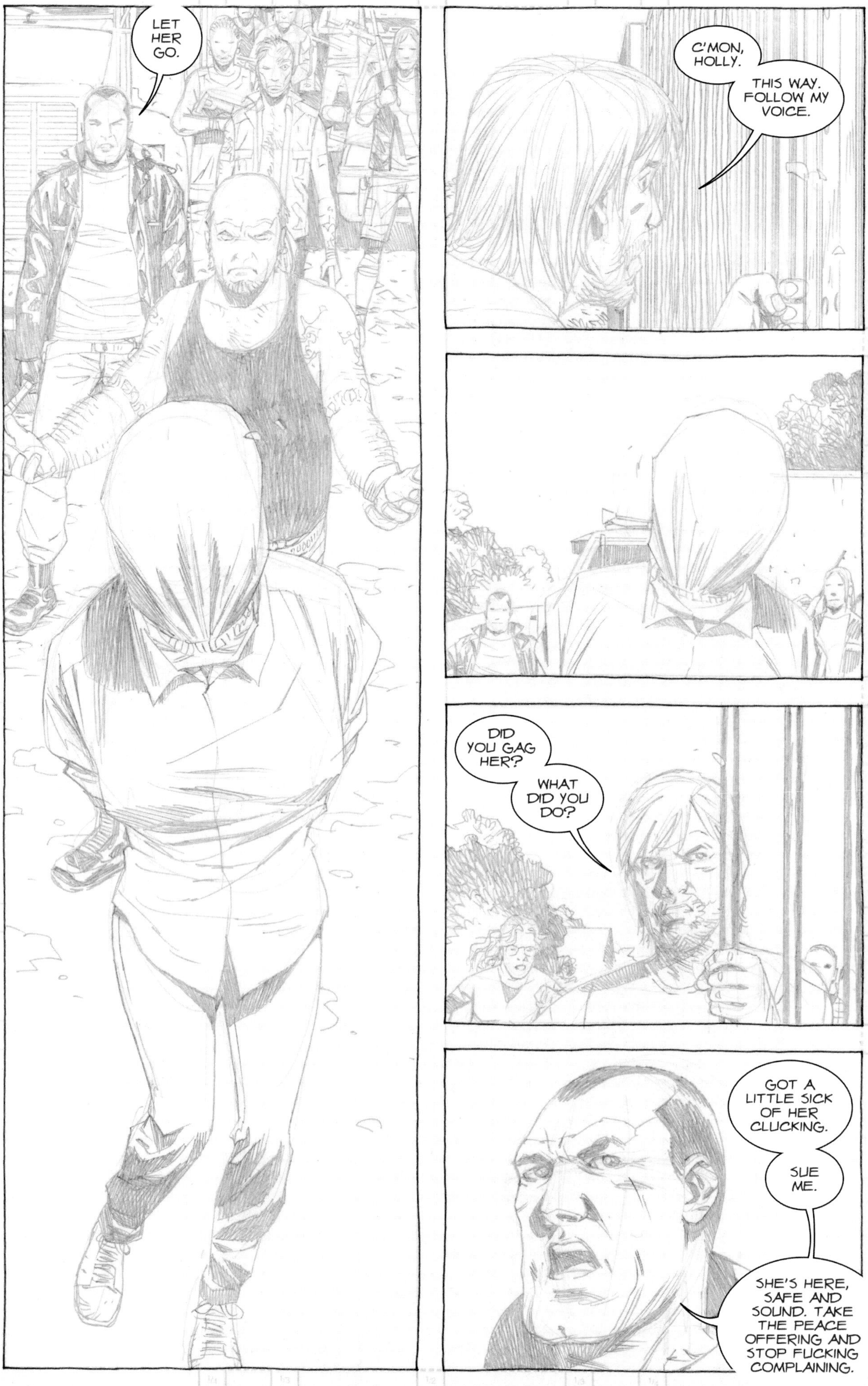
LET HER GO.
C'MON, HOLLY.
THIS WAY. FOLLOW MY VOICE.
DID YOU GAG HER?
WHAT DID YOU DO?
GOT A LITTLE SICK OF HER CLUCKING.
SUE ME.
SHE'S HERE, SAFE AND SOUND. TAKE THE PEACE OFFERING AND STOP FUCKING COMPLAINING.

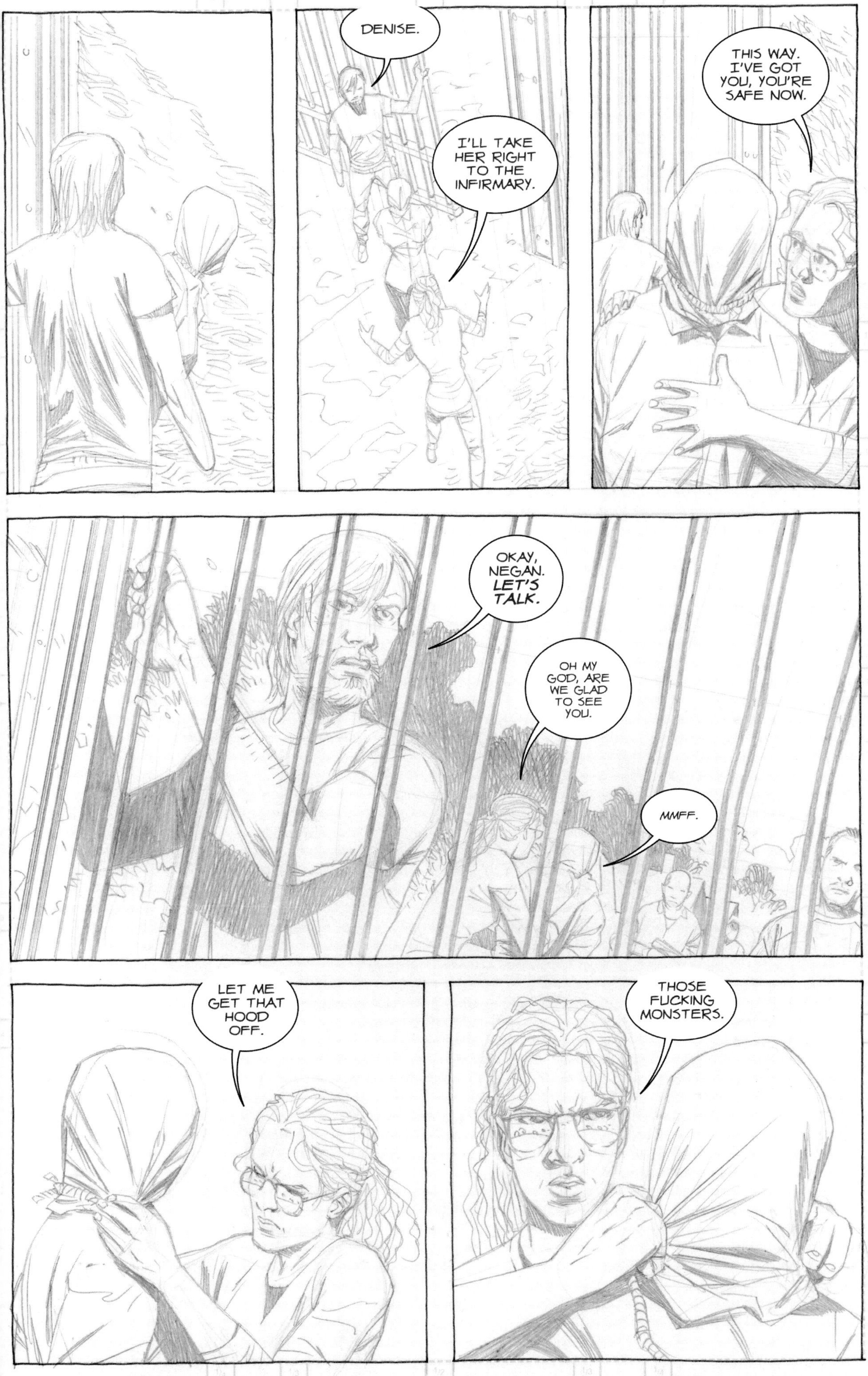
DENISE.
I'LL TAKE HER RIGHT TO THE INFIRMARY.
THIS WAY. I'VE GOT YOU, YOU'RE SAFE NOW.
OKAY, NEGAN. *LET'S TALK.*
OH MY GOD, ARE WE GLAD TO SEE YOU.
MMFF.
LET ME GET THAT HOOD OFF.
THOSE FUCKING MONSTERS.

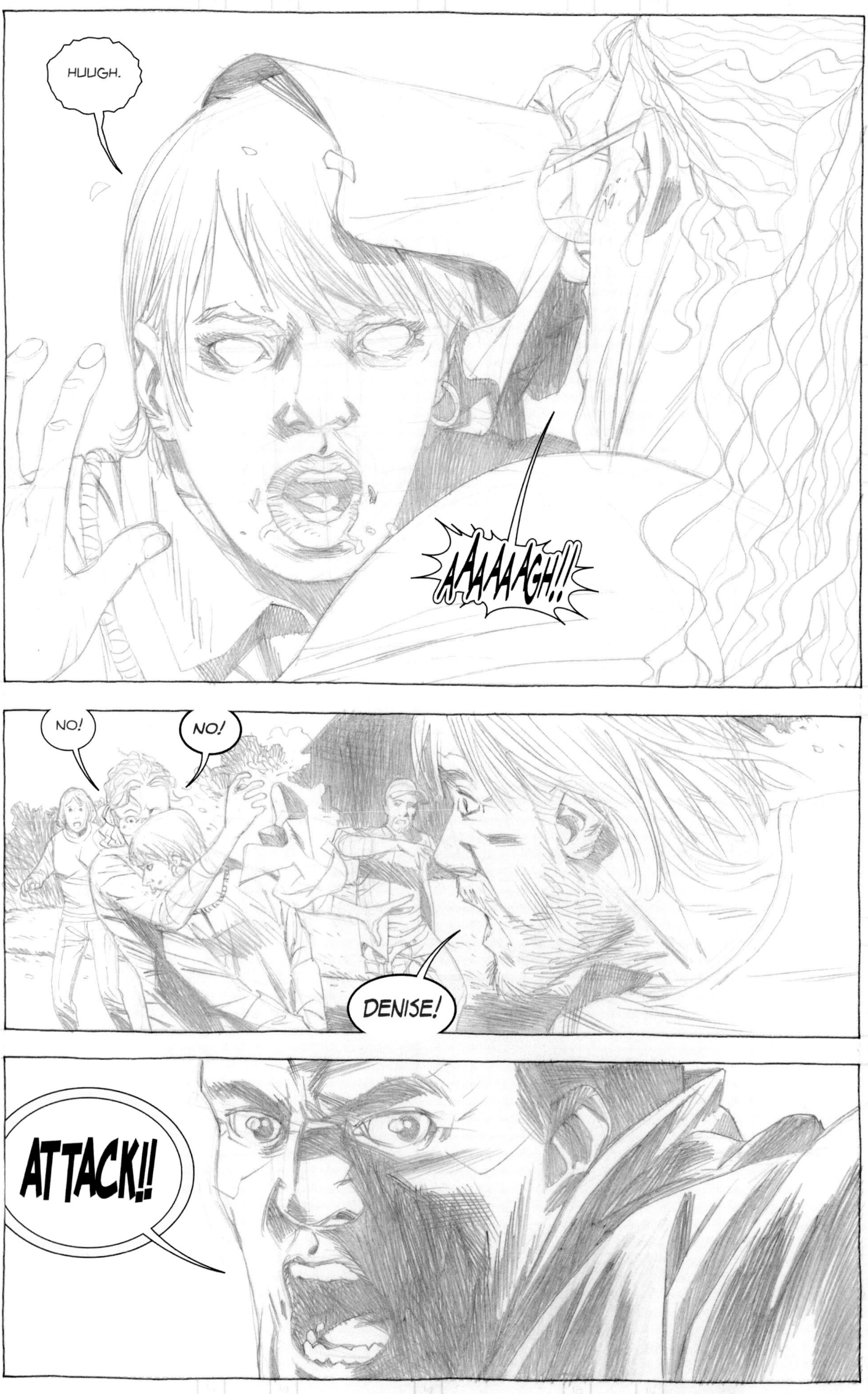
HUUGH.
AAAAAAGH!!
NO!
NO!
DENISE!
ATTACK!!

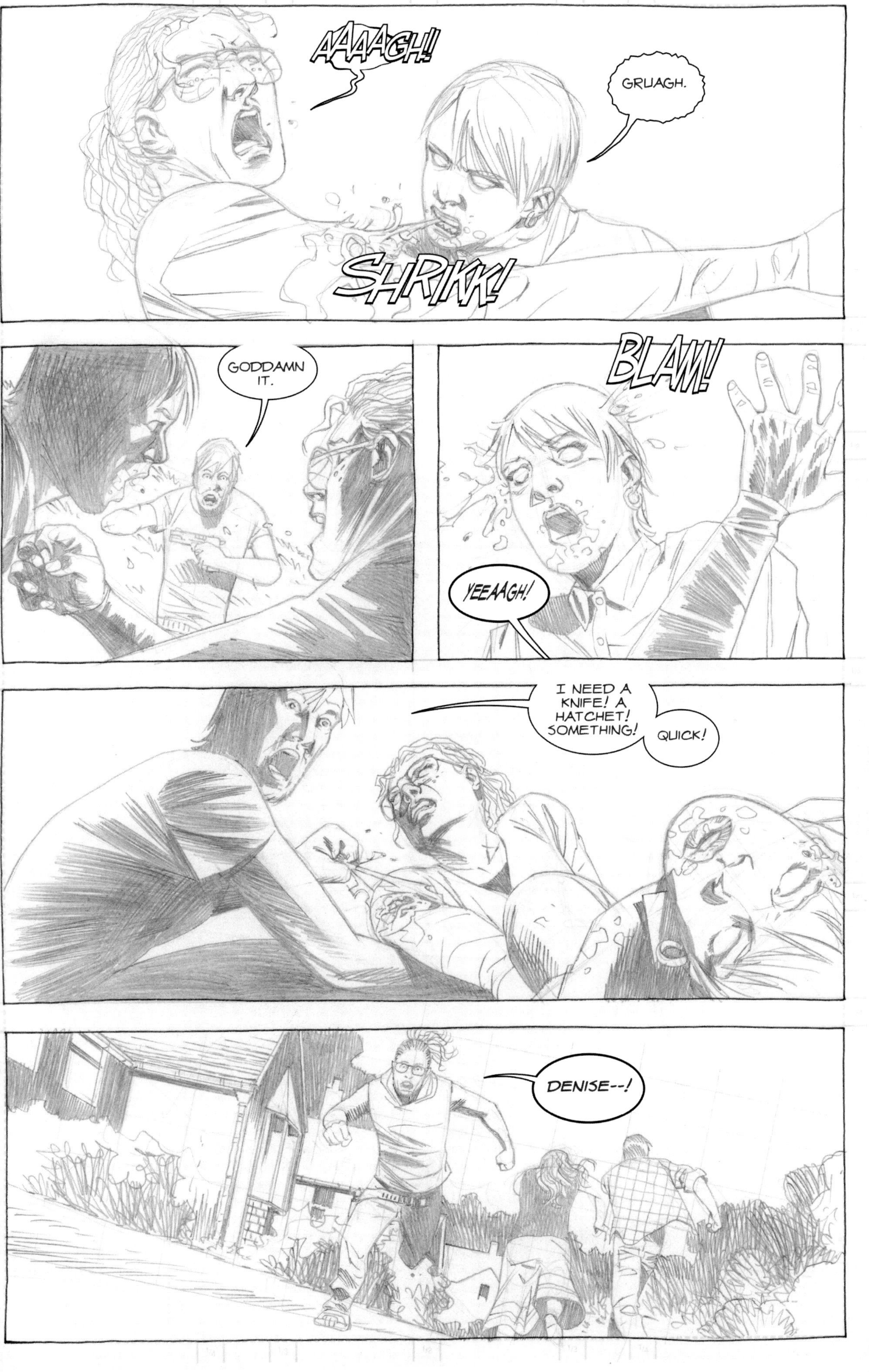
AAAAGH!!
GRUAGH.
SHRIKK!
GODDAMN IT.
BLAM!
YEEAAGH!
I NEED A KNIFE! A HATCHET! SOMETHING!
QUICK!
DENISE--!

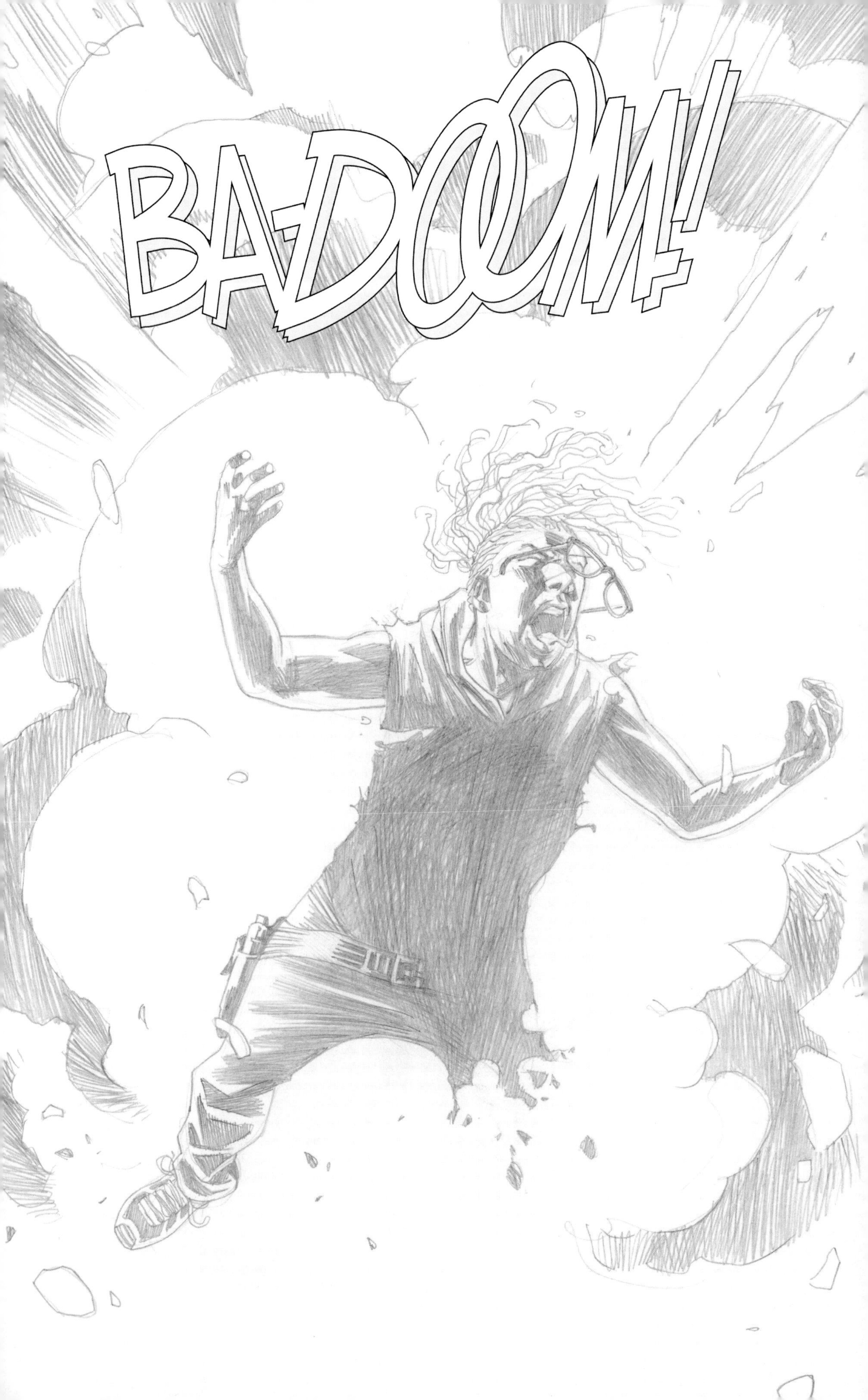
BA-DOOM!

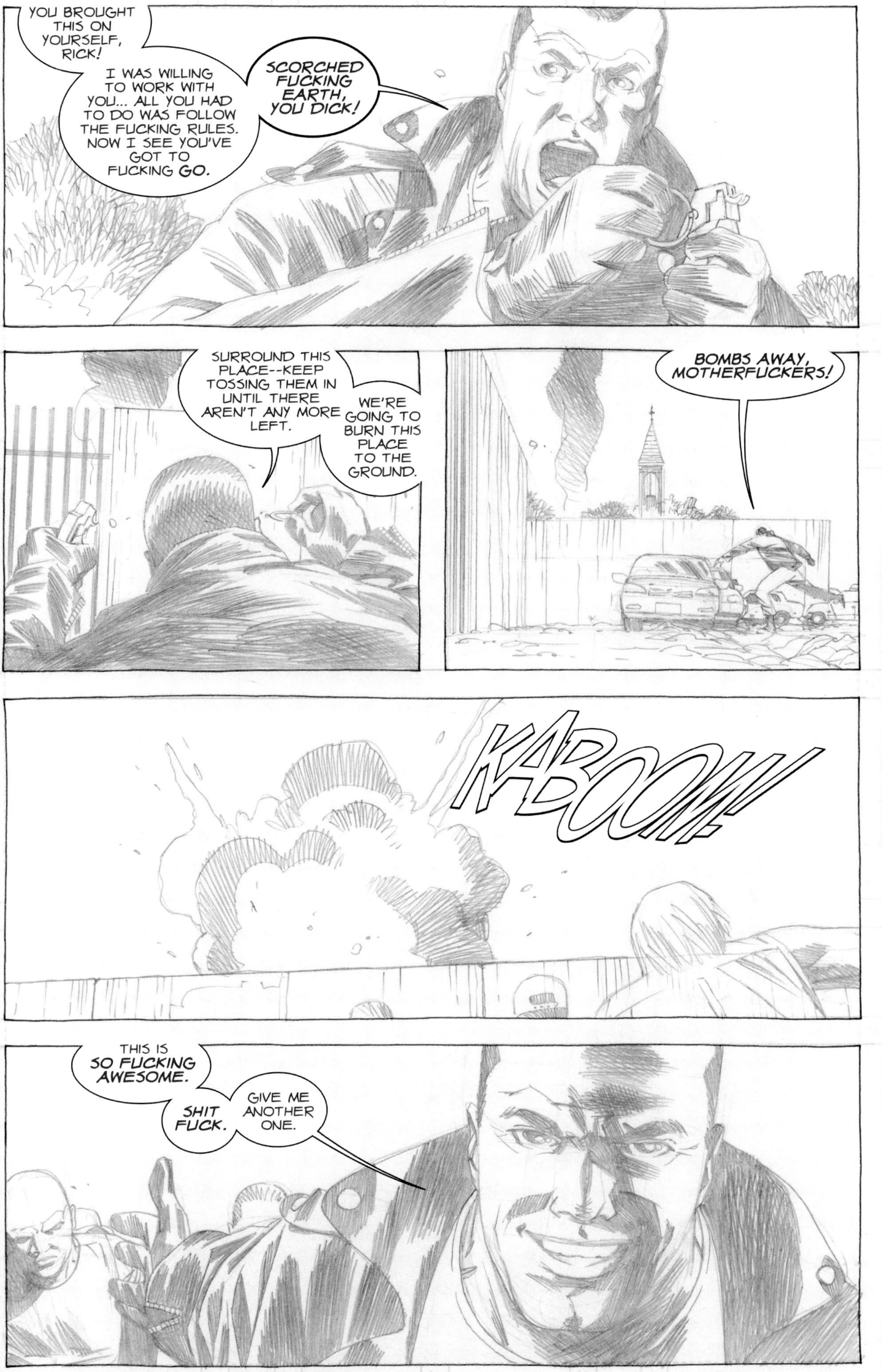
YOU BROUGHT THIS ON YOURSELF, RICK!
I WAS WILLING TO WORK WITH YOU... ALL YOU HAD TO DO WAS FOLLOW THE FUCKING RULES. NOW I SEE YOU'VE GOT TO FUCKING GO.
SCORCHED FUCKING EARTH, YOU DICK!
SURROUND THIS PLACE--KEEP TOSSING THEM IN UNTIL THERE AREN'T ANY MORE LEFT.
WE'RE GOING TO BURN THIS PLACE TO THE GROUND.
BOMBS AWAY, MOTHERFUCKERS!
KABOOM!
THIS IS SO FUCKING AWESOME.
SHIT FUCK.
GIVE ME ANOTHER ONE.

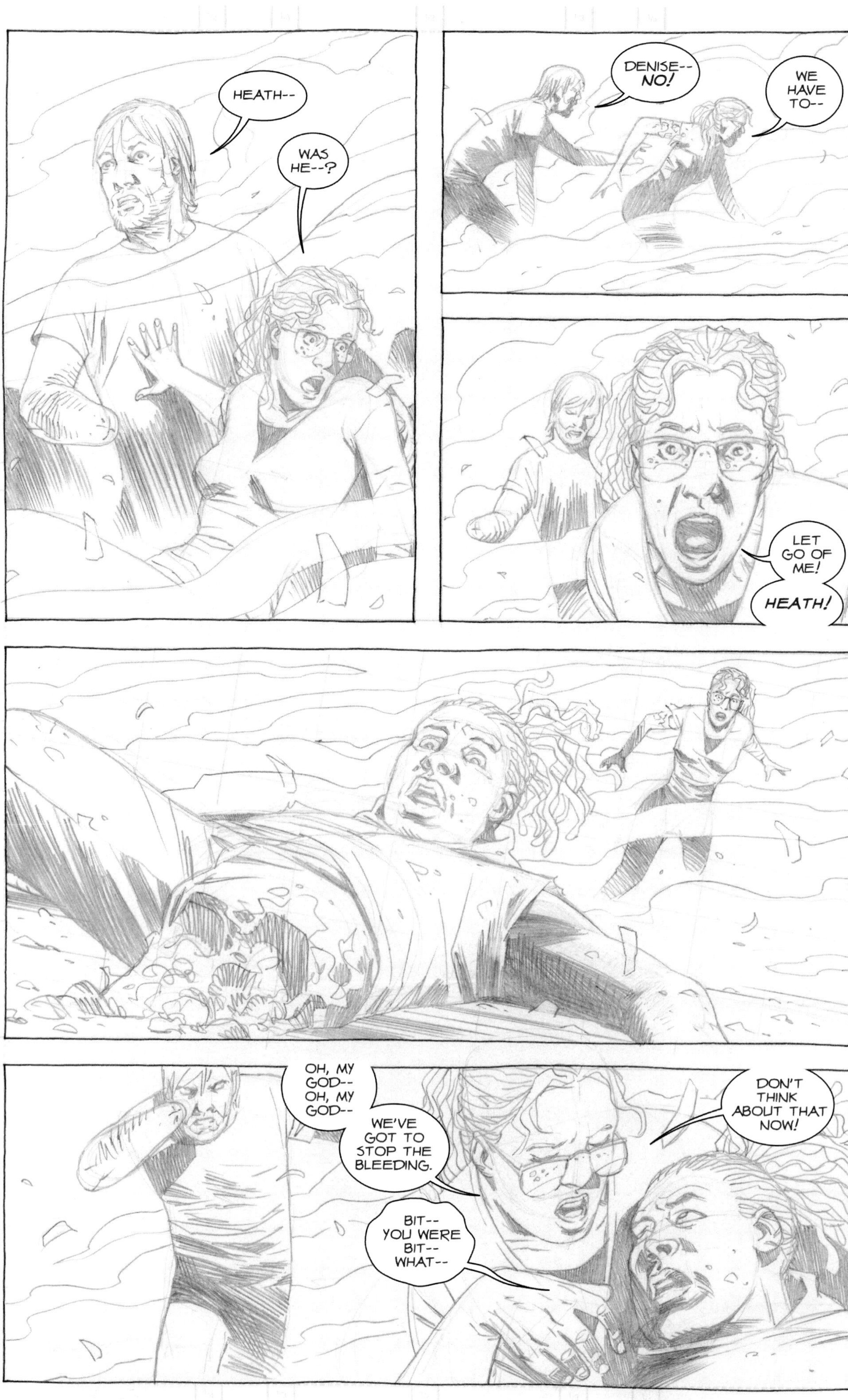
HEATH--
WAS HE--?
DENISE-- NO!
WE HAVE TO--
LET GO OF ME!
HEATH!
OH, MY GOD-- OH, MY GOD--
WE'VE GOT TO STOP THE BLEEDING.
DON'T THINK ABOUT THAT NOW!
BIT-- YOU WERE BIT-- WHAT--

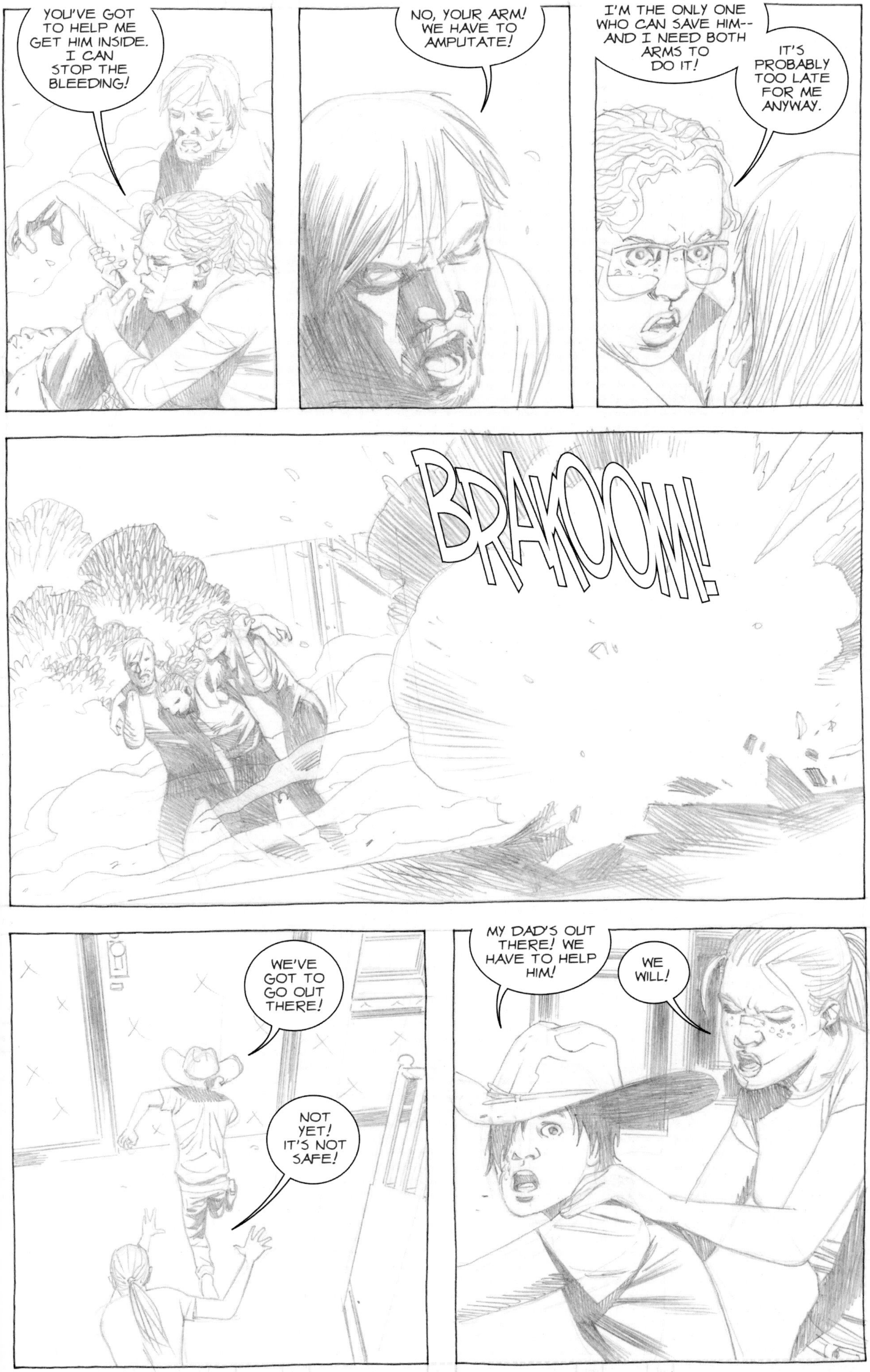
YOU'VE GOT TO HELP ME GET HIM INSIDE. I CAN STOP THE BLEEDING!
NO, YOUR ARM! WE HAVE TO AMPUTATE!
I'M THE ONLY ONE WHO CAN SAVE HIM-- AND I NEED BOTH ARMS TO DO IT!
IT'S PROBABLY TOO LATE FOR ME ANYWAY.
BRAKOOM!
WE'VE GOT TO GO OUT THERE!
NOT YET! IT'S NOT SAFE!
MY DAD'S OUT THERE! WE HAVE TO HELP HIM!
WE WILL!

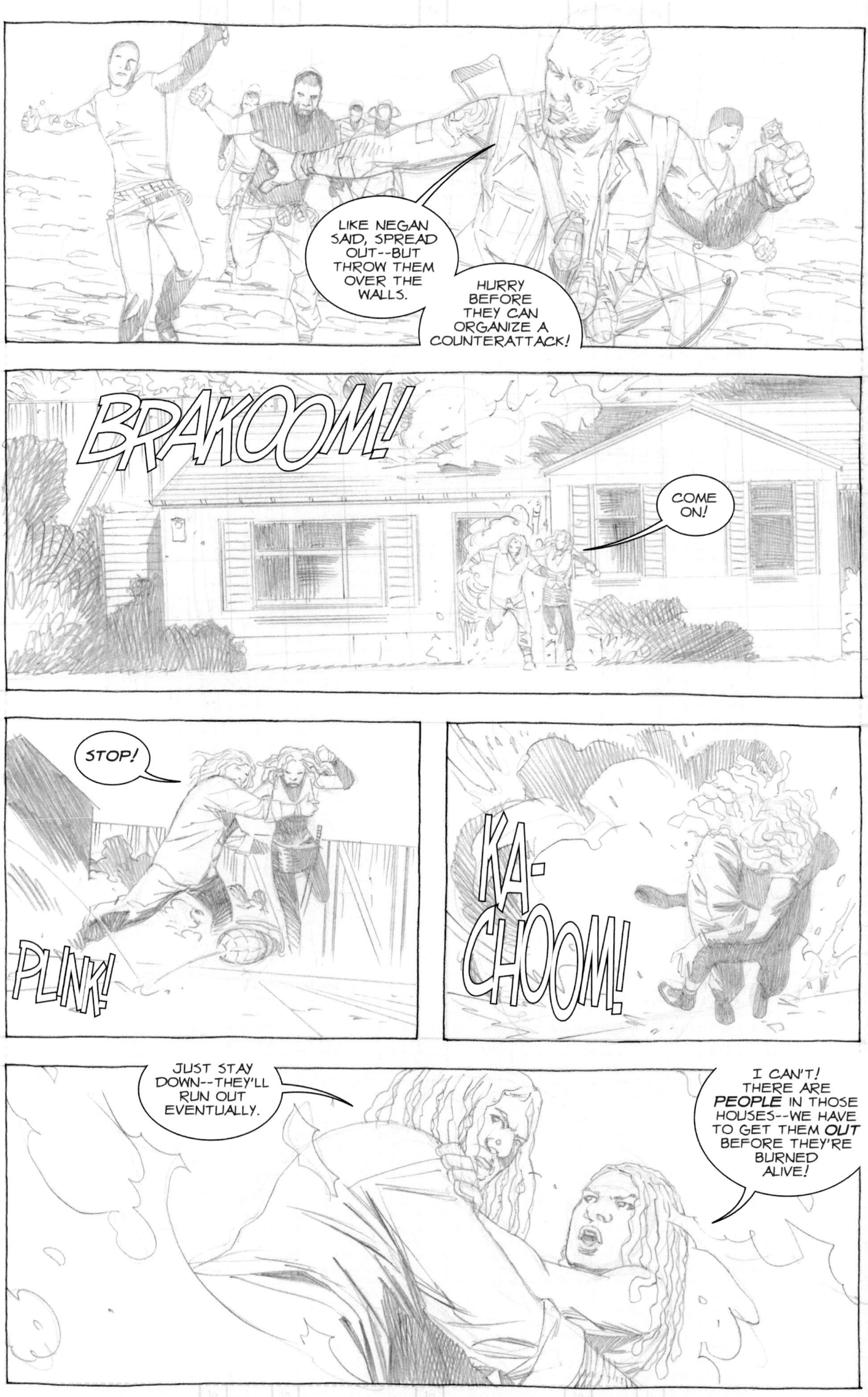
LIKE NEGAN SAID, SPREAD OUT--BUT THROW THEM OVER THE WALLS.
HURRY BEFORE THEY CAN ORGANIZE A COUNTERATTACK!
BRAKOOM!
COME ON!
STOP!
PLINK!
KA-CHOOM!
JUST STAY DOWN--THEY'LL RUN OUT EVENTUALLY.
I CAN'T! THERE ARE PEOPLE IN THOSE HOUSES--WE HAVE TO GET THEM OUT BEFORE THEY'RE BURNED ALIVE!

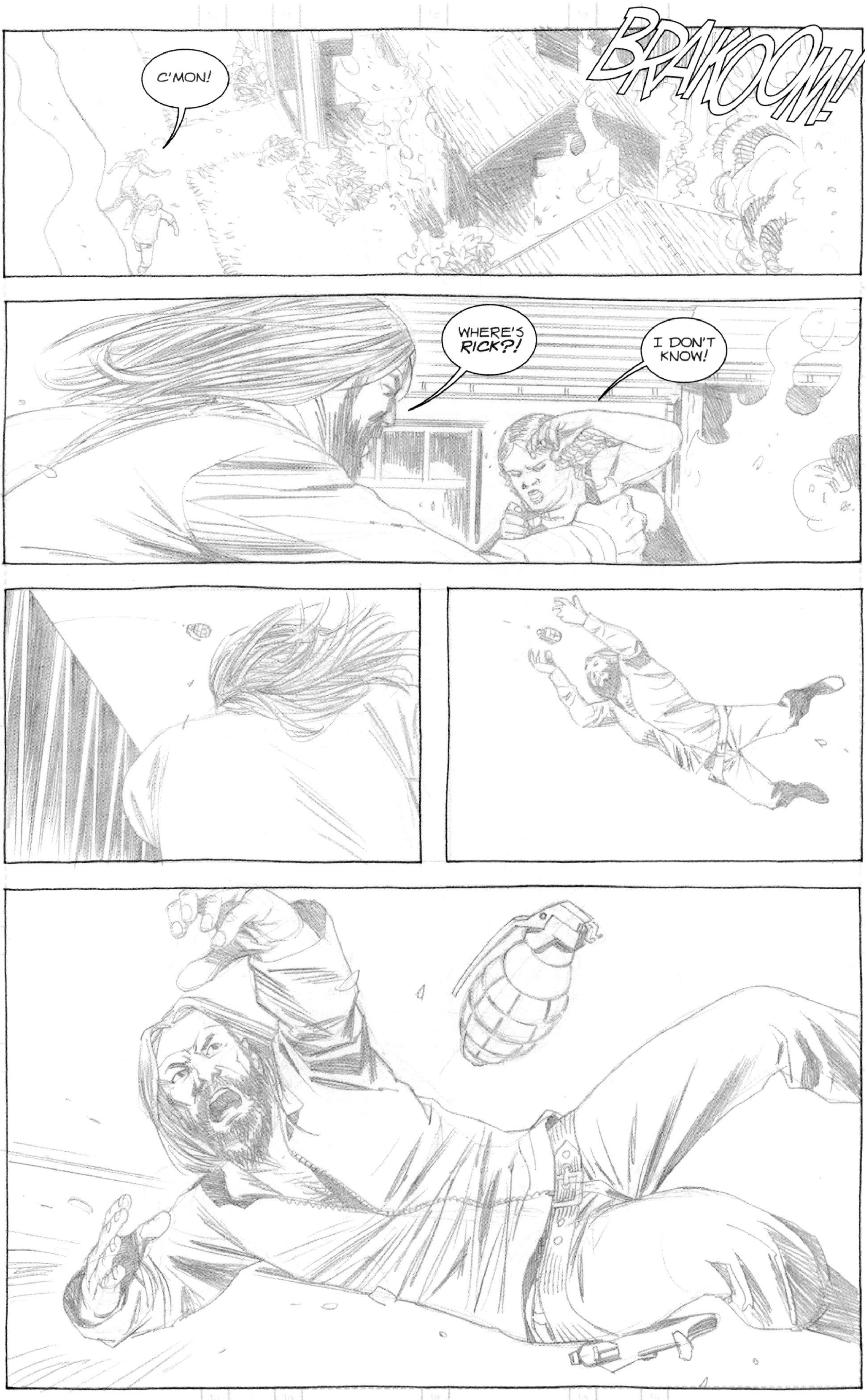
C'MON!
BRAKOOM!
WHERE'S RICK?!
I DON'T KNOW!

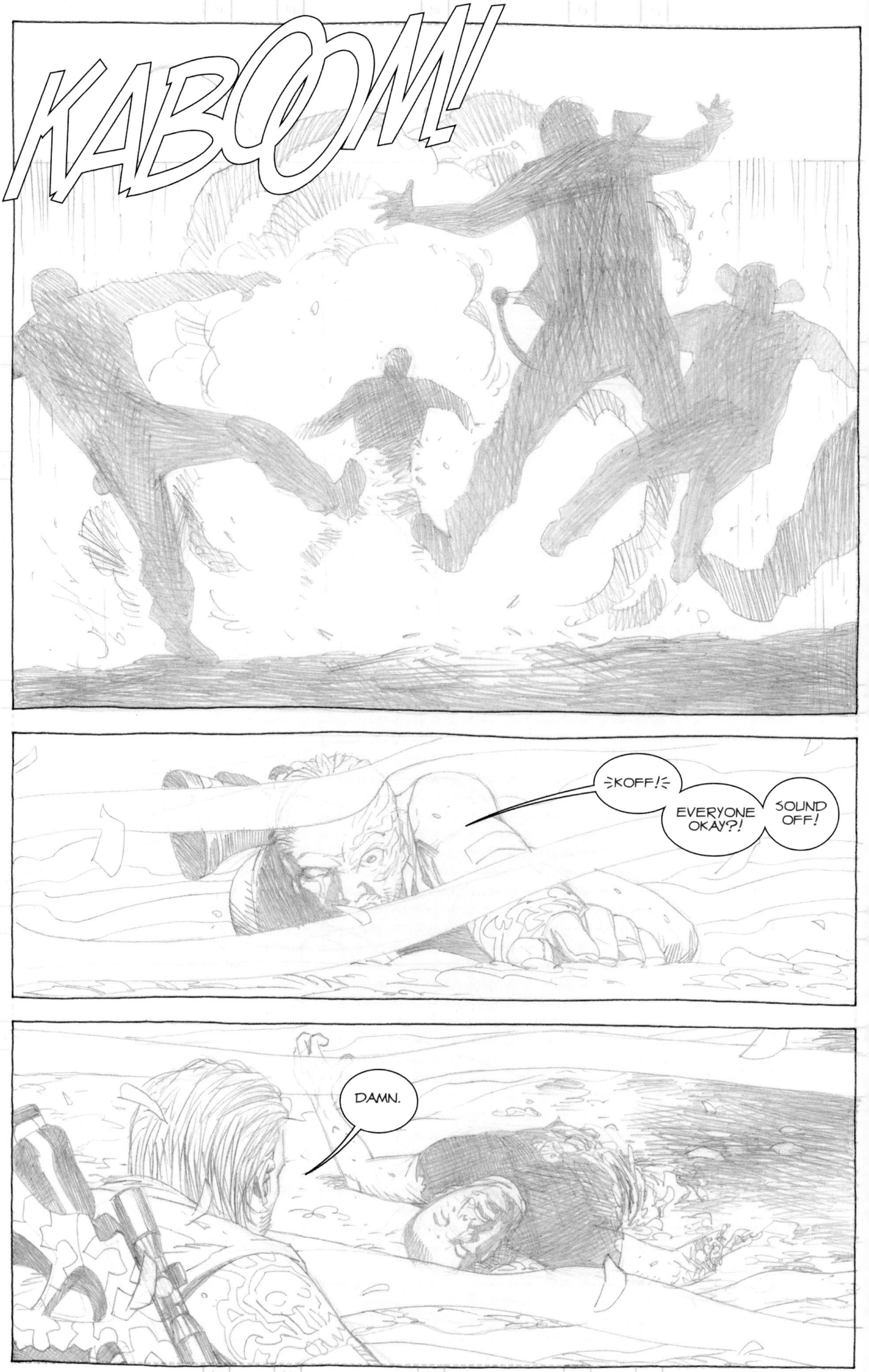
KABOOM!
KOFF!
EVERYONE OKAY?!
SOUND OFF!
DAMN.

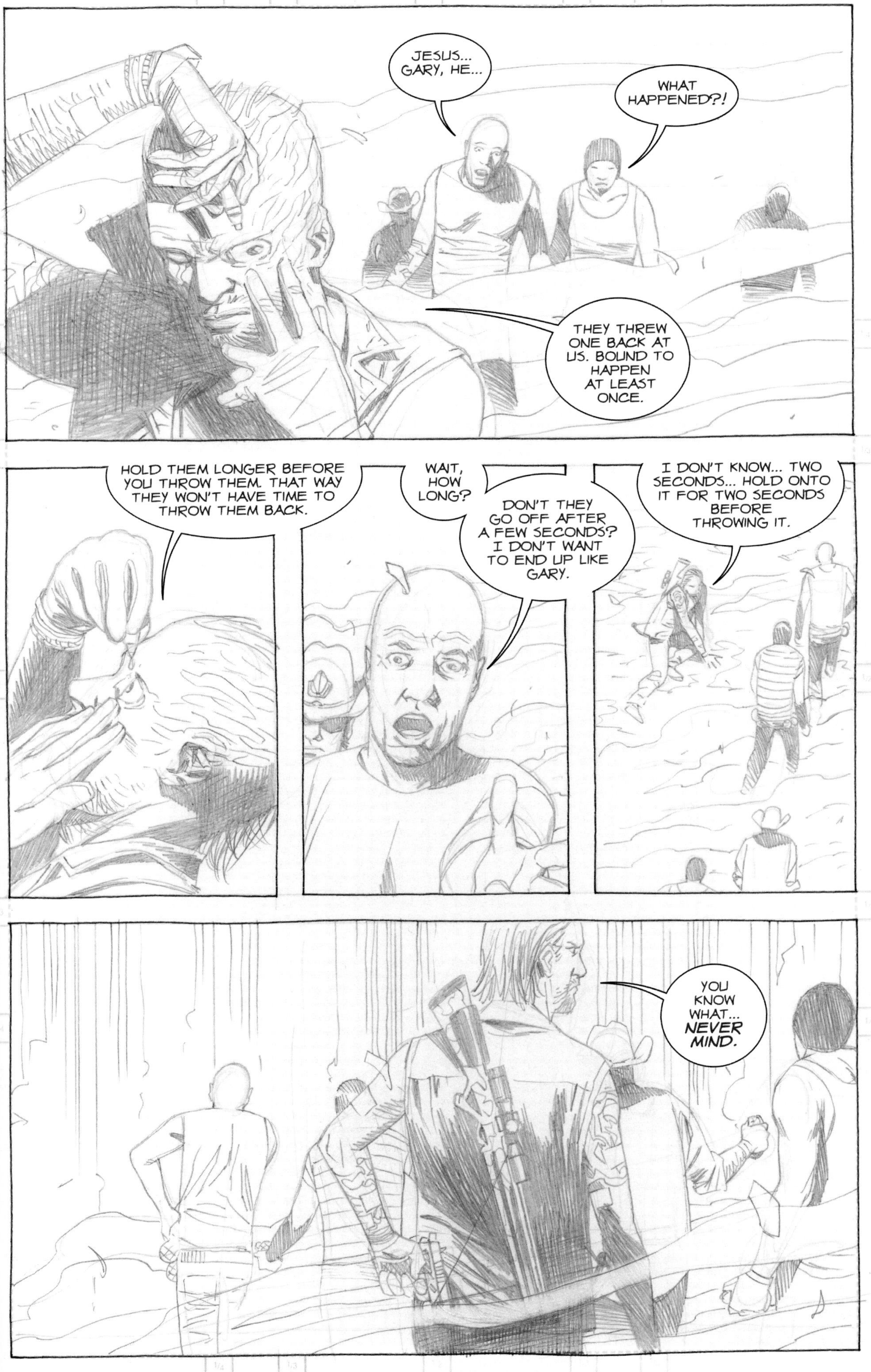
JESUS... GARY, HE...
WHAT HAPPENED?!
THEY THREW ONE BACK AT US. BOUND TO HAPPEN AT LEAST ONCE.
HOLD THEM LONGER BEFORE YOU THROW THEM. THAT WAY THEY WON'T HAVE TIME TO THROW THEM BACK.
WAIT, HOW LONG?
DON'T THEY GO OFF AFTER A FEW SECONDS? I DON'T WANT TO END UP LIKE GARY.
I DON'T KNOW... TWO SECONDS... HOLD ONTO IT FOR TWO SECONDS BEFORE THROWING IT.
YOU KNOW WHAT... NEVER MIND.

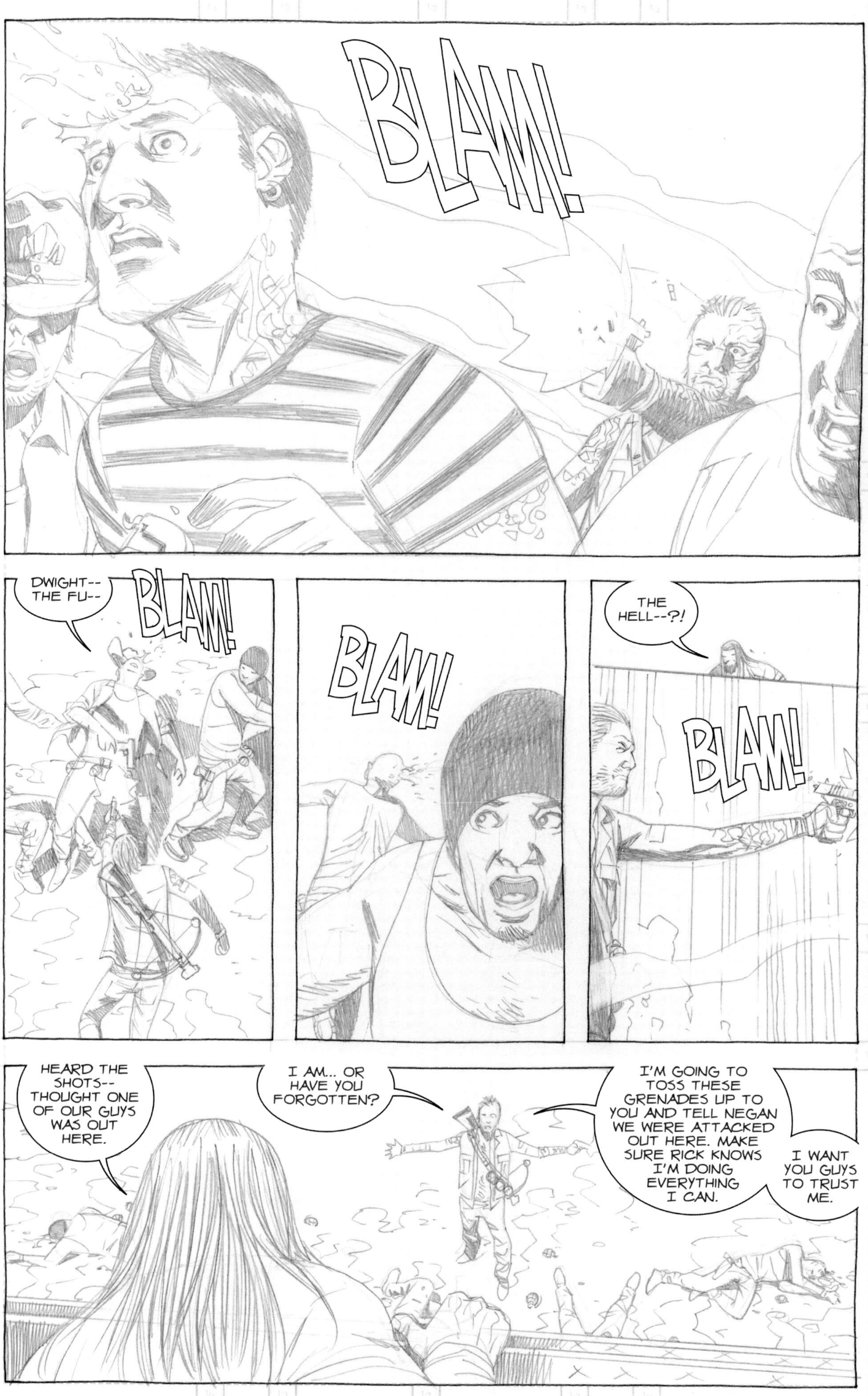
BLAM!
DWIGHT-- THE FU--
BLAM!
BLAM!
THE HELL--?!
BLAM!
HEARD THE SHOTS-- THOUGHT ONE OF OUR GUYS WAS OUT HERE.
I AM... OR HAVE YOU FORGOTTEN?
I'M GOING TO TOSS THESE GRENADES UP TO YOU AND TELL NEGAN WE WERE ATTACKED OUT HERE. MAKE SURE RICK KNOWS I'M DOING EVERYTHING I CAN.
I WANT YOU GUYS TO TRUST ME.

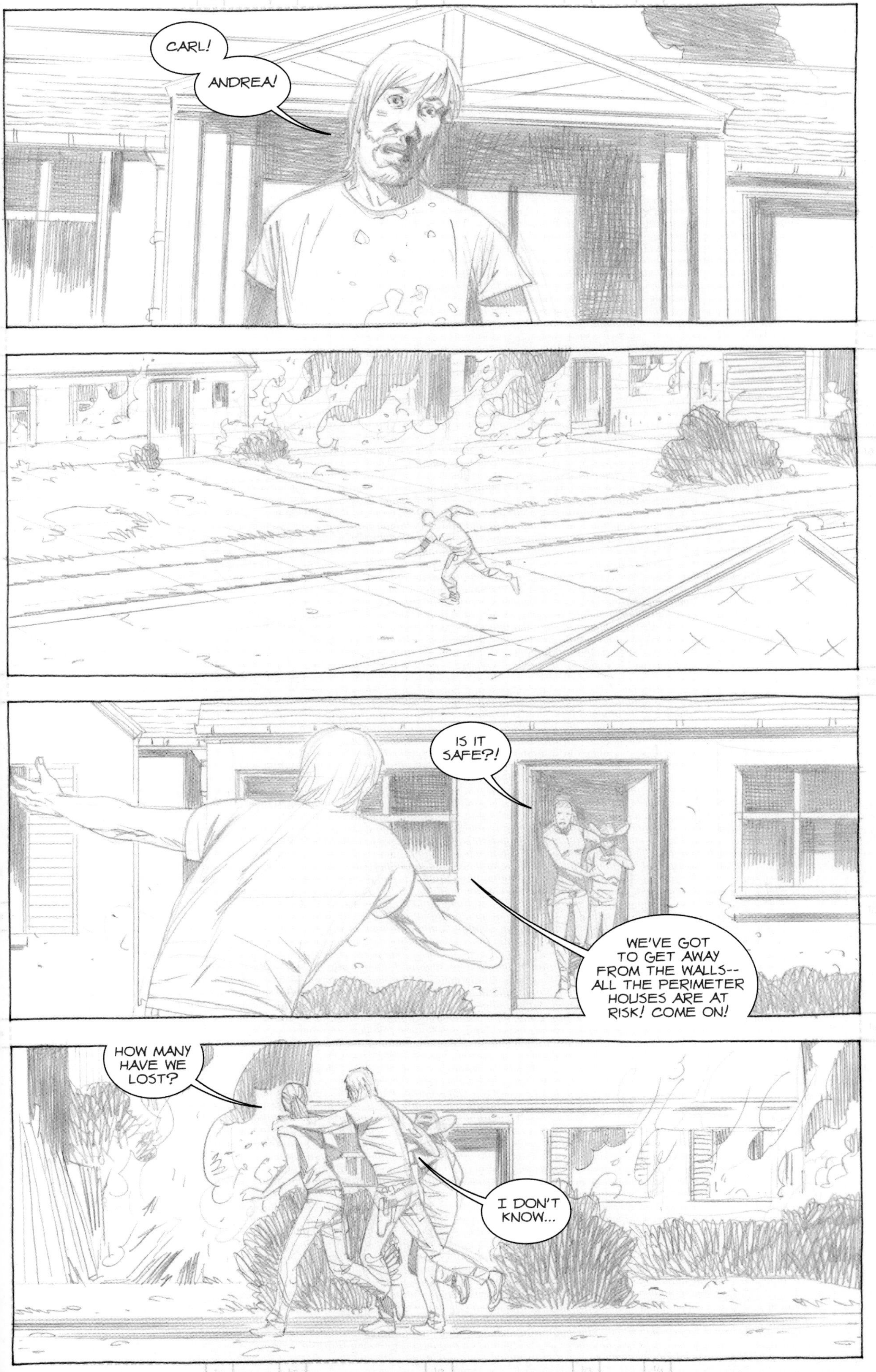

CARL!
ANDREA!
IS IT SAFE?!
WE'VE GOT TO GET AWAY FROM THE WALLS-- ALL THE PERIMETER HOUSES ARE AT RISK! COME ON!
HOW MANY HAVE WE LOST?
I DON'T KNOW...

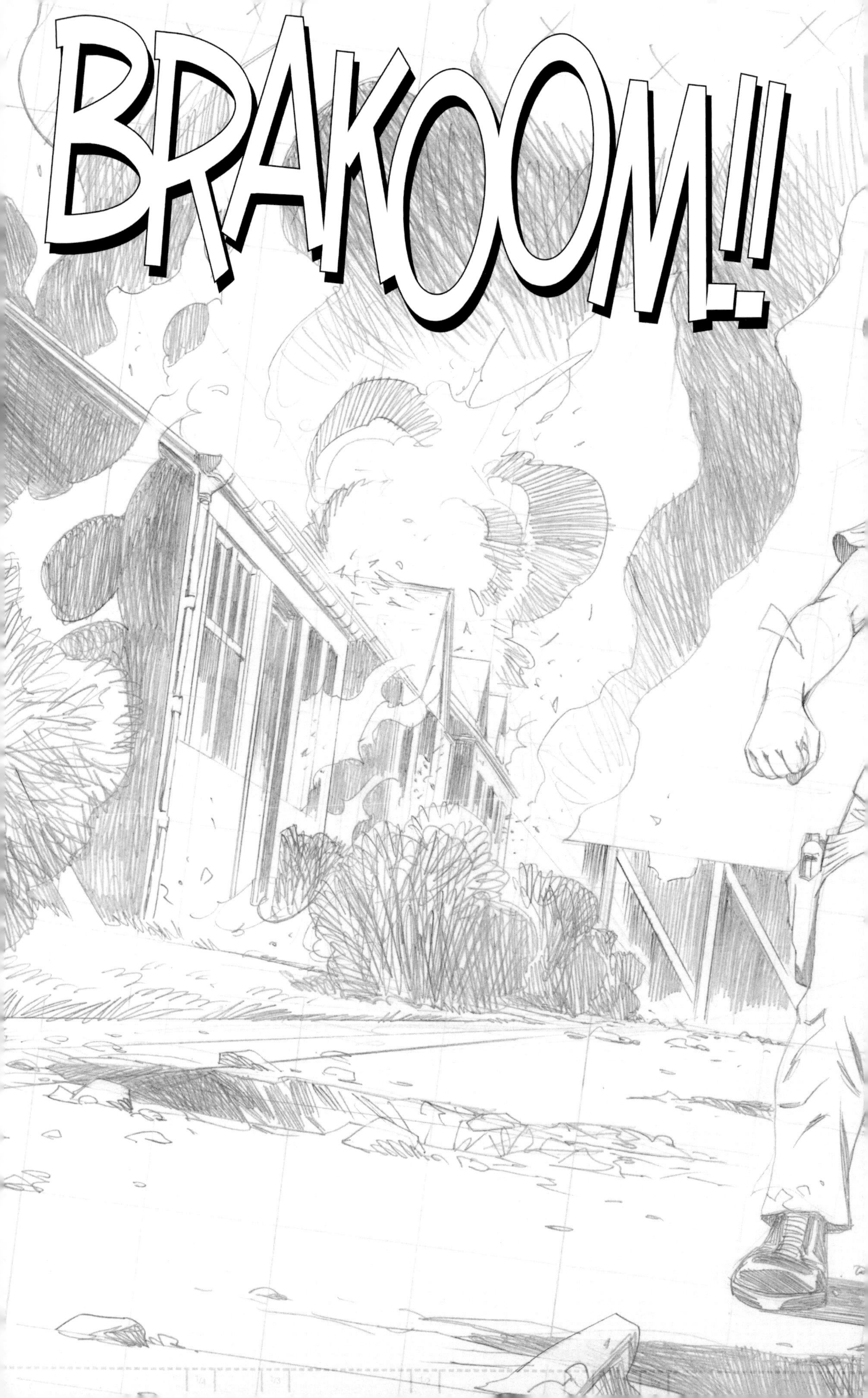
BRAKOOM!!

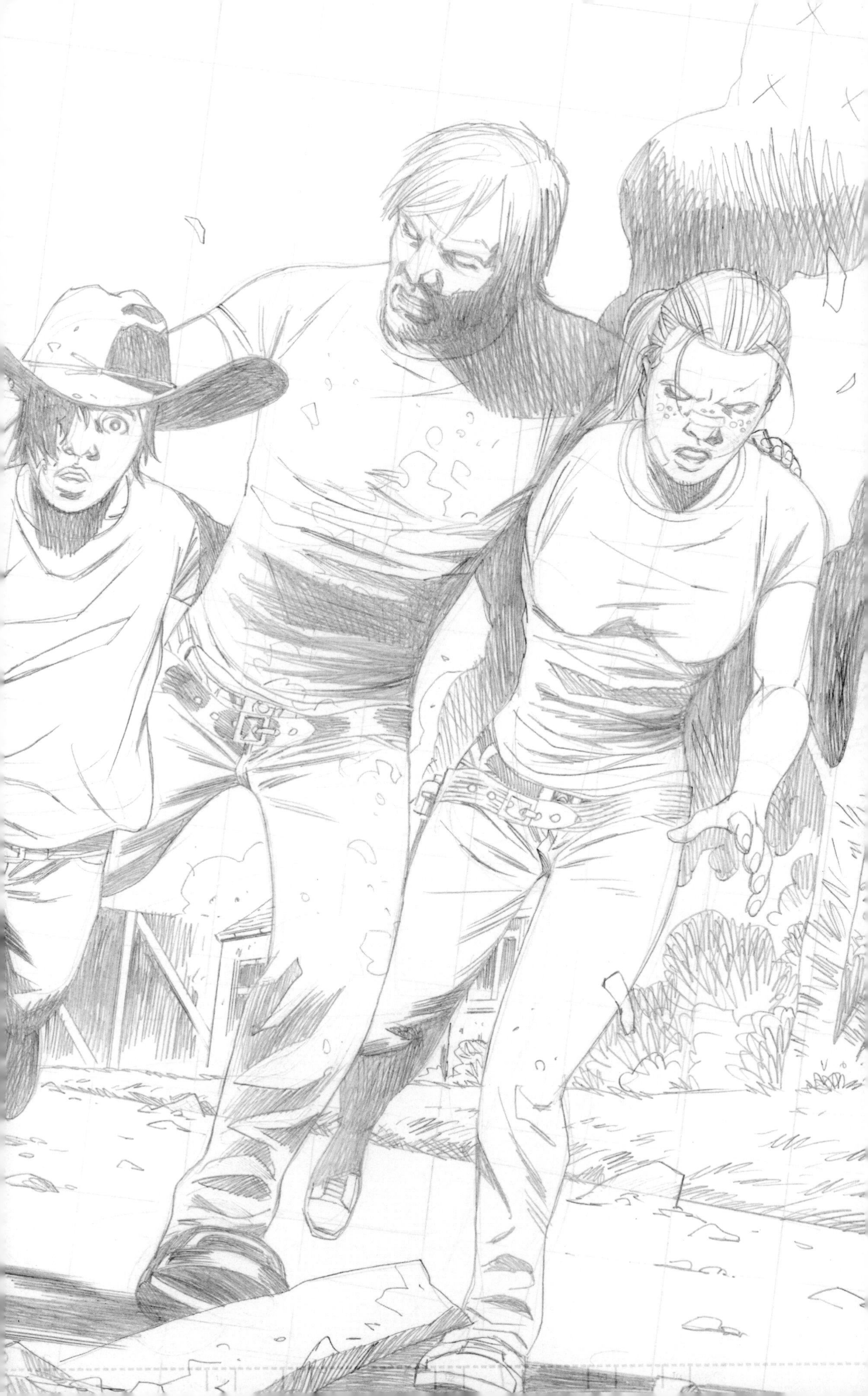

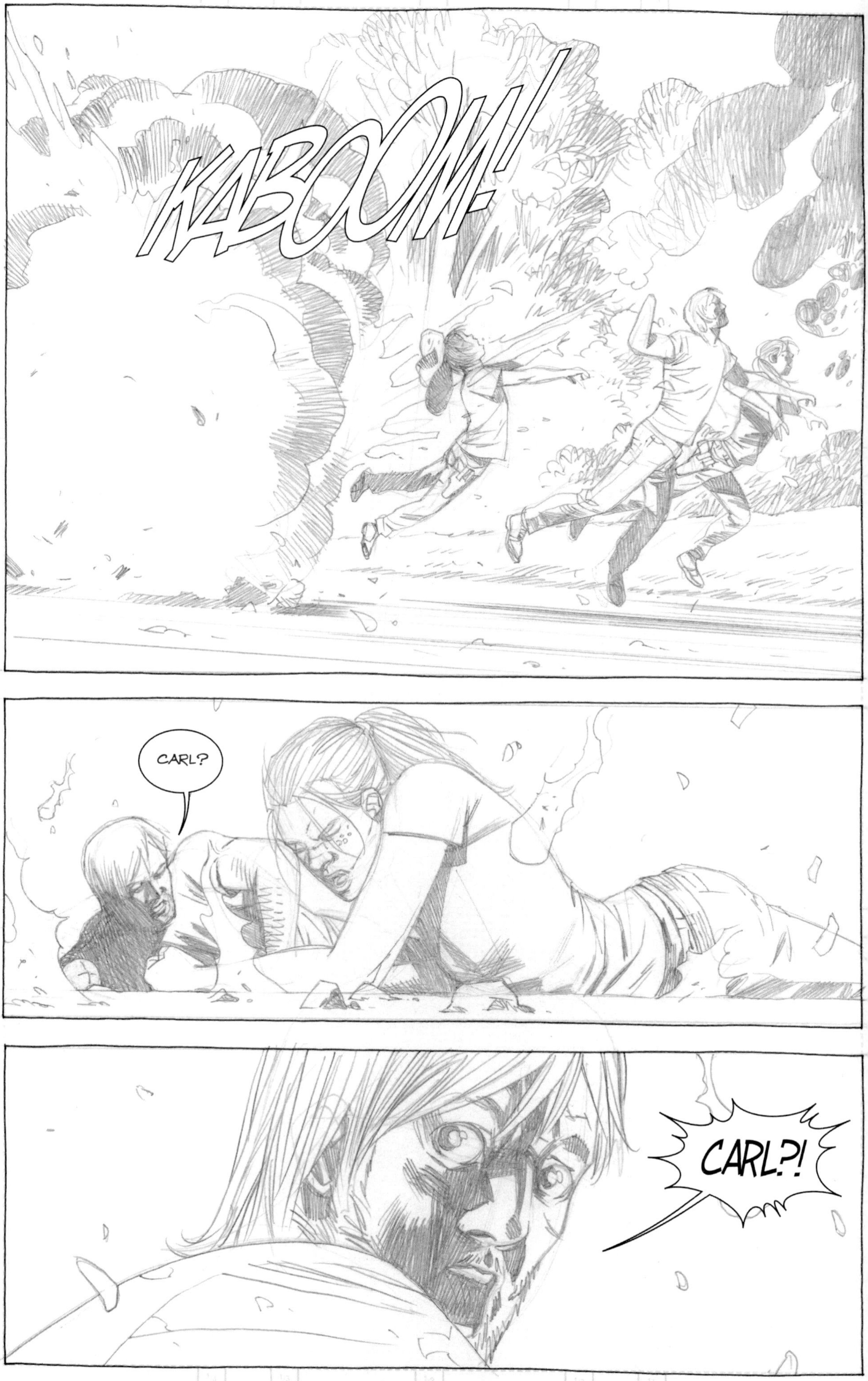
KABOOM!
CARL?
CARL?!

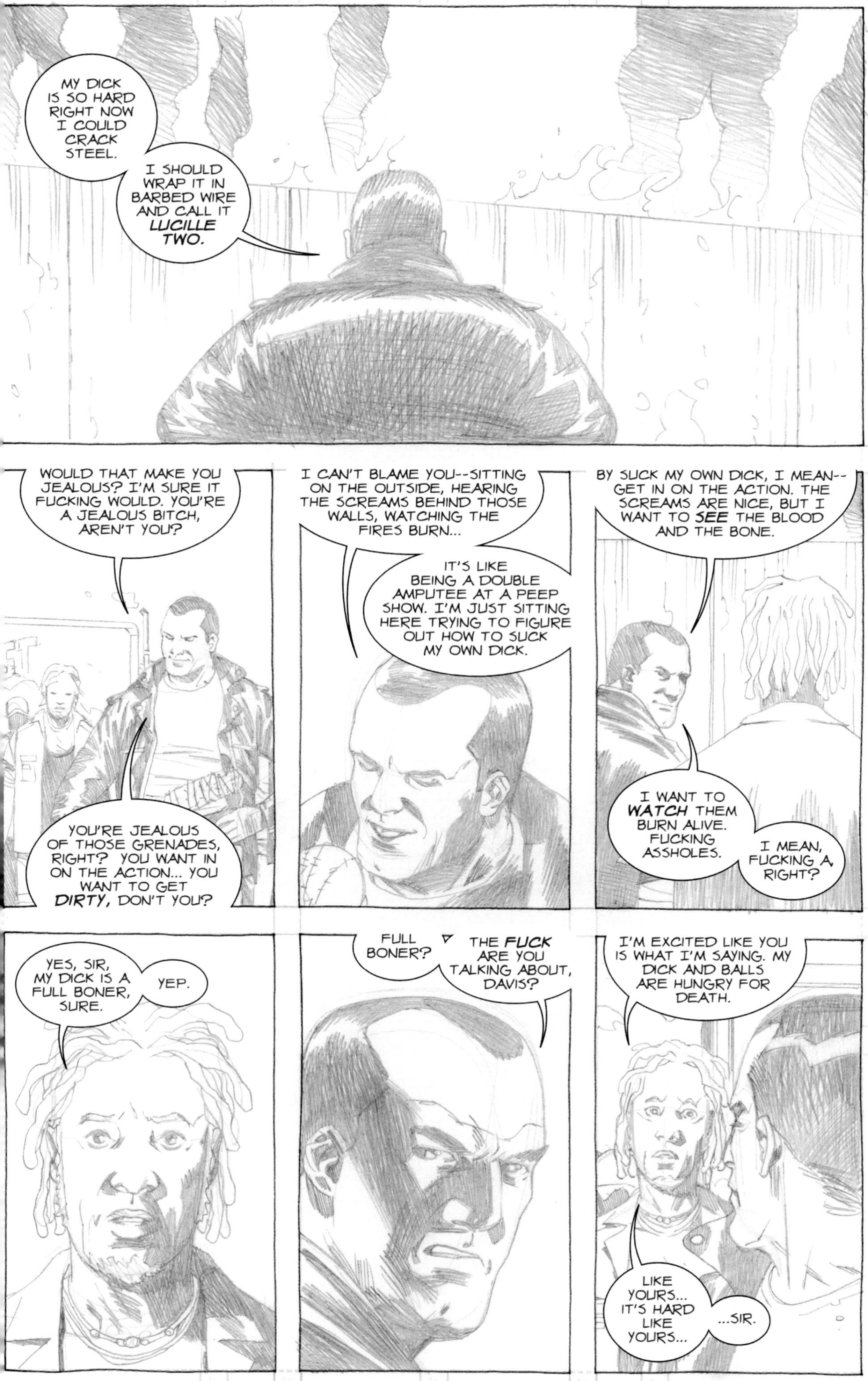
MY DICK IS SO HARD RIGHT NOW I COULD CRACK STEEL.
I SHOULD WRAP IT IN BARBED WIRE AND CALL IT *LUCILLE TWO.*
WOULD THAT MAKE YOU JEALOUS? I'M SURE IT FUCKING WOULD. YOU'RE A JEALOUS BITCH, AREN'T YOU?
YOU'RE JEALOUS OF THOSE GRENADES, RIGHT? YOU WANT IN ON THE ACTION... YOU WANT TO GET *DIRTY,* DON'T YOU?
I CAN'T BLAME YOU--SITTING ON THE OUTSIDE, HEARING THE SCREAMS BEHIND THOSE WALLS, WATCHING THE FIRES BURN...
IT'S LIKE BEING A DOUBLE AMPUTEE AT A PEEP SHOW. I'M JUST SITTING HERE TRYING TO FIGURE OUT HOW TO SUCK MY OWN DICK.
BY SUCK MY OWN DICK, I MEAN--GET IN ON THE ACTION. THE SCREAMS ARE NICE, BUT I WANT TO *SEE* THE BLOOD AND THE BONE.
I WANT TO *WATCH* THEM BURN ALIVE. FUCKING ASSHOLES.
I MEAN, FUCKING A, RIGHT?
YES, SIR, MY DICK IS A FULL BONER, SURE.
YEP.
FULL BONER?
THE *FUCK* ARE YOU TALKING ABOUT, DAVIS?
I'M EXCITED LIKE YOU IS WHAT I'M SAYING. MY DICK AND BALLS ARE HUNGRY FOR DEATH.
LIKE YOURS... IT'S HARD LIKE YOURS...
...SIR.

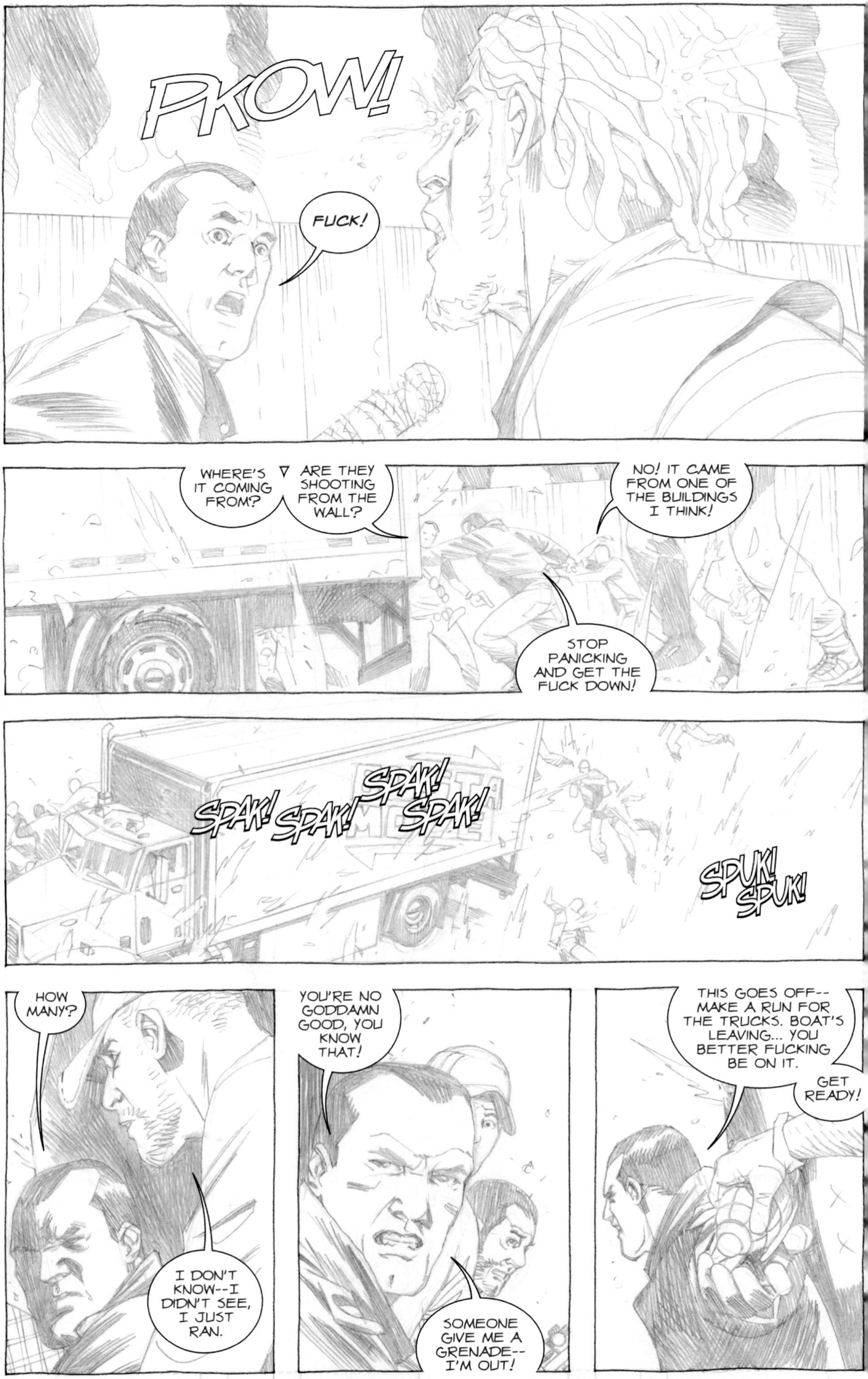
PKOW!
FUCK!
WHERE'S IT COMING FROM?
ARE THEY SHOOTING FROM THE WALL?
NO! IT CAME FROM ONE OF THE BUILDINGS I THINK!
STOP PANICKING AND GET THE FUCK DOWN!
SPAK! SPAK! SPAK! SPAK!
SPUK! SPUK!
HOW MANY?
I DON'T KNOW--I DIDN'T SEE, I JUST RAN.
YOU'RE NO GODDAMN GOOD, YOU KNOW THAT!
SOMEONE GIVE ME A GRENADE-- I'M OUT!
THIS GOES OFF-- MAKE A RUN FOR THE TRUCKS. BOAT'S LEAVING... YOU BETTER FUCKING BE ON IT.
GET READY!

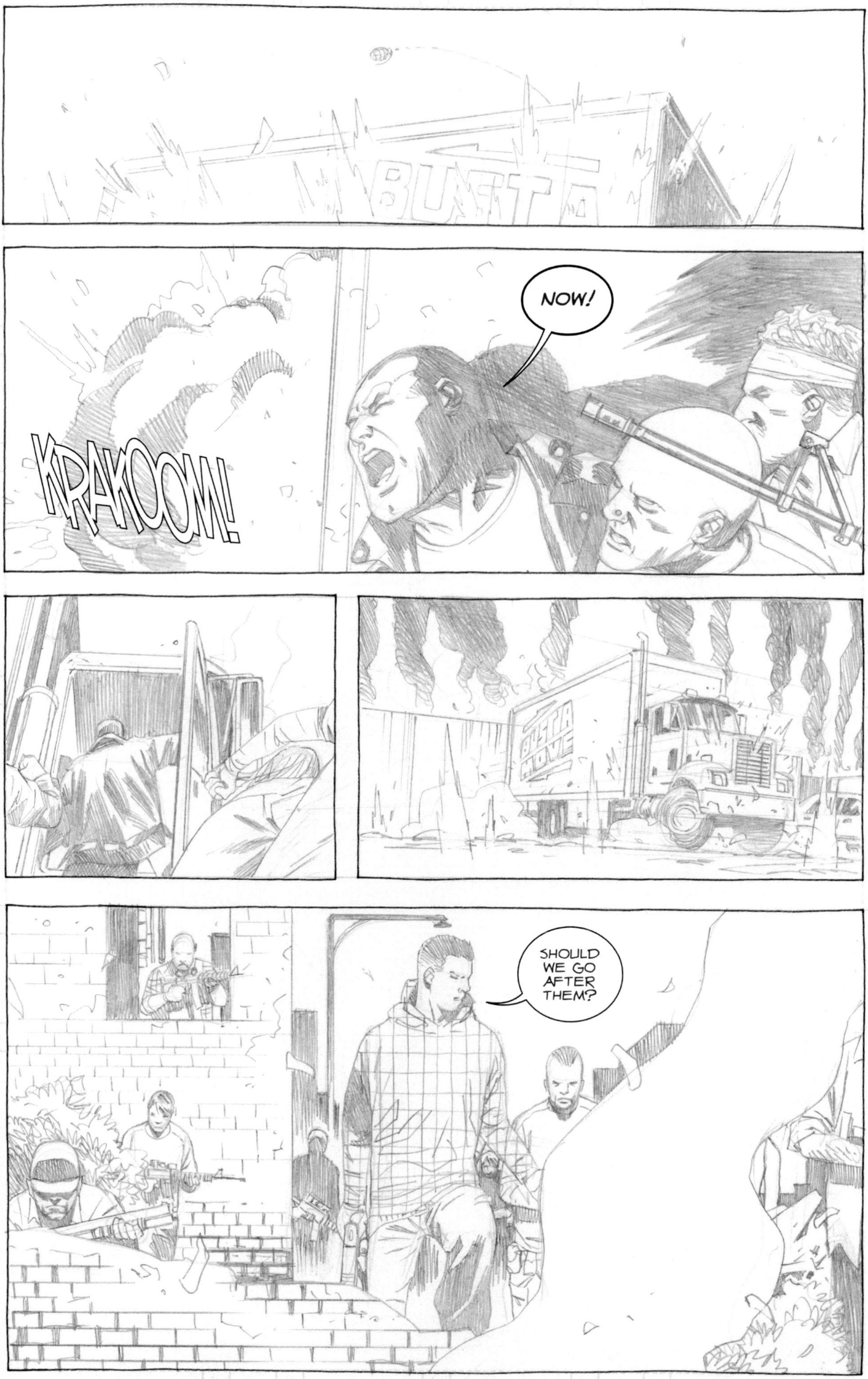
BUSTA
NOW!
KRAKOOM!
BUSTA MOVE
SHOULD WE GO AFTER THEM?

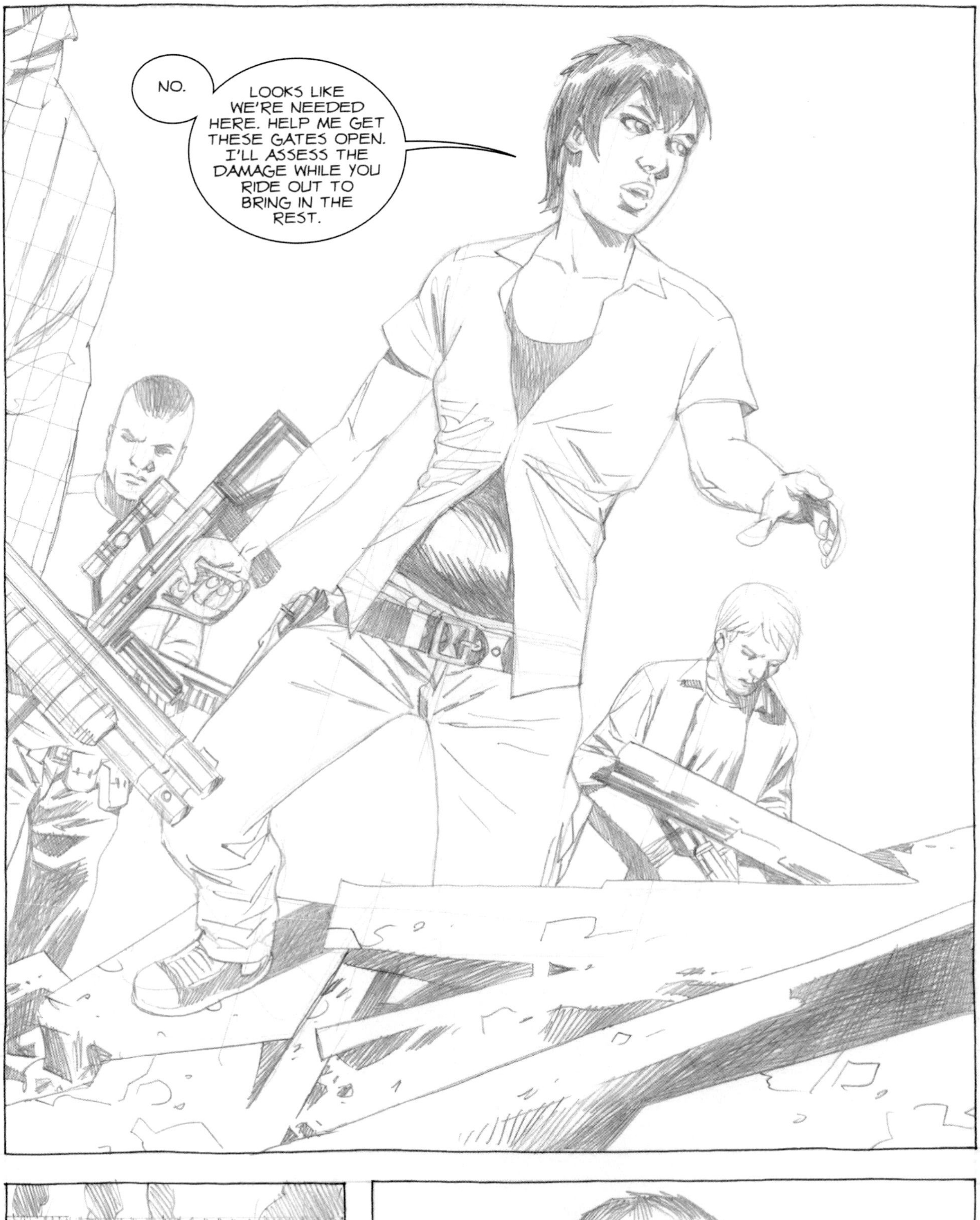
NO.
LOOKS LIKE WE'RE NEEDED HERE. HELP ME GET THESE GATES OPEN. I'LL ASSESS THE DAMAGE WHILE YOU RIDE OUT TO BRING IN THE REST.

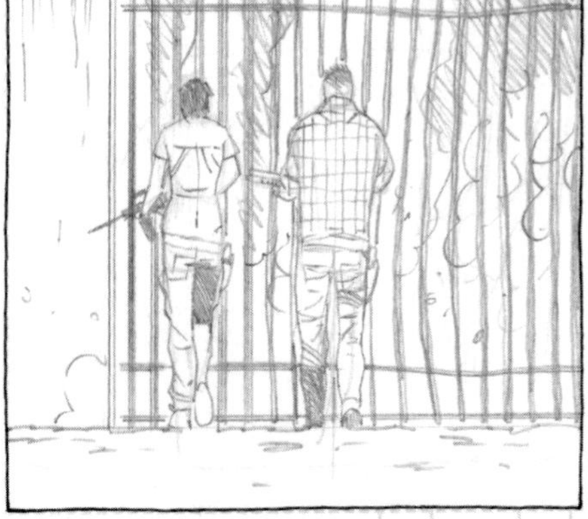

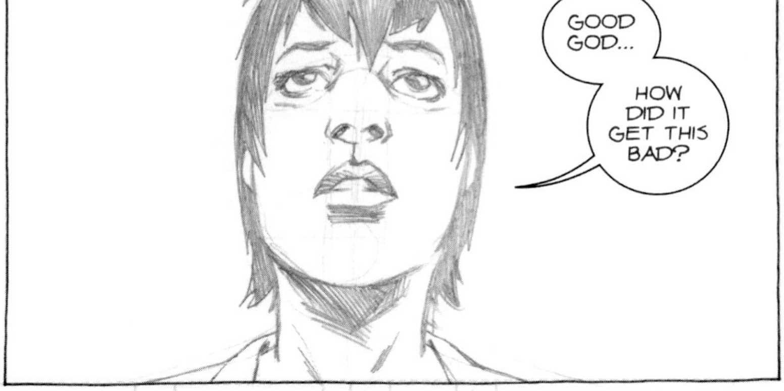
GOOD GOD...
HOW DID IT GET THIS BAD?

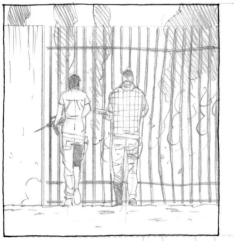

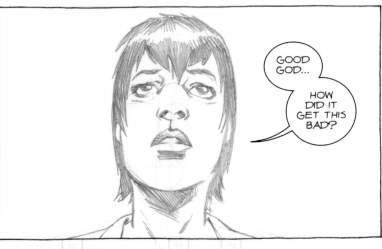

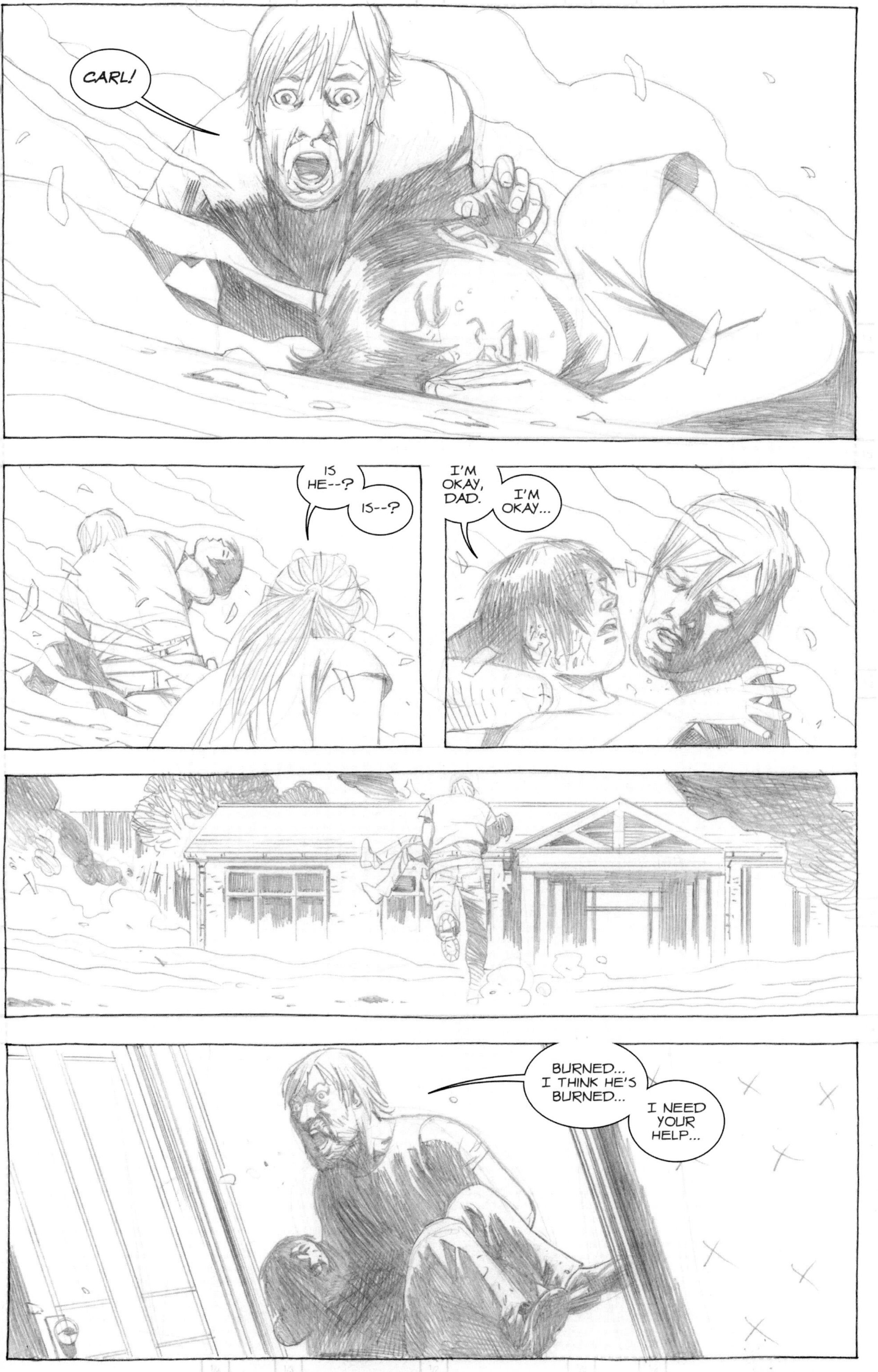
CARL!
IS HE--?
IS--?
I'M OKAY, DAD.
I'M OKAY...
BURNED... I THINK HE'S BURNED...
I NEED YOUR HELP...

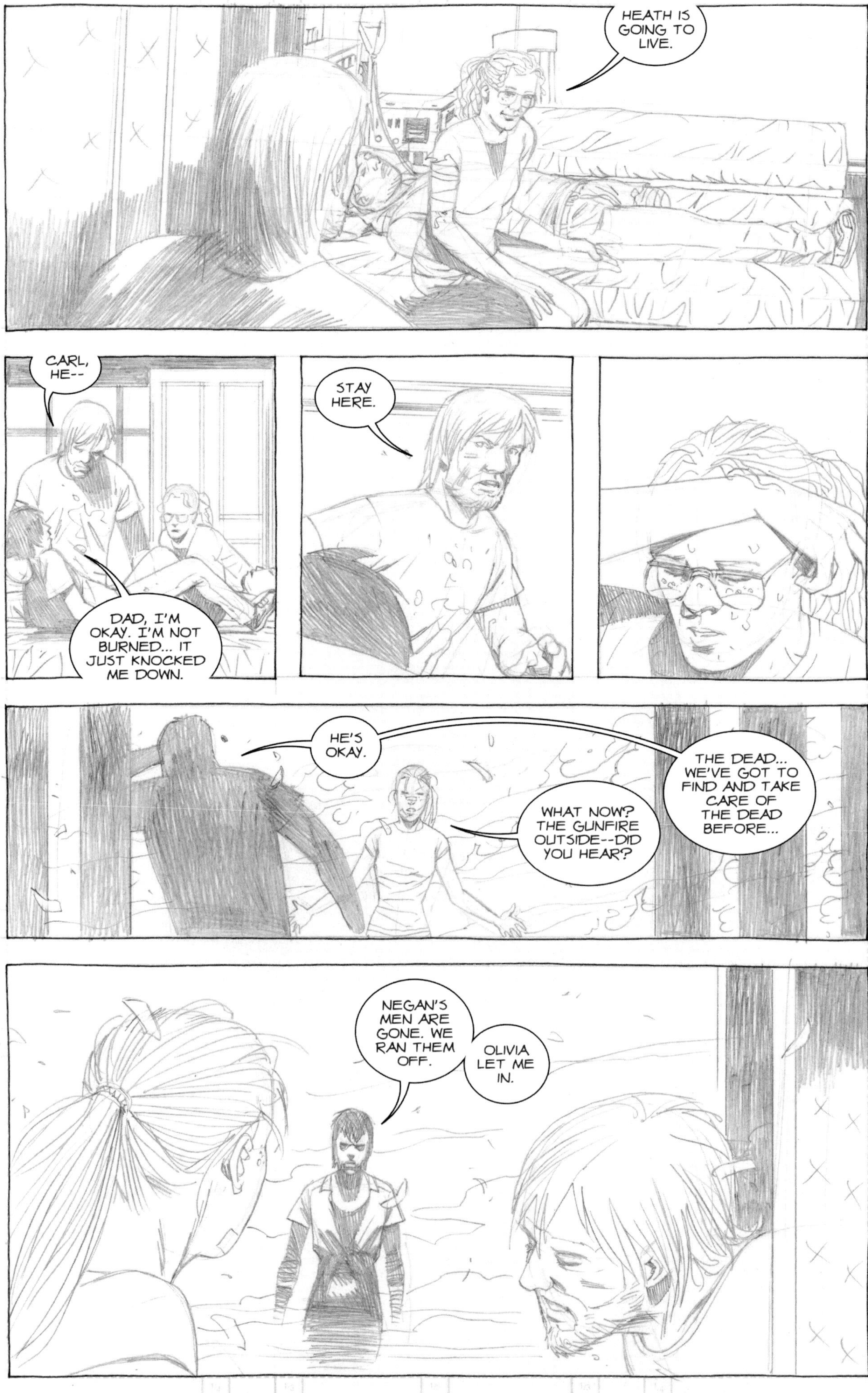
HEATH IS GOING TO LIVE.
CARL, HE--
DAD, I'M OKAY. I'M NOT BURNED... IT JUST KNOCKED ME DOWN.
STAY HERE.
HE'S OKAY.
WHAT NOW? THE GUNFIRE OUTSIDE--DID YOU HEAR?
THE DEAD... WE'VE GOT TO FIND AND TAKE CARE OF THE DEAD BEFORE...
NEGAN'S MEN ARE GONE. WE RAN THEM OFF.
OLIVIA LET ME IN.

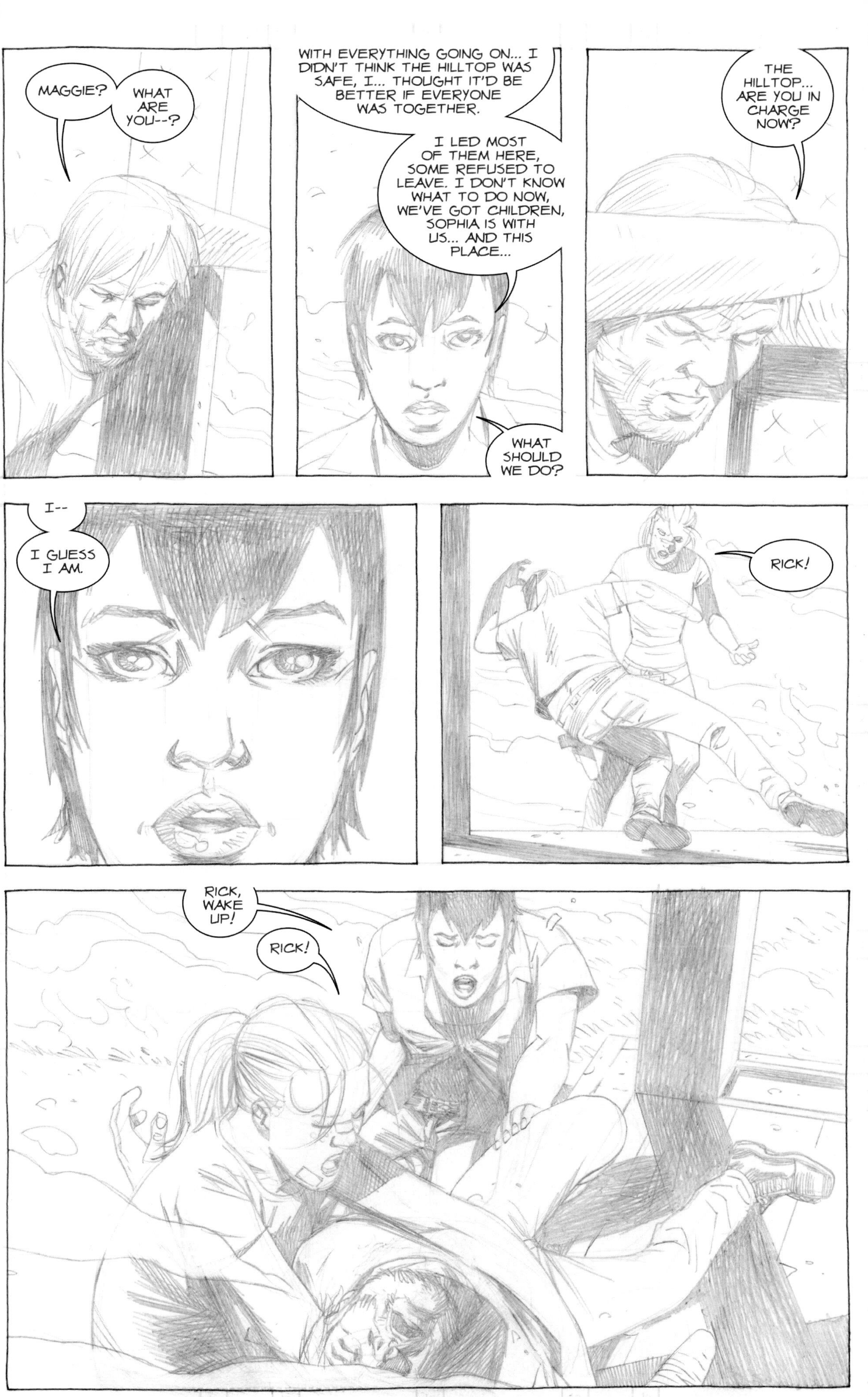
MAGGIE?
WHAT ARE YOU--?
WITH EVERYTHING GOING ON... I DIDN'T THINK THE HILLTOP WAS SAFE, I... THOUGHT IT'D BE BETTER IF EVERYONE WAS TOGETHER.
I LED MOST OF THEM HERE, SOME REFUSED TO LEAVE. I DON'T KNOW WHAT TO DO NOW, WE'VE GOT CHILDREN, SOPHIA IS WITH US... AND THIS PLACE...
WHAT SHOULD WE DO?
THE HILLTOP... ARE YOU IN CHARGE NOW?
I--
I GUESS I AM.
RICK!
RICK, WAKE UP!
RICK!

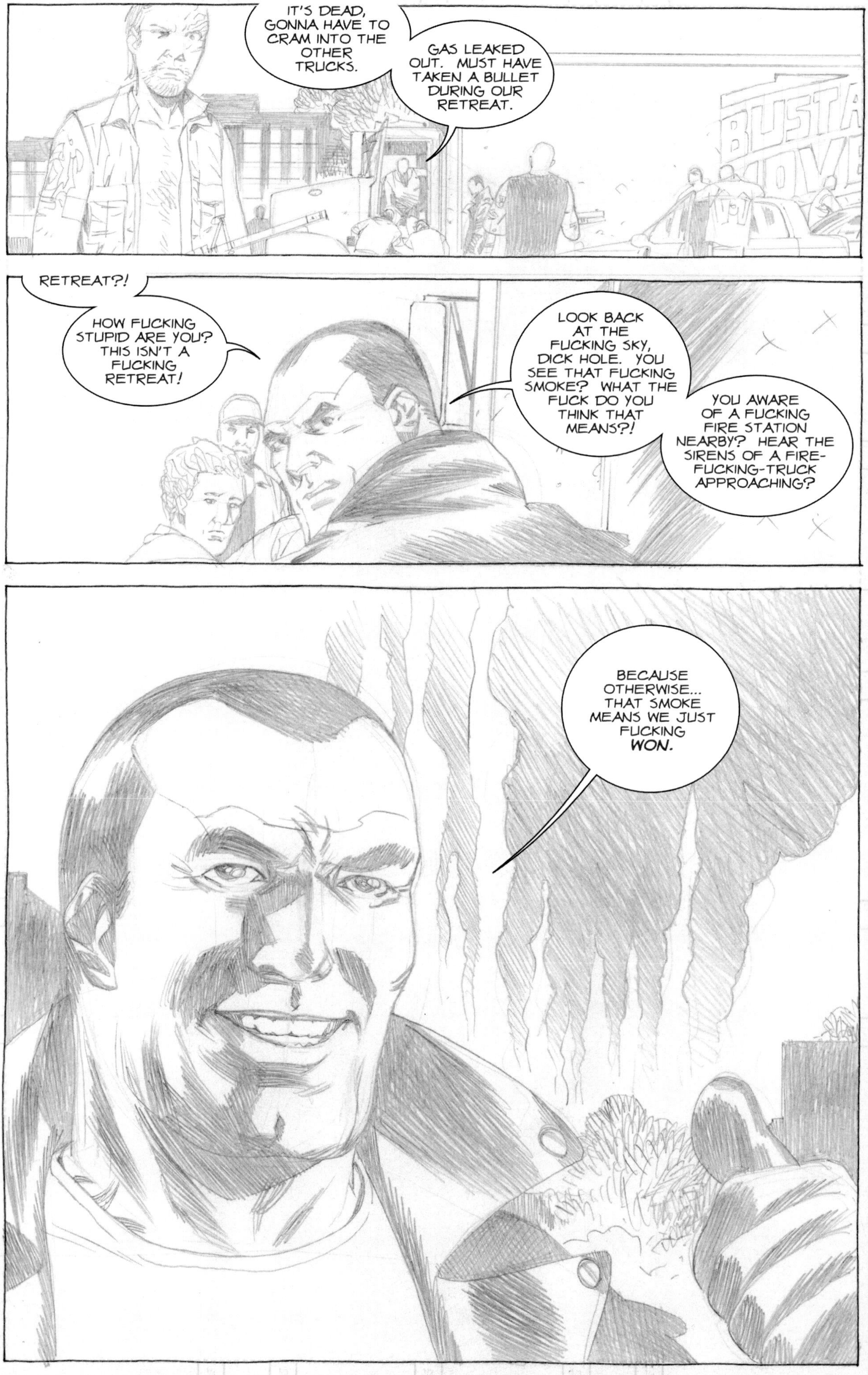
IT'S DEAD, GONNA HAVE TO CRAM INTO THE OTHER TRUCKS.
GAS LEAKED OUT. MUST HAVE TAKEN A BULLET DURING OUR RETREAT.
RETREAT?!
HOW FUCKING STUPID ARE YOU? THIS ISN'T A FUCKING RETREAT!
LOOK BACK AT THE FUCKING SKY, DICK HOLE. YOU SEE THAT FUCKING SMOKE? WHAT THE FUCK DO YOU THINK THAT MEANS?!
YOU AWARE OF A FUCKING FIRE STATION NEARBY? HEAR THE SIRENS OF A FIRE-FUCKING-TRUCK APPROACHING?
BECAUSE OTHERWISE... THAT SMOKE MEANS WE JUST FUCKING **WON.**

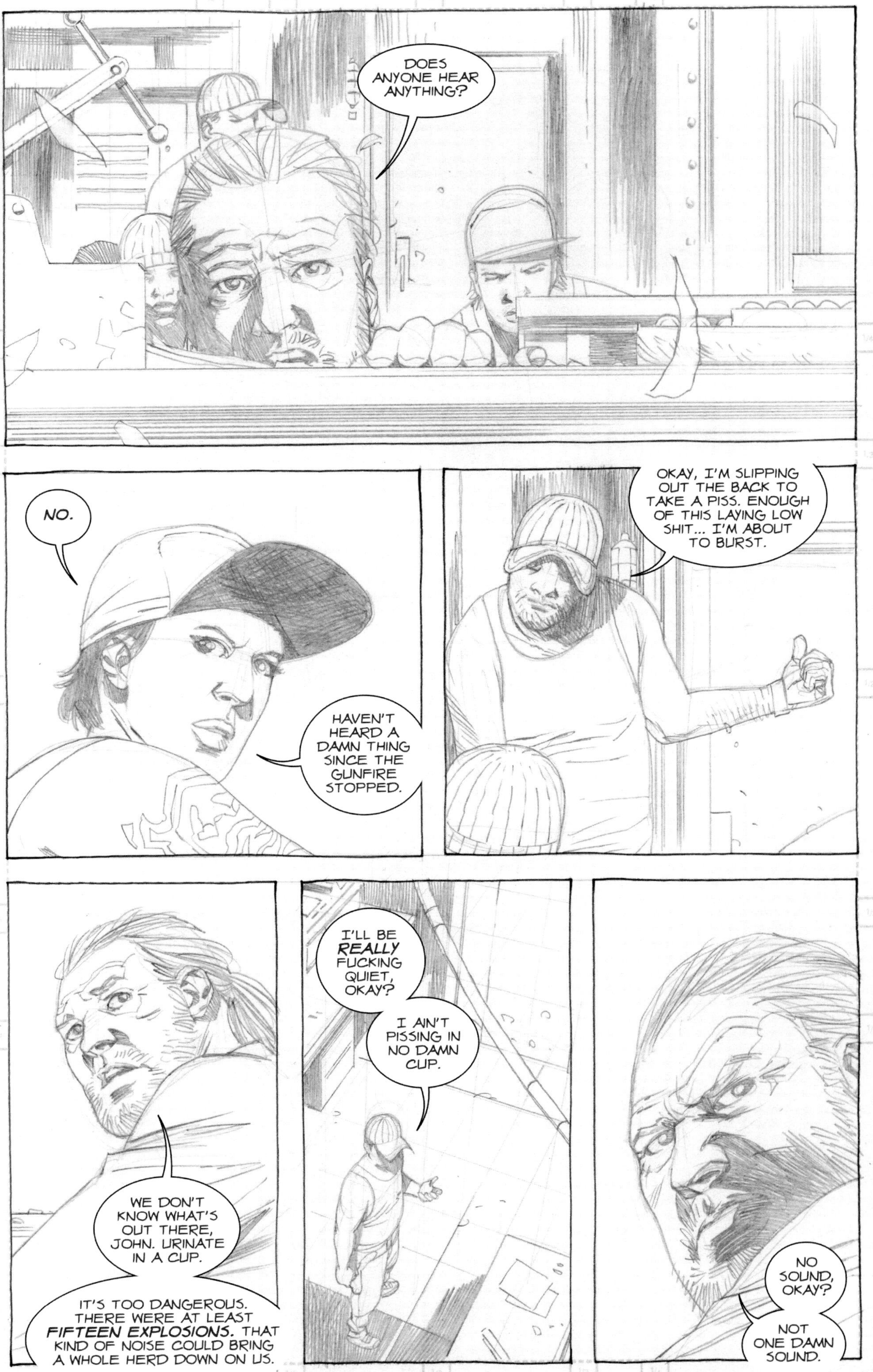
DOES ANYONE HEAR ANYTHING?
NO.
HAVEN'T HEARD A DAMN THING SINCE THE GUNFIRE STOPPED.
OKAY, I'M SLIPPING OUT THE BACK TO TAKE A PISS. ENOUGH OF THIS LAYING LOW SHIT... I'M ABOUT TO BURST.
WE DON'T KNOW WHAT'S OUT THERE, JOHN. URINATE IN A CUP.
IT'S TOO DANGEROUS. THERE WERE AT LEAST FIFTEEN EXPLOSIONS. THAT KIND OF NOISE COULD BRING A WHOLE HERD DOWN ON US.
I'LL BE REALLY FUCKING QUIET, OKAY?
I AIN'T PISSING IN NO DAMN CUP.
NO SOUND, OKAY?
NOT ONE DAMN SOUND.

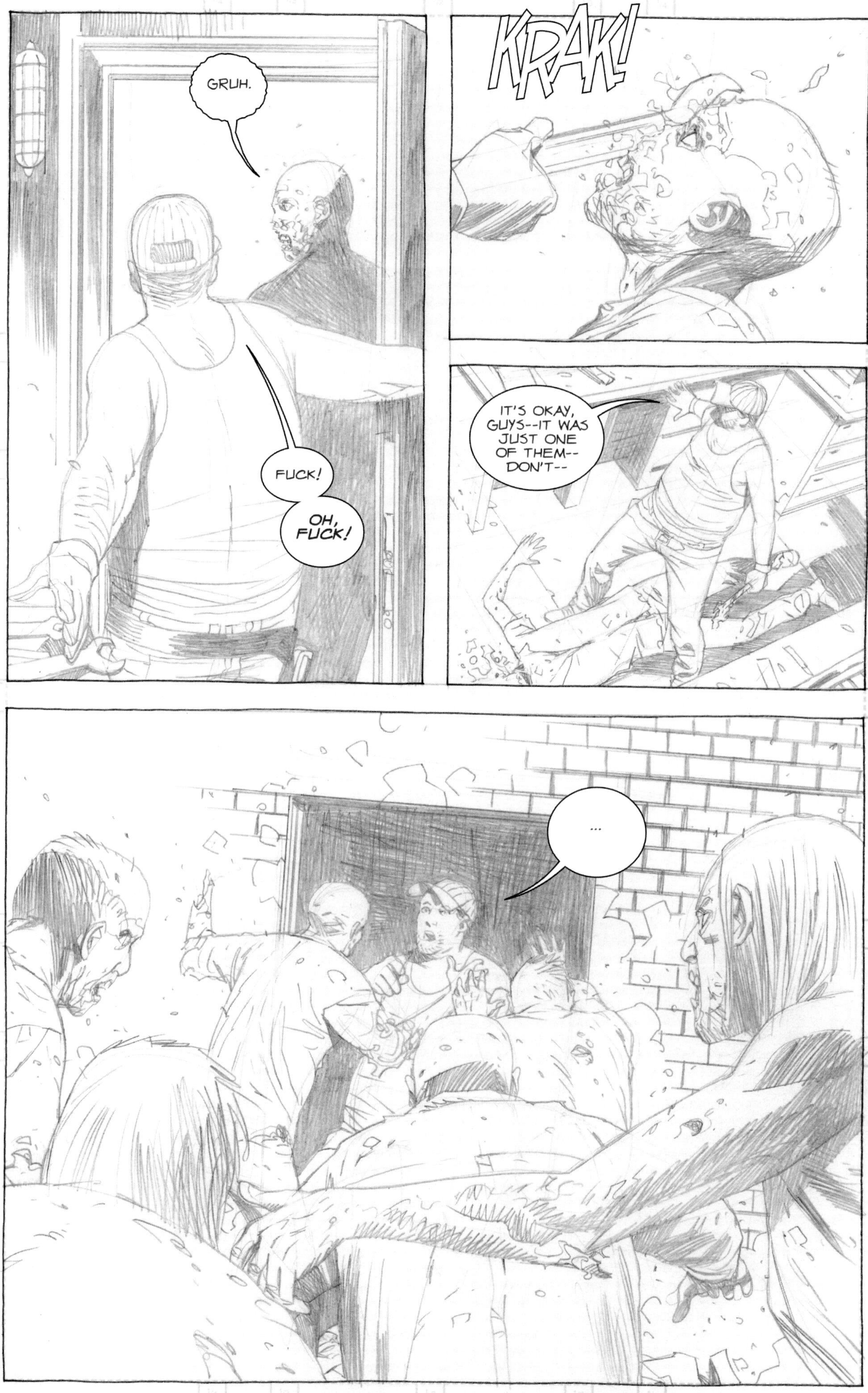
GRUH.
FUCK!
OH, FUCK!
KRAK!
IT'S OKAY, GUYS--IT WAS JUST ONE OF THEM--DON'T--
...

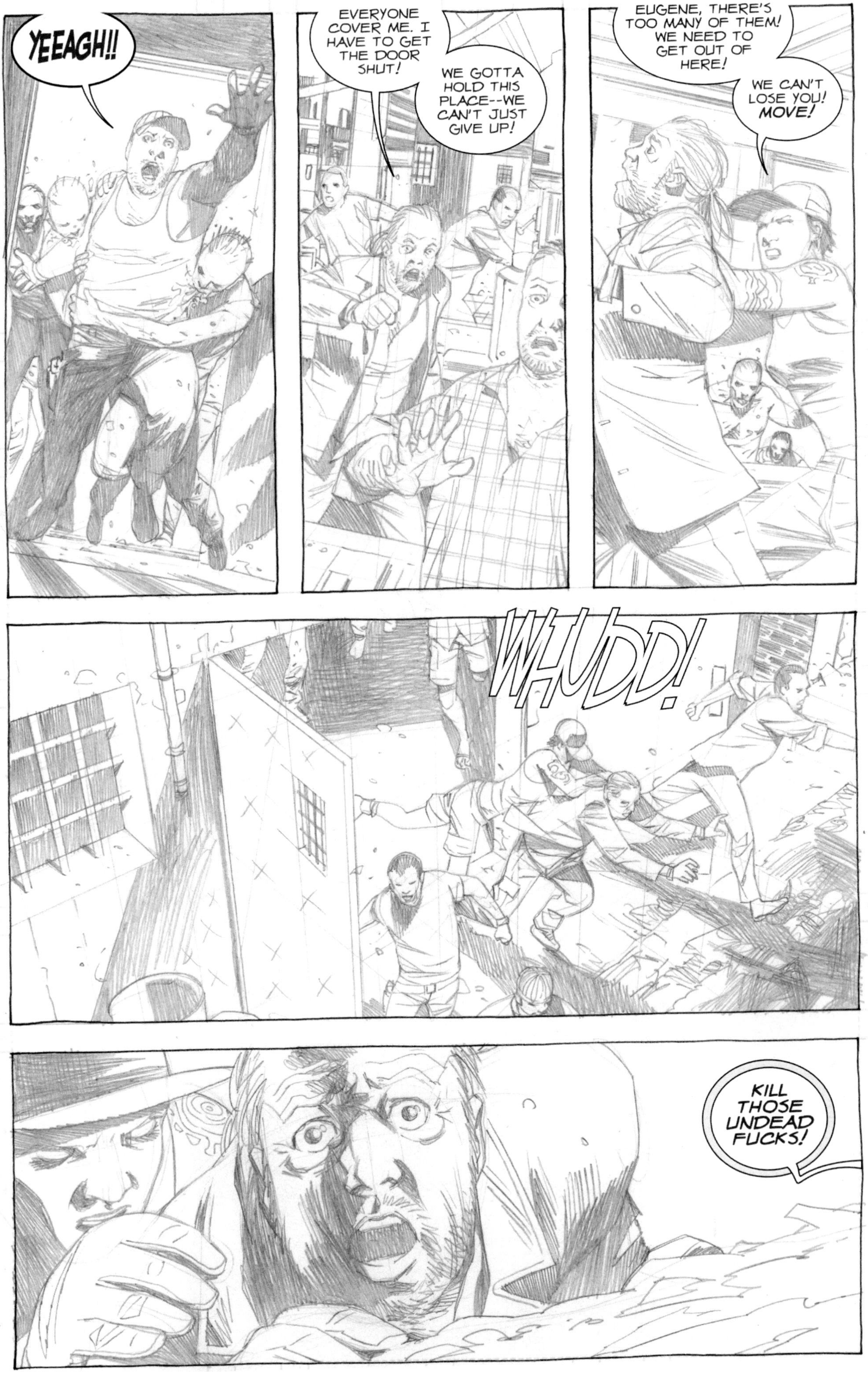
YEEAGH!!
EVERYONE COVER ME. I HAVE TO GET THE DOOR SHUT!
WE GOTTA HOLD THIS PLACE--WE CAN'T JUST GIVE UP!
EUGENE, THERE'S TOO MANY OF THEM! WE NEED TO GET OUT OF HERE!
WE CAN'T LOSE YOU! MOVE!
WHUDD!
KILL THOSE UNDEAD FUCKS!

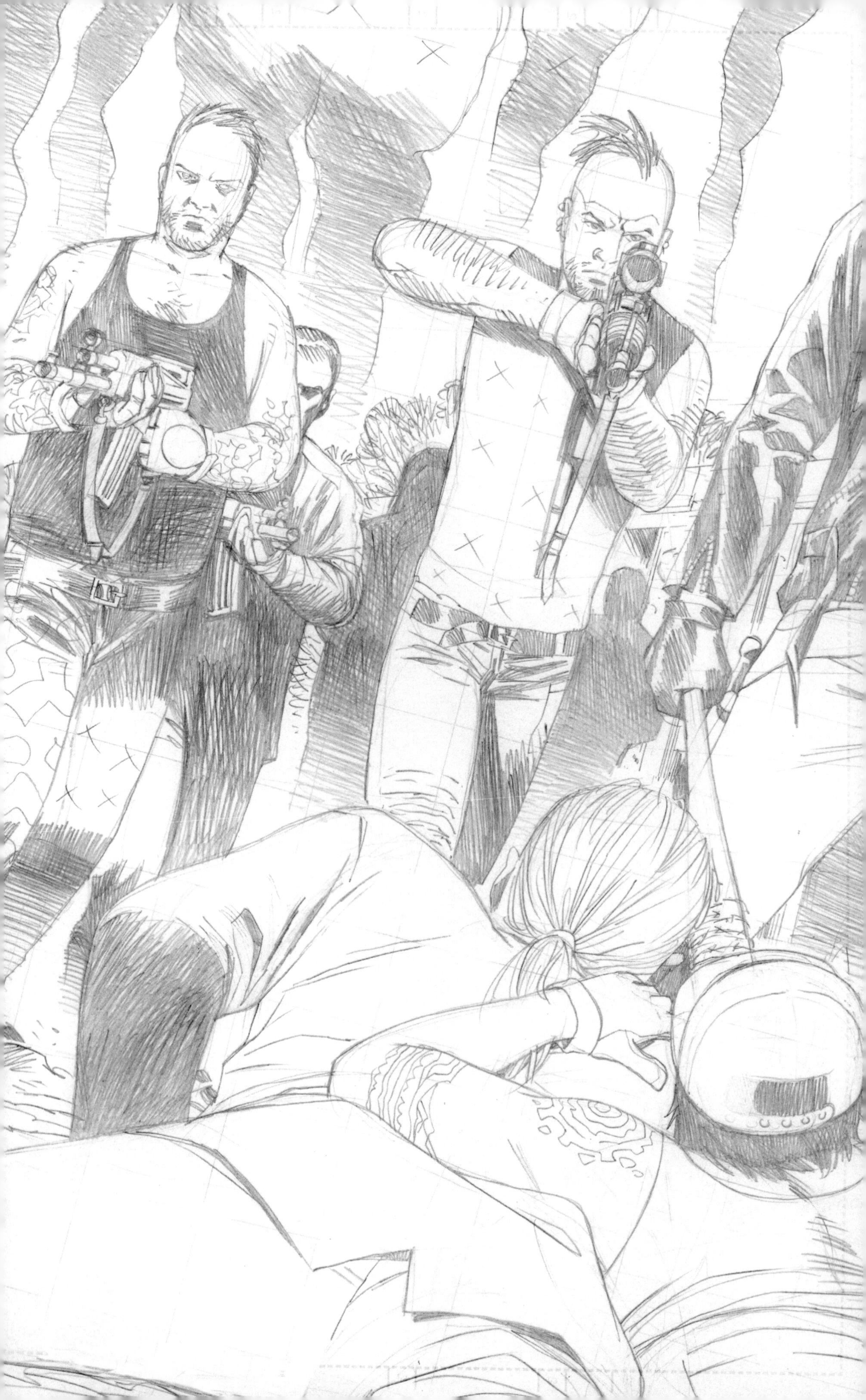

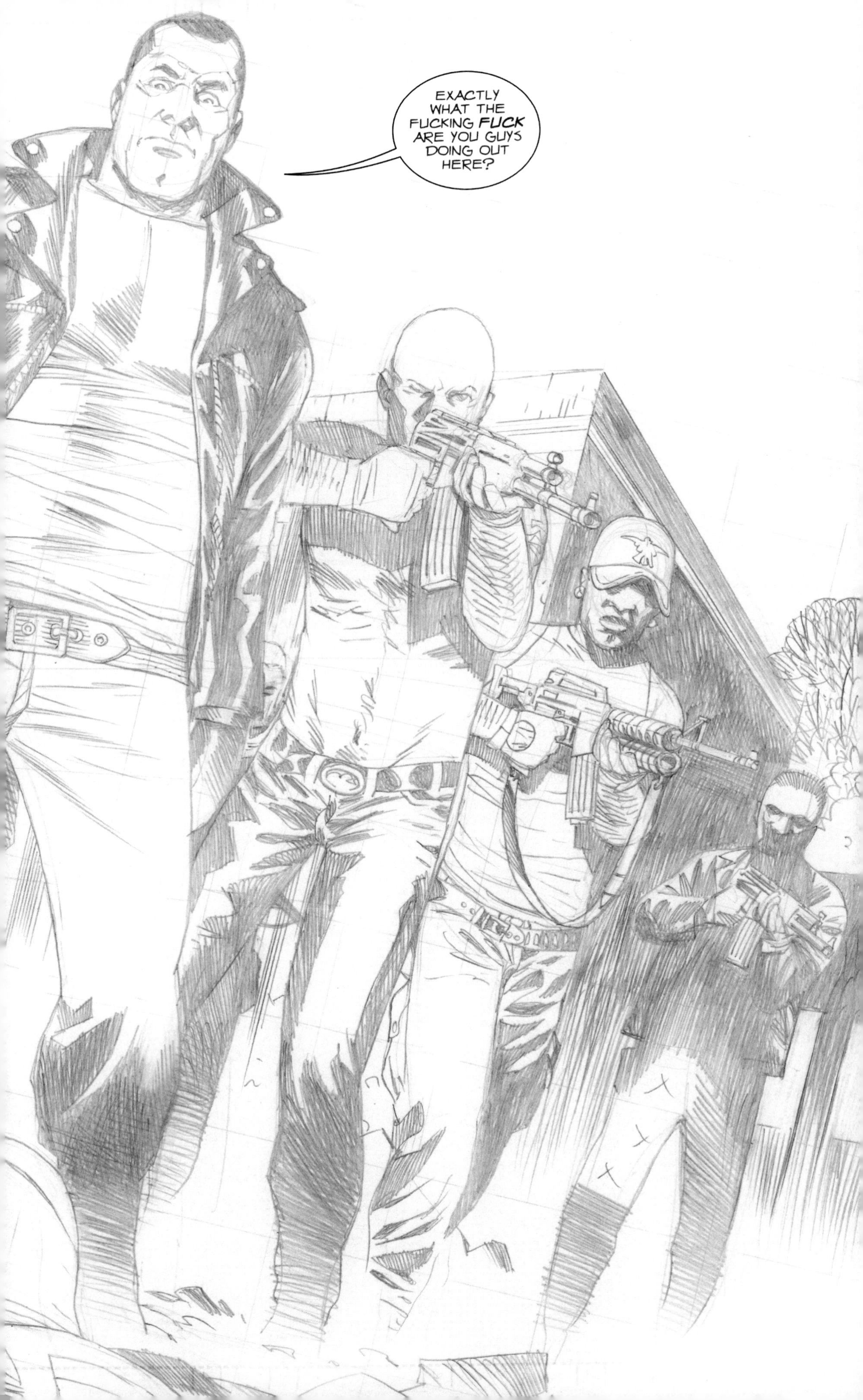
EXACTLY WHAT THE FUCKING FUCK ARE YOU GUYS DOING OUT HERE?

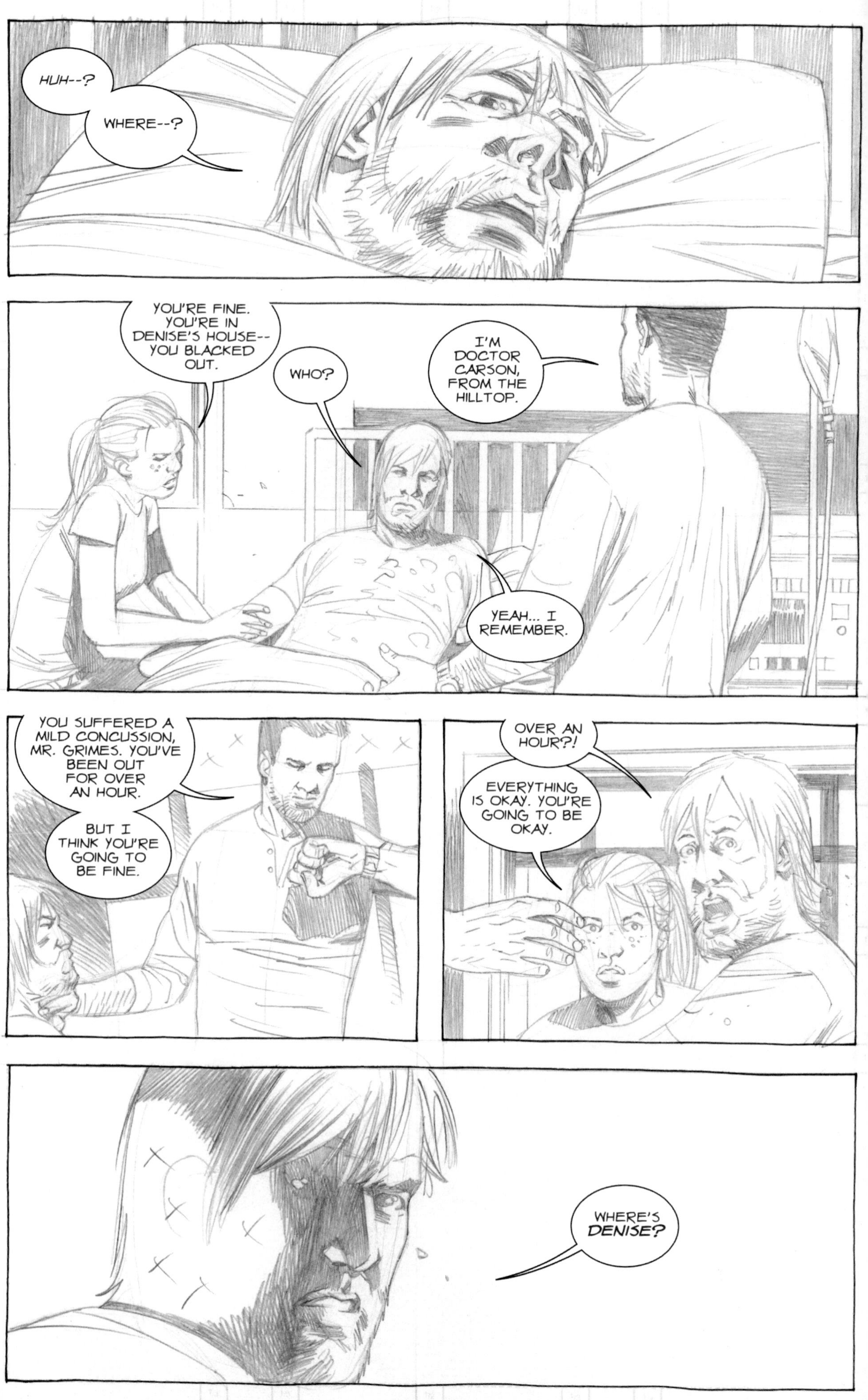
HUH--?
WHERE--?
YOU'RE FINE. YOU'RE IN DENISE'S HOUSE-- YOU BLACKED OUT.
WHO?
I'M DOCTOR CARSON, FROM THE HILLTOP.
YEAH... I REMEMBER.
YOU SUFFERED A MILD CONCUSSION, MR. GRIMES. YOU'VE BEEN OUT FOR OVER AN HOUR.
BUT I THINK YOU'RE GOING TO BE FINE.
OVER AN HOUR?!
EVERYTHING IS OKAY. YOU'RE GOING TO BE OKAY.
WHERE'S DENISE?

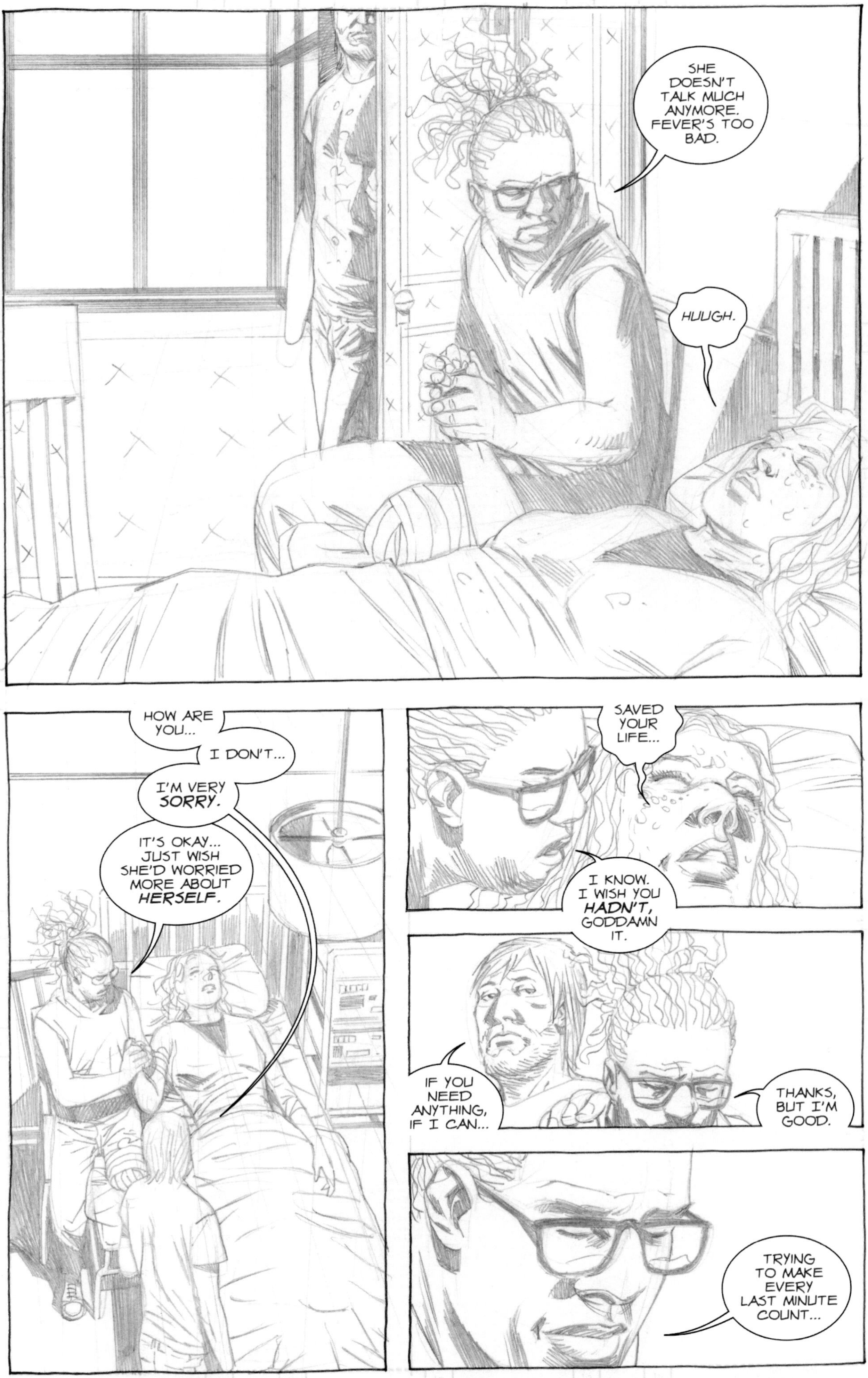
SHE DOESN'T TALK MUCH ANYMORE. FEVER'S TOO BAD.
HUUGH.
HOW ARE YOU...
I DON'T...
I'M VERY SORRY.
IT'S OKAY... JUST WISH SHE'D WORRIED MORE ABOUT HERSELF.
SAVED YOUR LIFE...
I KNOW. I WISH YOU HADN'T, GODDAMN IT.
IF YOU NEED ANYTHING, IF I CAN...
THANKS, BUT I'M GOOD.
TRYING TO MAKE EVERY LAST MINUTE COUNT...

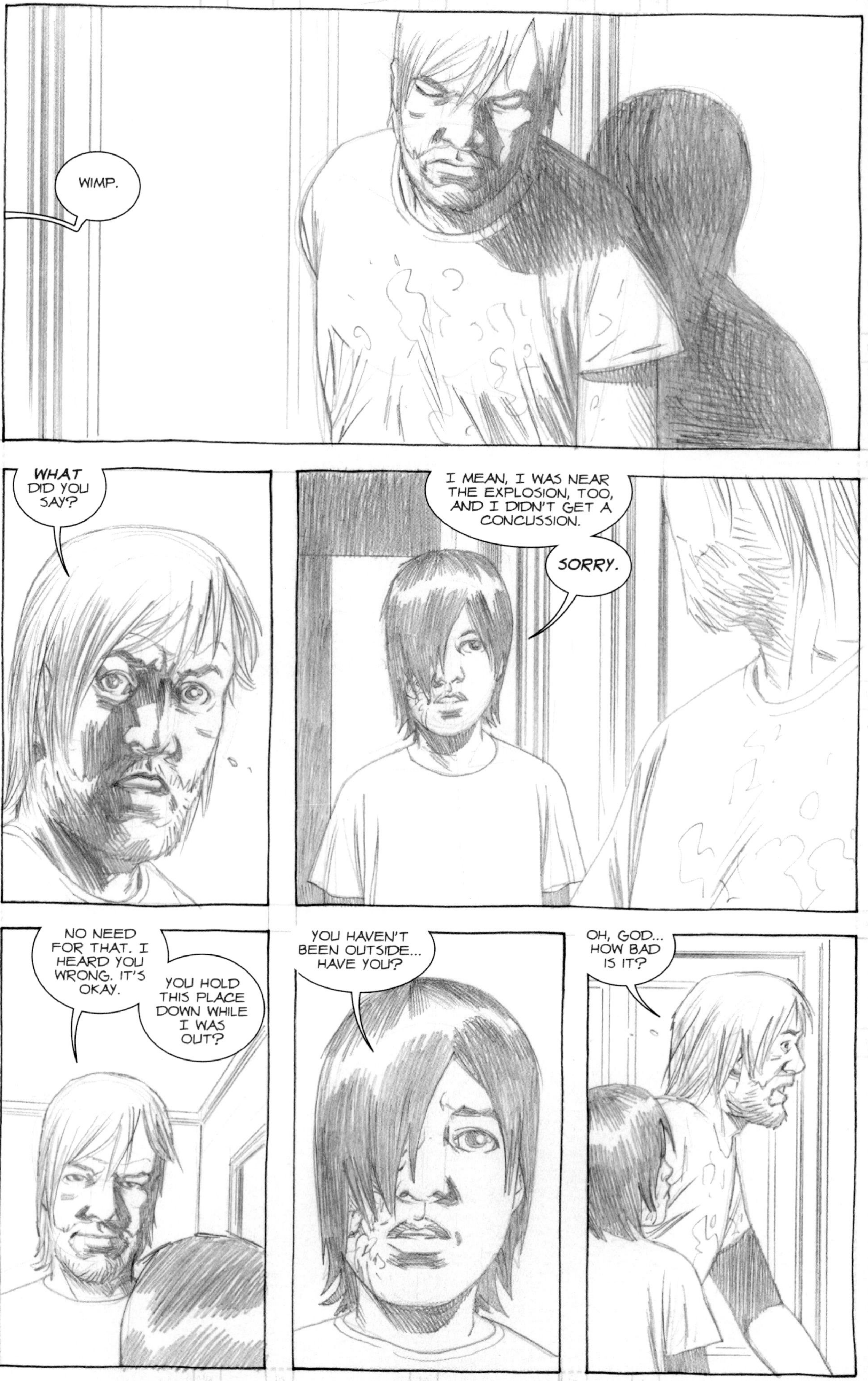
WIMP.
WHAT DID YOU SAY?
I MEAN, I WAS NEAR THE EXPLOSION, TOO, AND I DIDN'T GET A CONCUSSION.
SORRY.
NO NEED FOR THAT. I HEARD YOU WRONG. IT'S OKAY.
YOU HOLD THIS PLACE DOWN WHILE I WAS OUT?
YOU HAVEN'T BEEN OUTSIDE... HAVE YOU?
OH, GOD... HOW BAD IS IT?

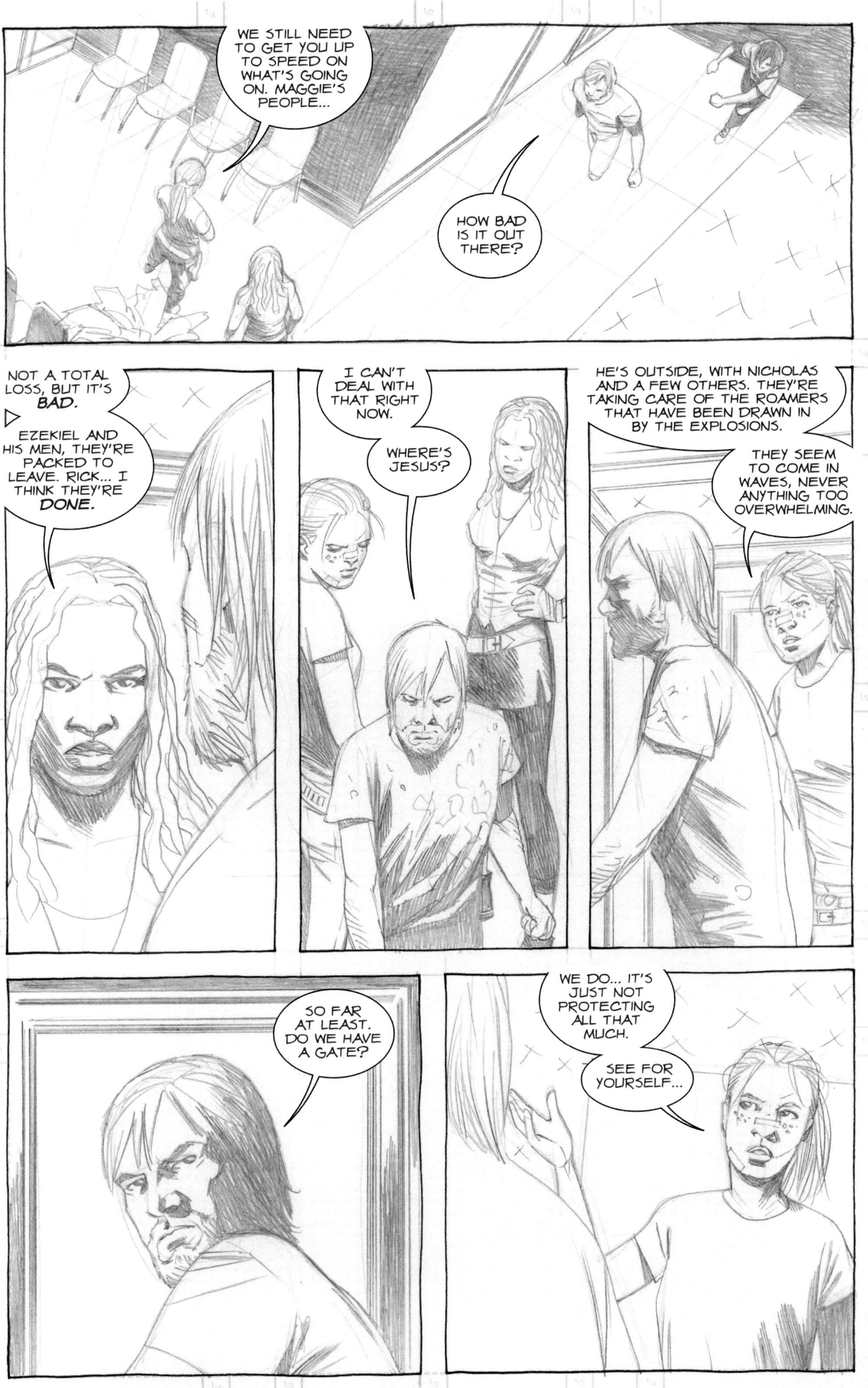

WE STILL NEED TO GET YOU UP TO SPEED ON WHAT'S GOING ON. MAGGIE'S PEOPLE...
HOW BAD IS IT OUT THERE?
NOT A TOTAL LOSS, BUT IT'S BAD.
EZEKIEL AND HIS MEN, THEY'RE PACKED TO LEAVE. RICK... I THINK THEY'RE DONE.
I CAN'T DEAL WITH THAT RIGHT NOW.
WHERE'S JESUS?
HE'S OUTSIDE, WITH NICHOLAS AND A FEW OTHERS. THEY'RE TAKING CARE OF THE ROAMERS THAT HAVE BEEN DRAWN IN BY THE EXPLOSIONS.
THEY SEEM TO COME IN WAVES, NEVER ANYTHING TOO OVERWHELMING.
SO FAR AT LEAST. DO WE HAVE A GATE?
WE DO... IT'S JUST NOT PROTECTING ALL THAT MUCH.
SEE FOR YOURSELF...

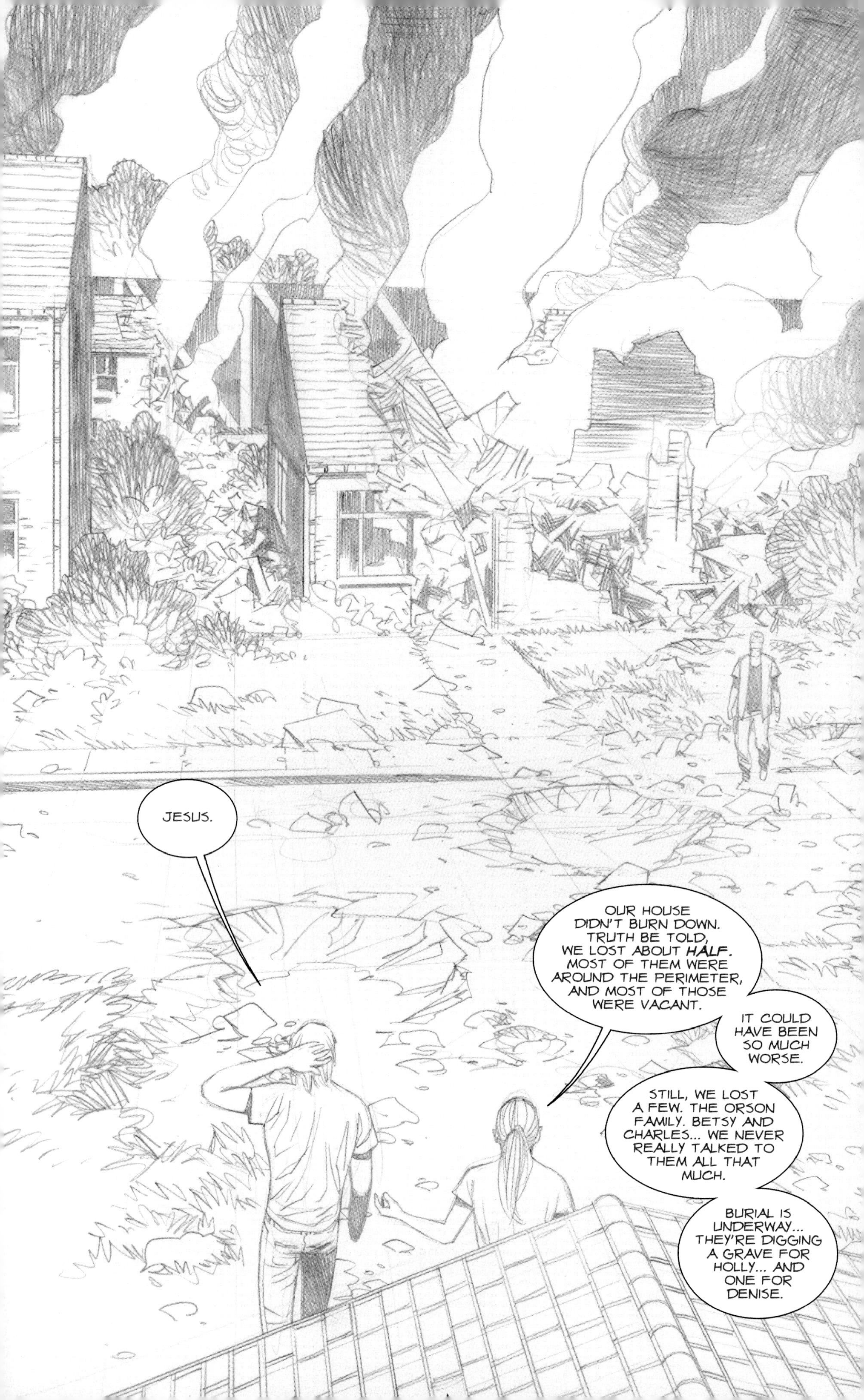
JESUS.
OUR HOUSE DIDN'T BURN DOWN. TRUTH BE TOLD, WE LOST ABOUT ***HALF.*** MOST OF THEM WERE AROUND THE PERIMETER, AND MOST OF THOSE WERE VACANT.
IT COULD HAVE BEEN SO MUCH WORSE.
STILL, WE LOST A FEW. THE ORSON FAMILY. BETSY AND CHARLES... WE NEVER REALLY TALKED TO THEM ALL THAT MUCH.
BURIAL IS UNDERWAY... THEY'RE DIGGING A GRAVE FOR HOLLY... AND ONE FOR DENISE.

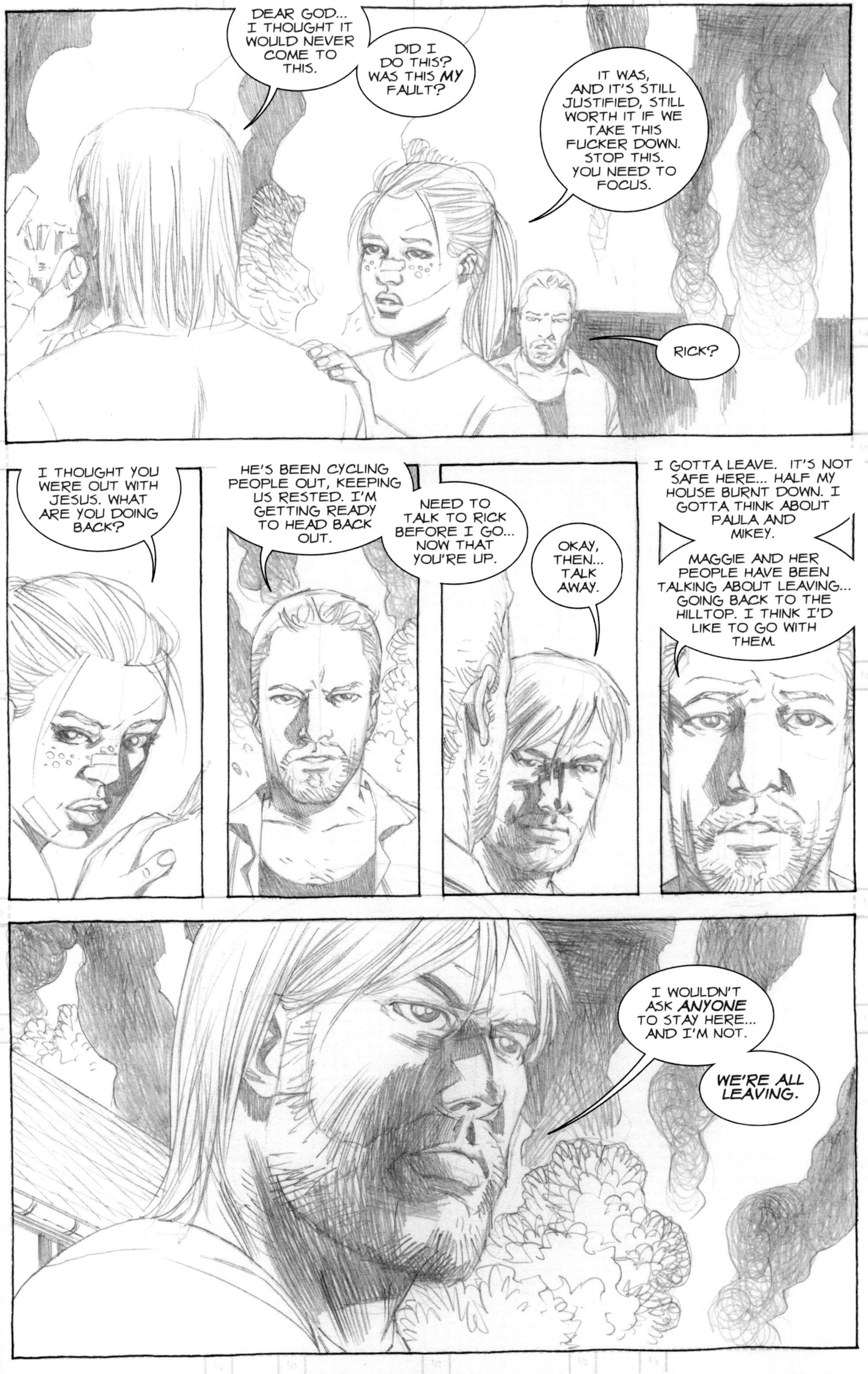
DEAR GOD... I THOUGHT IT WOULD NEVER COME TO THIS.
DID I DO THIS? WAS THIS MY FAULT?
IT WAS, AND IT'S STILL JUSTIFIED, STILL WORTH IT IF WE TAKE THIS FUCKER DOWN. STOP THIS. YOU NEED TO FOCUS.
RICK?
I THOUGHT YOU WERE OUT WITH JESUS. WHAT ARE YOU DOING BACK?
HE'S BEEN CYCLING PEOPLE OUT, KEEPING US RESTED. I'M GETTING READY TO HEAD BACK OUT.
NEED TO TALK TO RICK BEFORE I GO... NOW THAT YOU'RE UP.
OKAY, THEN... TALK AWAY.
I GOTTA LEAVE. IT'S NOT SAFE HERE... HALF MY HOUSE BURNT DOWN. I GOTTA THINK ABOUT PAULA AND MIKEY.
MAGGIE AND HER PEOPLE HAVE BEEN TALKING ABOUT LEAVING... GOING BACK TO THE HILLTOP. I THINK I'D LIKE TO GO WITH THEM.
I WOULDN'T ASK ANYONE TO STAY HERE... AND I'M NOT.
WE'RE ALL LEAVING.

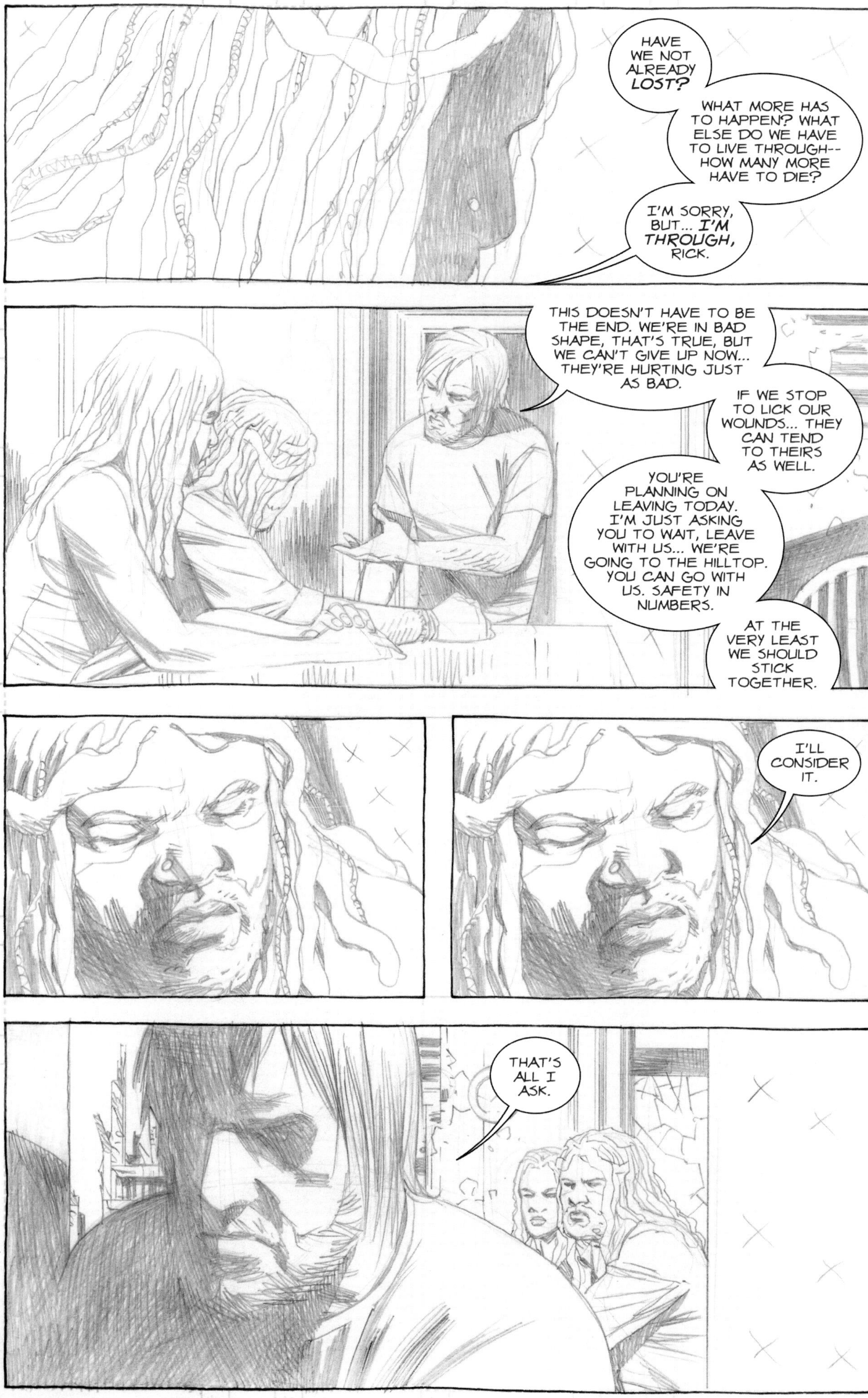
HAVE WE NOT ALREADY LOST?
WHAT MORE HAS TO HAPPEN? WHAT ELSE DO WE HAVE TO LIVE THROUGH-- HOW MANY MORE HAVE TO DIE?
I'M SORRY, BUT... I'M THROUGH, RICK.
THIS DOESN'T HAVE TO BE THE END. WE'RE IN BAD SHAPE, THAT'S TRUE, BUT WE CAN'T GIVE UP NOW... THEY'RE HURTING JUST AS BAD.
IF WE STOP TO LICK OUR WOUNDS... THEY CAN TEND TO THEIRS AS WELL.
YOU'RE PLANNING ON LEAVING TODAY. I'M JUST ASKING YOU TO WAIT, LEAVE WITH US... WE'RE GOING TO THE HILLTOP. YOU CAN GO WITH US. SAFETY IN NUMBERS.
AT THE VERY LEAST WE SHOULD STICK TOGETHER.
I'LL CONSIDER IT.
THAT'S ALL I ASK.

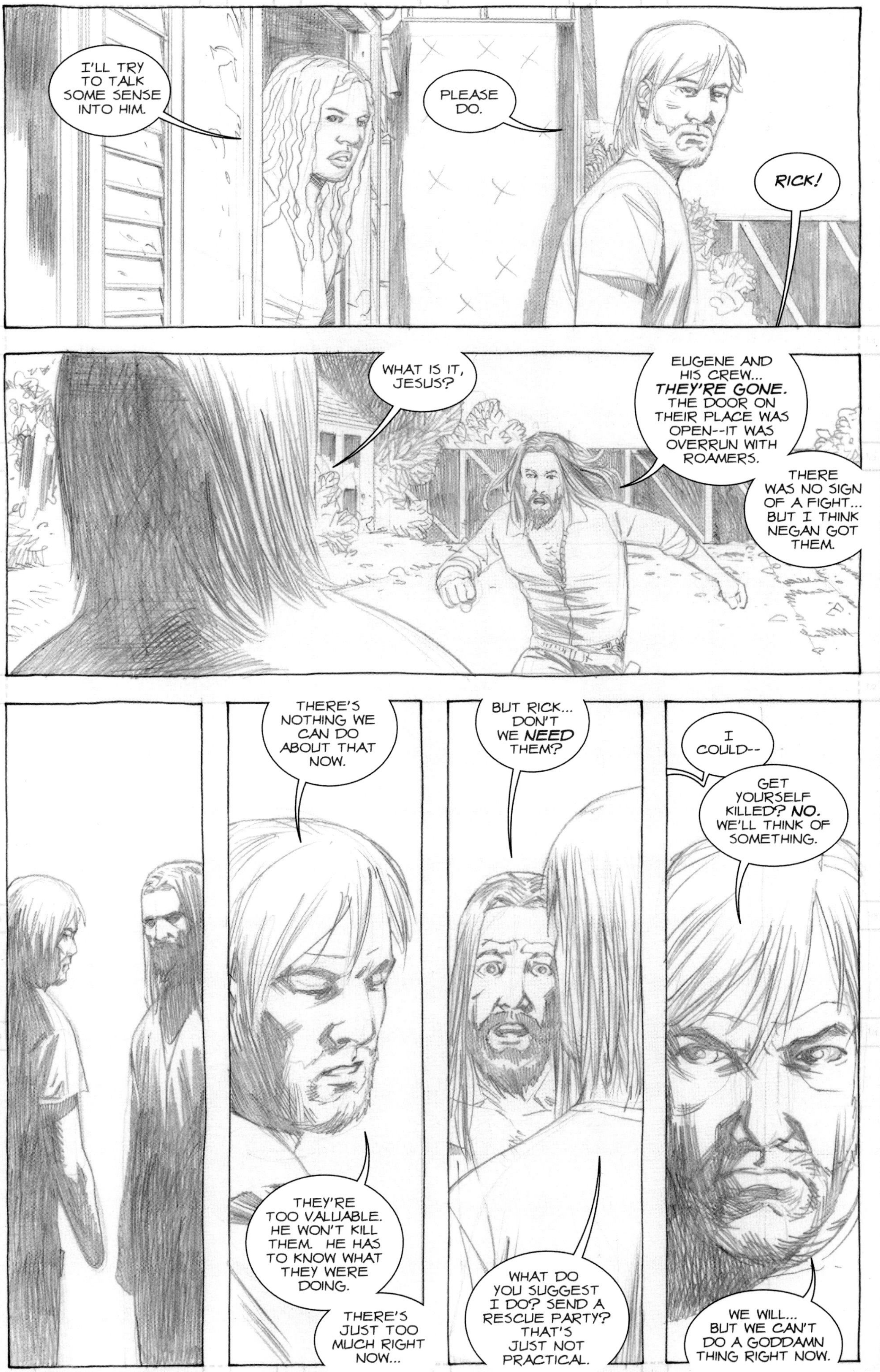
I'LL TRY TO TALK SOME SENSE INTO HIM.
PLEASE DO.
RICK!
WHAT IS IT, JESUS?
EUGENE AND HIS CREW... THEY'RE GONE. THE DOOR ON THEIR PLACE WAS OPEN--IT WAS OVERRUN WITH ROAMERS.
THERE WAS NO SIGN OF A FIGHT... BUT I THINK NEGAN GOT THEM.
THERE'S NOTHING WE CAN DO ABOUT THAT NOW.
THEY'RE TOO VALUABLE. HE WON'T KILL THEM. HE HAS TO KNOW WHAT THEY WERE DOING.
THERE'S JUST TOO MUCH RIGHT NOW...
BUT RICK... DON'T WE NEED THEM?
WHAT DO YOU SUGGEST I DO? SEND A RESCUE PARTY? THAT'S JUST NOT PRACTICAL.
I COULD--
GET YOURSELF KILLED? NO. WE'LL THINK OF SOMETHING.
WE WILL... BUT WE CAN'T DO A GODDAMN THING RIGHT NOW.

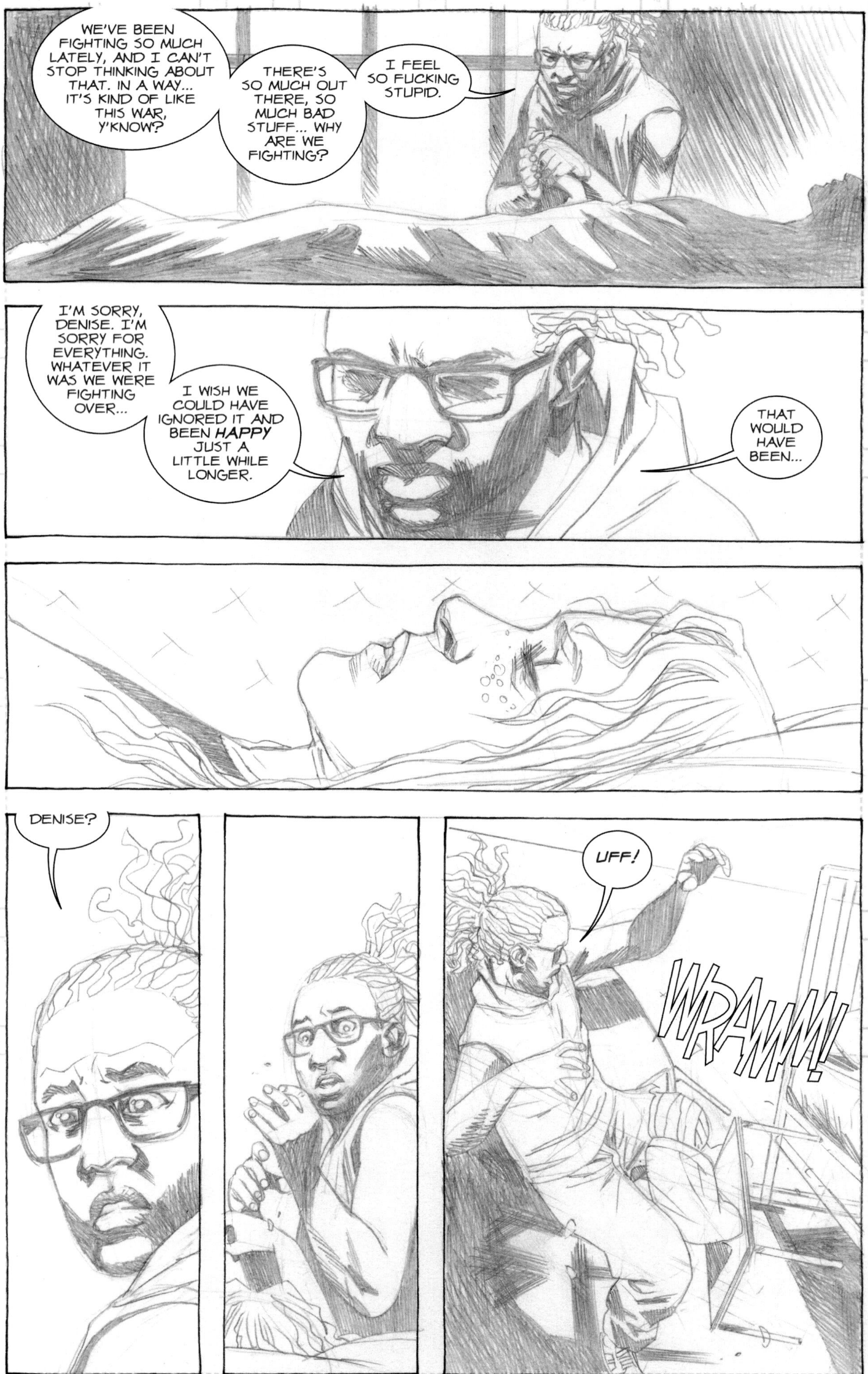
WE'VE BEEN FIGHTING SO MUCH LATELY, AND I CAN'T STOP THINKING ABOUT THAT. IN A WAY... IT'S KIND OF LIKE THIS WAR, Y'KNOW?
THERE'S SO MUCH OUT THERE, SO MUCH BAD STUFF... WHY ARE WE FIGHTING?
I FEEL SO FUCKING STUPID.
I'M SORRY, DENISE. I'M SORRY FOR EVERYTHING. WHATEVER IT WAS WE WERE FIGHTING OVER...
I WISH WE COULD HAVE IGNORED IT AND BEEN *HAPPY* JUST A LITTLE WHILE LONGER.
THAT WOULD HAVE BEEN...
DENISE?
UFF!
WRAMM!

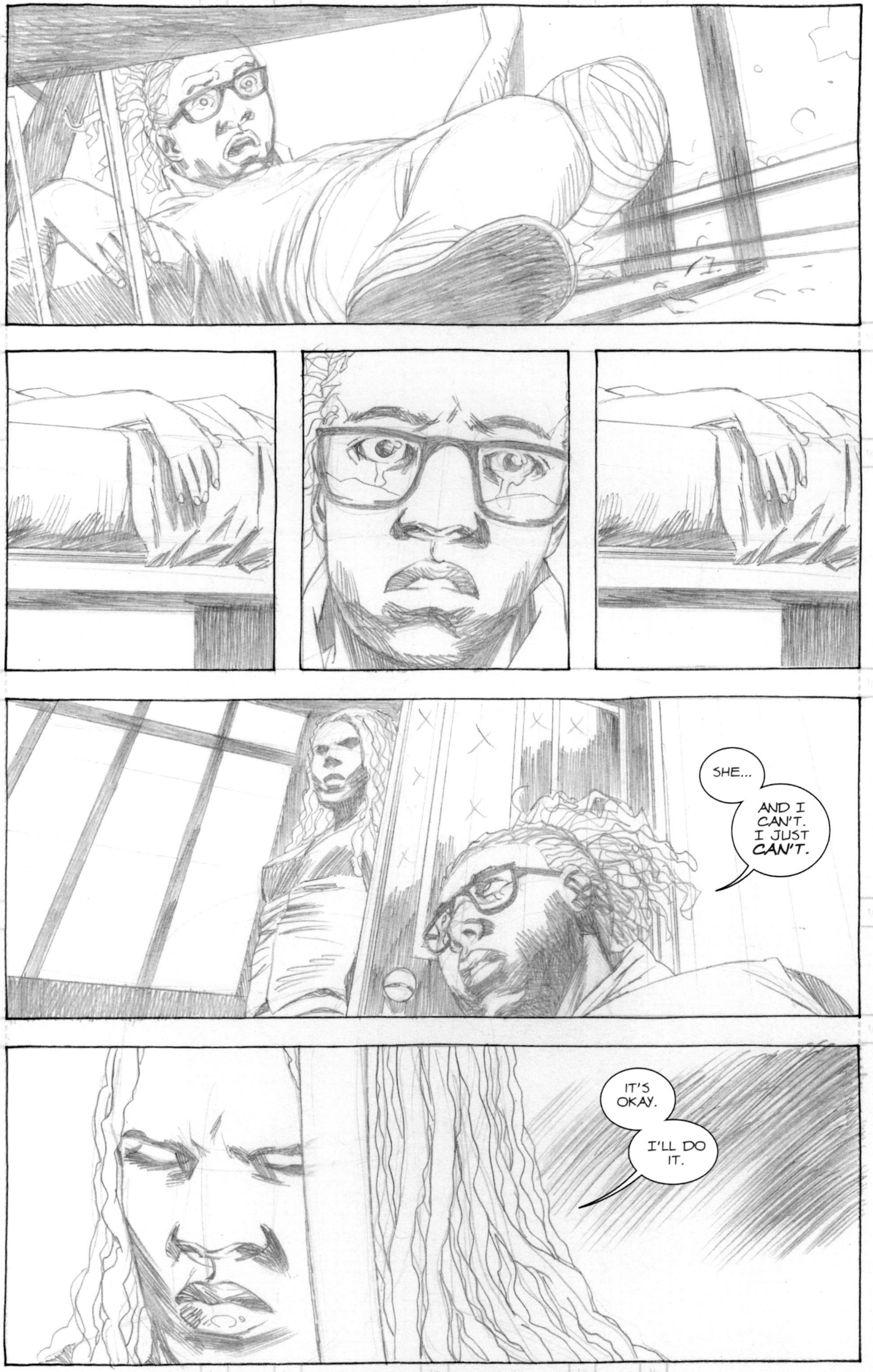
SHE...
AND I CAN'T. I JUST CAN'T.
IT'S OKAY.
I'LL DO IT.

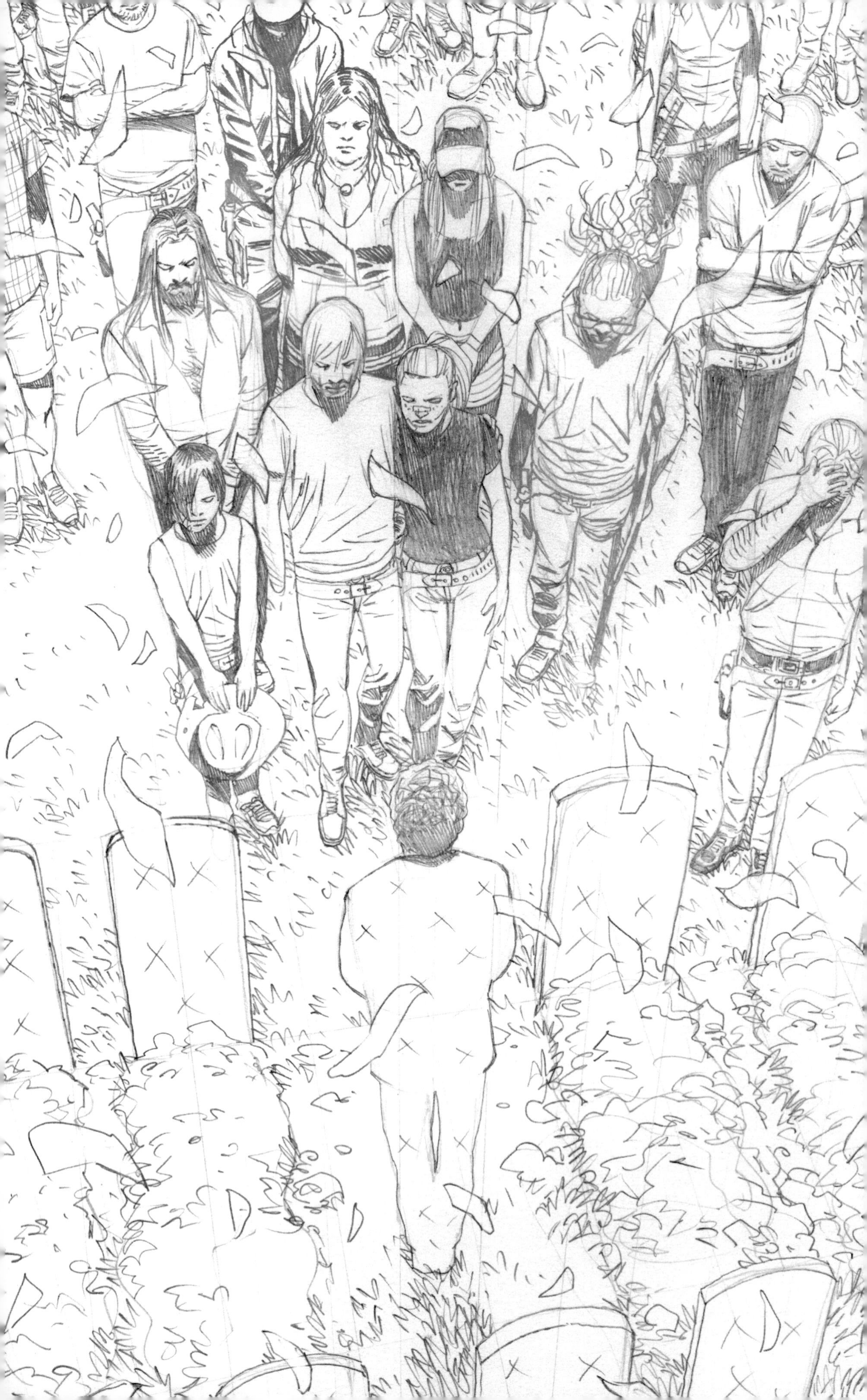

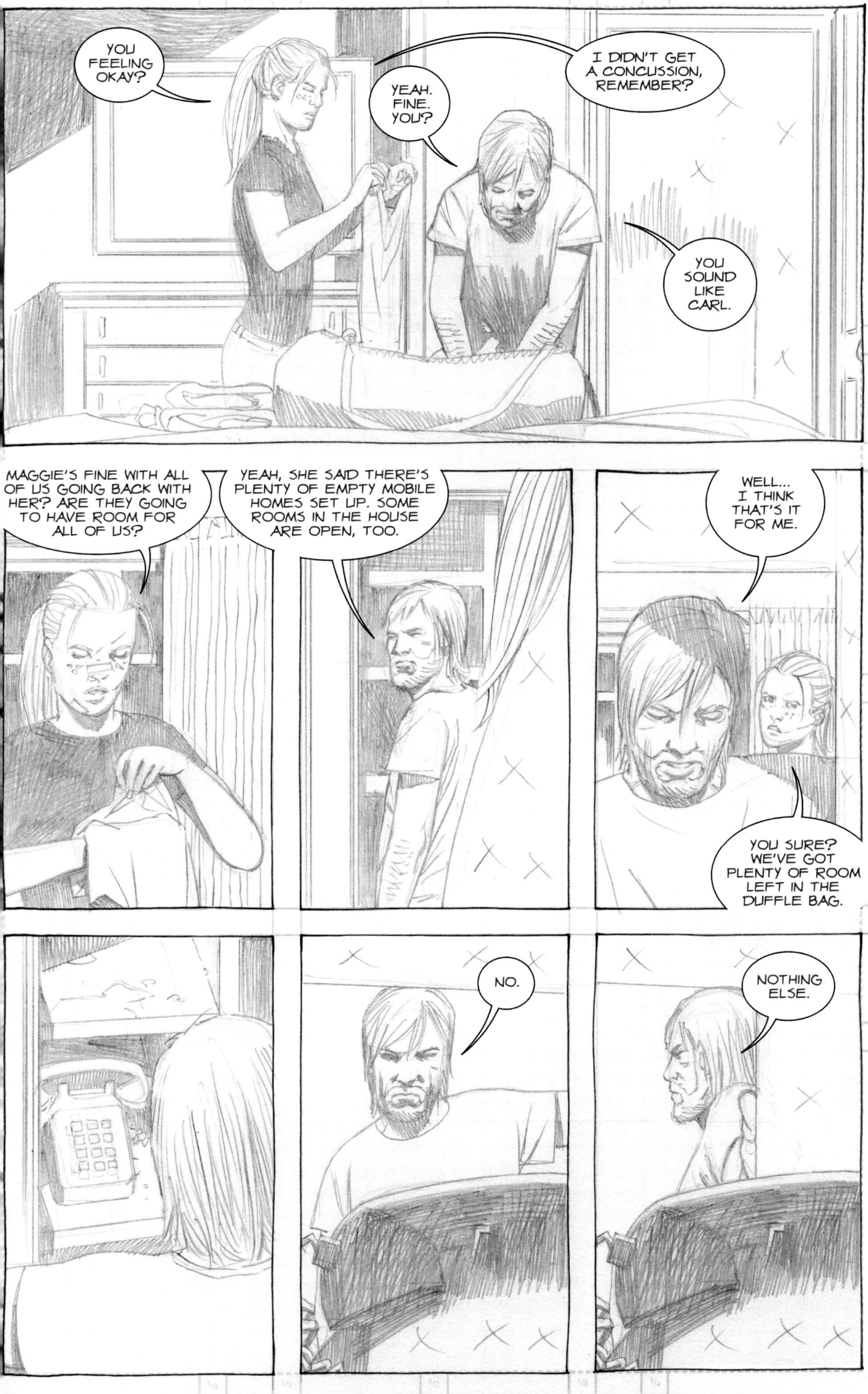
YOU FEELING OKAY?
YEAH. FINE. YOU?
I DIDN'T GET A CONCUSSION, REMEMBER?
YOU SOUND LIKE CARL.
MAGGIE'S FINE WITH ALL OF US GOING BACK WITH HER? ARE THEY GOING TO HAVE ROOM FOR ALL OF US?
YEAH, SHE SAID THERE'S PLENTY OF EMPTY MOBILE HOMES SET UP. SOME ROOMS IN THE HOUSE ARE OPEN, TOO.
WELL... I THINK THAT'S IT FOR ME.
YOU SURE? WE'VE GOT PLENTY OF ROOM LEFT IN THE DUFFLE BAG.
NO.
NOTHING ELSE.

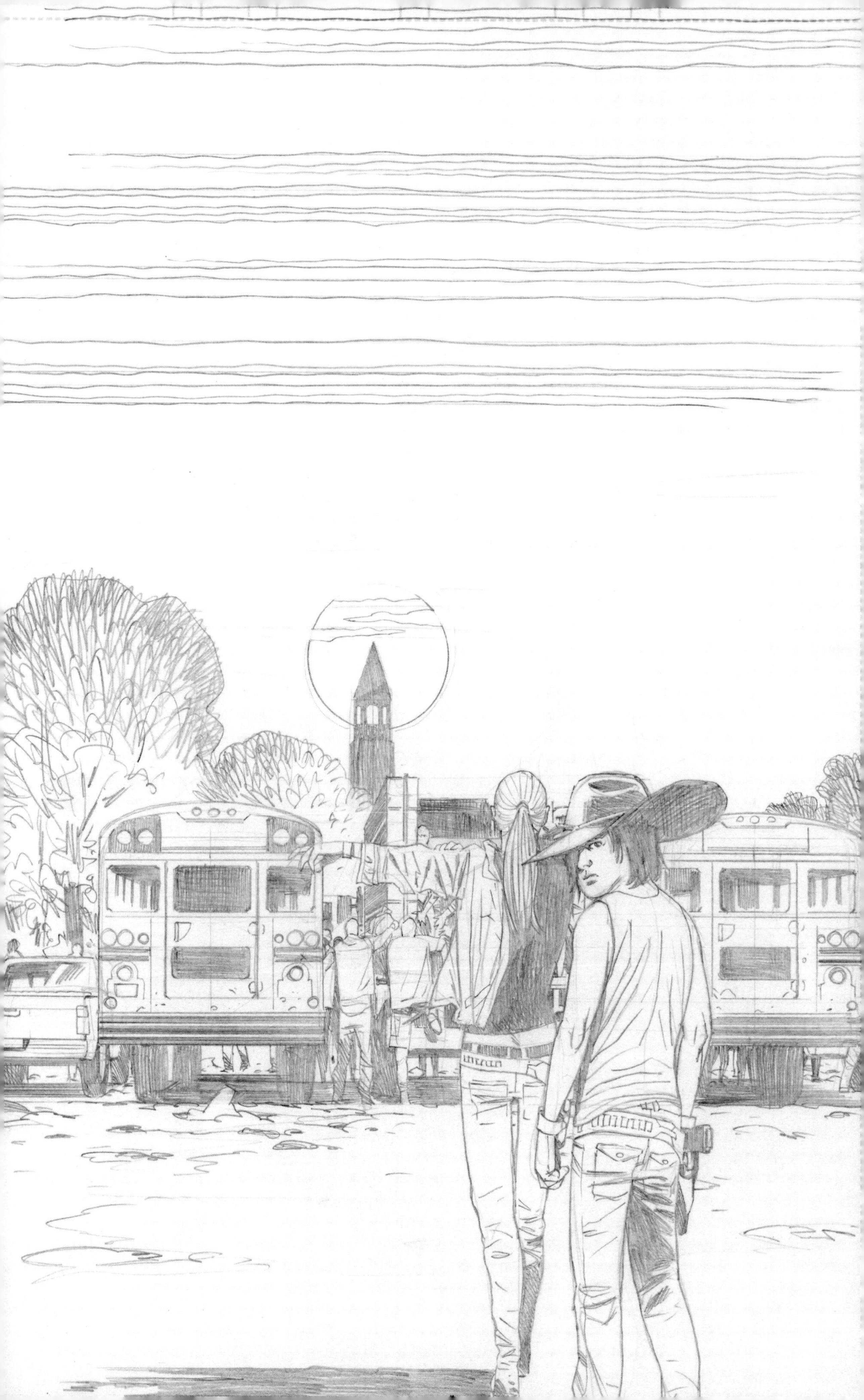

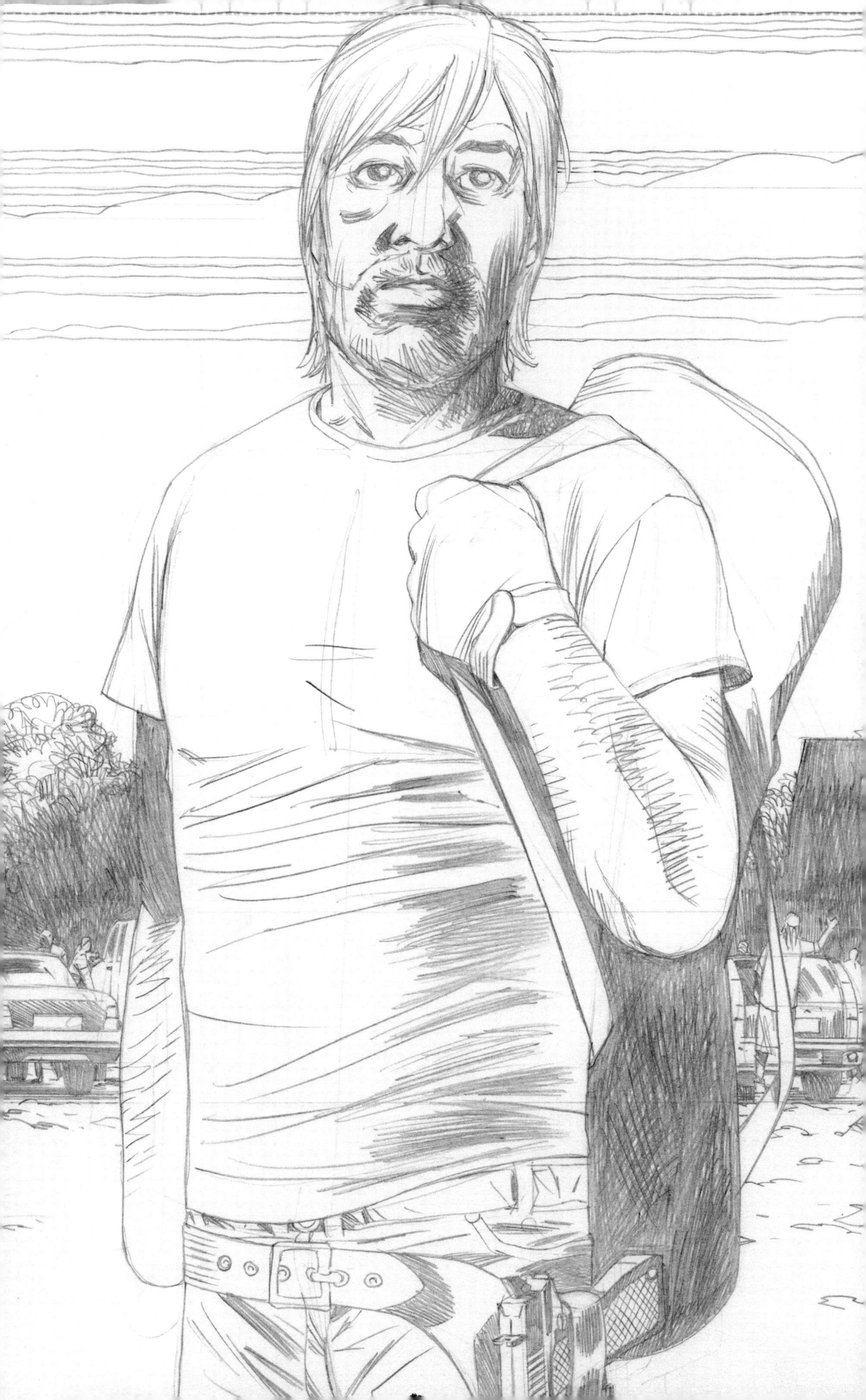

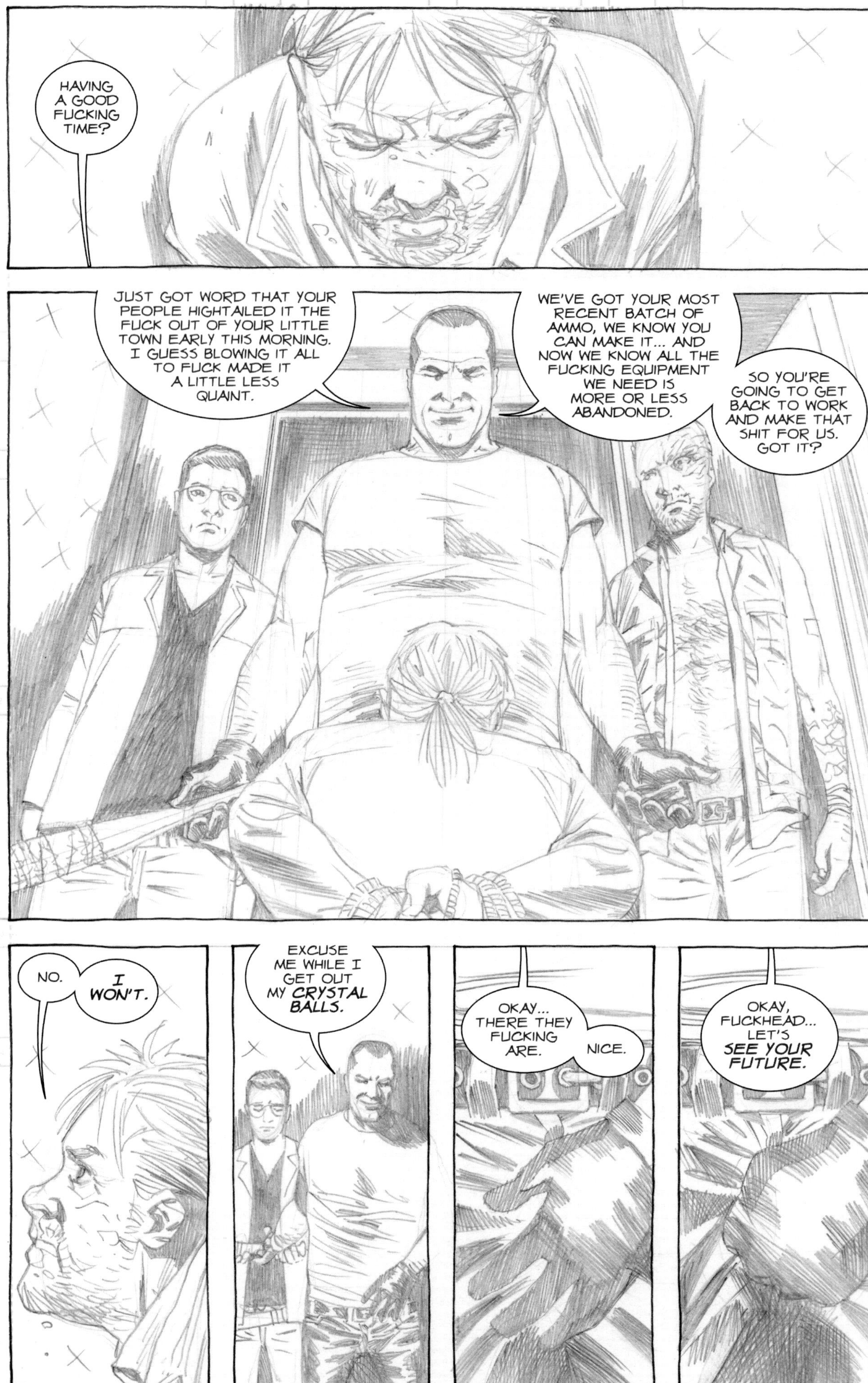
HAVING A GOOD FUCKING TIME?
JUST GOT WORD THAT YOUR PEOPLE HIGHTAILED IT THE FUCK OUT OF YOUR LITTLE TOWN EARLY THIS MORNING. I GUESS BLOWING IT ALL TO FUCK MADE IT A LITTLE LESS QUAINT.
WE'VE GOT YOUR MOST RECENT BATCH OF AMMO, WE KNOW YOU CAN MAKE IT... AND NOW WE KNOW ALL THE FUCKING EQUIPMENT WE NEED IS MORE OR LESS ABANDONED.
SO YOU'RE GOING TO GET BACK TO WORK AND MAKE THAT SHIT FOR US. GOT IT?
NO.
I WON'T.
EXCUSE ME WHILE I GET OUT MY CRYSTAL BALLS.
OKAY... THERE THEY FUCKING ARE.
NICE.
OKAY, FUCKHEAD... LET'S SEE YOUR FUTURE.

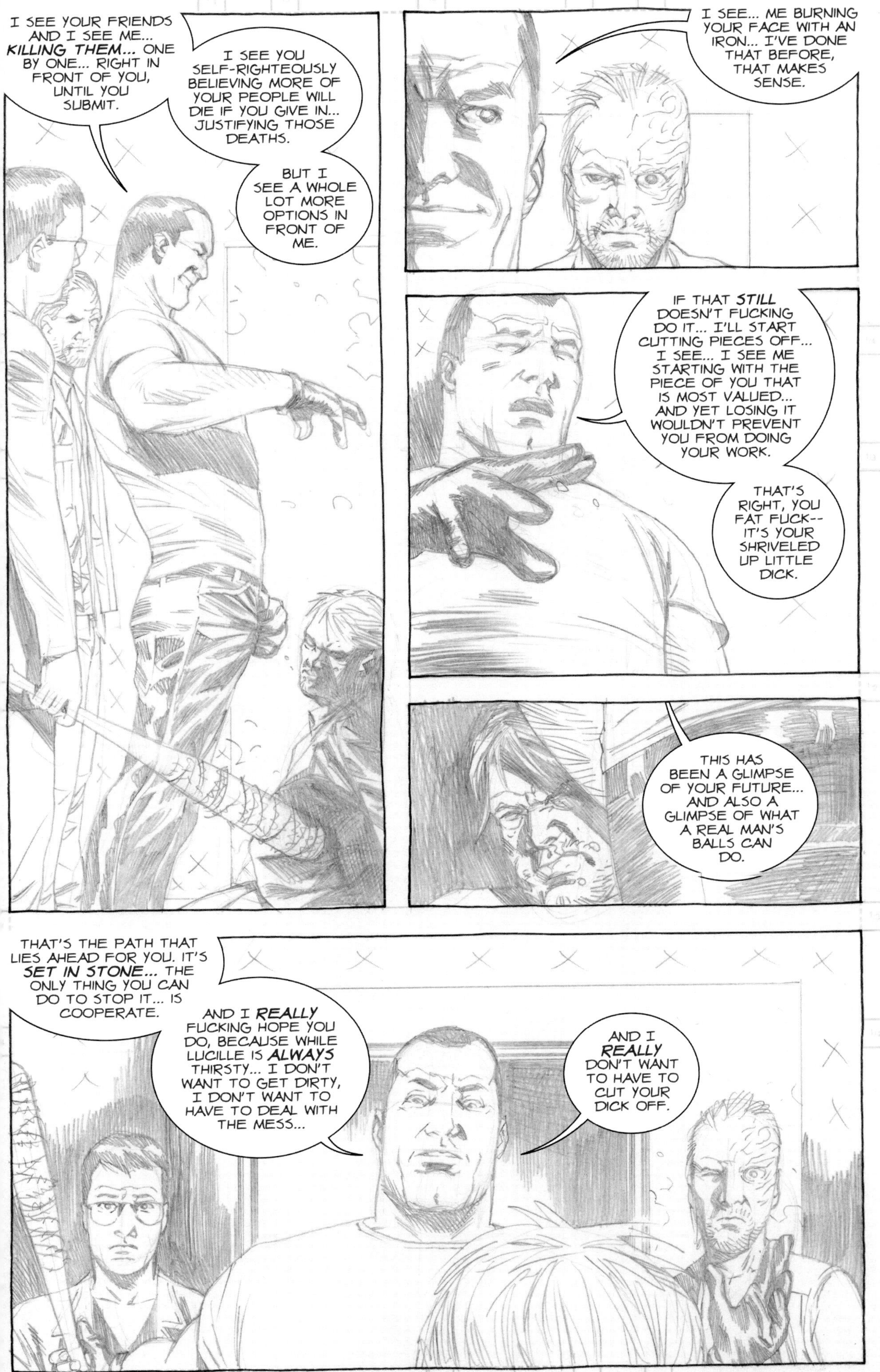
I SEE YOUR FRIENDS AND I SEE ME... KILLING THEM... ONE BY ONE... RIGHT IN FRONT OF YOU, UNTIL YOU SUBMIT.
I SEE YOU SELF-RIGHTEOUSLY BELIEVING MORE OF YOUR PEOPLE WILL DIE IF YOU GIVE IN... JUSTIFYING THOSE DEATHS.
BUT I SEE A WHOLE LOT MORE OPTIONS IN FRONT OF ME.
I SEE... ME BURNING YOUR FACE WITH AN IRON... I'VE DONE THAT BEFORE, THAT MAKES SENSE.
IF THAT STILL DOESN'T FUCKING DO IT... I'LL START CUTTING PIECES OFF... I SEE... I SEE ME STARTING WITH THE PIECE OF YOU THAT IS MOST VALUED... AND YET LOSING IT WOULDN'T PREVENT YOU FROM DOING YOUR WORK.
THAT'S RIGHT, YOU FAT FUCK-- IT'S YOUR SHRIVELED UP LITTLE DICK.
THIS HAS BEEN A GLIMPSE OF YOUR FUTURE... AND ALSO A GLIMPSE OF WHAT A REAL MAN'S BALLS CAN DO.
THAT'S THE PATH THAT LIES AHEAD FOR YOU. IT'S SET IN STONE... THE ONLY THING YOU CAN DO TO STOP IT... IS COOPERATE.
AND I REALLY FUCKING HOPE YOU DO, BECAUSE WHILE LUCILLE IS ALWAYS THIRSTY... I DON'T WANT TO GET DIRTY, I DON'T WANT TO HAVE TO DEAL WITH THE MESS...
AND I REALLY DON'T WANT TO HAVE TO CUT YOUR DICK OFF.

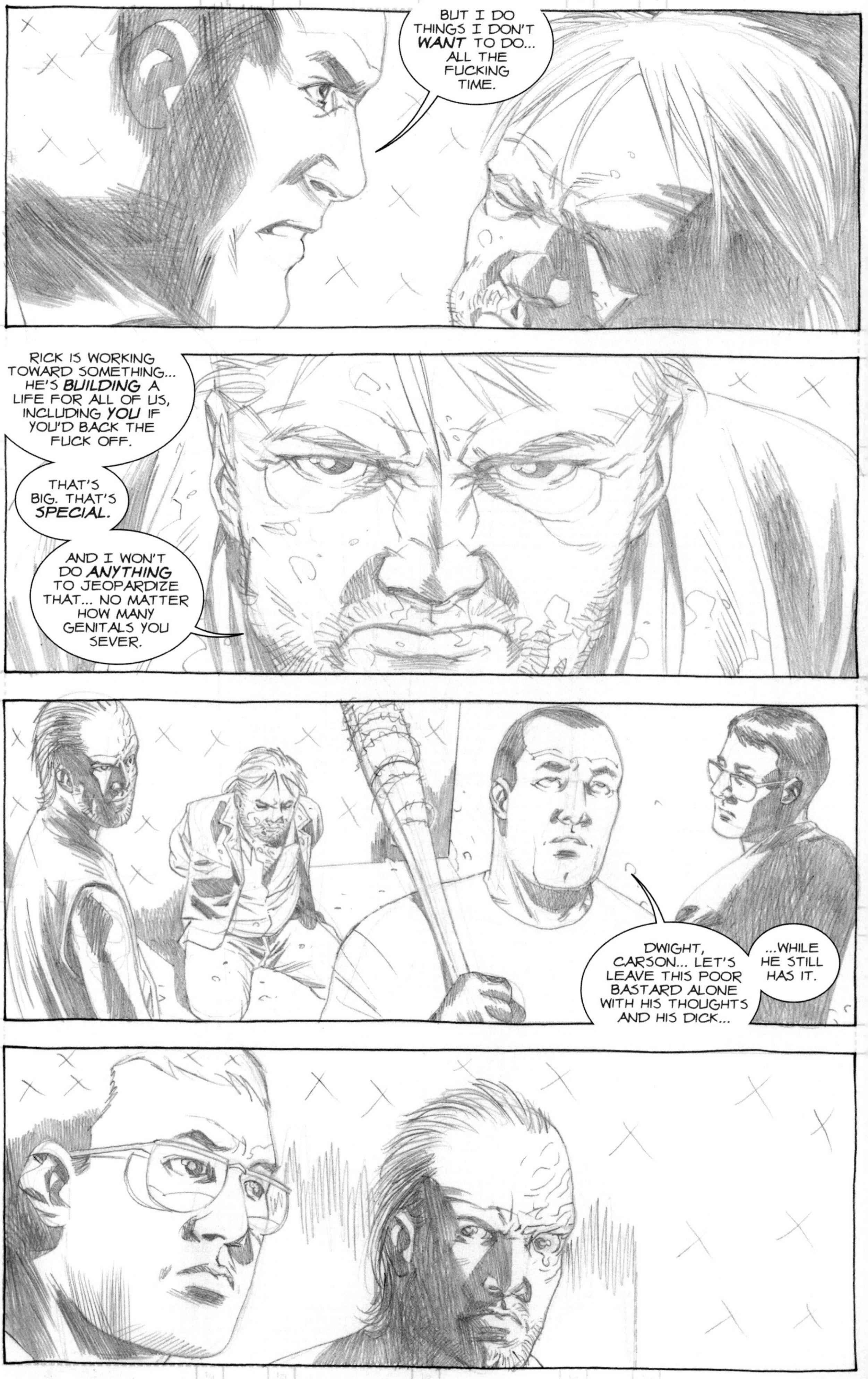
BUT I DO THINGS I DON'T WANT TO DO... ALL THE FUCKING TIME.
RICK IS WORKING TOWARD SOMETHING... HE'S BUILDING A LIFE FOR ALL OF US, INCLUDING YOU IF YOU'D BACK THE FUCK OFF.
THAT'S BIG. THAT'S SPECIAL.
AND I WON'T DO ANYTHING TO JEOPARDIZE THAT... NO MATTER HOW MANY GENITALS YOU SEVER.
DWIGHT, CARSON... LET'S LEAVE THIS POOR BASTARD ALONE WITH HIS THOUGHTS AND HIS DICK...
...WHILE HE STILL HAS IT.

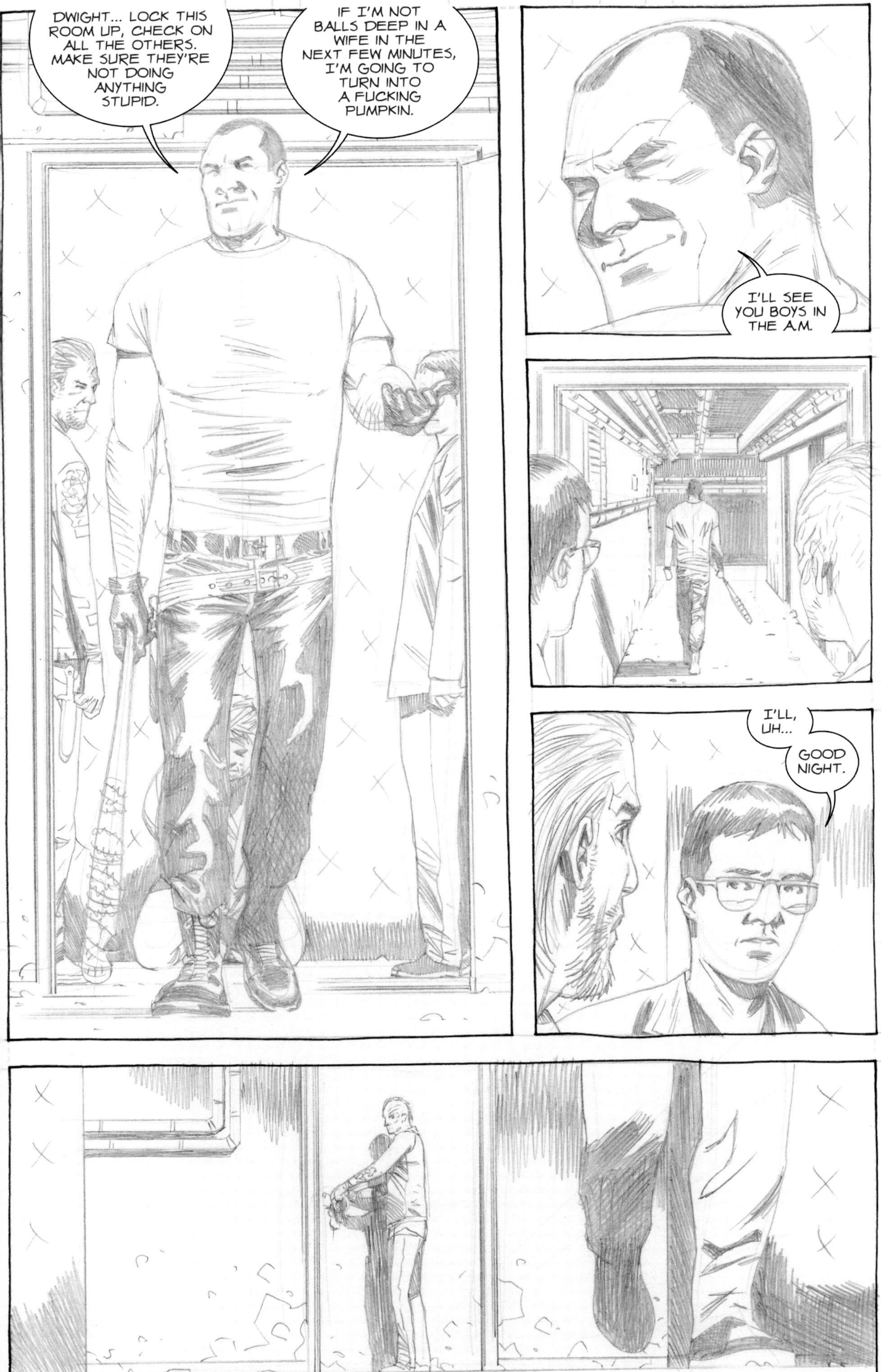
DWIGHT... LOCK THIS ROOM UP, CHECK ON ALL THE OTHERS. MAKE SURE THEY'RE NOT DOING ANYTHING STUPID.
IF I'M NOT BALLS DEEP IN A WIFE IN THE NEXT FEW MINUTES, I'M GOING TO TURN INTO A FUCKING PUMPKIN.
I'LL SEE YOU BOYS IN THE A.M.
I'LL, UH...
GOOD NIGHT.

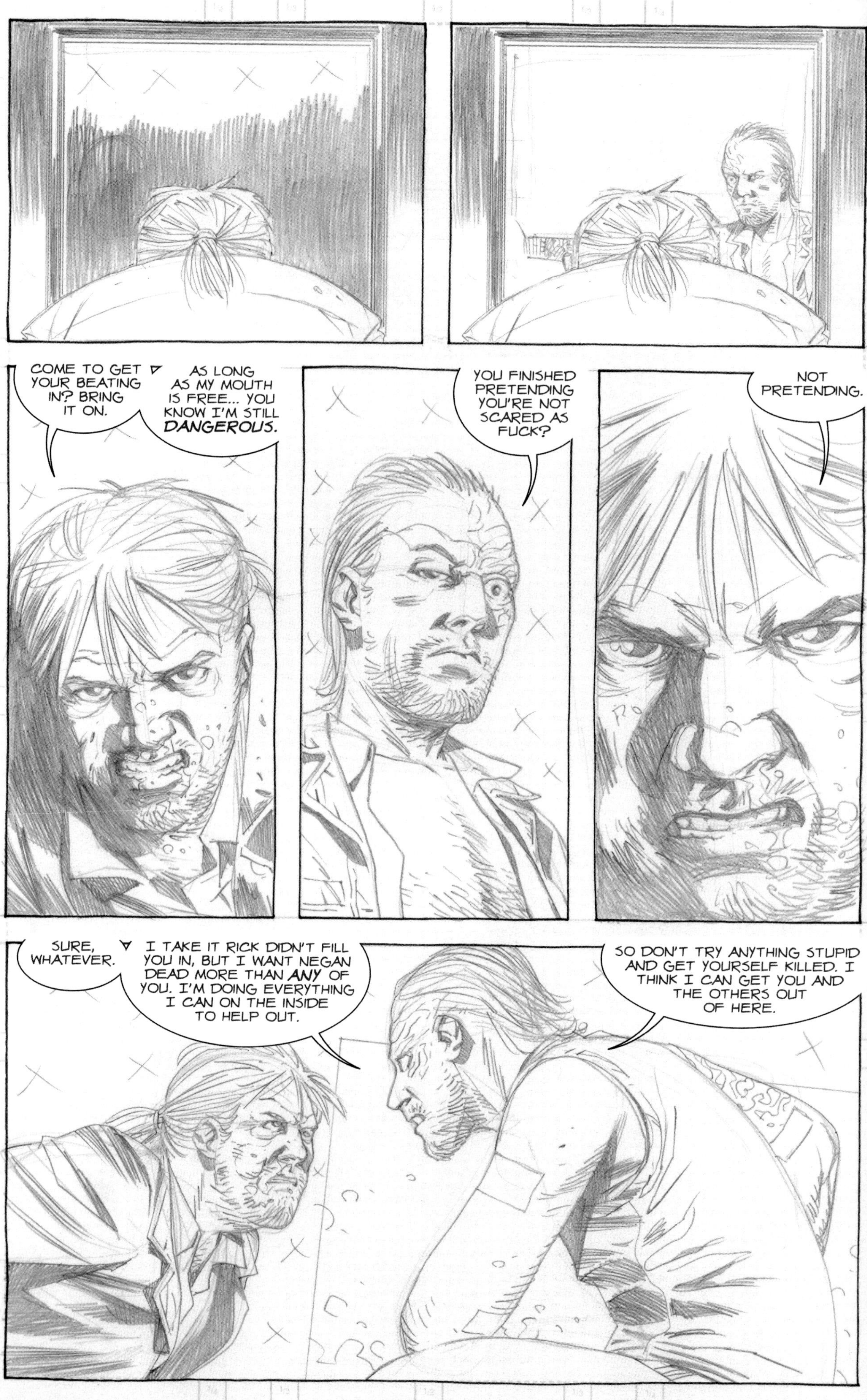
COME TO GET YOUR BEATING IN? BRING IT ON.
AS LONG AS MY MOUTH IS FREE... YOU KNOW I'M STILL DANGEROUS.
YOU FINISHED PRETENDING YOU'RE NOT SCARED AS FUCK?
NOT PRETENDING.
SURE, WHATEVER.
I TAKE IT RICK DIDN'T FILL YOU IN, BUT I WANT NEGAN DEAD MORE THAN ANY OF YOU. I'M DOING EVERYTHING I CAN ON THE INSIDE TO HELP OUT.
SO DON'T TRY ANYTHING STUPID AND GET YOURSELF KILLED. I THINK I CAN GET YOU AND THE OTHERS OUT OF HERE.

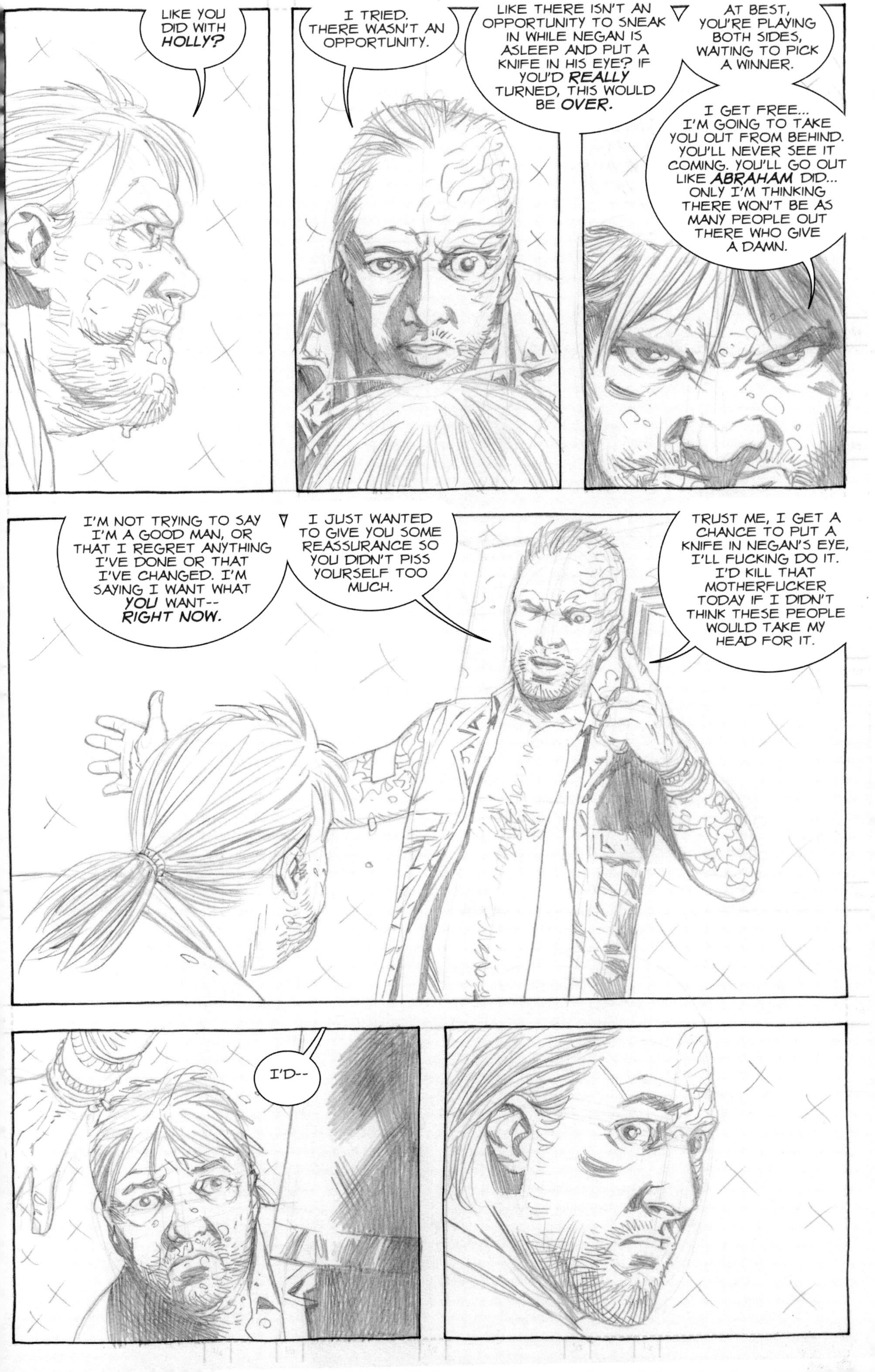
LIKE YOU DID WITH HOLLY?
I TRIED. THERE WASN'T AN OPPORTUNITY.
LIKE THERE ISN'T AN OPPORTUNITY TO SNEAK IN WHILE NEGAN IS ASLEEP AND PUT A KNIFE IN HIS EYE? IF YOU'D REALLY TURNED, THIS WOULD BE OVER.
AT BEST, YOU'RE PLAYING BOTH SIDES, WAITING TO PICK A WINNER.
I GET FREE... I'M GOING TO TAKE YOU OUT FROM BEHIND. YOU'LL NEVER SEE IT COMING. YOU'LL GO OUT LIKE ABRAHAM DID... ONLY I'M THINKING THERE WON'T BE AS MANY PEOPLE OUT THERE WHO GIVE A DAMN.
I'M NOT TRYING TO SAY I'M A GOOD MAN, OR THAT I REGRET ANYTHING I'VE DONE OR THAT I'VE CHANGED. I'M SAYING I WANT WHAT YOU WANT-- RIGHT NOW.
I JUST WANTED TO GIVE YOU SOME REASSURANCE SO YOU DIDN'T PISS YOURSELF TOO MUCH.
TRUST ME, I GET A CHANCE TO PUT A KNIFE IN NEGAN'S EYE, I'LL FUCKING DO IT. I'D KILL THAT MOTHERFUCKER TODAY IF I DIDN'T THINK THESE PEOPLE WOULD TAKE MY HEAD FOR IT.
I'D--

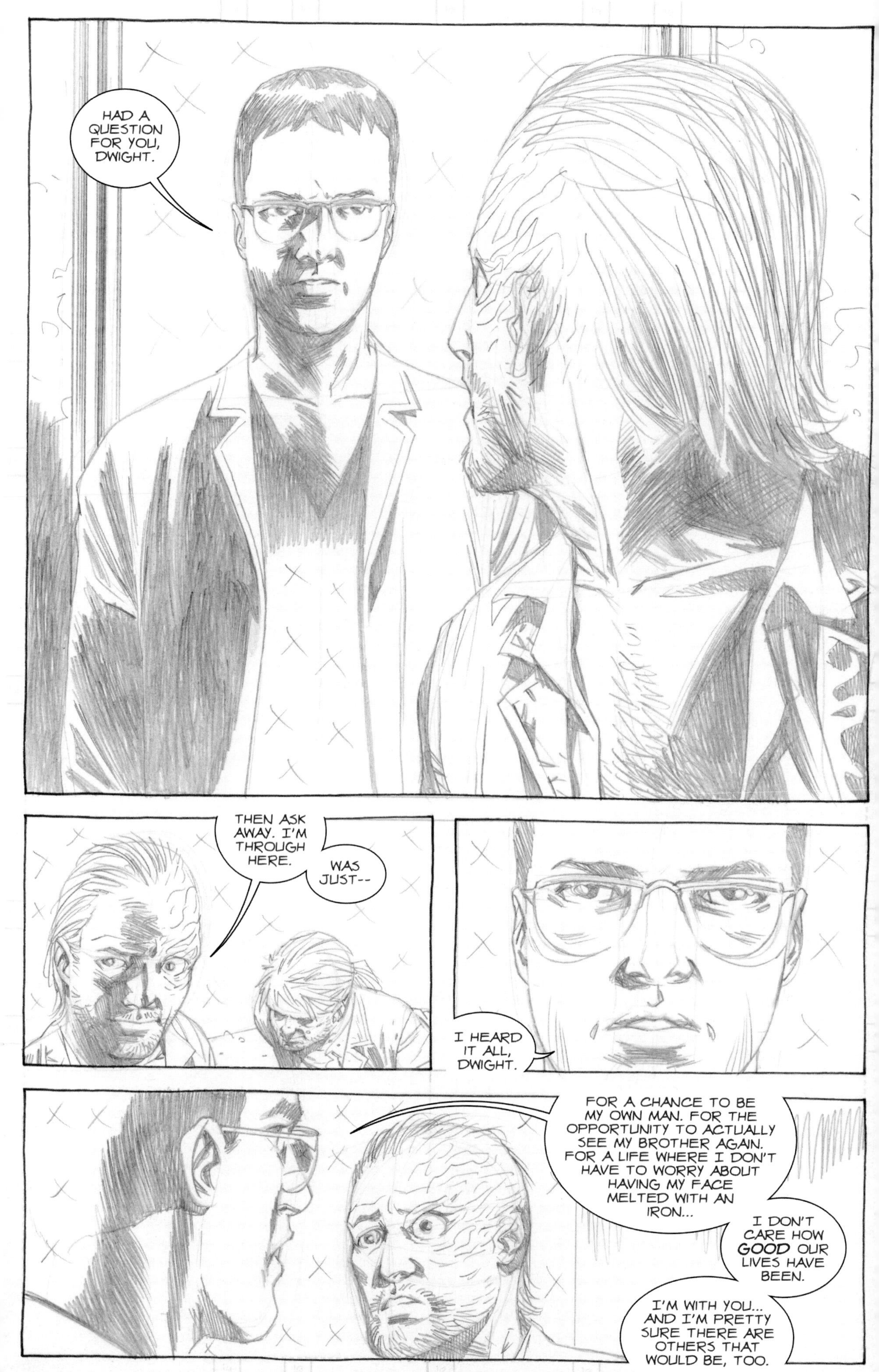
HAD A QUESTION FOR YOU, DWIGHT.
THEN ASK AWAY. I'M THROUGH HERE.
WAS JUST--
I HEARD IT ALL, DWIGHT.
FOR A CHANCE TO BE MY OWN MAN. FOR THE OPPORTUNITY TO ACTUALLY SEE MY BROTHER AGAIN. FOR A LIFE WHERE I DON'T HAVE TO WORRY ABOUT HAVING MY FACE MELTED WITH AN IRON...
I DON'T CARE HOW GOOD OUR LIVES HAVE BEEN.
I'M WITH YOU... AND I'M PRETTY SURE THERE ARE OTHERS THAT WOULD BE, TOO.

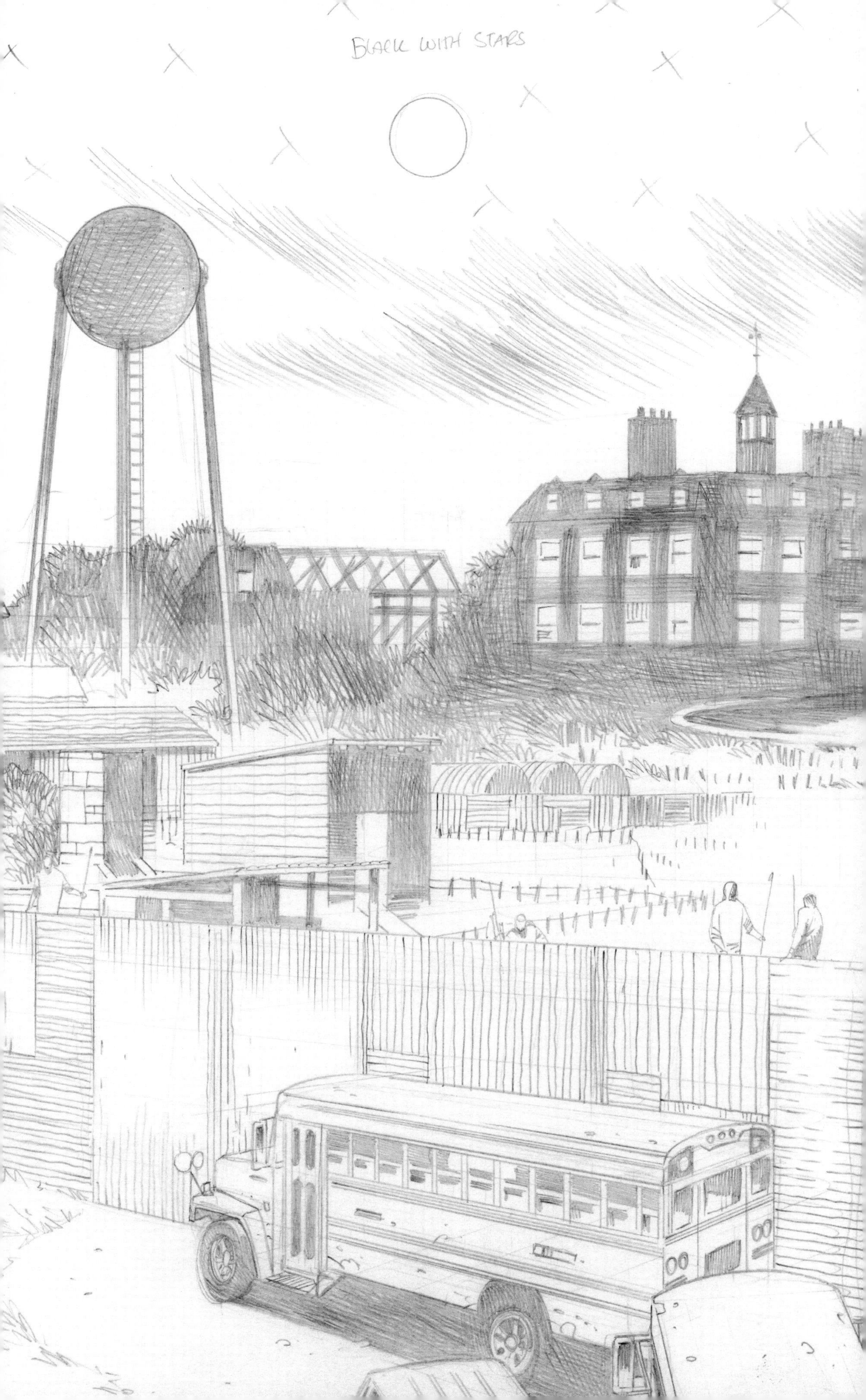
BLACK WITH STARS

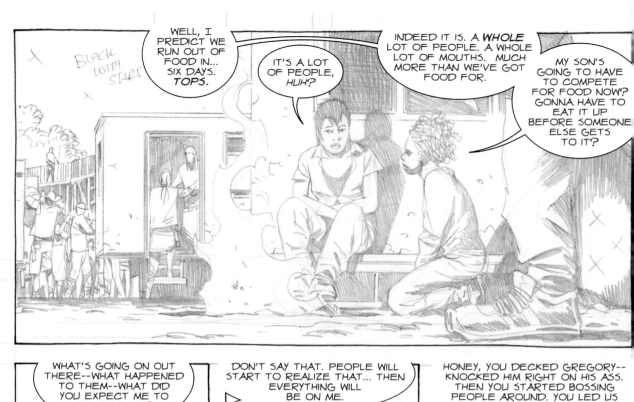

WELL, I PREDICT WE RUN OUT OF FOOD IN... SIX DAYS. *TOPS.*

IT'S A LOT OF PEOPLE, HUH?

INDEED IT IS. *A WHOLE* LOT OF PEOPLE. A WHOLE LOT OF MOUTHS. MUCH MORE THAN WE'VE GOT FOOD FOR.

MY SON'S GOING TO HAVE TO COMPETE FOR FOOD NOW? GONNA HAVE TO EAT IT UP BEFORE SOMEONE ELSE GETS TO IT?

BLACK WITH STARS

WHAT'S GOING ON OUT THERE--WHAT HAPPENED TO THEM--WHAT DID YOU EXPECT ME TO DO, BRIANNA?

WHATEVER YOU THINK IS *BEST* FOR US. YOU'RE IN CHARGE NOW... *REMEMBER?*

DON'T SAY THAT. PEOPLE WILL START TO REALIZE THAT... THEN EVERYTHING WILL BE ON ME.

I'M *NOT* IN CHARGE.

HONEY, YOU DECKED GREGORY-- KNOCKED HIM RIGHT ON HIS ASS. THEN YOU STARTED BOSSING PEOPLE AROUND. YOU LED US OUT OF HERE--AND YOU LED US BACK.

IT'S OFFICIAL. YOU'RE IN *CHARGE* AND *EVERYONE* KNOWS IT. NO ONE ELSE *WANTS* THE JOB... THEY'LL LET ANYONE BUT GREGORY DO IT... SO CONGRATULATIONS.

I'LL LET YOU SLIDE ON THE FOOD SITUATION BECAUSE I TRUST YOU KNOW WHAT YOU'RE DOING BUT DON'T YOU FORGET WHAT YOU SAID...

YOU BELIEVE IN RICK GRIMES... WELL, HOPEFULLY BY THE END OF ALL THIS... WE ALL WILL.

THEN I'LL BELIEVE IN MAGGIE GREENE, TOO.

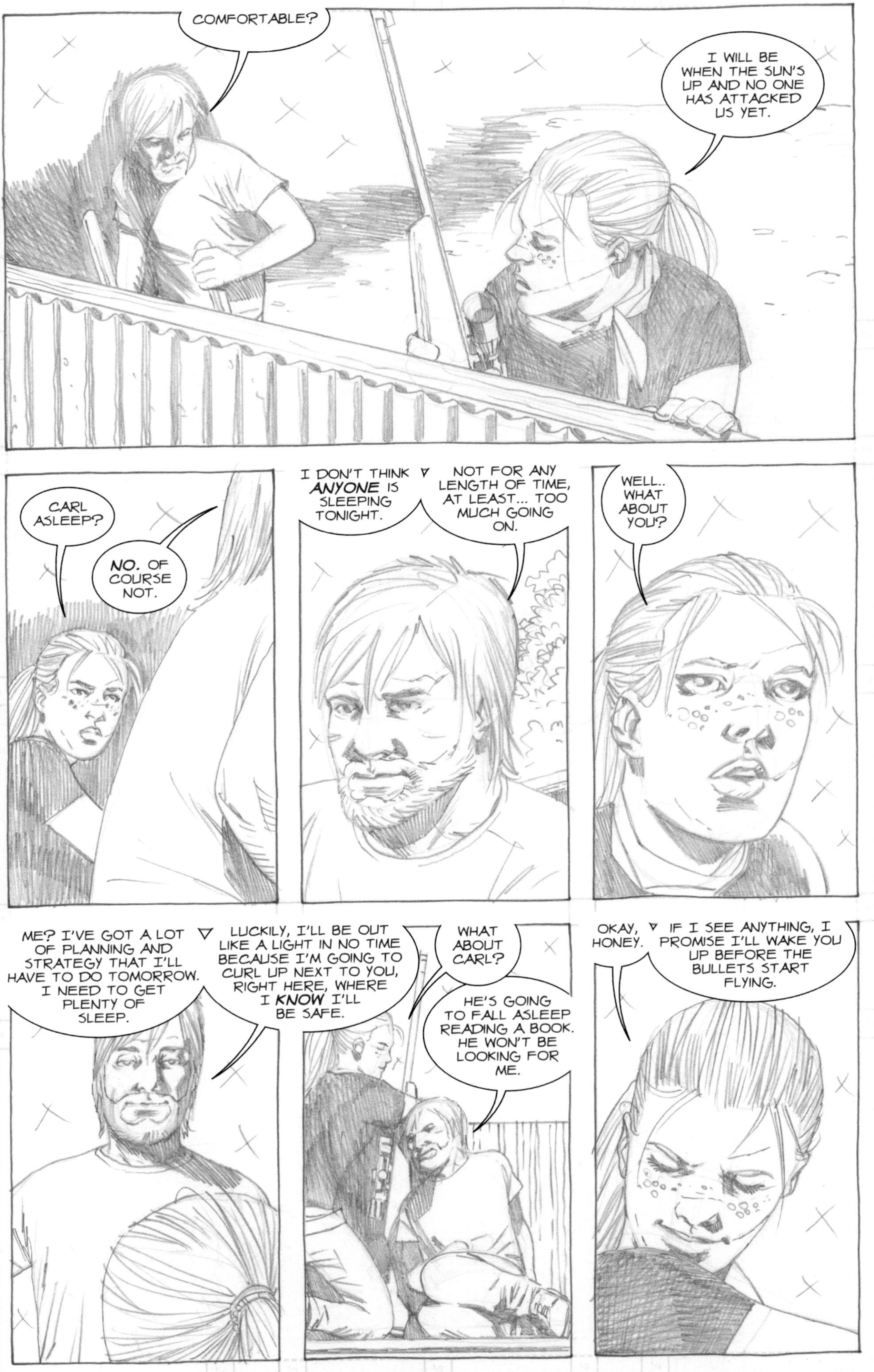
COMFORTABLE?
I WILL BE WHEN THE SUN'S UP AND NO ONE HAS ATTACKED US YET.
CARL ASLEEP?
NO. OF COURSE NOT.
I DON'T THINK ANYONE IS SLEEPING TONIGHT.
NOT FOR ANY LENGTH OF TIME, AT LEAST... TOO MUCH GOING ON.
WELL.. WHAT ABOUT YOU?
ME? I'VE GOT A LOT OF PLANNING AND STRATEGY THAT I'LL HAVE TO DO TOMORROW. I NEED TO GET PLENTY OF SLEEP.
LUCKILY, I'LL BE OUT LIKE A LIGHT IN NO TIME BECAUSE I'M GOING TO CURL UP NEXT TO YOU, RIGHT HERE, WHERE I KNOW I'LL BE SAFE.
WHAT ABOUT CARL?
HE'S GOING TO FALL ASLEEP READING A BOOK. HE WON'T BE LOOKING FOR ME.
OKAY, HONEY.
IF I SEE ANYTHING, I PROMISE I'LL WAKE YOU UP BEFORE THE BULLETS START FLYING.

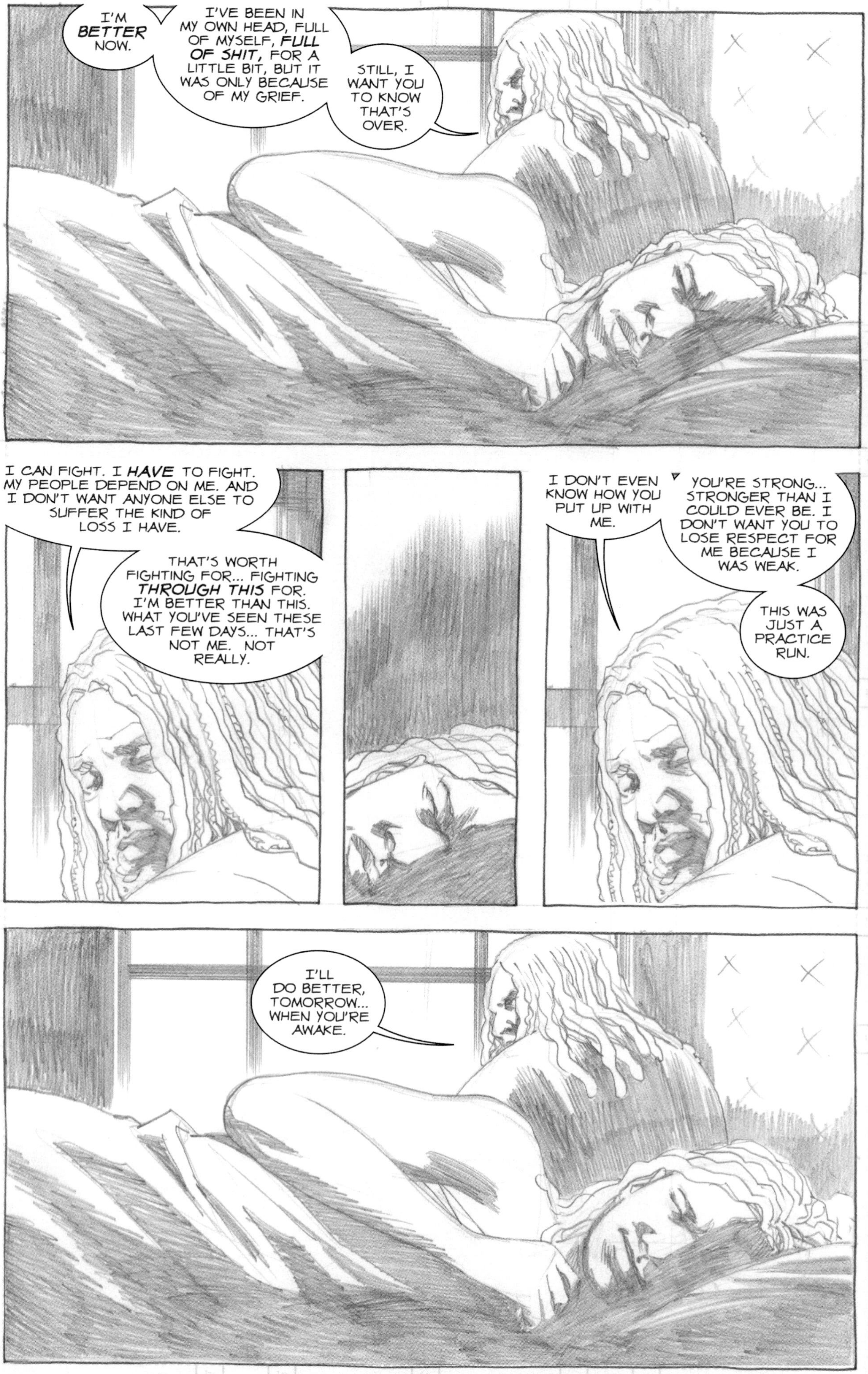
I'M *BETTER* NOW.
I'VE BEEN IN MY OWN HEAD, FULL OF MYSELF, *FULL OF SHIT,* FOR A LITTLE BIT, BUT IT WAS ONLY BECAUSE OF MY GRIEF.
STILL, I WANT YOU TO KNOW THAT'S OVER.
I CAN FIGHT. I *HAVE* TO FIGHT. MY PEOPLE DEPEND ON ME. AND I DON'T WANT ANYONE ELSE TO SUFFER THE KIND OF LOSS I HAVE.
THAT'S WORTH FIGHTING FOR... FIGHTING *THROUGH THIS* FOR. I'M BETTER THAN THIS. WHAT YOU'VE SEEN THESE LAST FEW DAYS... THAT'S NOT ME. NOT REALLY.
I DON'T EVEN KNOW HOW YOU PUT UP WITH ME.
YOU'RE STRONG... STRONGER THAN I COULD EVER BE. I DON'T WANT YOU TO LOSE RESPECT FOR ME BECAUSE I WAS WEAK.
THIS WAS JUST A PRACTICE RUN.
I'LL DO BETTER, TOMORROW... WHEN YOU'RE AWAKE.

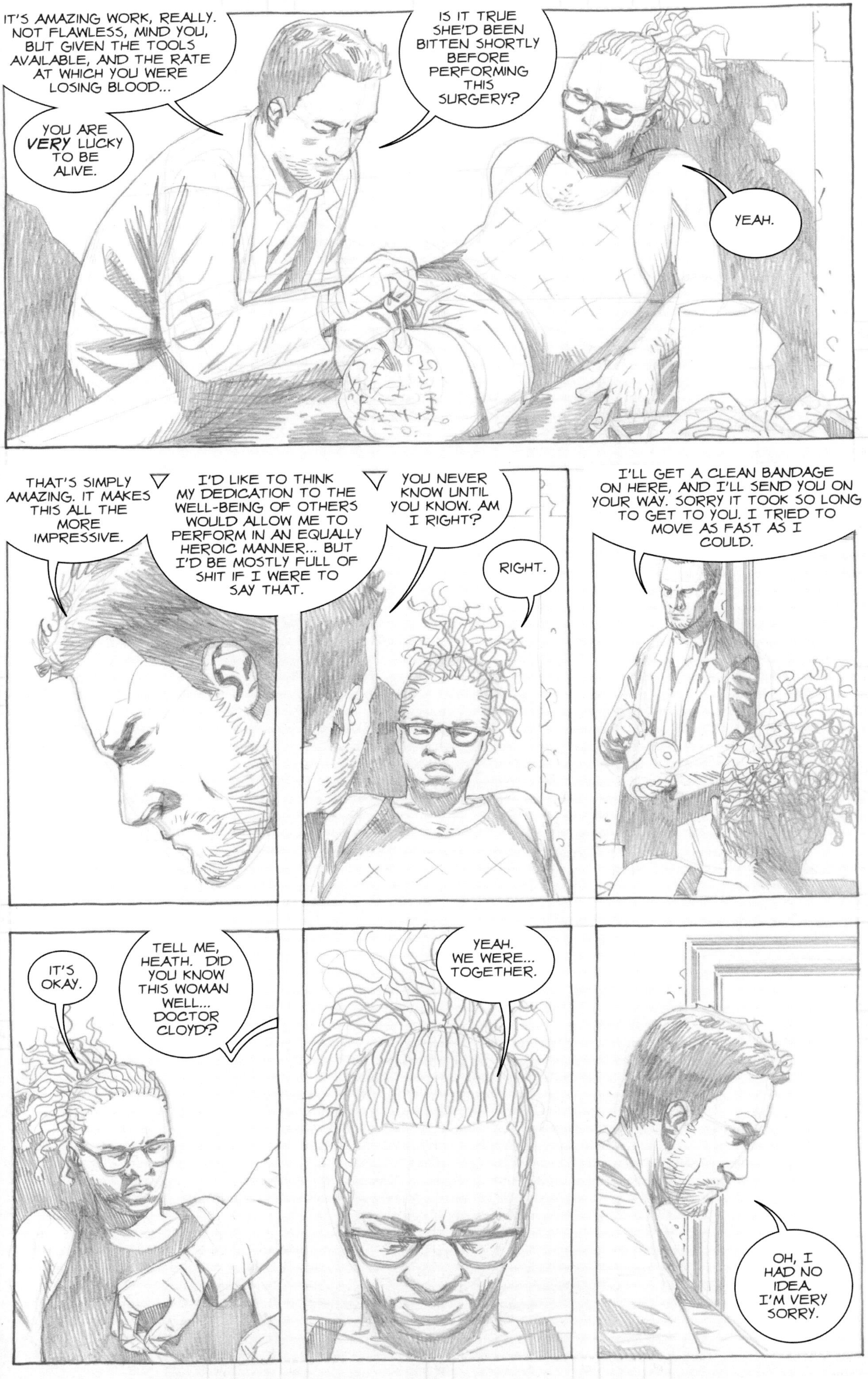
IT'S AMAZING WORK, REALLY. NOT FLAWLESS, MIND YOU, BUT GIVEN THE TOOLS AVAILABLE, AND THE RATE AT WHICH YOU WERE LOSING BLOOD...
YOU ARE VERY LUCKY TO BE ALIVE.
IS IT TRUE SHE'D BEEN BITTEN SHORTLY BEFORE PERFORMING THIS SURGERY?
YEAH.
THAT'S SIMPLY AMAZING. IT MAKES THIS ALL THE MORE IMPRESSIVE.
I'D LIKE TO THINK MY DEDICATION TO THE WELL-BEING OF OTHERS WOULD ALLOW ME TO PERFORM IN AN EQUALLY HEROIC MANNER... BUT I'D BE MOSTLY FULL OF SHIT IF I WERE TO SAY THAT.
YOU NEVER KNOW UNTIL YOU KNOW. AM I RIGHT?
RIGHT.
I'LL GET A CLEAN BANDAGE ON HERE, AND I'LL SEND YOU ON YOUR WAY. SORRY IT TOOK SO LONG TO GET TO YOU. I TRIED TO MOVE AS FAST AS I COULD.
IT'S OKAY.
TELL ME, HEATH. DID YOU KNOW THIS WOMAN WELL... DOCTOR CLOYD?
YEAH. WE WERE... TOGETHER.
OH, I HAD NO IDEA. I'M VERY SORRY.

BLACK WITH ST...

WORRIED ABOUT EUGENE?

AND THE OTHERS. ISN'T *EVERYONE?*

YEAH, BUT I KNOW YOU'RE A LITTLE SWEET ON THAT GUY. YOU DON'T HAVE TO HIDE IT FROM ME.

THIS AIN'T HIGH SCHOOL. YOU'RE NOT LESS COOL FOR LIKING THE FAT GUY.

HELL, *I* DO ALL RIGHT.

YEAH, GOOD... CONGRATULATIONS.

LISTEN, OLIVIA, CAN WE CATCH UP TOMORROW? IT'S LATE AND I JUST... I WANT TO BE ALONE WITH MY THOUGHTS, OKAY?

WHAT? SURE... YEAH. OKAY.

I HEAR YOU LOUD AND CLEAR. SORRY TO INTRUDE. YOU LOOKED SAD IS ALL. THOUGHT I COULD CHEER YOU UP.

GOOD NIGHT.

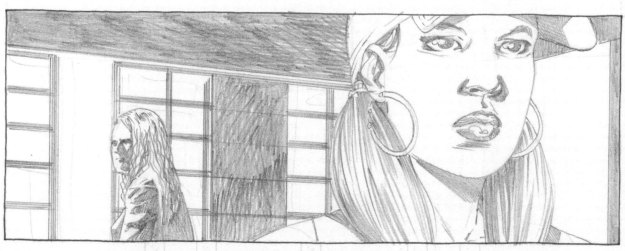

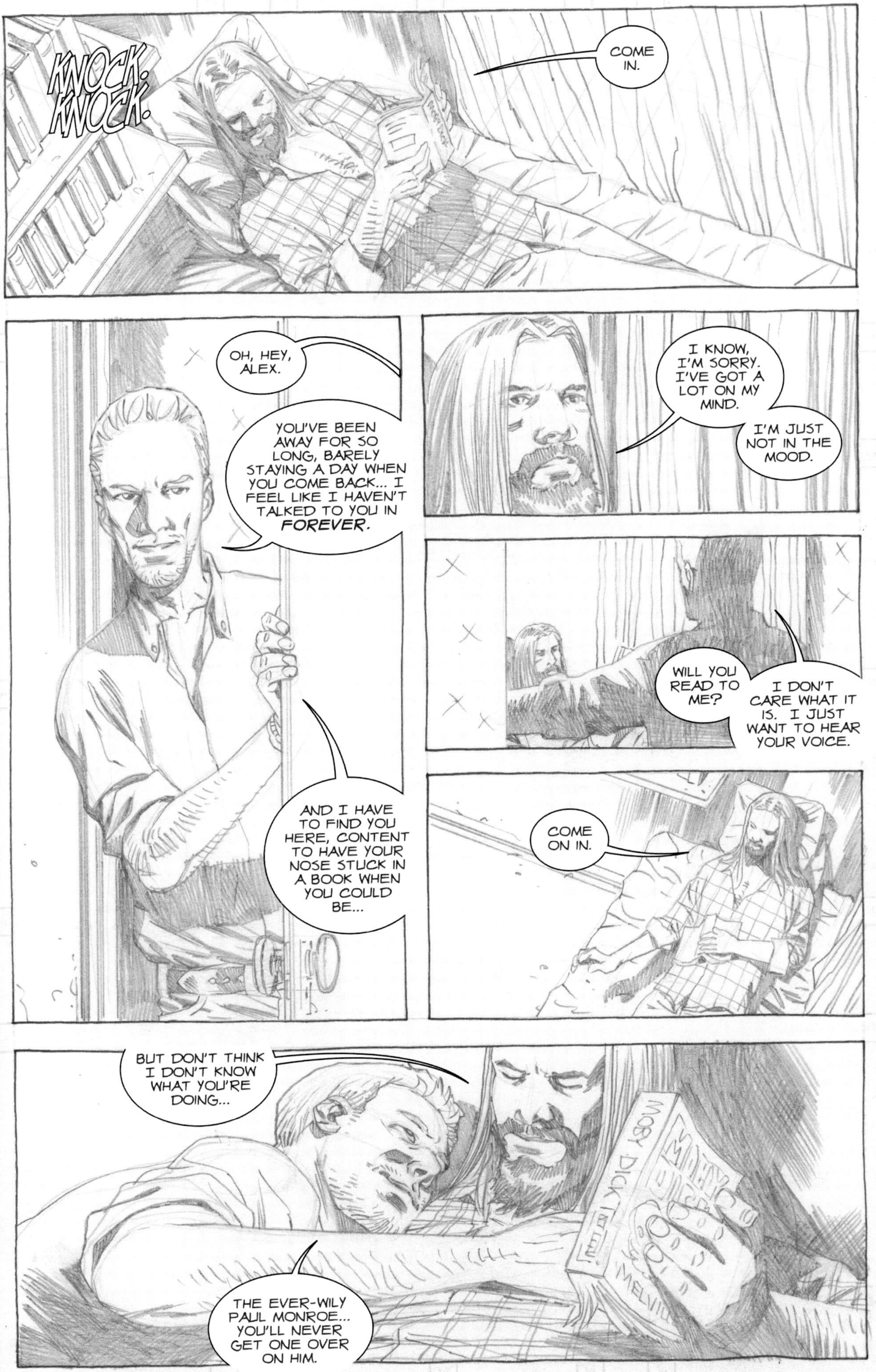
KNOCK. KNOCK.
COME IN.
OH, HEY, ALEX.
YOU'VE BEEN AWAY FOR SO LONG, BARELY STAYING A DAY WHEN YOU COME BACK... I FEEL LIKE I HAVEN'T TALKED TO YOU IN FOREVER.
AND I HAVE TO FIND YOU HERE, CONTENT TO HAVE YOUR NOSE STUCK IN A BOOK WHEN YOU COULD BE...
I KNOW, I'M SORRY. I'VE GOT A LOT ON MY MIND.
I'M JUST NOT IN THE MOOD.
WILL YOU READ TO ME?
I DON'T CARE WHAT IT IS. I JUST WANT TO HEAR YOUR VOICE.
COME ON IN.
BUT DON'T THINK I DON'T KNOW WHAT YOU'RE DOING...
THE EVER-WILY PAUL MONROE... YOU'LL NEVER GET ONE OVER ON HIM.

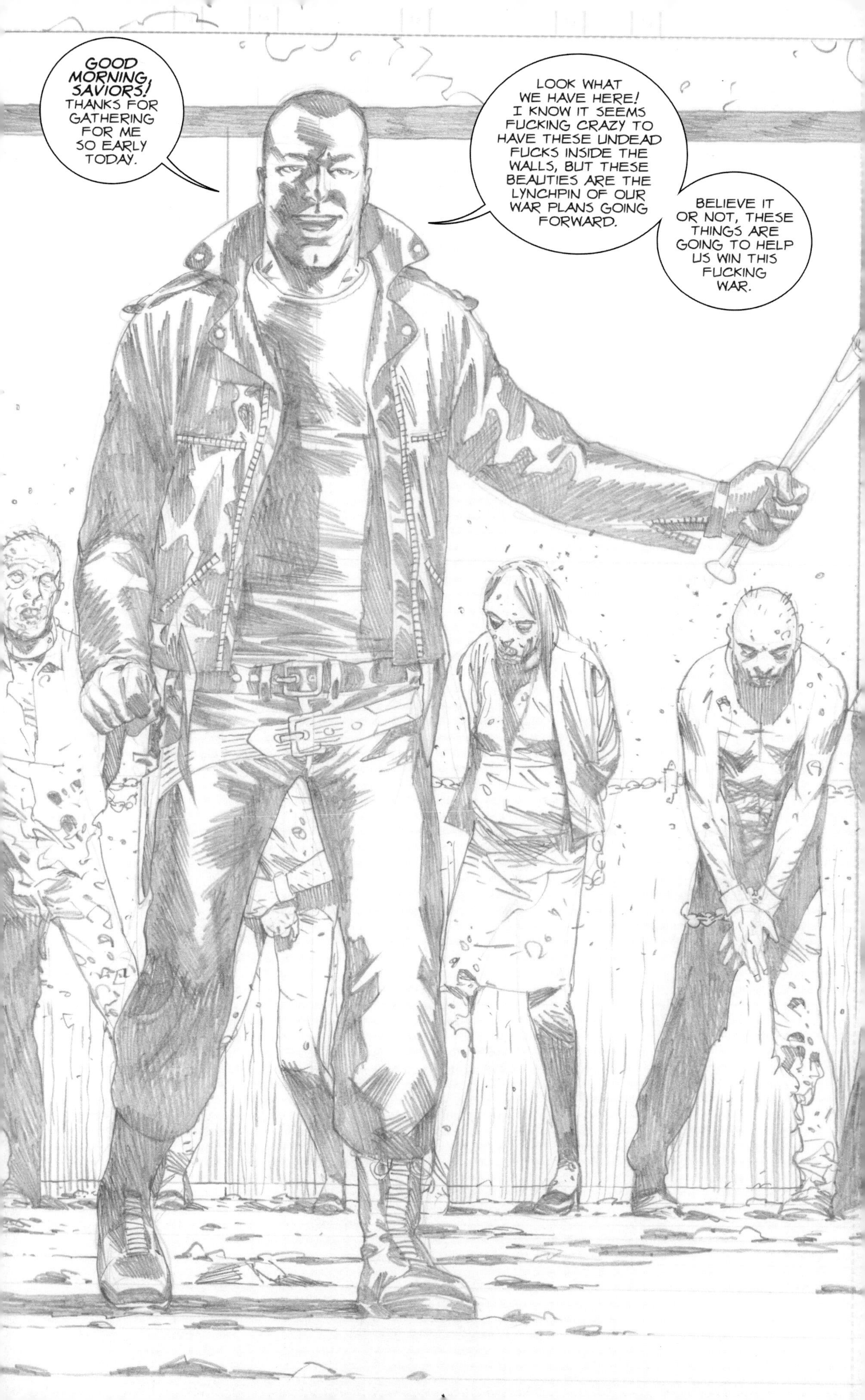
GOOD MORNING, SAVIORS! THANKS FOR GATHERING FOR ME SO EARLY TODAY.
LOOK WHAT WE HAVE HERE! I KNOW IT SEEMS FUCKING CRAZY TO HAVE THESE UNDEAD FUCKS INSIDE THE WALLS, BUT THESE BEAUTIES ARE THE LYNCHPIN OF OUR WAR PLANS GOING FORWARD.
BELIEVE IT OR NOT, THESE THINGS ARE GOING TO HELP US WIN THIS FUCKING WAR.

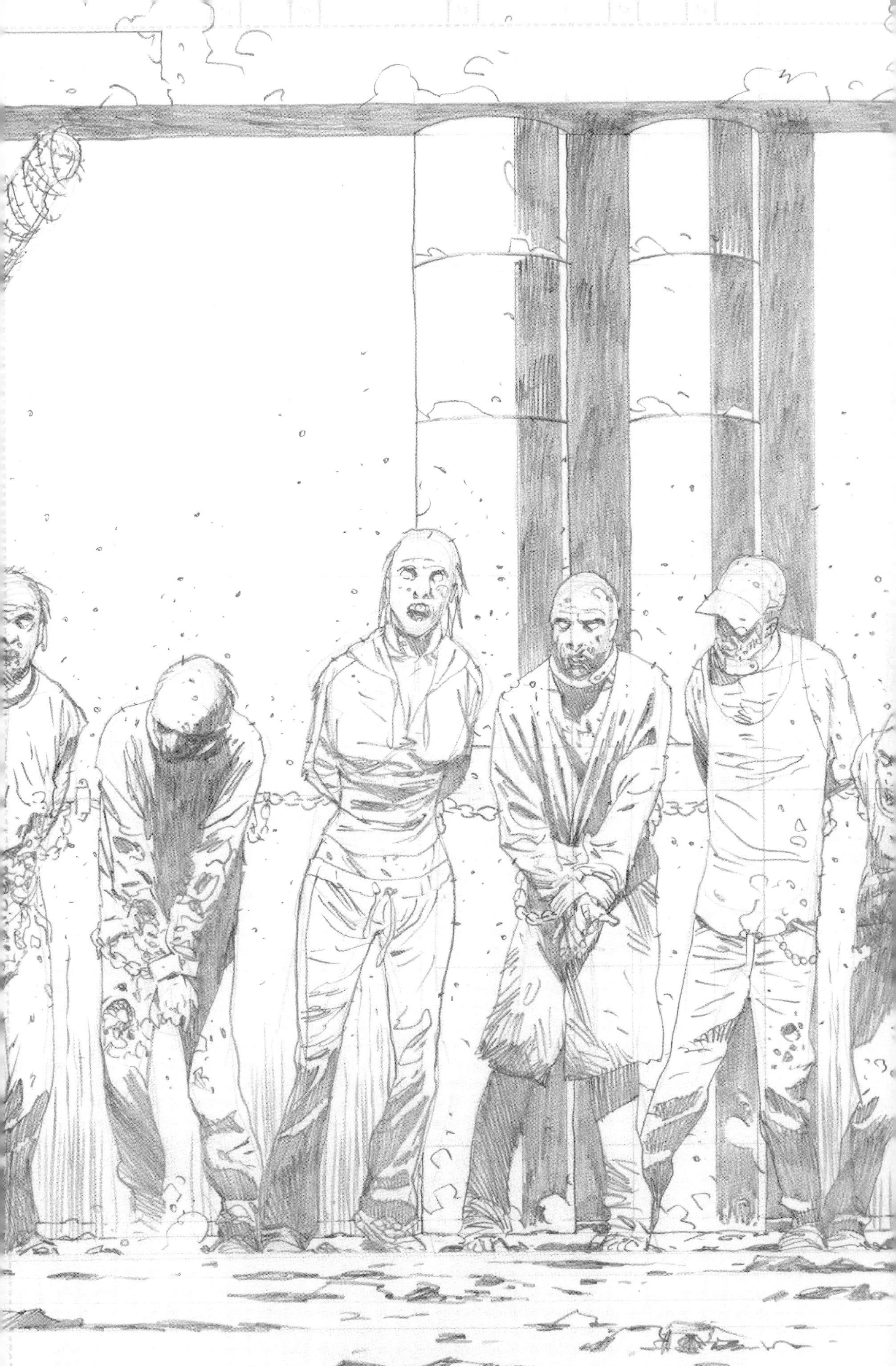

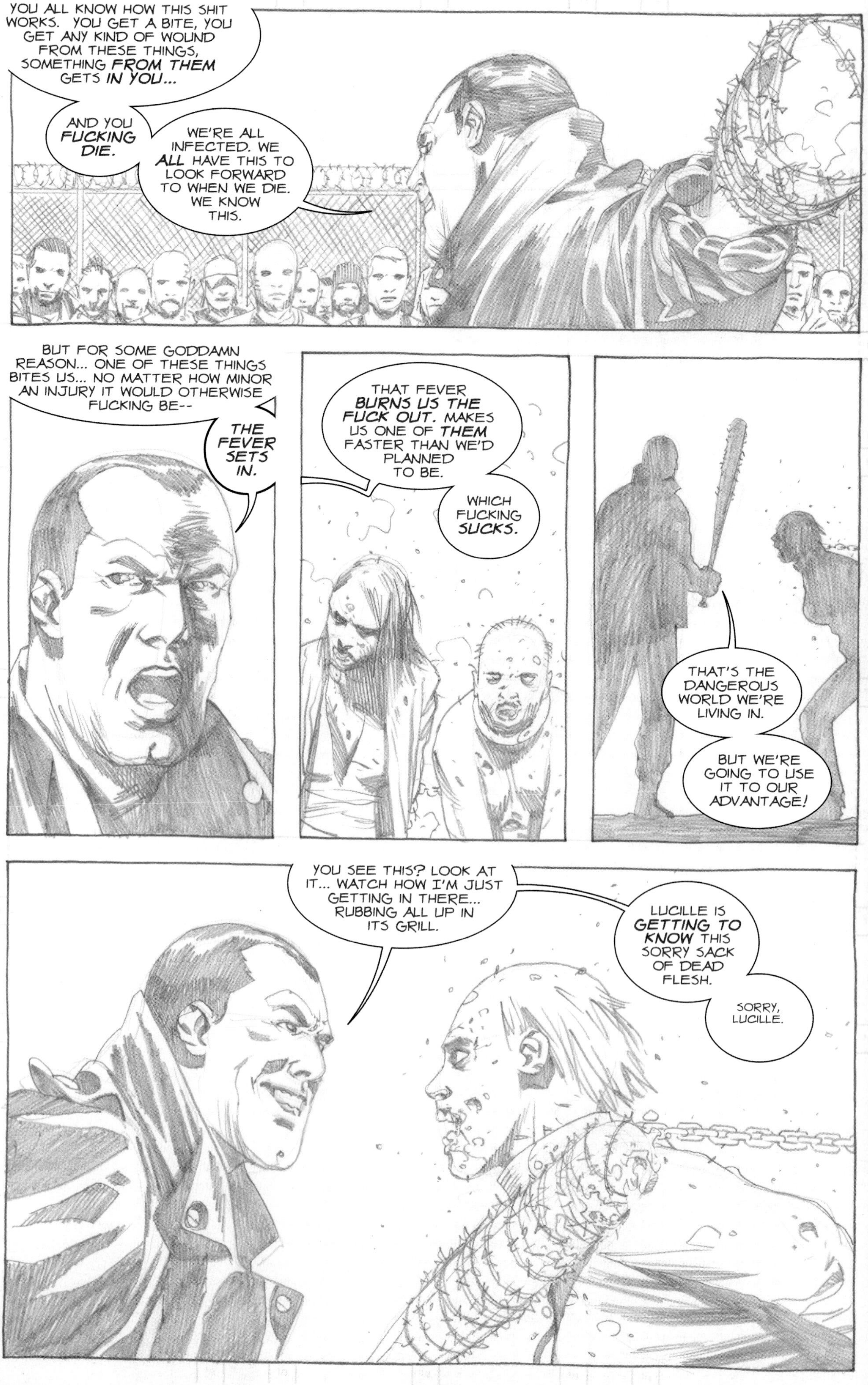

YOU ALL KNOW HOW THIS SHIT WORKS. YOU GET A BITE, YOU GET ANY KIND OF WOUND FROM THESE THINGS, SOMETHING FROM THEM GETS IN YOU...
AND YOU FUCKING DIE.
WE'RE ALL INFECTED. WE ALL HAVE THIS TO LOOK FORWARD TO WHEN WE DIE. WE KNOW THIS.
BUT FOR SOME GODDAMN REASON... ONE OF THESE THINGS BITES US... NO MATTER HOW MINOR AN INJURY IT WOULD OTHERWISE FUCKING BE--
THE FEVER SETS IN.
THAT FEVER BURNS US THE FUCK OUT. MAKES US ONE OF THEM FASTER THAN WE'D PLANNED TO BE.
WHICH FUCKING SUCKS.
THAT'S THE DANGEROUS WORLD WE'RE LIVING IN.
BUT WE'RE GOING TO USE IT TO OUR ADVANTAGE!
YOU SEE THIS? LOOK AT IT... WATCH HOW I'M JUST GETTING IN THERE... RUBBING ALL UP IN ITS GRILL.
LUCILLE IS GETTING TO KNOW THIS SORRY SACK OF DEAD FLESH.
SORRY, LUCILLE.

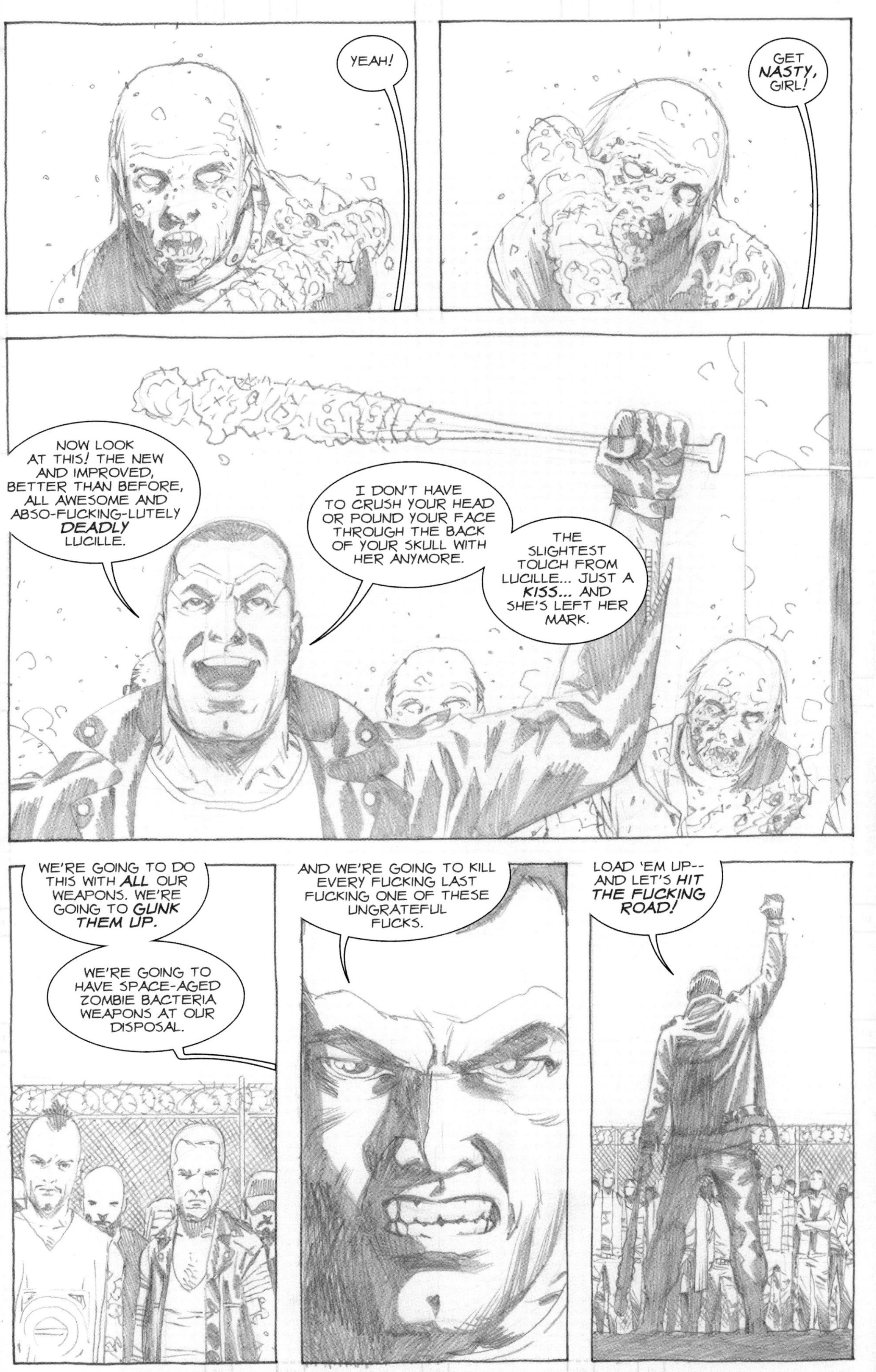
YEAH!
GET NASTY, GIRL!
NOW LOOK AT THIS! THE NEW AND IMPROVED, BETTER THAN BEFORE, ALL AWESOME AND ABSO-FUCKING-LUTELY DEADLY LUCILLE.
I DON'T HAVE TO CRUSH YOUR HEAD OR POUND YOUR FACE THROUGH THE BACK OF YOUR SKULL WITH HER ANYMORE.
THE SLIGHTEST TOUCH FROM LUCILLE... JUST A KISS... AND SHE'S LEFT HER MARK.
WE'RE GOING TO DO THIS WITH ALL OUR WEAPONS. WE'RE GOING TO GUNK THEM UP.
WE'RE GOING TO HAVE SPACE-AGED ZOMBIE BACTERIA WEAPONS AT OUR DISPOSAL.
AND WE'RE GOING TO KILL EVERY FUCKING LAST FUCKING ONE OF THESE UNGRATEFUL FUCKS.
LOAD 'EM UP-- AND LET'S HIT THE FUCKING ROAD!

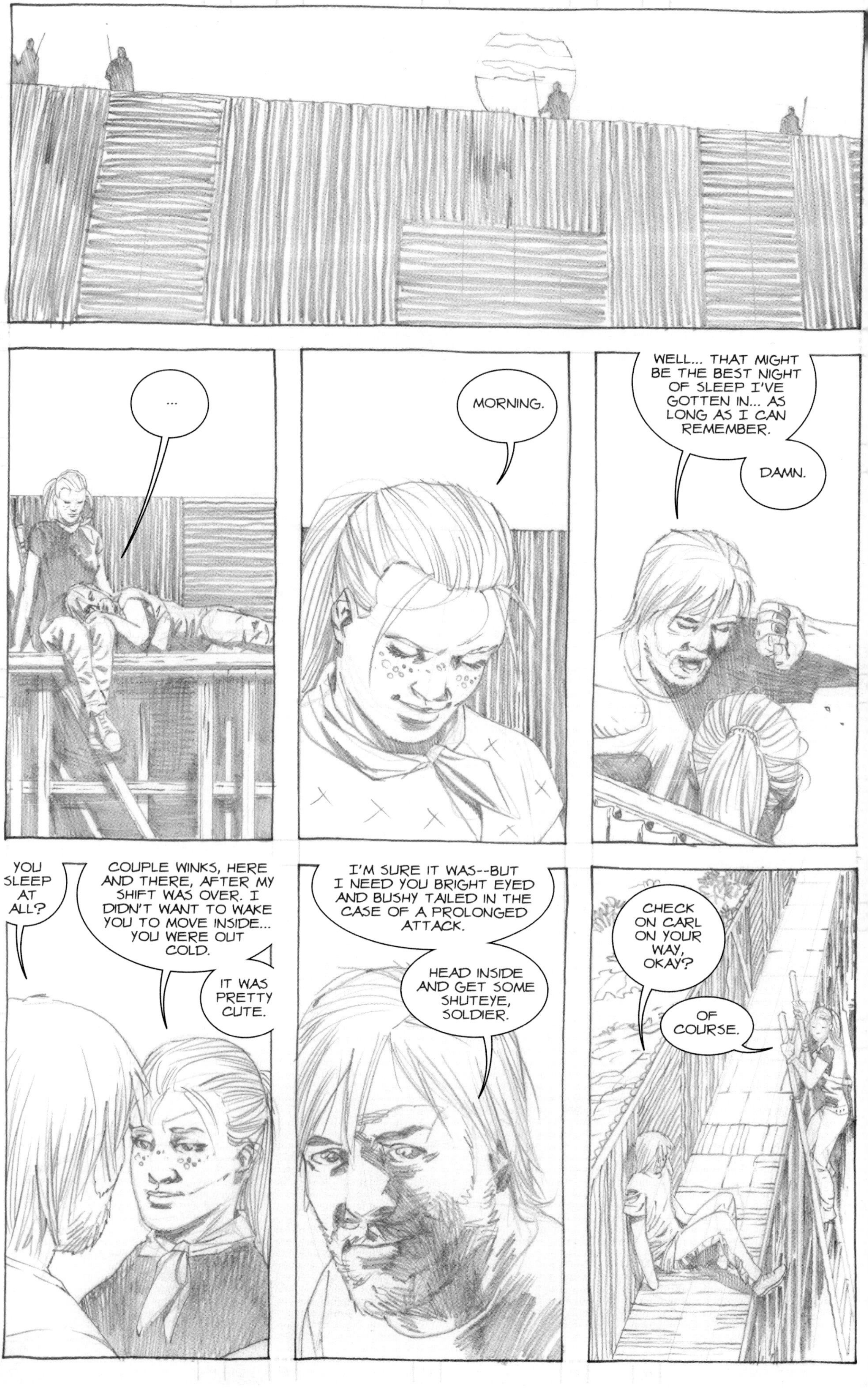
...
MORNING.
WELL... THAT MIGHT BE THE BEST NIGHT OF SLEEP I'VE GOTTEN IN... AS LONG AS I CAN REMEMBER.
DAMN.
YOU SLEEP AT ALL?
COUPLE WINKS, HERE AND THERE, AFTER MY SHIFT WAS OVER. I DIDN'T WANT TO WAKE YOU TO MOVE INSIDE... YOU WERE OUT COLD.
IT WAS PRETTY CUTE.
I'M SURE IT WAS--BUT I NEED YOU BRIGHT EYED AND BUSHY TAILED IN THE CASE OF A PROLONGED ATTACK.
HEAD INSIDE AND GET SOME SHUTEYE, SOLDIER.
CHECK ON CARL ON YOUR WAY, OKAY?
OF COURSE.

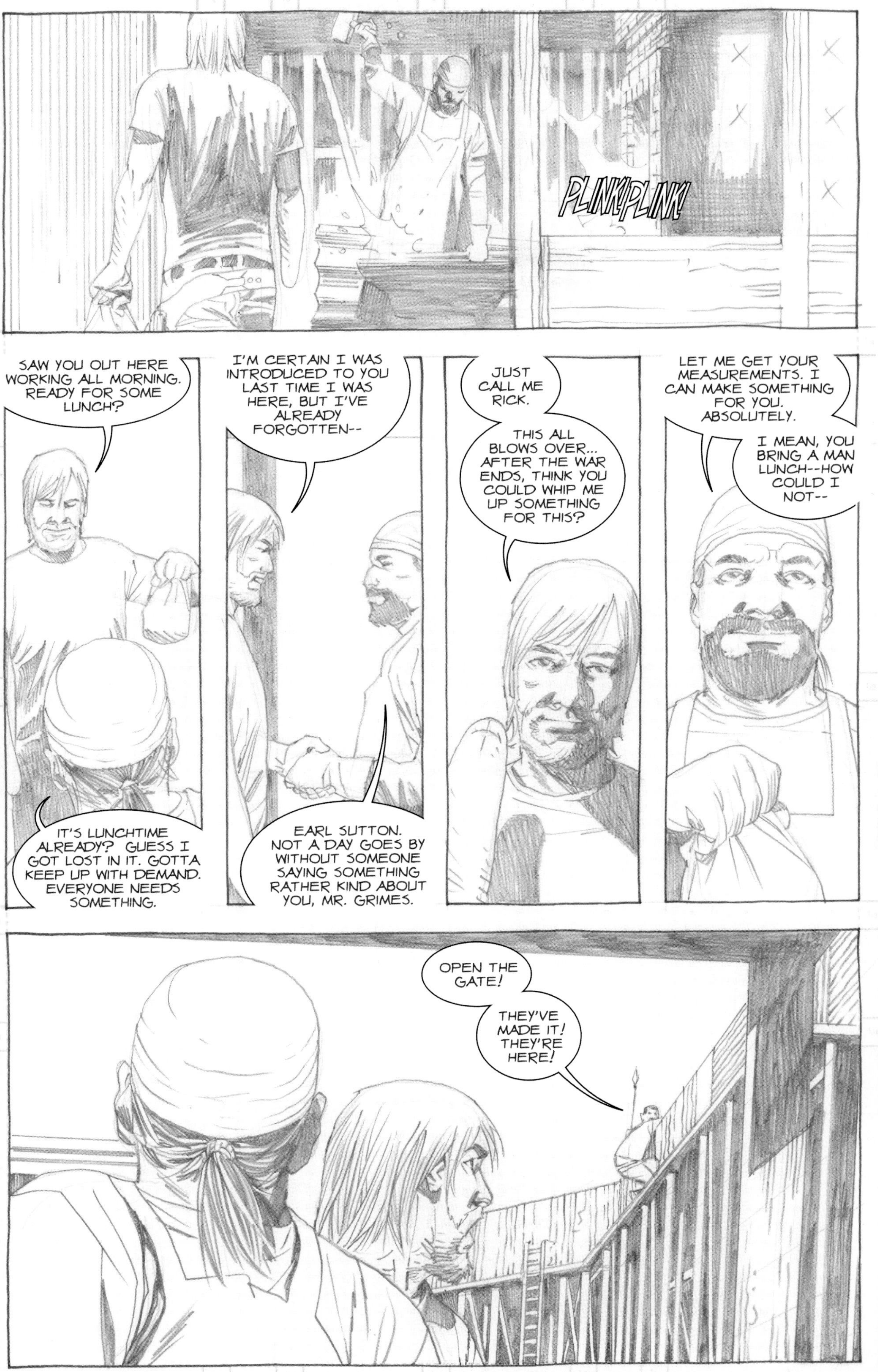
PLINK! PLINK!
SAW YOU OUT HERE WORKING ALL MORNING. READY FOR SOME LUNCH?
IT'S LUNCHTIME ALREADY? GUESS I GOT LOST IN IT. GOTTA KEEP UP WITH DEMAND. EVERYONE NEEDS SOMETHING.
I'M CERTAIN I WAS INTRODUCED TO YOU LAST TIME I WAS HERE, BUT I'VE ALREADY FORGOTTEN--
EARL SUTTON. NOT A DAY GOES BY WITHOUT SOMEONE SAYING SOMETHING RATHER KIND ABOUT YOU, MR. GRIMES.
JUST CALL ME RICK.
THIS ALL BLOWS OVER... AFTER THE WAR ENDS, THINK YOU COULD WHIP ME UP SOMETHING FOR THIS?
LET ME GET YOUR MEASUREMENTS. I CAN MAKE SOMETHING FOR YOU. ABSOLUTELY.
I MEAN, YOU BRING A MAN LUNCH--HOW COULD I NOT--
OPEN THE GATE!
THEY'VE MADE IT! THEY'RE HERE!

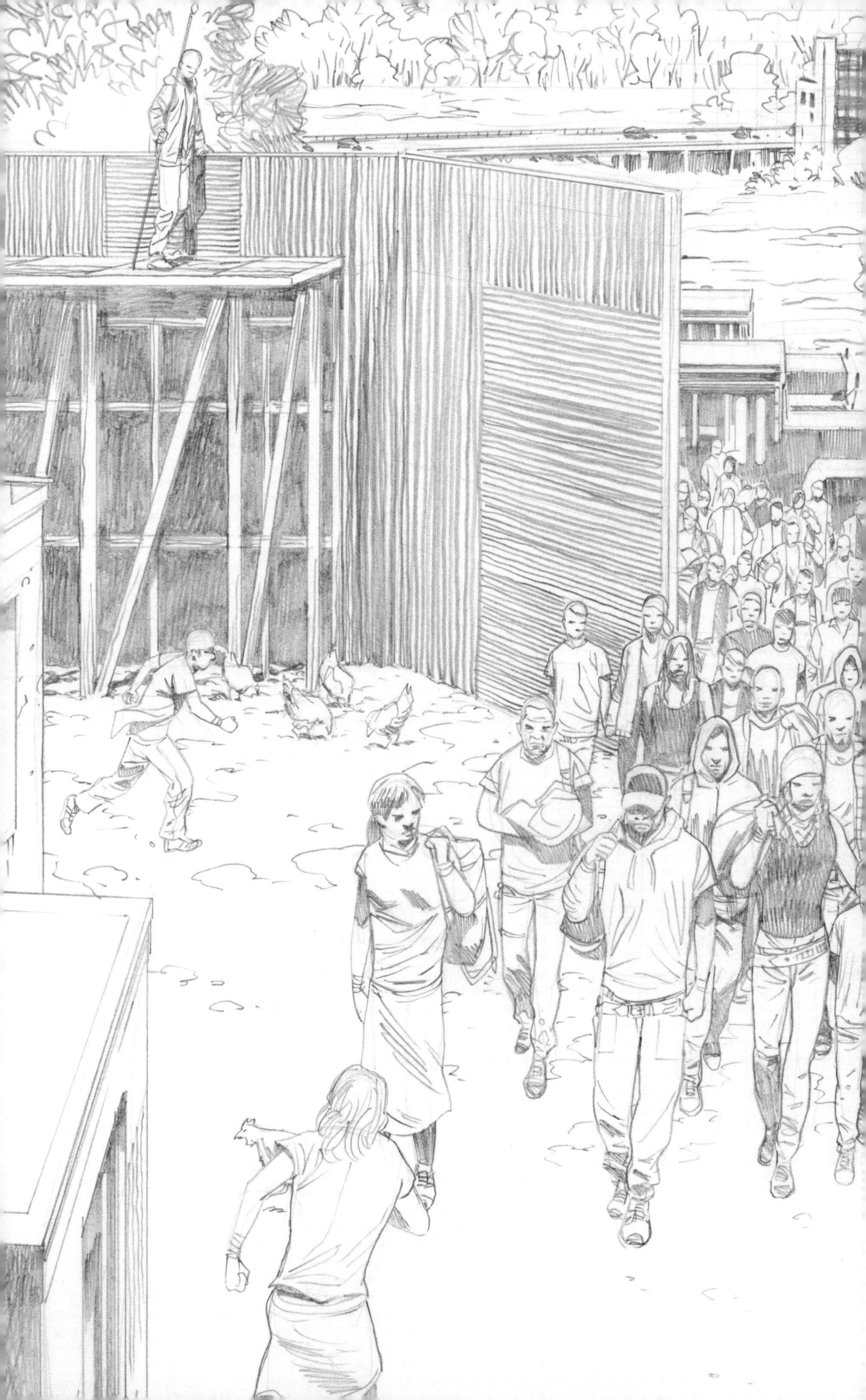

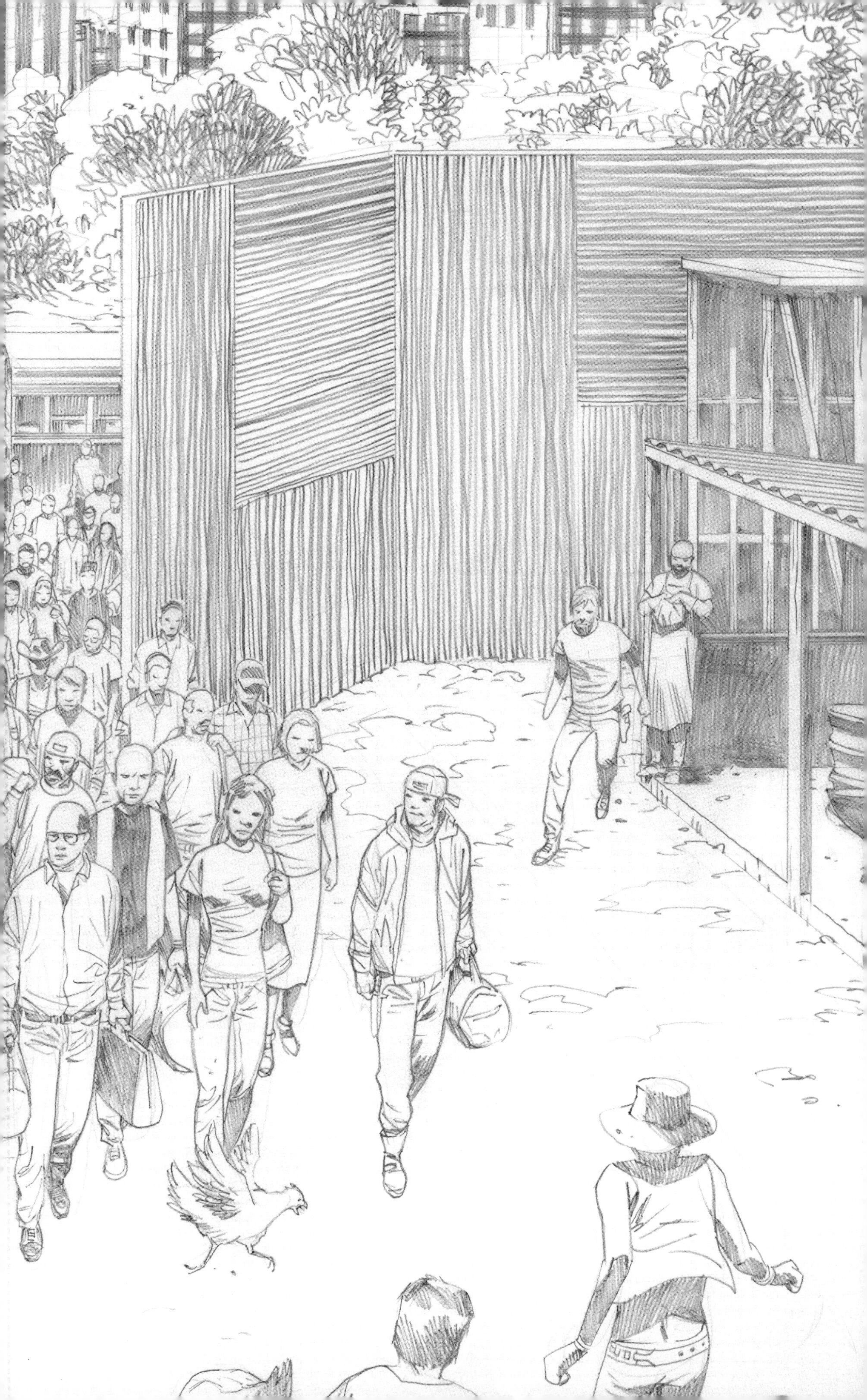

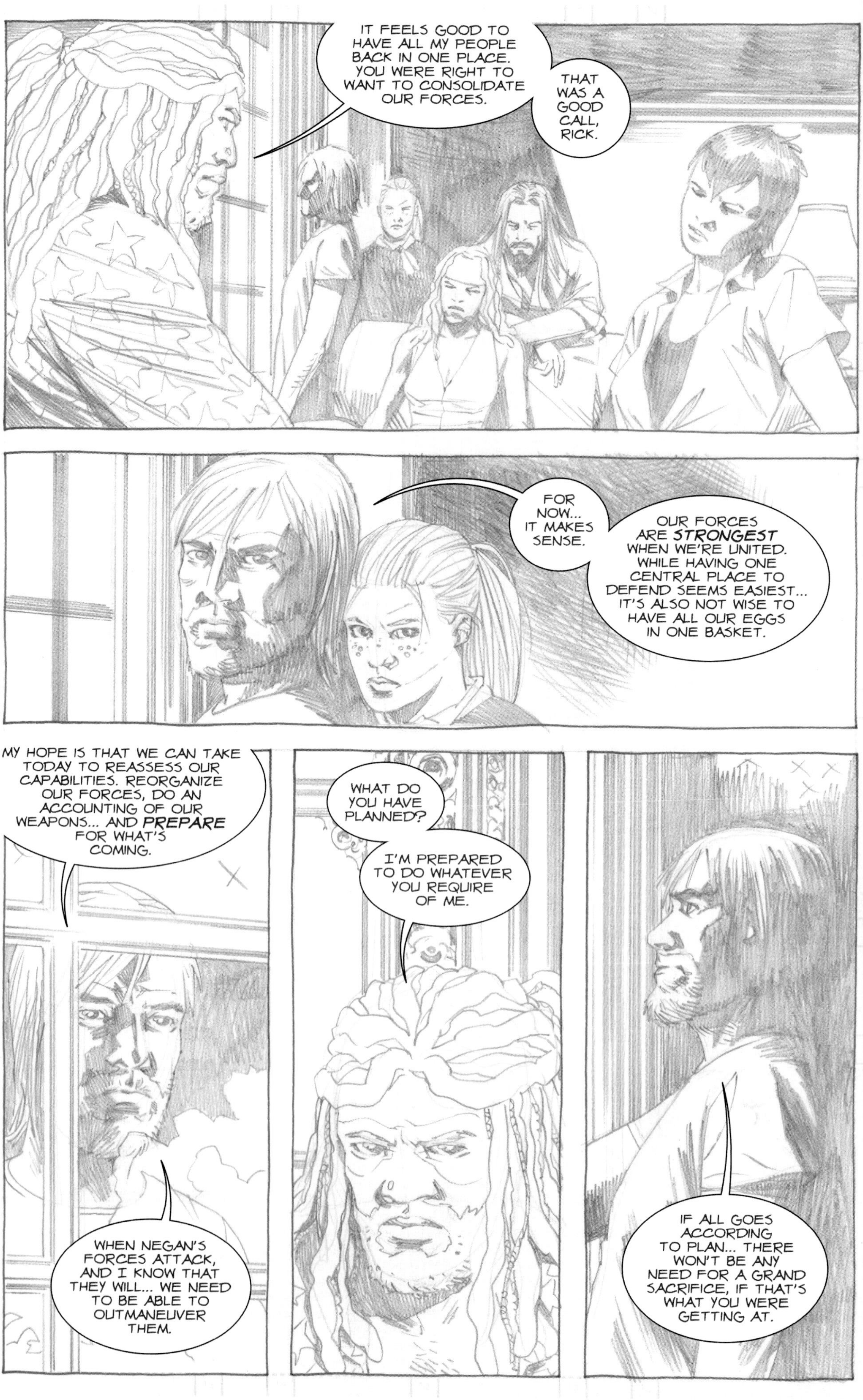
IT FEELS GOOD TO HAVE ALL MY PEOPLE BACK IN ONE PLACE. YOU WERE RIGHT TO WANT TO CONSOLIDATE OUR FORCES.
THAT WAS A GOOD CALL, RICK.
FOR NOW... IT MAKES SENSE.
OUR FORCES ARE STRONGEST WHEN WE'RE UNITED. WHILE HAVING ONE CENTRAL PLACE TO DEFEND SEEMS EASIEST... IT'S ALSO NOT WISE TO HAVE ALL OUR EGGS IN ONE BASKET.
MY HOPE IS THAT WE CAN TAKE TODAY TO REASSESS OUR CAPABILITIES. REORGANIZE OUR FORCES, DO AN ACCOUNTING OF OUR WEAPONS... AND PREPARE FOR WHAT'S COMING.
WHEN NEGAN'S FORCES ATTACK, AND I KNOW THAT THEY WILL... WE NEED TO BE ABLE TO OUTMANEUVER THEM.
WHAT DO YOU HAVE PLANNED?
I'M PREPARED TO DO WHATEVER YOU REQUIRE OF ME.
IF ALL GOES ACCORDING TO PLAN... THERE WON'T BE ANY NEED FOR A GRAND SACRIFICE, IF THAT'S WHAT YOU WERE GETTING AT.

JESUS WAS TELLING ME ABOUT A PLACE ABOUT HALF A MILE FROM HERE.

RIGHT DOWN THE ROAD, A SMALL TOWN. A FEW SHOPS, BUNCH OF HOUSES. WE CLEANED IT OUT FOR SUPPLIES.

NOT THE WORST STAGING GROUND.

RIGHT. I THINK IT'D BE A GOOD PLACE TO MOVE OUR MOST VULNERABLE PEOPLE. KEEP ALL THE BUSSES THERE, KEEP THEM MOBILE IF NEED BE.

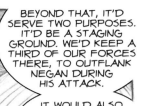
BEYOND THAT, IT'D SERVE TWO PURPOSES. IT'D BE A STAGING GROUND. WE'D KEEP A THIRD OF OUR FORCES THERE, TO OUTFLANK NEGAN DURING HIS ATTACK.

IT WOULD ALSO BE A RENDEZVOUS POINT IF THE HILLTOP FALLS.

I JUST WANT TO BE PREPARED FOR THE WORST.

ALL WE NEED IS TIME. IT'S GOING TO TAKE AT LEAST ANOTHER DAY TO SET THIS ALL IN MOTION.

LET'S HOPE NEGAN AND HIS MEN TAKE LONGER THAN THAT TO COME AFTER US.

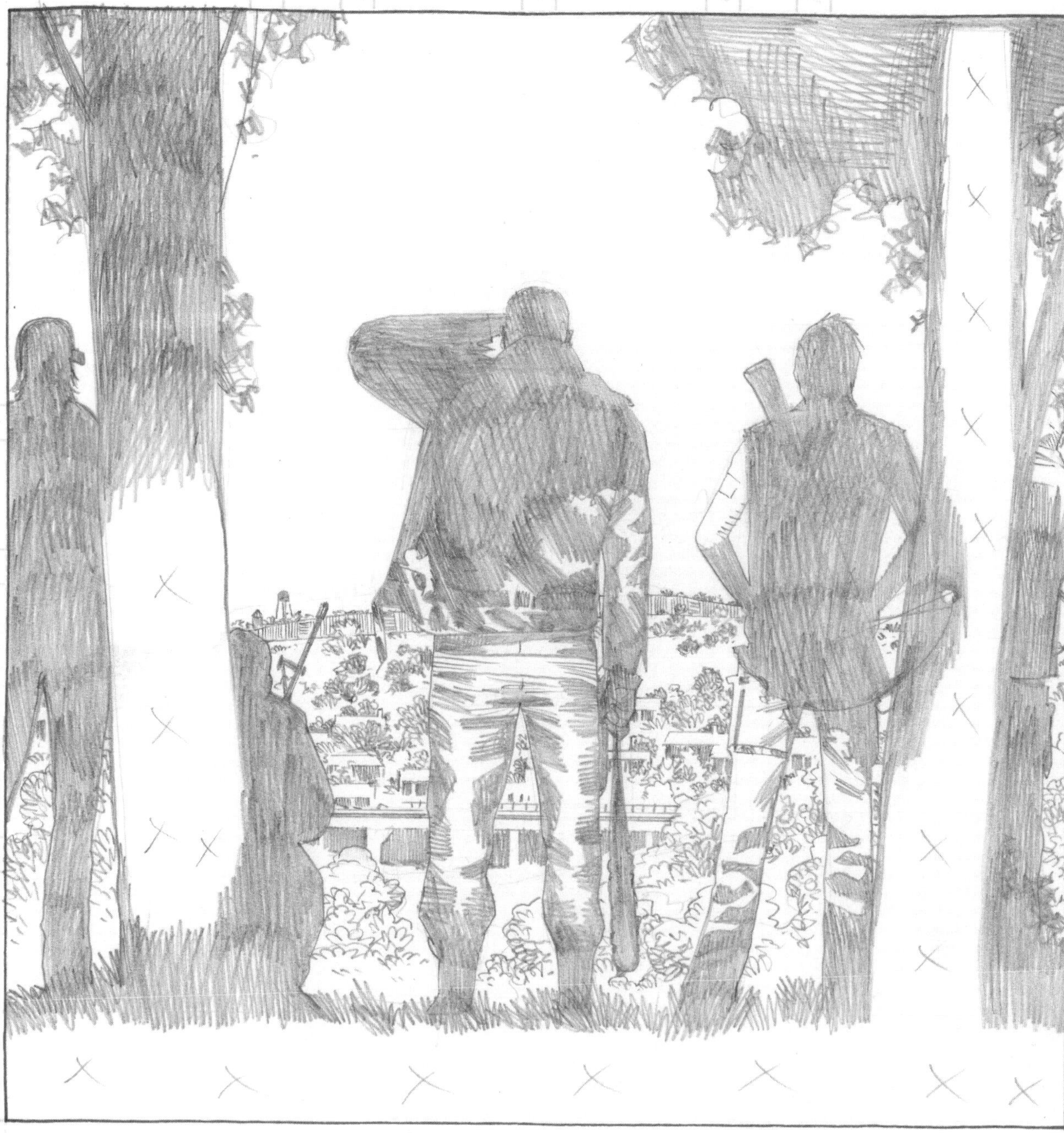

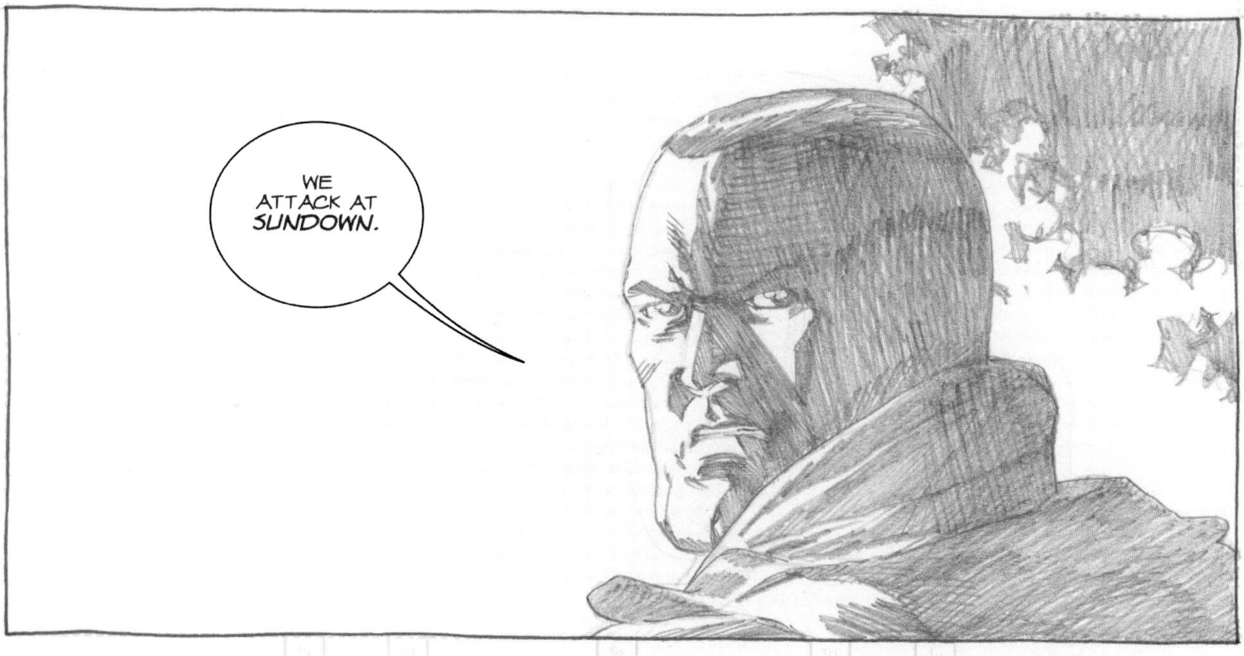
WE ATTACK AT SUNDOWN.

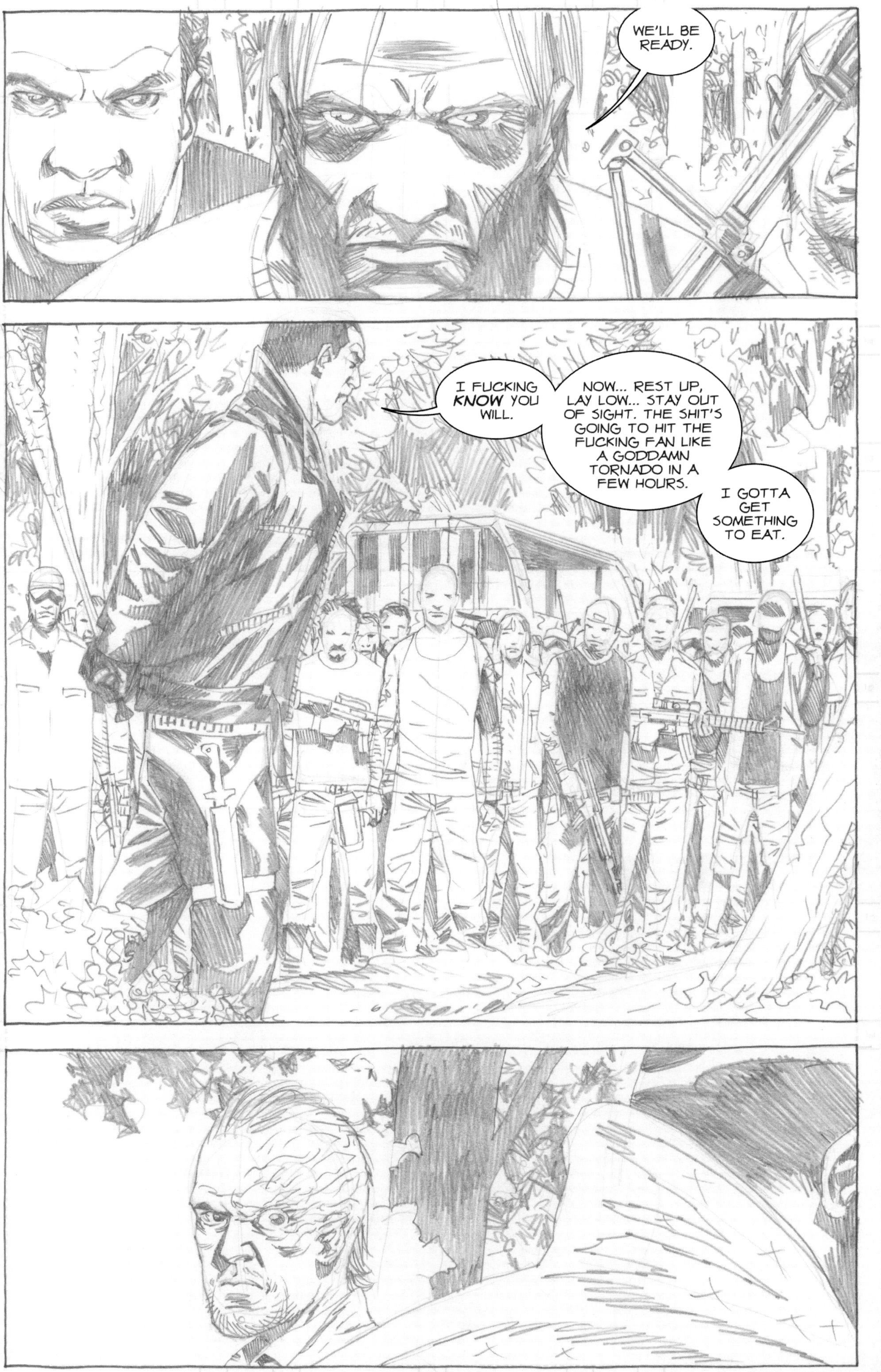
WE'LL BE READY.
I FUCKING KNOW YOU WILL.
NOW... REST UP, LAY LOW... STAY OUT OF SIGHT. THE SHIT'S GOING TO HIT THE FUCKING FAN LIKE A GODDAMN TORNADO IN A FEW HOURS.
I GOTTA GET SOMETHING TO EAT.

HUH?

COME ON... WE'RE GOING TO HAVE TO HURRY. THERE'S BARELY ANYONE HERE, BUT IT'D STILL BE BETTER IF WE SLIPPED OUT UNSEEN.

WHAT? WHY ARE YOU DOING THIS?

IN THE GRAND SCHEME OF THINGS... DOES THAT REALLY MATTER RIGHT NOW?

AN EXCELLENT POINT.

WHERE ARE MY FRIENDS?

THIS WAY.

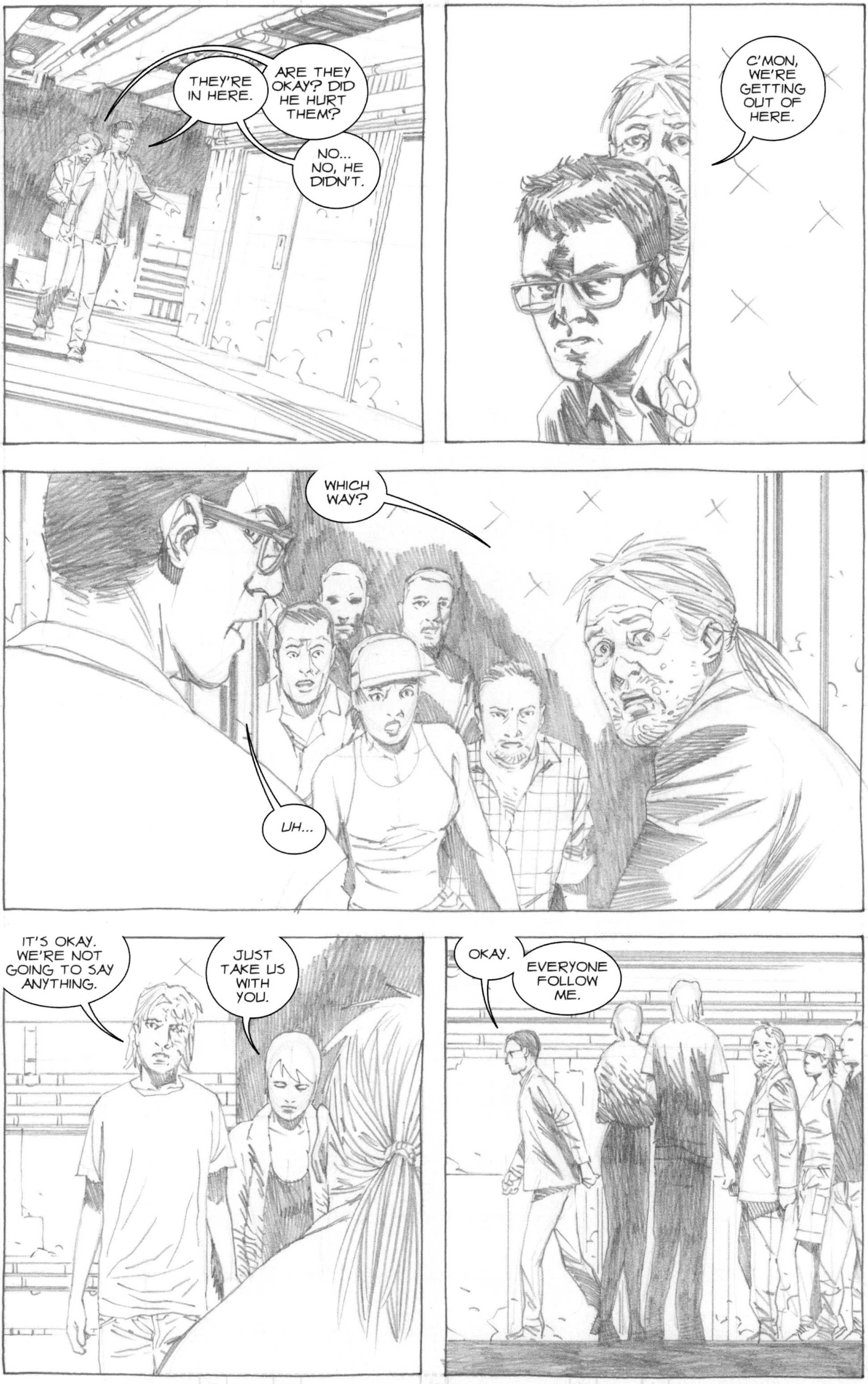
THEY'RE IN HERE.
ARE THEY OKAY? DID HE HURT THEM?
NO... NO, HE DIDN'T.
C'MON, WE'RE GETTING OUT OF HERE.
WHICH WAY?
UH...
IT'S OKAY. WE'RE NOT GOING TO SAY ANYTHING.
JUST TAKE US WITH YOU.
OKAY.
EVERYONE FOLLOW ME.

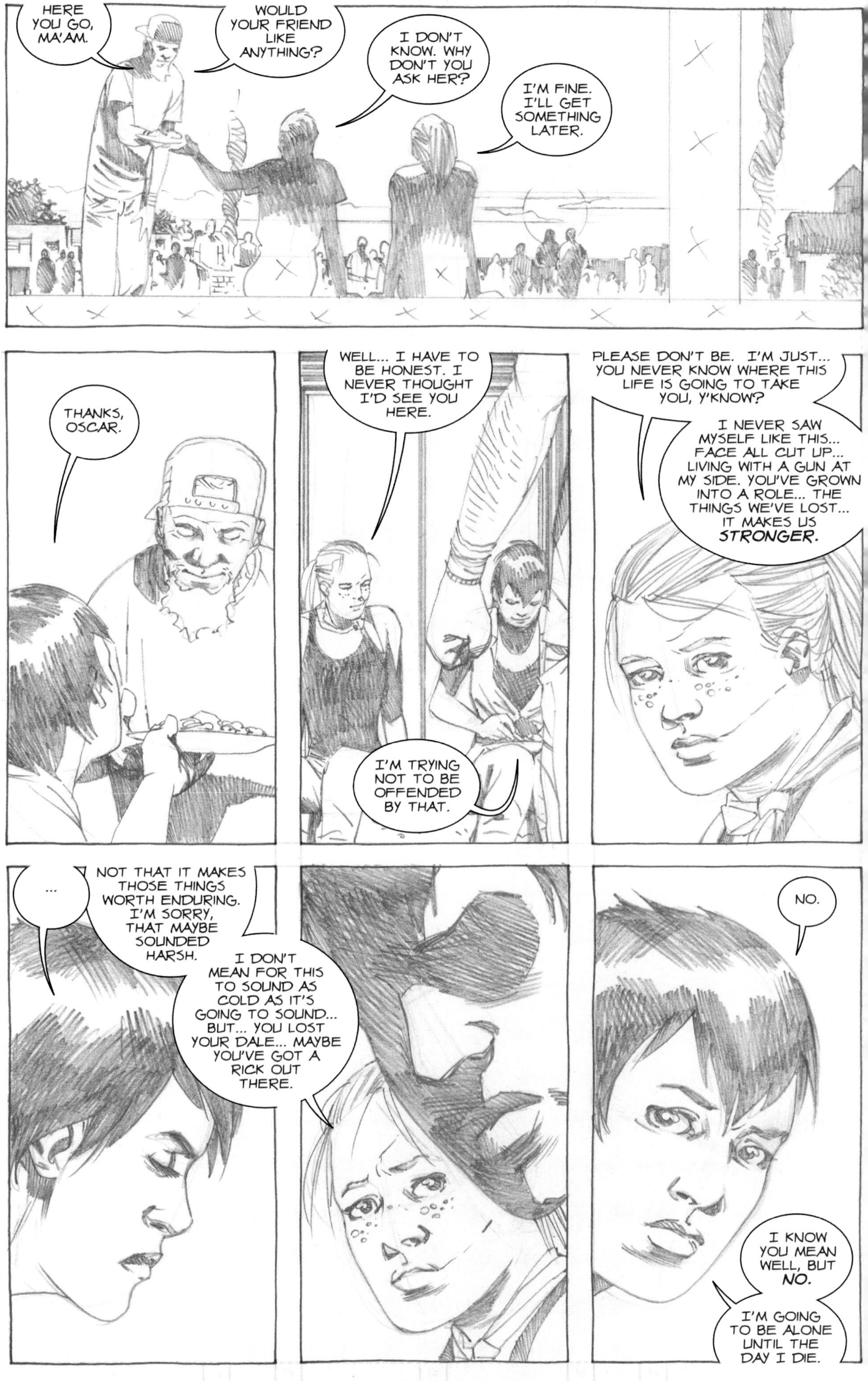
HERE YOU GO, MA'AM.
WOULD YOUR FRIEND LIKE ANYTHING?
I DON'T KNOW. WHY DON'T YOU ASK HER?
I'M FINE. I'LL GET SOMETHING LATER.
THANKS, OSCAR.
WELL... I HAVE TO BE HONEST. I NEVER THOUGHT I'D SEE YOU HERE.
I'M TRYING NOT TO BE OFFENDED BY THAT.
PLEASE DON'T BE. I'M JUST... YOU NEVER KNOW WHERE THIS LIFE IS GOING TO TAKE YOU, Y'KNOW?
I NEVER SAW MYSELF LIKE THIS... FACE ALL CUT UP... LIVING WITH A GUN AT MY SIDE. YOU'VE GROWN INTO A ROLE... THE THINGS WE'VE LOST... IT MAKES US STRONGER.
...
NOT THAT IT MAKES THOSE THINGS WORTH ENDURING. I'M SORRY, THAT MAYBE SOUNDED HARSH.
I DON'T MEAN FOR THIS TO SOUND AS COLD AS IT'S GOING TO SOUND... BUT... YOU LOST YOUR DALE... MAYBE YOU'VE GOT A RICK OUT THERE.
NO.
I KNOW YOU MEAN WELL, BUT NO.
I'M GOING TO BE ALONE UNTIL THE DAY I DIE.

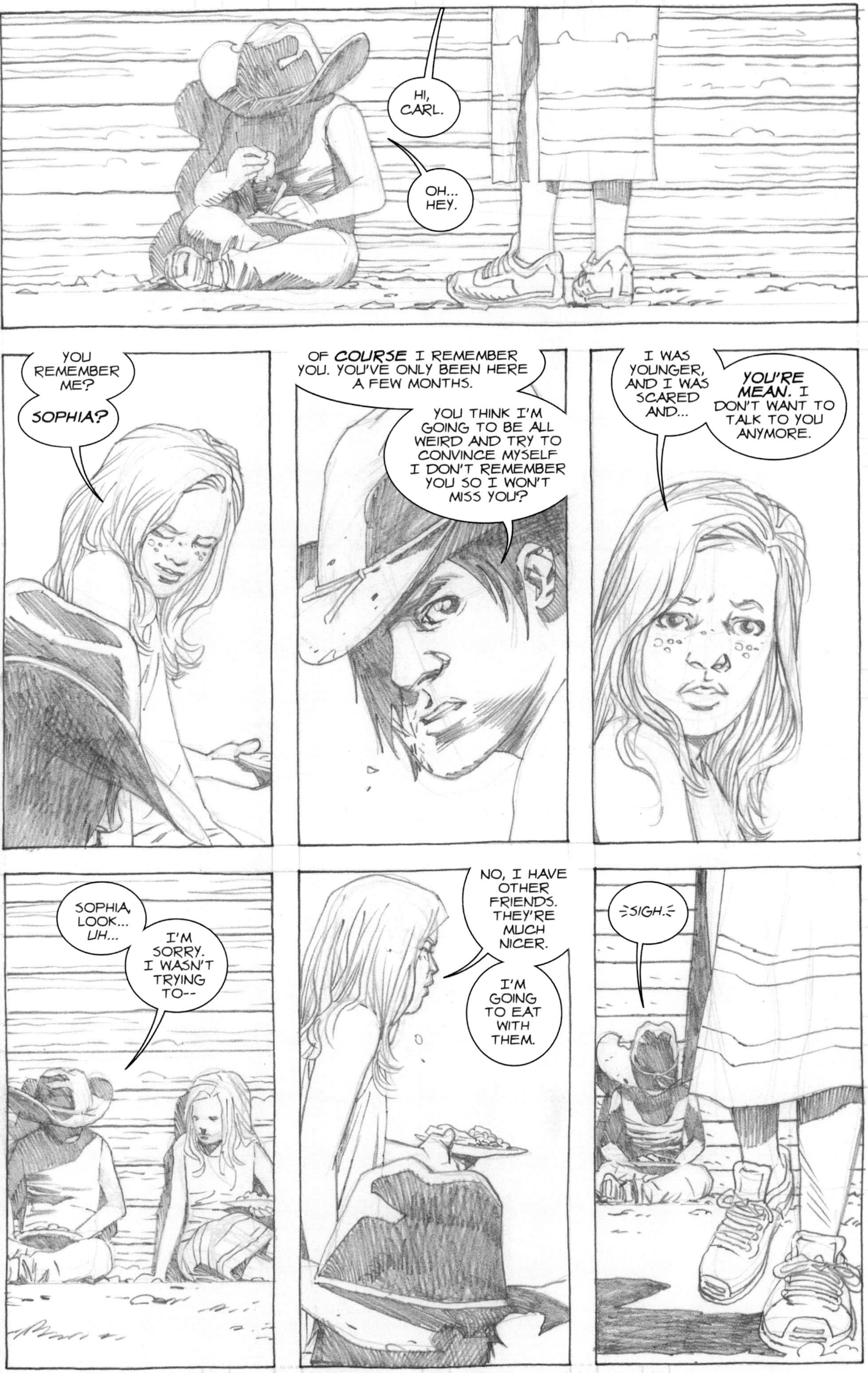
HI, CARL.
OH... HEY.
YOU REMEMBER ME?
SOPHIA?
OF COURSE I REMEMBER YOU. YOU'VE ONLY BEEN HERE A FEW MONTHS.
YOU THINK I'M GOING TO BE ALL WEIRD AND TRY TO CONVINCE MYSELF I DON'T REMEMBER YOU SO I WON'T MISS YOU?
I WAS YOUNGER, AND I WAS SCARED AND...
YOU'RE MEAN. I DON'T WANT TO TALK TO YOU ANYMORE.
SOPHIA, LOOK... UH...
I'M SORRY. I WASN'T TRYING TO--
NO, I HAVE OTHER FRIENDS. THEY'RE MUCH NICER.
I'M GOING TO EAT WITH THEM.
SIGH.

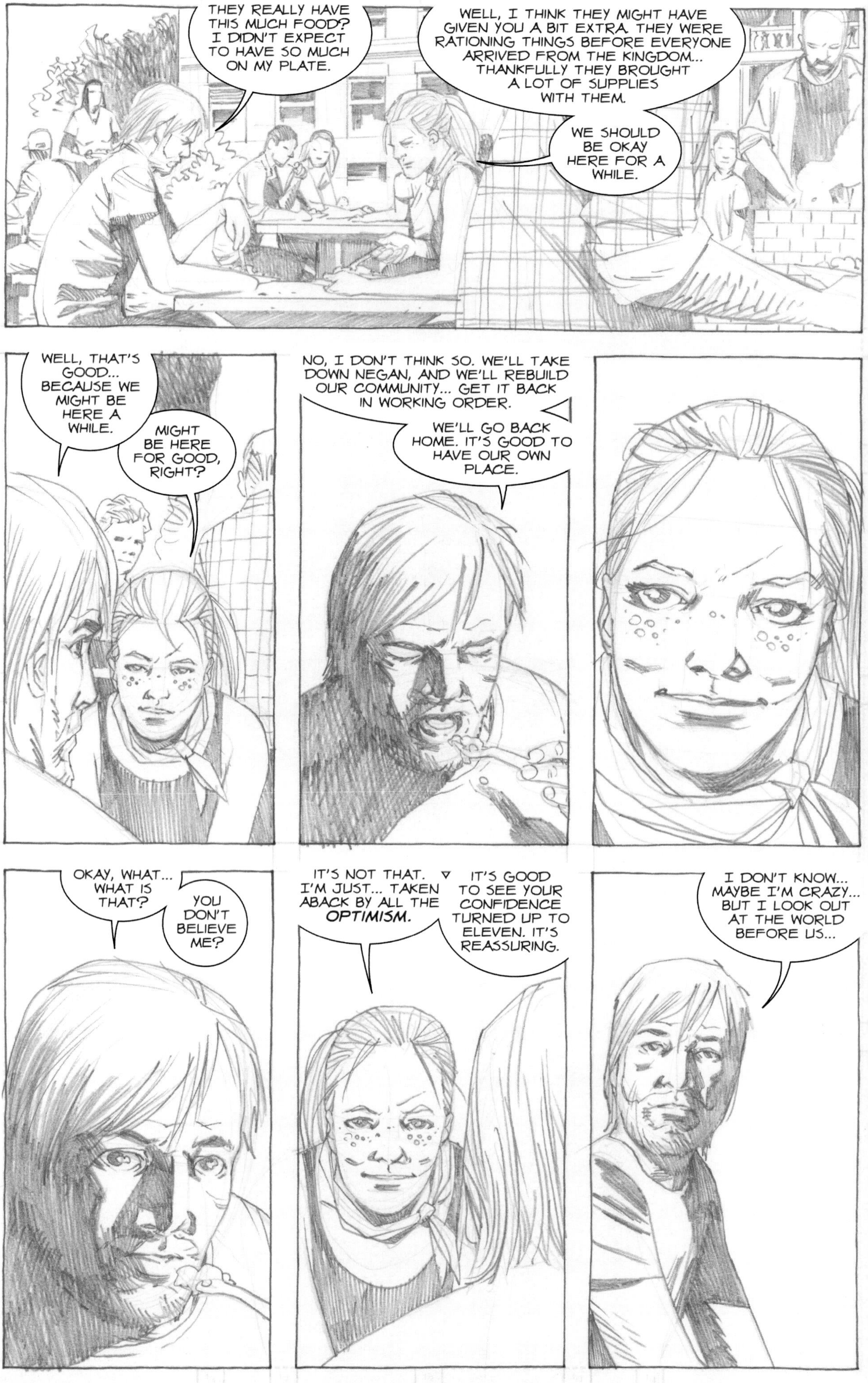
THEY REALLY HAVE THIS MUCH FOOD? I DIDN'T EXPECT TO HAVE SO MUCH ON MY PLATE.
WELL, I THINK THEY MIGHT HAVE GIVEN YOU A BIT EXTRA. THEY WERE RATIONING THINGS BEFORE EVERYONE ARRIVED FROM THE KINGDOM... THANKFULLY THEY BROUGHT A LOT OF SUPPLIES WITH THEM.
WE SHOULD BE OKAY HERE FOR A WHILE.
WELL, THAT'S GOOD... BECAUSE WE MIGHT BE HERE A WHILE.
MIGHT BE HERE FOR GOOD, RIGHT?
NO, I DON'T THINK SO. WE'LL TAKE DOWN NEGAN, AND WE'LL REBUILD OUR COMMUNITY... GET IT BACK IN WORKING ORDER.
WE'LL GO BACK HOME. IT'S GOOD TO HAVE OUR OWN PLACE.
OKAY, WHAT... WHAT IS THAT?
YOU DON'T BELIEVE ME?
IT'S NOT THAT. I'M JUST... TAKEN ABACK BY ALL THE *OPTIMISM.*
IT'S GOOD TO SEE YOUR CONFIDENCE TURNED UP TO ELEVEN. IT'S REASSURING.
I DON'T KNOW... MAYBE I'M CRAZY... BUT I LOOK OUT AT THE WORLD BEFORE US...

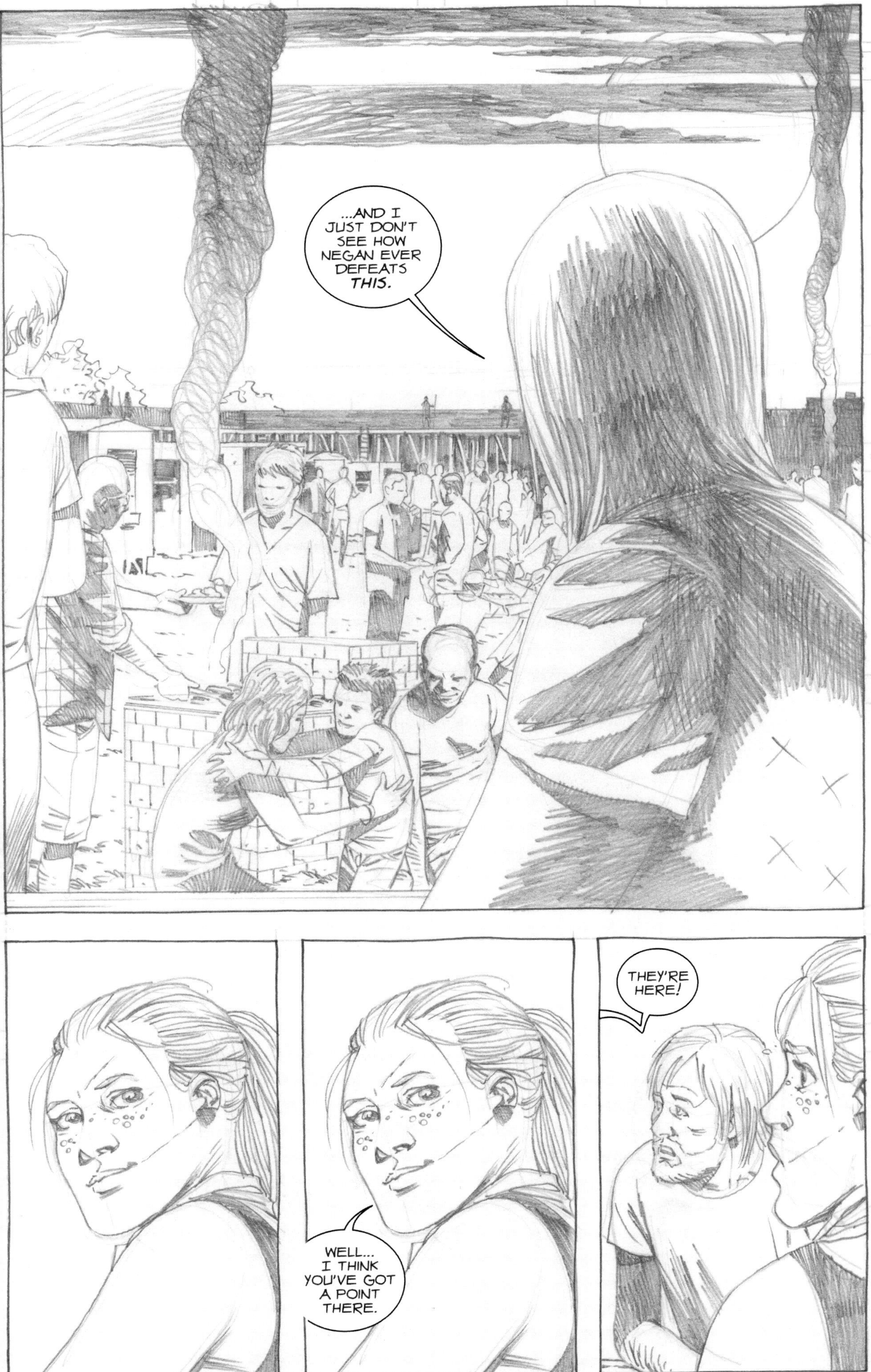
...AND I JUST DON'T SEE HOW NEGAN EVER DEFEATS *THIS.*
WELL... I THINK YOU'VE GOT A POINT THERE.
THEY'RE HERE!

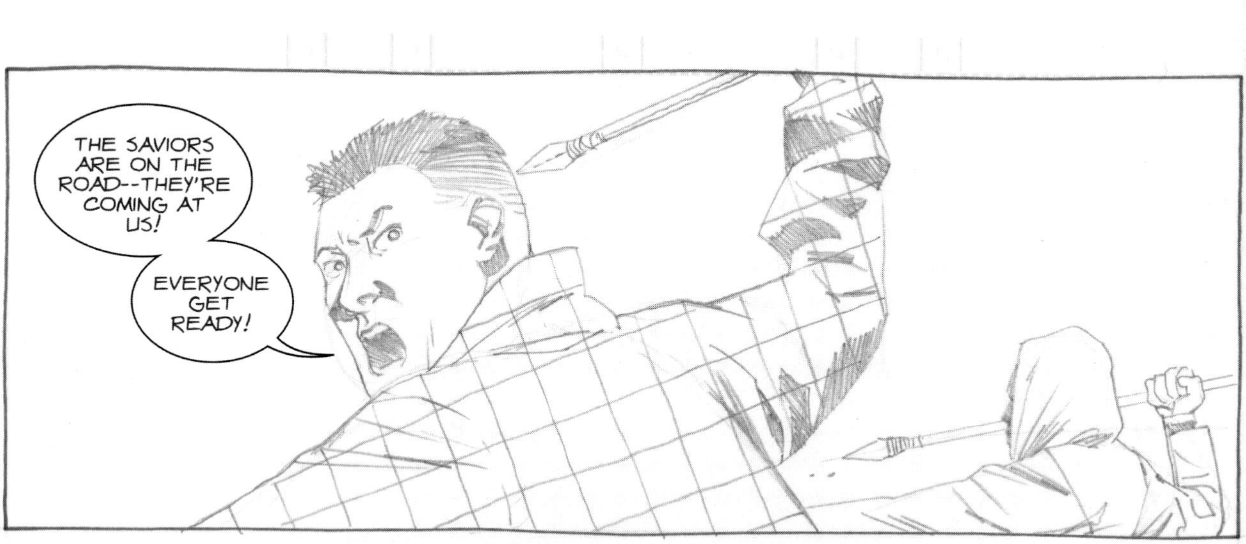
THE SAVIORS ARE ON THE ROAD--THEY'RE COMING AT US!
EVERYONE GET READY!

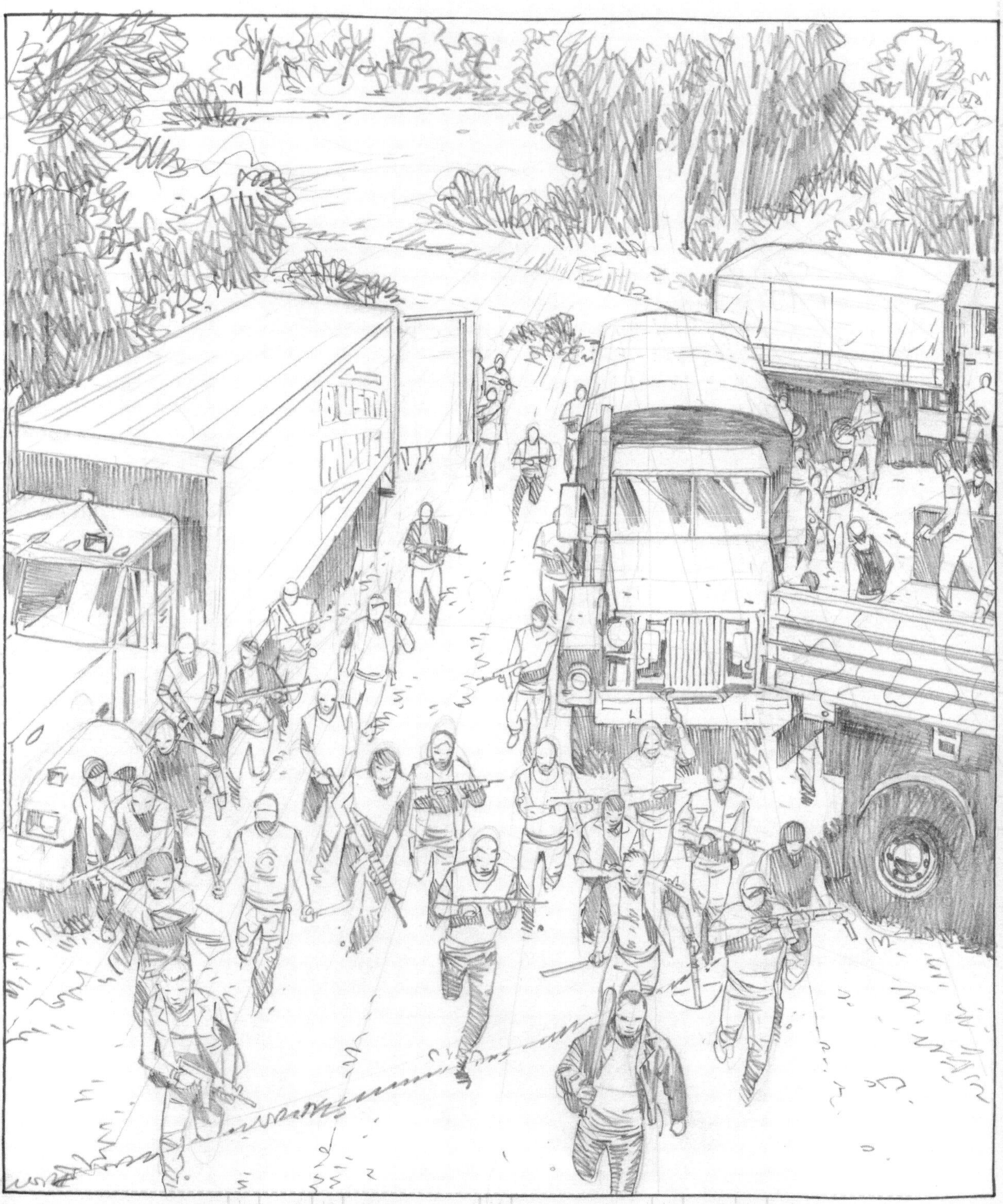

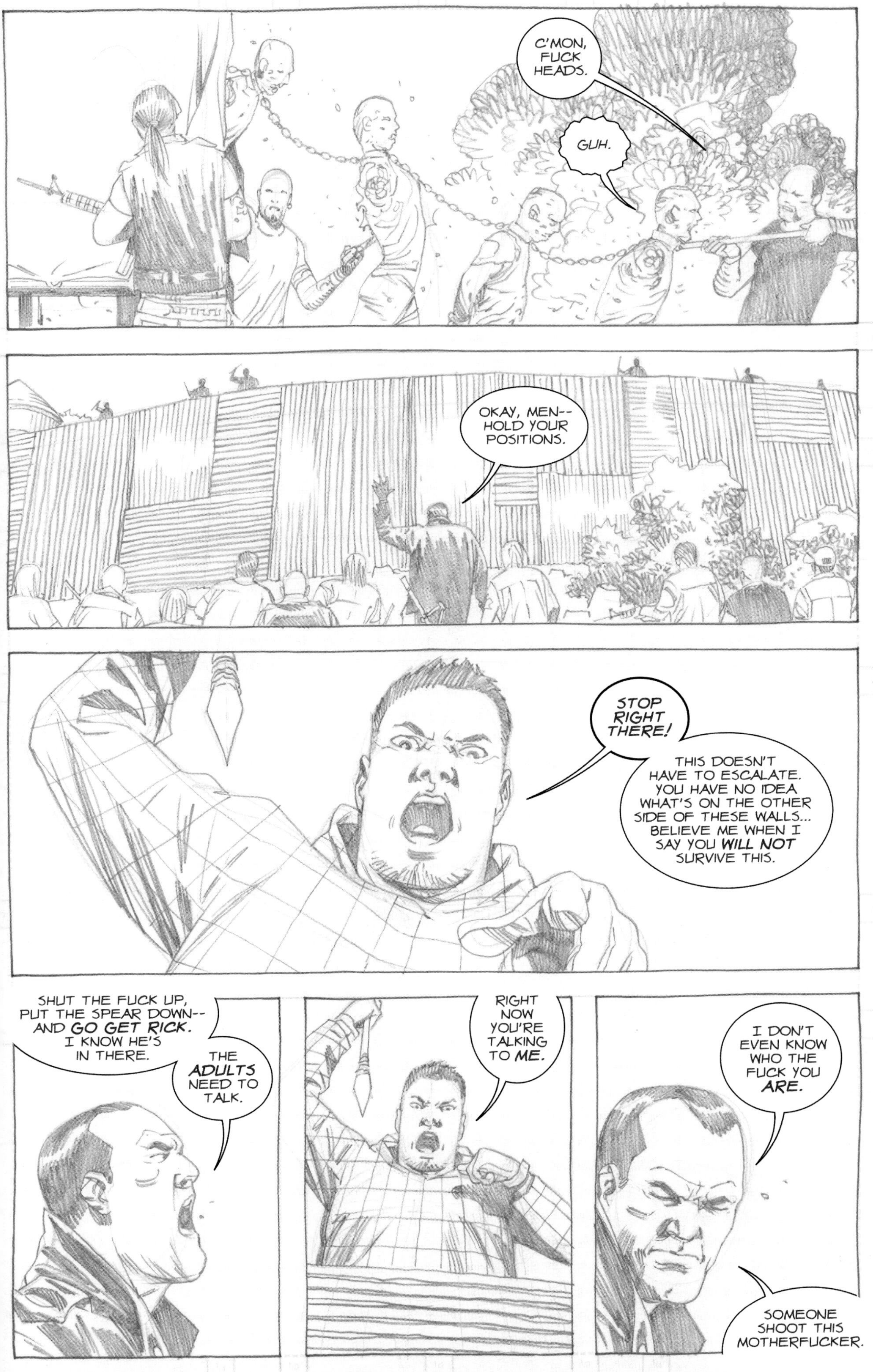
C'MON, FUCK HEADS.
GUH.
OKAY, MEN-- HOLD YOUR POSITIONS.
STOP RIGHT THERE!
THIS DOESN'T HAVE TO ESCALATE. YOU HAVE NO IDEA WHAT'S ON THE OTHER SIDE OF THESE WALLS... BELIEVE ME WHEN I SAY YOU WILL NOT SURVIVE THIS.
SHUT THE FUCK UP, PUT THE SPEAR DOWN-- AND GO GET RICK. I KNOW HE'S IN THERE.
THE ADULTS NEED TO TALK.
RIGHT NOW YOU'RE TALKING TO ME.
I DON'T EVEN KNOW WHO THE FUCK YOU ARE.
SOMEONE SHOOT THIS MOTHERFUCKER.

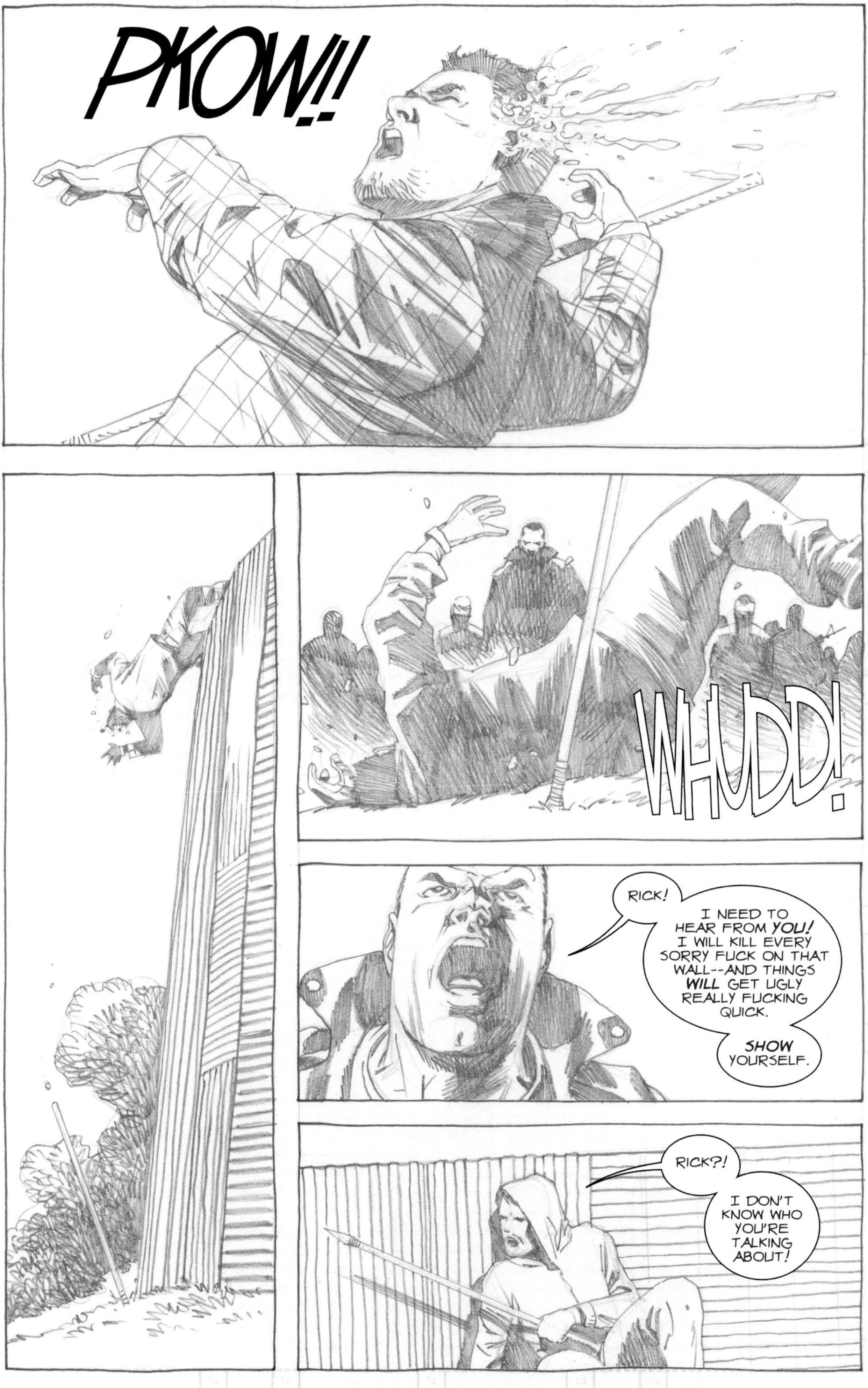
PKOW!!
WHUDD!
RICK!
I NEED TO HEAR FROM YOU! I WILL KILL EVERY SORRY FUCK ON THAT WALL--AND THINGS WILL GET UGLY REALLY FUCKING QUICK.
SHOW YOURSELF.
RICK?!
I DON'T KNOW WHO YOU'RE TALKING ABOUT!

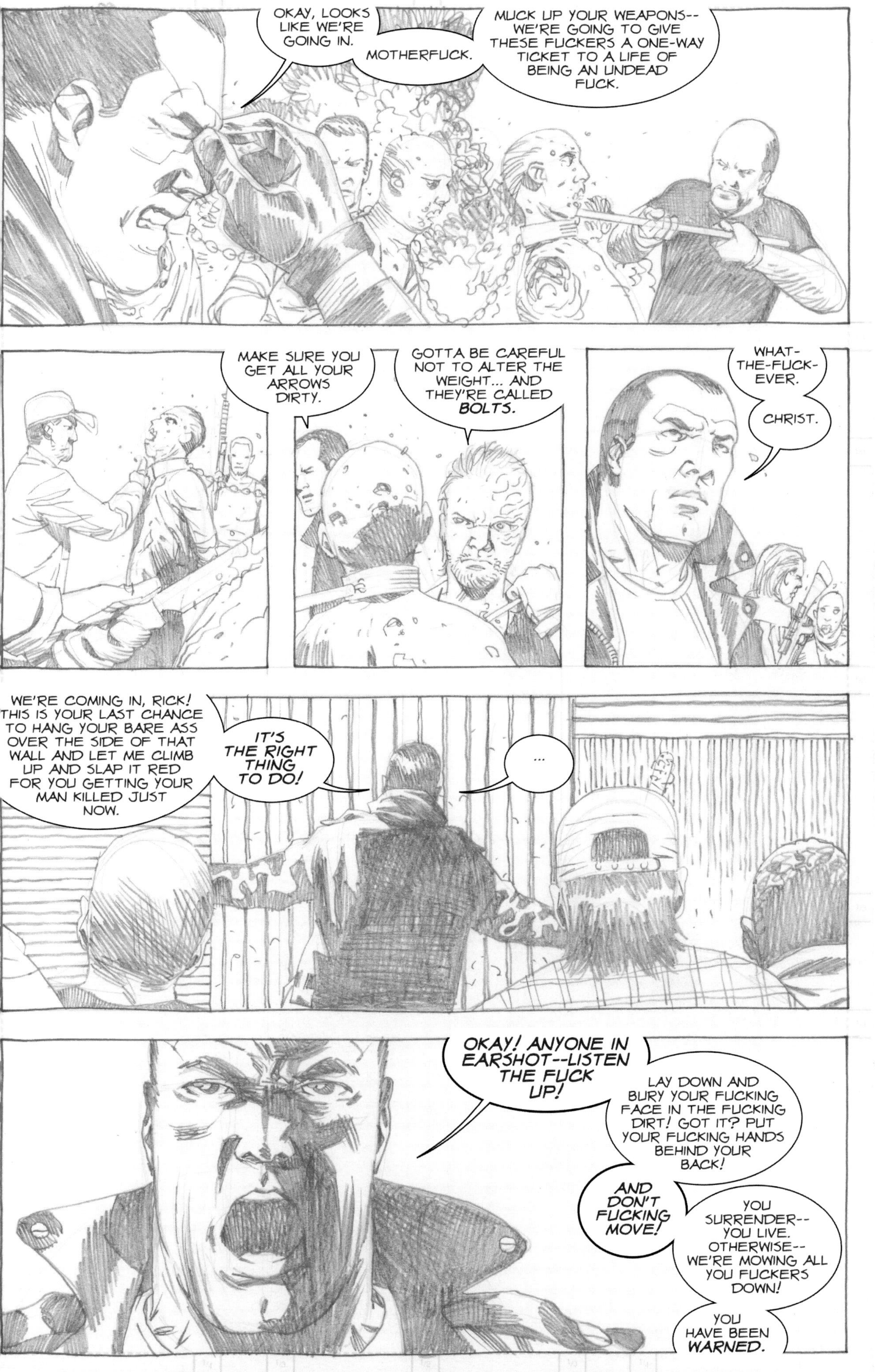
OKAY, LOOKS LIKE WE'RE GOING IN.
MOTHERFUCK.
MUCK UP YOUR WEAPONS-- WE'RE GOING TO GIVE THESE FUCKERS A ONE-WAY TICKET TO A LIFE OF BEING AN UNDEAD FUCK.
MAKE SURE YOU GET ALL YOUR ARROWS DIRTY.
GOTTA BE CAREFUL NOT TO ALTER THE WEIGHT... AND THEY'RE CALLED BOLTS.
WHAT-THE-FUCK-EVER.
CHRIST.
WE'RE COMING IN, RICK! THIS IS YOUR LAST CHANCE TO HANG YOUR BARE ASS OVER THE SIDE OF THAT WALL AND LET ME CLIMB UP AND SLAP IT RED FOR YOU GETTING YOUR MAN KILLED JUST NOW.
IT'S THE RIGHT THING TO DO!
...
OKAY! ANYONE IN EARSHOT--LISTEN THE FUCK UP!
LAY DOWN AND BURY YOUR FUCKING FACE IN THE FUCKING DIRT! GOT IT? PUT YOUR FUCKING HANDS BEHIND YOUR BACK!
AND DON'T FUCKING MOVE!
YOU SURRENDER-- YOU LIVE. OTHERWISE-- WE'RE MOWING ALL YOU FUCKERS DOWN!
YOU HAVE BEEN WARNED.

TAKE IT
DOWN!

WRAMM!

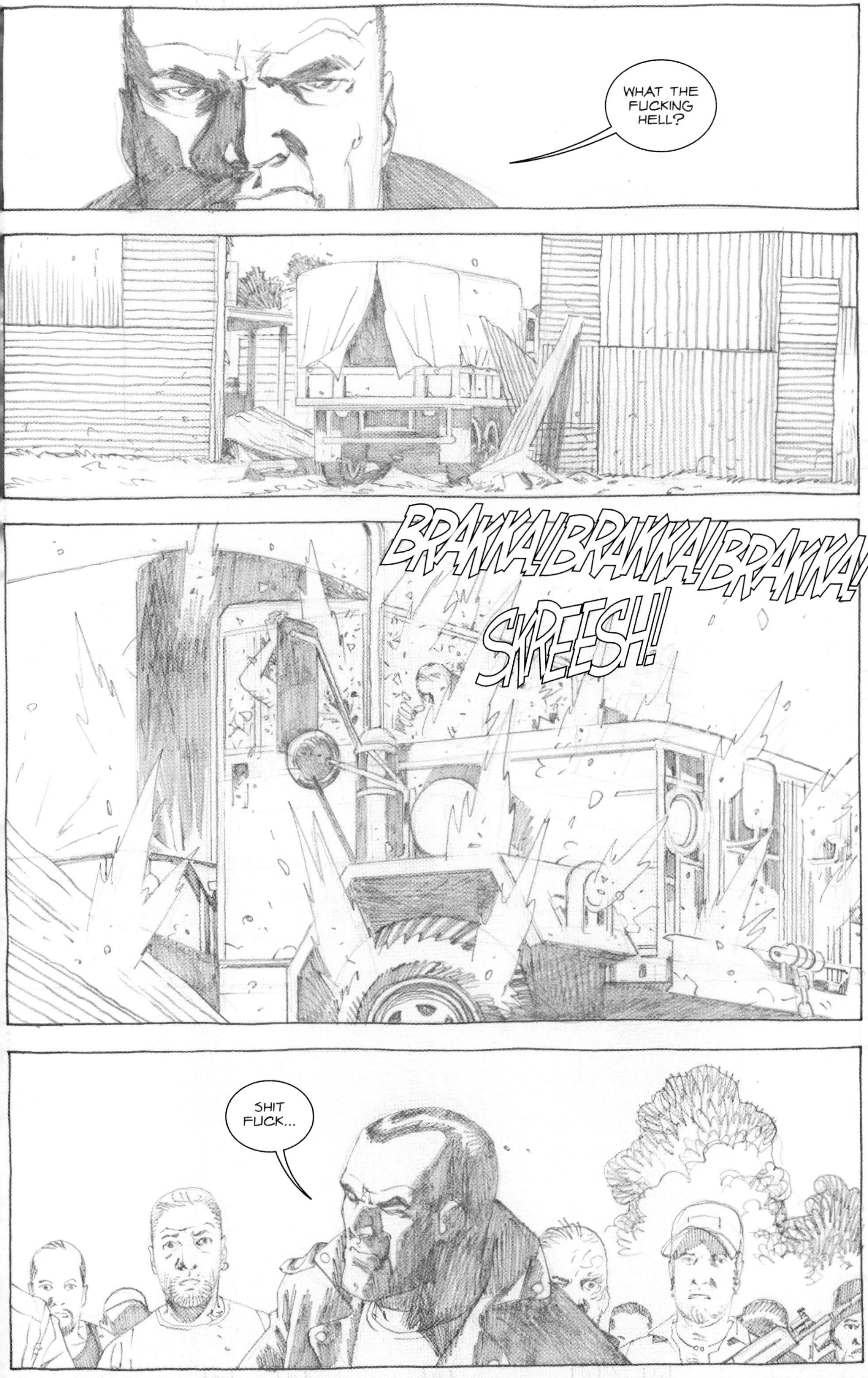
WHAT THE FUCKING HELL?
BRAKKA! BRAKKA! BRAKKA!
SKREESH!
SHIT FUCK...

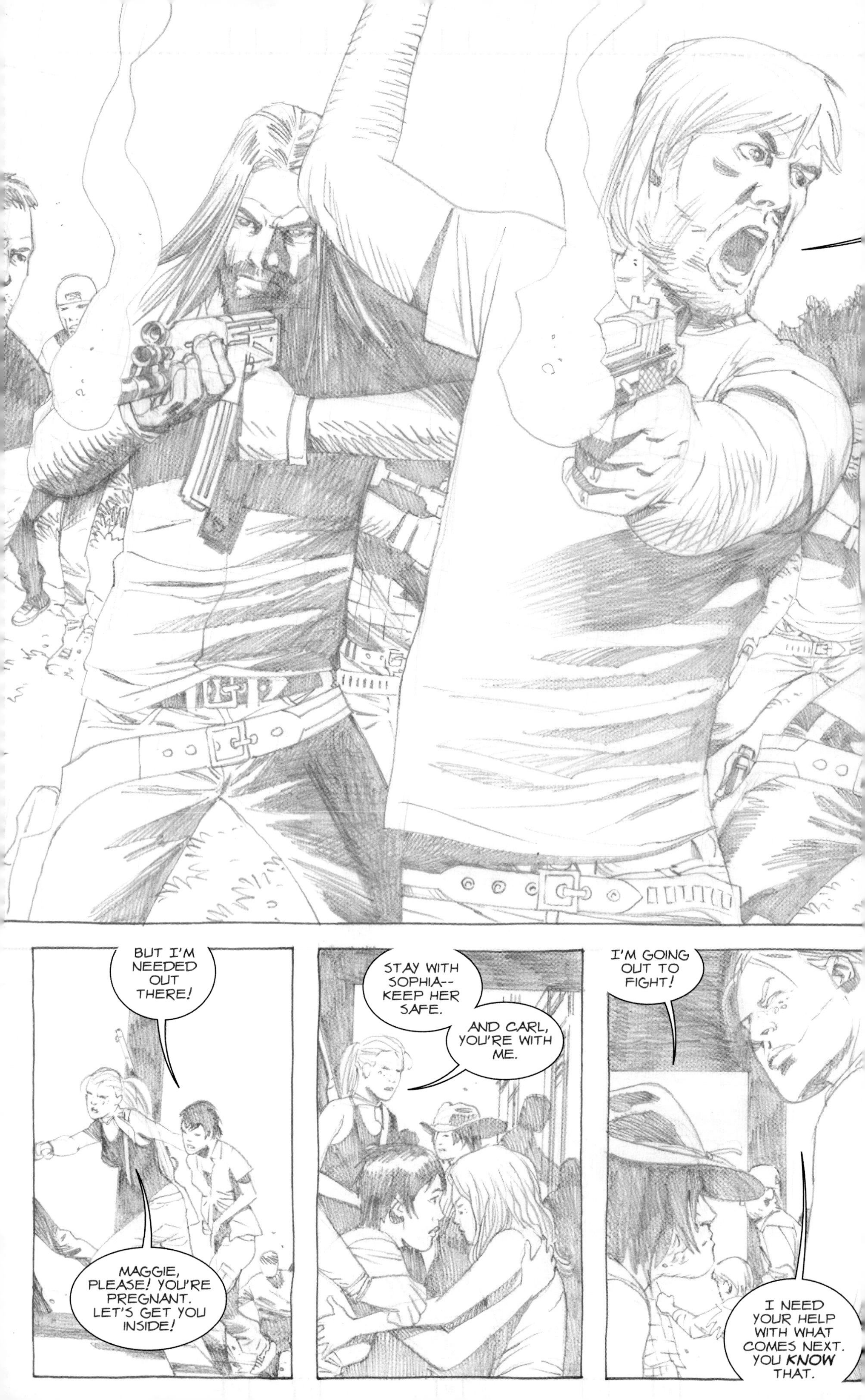
BUT I'M NEEDED OUT THERE!
MAGGIE, PLEASE! YOU'RE PREGNANT. LET'S GET YOU INSIDE!
STAY WITH SOPHIA-- KEEP HER SAFE.
AND CARL, YOU'RE WITH ME.
I'M GOING OUT TO FIGHT!
I NEED YOUR HELP WITH WHAT COMES NEXT. YOU KNOW THAT.

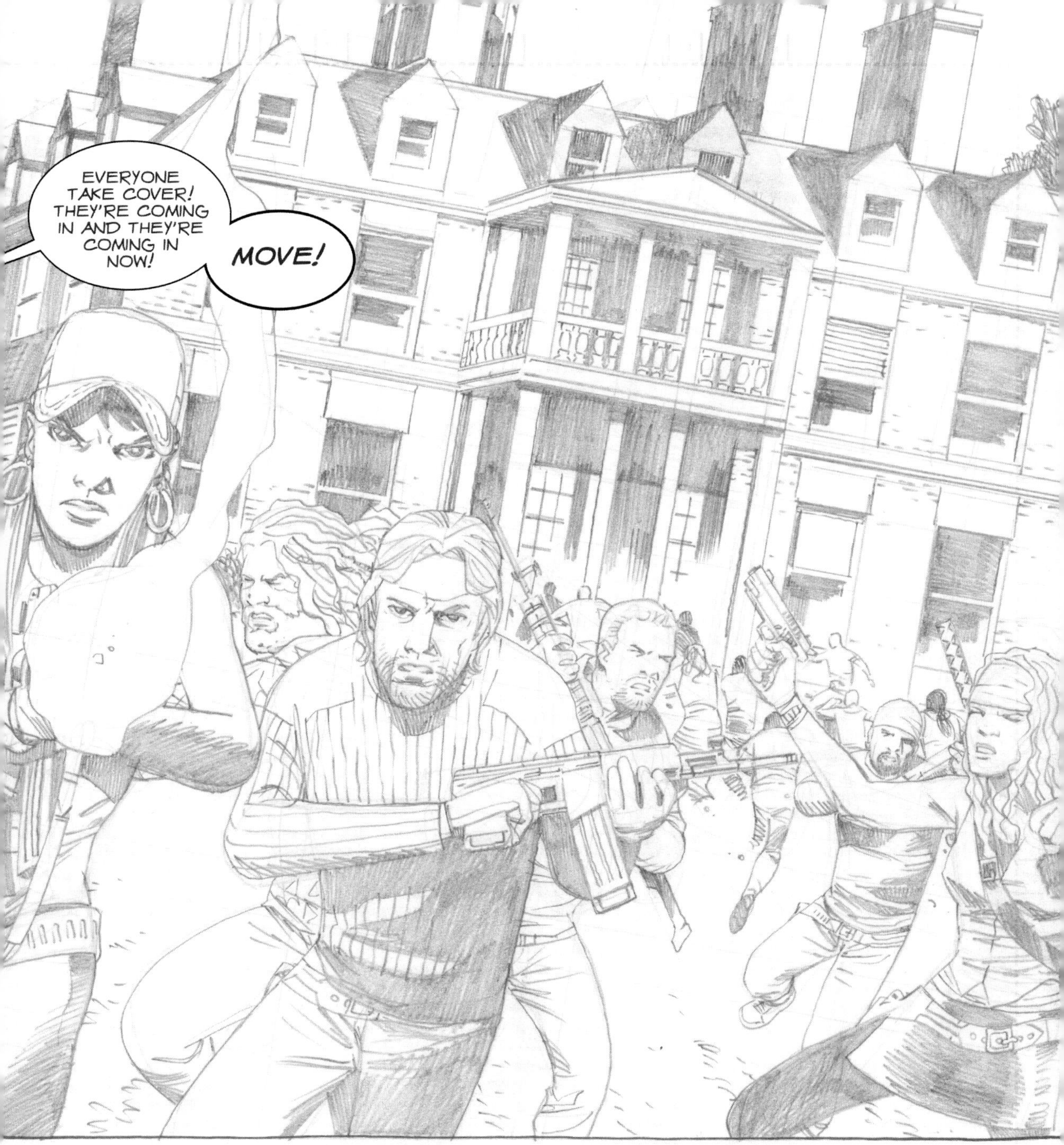
EVERYONE TAKE COVER! THEY'RE COMING IN AND THEY'RE COMING IN NOW!
MOVE!

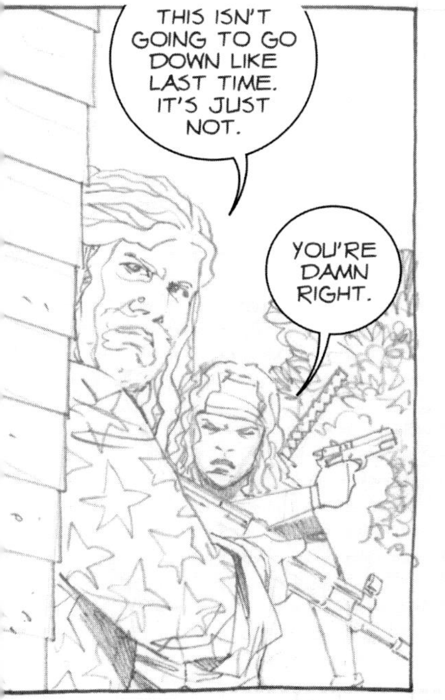
THIS ISN'T GOING TO GO DOWN LIKE LAST TIME. IT'S JUST NOT.
YOU'RE DAMN RIGHT.

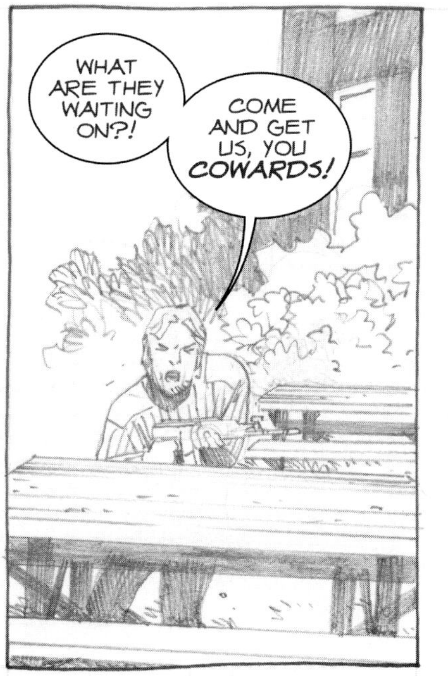
WHAT ARE THEY WAITING ON?!
COME AND GET US, YOU COWARDS!

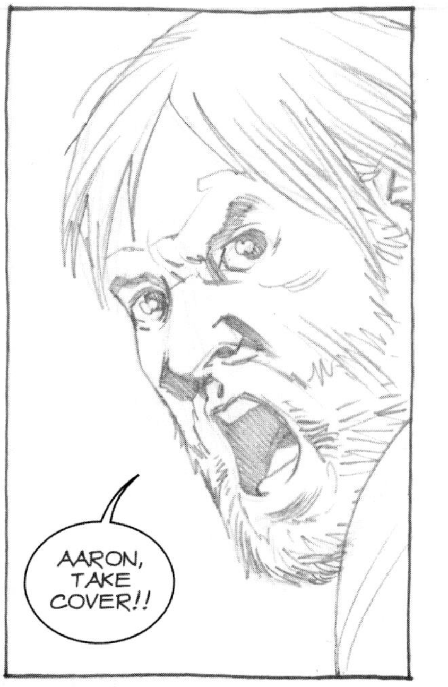
AARON, TAKE COVER!!

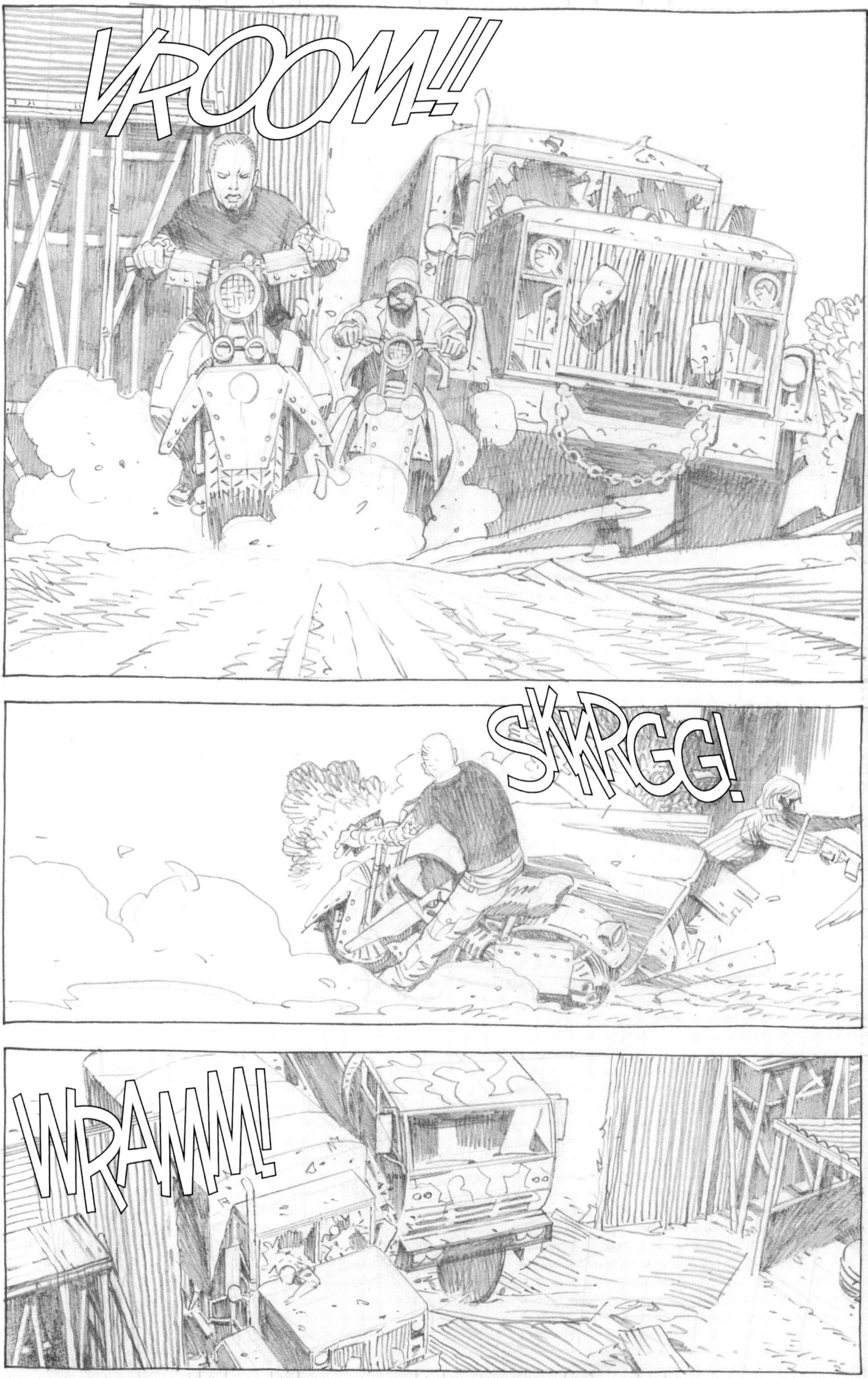
VROOM!!
SKRGG!
WRAMM!

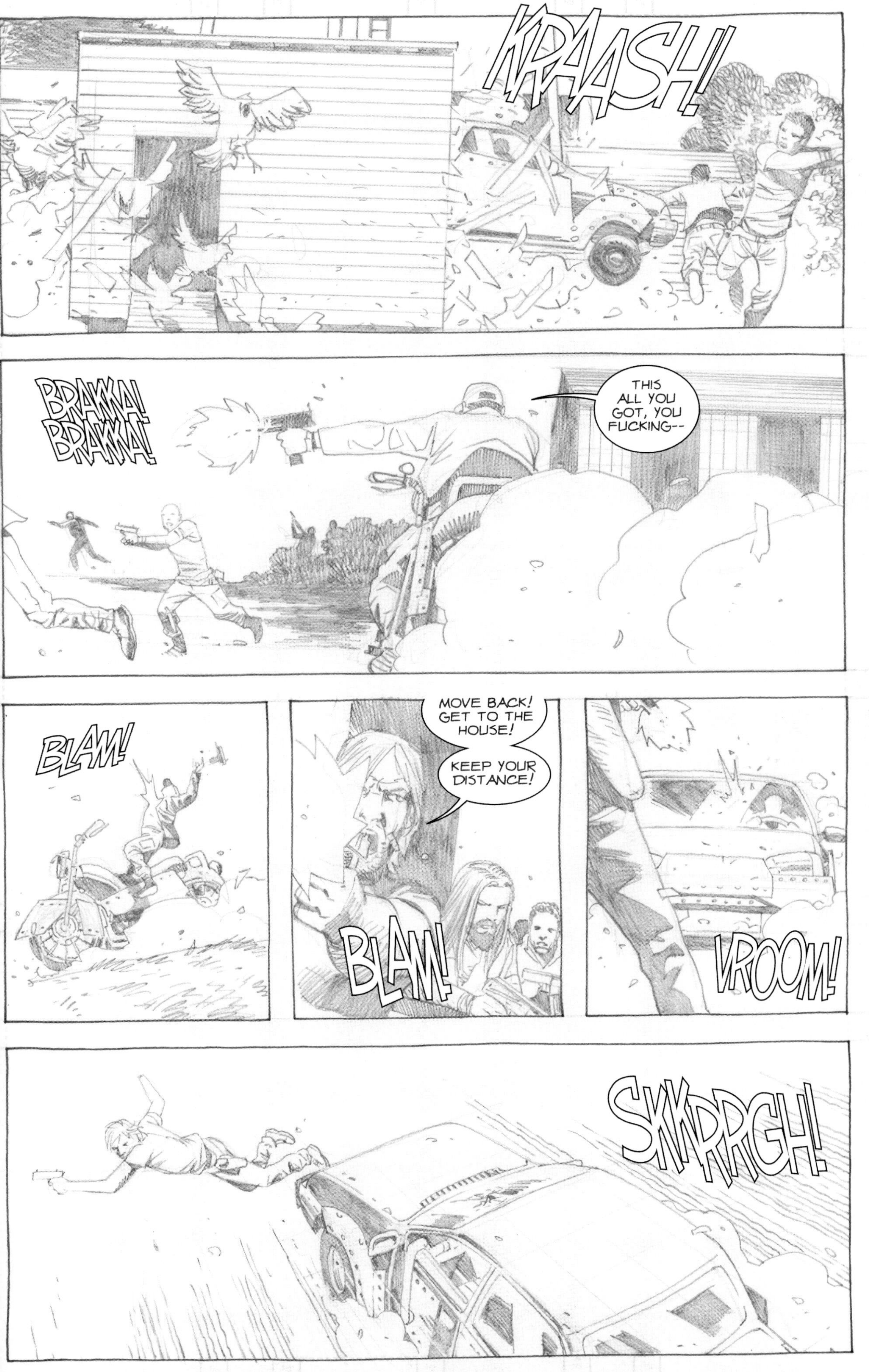
KRAASH!
BRAKKA! BRAKKA!
THIS ALL YOU GOT, YOU FUCKING--
BLAM!
MOVE BACK! GET TO THE HOUSE!
KEEP YOUR DISTANCE!
BLAM!
VROOM!
SKKRRGH!

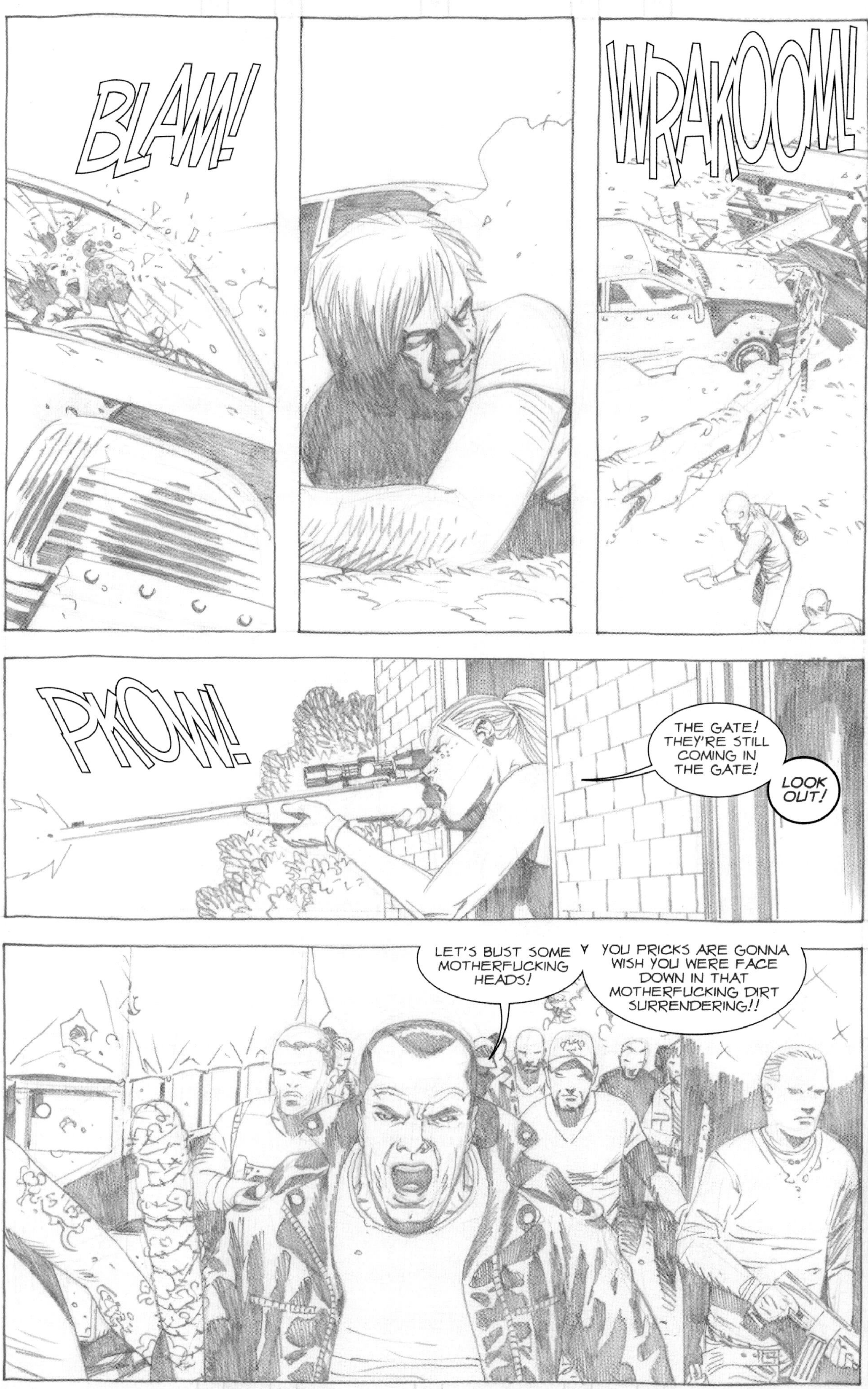
BLAM!
WRAKOOM!
PKOW!
THE GATE! THEY'RE STILL COMING IN THE GATE!
LOOK OUT!
LET'S BUST SOME MOTHERFUCKING HEADS!
YOU PRICKS ARE GONNA WISH YOU WERE FACE DOWN IN THAT MOTHERFUCKING DIRT SURRENDERING!!

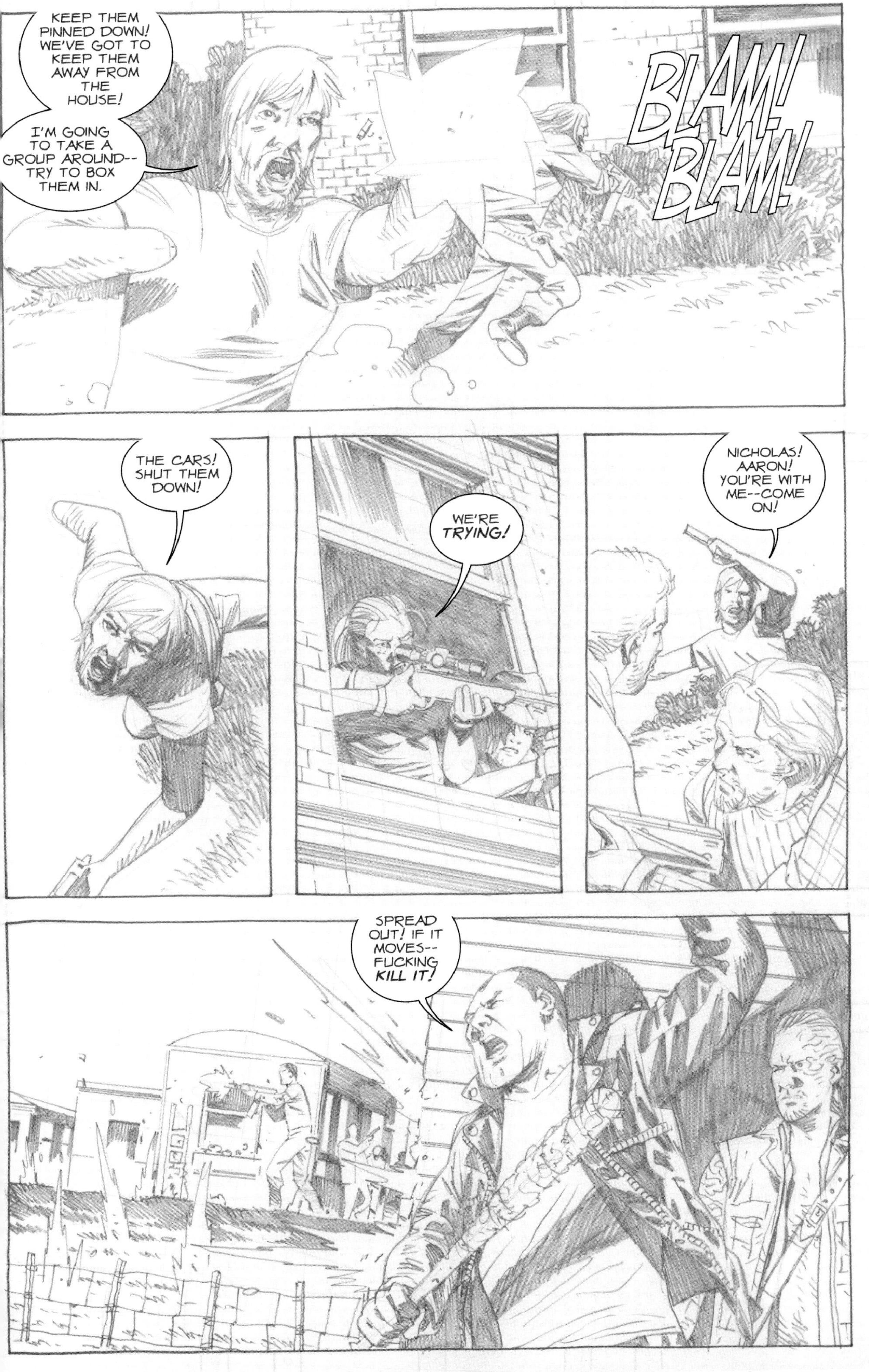
KEEP THEM PINNED DOWN! WE'VE GOT TO KEEP THEM AWAY FROM THE HOUSE!
I'M GOING TO TAKE A GROUP AROUND-- TRY TO BOX THEM IN.
BLAM! BLAM!
THE CARS! SHUT THEM DOWN!
WE'RE TRYING!
NICHOLAS! AARON! YOU'RE WITH ME--COME ON!
SPREAD OUT! IF IT MOVES-- FUCKING KILL IT!

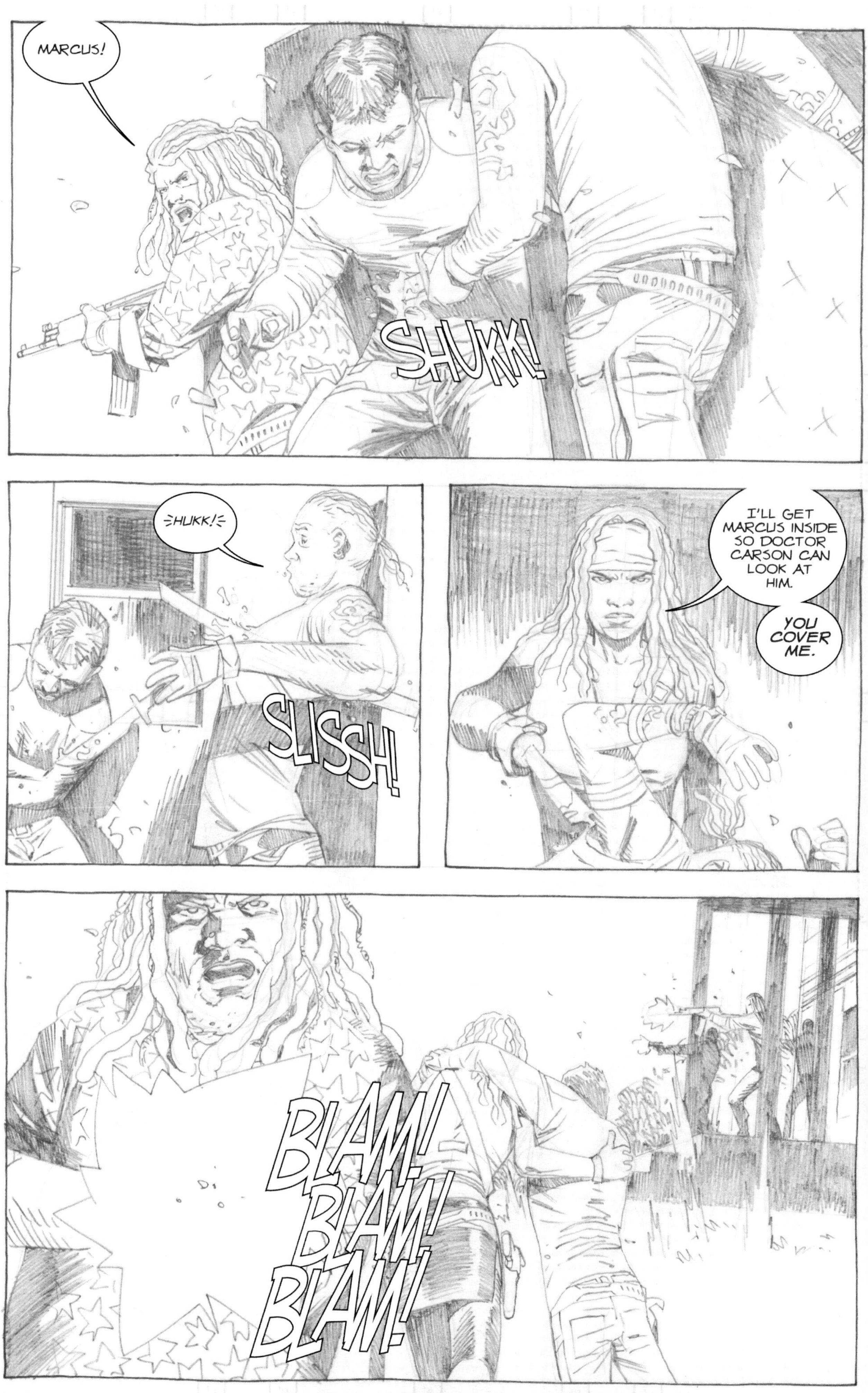

MARCUS!
SHUKK!
HUKK!
SLISSH!
I'LL GET MARCUS INSIDE SO DOCTOR CARSON CAN LOOK AT HIM.
YOU COVER ME.
BLAM! BLAM! BLAM!

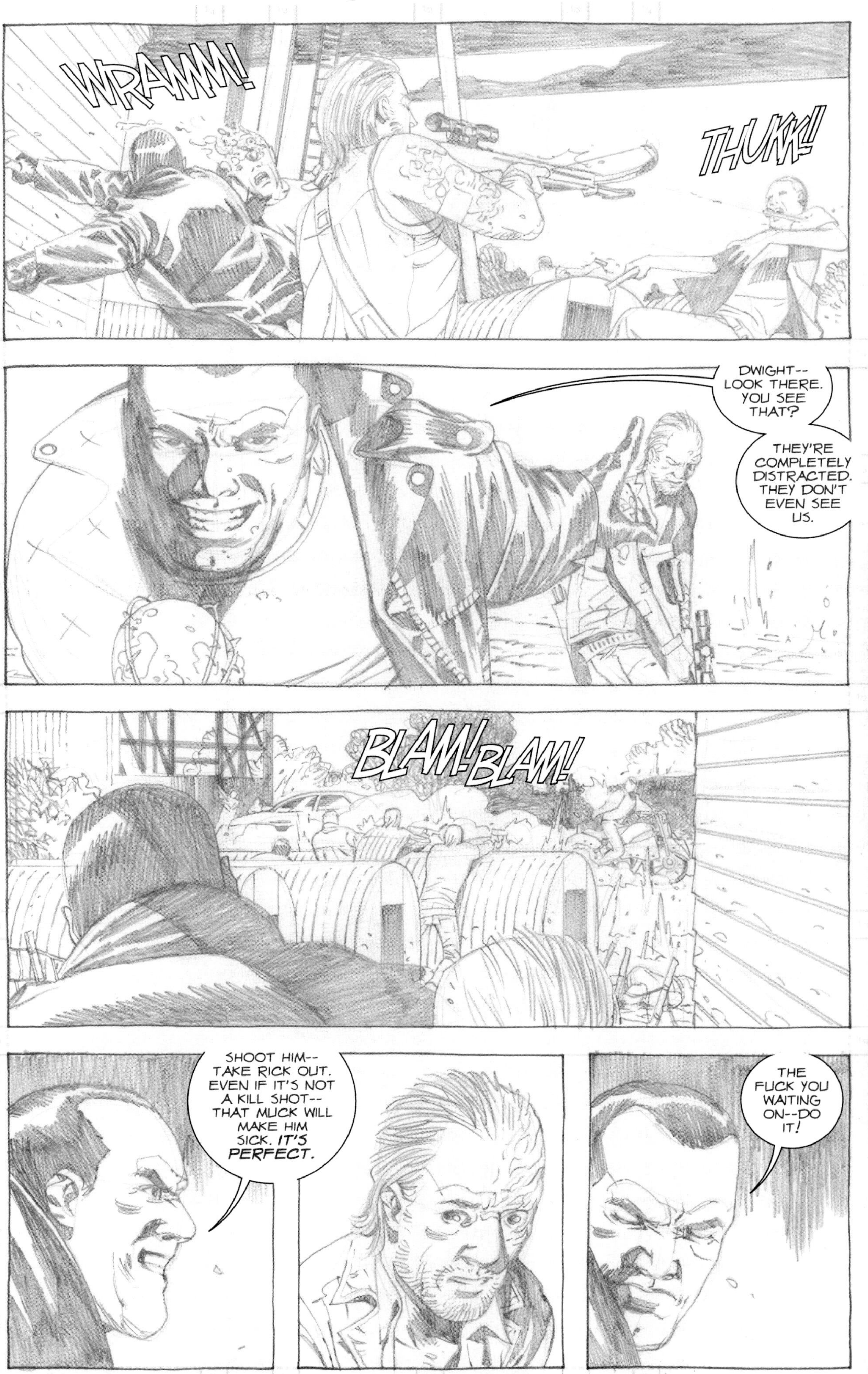
WRAMM!
THUKK!!
DWIGHT-- LOOK THERE. YOU SEE THAT?
THEY'RE COMPLETELY DISTRACTED. THEY DON'T EVEN SEE US.
BLAM! BLAM!
SHOOT HIM-- TAKE RICK OUT. EVEN IF IT'S NOT A KILL SHOT-- THAT MUCK WILL MAKE HIM SICK. IT'S PERFECT.
THE FUCK YOU WAITING ON--DO IT!

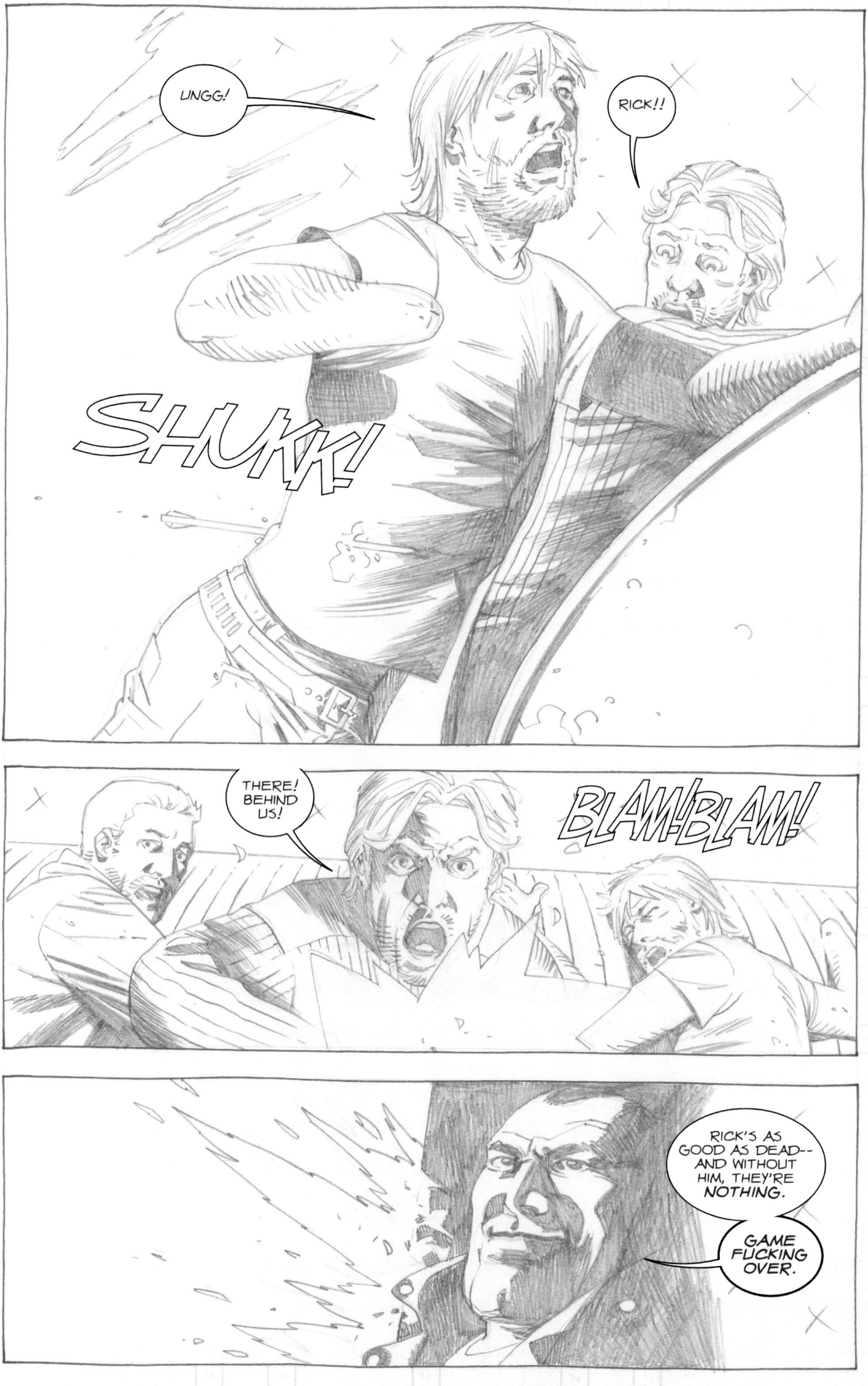
UNGG!
RICK!!
SHUKK!
THERE! BEHIND US!
BLAM-BLAM!
RICK'S AS GOOD AS DEAD-- AND WITHOUT HIM, THEY'RE NOTHING.
GAME FUCKING OVER.

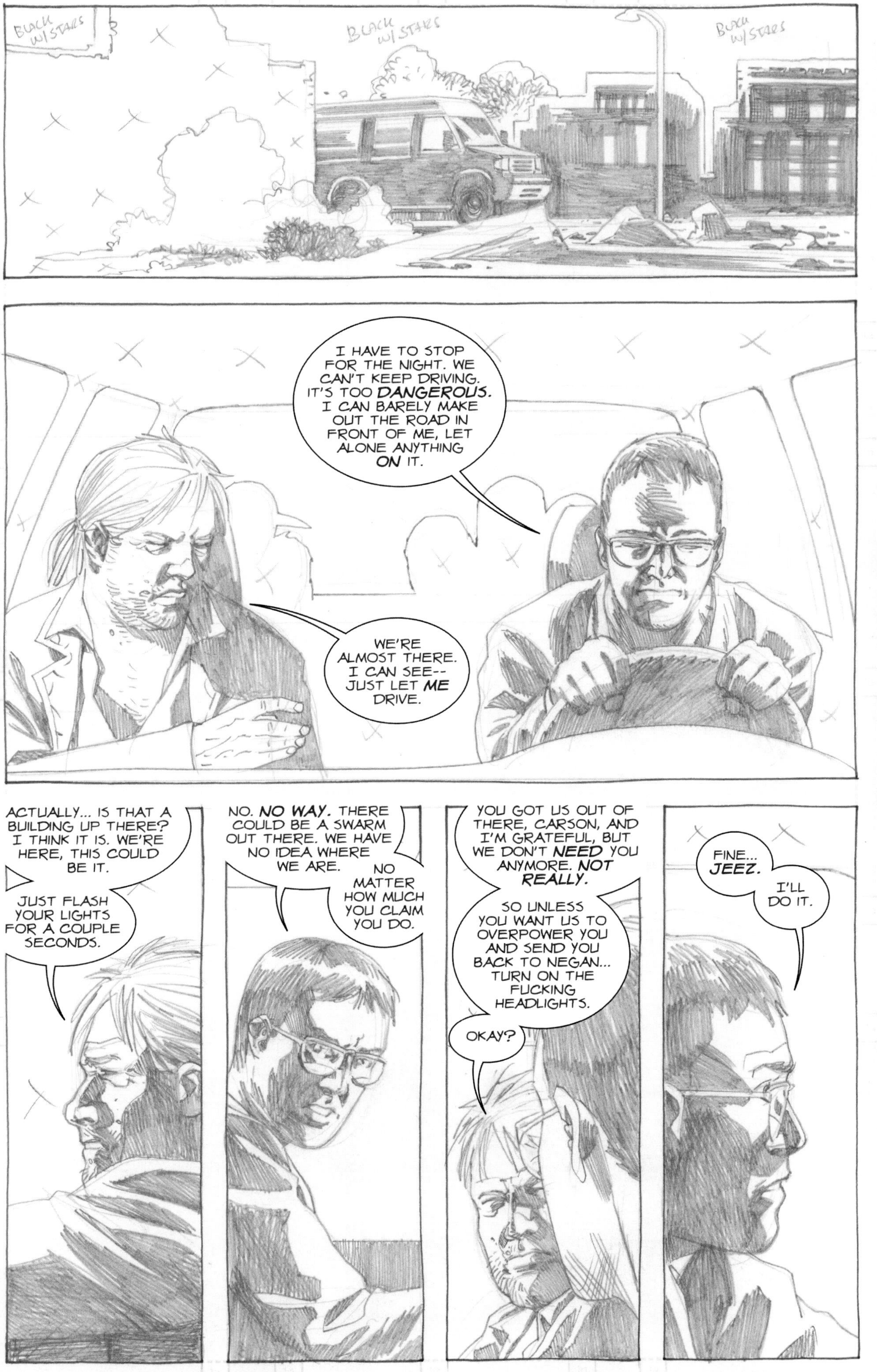
BLACK W/STARS
BLACK W/STARS
BLACK W/STARS
I HAVE TO STOP FOR THE NIGHT. WE CAN'T KEEP DRIVING. IT'S TOO DANGEROUS. I CAN BARELY MAKE OUT THE ROAD IN FRONT OF ME, LET ALONE ANYTHING ON IT.
WE'RE ALMOST THERE. I CAN SEE-- JUST LET ME DRIVE.
ACTUALLY... IS THAT A BUILDING UP THERE? I THINK IT IS. WE'RE HERE, THIS COULD BE IT.
JUST FLASH YOUR LIGHTS FOR A COUPLE SECONDS.
NO. NO WAY. THERE COULD BE A SWARM OUT THERE. WE HAVE NO IDEA WHERE WE ARE.
NO MATTER HOW MUCH YOU CLAIM YOU DO.
YOU GOT US OUT OF THERE, CARSON, AND I'M GRATEFUL, BUT WE DON'T NEED YOU ANYMORE. NOT REALLY.
SO UNLESS YOU WANT US TO OVERPOWER YOU AND SEND YOU BACK TO NEGAN... TURN ON THE FUCKING HEADLIGHTS.
OKAY?
FINE... JEEZ.
I'LL DO IT.

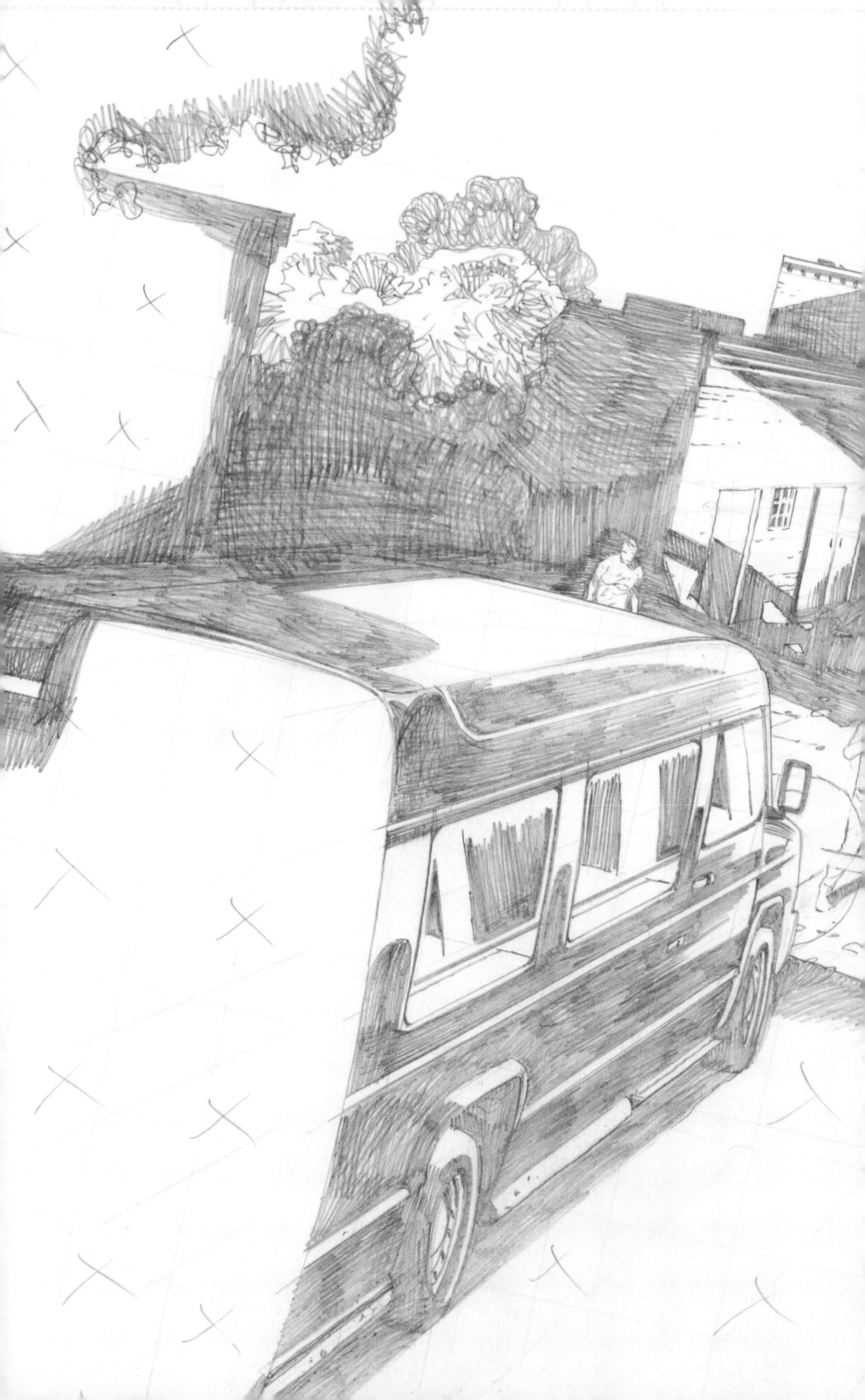

BLACK W/ STARS
(GREY? FOR CLIFF)

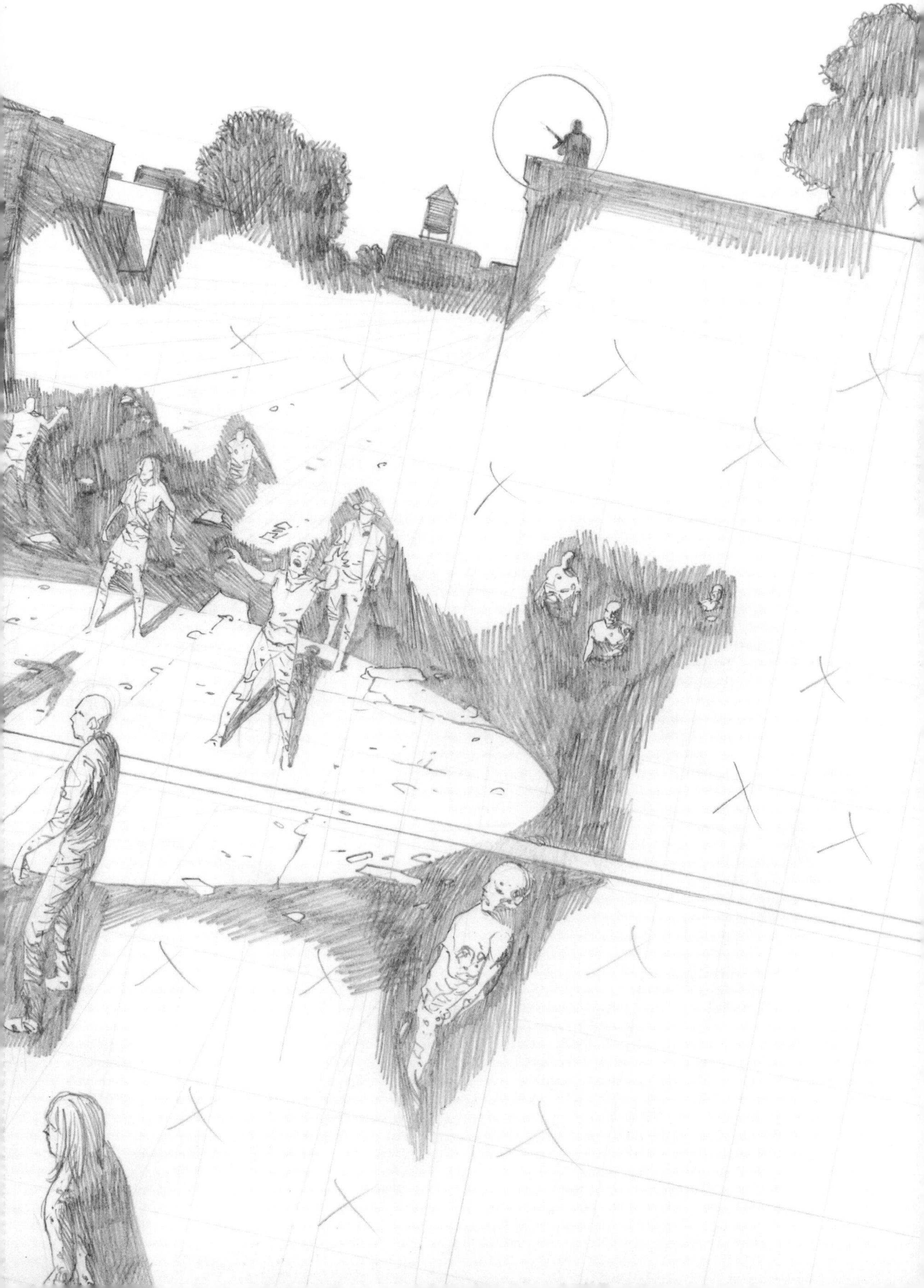

OKAY-- WE'RE OUT OF HERE!

THE LIGHTS! TURN OFF THE LIGHTS!

SKREECH!

I NEED THE LIGHTS TO SEE! I HAVE TO GET AWAY!

DIDN'T YOU SEE?! THERE WAS A MAN ON THE ROOF!

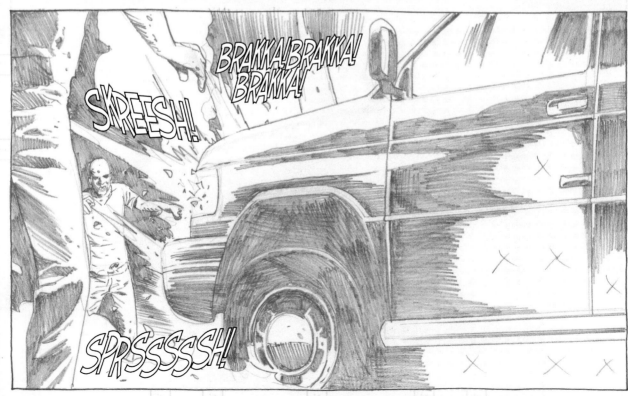

SKREESH!

BRAKKA! BRAKKA! BRAKKA!

SPRSSSSH!

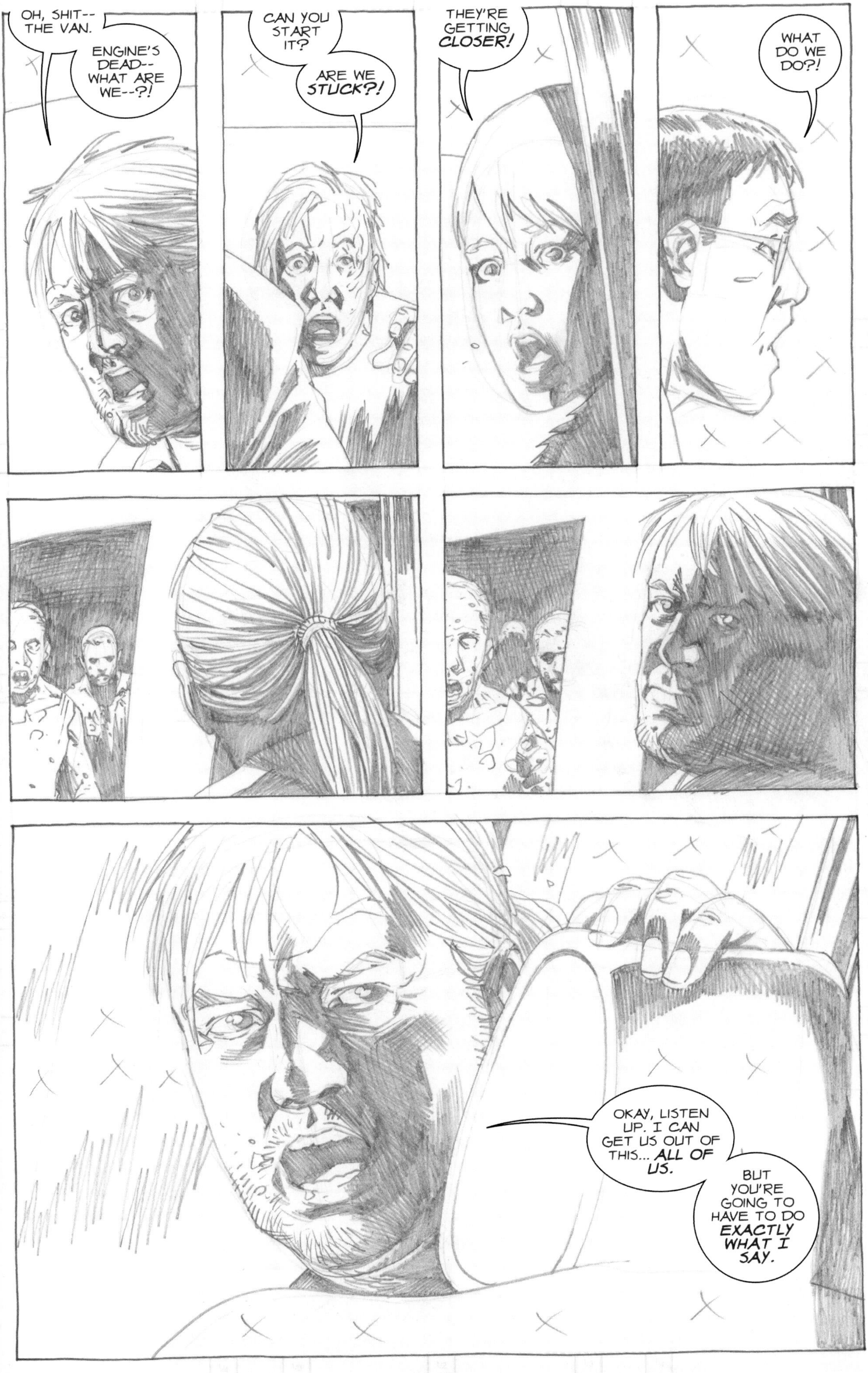

OH, SHIT-- THE VAN.
ENGINE'S DEAD-- WHAT ARE WE--?!
CAN YOU START IT?
ARE WE STUCK?!
THEY'RE GETTING CLOSER!
WHAT DO WE DO?!
OKAY, LISTEN UP. I CAN GET US OUT OF THIS... ALL OF US.
BUT YOU'RE GOING TO HAVE TO DO EXACTLY WHAT I SAY.

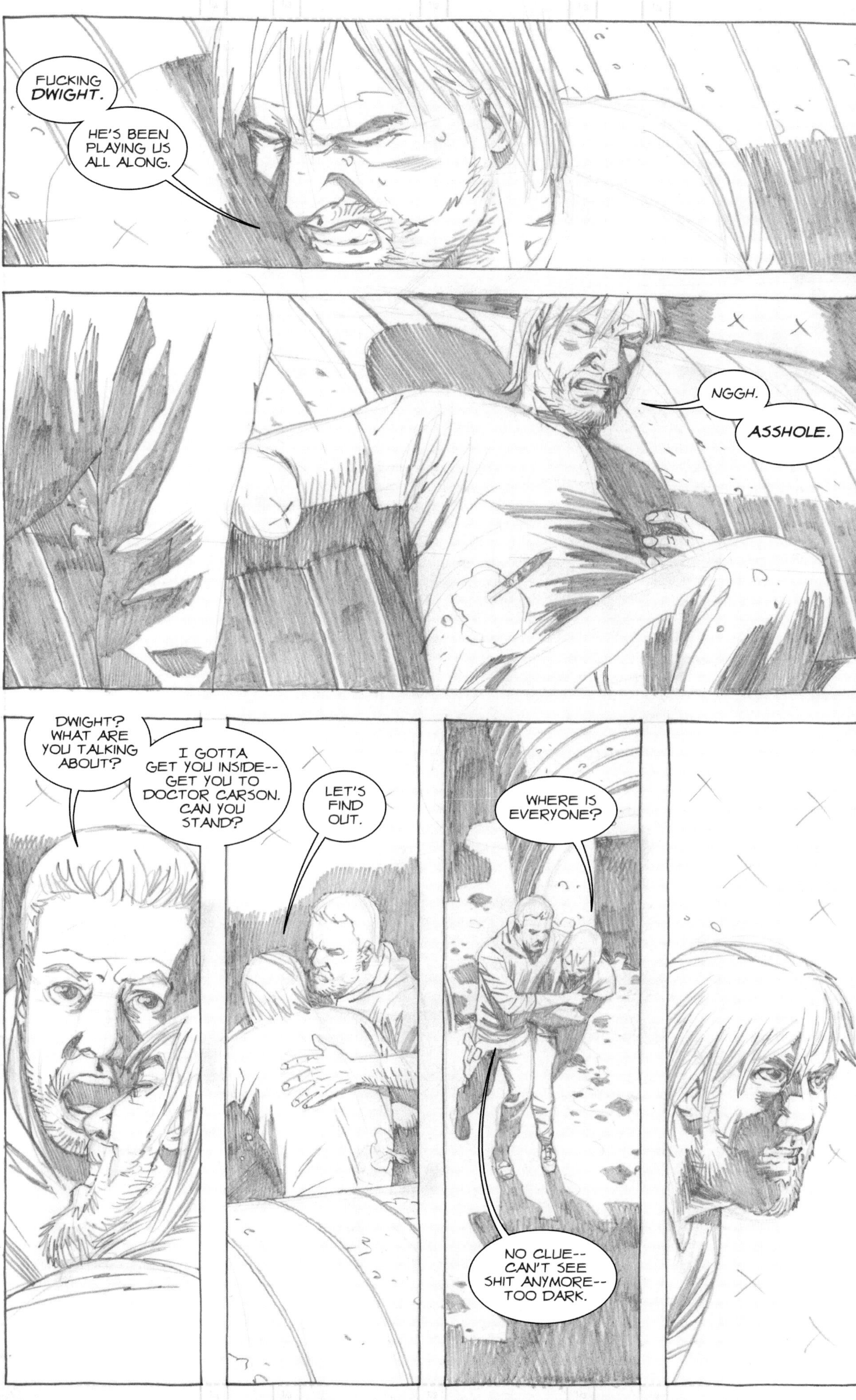
FUCKING DWIGHT.
HE'S BEEN PLAYING US ALL ALONG.
NGGH.
ASSHOLE.
DWIGHT? WHAT ARE YOU TALKING ABOUT?
I GOTTA GET YOU INSIDE-- GET YOU TO DOCTOR CARSON. CAN YOU STAND?
LET'S FIND OUT.
WHERE IS EVERYONE?
NO CLUE-- CAN'T SEE SHIT ANYMORE-- TOO DARK.

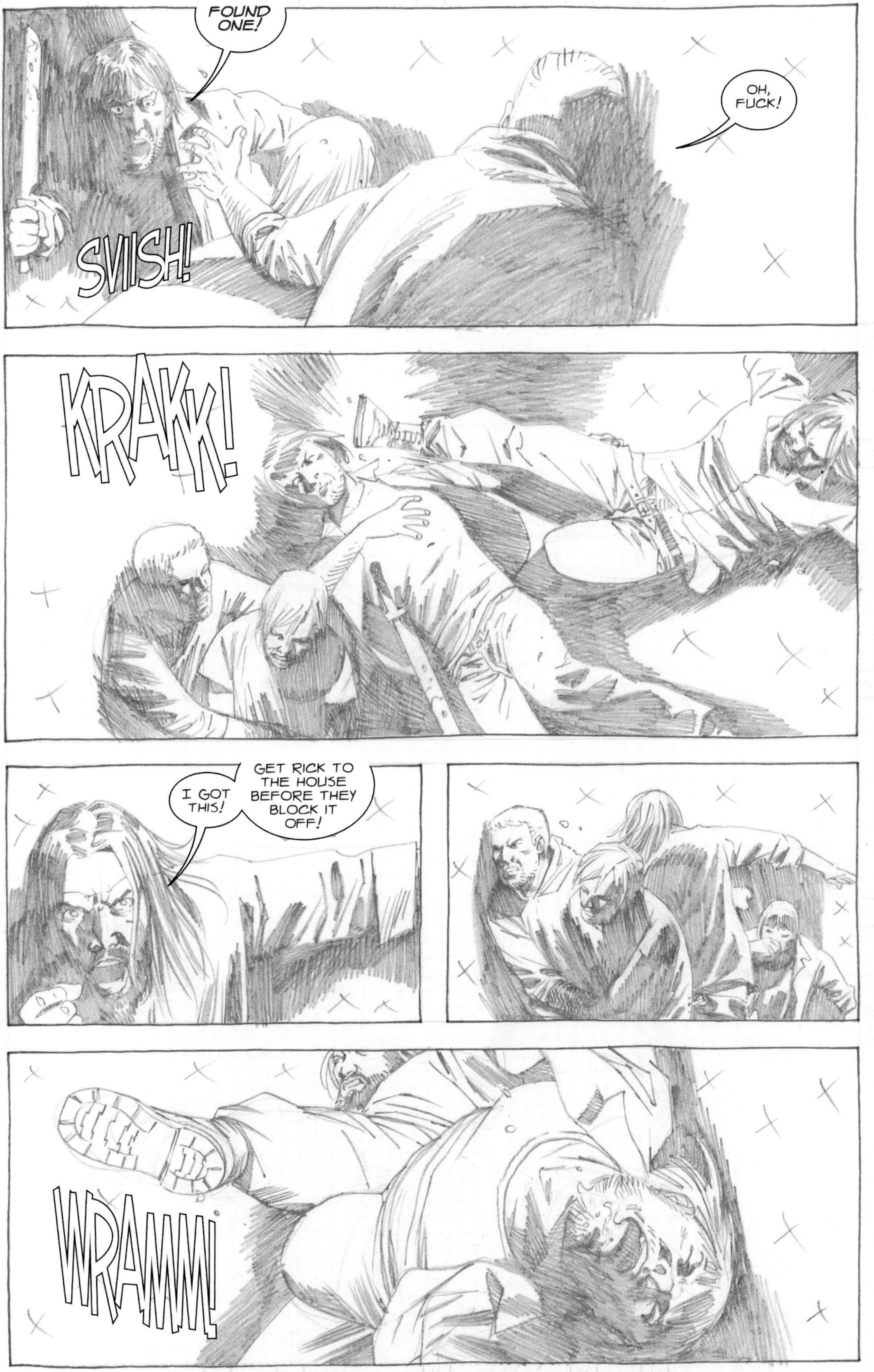
FOUND ONE!
OH, FUCK!
SVIISH!
KRAKK!
I GOT THIS!
GET RICK TO THE HOUSE BEFORE THEY BLOCK IT OFF!
WRAMM!

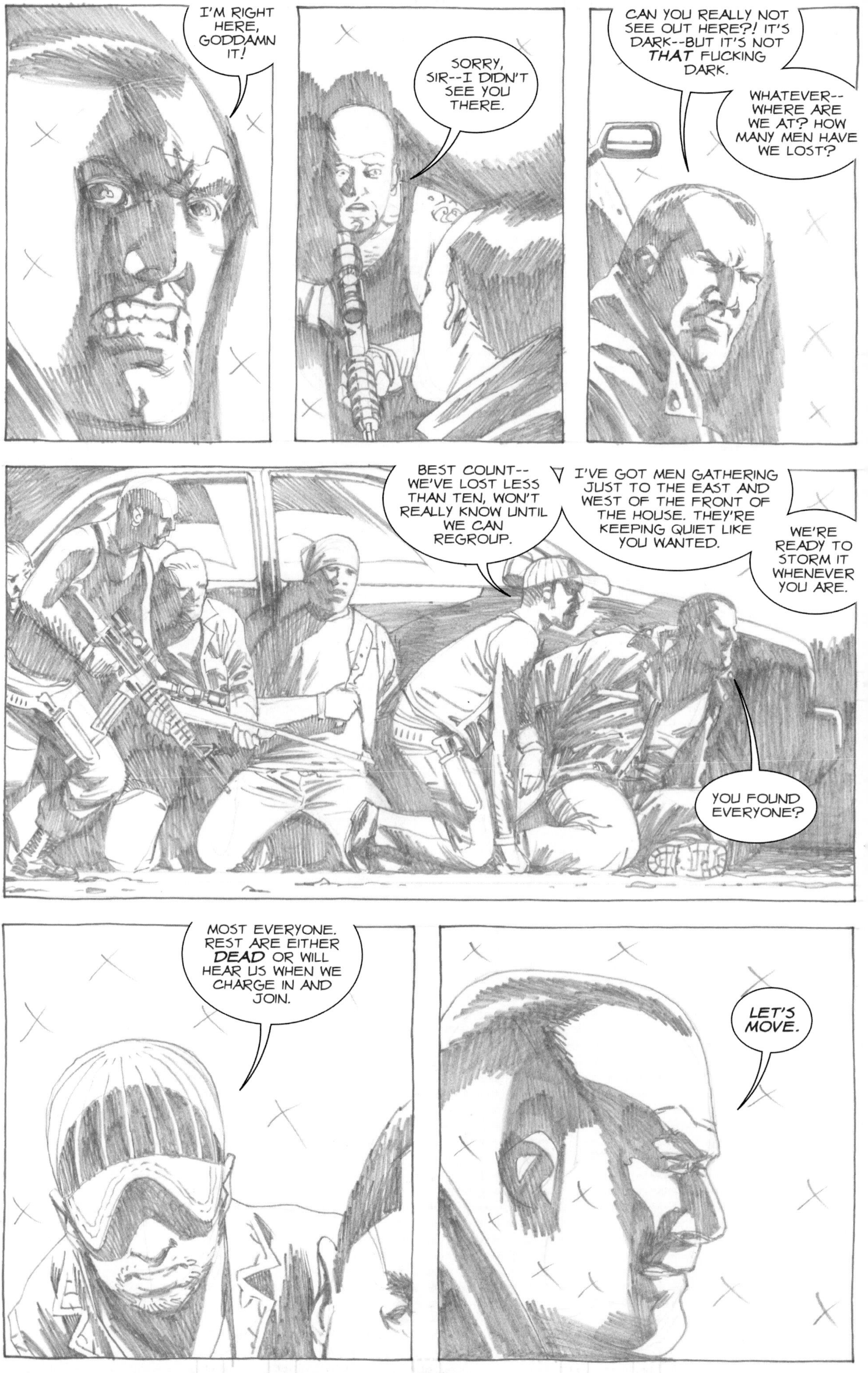
I'M RIGHT HERE, GODDAMN IT!
SORRY, SIR--I DIDN'T SEE YOU THERE.
CAN YOU REALLY NOT SEE OUT HERE?! IT'S DARK--BUT IT'S NOT THAT FUCKING DARK.
WHATEVER--WHERE ARE WE AT? HOW MANY MEN HAVE WE LOST?
BEST COUNT--WE'VE LOST LESS THAN TEN, WON'T REALLY KNOW UNTIL WE CAN REGROUP.
I'VE GOT MEN GATHERING JUST TO THE EAST AND WEST OF THE FRONT OF THE HOUSE. THEY'RE KEEPING QUIET LIKE YOU WANTED.
WE'RE READY TO STORM IT WHENEVER YOU ARE.
YOU FOUND EVERYONE?
MOST EVERYONE. REST ARE EITHER DEAD OR WILL HEAR US WHEN WE CHARGE IN AND JOIN.
LET'S MOVE.

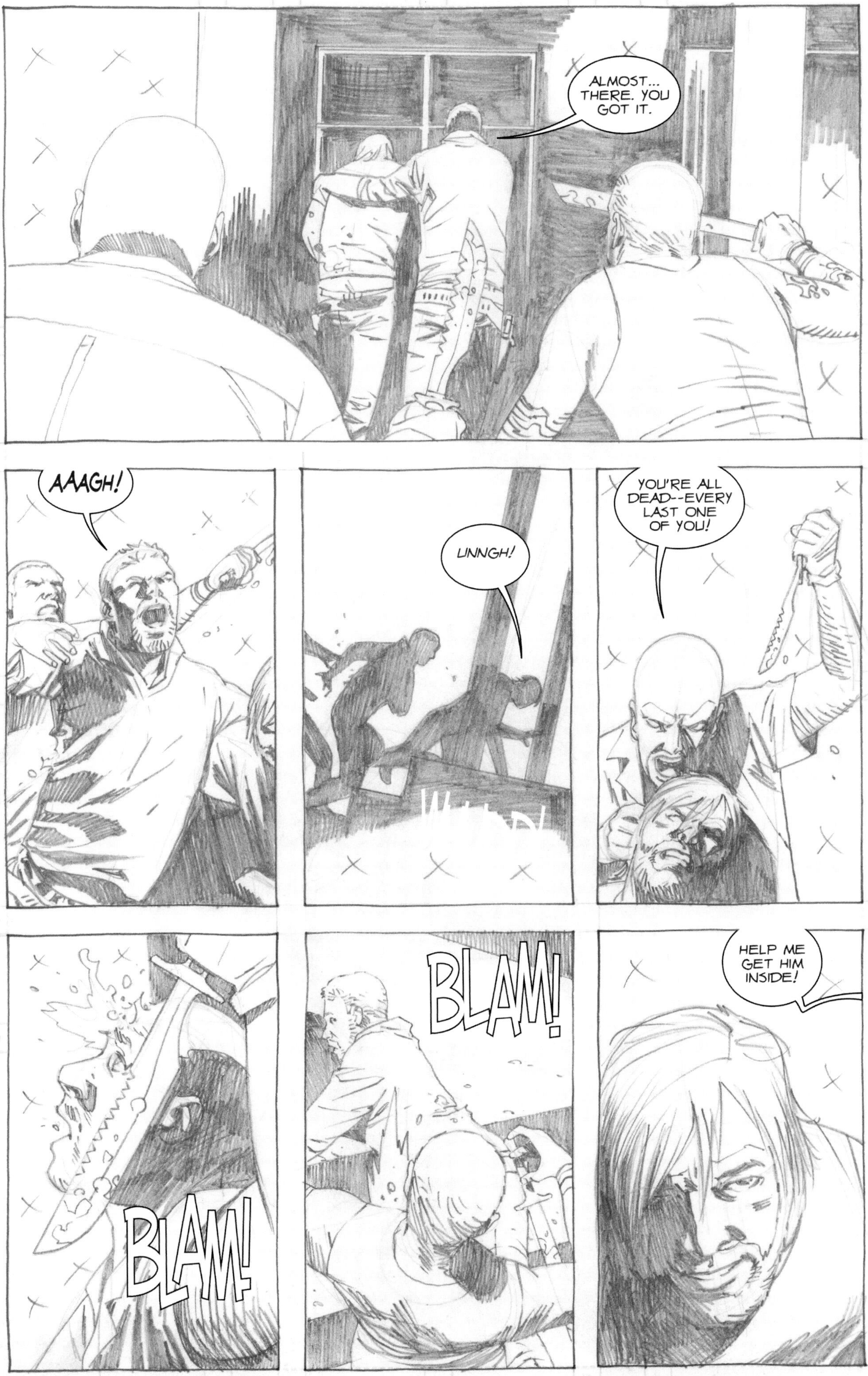
ALMOST... THERE. YOU GOT IT.
AAAGH!
UNNGH!
YOU'RE ALL DEAD--EVERY LAST ONE OF YOU!
BLAM!
BLAM!
HELP ME GET HIM INSIDE!

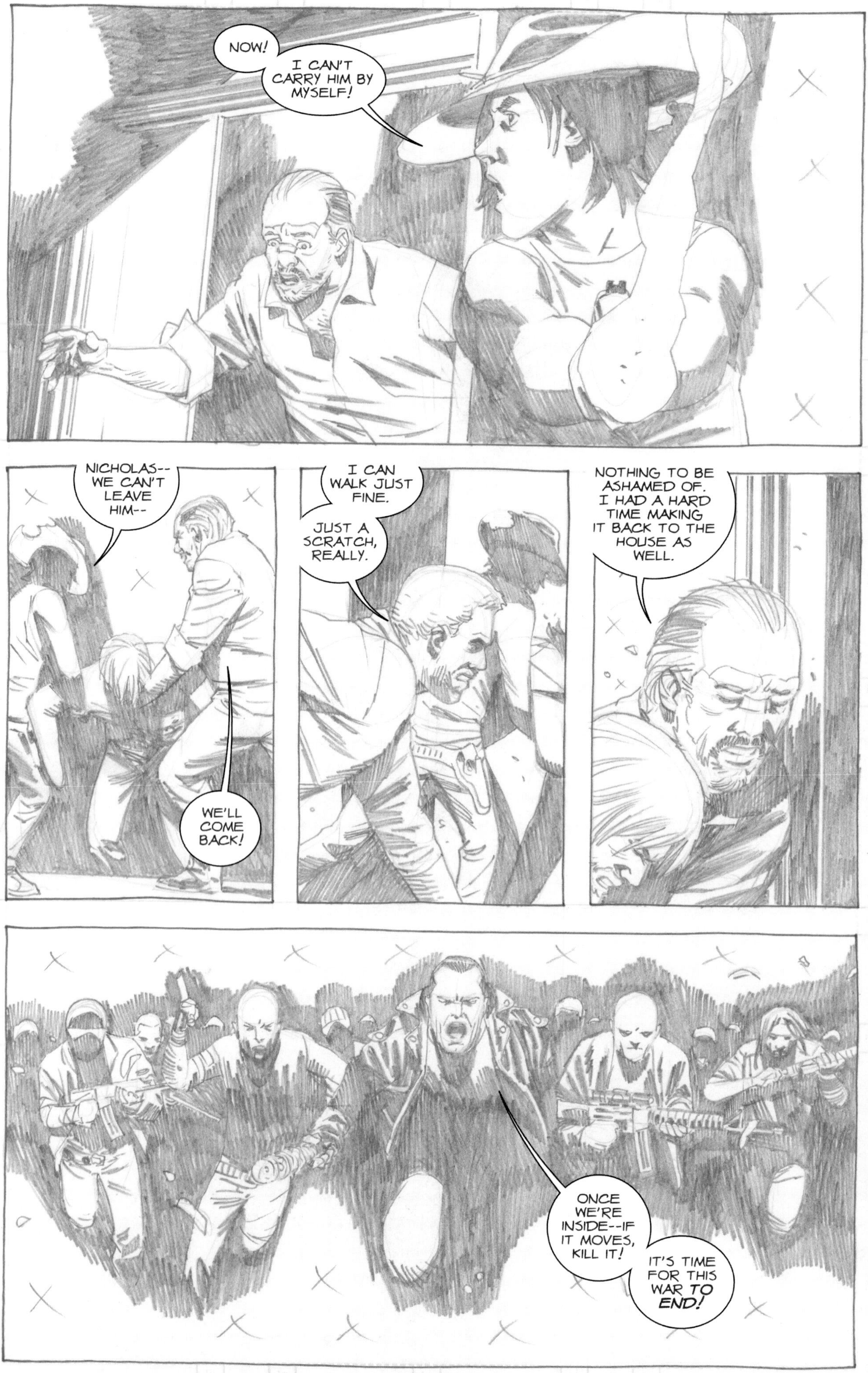
NOW!
I CAN'T CARRY HIM BY MYSELF!
NICHOLAS-- WE CAN'T LEAVE HIM--
WE'LL COME BACK!
I CAN WALK JUST FINE.
JUST A SCRATCH, REALLY.
NOTHING TO BE ASHAMED OF. I HAD A HARD TIME MAKING IT BACK TO THE HOUSE AS WELL.
ONCE WE'RE INSIDE--IF IT MOVES, KILL IT!
IT'S TIME FOR THIS WAR TO END!

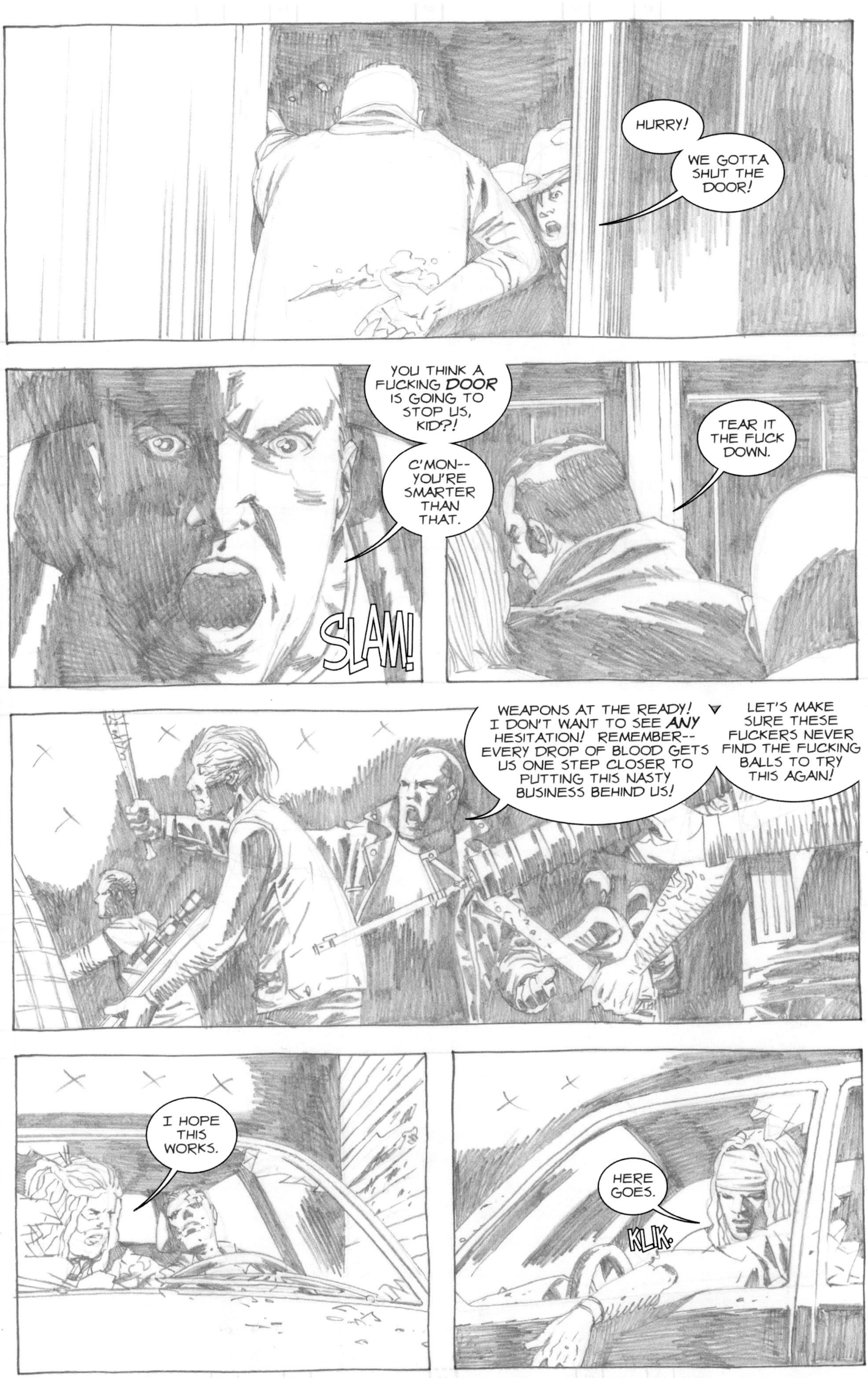
HURRY!
WE GOTTA SHUT THE DOOR!
YOU THINK A FUCKING DOOR IS GOING TO STOP US, KID?!
C'MON-- YOU'RE SMARTER THAN THAT.
SLAM!
TEAR IT THE FUCK DOWN.
WEAPONS AT THE READY! I DON'T WANT TO SEE ANY HESITATION! REMEMBER-- EVERY DROP OF BLOOD GETS US ONE STEP CLOSER TO PUTTING THIS NASTY BUSINESS BEHIND US!
LET'S MAKE SURE THESE FUCKERS NEVER FIND THE FUCKING BALLS TO TRY THIS AGAIN!
I HOPE THIS WORKS.
HERE GOES.
KLIK.

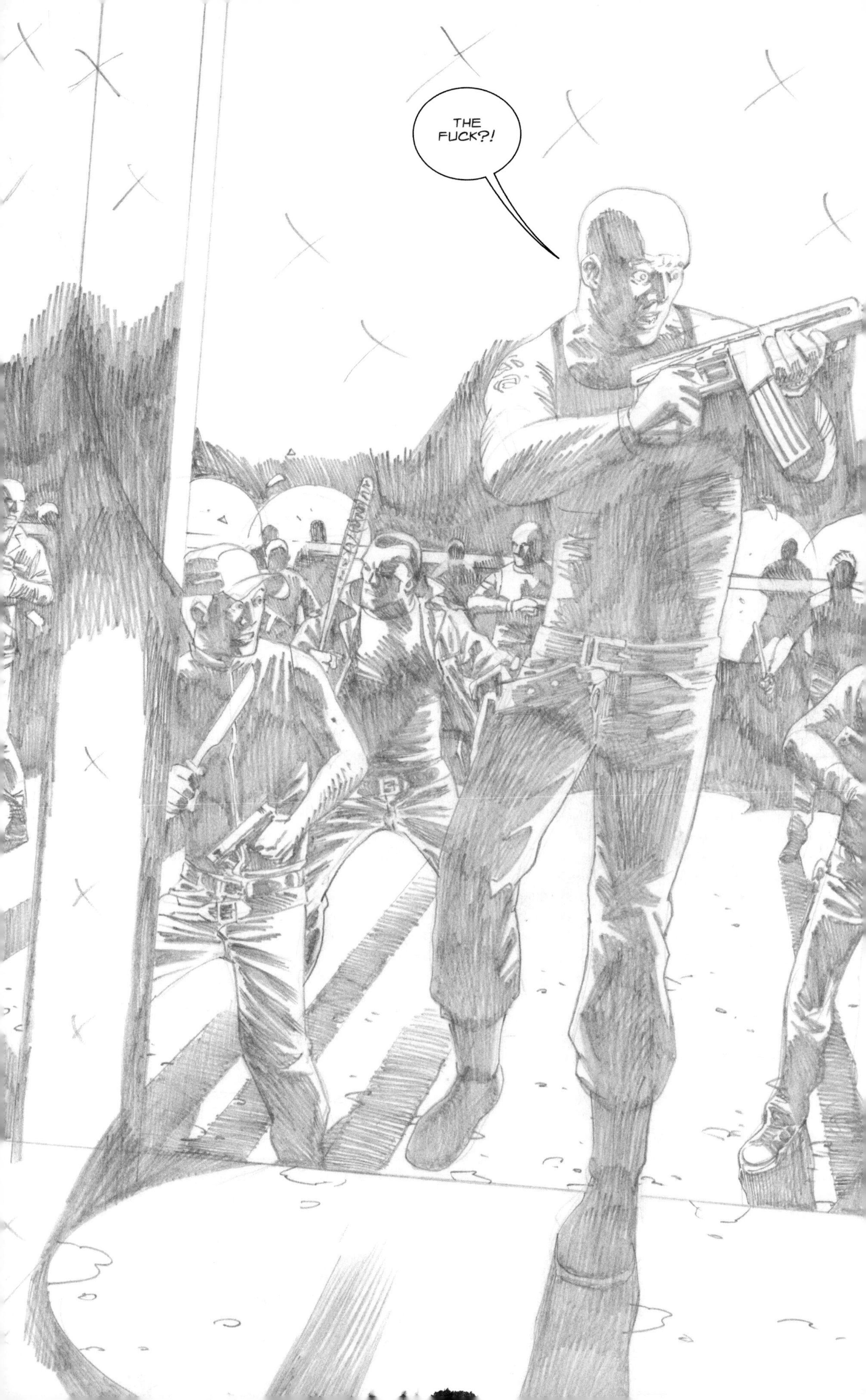
THE FUCK?!

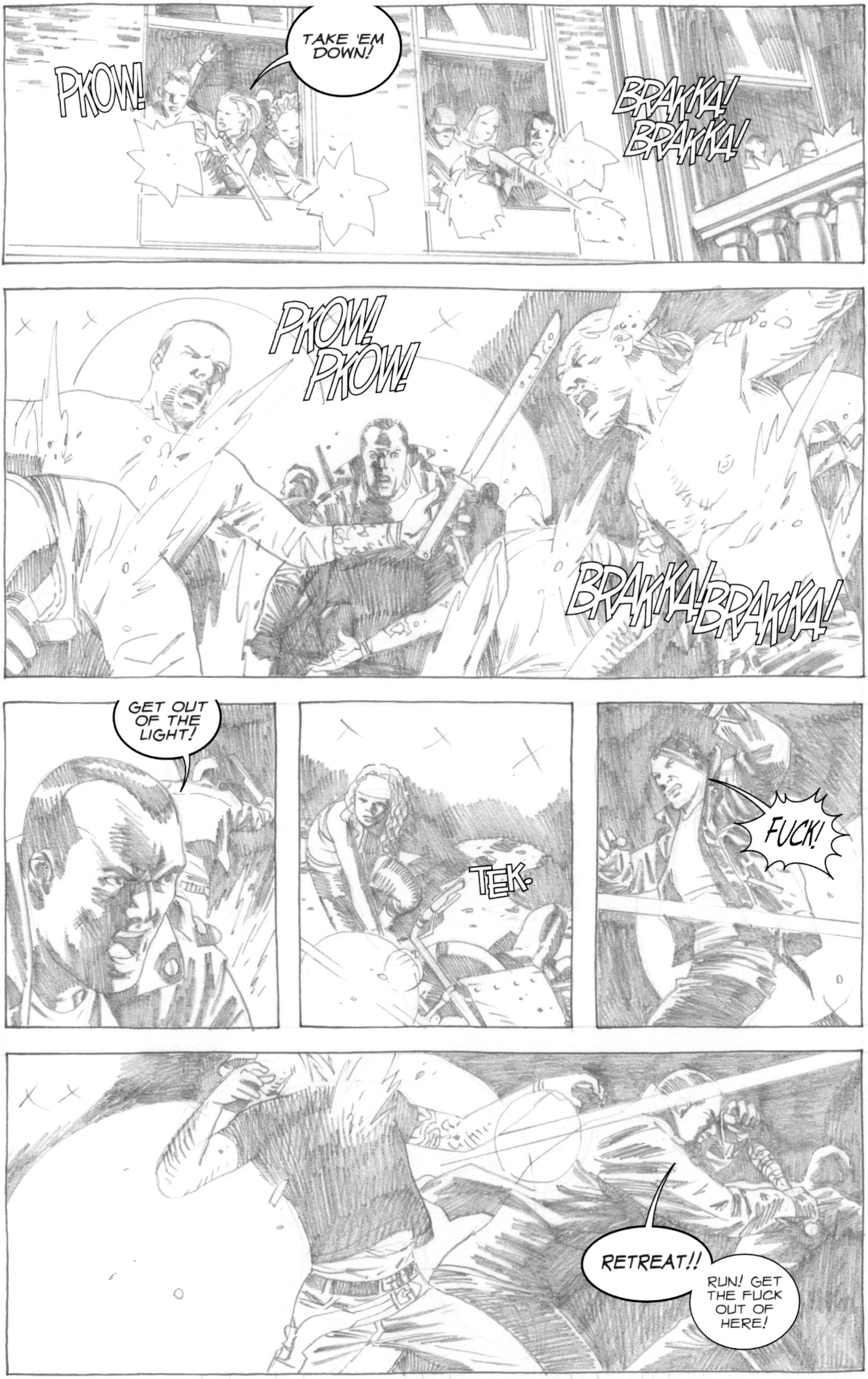
PKOW!
TAKE 'EM DOWN!
BRAKKA! BRAKKA!
PKOW! PKOW!
BRAKKA-BRAKKA!
GET OUT OF THE LIGHT!
TEK.
FUCK!
RETREAT!!
RUN! GET THE FUCK OUT OF HERE!

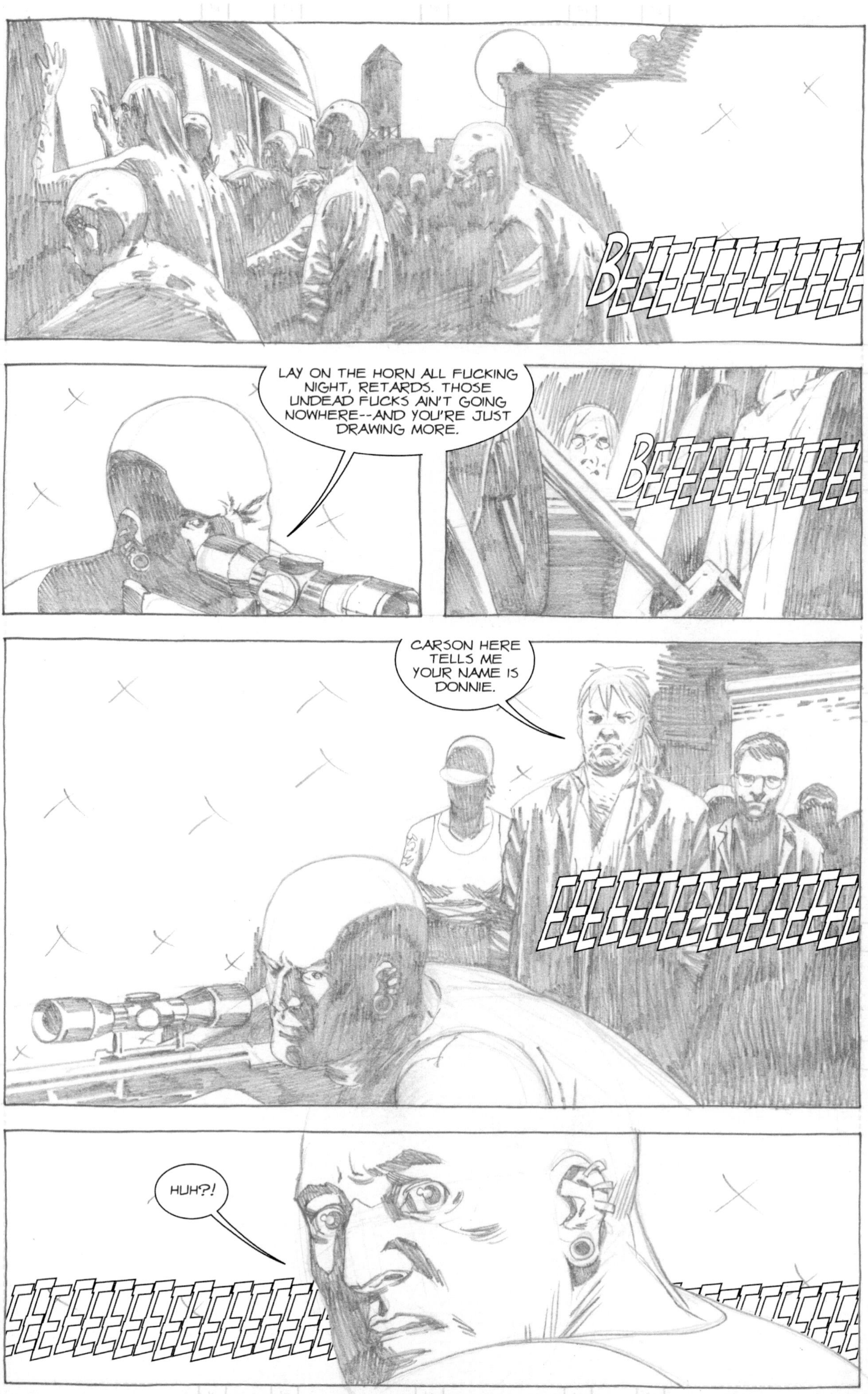

BEEEEEEEEEEEEEEE
LAY ON THE HORN ALL FUCKING NIGHT, RETARDS. THOSE UNDEAD FUCKS AIN'T GOING NOWHERE--AND YOU'RE JUST DRAWING MORE.
BEEEEEEEEEEEE
CARSON HERE TELLS ME YOUR NAME IS DONNIE.
EEEEEEEEEEEEEEEE
HUH?!
EEEEEEEEEEEEEEEEEEEEEEEEEEEE

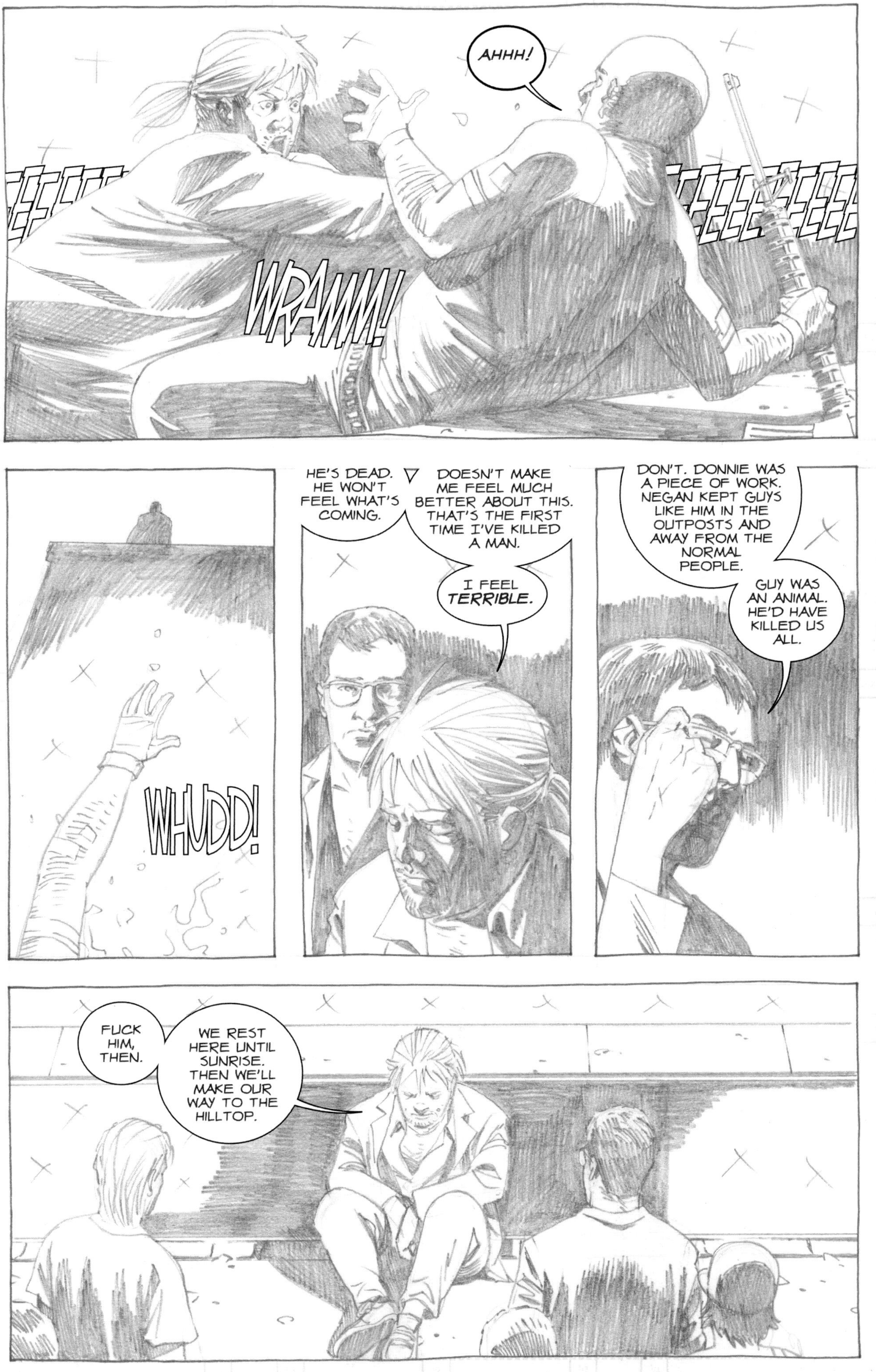
AHHH!
EEEEEEE
EEEEEEEEEEEE
WRAMM!
WHUDD!
HE'S DEAD. HE WON'T FEEL WHAT'S COMING.
DOESN'T MAKE ME FEEL MUCH BETTER ABOUT THIS. THAT'S THE FIRST TIME I'VE KILLED A MAN.
I FEEL TERRIBLE.
DON'T. DONNIE WAS A PIECE OF WORK. NEGAN KEPT GUYS LIKE HIM IN THE OUTPOSTS AND AWAY FROM THE NORMAL PEOPLE.
GUY WAS AN ANIMAL. HE'D HAVE KILLED US ALL.
FUCK HIM, THEN.
WE REST HERE UNTIL SUNRISE. THEN WE'LL MAKE OUR WAY TO THE HILLTOP.

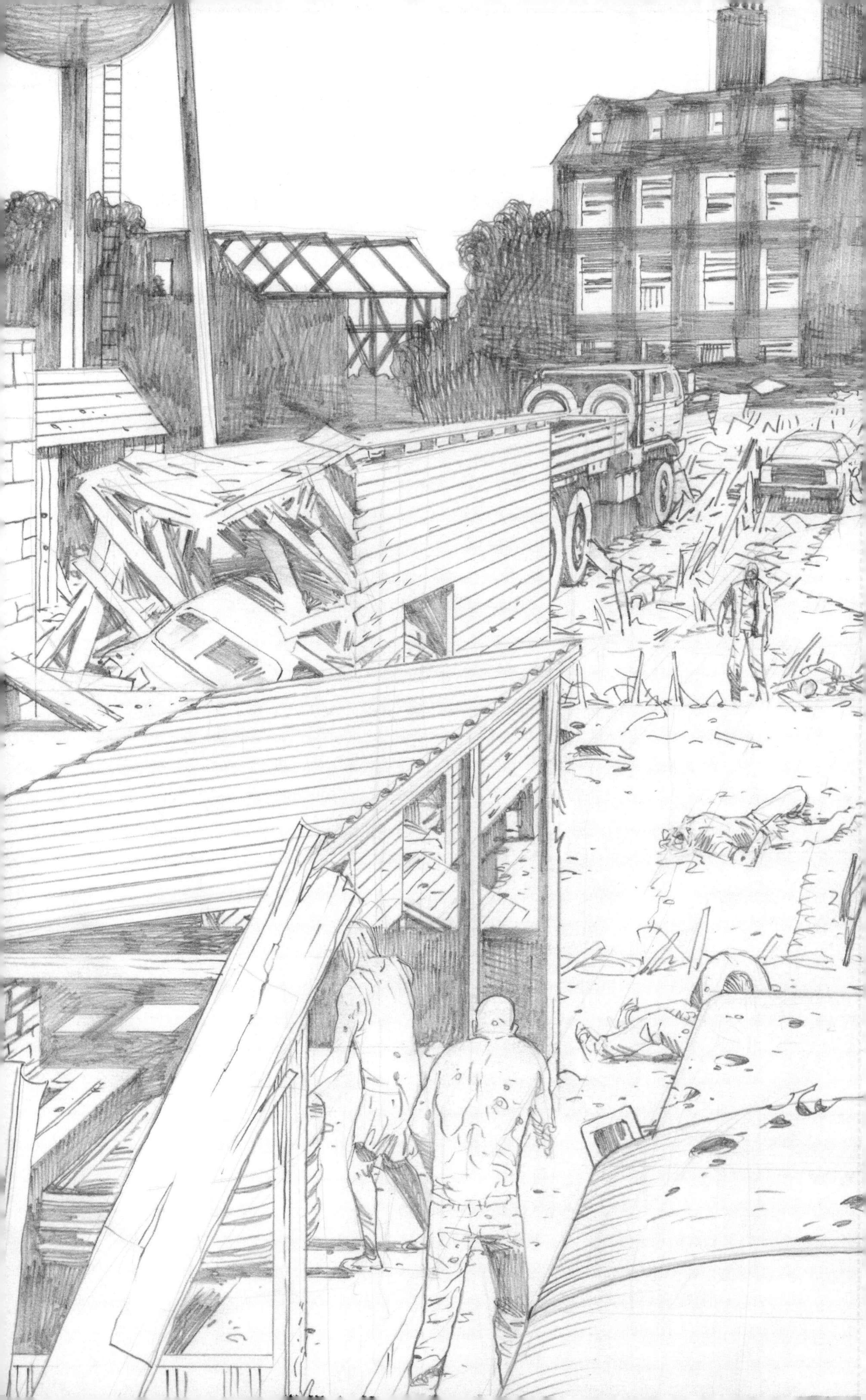

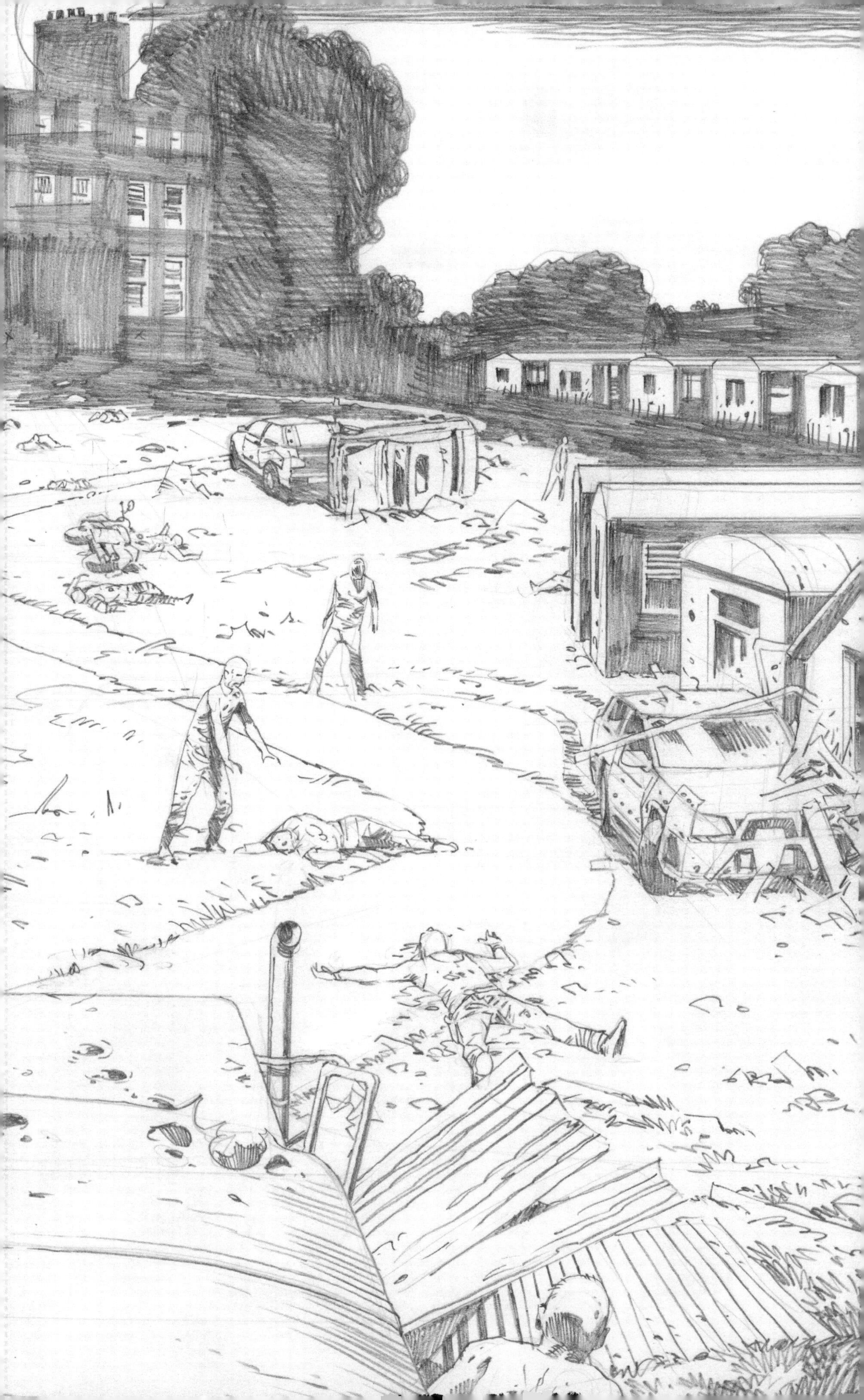

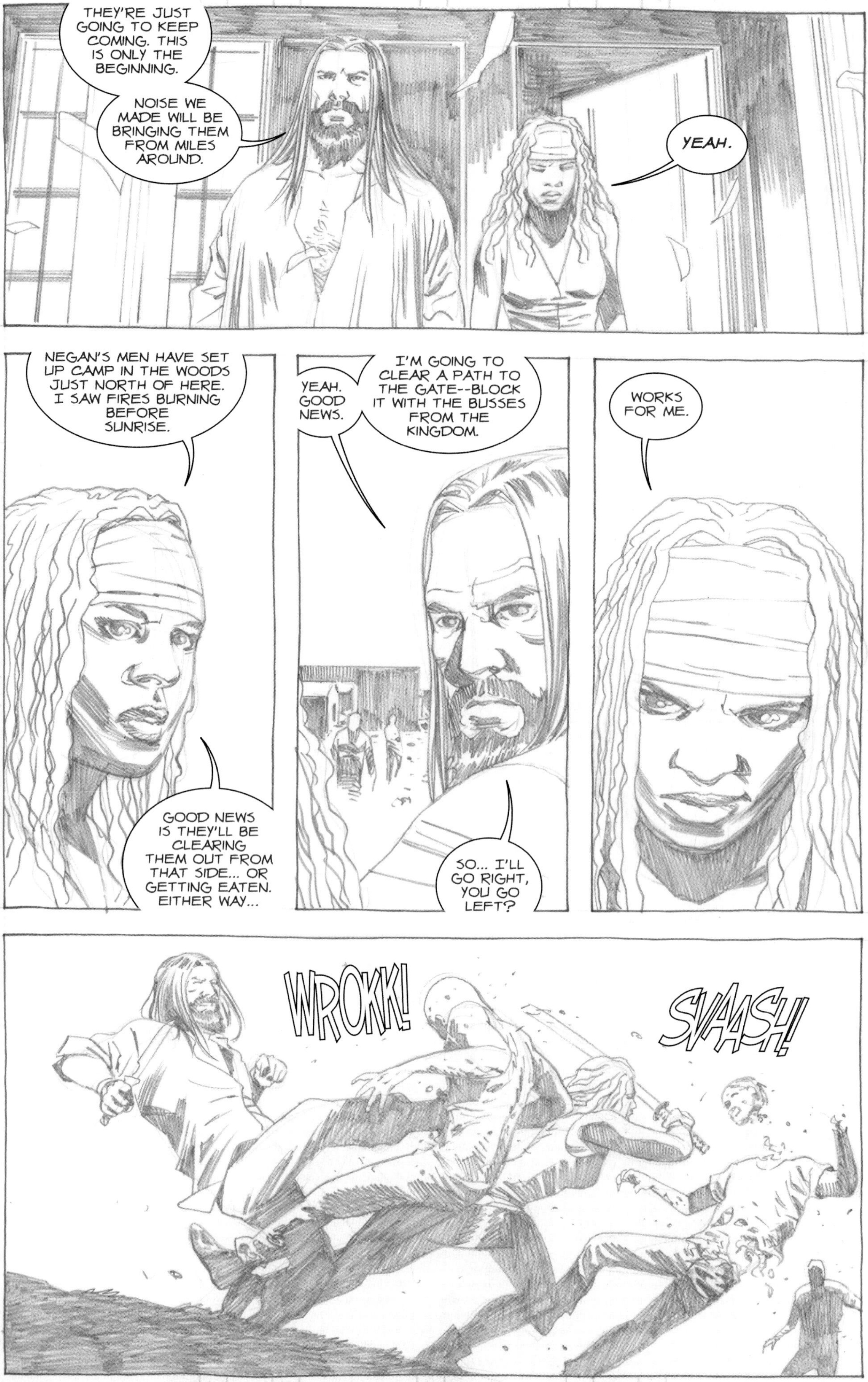
THEY'RE JUST GOING TO KEEP COMING. THIS IS ONLY THE BEGINNING.
NOISE WE MADE WILL BE BRINGING THEM FROM MILES AROUND.
YEAH.
NEGAN'S MEN HAVE SET UP CAMP IN THE WOODS JUST NORTH OF HERE. I SAW FIRES BURNING BEFORE SUNRISE.
GOOD NEWS IS THEY'LL BE CLEARING THEM OUT FROM THAT SIDE... OR GETTING EATEN. EITHER WAY...
YEAH. GOOD NEWS.
I'M GOING TO CLEAR A PATH TO THE GATE--BLOCK IT WITH THE BUSSES FROM THE KINGDOM.
SO... I'LL GO RIGHT, YOU GO LEFT?
WORKS FOR ME.
WROKK!
SVAASH!

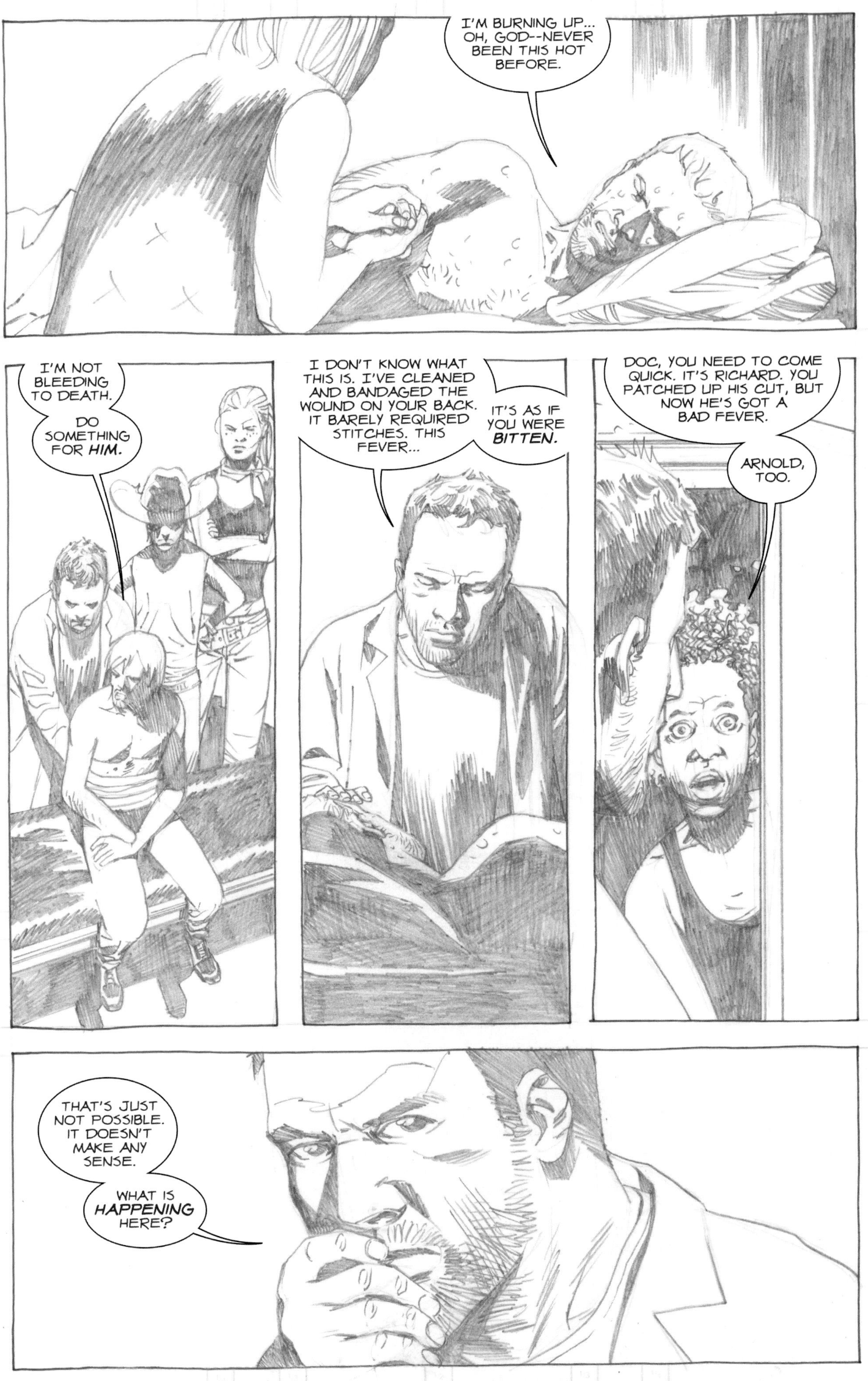
I'M BURNING UP... OH, GOD--NEVER BEEN THIS HOT BEFORE.
I'M NOT BLEEDING TO DEATH.
DO SOMETHING FOR *HIM.*
I DON'T KNOW WHAT THIS IS. I'VE CLEANED AND BANDAGED THE WOUND ON YOUR BACK. IT BARELY REQUIRED STITCHES. THIS FEVER...
IT'S AS IF YOU WERE *BITTEN.*
DOC, YOU NEED TO COME QUICK. IT'S RICHARD. YOU PATCHED UP HIS CUT, BUT NOW HE'S GOT A BAD FEVER.
ARNOLD, TOO.
THAT'S JUST NOT POSSIBLE. IT DOESN'T MAKE ANY SENSE.
WHAT IS *HAPPENING* HERE?

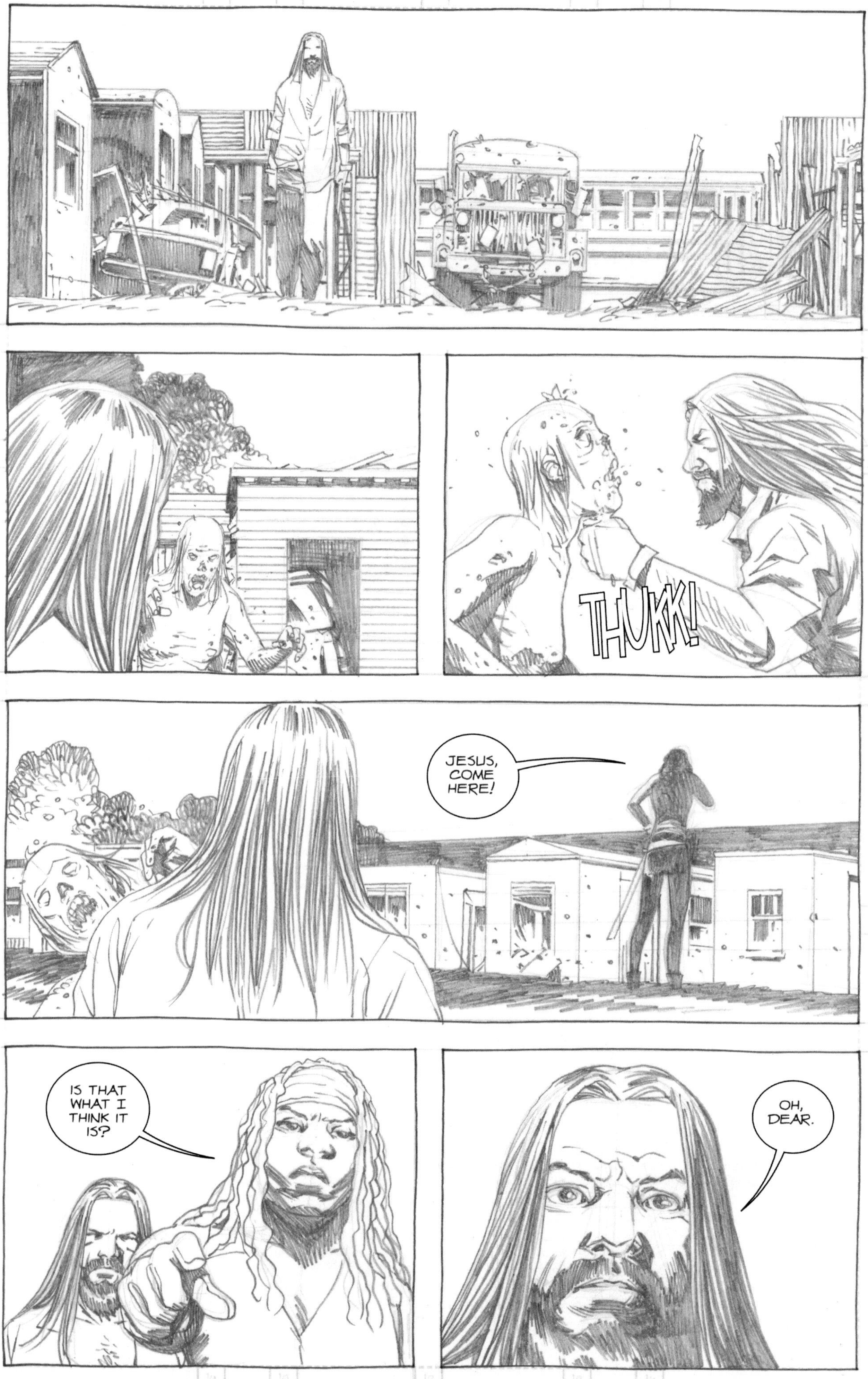
THUKK!
JESUS, COME HERE!
IS THAT WHAT I THINK IT IS?
OH, DEAR.

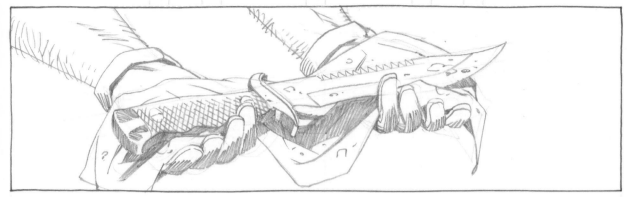

WHAT IS THAT? IT'S TOO DRY TO HAVE BEEN FROM LAST NIGHT.

RIGHT.

I CHECKED ALL THE SAVIORS' WEAPONS THAT WERE LEFT IN THE YARD-- THEY'RE **ALL** LIKE THIS.

I BELIEVE IT'S RESIDUE FROM THE ROAMERS--THEY CONTAMINATED THEIR WEAPONS BEFORE THEY ATTACKED.

DEAR GOD... THEN ANYONE WHO WAS INJURED BY ONE OF THEIR WEAPONS... NO MATTER HOW MINOR THE WOUND... WILL...

...DIE.

DAD?

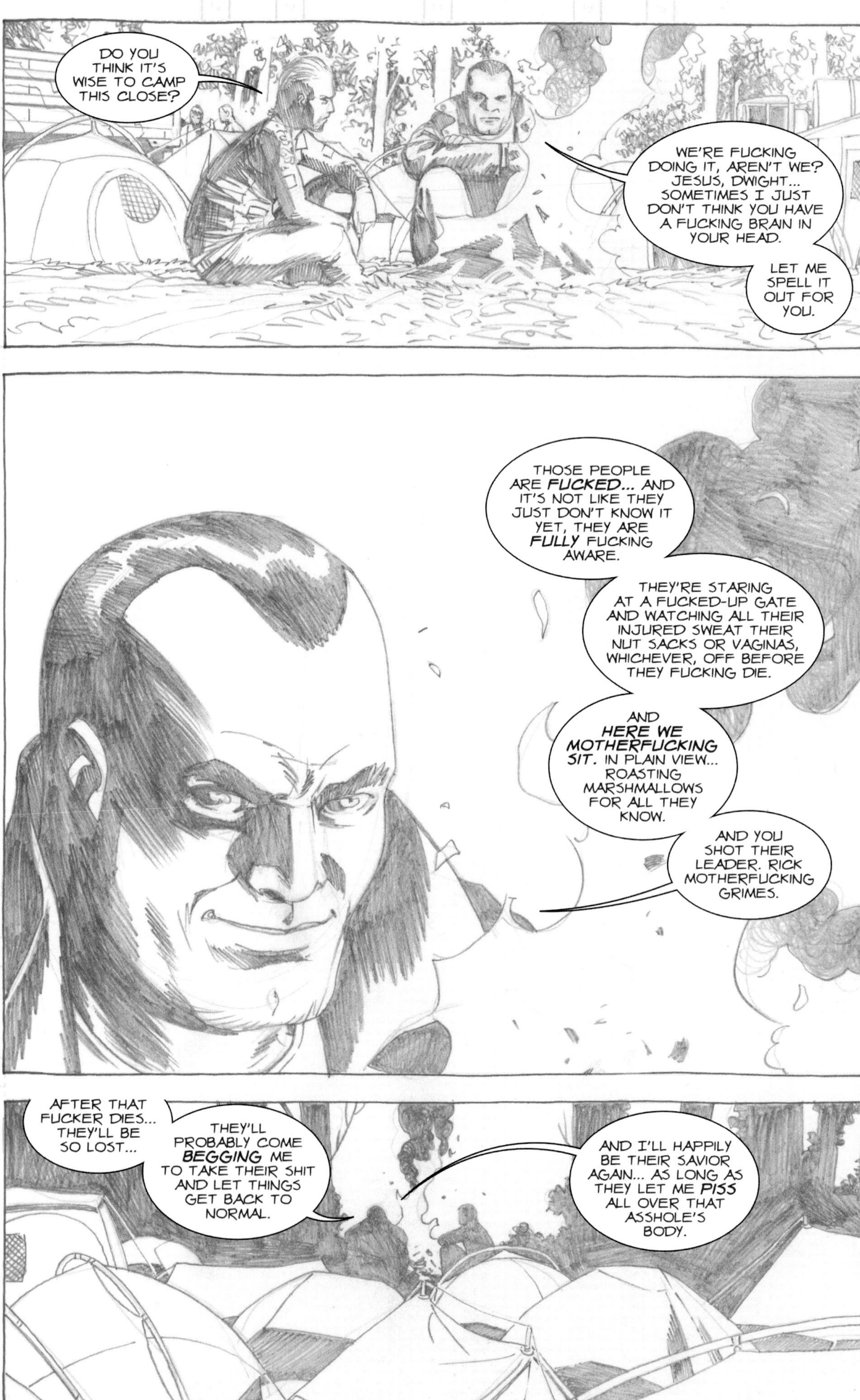
DO YOU THINK IT'S WISE TO CAMP THIS CLOSE?
WE'RE FUCKING DOING IT, AREN'T WE? JESUS, DWIGHT... SOMETIMES I JUST DON'T THINK YOU HAVE A FUCKING BRAIN IN YOUR HEAD.
LET ME SPELL IT OUT FOR YOU.
THOSE PEOPLE ARE FUCKED... AND IT'S NOT LIKE THEY JUST DON'T KNOW IT YET, THEY ARE FULLY FUCKING AWARE.
THEY'RE STARING AT A FUCKED-UP GATE AND WATCHING ALL THEIR INJURED SWEAT THEIR NUT SACKS OR VAGINAS, WHICHEVER, OFF BEFORE THEY FUCKING DIE.
AND HERE WE MOTHERFUCKING SIT. IN PLAIN VIEW... ROASTING MARSHMALLOWS FOR ALL THEY KNOW.
AND YOU SHOT THEIR LEADER. RICK MOTHERFUCKING GRIMES.
AFTER THAT FUCKER DIES... THEY'LL BE SO LOST...
THEY'LL PROBABLY COME BEGGING ME TO TAKE THEIR SHIT AND LET THINGS GET BACK TO NORMAL.
AND I'LL HAPPILY BE THEIR SAVIOR AGAIN... AS LONG AS THEY LET ME PISS ALL OVER THAT ASSHOLE'S BODY.

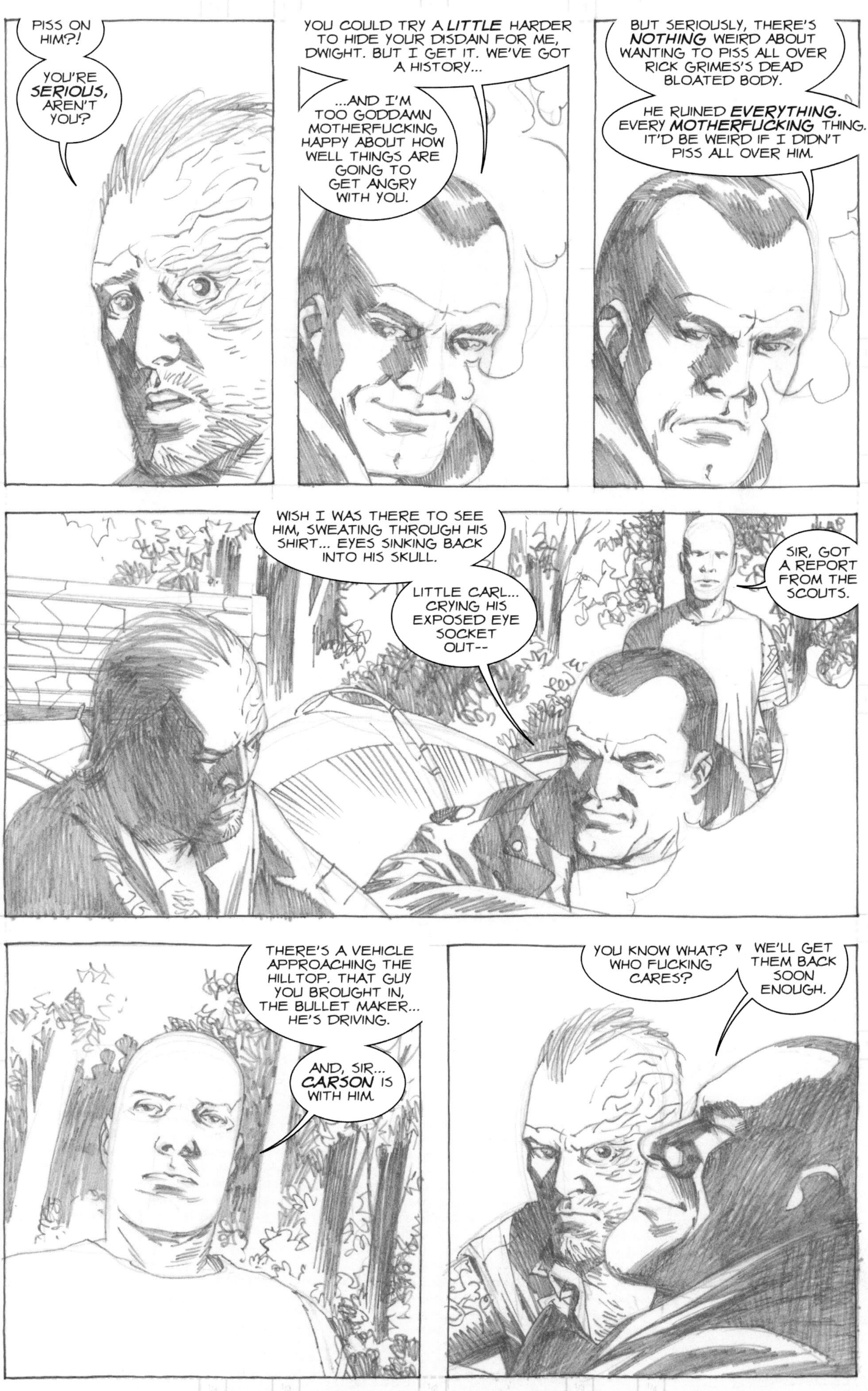
PISS ON HIM?!
YOU'RE SERIOUS, AREN'T YOU?
YOU COULD TRY A LITTLE HARDER TO HIDE YOUR DISDAIN FOR ME, DWIGHT. BUT I GET IT. WE'VE GOT A HISTORY...
...AND I'M TOO GODDAMN MOTHERFUCKING HAPPY ABOUT HOW WELL THINGS ARE GOING TO GET ANGRY WITH YOU.
BUT SERIOUSLY, THERE'S NOTHING WEIRD ABOUT WANTING TO PISS ALL OVER RICK GRIMES'S DEAD BLOATED BODY.
HE RUINED EVERYTHING. EVERY MOTHERFUCKING THING. IT'D BE WEIRD IF I DIDN'T PISS ALL OVER HIM.
WISH I WAS THERE TO SEE HIM, SWEATING THROUGH HIS SHIRT... EYES SINKING BACK INTO HIS SKULL.
LITTLE CARL... CRYING HIS EXPOSED EYE SOCKET OUT--
SIR, GOT A REPORT FROM THE SCOUTS.
THERE'S A VEHICLE APPROACHING THE HILLTOP. THAT GUY YOU BROUGHT IN, THE BULLET MAKER... HE'S DRIVING.
AND, SIR... CARSON IS WITH HIM.
YOU KNOW WHAT? WHO FUCKING CARES?
WE'LL GET THEM BACK SOON ENOUGH.

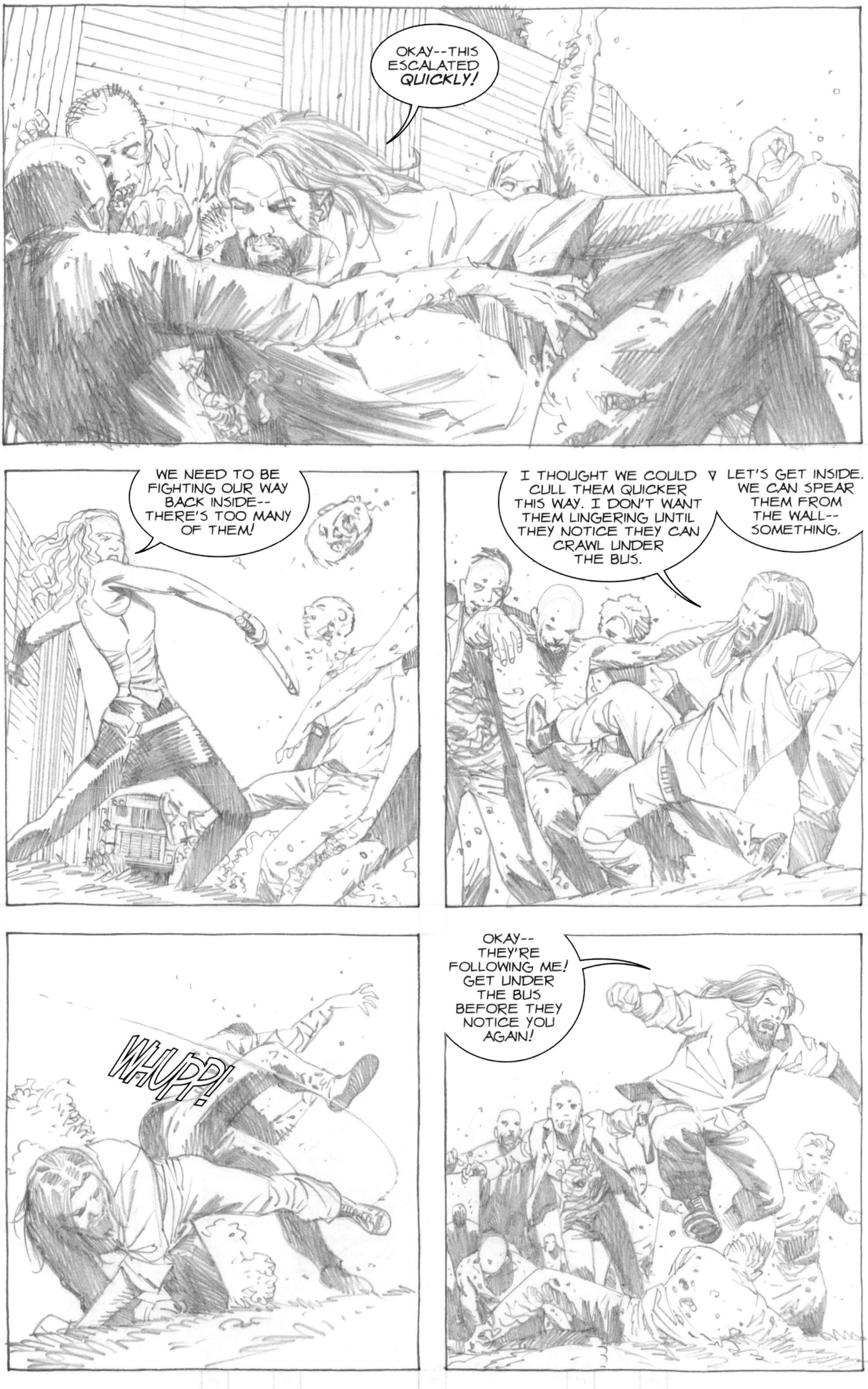
OKAY--THIS ESCALATED QUICKLY!
WE NEED TO BE FIGHTING OUR WAY BACK INSIDE-- THERE'S TOO MANY OF THEM!
I THOUGHT WE COULD CULL THEM QUICKER THIS WAY. I DON'T WANT THEM LINGERING UNTIL THEY NOTICE THEY CAN CRAWL UNDER THE BUS.
LET'S GET INSIDE. WE CAN SPEAR THEM FROM THE WALL-- SOMETHING.
WHUPP!
OKAY-- THEY'RE FOLLOWING ME! GET UNDER THE BUS BEFORE THEY NOTICE YOU AGAIN!

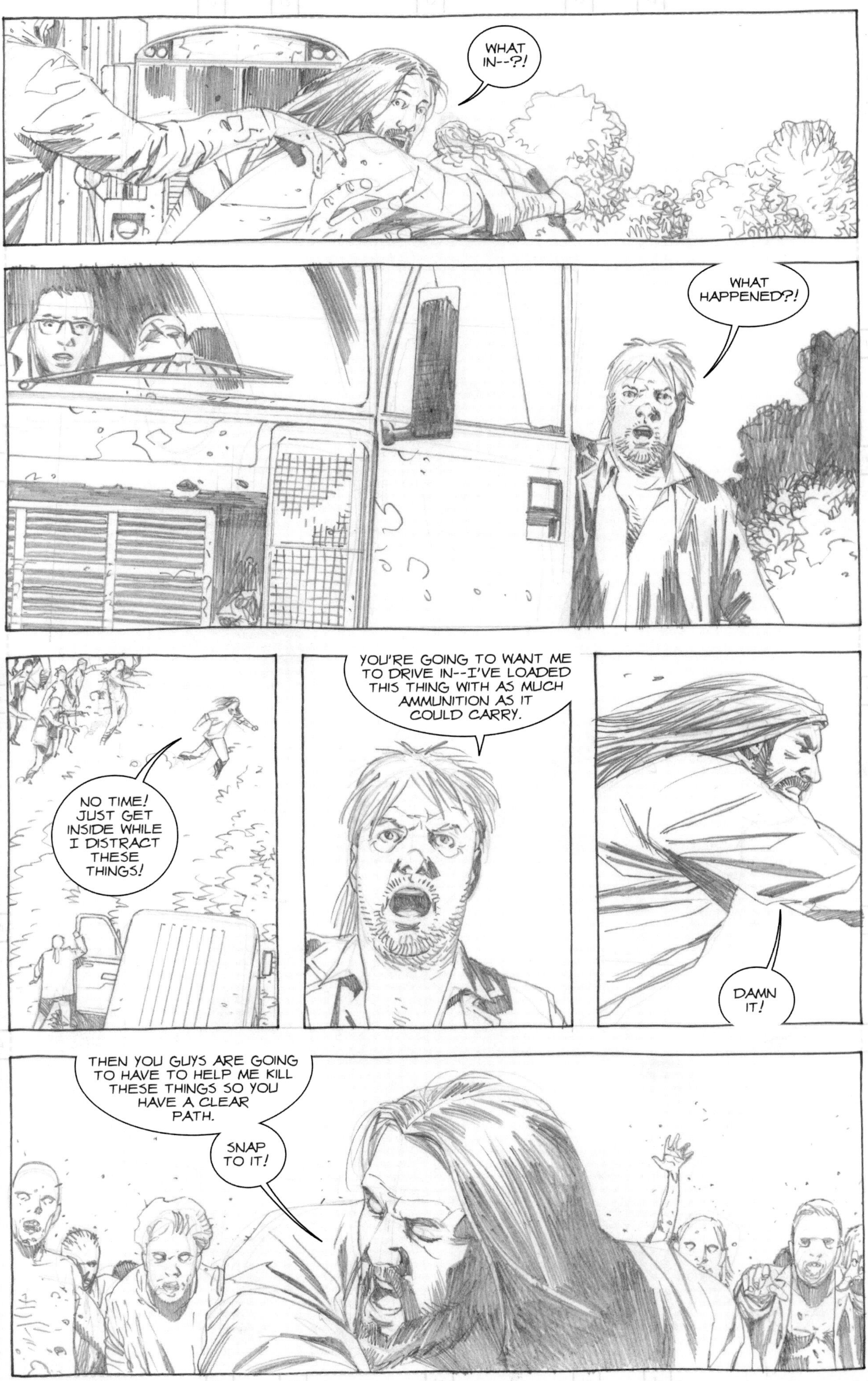
WHAT IN--?!
WHAT HAPPENED?!
NO TIME! JUST GET INSIDE WHILE I DISTRACT THESE THINGS!
YOU'RE GOING TO WANT ME TO DRIVE IN--I'VE LOADED THIS THING WITH AS MUCH AMMUNITION AS IT COULD CARRY.
DAMN IT!
THEN YOU GUYS ARE GOING TO HAVE TO HELP ME KILL THESE THINGS SO YOU HAVE A CLEAR PATH.
SNAP TO IT!

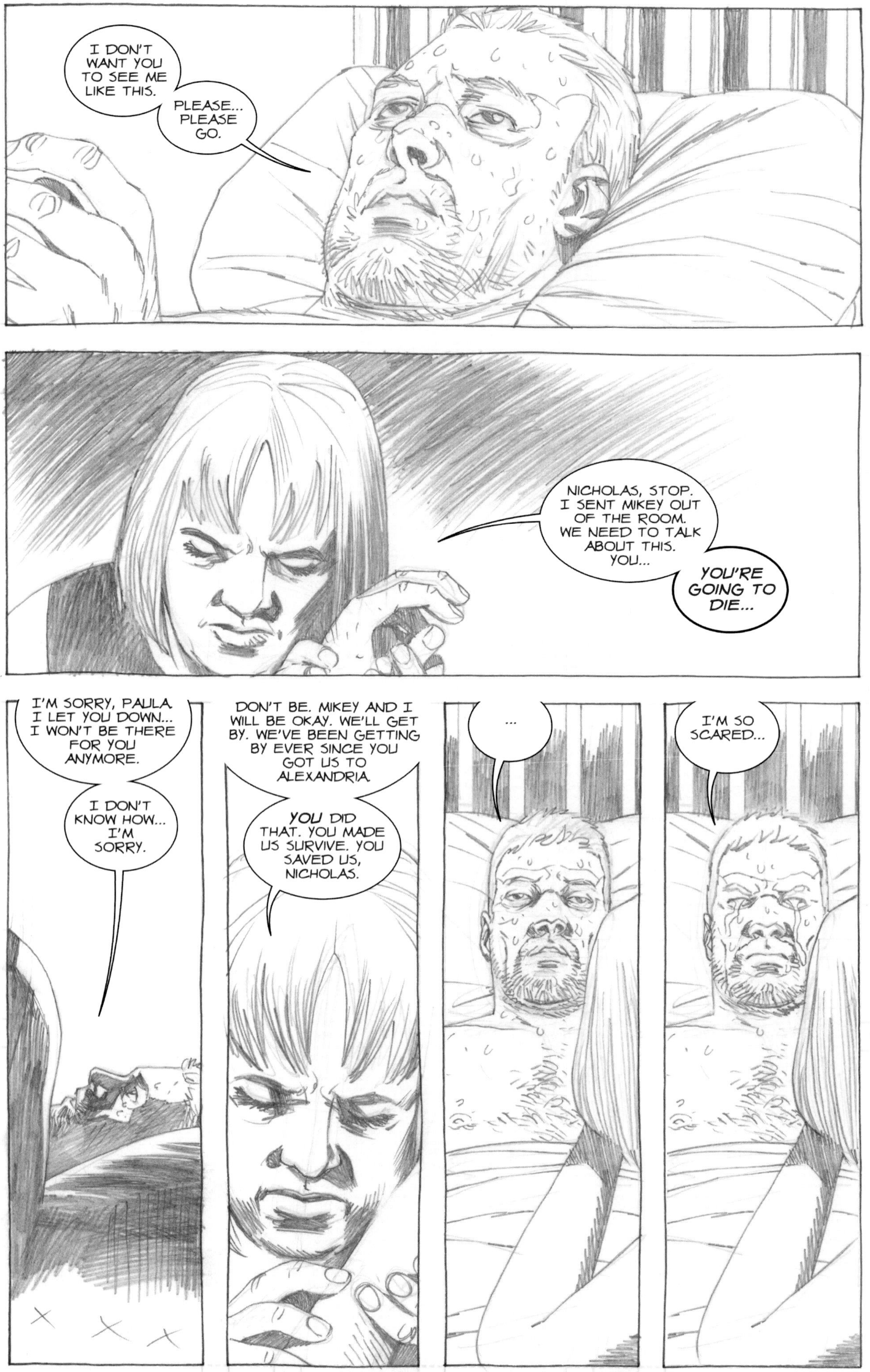
I DON'T WANT YOU TO SEE ME LIKE THIS.
PLEASE... PLEASE GO.
NICHOLAS, STOP. I SENT MIKEY OUT OF THE ROOM. WE NEED TO TALK ABOUT THIS. YOU...
YOU'RE GOING TO DIE...
I'M SORRY, PAULA. I LET YOU DOWN... I WON'T BE THERE FOR YOU ANYMORE.
I DON'T KNOW HOW... I'M SORRY.
DON'T BE. MIKEY AND I WILL BE OKAY. WE'LL GET BY. WE'VE BEEN GETTING BY EVER SINCE YOU GOT US TO ALEXANDRIA.
YOU DID THAT. YOU MADE US SURVIVE. YOU SAVED US, NICHOLAS.
...
I'M SO SCARED...

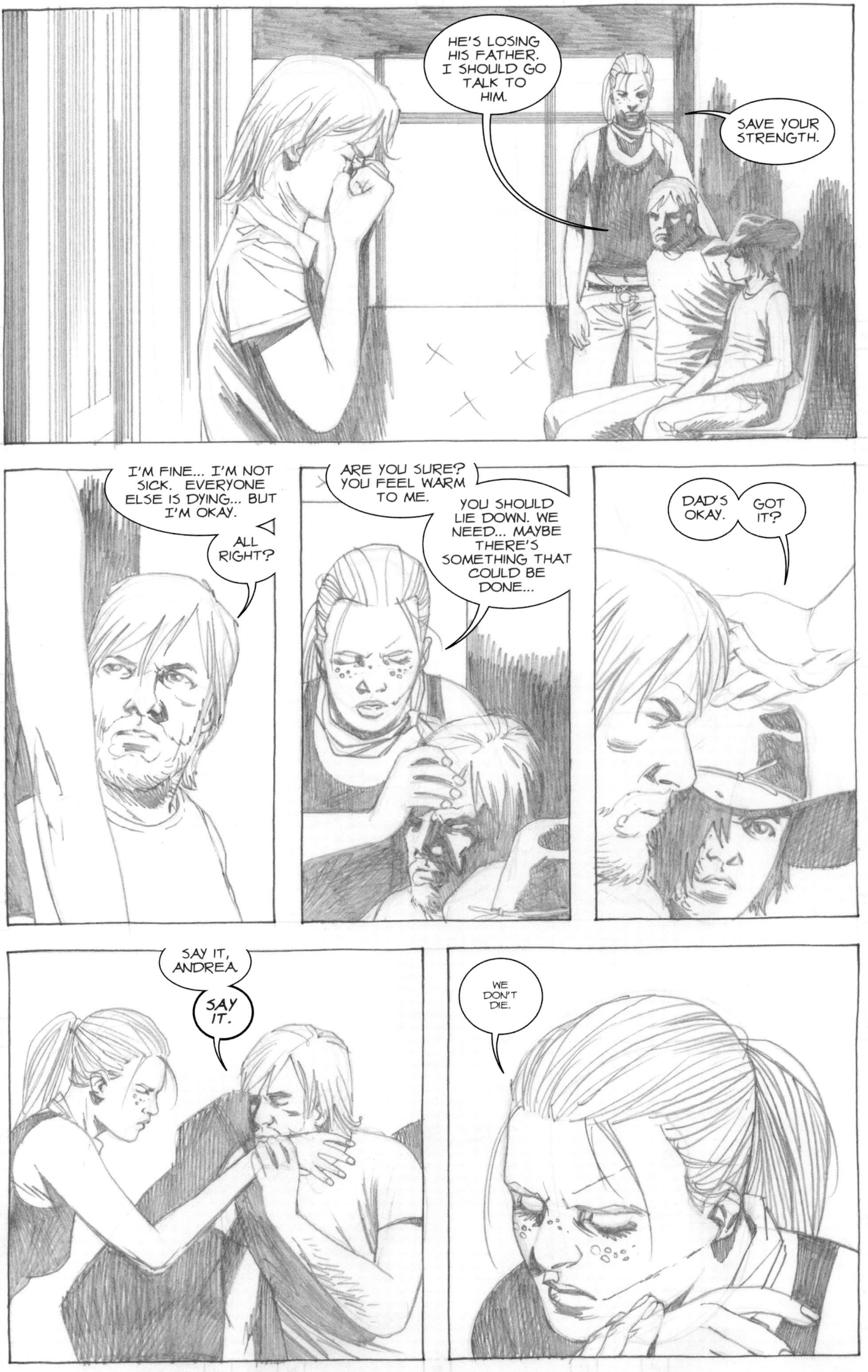
HE'S LOSING HIS FATHER. I SHOULD GO TALK TO HIM.
SAVE YOUR STRENGTH.
I'M FINE... I'M NOT SICK. EVERYONE ELSE IS DYING... BUT I'M OKAY.
ALL RIGHT?
ARE YOU SURE? YOU FEEL WARM TO ME.
YOU SHOULD LIE DOWN. WE NEED... MAYBE THERE'S SOMETHING THAT COULD BE DONE...
DAD'S OKAY.
GOT IT?
SAY IT, ANDREA.
SAY IT.
WE DON'T DIE.

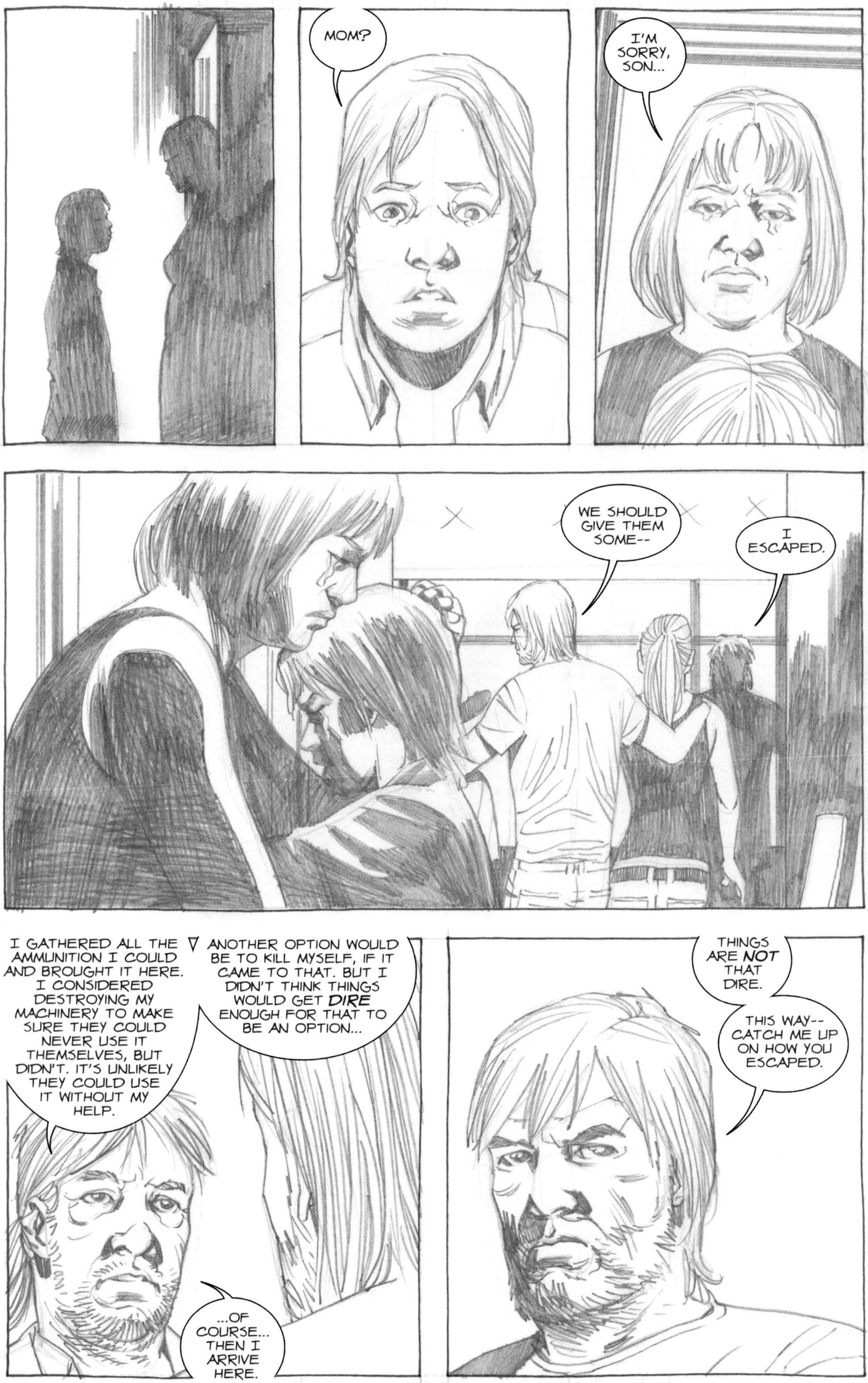
MOM?
I'M SORRY, SON...
WE SHOULD GIVE THEM SOME--
I ESCAPED.
I GATHERED ALL THE AMMUNITION I COULD AND BROUGHT IT HERE. I CONSIDERED DESTROYING MY MACHINERY TO MAKE SURE THEY COULD NEVER USE IT THEMSELVES, BUT DIDN'T. IT'S UNLIKELY THEY COULD USE IT WITHOUT MY HELP.
ANOTHER OPTION WOULD BE TO KILL MYSELF, IF IT CAME TO THAT. BUT I DIDN'T THINK THINGS WOULD GET DIRE ENOUGH FOR THAT TO BE AN OPTION...
...OF COURSE... THEN I ARRIVE HERE.
THINGS ARE NOT THAT DIRE.
THIS WAY-- CATCH ME UP ON HOW YOU ESCAPED.

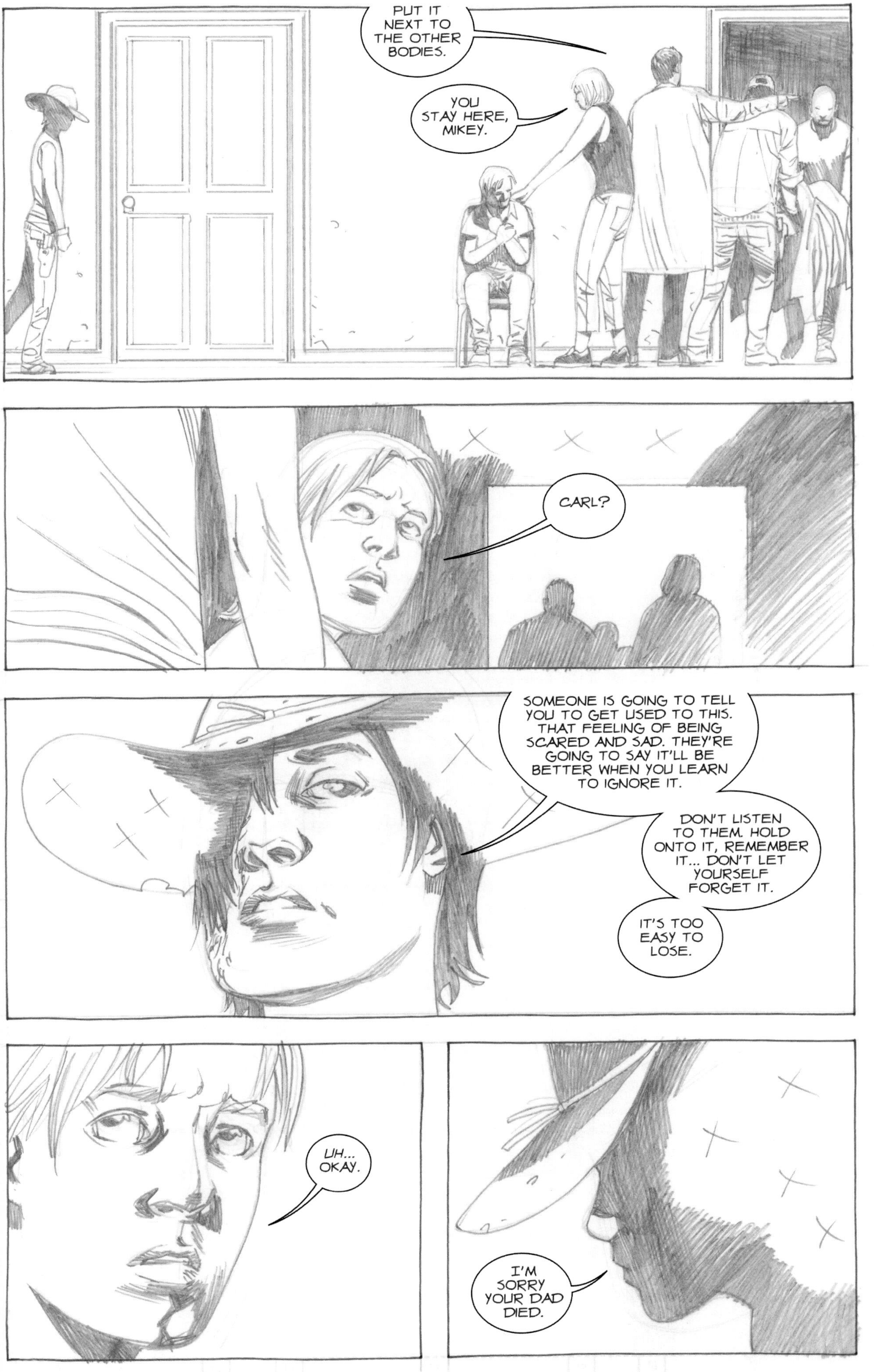
PUT IT NEXT TO THE OTHER BODIES.
YOU STAY HERE, MIKEY.
CARL?
SOMEONE IS GOING TO TELL YOU TO GET USED TO THIS. THAT FEELING OF BEING SCARED AND SAD. THEY'RE GOING TO SAY IT'LL BE BETTER WHEN YOU LEARN TO IGNORE IT.
DON'T LISTEN TO THEM. HOLD ONTO IT, REMEMBER IT... DON'T LET YOURSELF FORGET IT.
IT'S TOO EASY TO LOSE.
UH... OKAY.
I'M SORRY YOUR DAD DIED.

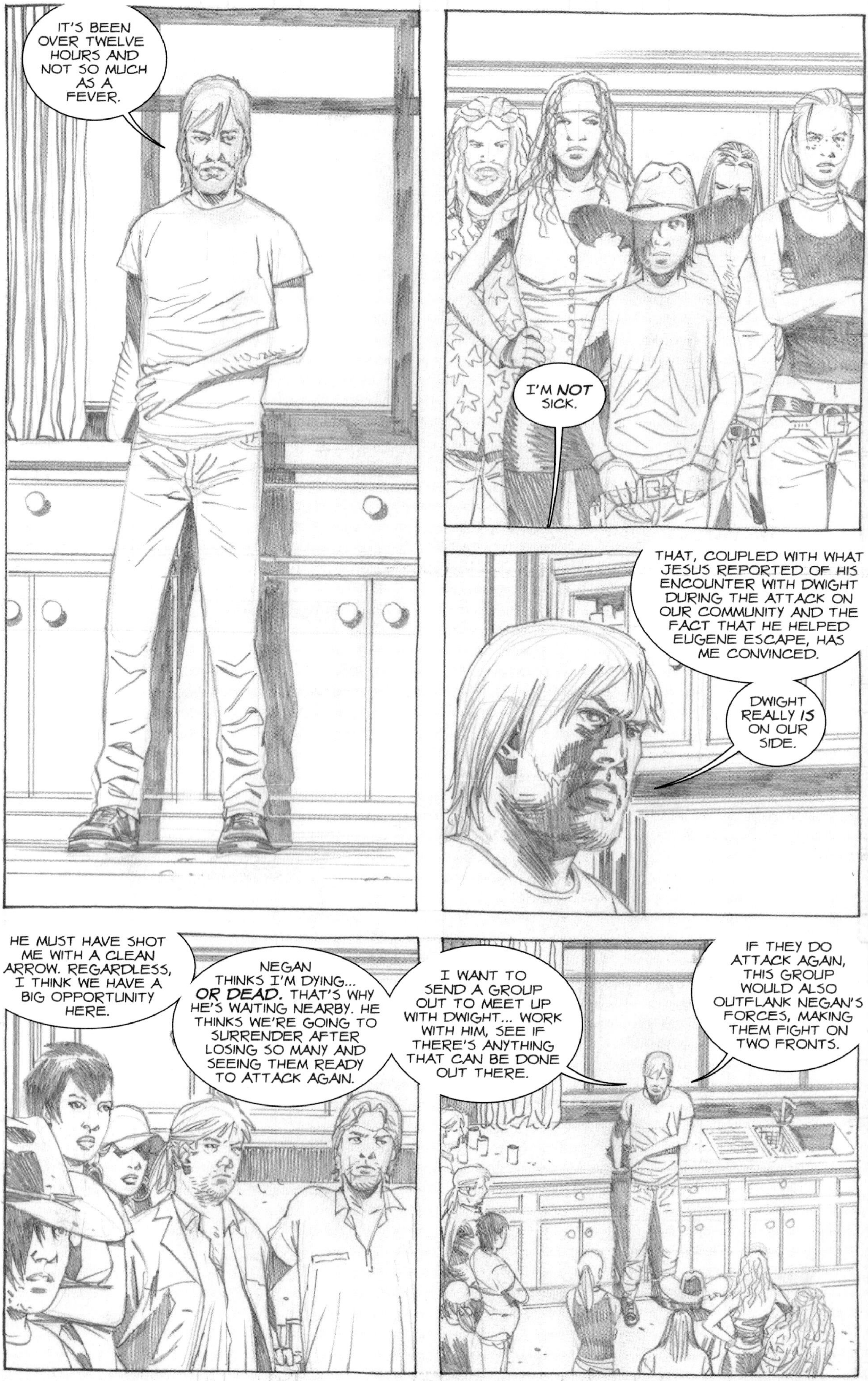
IT'S BEEN OVER TWELVE HOURS AND NOT SO MUCH AS A FEVER.
I'M **NOT** SICK.
THAT, COUPLED WITH WHAT JESUS REPORTED OF HIS ENCOUNTER WITH DWIGHT DURING THE ATTACK ON OUR COMMUNITY AND THE FACT THAT HE HELPED EUGENE ESCAPE, HAS ME CONVINCED.
DWIGHT REALLY ***IS*** ON OUR SIDE.
HE MUST HAVE SHOT ME WITH A CLEAN ARROW. REGARDLESS, I THINK WE HAVE A BIG OPPORTUNITY HERE.
NEGAN THINKS I'M DYING... ***OR DEAD.*** THAT'S WHY HE'S WAITING NEARBY. HE THINKS WE'RE GOING TO SURRENDER AFTER LOSING SO MANY AND SEEING THEM READY TO ATTACK AGAIN.
I WANT TO SEND A GROUP OUT TO MEET UP WITH DWIGHT... WORK WITH HIM, SEE IF THERE'S ANYTHING THAT CAN BE DONE OUT THERE.
IF THEY DO ATTACK AGAIN, THIS GROUP WOULD ALSO OUTFLANK NEGAN'S FORCES, MAKING THEM FIGHT ON TWO FRONTS.

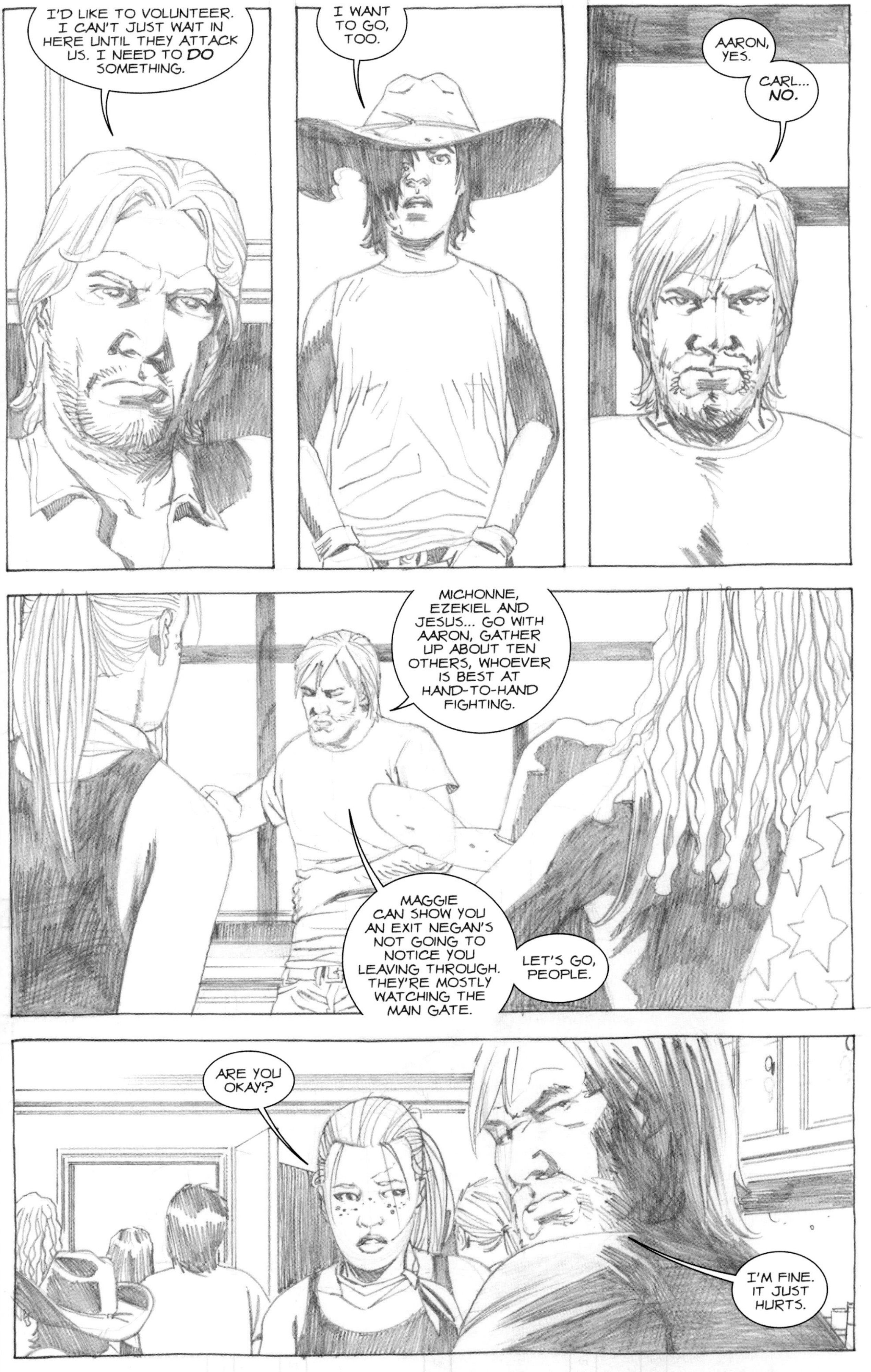
I'D LIKE TO VOLUNTEER. I CAN'T JUST WAIT IN HERE UNTIL THEY ATTACK US. I NEED TO DO SOMETHING.
I WANT TO GO, TOO.
AARON, YES.
CARL... NO.
MICHONNE, EZEKIEL AND JESUS... GO WITH AARON, GATHER UP ABOUT TEN OTHERS, WHOEVER IS BEST AT HAND-TO-HAND FIGHTING.
MAGGIE CAN SHOW YOU AN EXIT NEGAN'S NOT GOING TO NOTICE YOU LEAVING THROUGH. THEY'RE MOSTLY WATCHING THE MAIN GATE.
LET'S GO, PEOPLE.
ARE YOU OKAY?
I'M FINE. IT JUST HURTS.

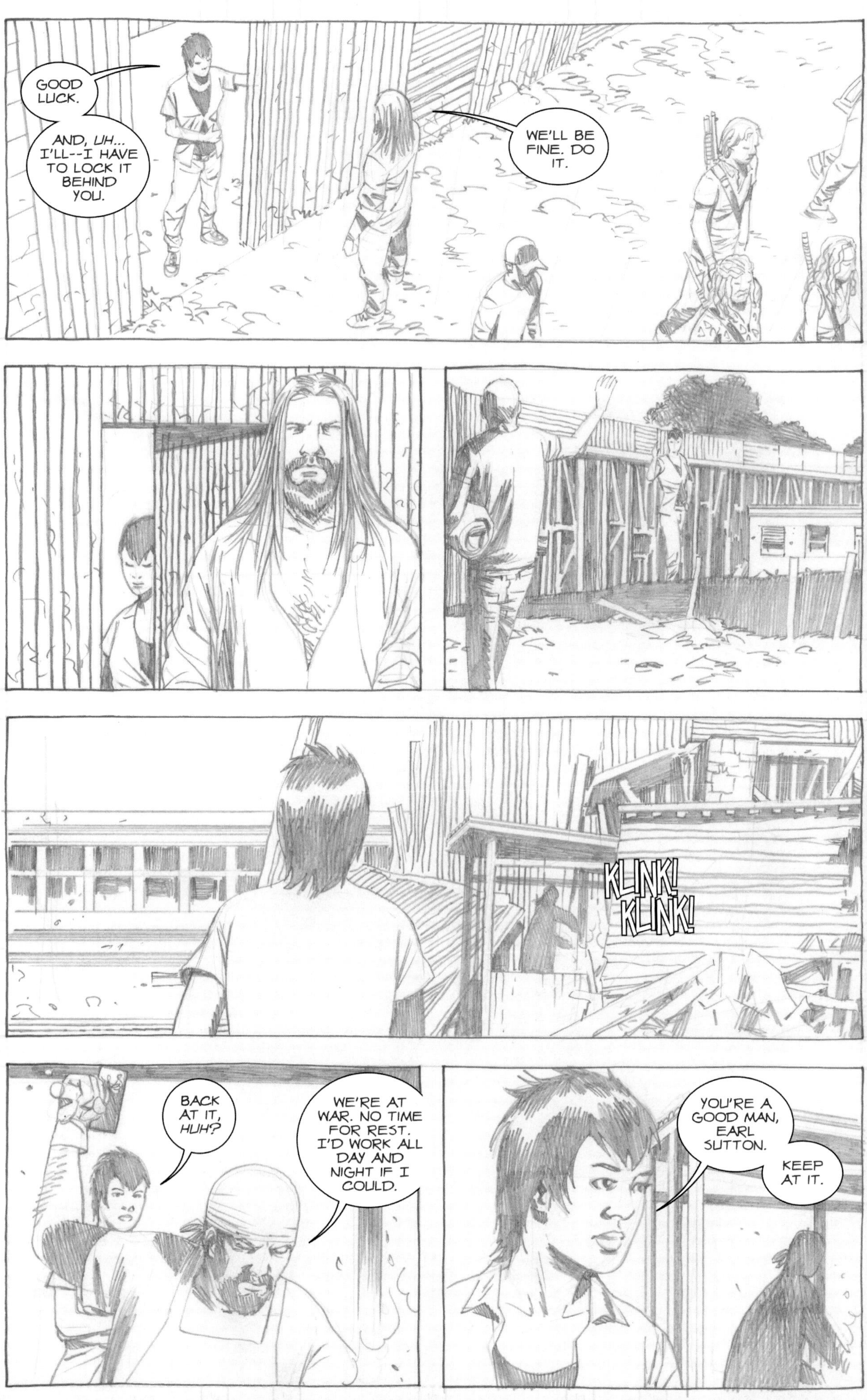
GOOD LUCK.
AND, UH... I'LL--I HAVE TO LOCK IT BEHIND YOU.
WE'LL BE FINE. DO IT.
KLINK! KLINK!
BACK AT IT, HUH?
WE'RE AT WAR. NO TIME FOR REST. I'D WORK ALL DAY AND NIGHT IF I COULD.
YOU'RE A GOOD MAN, EARL SUTTON.
KEEP AT IT.

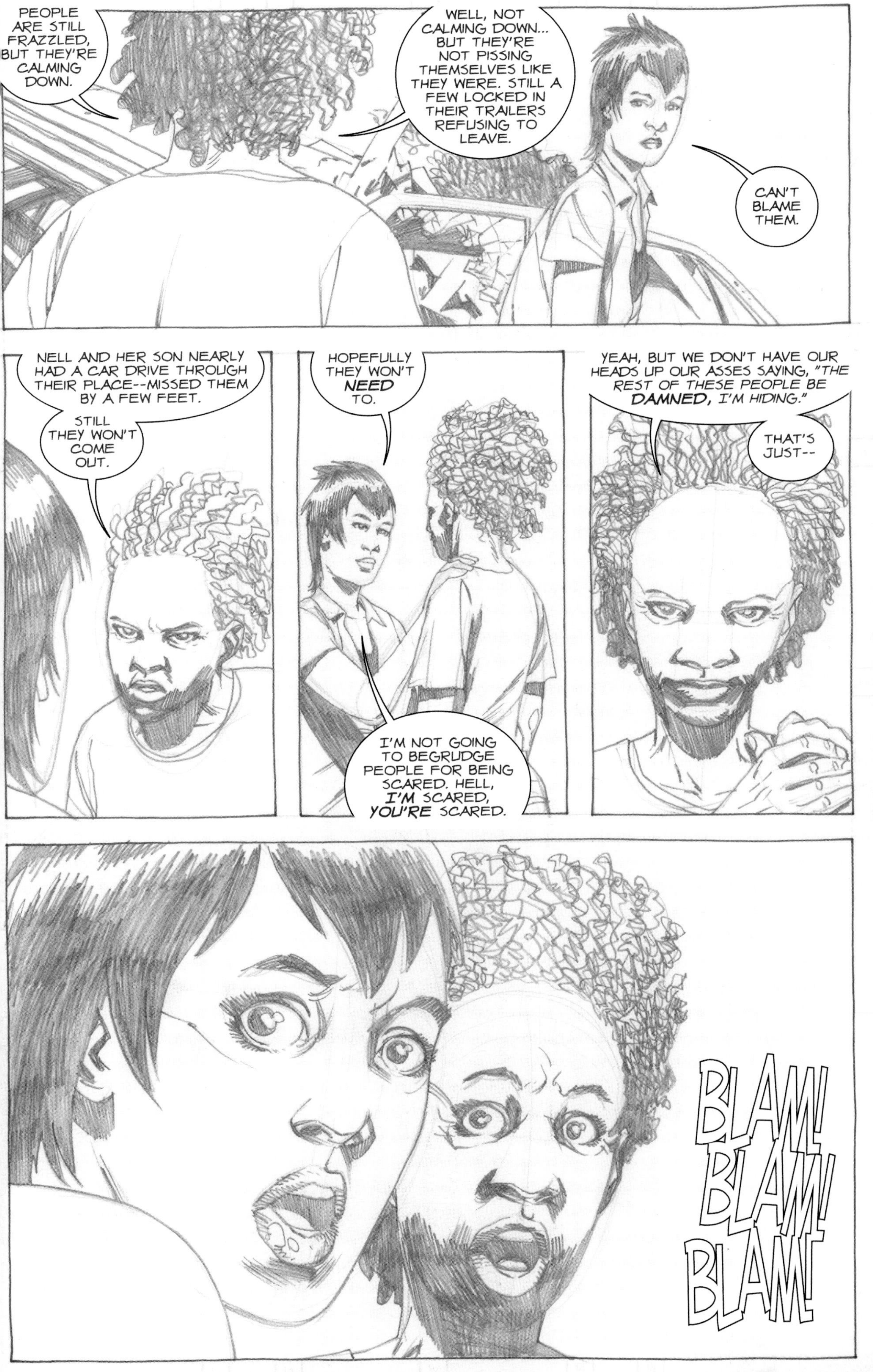

PEOPLE ARE STILL FRAZZLED, BUT THEY'RE CALMING DOWN.
WELL, NOT CALMING DOWN... BUT THEY'RE NOT PISSING THEMSELVES LIKE THEY WERE. STILL A FEW LOCKED IN THEIR TRAILERS REFUSING TO LEAVE.
CAN'T BLAME THEM.
NELL AND HER SON NEARLY HAD A CAR DRIVE THROUGH THEIR PLACE--MISSED THEM BY A FEW FEET.
STILL THEY WON'T COME OUT.
HOPEFULLY THEY WON'T NEED TO.
I'M NOT GOING TO BEGRUDGE PEOPLE FOR BEING SCARED. HELL, I'M SCARED, YOU'RE SCARED.
YEAH, BUT WE DON'T HAVE OUR HEADS UP OUR ASSES SAYING, "THE REST OF THESE PEOPLE BE DAMNED, I'M HIDING."
THAT'S JUST--
BLAM! BLAM! BLAM!

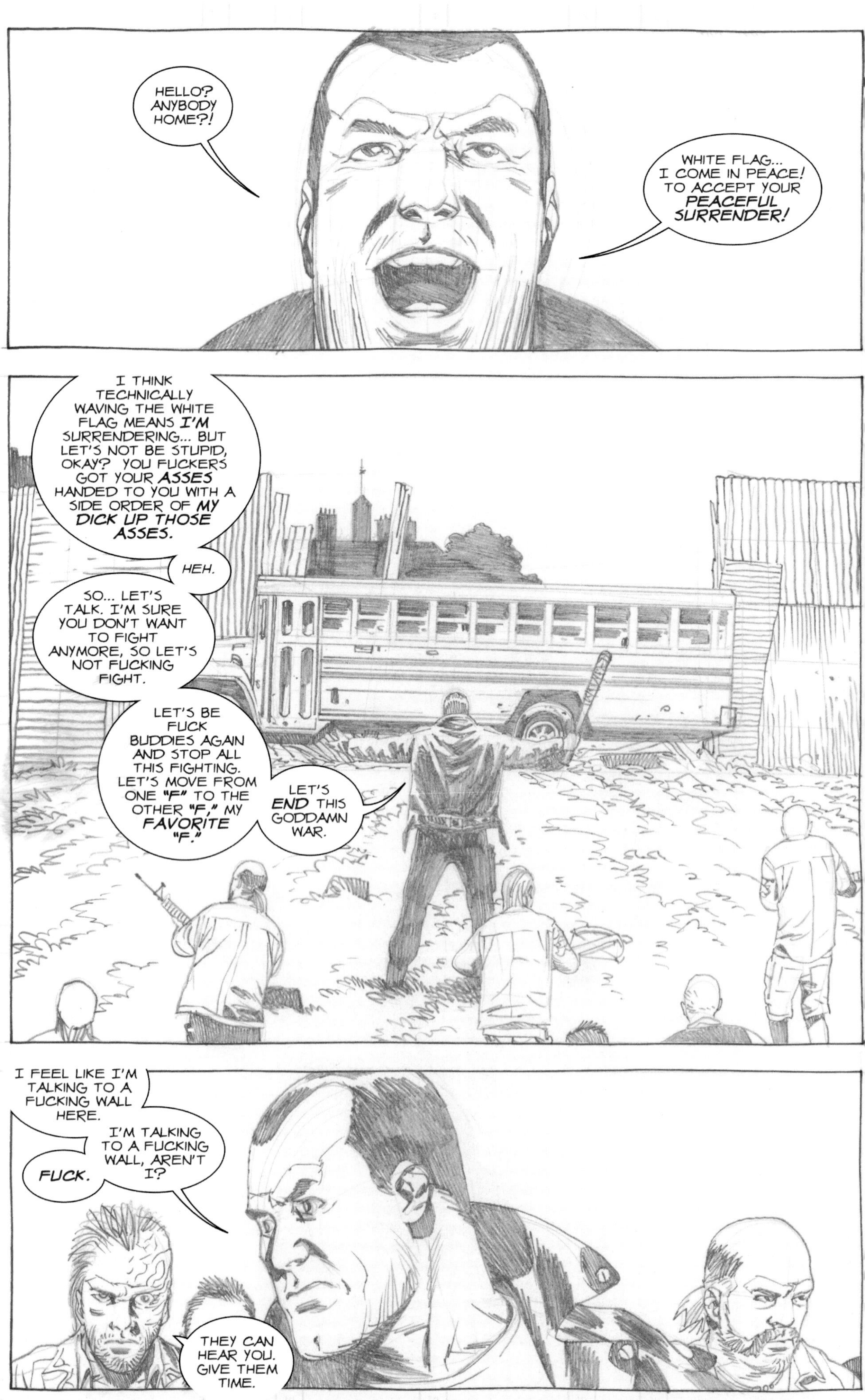
HELLO? ANYBODY HOME?!
WHITE FLAG... I COME IN PEACE! TO ACCEPT YOUR PEACEFUL SURRENDER!
I THINK TECHNICALLY WAVING THE WHITE FLAG MEANS I'M SURRENDERING... BUT LET'S NOT BE STUPID, OKAY? YOU FUCKERS GOT YOUR ASSES HANDED TO YOU WITH A SIDE ORDER OF MY DICK UP THOSE ASSES.
HEH.
SO... LET'S TALK. I'M SURE YOU DON'T WANT TO FIGHT ANYMORE, SO LET'S NOT FUCKING FIGHT.
LET'S BE FUCK BUDDIES AGAIN AND STOP ALL THIS FIGHTING. LET'S MOVE FROM ONE "F" TO THE OTHER "F," MY FAVORITE "F."
LET'S END THIS GODDAMN WAR.
I FEEL LIKE I'M TALKING TO A FUCKING WALL HERE.
I'M TALKING TO A FUCKING WALL, AREN'T I?
FUCK.
THEY CAN HEAR YOU. GIVE THEM TIME.

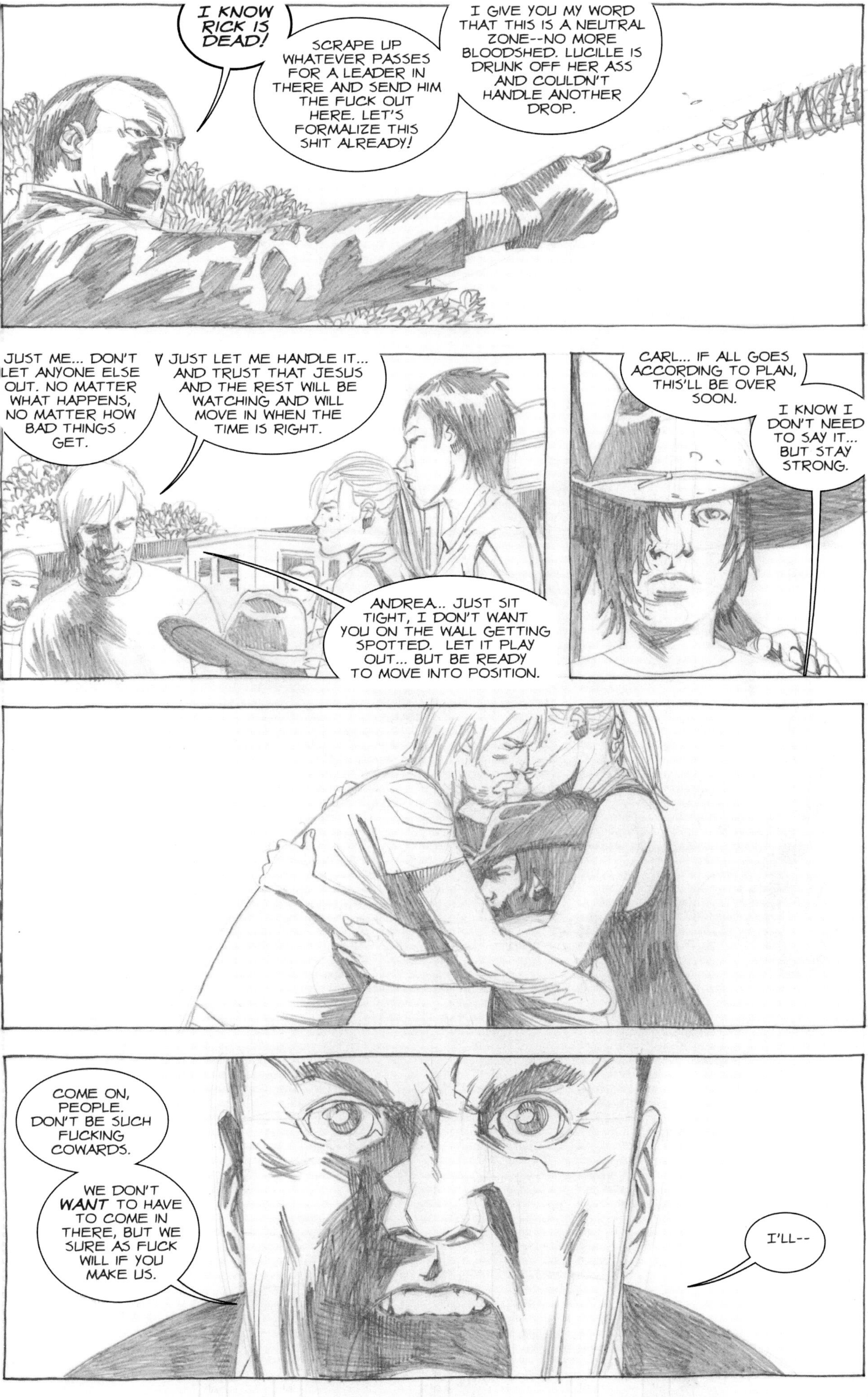

I KNOW RICK IS DEAD!
SCRAPE UP WHATEVER PASSES FOR A LEADER IN THERE AND SEND HIM THE FUCK OUT HERE. LET'S FORMALIZE THIS SHIT ALREADY!
I GIVE YOU MY WORD THAT THIS IS A NEUTRAL ZONE--NO MORE BLOODSHED. LUCILLE IS DRUNK OFF HER ASS AND COULDN'T HANDLE ANOTHER DROP.
JUST ME... DON'T LET ANYONE ELSE OUT. NO MATTER WHAT HAPPENS, NO MATTER HOW BAD THINGS GET.
JUST LET ME HANDLE IT... AND TRUST THAT JESUS AND THE REST WILL BE WATCHING AND WILL MOVE IN WHEN THE TIME IS RIGHT.
ANDREA... JUST SIT TIGHT, I DON'T WANT YOU ON THE WALL GETTING SPOTTED. LET IT PLAY OUT... BUT BE READY TO MOVE INTO POSITION.
CARL... IF ALL GOES ACCORDING TO PLAN, THIS'LL BE OVER SOON.
I KNOW I DON'T NEED TO SAY IT... BUT STAY STRONG.
COME ON, PEOPLE. DON'T BE SUCH FUCKING COWARDS.
WE DON'T WANT TO HAVE TO COME IN THERE, BUT WE SURE AS FUCK WILL IF YOU MAKE US.
I'LL--

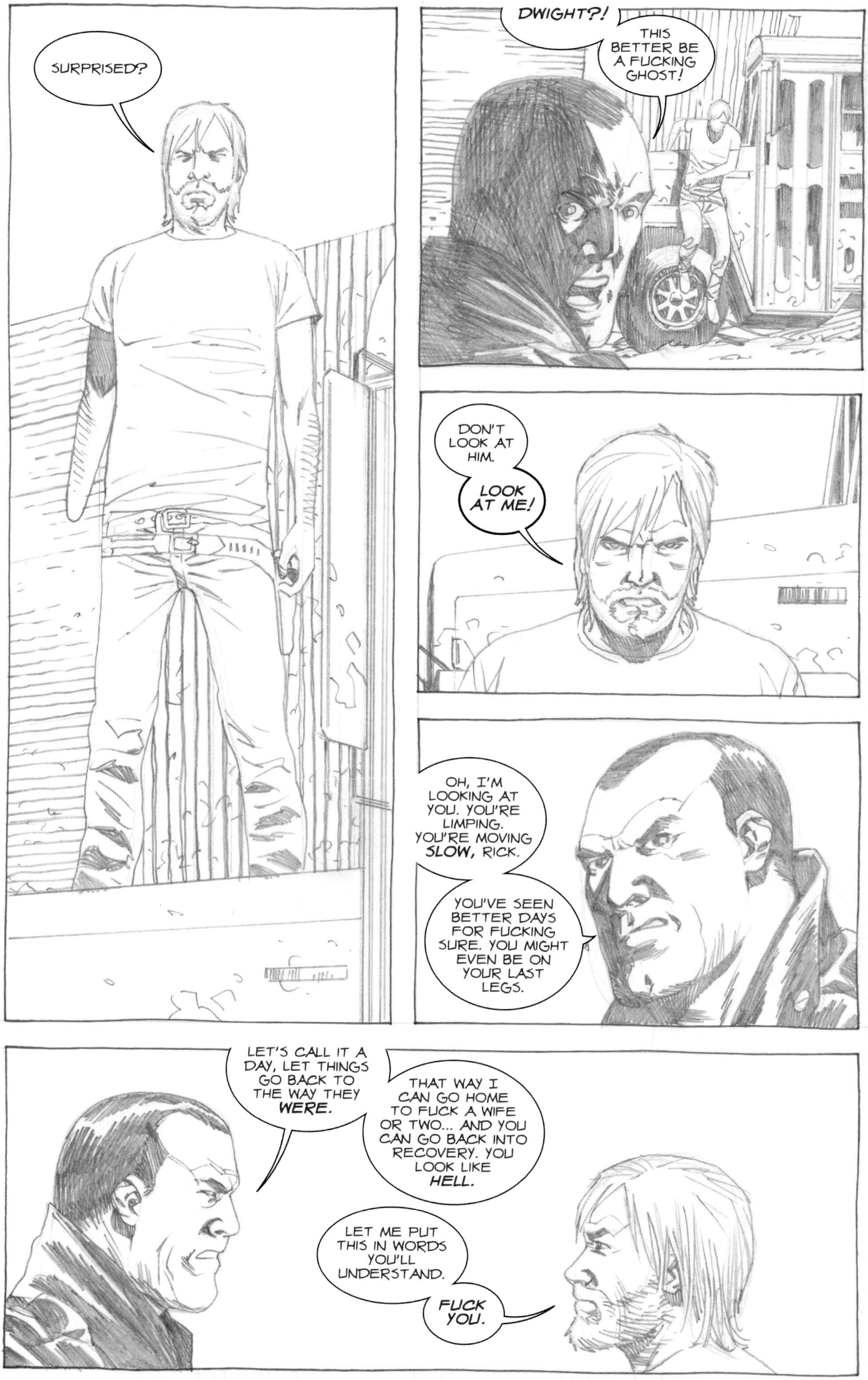
SURPRISED?
DWIGHT?!
THIS BETTER BE A FUCKING GHOST!
DON'T LOOK AT HIM.
LOOK AT ME!
OH, I'M LOOKING AT YOU. YOU'RE LIMPING. YOU'RE MOVING SLOW, RICK.
YOU'VE SEEN BETTER DAYS FOR FUCKING SURE. YOU MIGHT EVEN BE ON YOUR LAST LEGS.
LET'S CALL IT A DAY, LET THINGS GO BACK TO THE WAY THEY WERE.
THAT WAY I CAN GO HOME TO FUCK A WIFE OR TWO... AND YOU CAN GO BACK INTO RECOVERY. YOU LOOK LIKE HELL.
LET ME PUT THIS IN WORDS YOU'LL UNDERSTAND.
FUCK YOU.

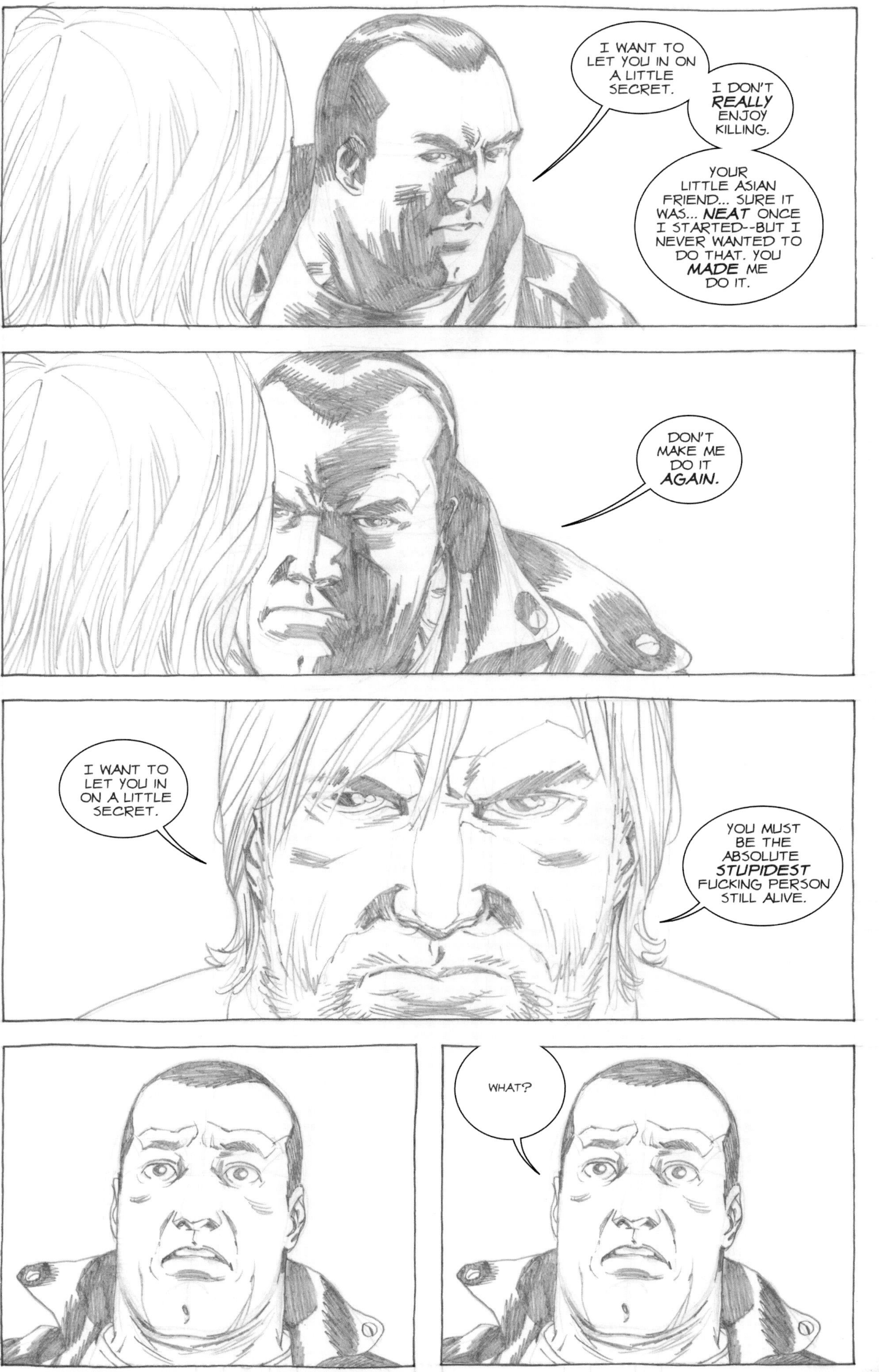
I WANT TO LET YOU IN ON A LITTLE SECRET.
I DON'T REALLY ENJOY KILLING.
YOUR LITTLE ASIAN FRIEND... SURE IT WAS... NEAT ONCE I STARTED--BUT I NEVER WANTED TO DO THAT. YOU MADE ME DO IT.
DON'T MAKE ME DO IT AGAIN.
I WANT TO LET YOU IN ON A LITTLE SECRET.
YOU MUST BE THE ABSOLUTE STUPIDEST FUCKING PERSON STILL ALIVE.
WHAT?

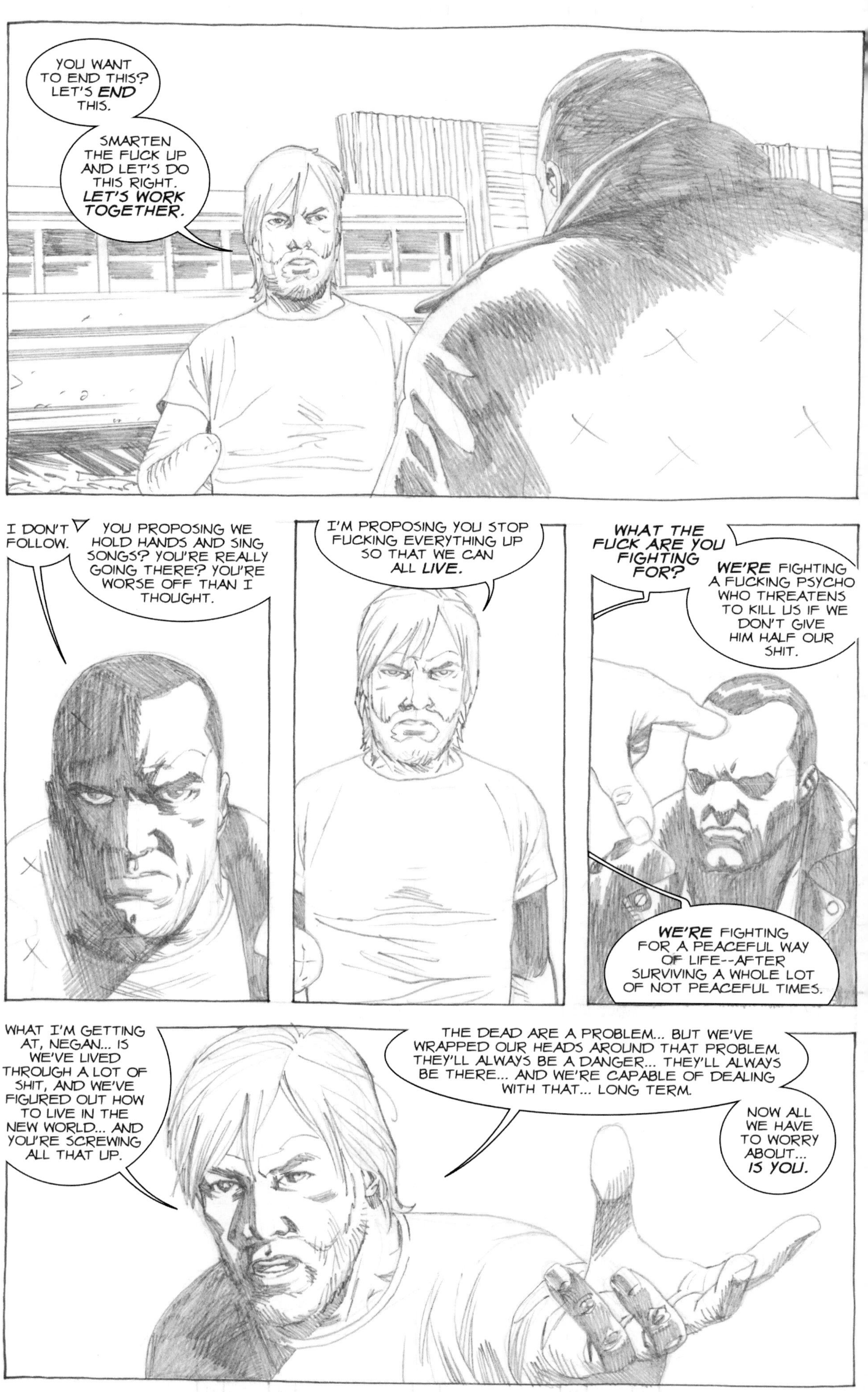
YOU WANT TO END THIS? LET'S END THIS.
SMARTEN THE FUCK UP AND LET'S DO THIS RIGHT. LET'S WORK TOGETHER.
I DON'T FOLLOW.
YOU PROPOSING WE HOLD HANDS AND SING SONGS? YOU'RE REALLY GOING THERE? YOU'RE WORSE OFF THAN I THOUGHT.
I'M PROPOSING YOU STOP FUCKING EVERYTHING UP SO THAT WE CAN ALL LIVE.
WHAT THE FUCK ARE YOU FIGHTING FOR?
WE'RE FIGHTING A FUCKING PSYCHO WHO THREATENS TO KILL US IF WE DON'T GIVE HIM HALF OUR SHIT.
WE'RE FIGHTING FOR A PEACEFUL WAY OF LIFE--AFTER SURVIVING A WHOLE LOT OF NOT PEACEFUL TIMES.
WHAT I'M GETTING AT, NEGAN... IS WE'VE LIVED THROUGH A LOT OF SHIT, AND WE'VE FIGURED OUT HOW TO LIVE IN THE NEW WORLD... AND YOU'RE SCREWING ALL THAT UP.
THE DEAD ARE A PROBLEM... BUT WE'VE WRAPPED OUR HEADS AROUND THAT PROBLEM. THEY'LL ALWAYS BE A DANGER... THEY'LL ALWAYS BE THERE... AND WE'RE CAPABLE OF DEALING WITH THAT... LONG TERM.
NOW ALL WE HAVE TO WORRY ABOUT... IS YOU.

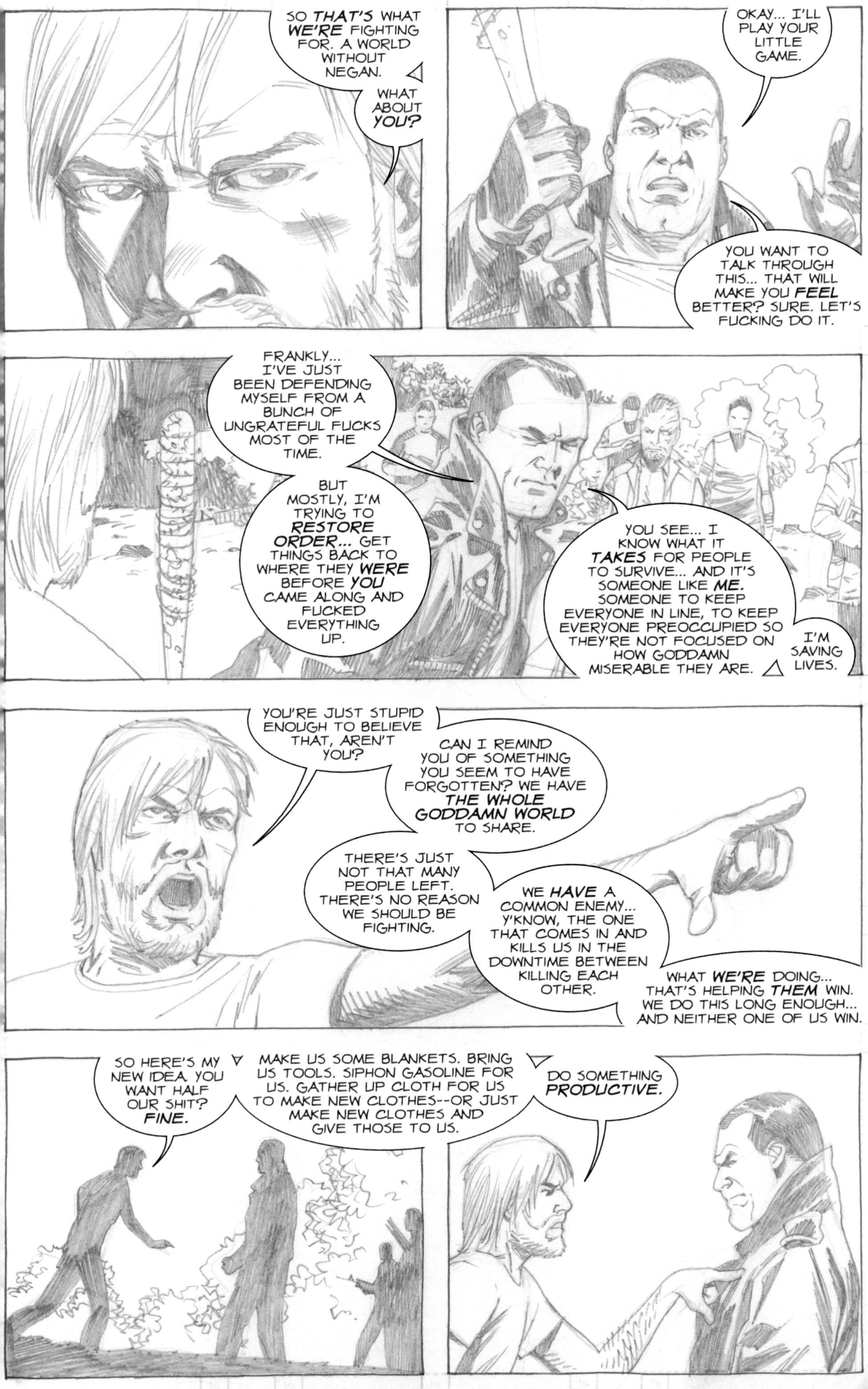
SO THAT'S WHAT WE'RE FIGHTING FOR. A WORLD WITHOUT NEGAN.
WHAT ABOUT YOU?
OKAY... I'LL PLAY YOUR LITTLE GAME.
YOU WANT TO TALK THROUGH THIS... THAT WILL MAKE YOU FEEL BETTER? SURE. LET'S FUCKING DO IT.
FRANKLY... I'VE JUST BEEN DEFENDING MYSELF FROM A BUNCH OF UNGRATEFUL FUCKS MOST OF THE TIME.
BUT MOSTLY, I'M TRYING TO RESTORE ORDER... GET THINGS BACK TO WHERE THEY WERE BEFORE YOU CAME ALONG AND FUCKED EVERYTHING UP.
YOU SEE... I KNOW WHAT IT TAKES FOR PEOPLE TO SURVIVE... AND IT'S SOMEONE LIKE ME. SOMEONE TO KEEP EVERYONE IN LINE, TO KEEP EVERYONE PREOCCUPIED SO THEY'RE NOT FOCUSED ON HOW GODDAMN MISERABLE THEY ARE.
I'M SAVING LIVES.
YOU'RE JUST STUPID ENOUGH TO BELIEVE THAT, AREN'T YOU?
CAN I REMIND YOU OF SOMETHING YOU SEEM TO HAVE FORGOTTEN? WE HAVE THE WHOLE GODDAMN WORLD TO SHARE.
THERE'S JUST NOT THAT MANY PEOPLE LEFT. THERE'S NO REASON WE SHOULD BE FIGHTING.
WE HAVE A COMMON ENEMY... Y'KNOW, THE ONE THAT COMES IN AND KILLS US IN THE DOWNTIME BETWEEN KILLING EACH OTHER.
WHAT WE'RE DOING... THAT'S HELPING THEM WIN. WE DO THIS LONG ENOUGH... AND NEITHER ONE OF US WIN.
SO HERE'S MY NEW IDEA. YOU WANT HALF OUR SHIT? FINE.
MAKE US SOME BLANKETS. BRING US TOOLS. SIPHON GASOLINE FOR US. GATHER UP CLOTH FOR US TO MAKE NEW CLOTHES--OR JUST MAKE NEW CLOTHES AND GIVE THOSE TO US.
DO SOMETHING PRODUCTIVE.

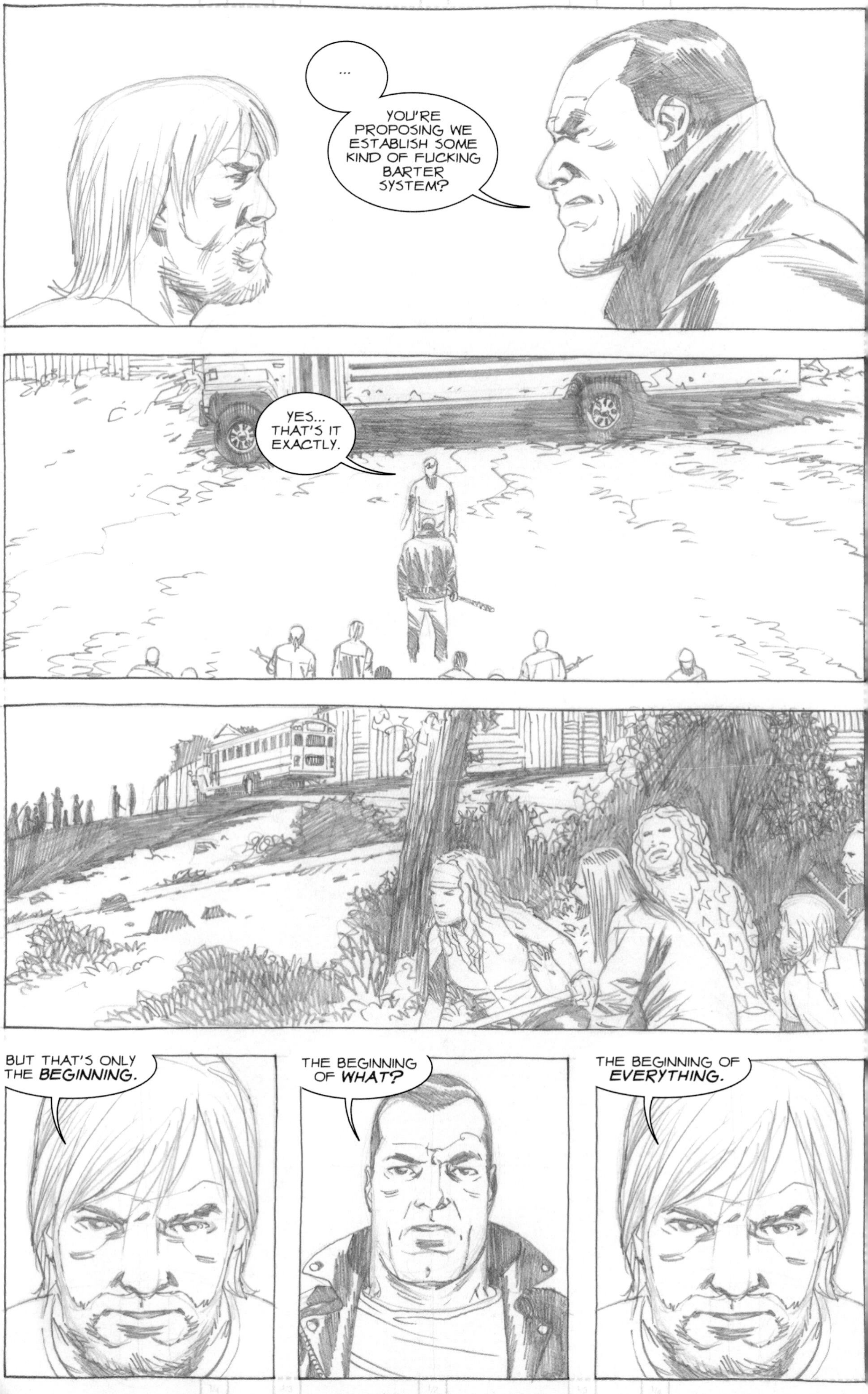
...
YOU'RE PROPOSING WE ESTABLISH SOME KIND OF FUCKING BARTER SYSTEM?
YES... THAT'S IT EXACTLY.
BUT THAT'S ONLY THE BEGINNING.
THE BEGINNING OF WHAT?
THE BEGINNING OF EVERYTHING.

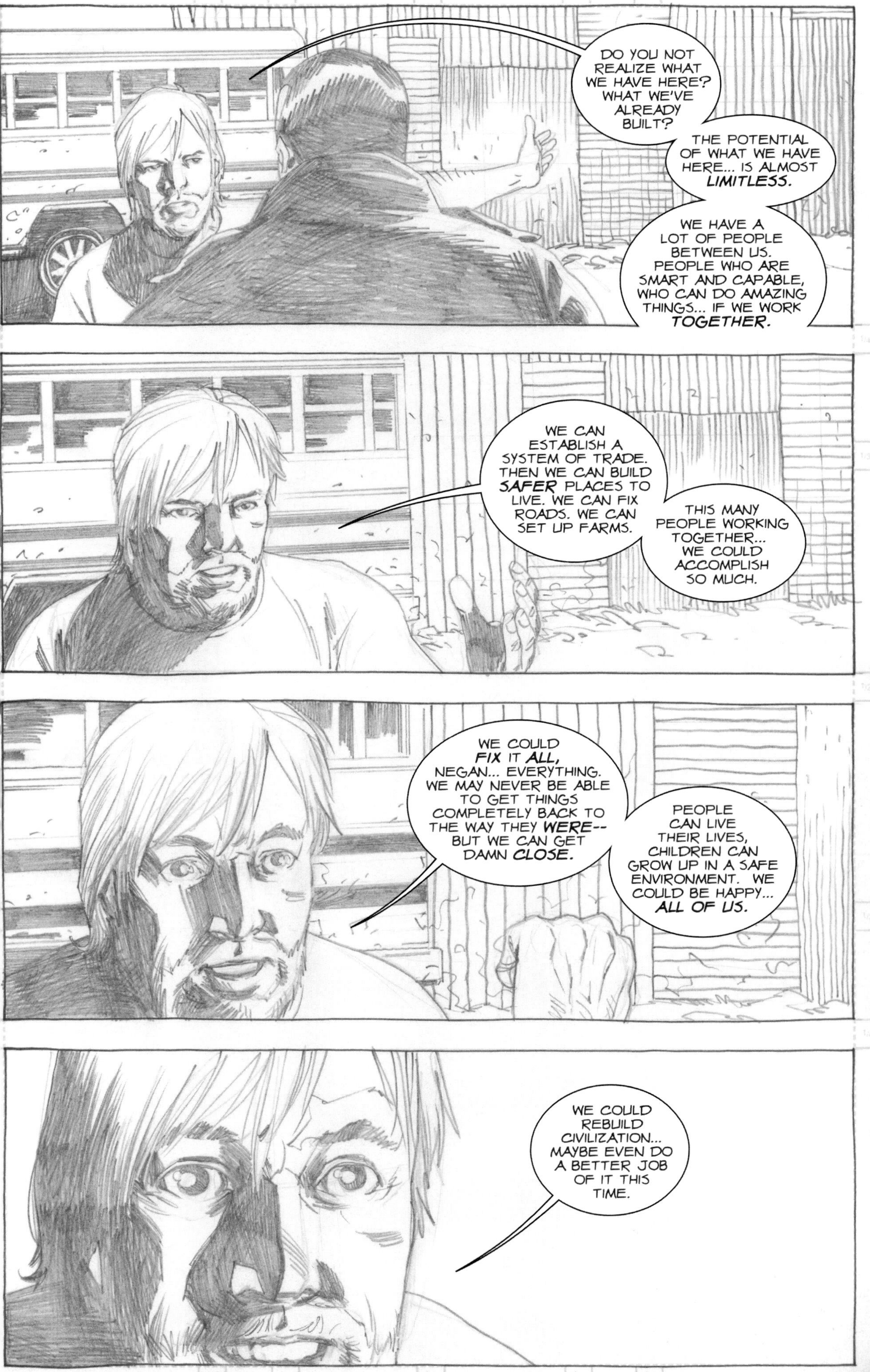
DO YOU NOT REALIZE WHAT WE HAVE HERE? WHAT WE'VE ALREADY BUILT?
THE POTENTIAL OF WHAT WE HAVE HERE... IS ALMOST LIMITLESS.
WE HAVE A LOT OF PEOPLE BETWEEN US. PEOPLE WHO ARE SMART AND CAPABLE, WHO CAN DO AMAZING THINGS... IF WE WORK TOGETHER.
WE CAN ESTABLISH A SYSTEM OF TRADE. THEN WE CAN BUILD SAFER PLACES TO LIVE. WE CAN FIX ROADS. WE CAN SET UP FARMS.
THIS MANY PEOPLE WORKING TOGETHER... WE COULD ACCOMPLISH SO MUCH.
WE COULD FIX IT ALL, NEGAN... EVERYTHING. WE MAY NEVER BE ABLE TO GET THINGS COMPLETELY BACK TO THE WAY THEY WERE-- BUT WE CAN GET DAMN CLOSE.
PEOPLE CAN LIVE THEIR LIVES, CHILDREN CAN GROW UP IN A SAFE ENVIRONMENT. WE COULD BE HAPPY... ALL OF US.
WE COULD REBUILD CIVILIZATION... MAYBE EVEN DO A BETTER JOB OF IT THIS TIME.

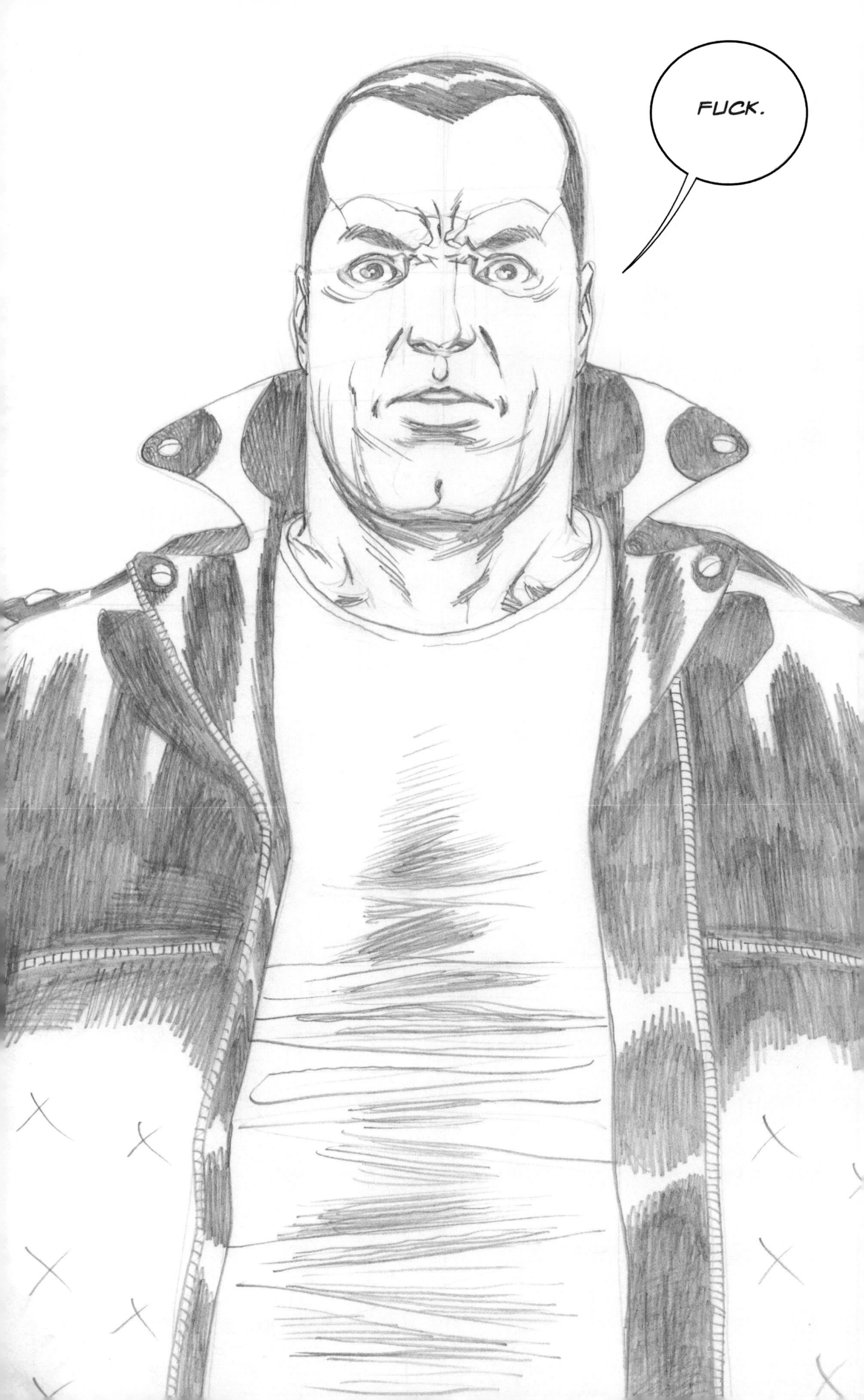
FUCK.

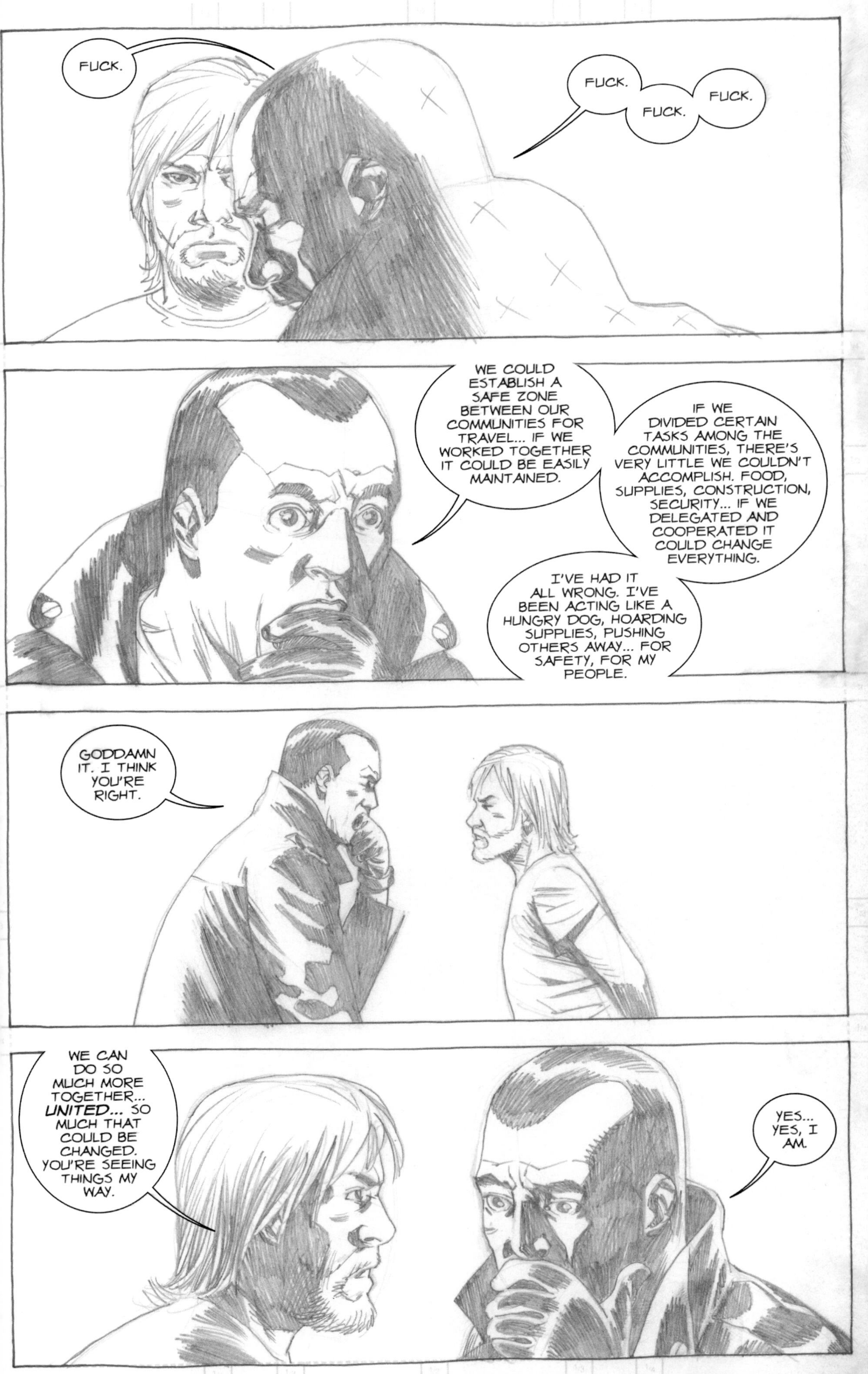
FUCK.
FUCK.
FUCK.
FUCK.
WE COULD ESTABLISH A SAFE ZONE BETWEEN OUR COMMUNITIES FOR TRAVEL... IF WE WORKED TOGETHER IT COULD BE EASILY MAINTAINED.
IF WE DIVIDED CERTAIN TASKS AMONG THE COMMUNITIES, THERE'S VERY LITTLE WE COULDN'T ACCOMPLISH. FOOD, SUPPLIES, CONSTRUCTION, SECURITY... IF WE DELEGATED AND COOPERATED IT COULD CHANGE EVERYTHING.
I'VE HAD IT ALL WRONG. I'VE BEEN ACTING LIKE A HUNGRY DOG, HOARDING SUPPLIES, PUSHING OTHERS AWAY... FOR SAFETY, FOR MY PEOPLE.
GODDAMN IT. I THINK YOU'RE RIGHT.
WE CAN DO SO MUCH MORE TOGETHER... ***UNITED...*** SO MUCH THAT COULD BE CHANGED. YOU'RE SEEING THINGS MY WAY.
YES... YES, I AM.

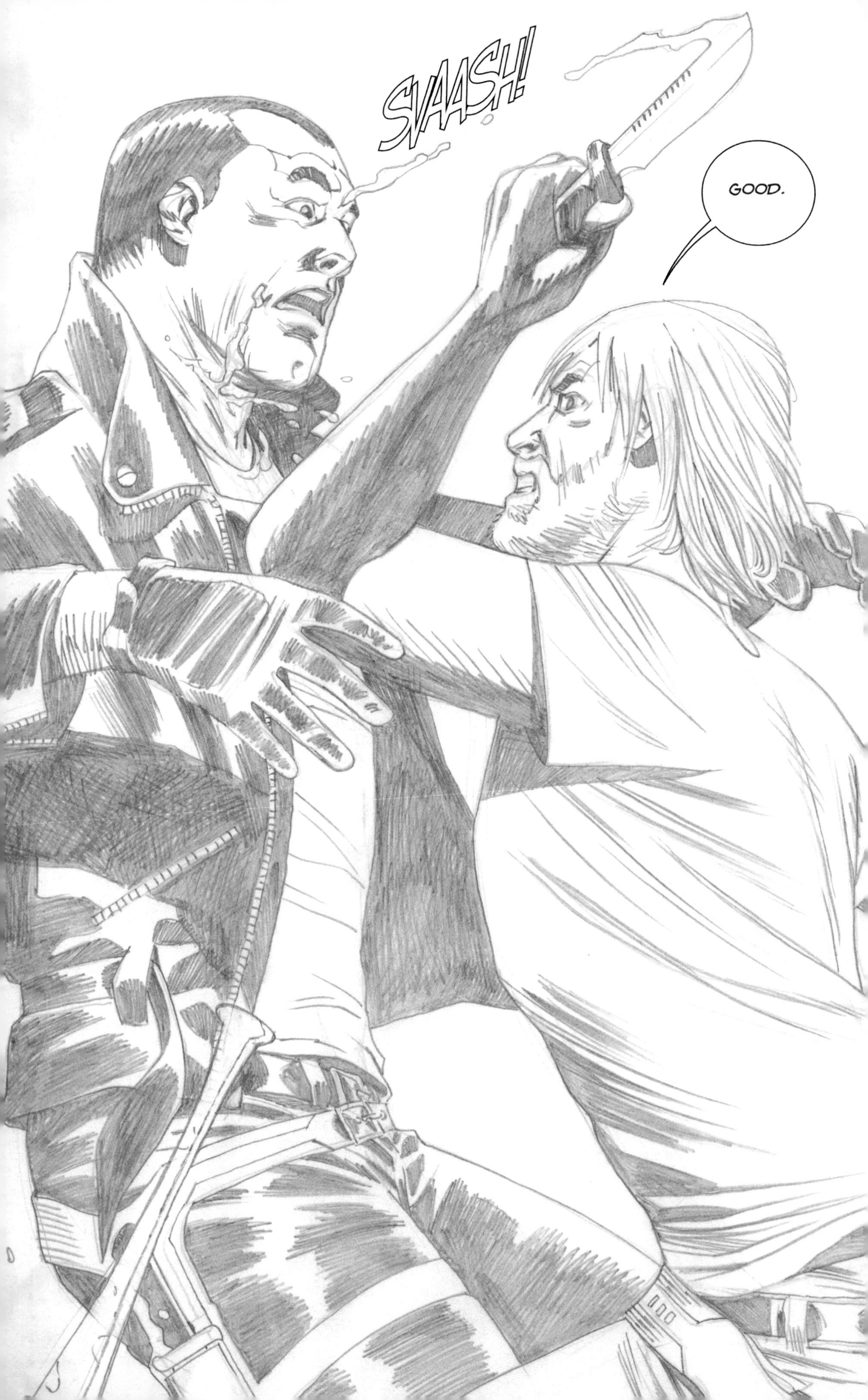
SVAASH!
GOOD.

=HUGK.=

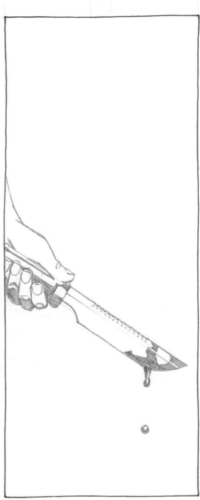

IT'S **DONE!** THIS WAR IS **OVER!**

WE HAVE A DOCTOR WHO CAN SAVE HIS LIFE!

SURRENDER AND ALLOW US TO TAKE HIM, AND WE WILL NOT ATTACK. YOU CAN APPOINT A NEW LEADER AND RETURN HOME.

DECIDE **NOW** BEFORE HE DIES!

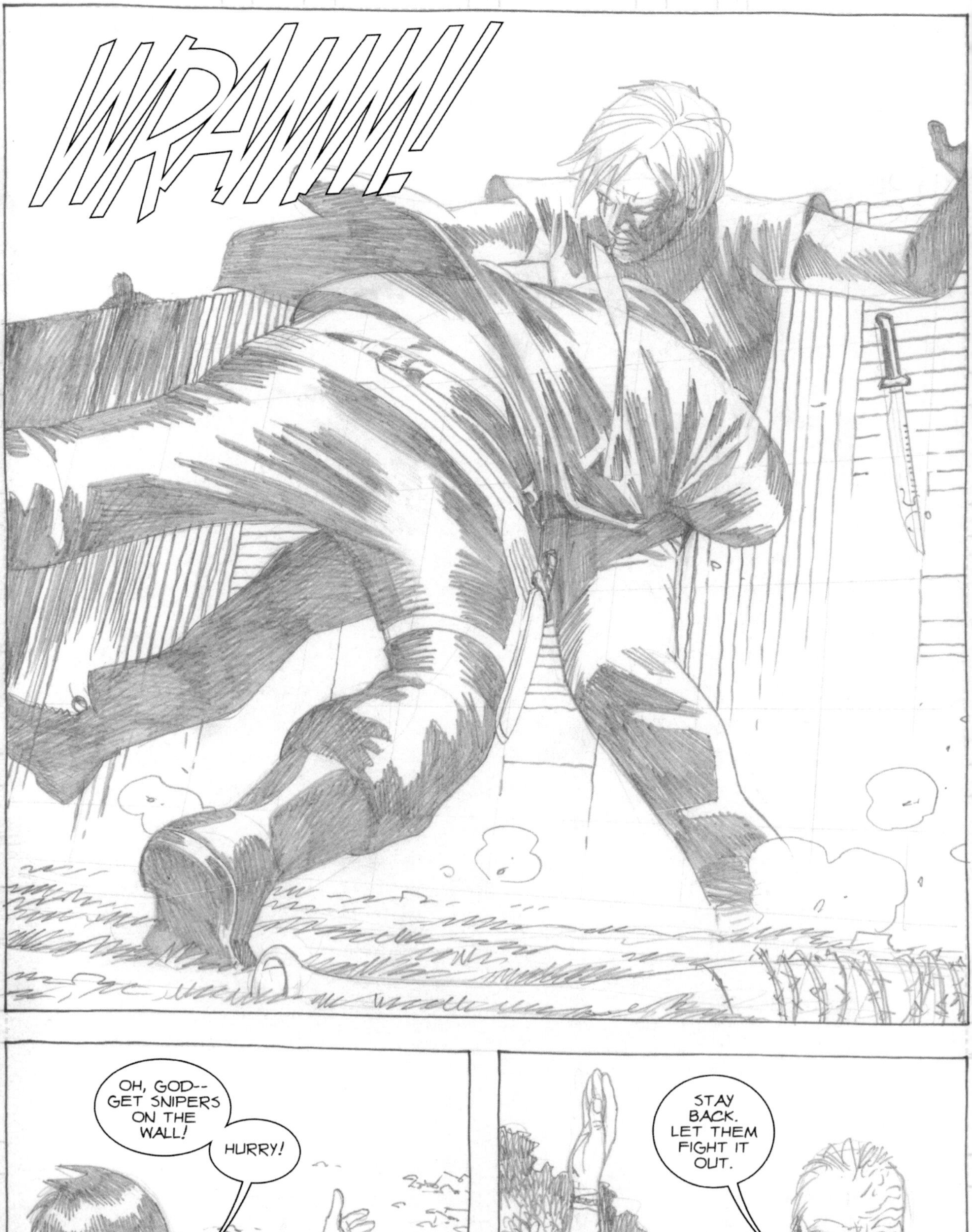
WRAMM!

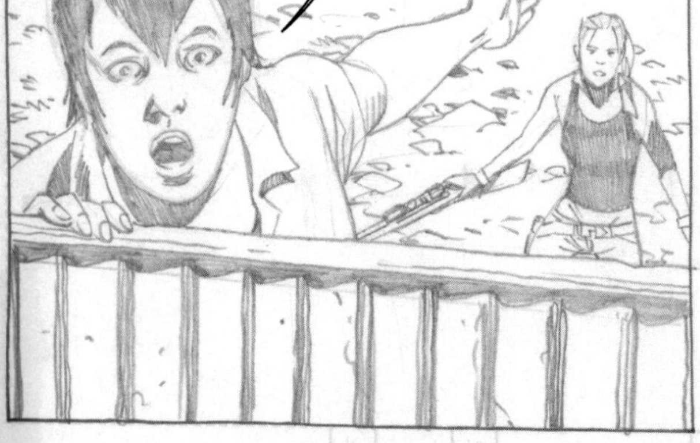
OH, GOD-- GET SNIPERS ON THE WALL!
HURRY!

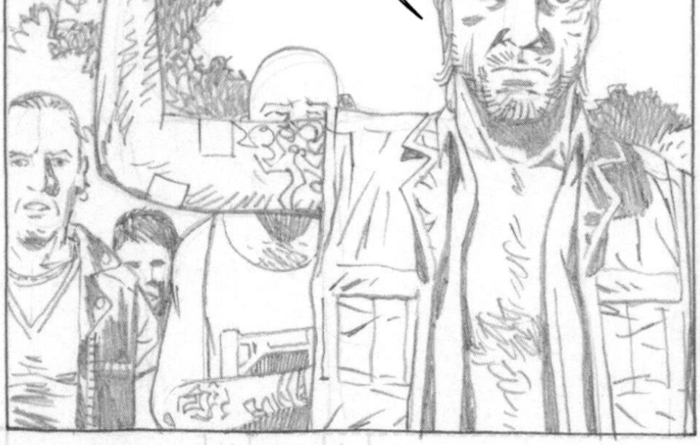
STAY BACK. LET THEM FIGHT IT OUT.

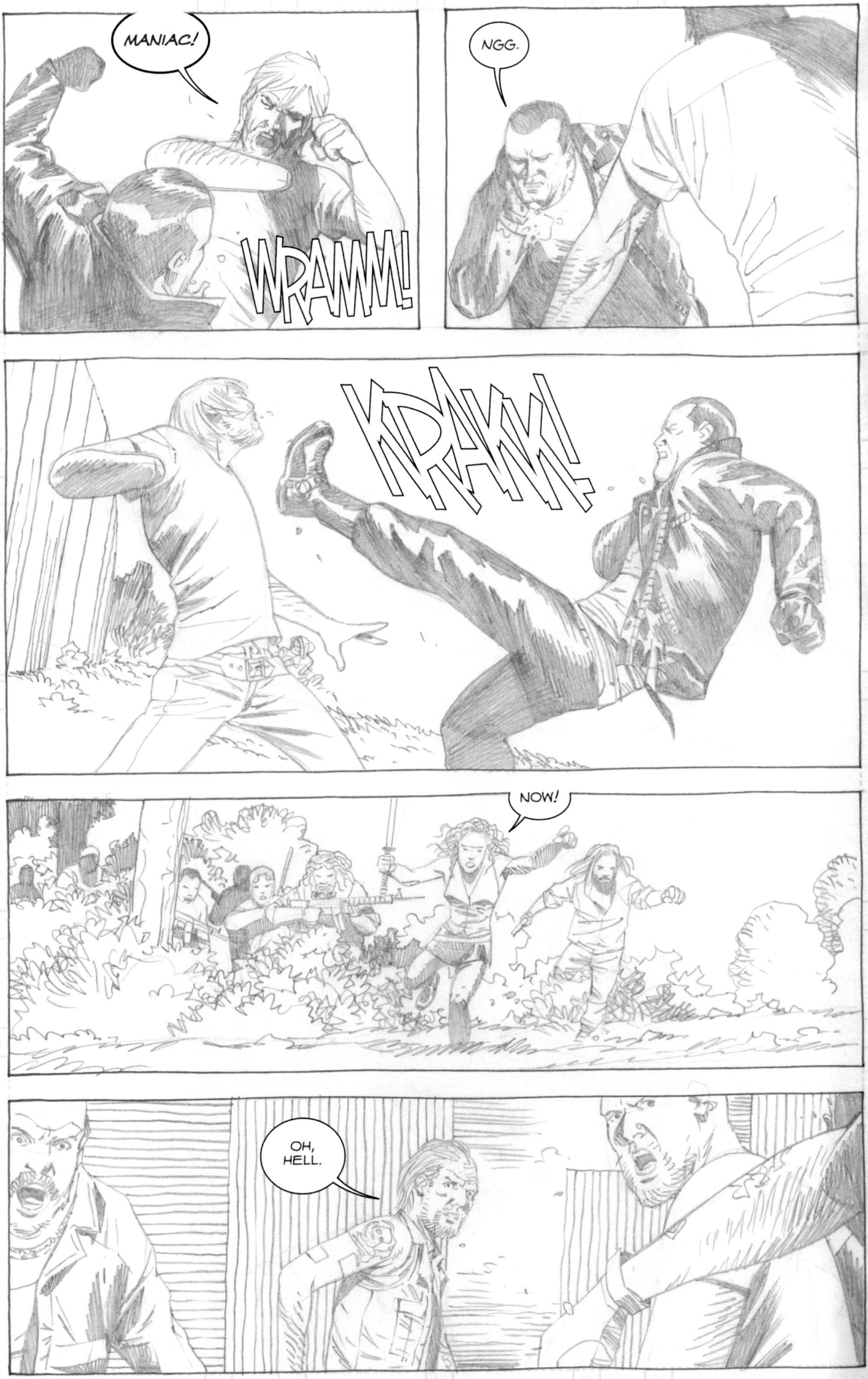

MANIAC!
WRAMM!
NGG.
KRAKK!
NOW!
OH, HELL.

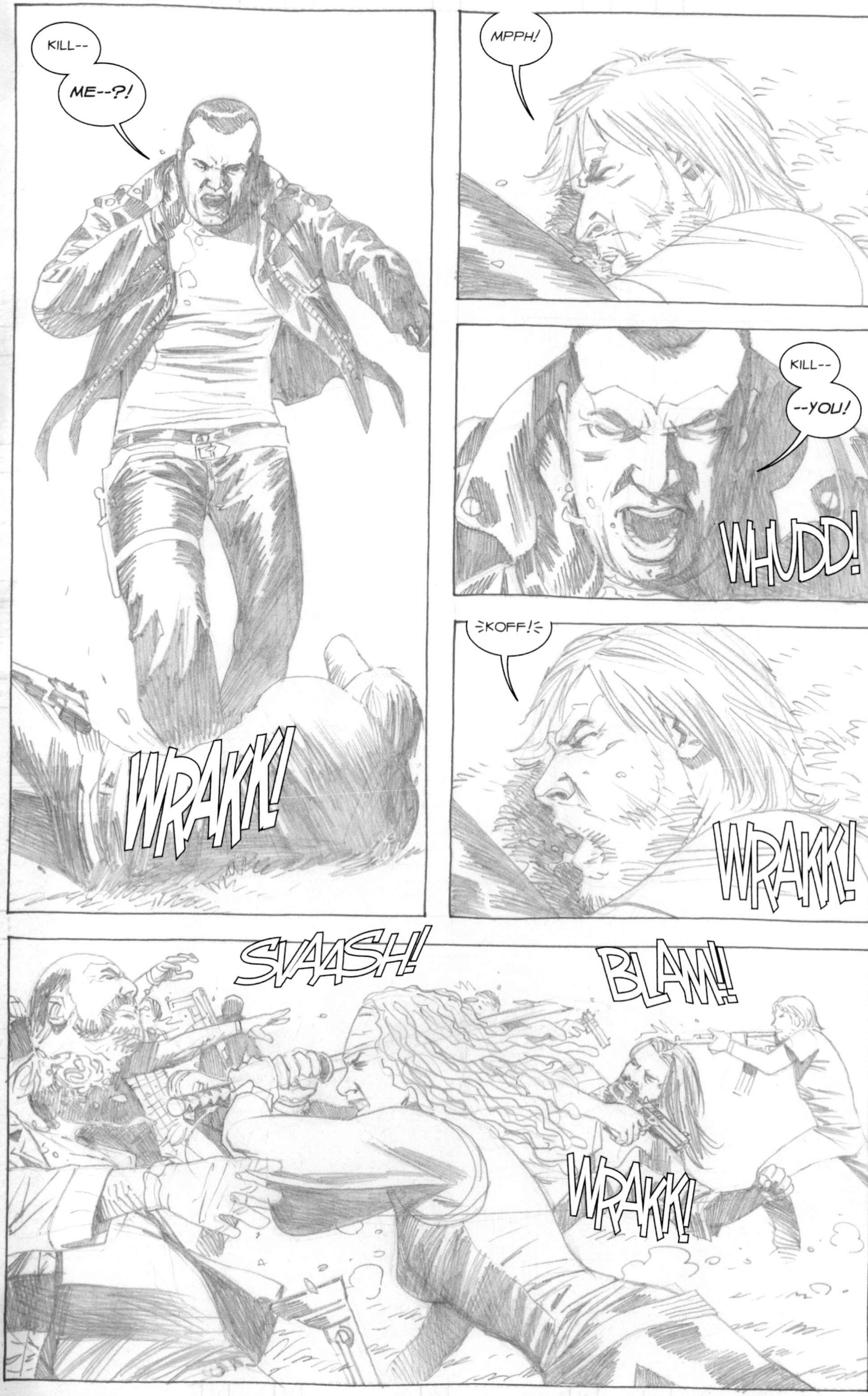
KILL--
ME--?!
WRAKK!
MPPH!
KILL--
--YOU!
WHUDD!
KOFF!
WRAKK!
SVAASH!
BLAM!
WRAKK!

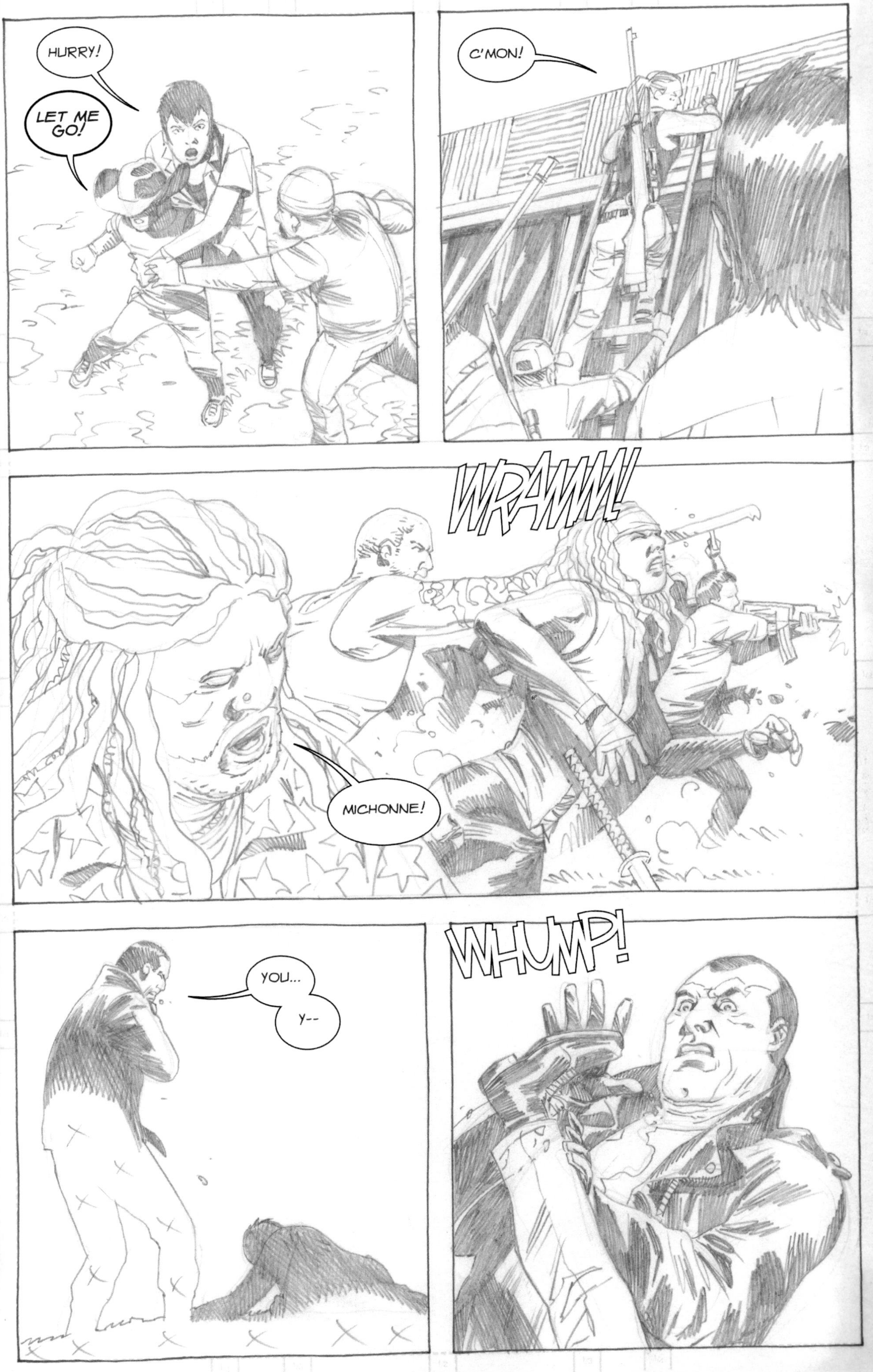
HURRY!
LET ME GO!
C'MON!
WRAMM!
MICHONNE!
YOU...
Y--
WHUMP!

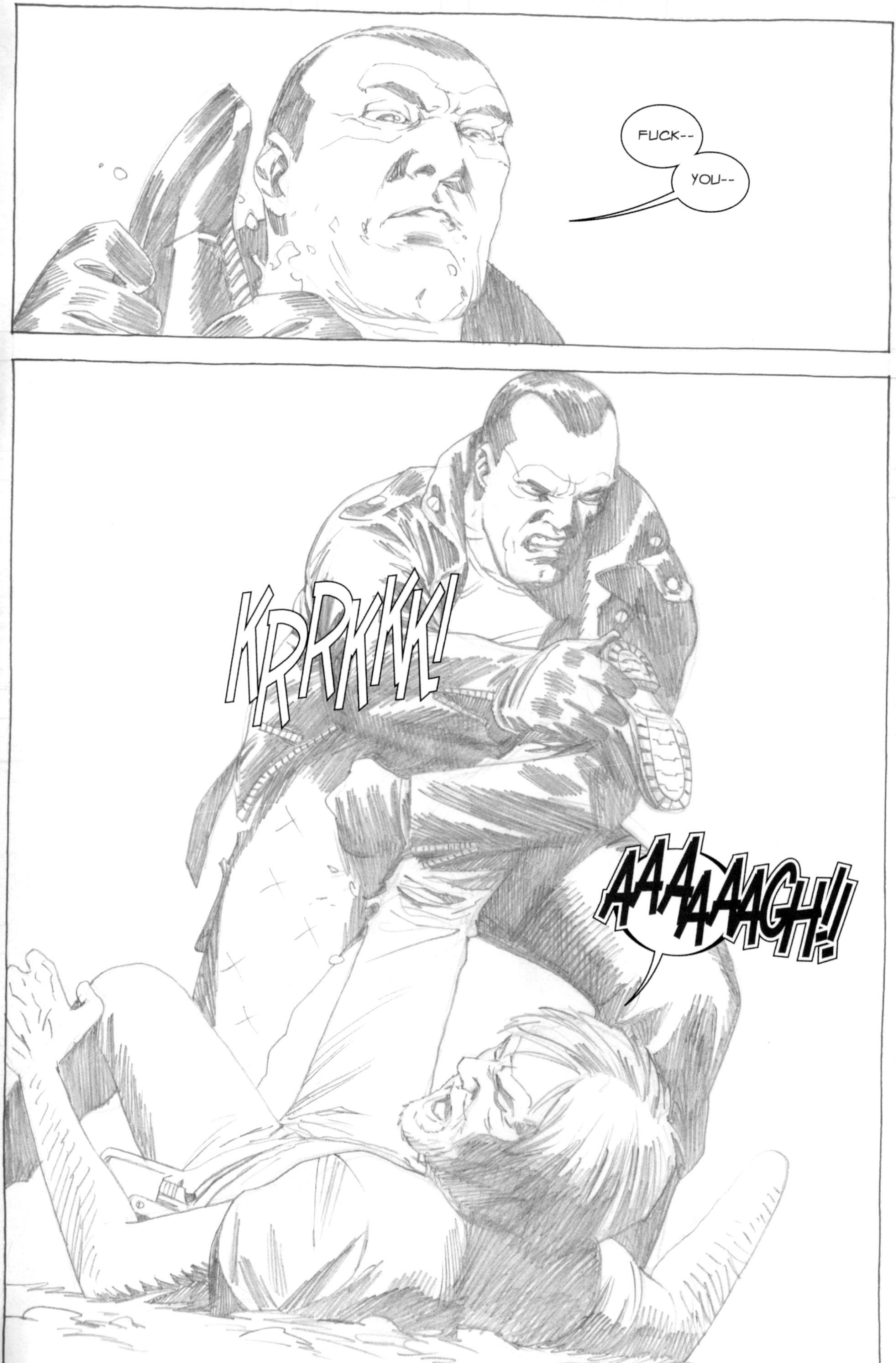
FUCK--
YOU--
KRRKKK!
AAAAAAGH!!

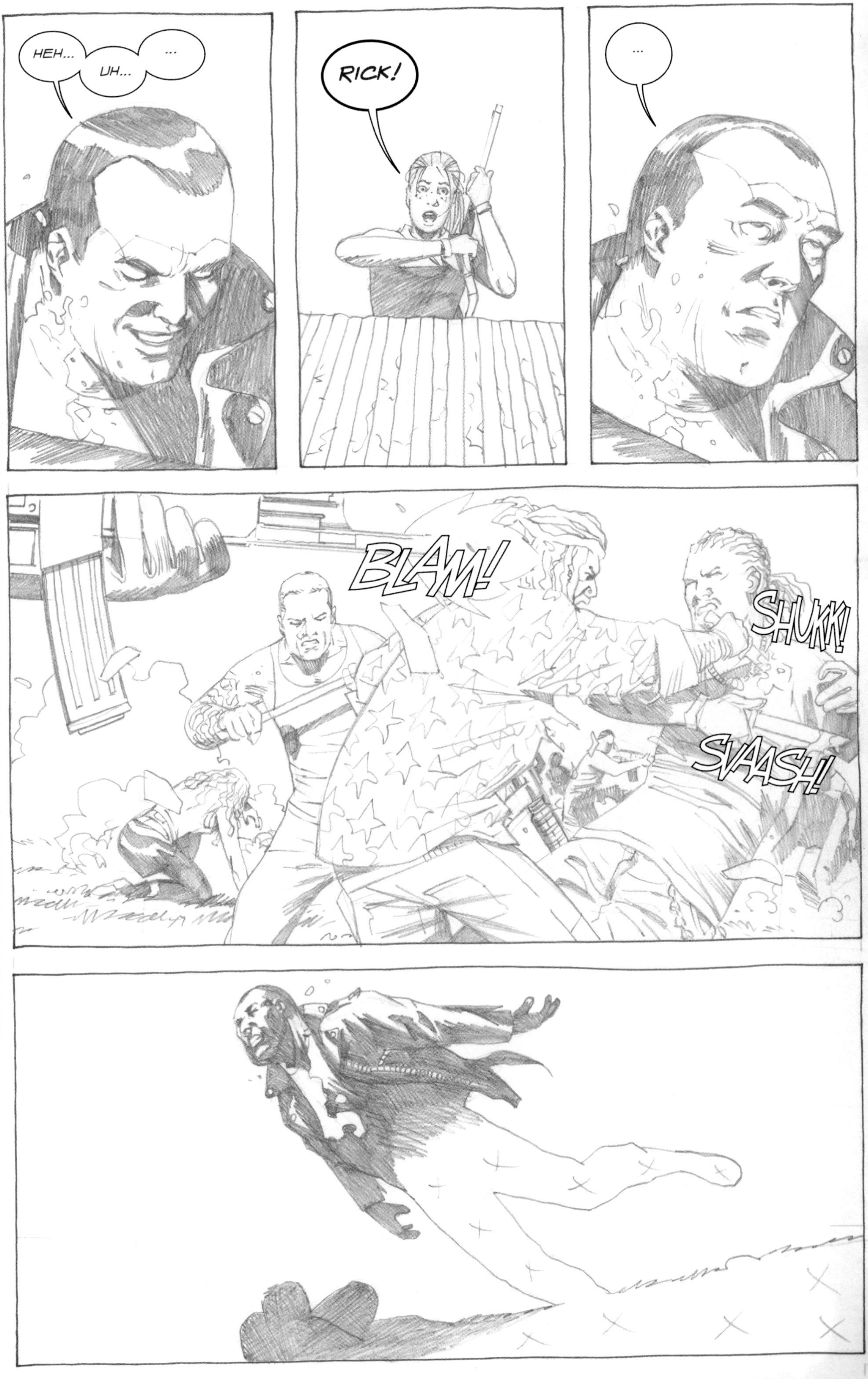
HEH...
UH...
...
RICK!
...
BLAM!
SHUKK!
SVAASH!

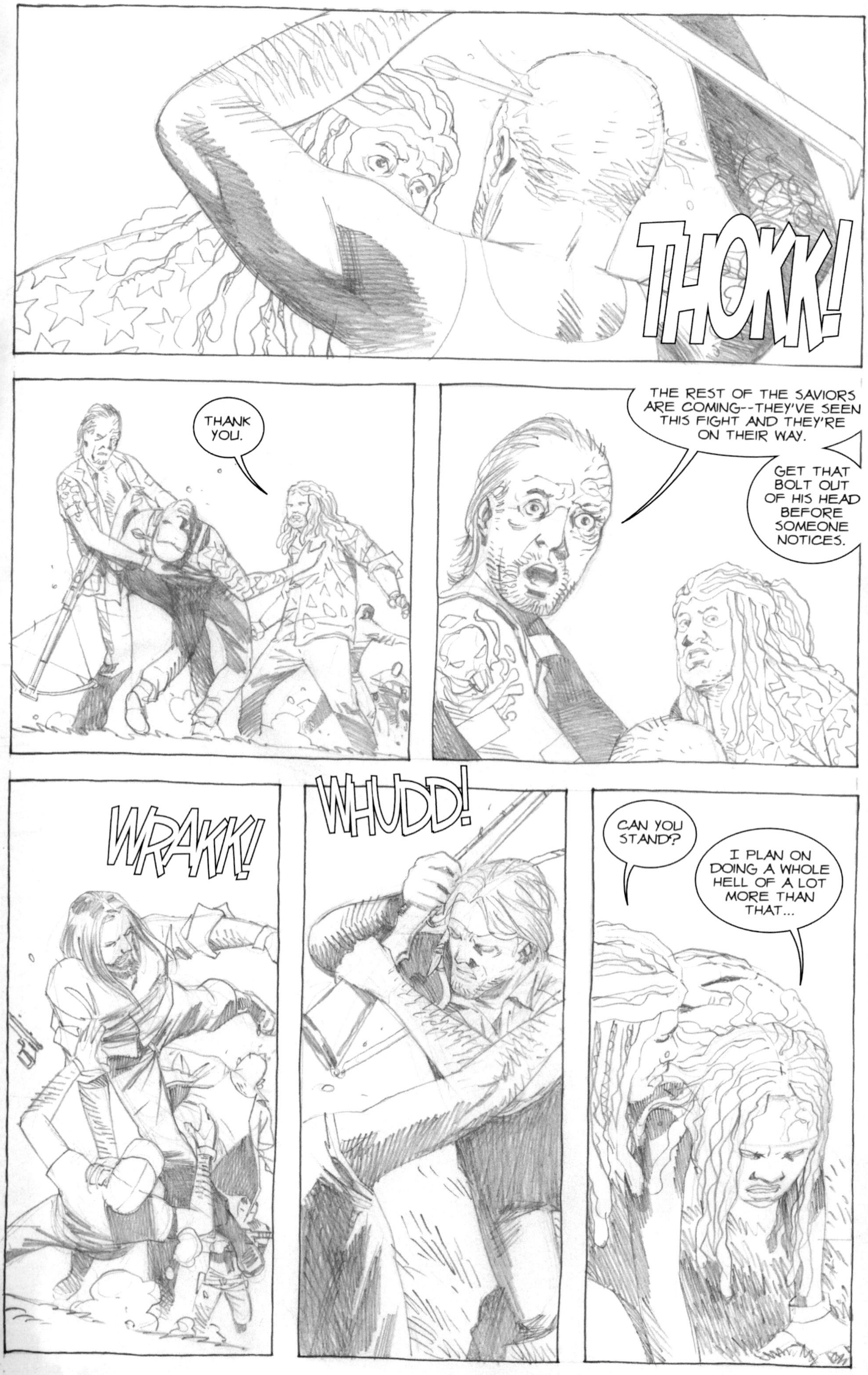
THOKK!
THANK YOU.
THE REST OF THE SAVIORS ARE COMING--THEY'VE SEEN THIS FIGHT AND THEY'RE ON THEIR WAY.
GET THAT BOLT OUT OF HIS HEAD BEFORE SOMEONE NOTICES.
WRAKK!
WHUDD!
CAN YOU STAND?
I PLAN ON DOING A WHOLE HELL OF A LOT MORE THAN THAT...

NNG.

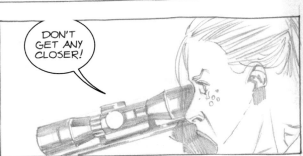

DON'T GET ANY CLOSER!

I'M ON *YOUR* SIDE.

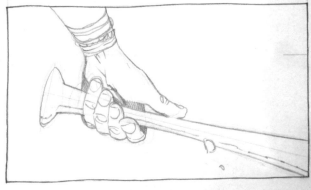

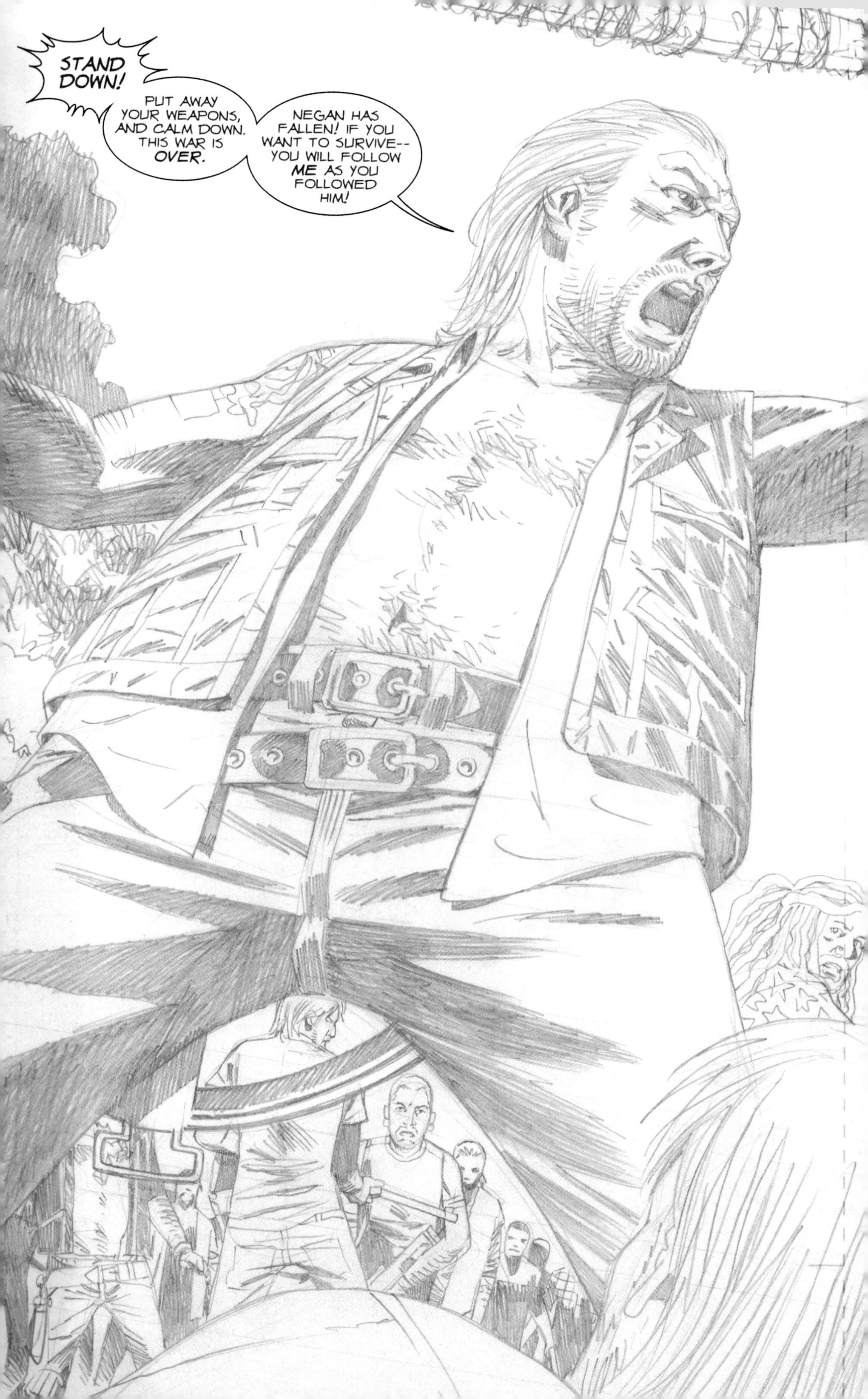
STAND DOWN!
PUT AWAY YOUR WEAPONS, AND CALM DOWN. THIS WAR IS OVER.
NEGAN HAS FALLEN! IF YOU WANT TO SURVIVE-- YOU WILL FOLLOW ME AS YOU FOLLOWED HIM!

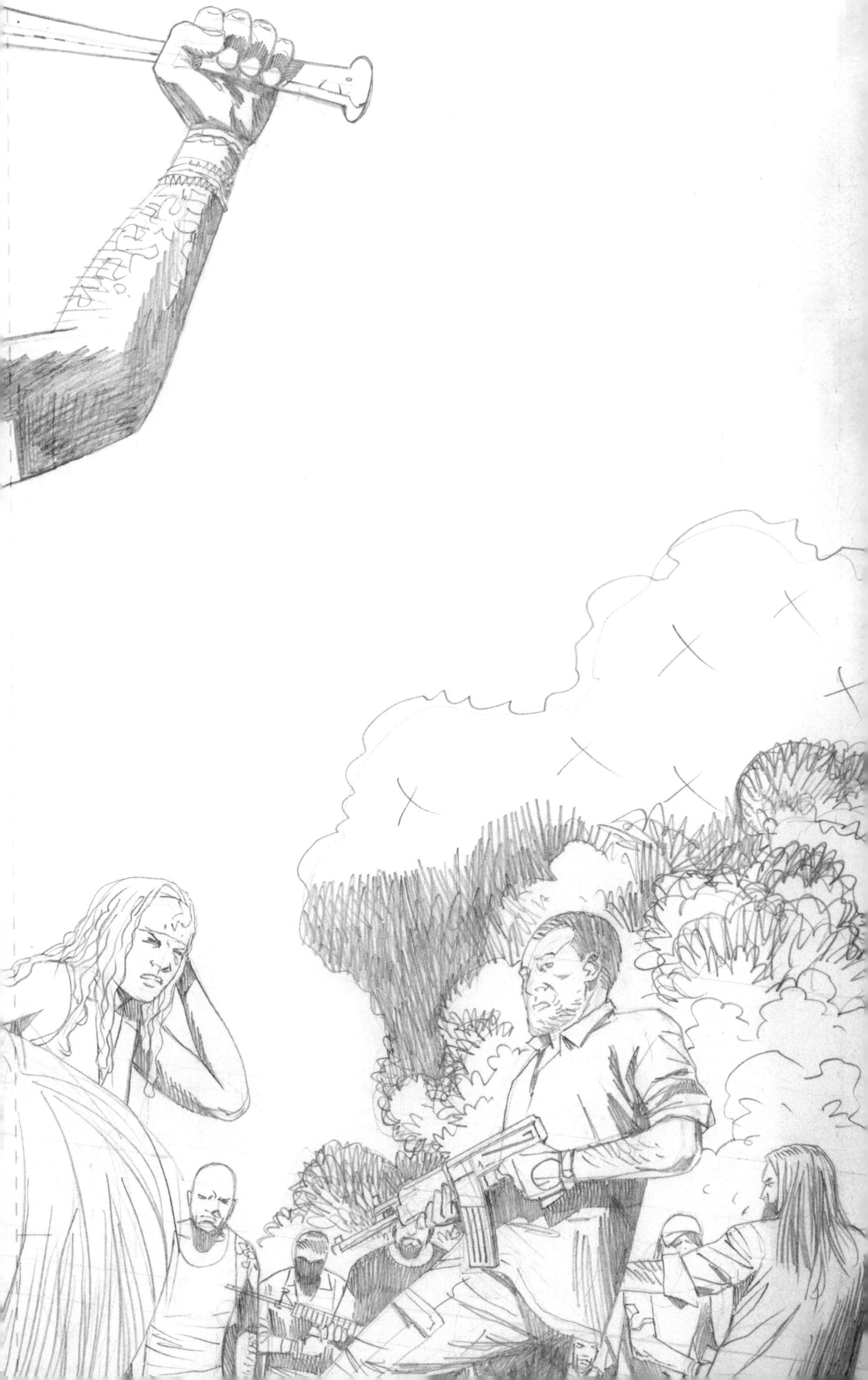

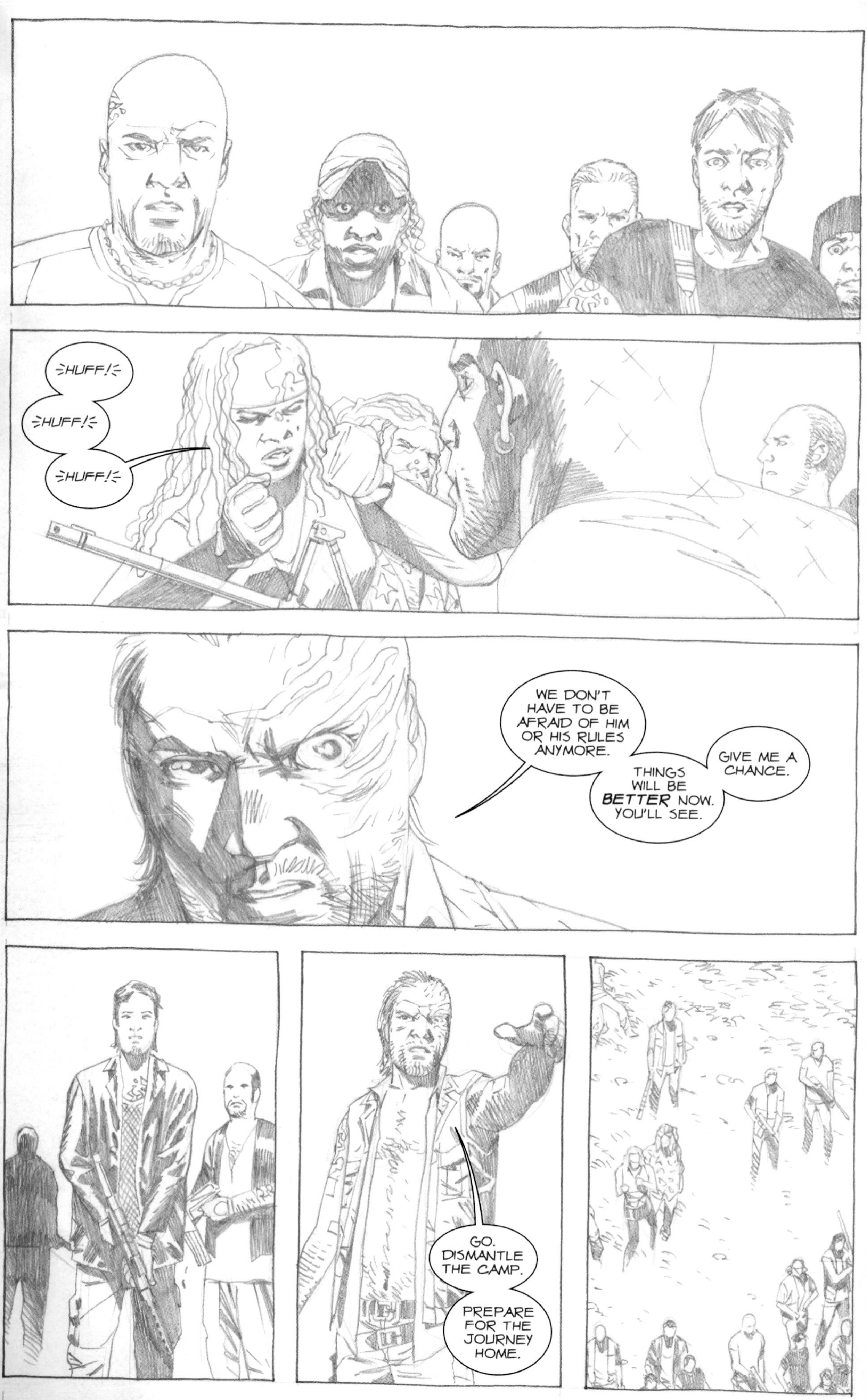

HUFF!
HUFF!
HUFF!
WE DON'T HAVE TO BE AFRAID OF HIM OR HIS RULES ANYMORE.
THINGS WILL BE BETTER NOW. YOU'LL SEE.
GIVE ME A CHANCE.
GO. DISMANTLE THE CAMP.
PREPARE FOR THE JOURNEY HOME.

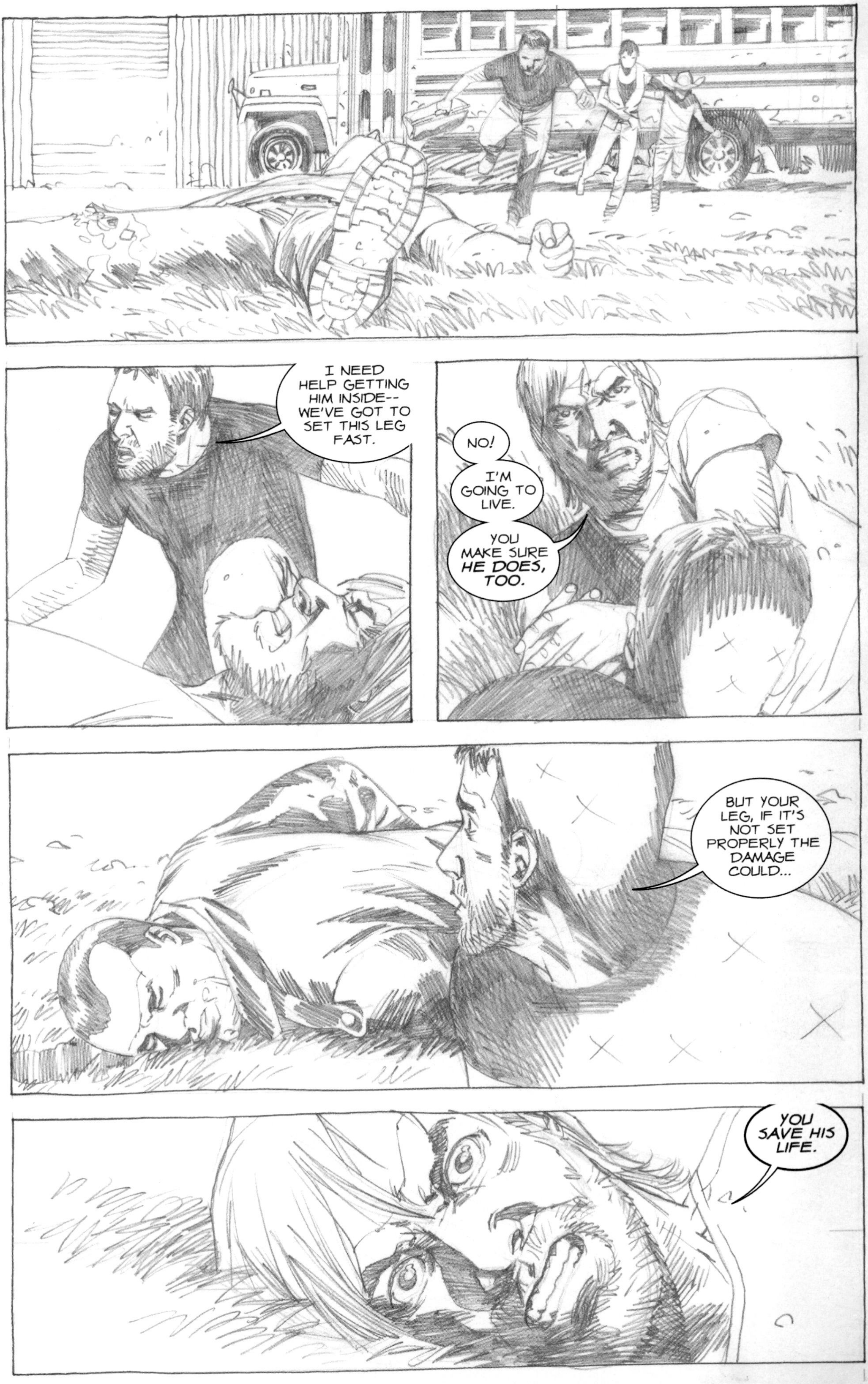
I NEED HELP GETTING HIM INSIDE-- WE'VE GOT TO SET THIS LEG FAST.
NO!
I'M GOING TO LIVE.
YOU MAKE SURE *HE DOES,* *TOO.*
BUT YOUR LEG, IF IT'S NOT SET PROPERLY THE DAMAGE COULD...
YOU SAVE HIS LIFE.

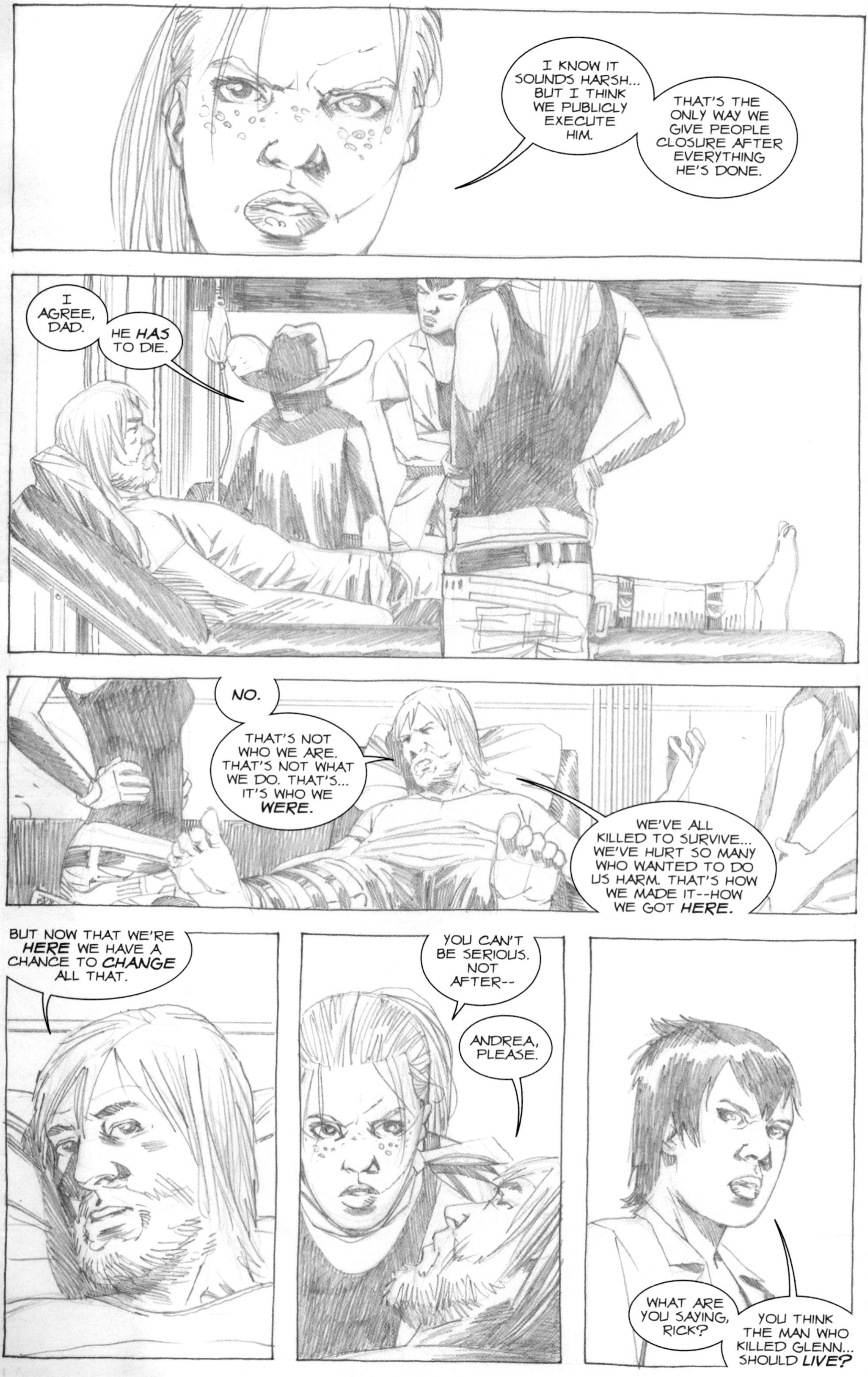
I KNOW IT SOUNDS HARSH... BUT I THINK WE PUBLICLY EXECUTE HIM.
THAT'S THE ONLY WAY WE GIVE PEOPLE CLOSURE AFTER EVERYTHING HE'S DONE.
I AGREE, DAD.
HE **HAS** TO DIE.
NO.
THAT'S NOT WHO WE ARE. THAT'S NOT WHAT WE DO. THAT'S... IT'S WHO WE **WERE.**
WE'VE ALL KILLED TO SURVIVE... WE'VE HURT SO MANY WHO WANTED TO DO US HARM. THAT'S HOW WE MADE IT--HOW WE GOT **HERE.**
BUT NOW THAT WE'RE **HERE** WE HAVE A CHANCE TO **CHANGE** ALL THAT.
YOU **CAN'T** BE SERIOUS. NOT AFTER--
ANDREA, PLEASE.
WHAT ARE YOU SAYING, RICK?
YOU THINK THE MAN WHO KILLED GLENN... SHOULD **LIVE?**

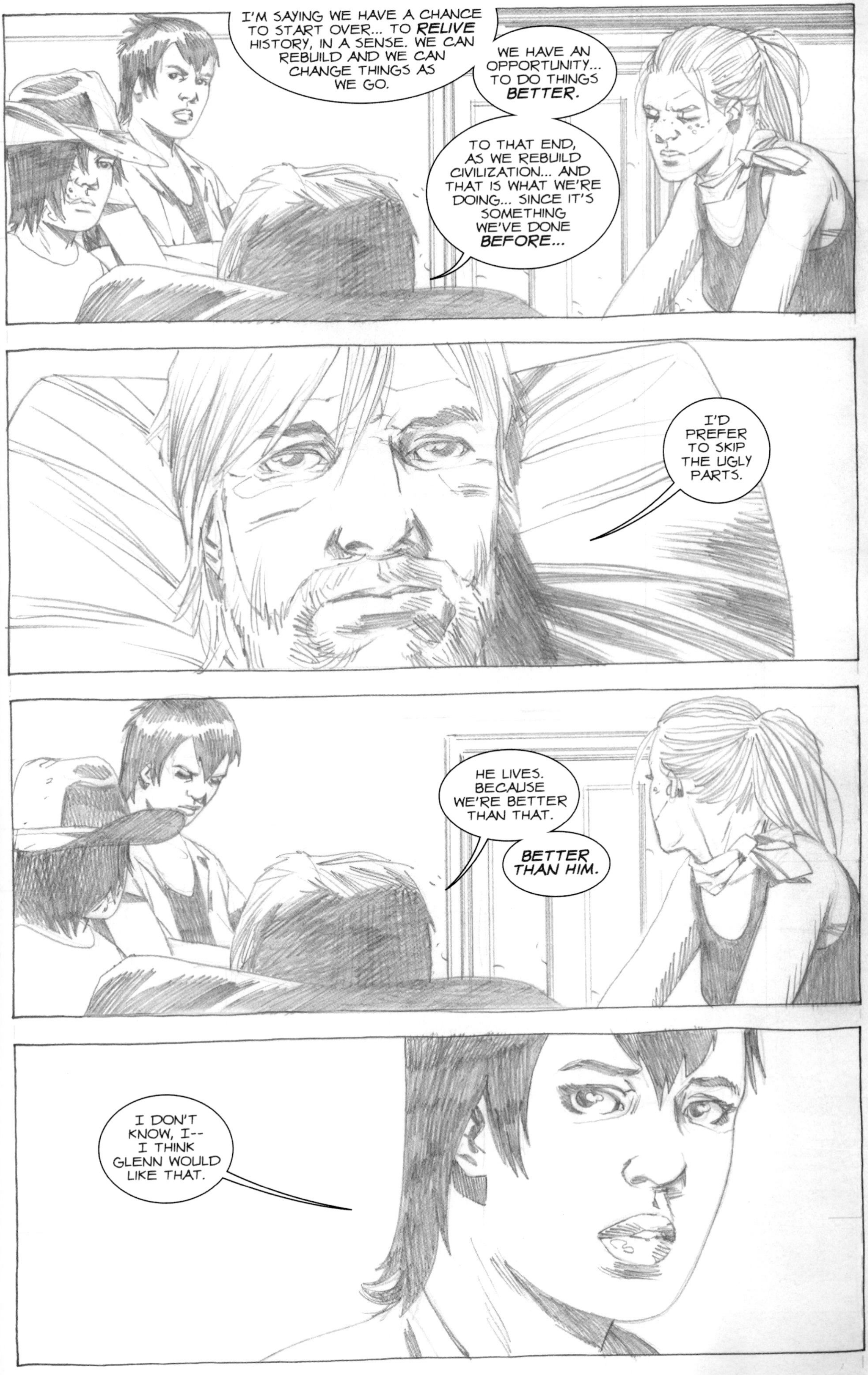
I'M SAYING WE HAVE A CHANCE TO START OVER... TO RELIVE HISTORY, IN A SENSE. WE CAN REBUILD AND WE CAN CHANGE THINGS AS WE GO.
WE HAVE AN OPPORTUNITY... TO DO THINGS BETTER.
TO THAT END, AS WE REBUILD CIVILIZATION... AND THAT IS WHAT WE'RE DOING... SINCE IT'S SOMETHING WE'VE DONE BEFORE...
I'D PREFER TO SKIP THE UGLY PARTS.
HE LIVES. BECAUSE WE'RE BETTER THAN THAT.
BETTER THAN HIM.
I DON'T KNOW, I-- I THINK GLENN WOULD LIKE THAT.

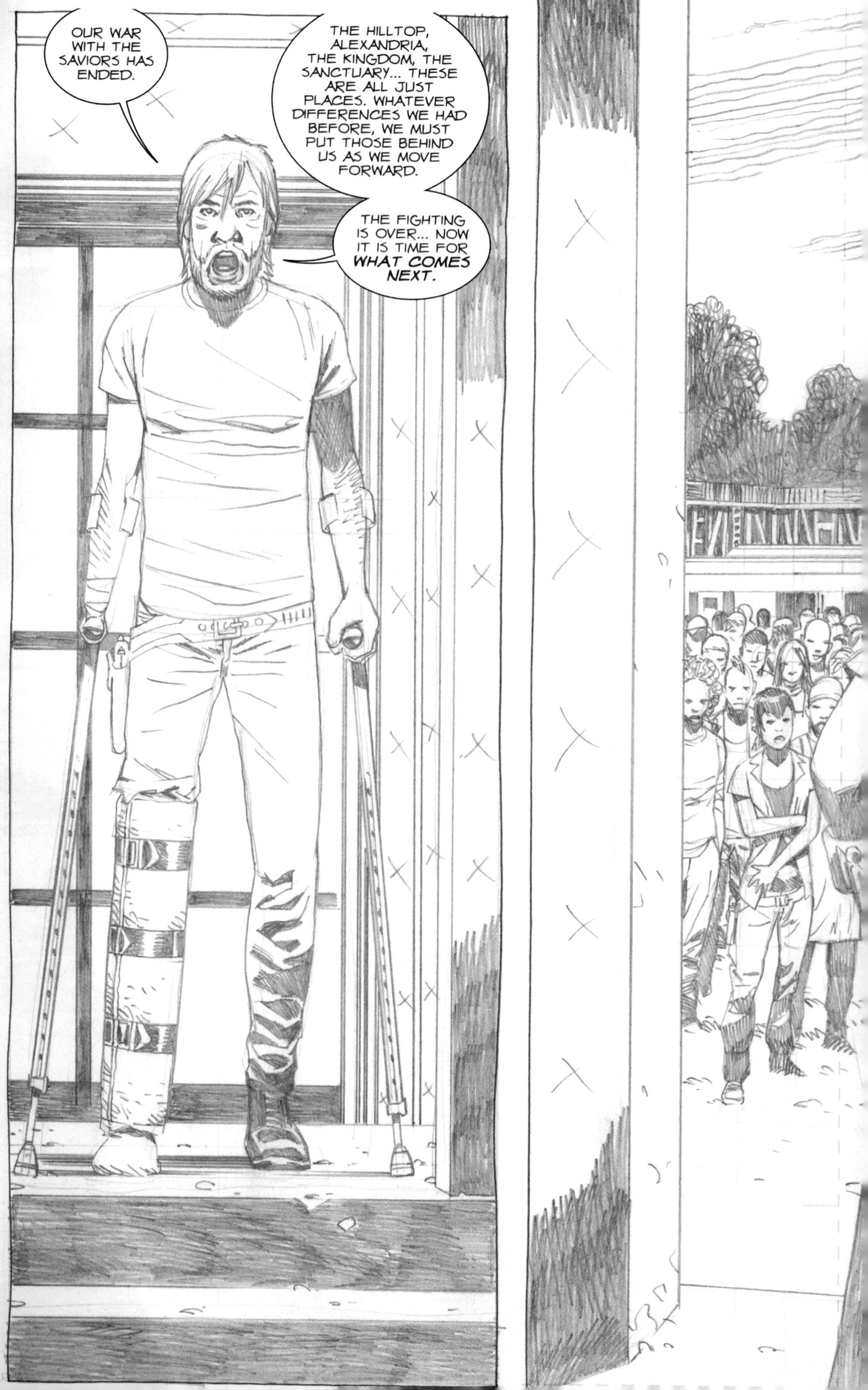
OUR WAR WITH THE SAVIORS HAS ENDED.
THE HILLTOP, ALEXANDRIA, THE KINGDOM, THE SANCTUARY... THESE ARE ALL JUST PLACES. WHATEVER DIFFERENCES WE HAD BEFORE, WE MUST PUT THOSE BEHIND US AS WE MOVE FORWARD.
THE FIGHTING IS OVER... NOW IT IS TIME FOR WHAT COMES NEXT.

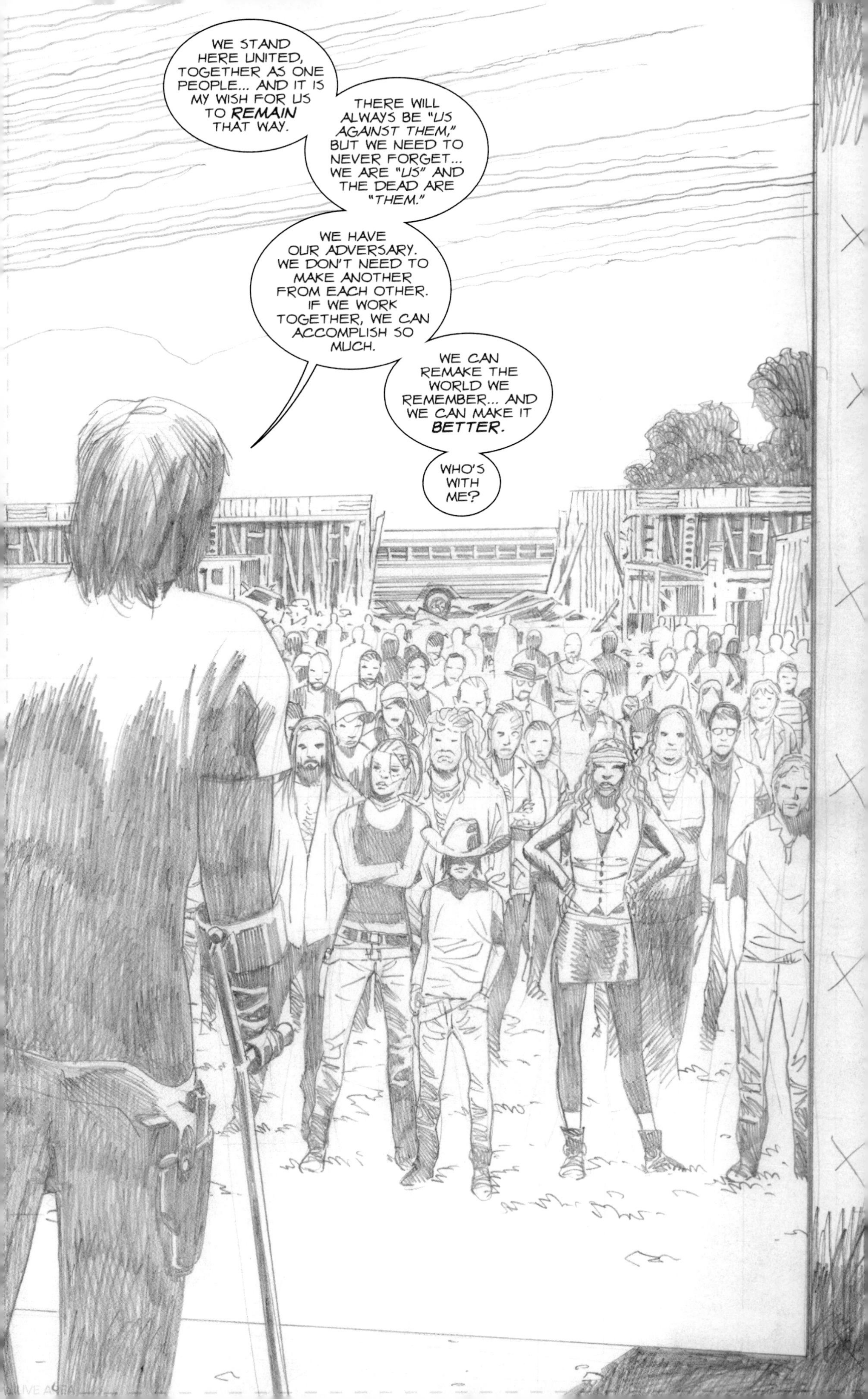
WE STAND HERE UNITED, TOGETHER AS ONE PEOPLE... AND IT IS MY WISH FOR US TO ***REMAIN*** THAT WAY.
THERE WILL ALWAYS BE "*US AGAINST THEM,*" BUT WE NEED TO NEVER FORGET... WE ARE "*US*" AND THE DEAD ARE "*THEM.*"
WE HAVE OUR ADVERSARY. WE DON'T NEED TO MAKE ANOTHER FROM EACH OTHER. IF WE WORK TOGETHER, WE CAN ACCOMPLISH SO MUCH.
WE CAN REMAKE THE WORLD WE REMEMBER... AND WE CAN MAKE IT ***BETTER.***
WHO'S WITH ME?

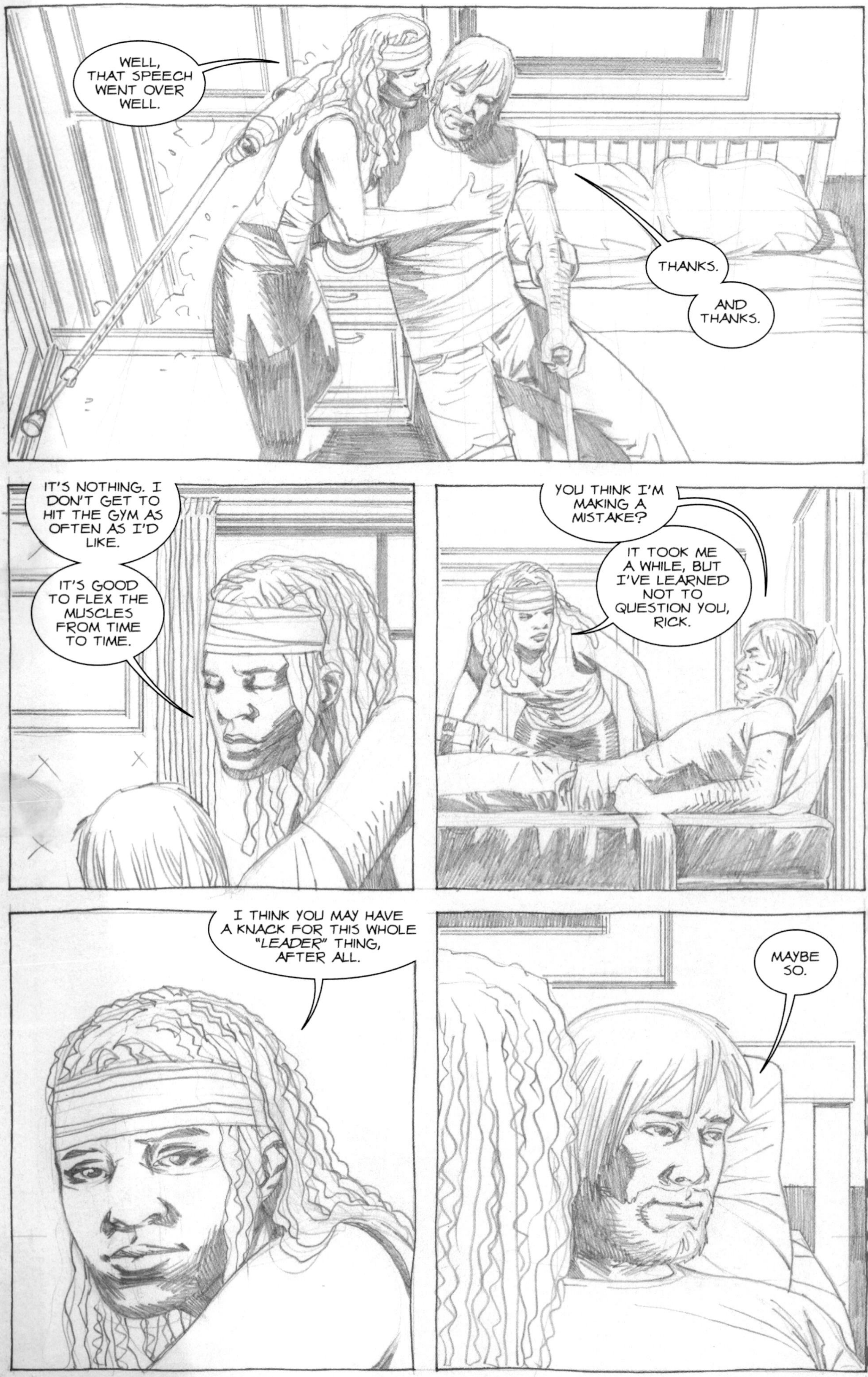
WELL, THAT SPEECH WENT OVER WELL.
THANKS.
AND THANKS.
IT'S NOTHING. I DON'T GET TO HIT THE GYM AS OFTEN AS I'D LIKE.
IT'S GOOD TO FLEX THE MUSCLES FROM TIME TO TIME.
YOU THINK I'M MAKING A MISTAKE?
IT TOOK ME A WHILE, BUT I'VE LEARNED NOT TO QUESTION YOU, RICK.
I THINK YOU MAY HAVE A KNACK FOR THIS WHOLE "LEADER" THING, AFTER ALL.
MAYBE SO.

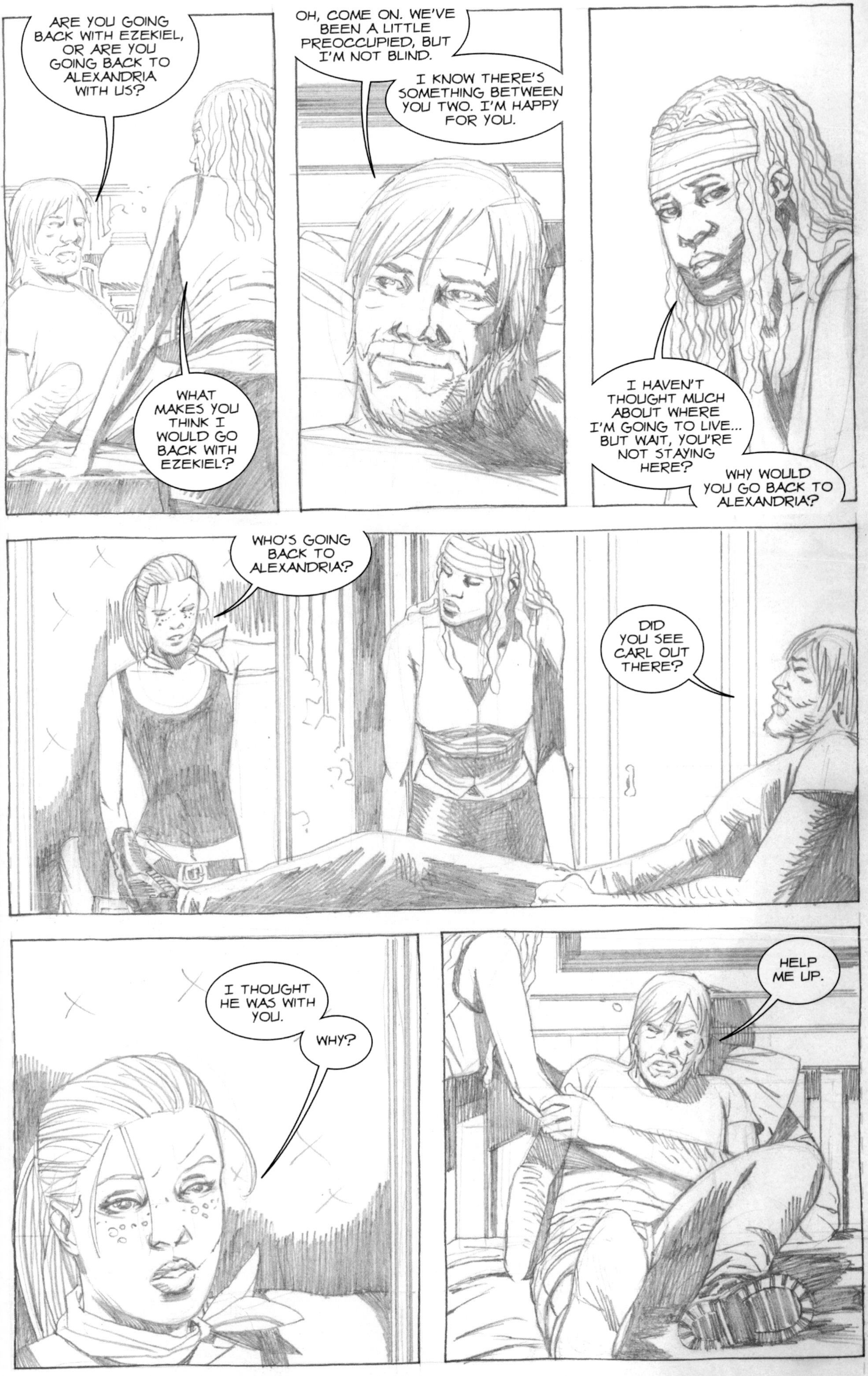
ARE YOU GOING BACK WITH EZEKIEL, OR ARE YOU GOING BACK TO ALEXANDRIA WITH US?
WHAT MAKES YOU THINK I WOULD GO BACK WITH EZEKIEL?
OH, COME ON. WE'VE BEEN A LITTLE PREOCCUPIED, BUT I'M NOT BLIND.
I KNOW THERE'S SOMETHING BETWEEN YOU TWO. I'M HAPPY FOR YOU.
I HAVEN'T THOUGHT MUCH ABOUT WHERE I'M GOING TO LIVE... BUT WAIT, YOU'RE NOT STAYING HERE?
WHY WOULD YOU GO BACK TO ALEXANDRIA?
WHO'S GOING BACK TO ALEXANDRIA?
DID YOU SEE CARL OUT THERE?
I THOUGHT HE WAS WITH YOU.
WHY?
HELP ME UP.

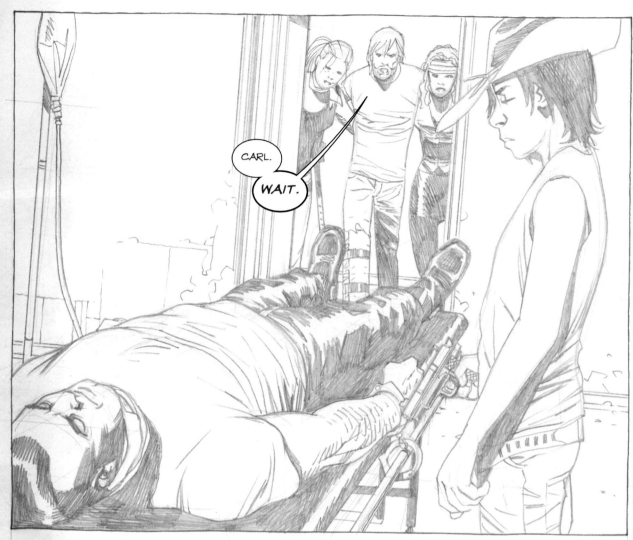

CARL.

WAIT.

DAD, I HAVE TO DO THIS.

YOU'RE WRONG.

LEAVE US ALONE.

IF WE KILL HIM, CARL... WE'RE NO BETTER THAN HE IS.

IN FACT, WE'RE WORSE. HE LET BOTH OF US LIVE WHEN HE HAD THE CHANCE TO KILL US.

YOU HAVE TO TRUST ME ON THIS. TAKING SOMEONE'S LIFE, IT'S SOMETHING WE DID WHEN WE HAD TO DO IT. BUT THINGS ARE DIFFERENT NOW. SO THE RULES ARE CHANGING.

SO HE GETS TO KILL PEOPLE AND GET AWAY WITH IT?

NO. HE'S GOING TO BE *PUNISHED* FOR WHAT HE DID... BUT WE'RE GOING TO DO IT IN A *CIVILIZED* WAY.

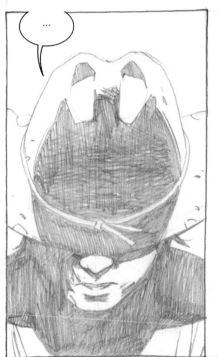

...

OKAY.

WAIT FOR ME OUTSIDE.

YOU'RE *AWAKE*, AREN'T YOU?

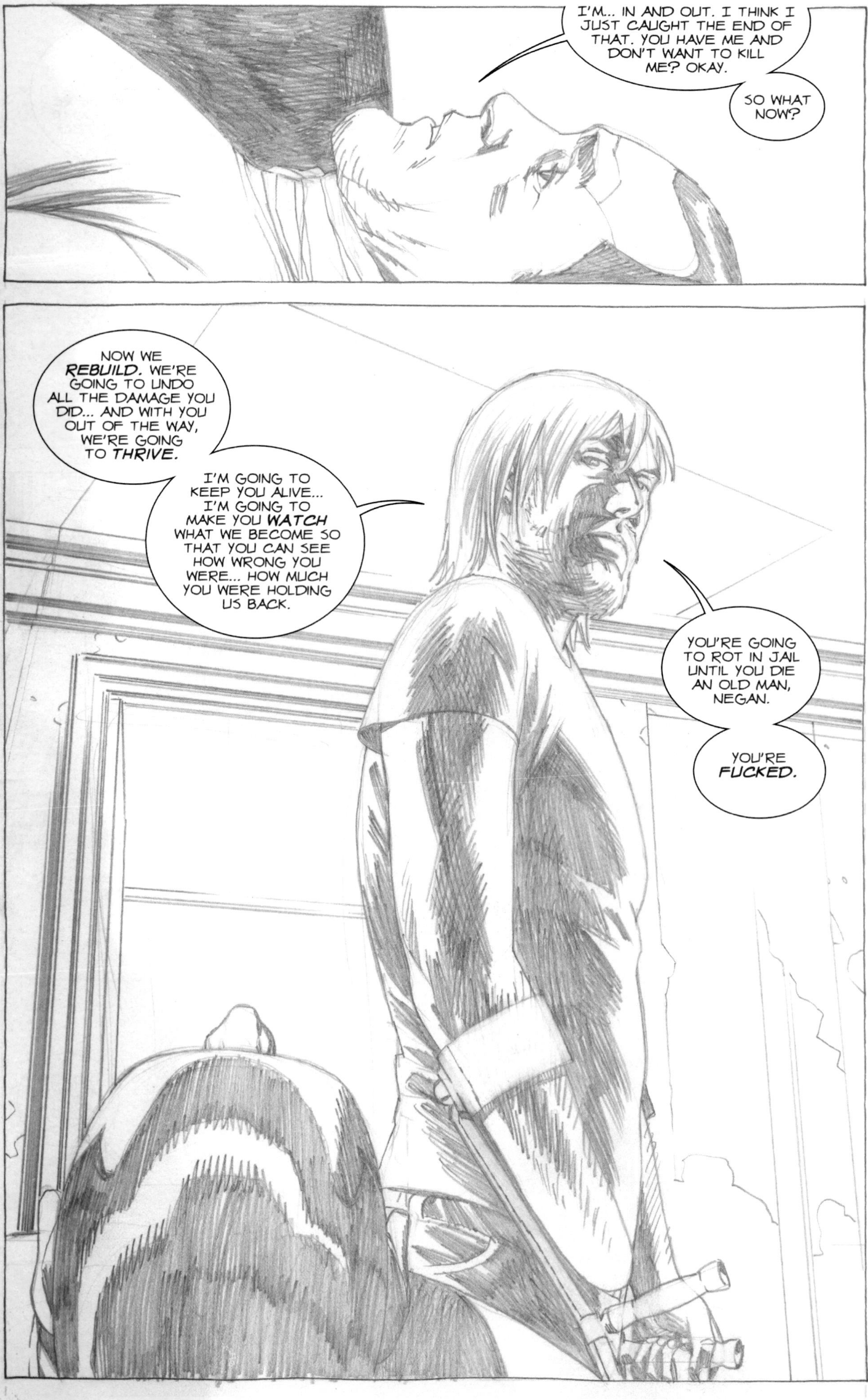

I'M... IN AND OUT. I THINK I JUST CAUGHT THE END OF THAT. YOU HAVE ME AND DON'T WANT TO KILL ME? OKAY.
SO WHAT NOW?
NOW WE **REBUILD.** WE'RE GOING TO UNDO ALL THE DAMAGE YOU DID... AND WITH YOU OUT OF THE WAY, WE'RE GOING TO ***THRIVE.***
I'M GOING TO KEEP YOU ALIVE... I'M GOING TO MAKE YOU **WATCH** WHAT WE BECOME SO THAT YOU CAN SEE HOW WRONG YOU WERE... HOW MUCH YOU WERE HOLDING US BACK.
YOU'RE GOING TO ROT IN JAIL UNTIL YOU DIE AN OLD MAN, NEGAN.
YOU'RE ***FUCKED.***

OR MORE OF THE WALKING DEAD

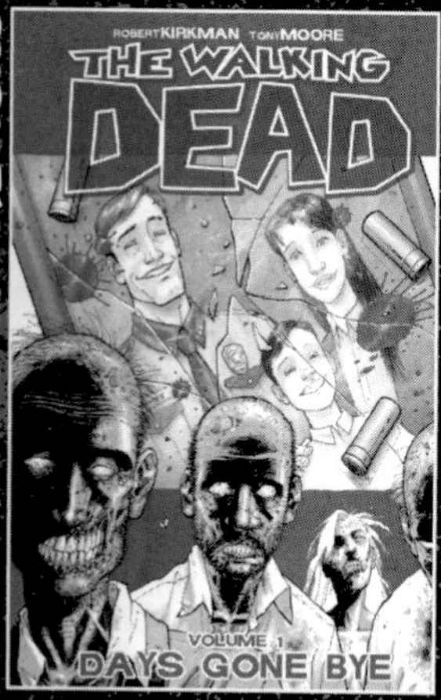

ROBERT KIRKMAN TONY MOORE
THE WALKING DEAD
VOLUME 1
DAYS GONE BYE

VOL. 1: DAYS GONE BYE TP
ISBN: 978-1-58240-672-5
$14.99
VOL. 2: MILES BEHIND US TP
ISBN: 978-1-58240-775-3
$14.99
VOL. 3: SAFETY BEHIND BARS TP
ISBN: 978-1-58240-805-7
$14.99
VOL. 4: THE HEART'S DESIRE TP
ISBN: 978-1-58240-530-8
$14.99
VOL. 5: THE BEST DEFENSE TP
ISBN: 978-1-58240-612-1
$14.99
VOL. 6: THIS SORROWFUL LIFE TP
ISBN: 978-1-58240-684-8
$14.99
VOL. 7: THE CALM BEFORE TP
ISBN: 978-1-58240-828-6
$14.99

VOL. 8: MADE TO SUFFER TP
ISBN: 978-1-58240-883-5
$14.99
VOL. 9: HERE WE REMAIN TP
ISBN: 978-1-60706-022-2
$14.99
VOL. 10: WHAT WE BECOME TP
ISBN: 978-1-60706-075-8
$14.99
VOL. 11: FEAR THE HUNTERS TP
ISBN: 978-1-60706-181-6
$14.99
VOL. 12: LIFE AMONG THEM TP
ISBN: 978-1-60706-254-7
$14.99
VOL. 13: TOO FAR GONE TP
ISBN: 978-1-60706-329-2
$14.99
VOL. 14: NO WAY OUT TP
ISBN: 978-1-60706-392-6
$14.99

VOL. 15: WE FIND OURSELVES TP
ISBN: 978-1-60706-440-4
$14.99
VOL. 16: A LARGER WORLD TP
ISBN: 978-1-60706-559-3
$14.99
VOL. 17: SOMETHING TO FEAR TP
ISBN: 978-1-60706-615-6
$14.99
VOL. 18: WHAT COMES AFTER TP
ISBN: 978-1-60706-687-3
$14.99
VOL. 19: MARCH TO WAR TP
ISBN: 978-1-60706-818-1
$14.99
VOL. 20: ALL OUT WAR PART ONE TP
ISBN: 978-1-60706-882-2
$14.99
VOL. 21: ALL OUT WAR PART TWO TP
ISBN: 978-1-63215-030-1
$14.99

VOL. 1: SPANISH EDITION TP
ISBN: 978-1-60706-797-9
$14.99
VOL. 2: SPANISH EDITION TP
ISBN: 978-1-60706-845-7
$14.99
VOL. 3: SPANISH EDITION TP
ISBN: 978-1-60706-883-9
$14.99
VOL. 4: SPANISH EDITION TP
ISBN: 978-1-63215-035-6
$14.99

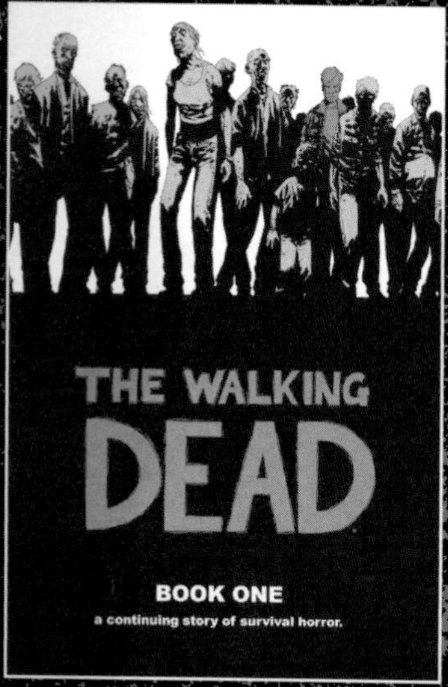

THE WALKING DEAD
BOOK ONE
a continuing story of survival horror.

BOOK ONE HC
ISBN: 978-1-58240-619-0
$34.99
BOOK TWO HC
ISBN: 978-1-58240-698-5
$34.99
BOOK THREE HC
ISBN: 978-1-58240-825-5
$34.99
BOOK FOUR HC
ISBN: 978-1-60706-000-0
$34.99
BOOK FIVE HC
ISBN: 978-1-60706-171-7
$34.99
BOOK SIX HC
ISBN: 978-1-60706-327-8
$34.99
BOOK SEVEN HC
ISBN: 978-1-60706-439-8
$34.99
BOOK EIGHT HC
ISBN: 978-1-60706-593-7
$34.99
BOOK NINE HC
ISBN: 978-1-60706-798-6
$34.99
BOOK TEN HC
ISBN: 978-1-63215-034-9
$34.99

COMPENDIUMS

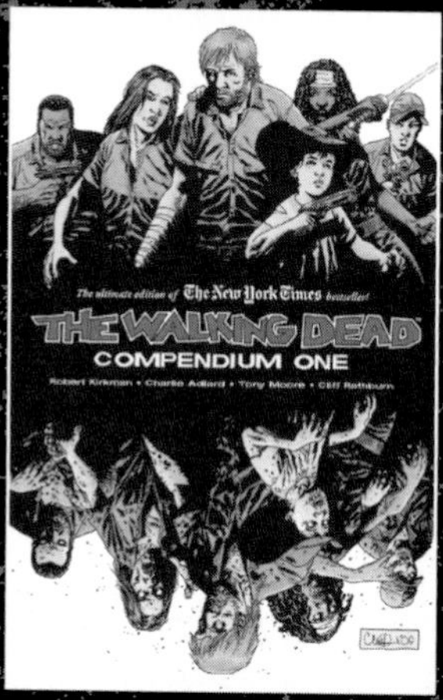

The ultimate edition of The New York Times bestseller!
THE WALKING DEAD
COMPENDIUM ONE
Robert Kirkman • Charlie Adlard • Tony Moore • Cliff Rathburn

COMPENDIUM TP, VOL. 1
ISBN: 978-1-60706-076-5
$59.99
COMPENDIUM TP, VOL. 2
ISBN: 978-1-60706-596-8
$59.99

SPECIALTY BOOKS

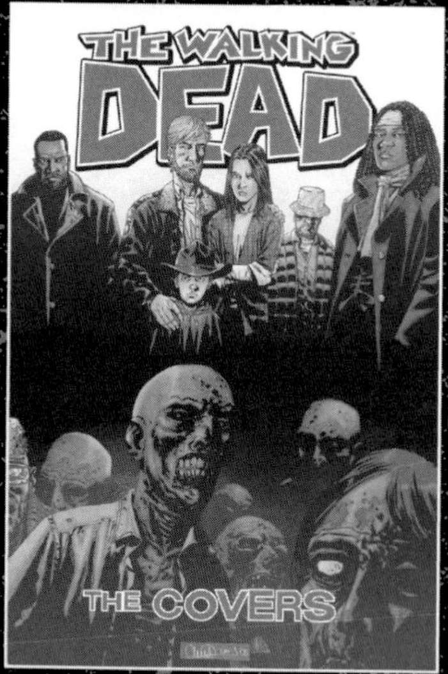

THE WALKING DEAD
THE COVERS

THE WALKING DEAD: THE COVERS, VOL. 1 HC
ISBN: 978-1-60706-002-4
$24.99
THE WALKING DEAD SURVIVORS' GUIDE
ISBN: 978-1-60706-458-9
$12.99

OMNIBUS

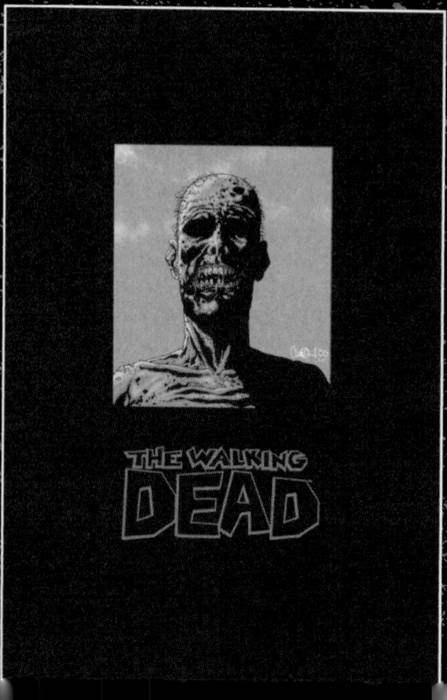

THE WALKING DEAD

OMNIBUS, VOL. 1
ISBN: 978-1-60706-503-6
$100.00
OMNIBUS, VOL. 2
ISBN: 978-1-60706-515-9
$100.00
OMNIBUS, VOL. 3
ISBN: 978-1-60706-330-8
$100.00
OMNIBUS, VOL. 4
ISBN: 978-1-60706-616-3
$100.00

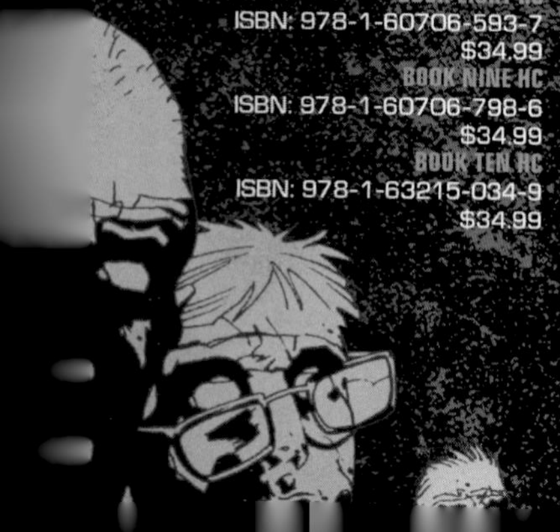

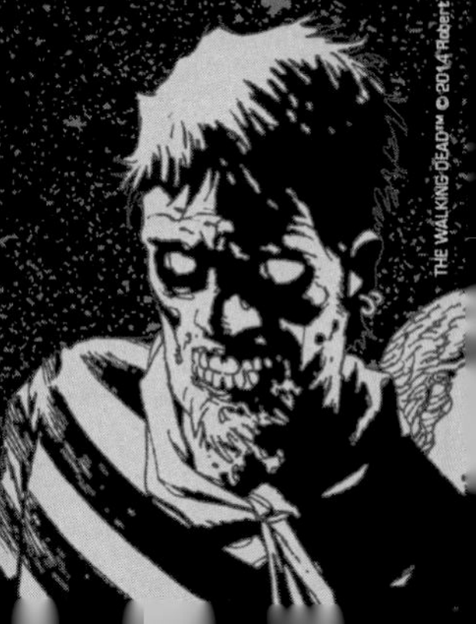

FOR MORE OF INVINCIBLE

TRADEPAPERBACKS

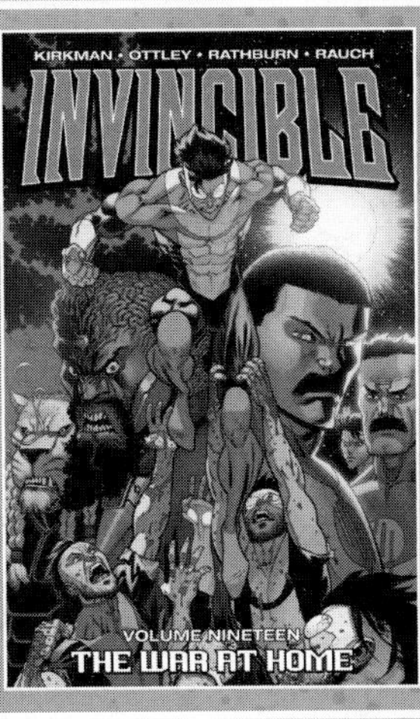
KIRKMAN · OTTLEY · RATHBURN · RAUCH
INVINCIBLE
VOLUME NINETEEN
THE WAR AT HOME

VOL. 1: FAMILY MATTERS TP
ISBN: 978-1-58240-711-1
$12.99
VOL. 2: EIGHT IS ENOUGH TP
ISBN: 978-1-58240-347-2
$12.99
VOL. 3: PERFECT STRANGERS TP
ISBN: 978-1-58240-793-7
$12.99
VOL. 4: HEAD OF THE CLASS TP
ISBN: 978-1-58240-440-2
$14.95
VOL. 5: THE FACTS OF LIFE TP
ISBN: 978-1-58240-554-4
$14.99
VOL. 6: A DIFFERENT WORLD TP
ISBN: 978-1-58240-579-7
$14.99
VOL. 7: THREE'S COMPANY TP
ISBN: 978-1-58240-656-5
$14.99
VOL. 8: MY FAVORITE MARTIAN TP
ISBN: 978-1-58240-683-1
$14.99
VOL. 9: OUT OF THIS WORLD TP
ISBN: 978-1-58240-827-9
$14.99
VOL. 10: WHO'S THE BOSS TP
ISBN: 978-1-60706-013-0
$16.99
VOL. 11: HAPPY DAYS TP
ISBN: 978-1-60706-062-8
$16.99
VOL. 12: STILL STANDING TP
ISBN: 978-1-60706-166-3
$16.99
VOL. 13: GROWING PAINS TP
ISBN: 978-1-60706-251-6
$16.99
VOL. 14: THE VILTRUMITE WAR TP
ISBN: 978-1-60706-367-4
$19.99
VOL. 15: GET SMART TP
ISBN: 978-1-60706-498-5
$16.99
VOL. 16: FAMILY TIES TP
ISBN: 978-1-60706-579-1
$16.99
VOL. 17: WHAT'S HAPPENING TP
ISBN: 978-1-60706-662-0
$16.99
VOL. 18: DEATH OF EVERYONE TP
ISBN: 978-1-60706-762-7
$16.99
VOL. 19: THE WAR AT HOME TP
ISBN: 978-1-60706-856-3
$16.99
THE OFFICIAL HANDBOOK OF
THE INVINCIBLE UNIVERSE TP
ISBN: 978-1-58240-831-6
$12.99
INVINCIBLE PRESENTS,
VOL. 1: ATOM EVE & REX SPLODE TP
ISBN: 978-1-60706-255-4
$14.99

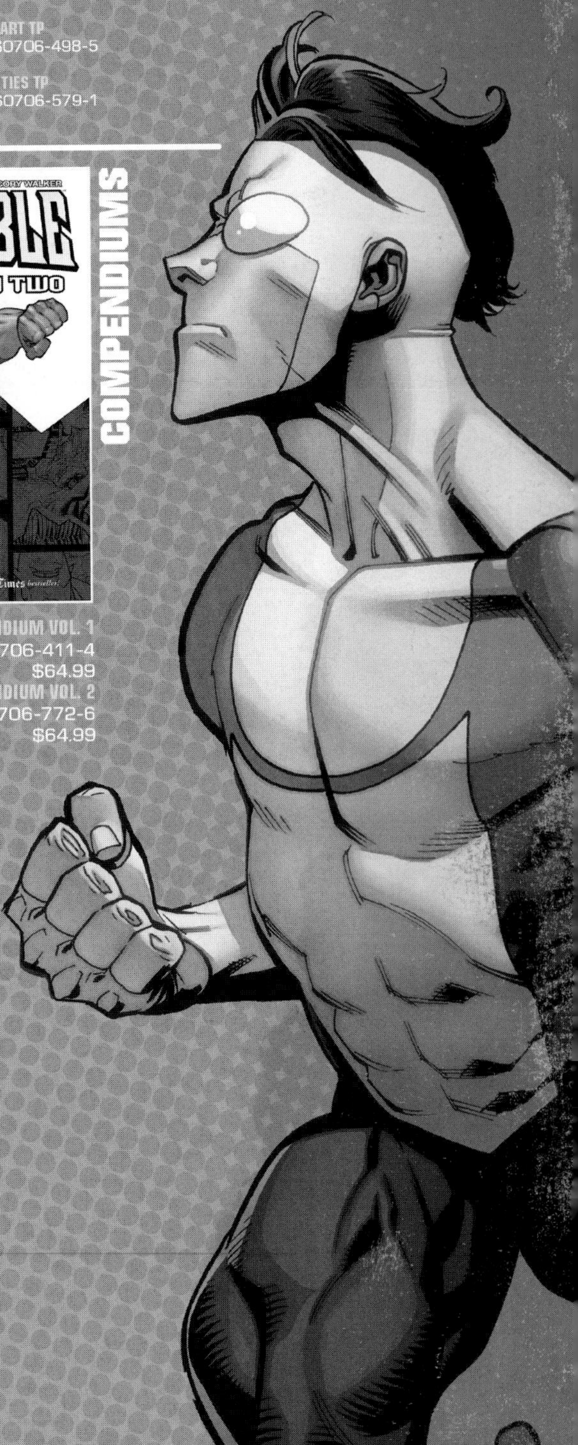

COMPLETE LIBRARY

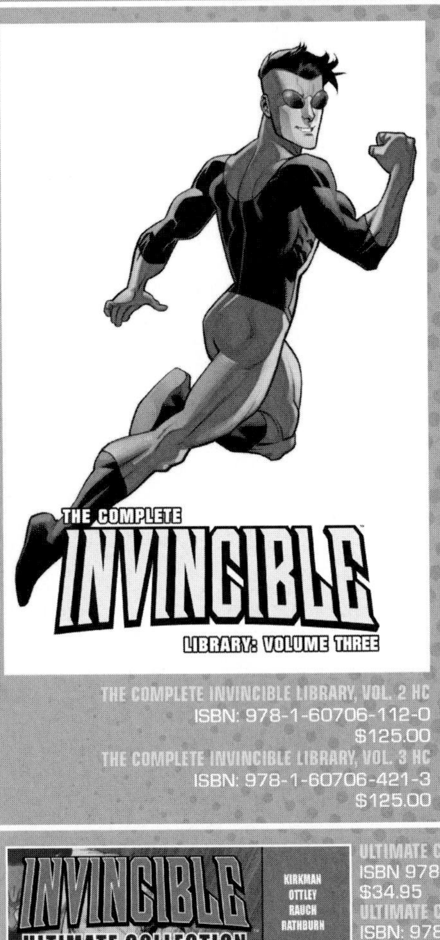
THE COMPLETE
INVINCIBLE
LIBRARY: VOLUME THREE

THE COMPLETE INVINCIBLE LIBRARY, VOL. 2 HC
ISBN: 978-1-60706-112-0
$125.00
THE COMPLETE INVINCIBLE LIBRARY, VOL. 3 HC
ISBN: 978-1-60706-421-3
$125.00

COMPENDIUMS

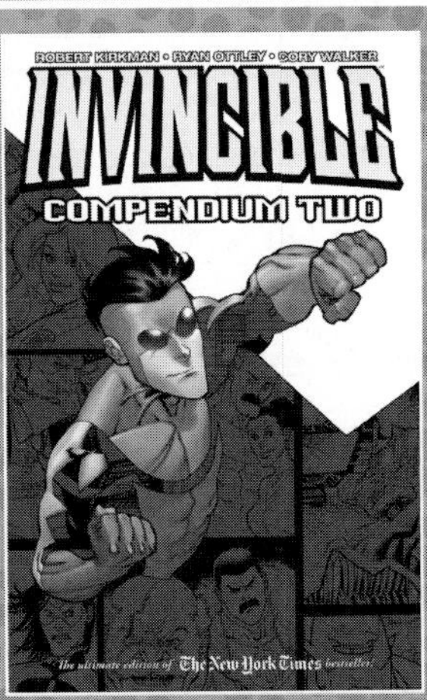
ROBERT KIRKMAN · RYAN OTTLEY · CORY WALKER
INVINCIBLE
COMPENDIUM TWO
The ultimate edition of The New York Times bestseller!

COMPENDIUM VOL. 1
ISBN: 978-1-60706-411-4
$64.99
COMPENDIUM VOL. 2
ISBN: 978-1-60706-772-6
$64.99

ULTIMATE COLLECTIONS

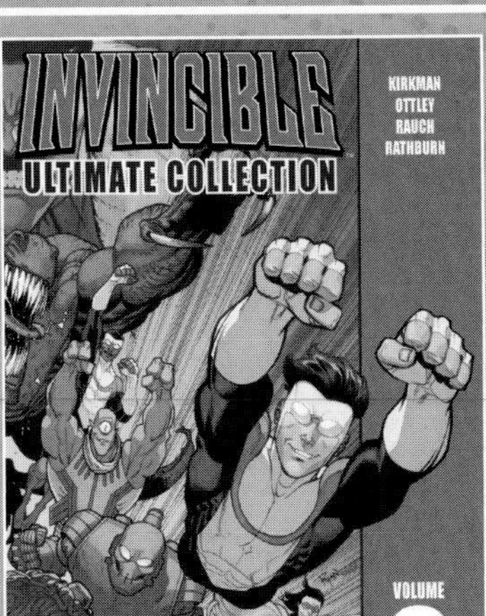
INVINCIBLE
ULTIMATE COLLECTION
KIRKMAN
OTTLEY
RAUCH
RATHBURN
VOLUME
9

ULTIMATE COLLECTION, VOL. 1 HC
ISBN 978-1-58240-500-1
$34.95
ULTIMATE COLLECTION, VOL. 2 HC
ISBN: 978-1-58240-594-0
$34.99
ULTIMATE COLLECTION, VOL. 3 HC
ISBN: 978-1-58240-763-0
$34.99
ULTIMATE COLLECTION, VOL. 4 HC
ISBN: 978-1-58240-989-4
$34.99
ULTIMATE COLLECTION, VOL. 5 HC
ISBN: 978-1-60706-116-8
$34.99
ULTIMATE COLLECTION, VOL. 6 HC
ISBN: 978-1-60706-360-5
$34.99
ULTIMATE COLLECTION, VOL. 7 HC
ISBN: 978-1-60706-509-8
$39.99
ULTIMATE COLLECTION, VOL. 8 HC
ISBN: 978-1-60706-680-4
$39.99
ULTIMATE COLLECTION, VOL. 9 HC
ISBN: 978-1-63215-032-5
$39.99

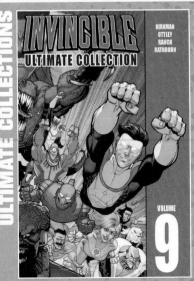

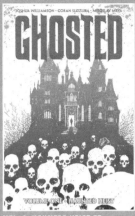